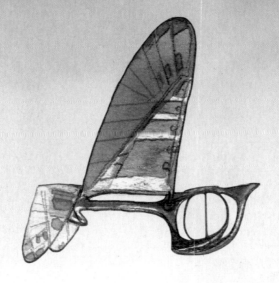

FROM THE IMAGINATION OF B.C. PETERSCHMIDT

AMELIA ERROWAY

CASTAWAY COMMANDER

An Imprint of

SCHOLASTIC

Library of Congress Control Number: 2020943075

ISBN 978-1-338-18614-7 (hardcover)
ISBN 978-1-338-18612-3 (paperback)

10 9 8 7 6 5 4 3 2 1   21 22 23 24 25

Printed in China   62
First edition, August 2021

Book design by Steve Ponzo
Creative Director: Phil Falco
Publisher: David Saylor

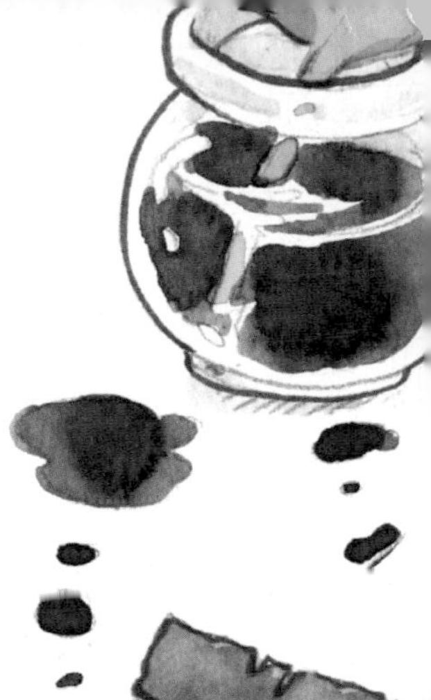

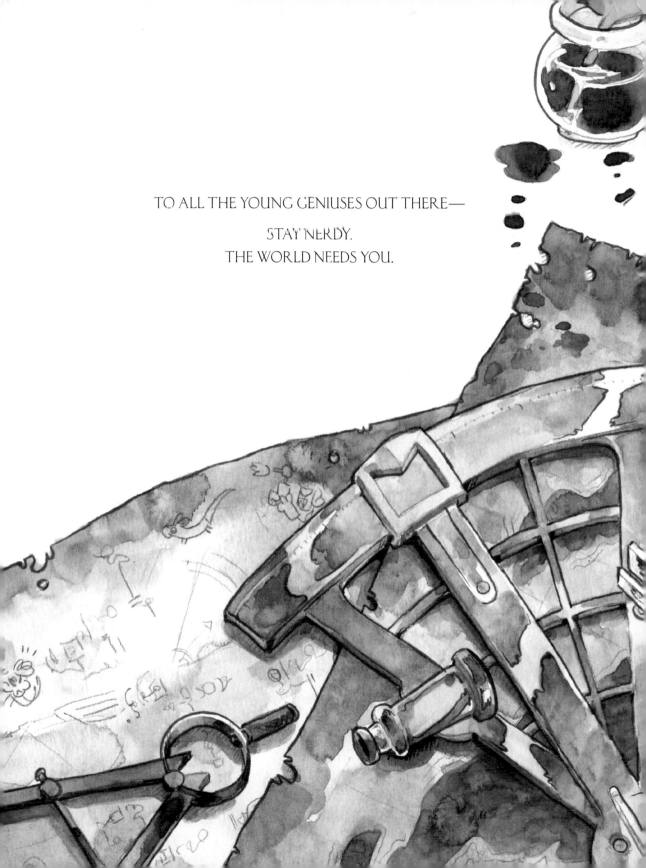

TO ALL THE YOUNG GENIUSES OUT THERE—

STAY NERDY.
THE WORLD NEEDS YOU.

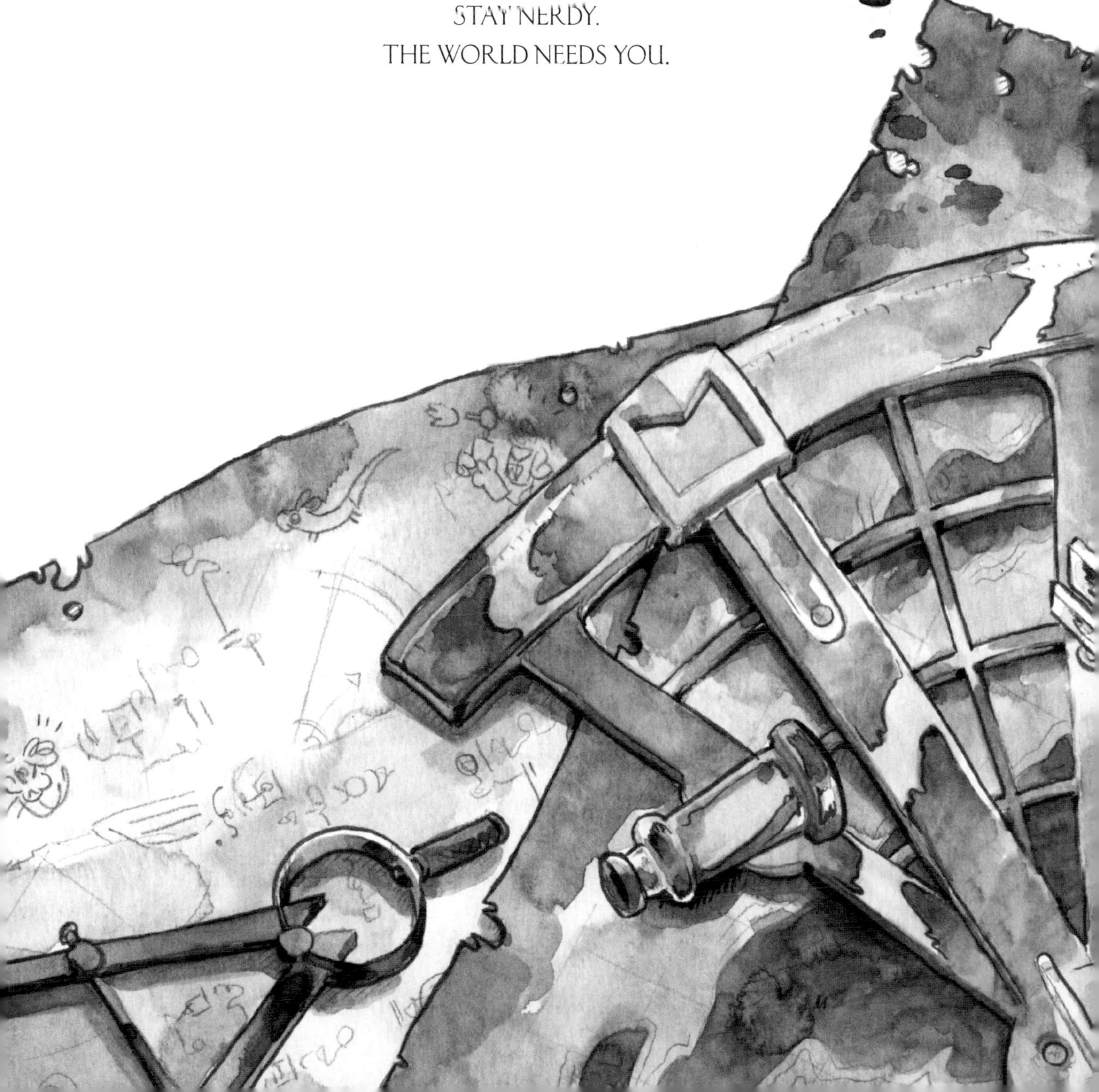

SOMETIMES, THINGS
DON'T GO THE WAY
YOU WANT—

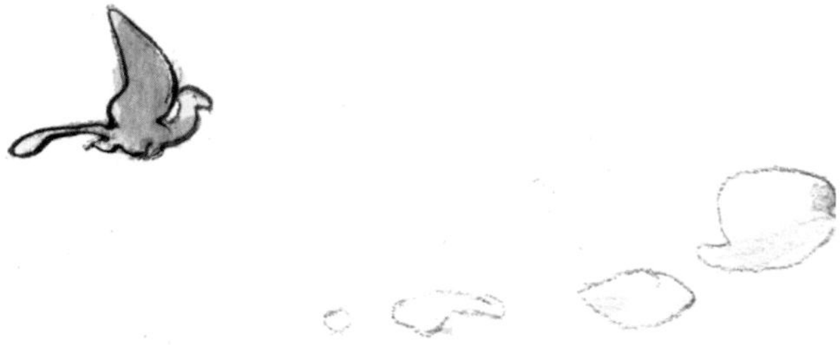

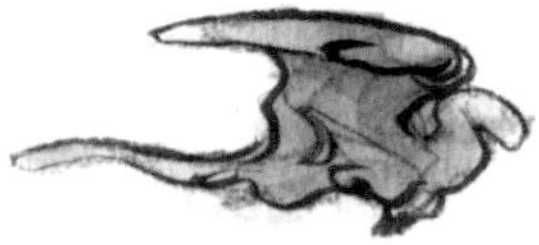

BUT THAT DOESN'T MEAN YOU
CAN'T ***STILL*** CHOOSE HAPPINESS.

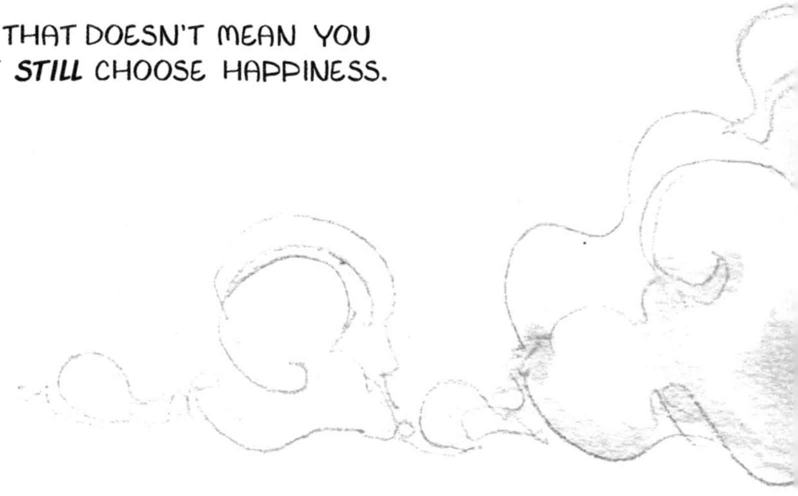

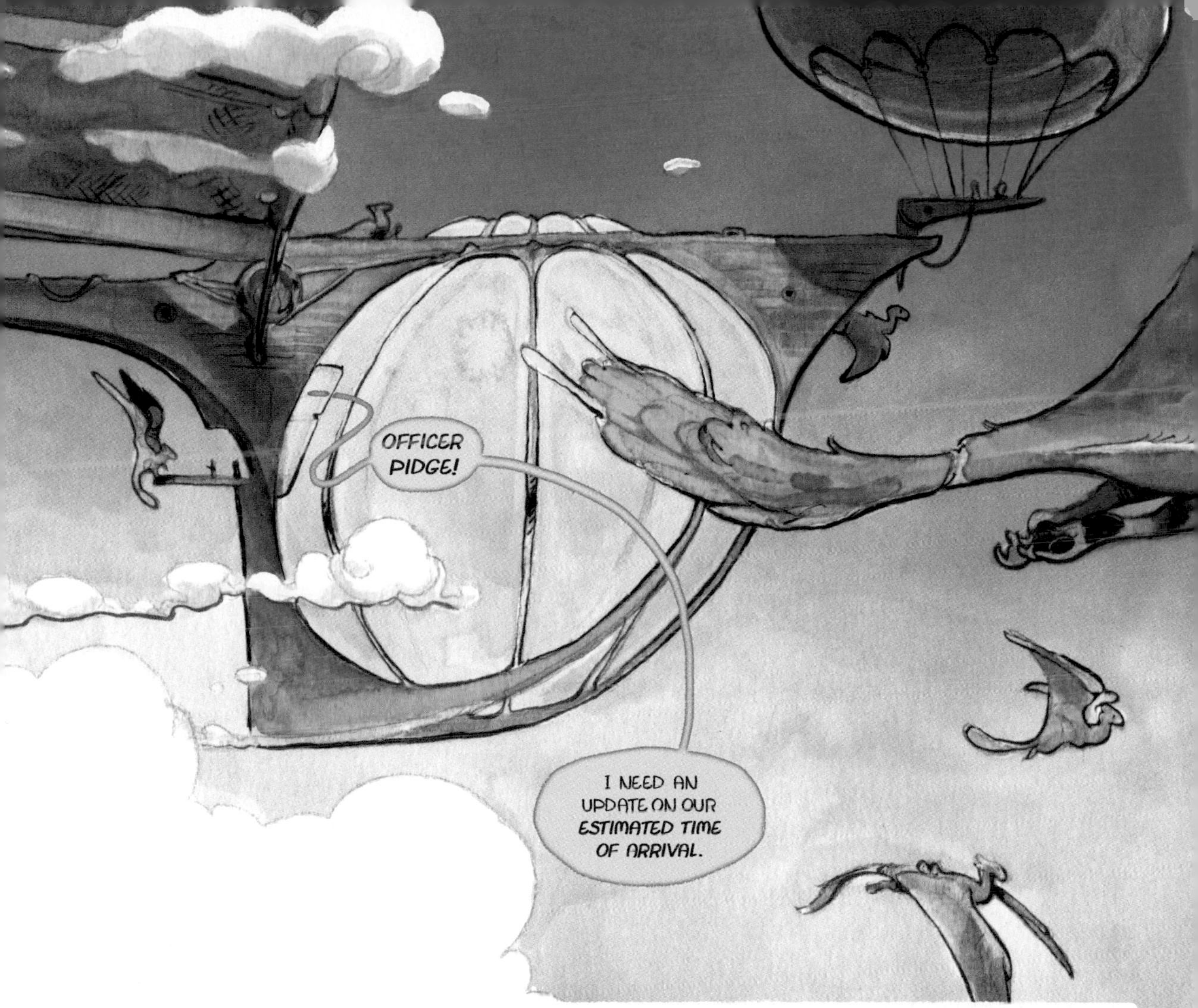
OFFICER PIDGE!
I NEED AN UPDATE ON OUR ESTIMATED TIME OF ARRIVAL.

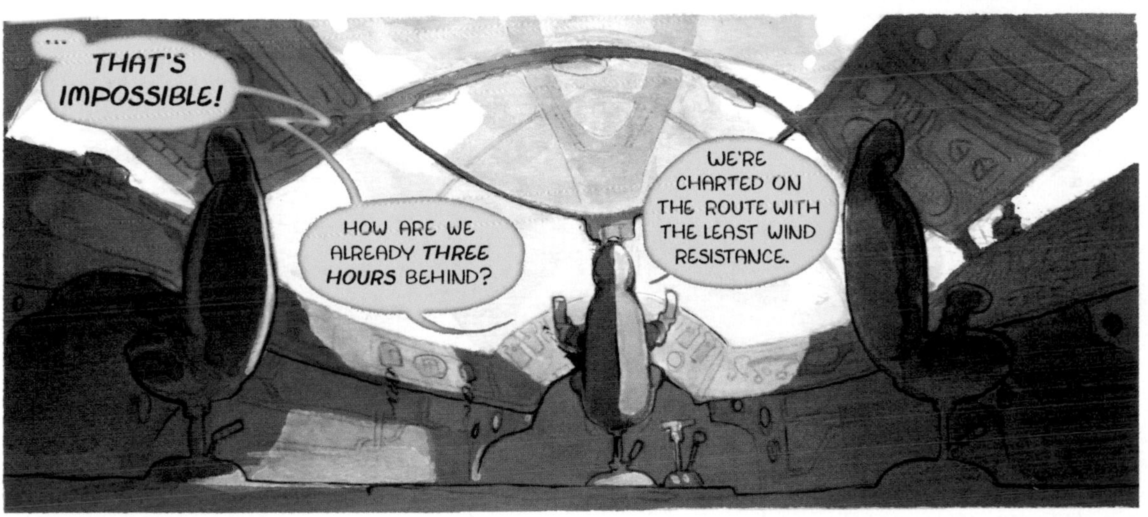
... THAT'S IMPOSSIBLE!
HOW ARE WE ALREADY THREE HOURS BEHIND?
WE'RE CHARTED ON THE ROUTE WITH THE LEAST WIND RESISTANCE.

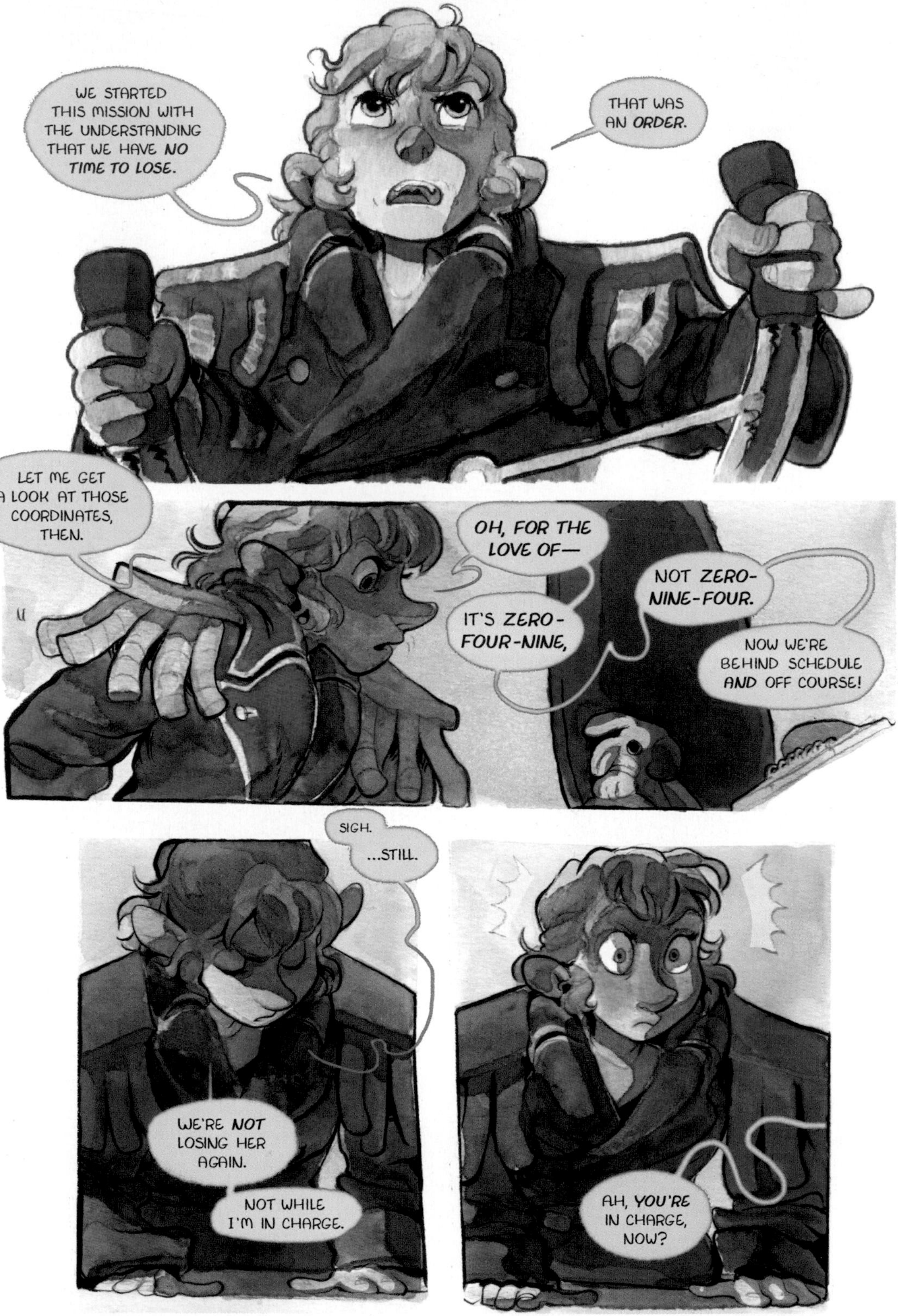
WE STARTED THIS MISSION WITH THE UNDERSTANDING THAT WE HAVE NO TIME TO LOSE.
THAT WAS AN ORDER.
LET ME GET A LOOK AT THOSE COORDINATES, THEN.
OH, FOR THE LOVE OF—
IT'S ZERO-FOUR-NINE,
NOT ZERO-NINE-FOUR.
NOW WE'RE BEHIND SCHEDULE AND OFF COURSE!
SIGH.
...STILL.
WE'RE NOT LOSING HER AGAIN.
NOT WHILE I'M IN CHARGE.
AH, YOU'RE IN CHARGE, NOW?

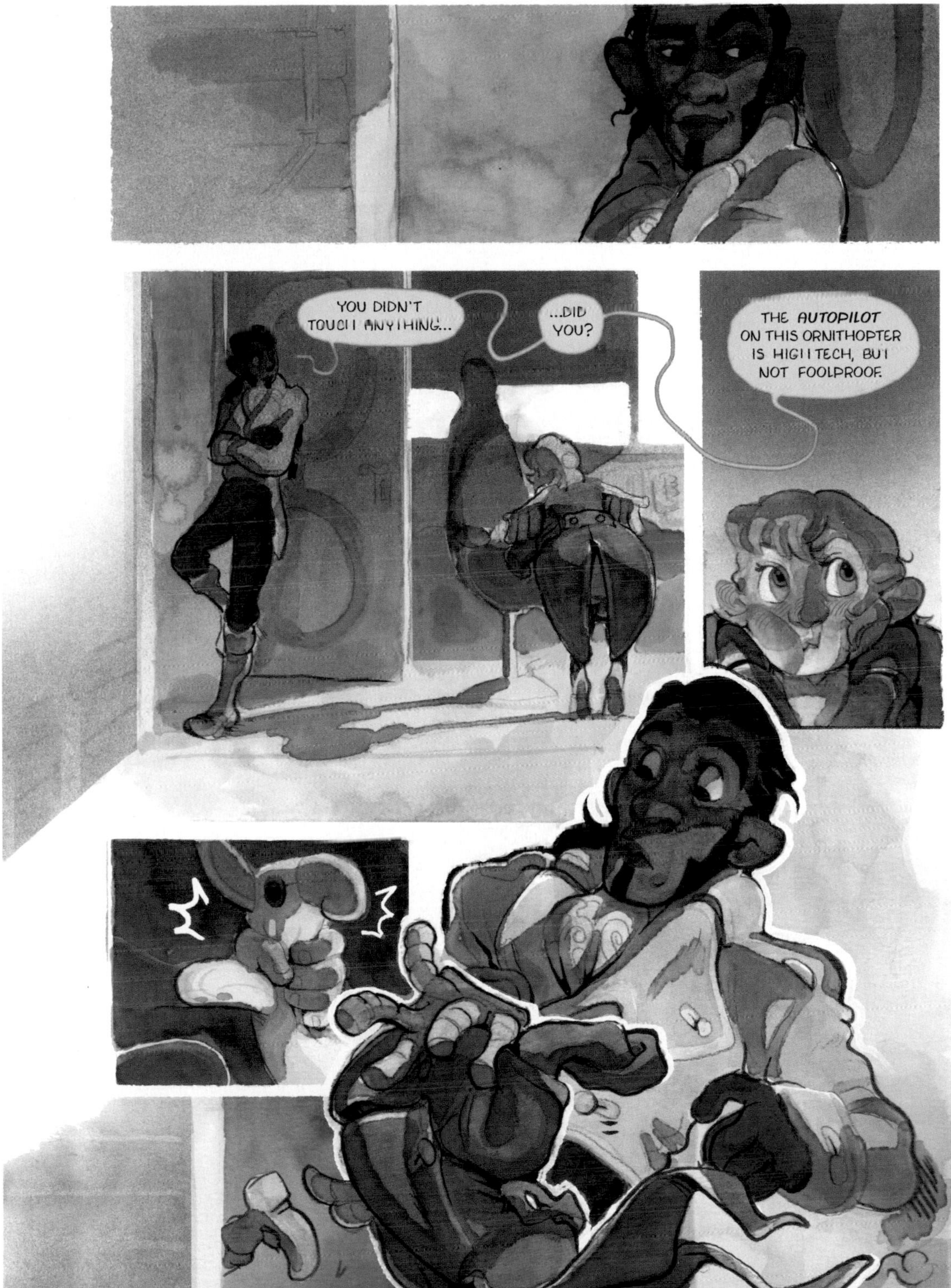
YOU DIDN'T TOUCH ANYTHING...
...DID YOU?
THE *AUTOPILOT* ON THIS ORNITHOPTER IS HIGH TECH, BUT NOT FOOLPROOF.

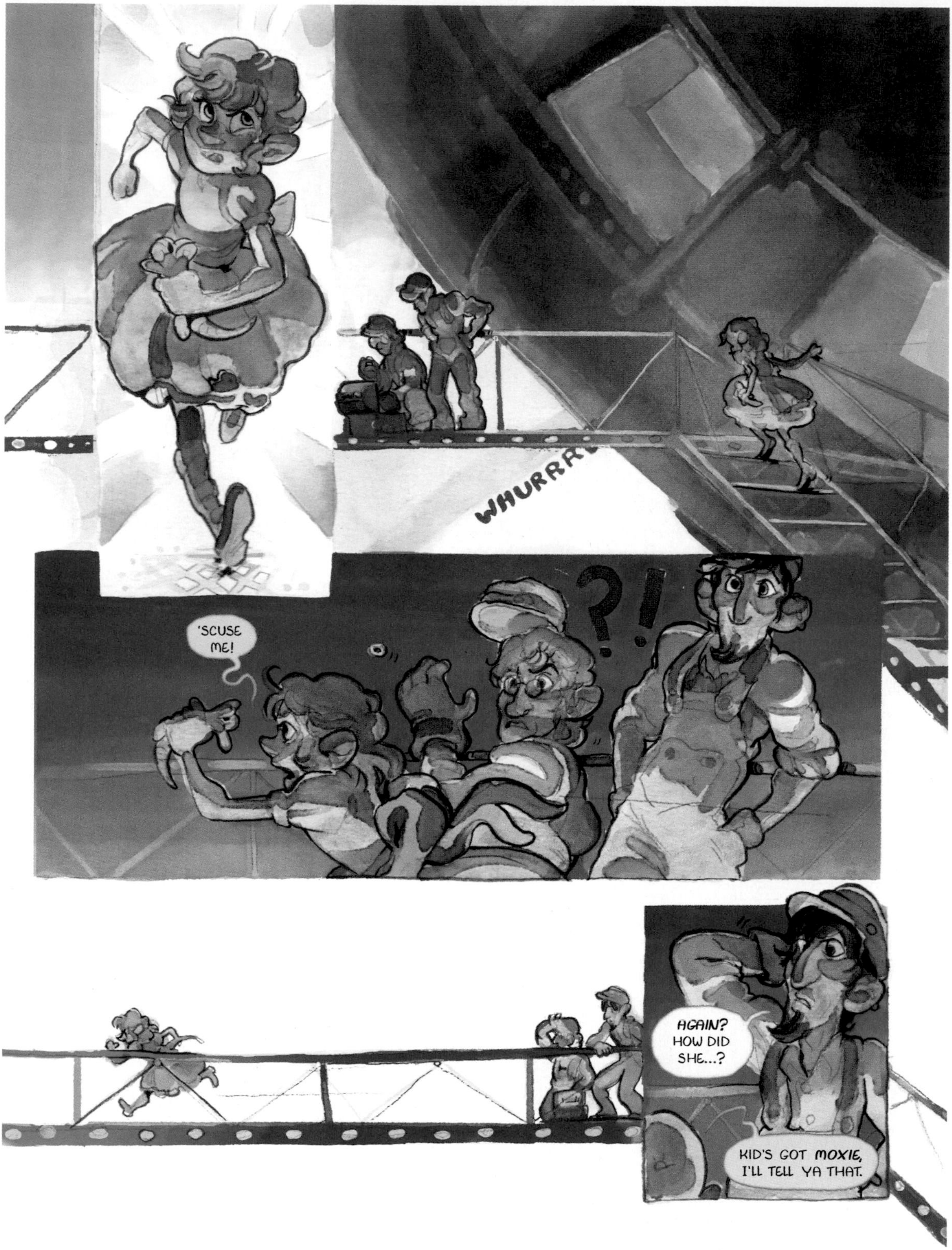
WHURRR
'SCUSE ME!
?!
AGAIN? HOW DID SHE...?
KID'S GOT MOXIE, I'LL TELL YA THAT.

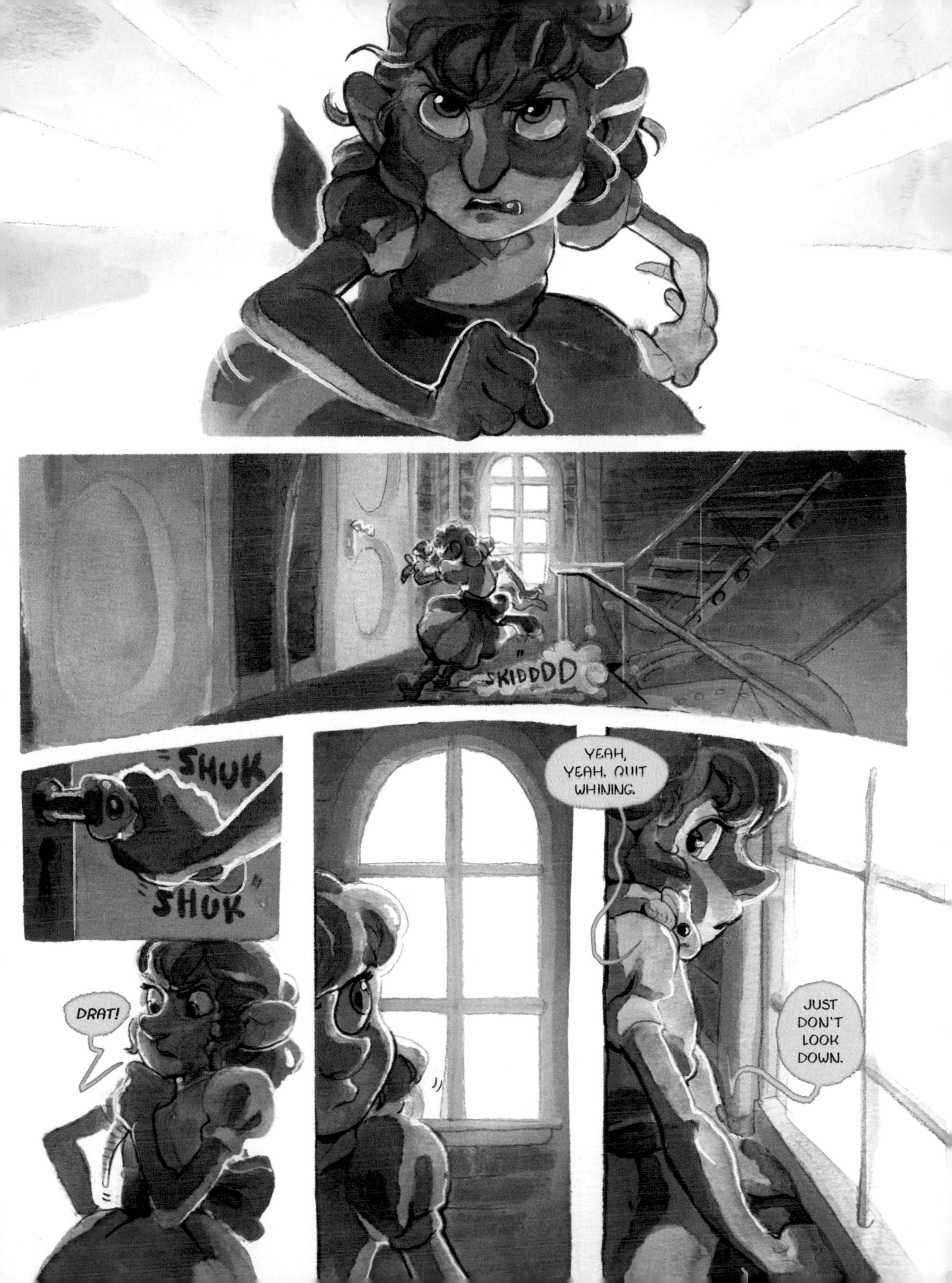
SKIDDDD
SHUK
SHUK
DRAT!
YEAH, YEAH. QUIT WHINING.
JUST DON'T LOOK DOWN.

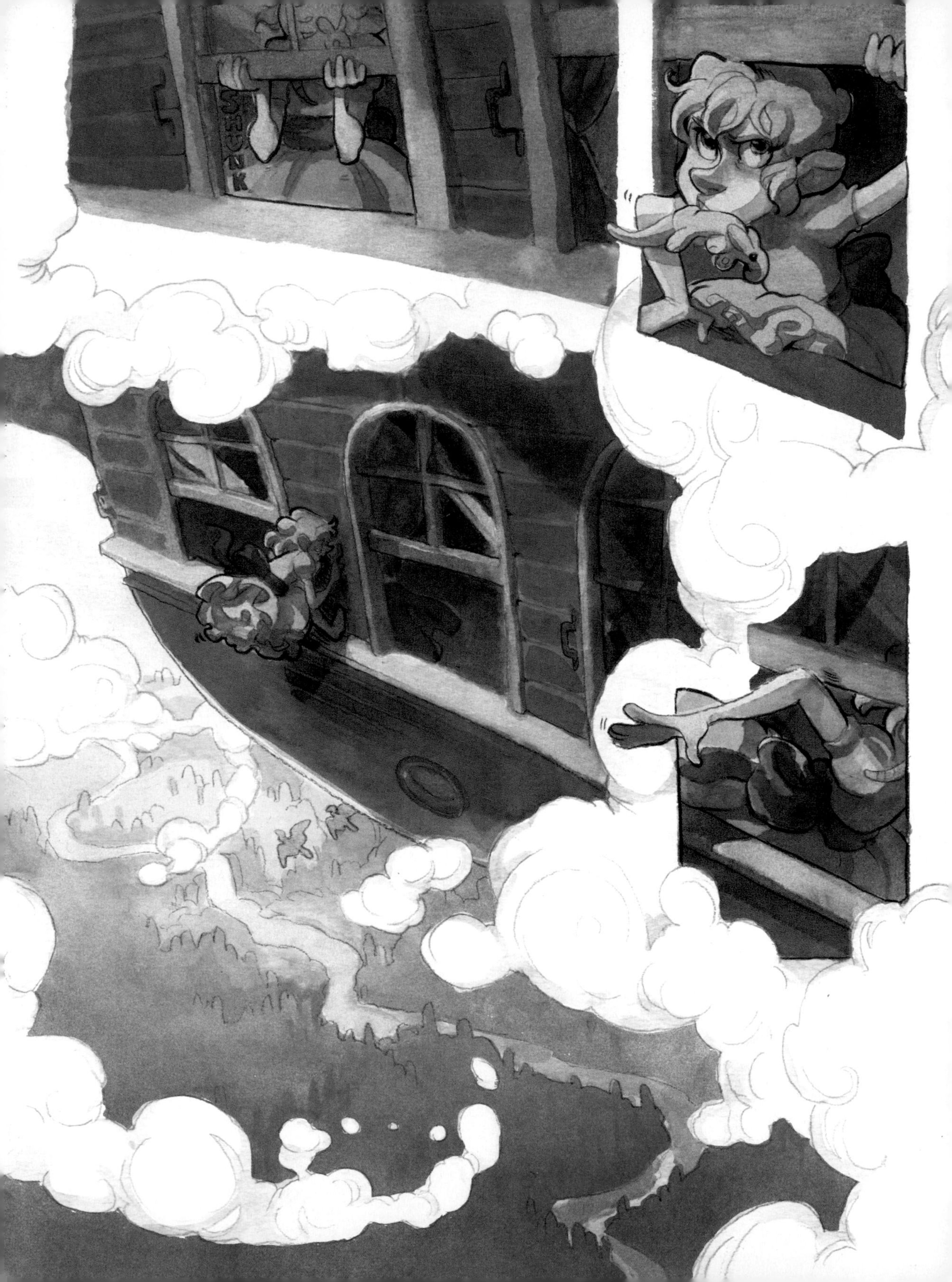
SHUNK

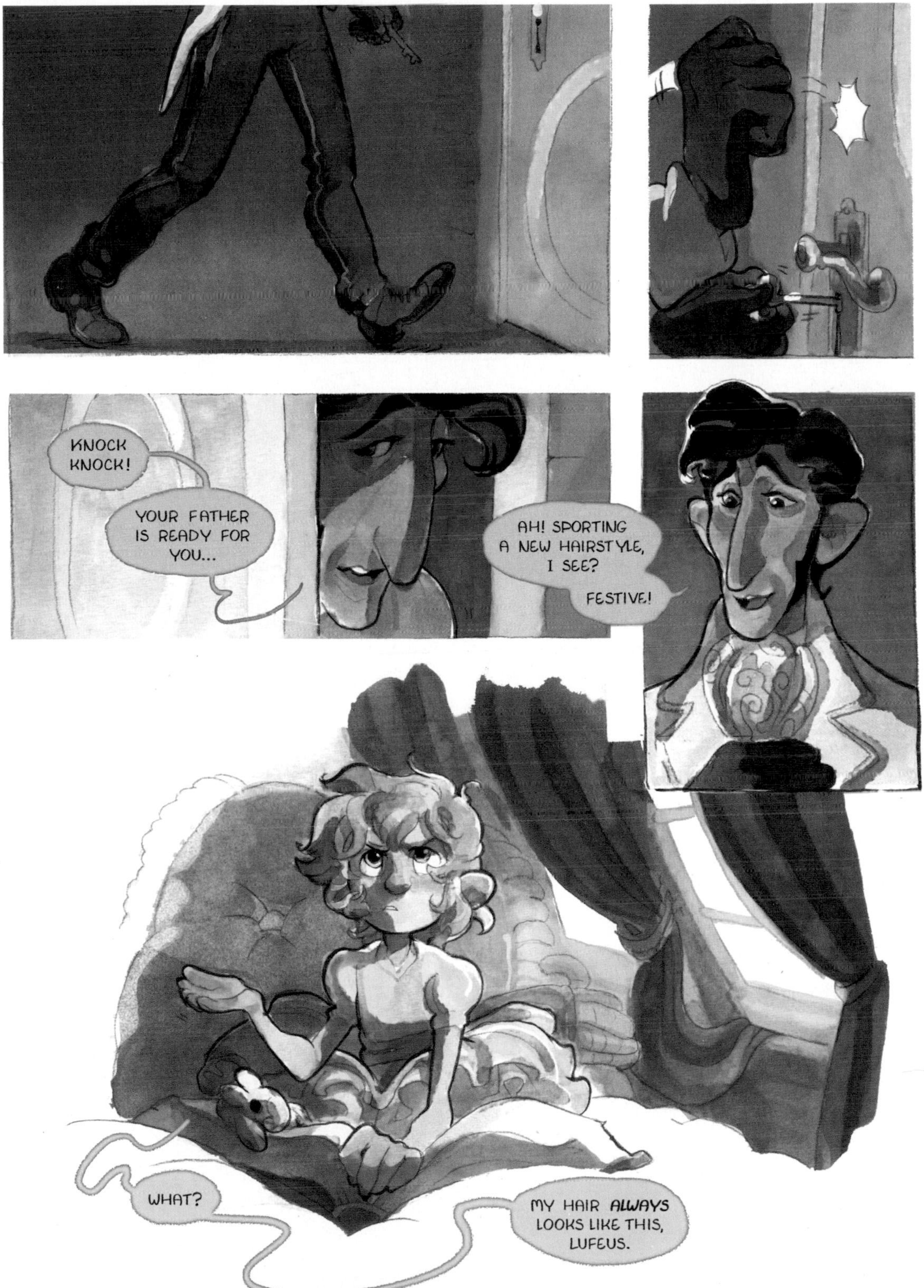
KNOCK KNOCK!
YOUR FATHER IS READY FOR YOU...
AH! SPORTING A NEW HAIRSTYLE, I SEE?
FESTIVE!
WHAT?
MY HAIR ALWAYS LOOKS LIKE THIS, LUFEUS.

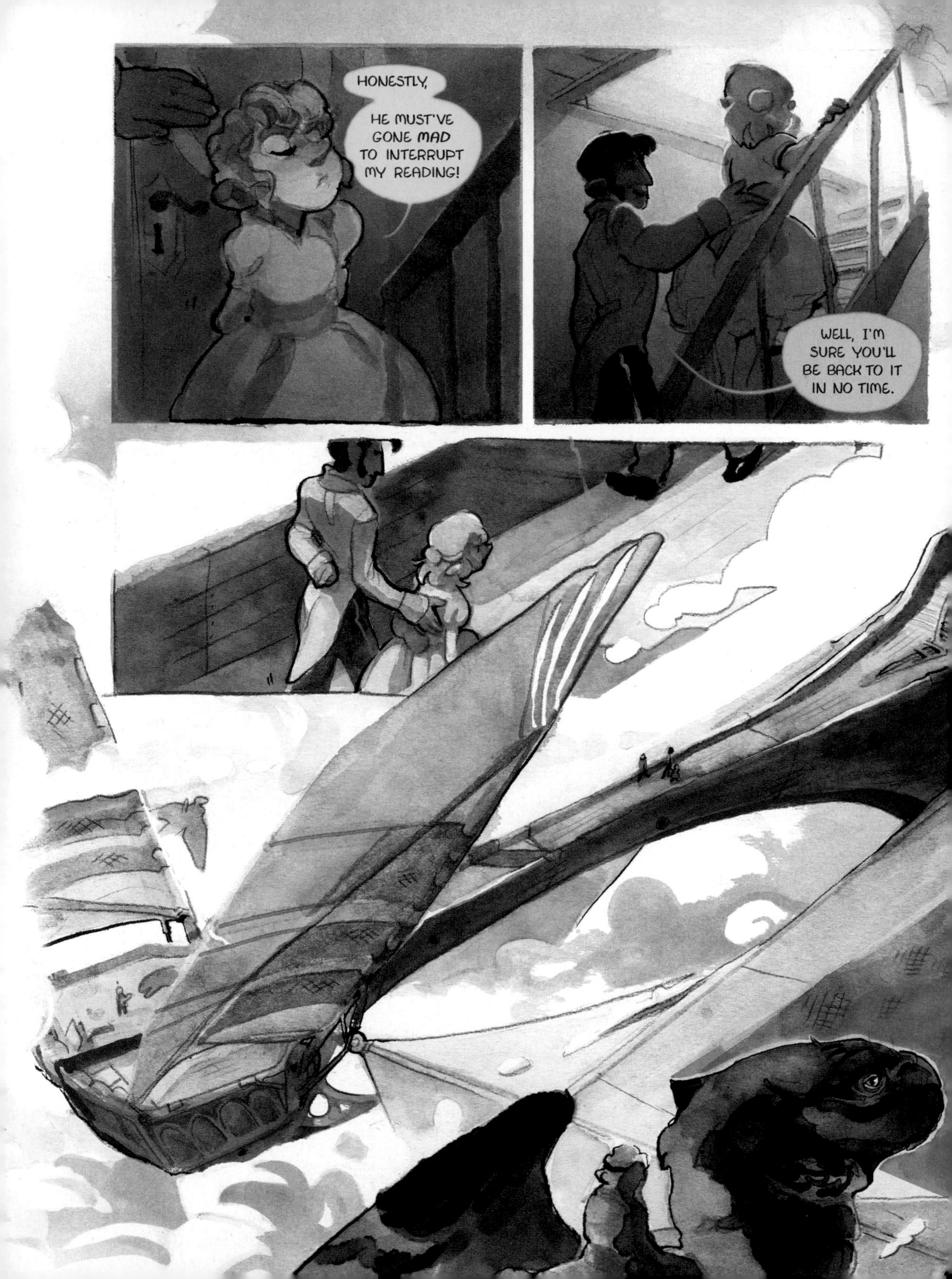
HONESTLY,
HE MUST'VE GONE *MAD* TO INTERRUPT MY READING!
WELL, I'M SURE YOU'LL BE BACK TO IT IN NO TIME.

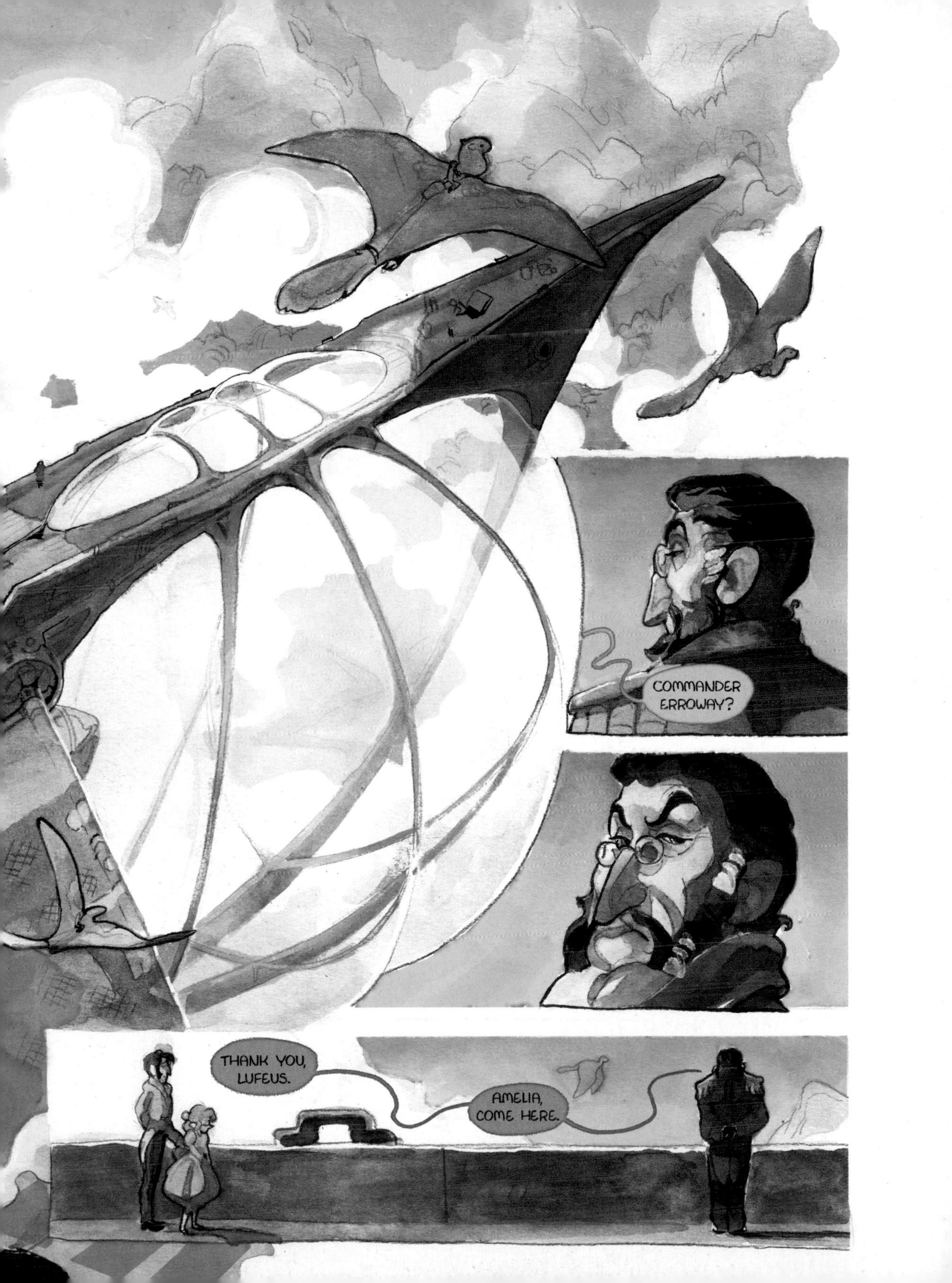
COMMANDER ERROWAY?
THANK YOU, LUFEUS.
AMELIA, COME HERE.

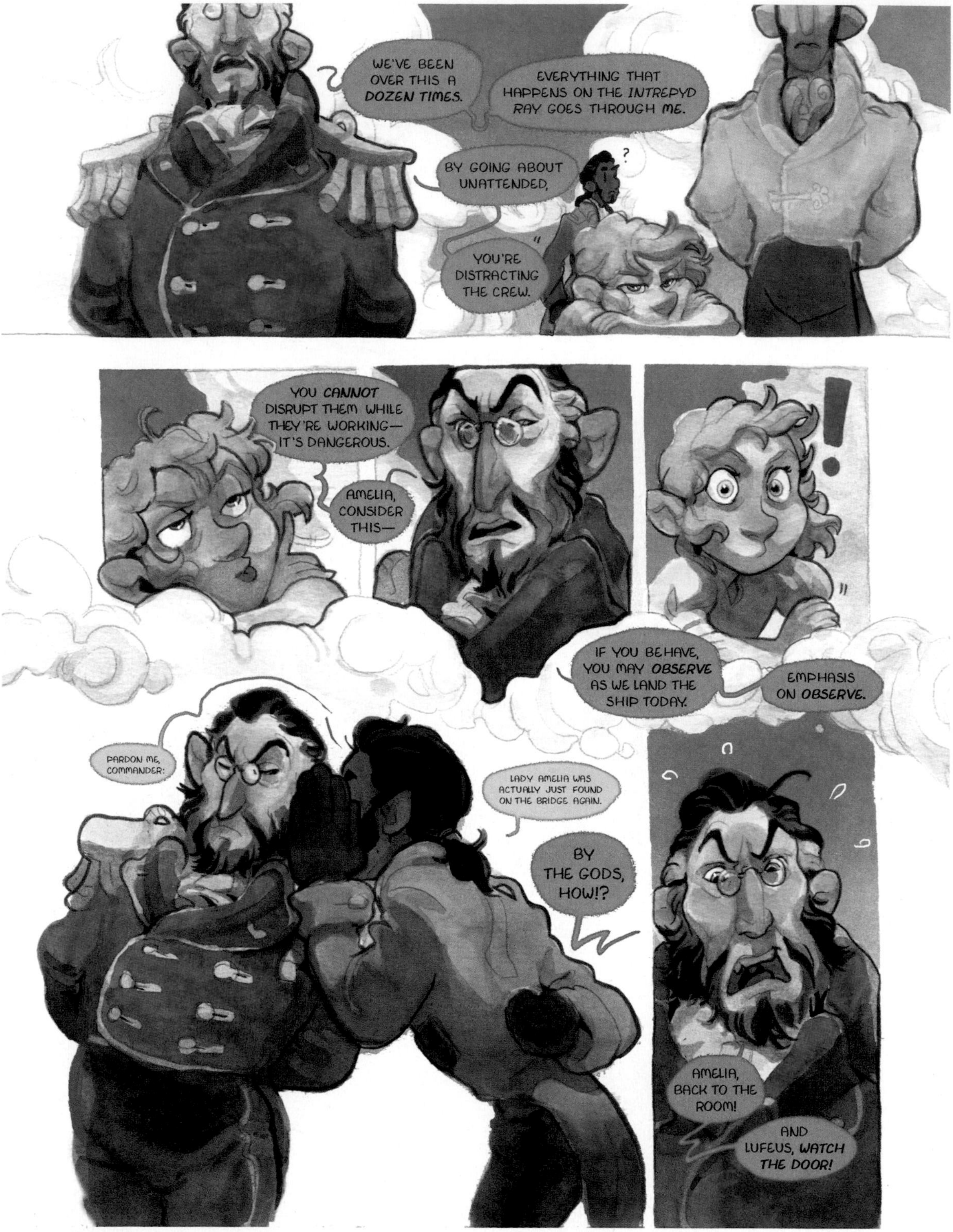

WE'VE BEEN OVER THIS A DOZEN TIMES.
EVERYTHING THAT HAPPENS ON THE INTREPYD RAY GOES THROUGH ME.
?
BY GOING ABOUT UNATTENDED,
YOU'RE DISTRACTING THE CREW.
YOU CANNOT DISRUPT THEM WHILE THEY'RE WORKING—IT'S DANGEROUS.
AMELIA, CONSIDER THIS—
!
IF YOU BEHAVE, YOU MAY OBSERVE AS WE LAND THE SHIP TODAY.
EMPHASIS ON OBSERVE.
PARDON ME, COMMANDER:
LADY AMELIA WAS ACTUALLY JUST FOUND ON THE BRIDGE AGAIN.
BY THE GODS, HOW!?
AMELIA, BACK TO THE ROOM!
AND LUFEUS, WATCH THE DOOR!

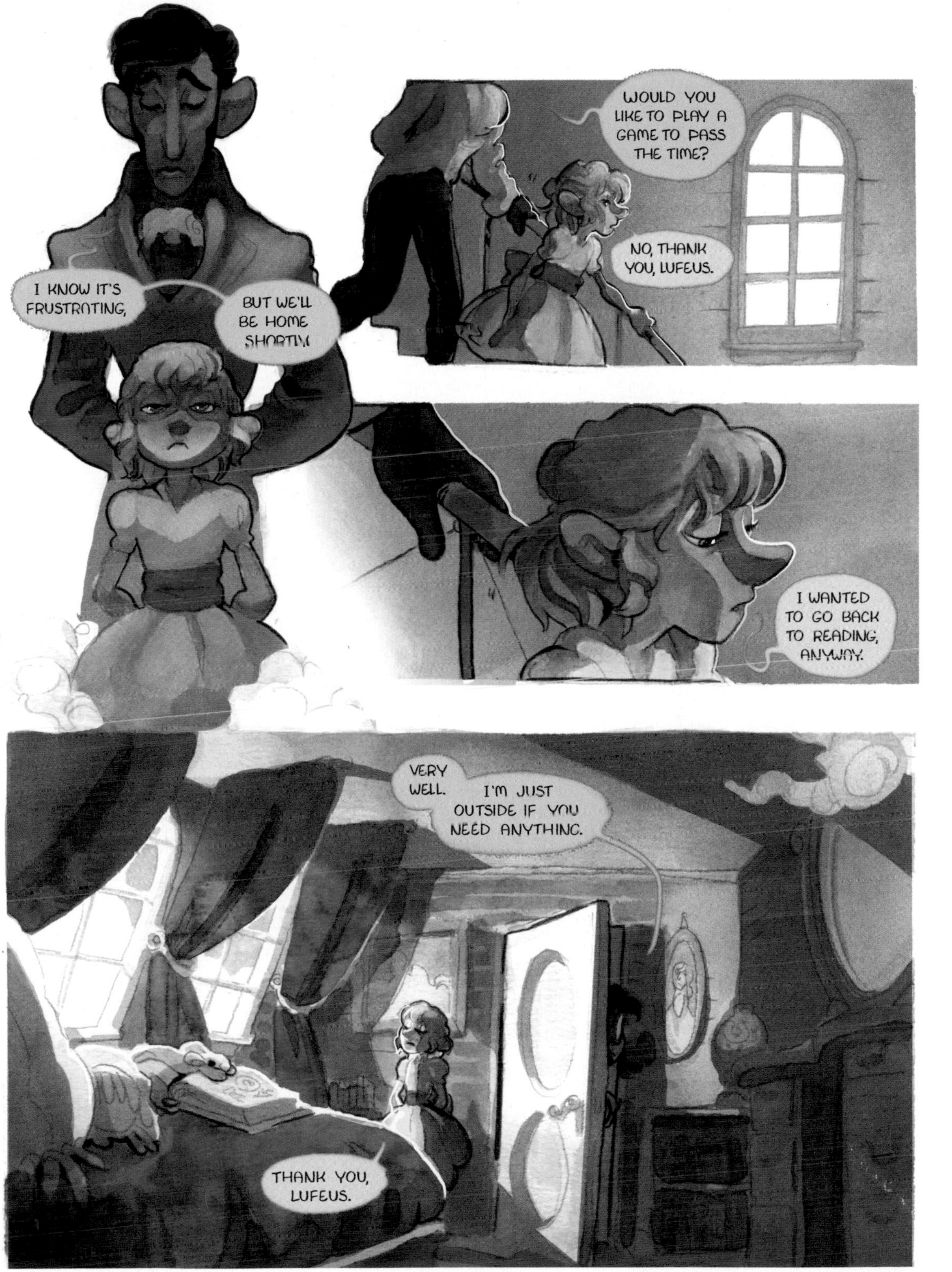
WOULD YOU LIKE TO PLAY A GAME TO PASS THE TIME?
NO, THANK YOU, LUFEUS.
I KNOW IT'S FRUSTRATING,
BUT WE'LL BE HOME SHORTLY.
I WANTED TO GO BACK TO READING, ANYWAY.
VERY WELL.
I'M JUST OUTSIDE IF YOU NEED ANYTHING.
THANK YOU, LUFEUS.

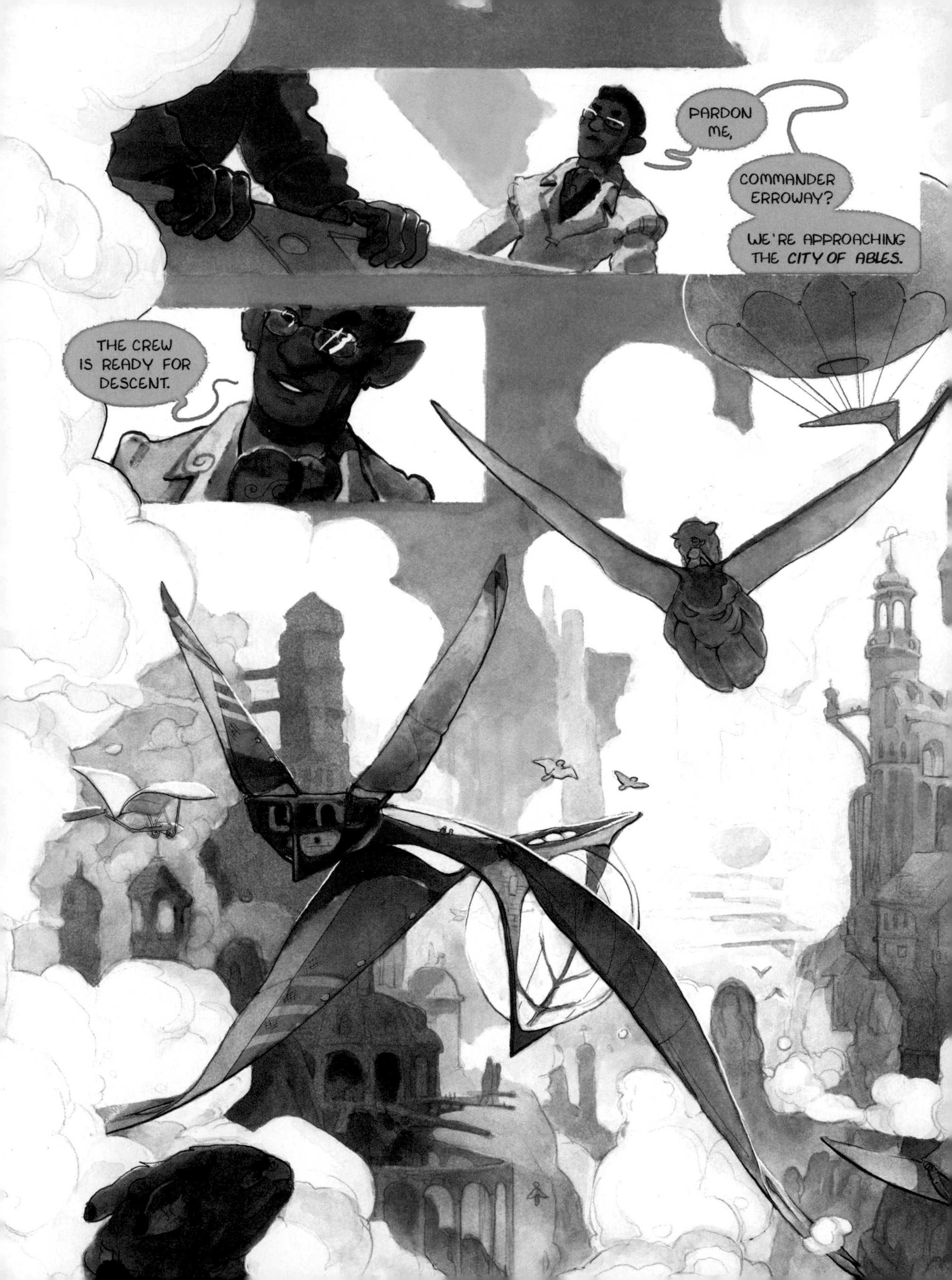
PARDON ME,
COMMANDER ERROWAY?
WE'RE APPROACHING THE *CITY OF ABLES.*
THE CREW IS READY FOR DESCENT.

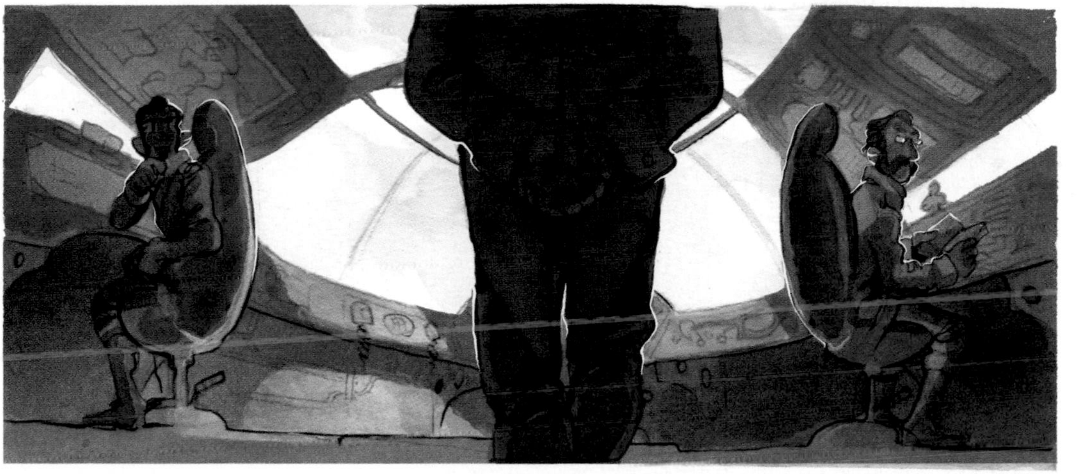

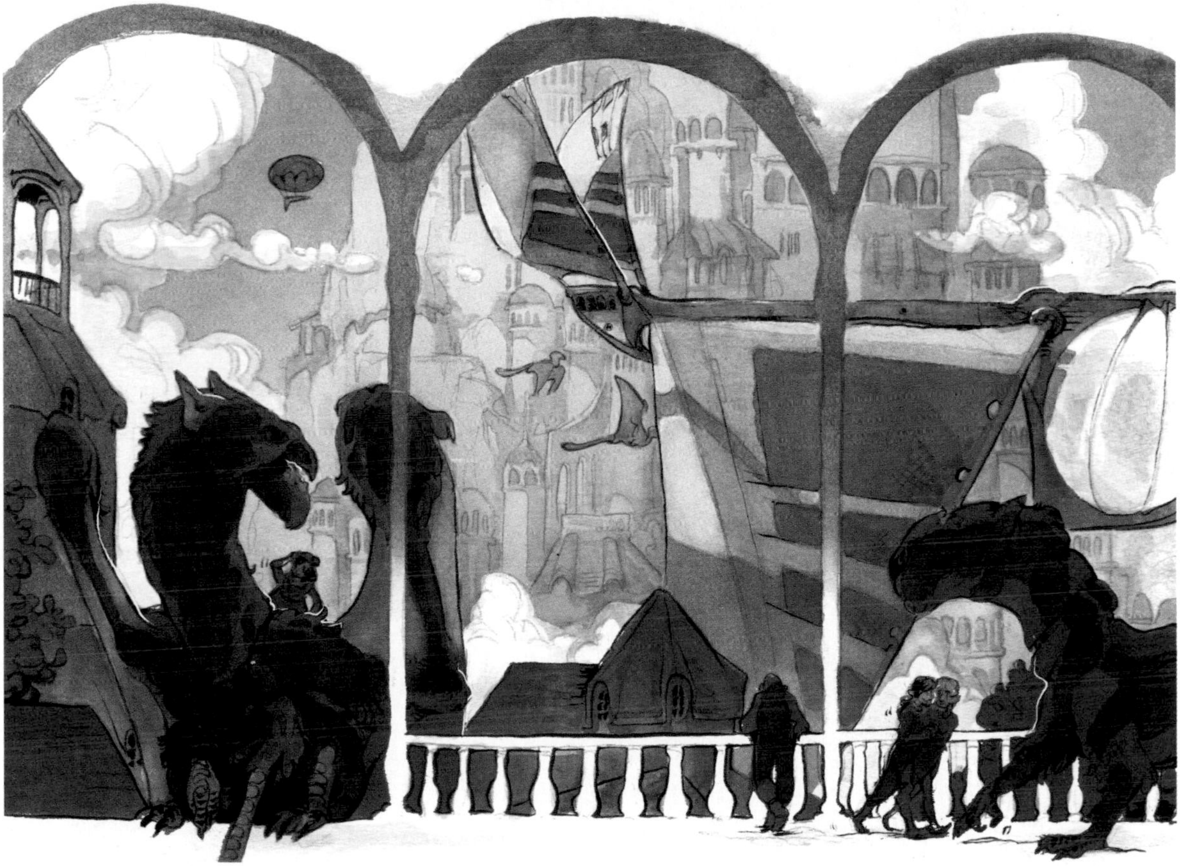

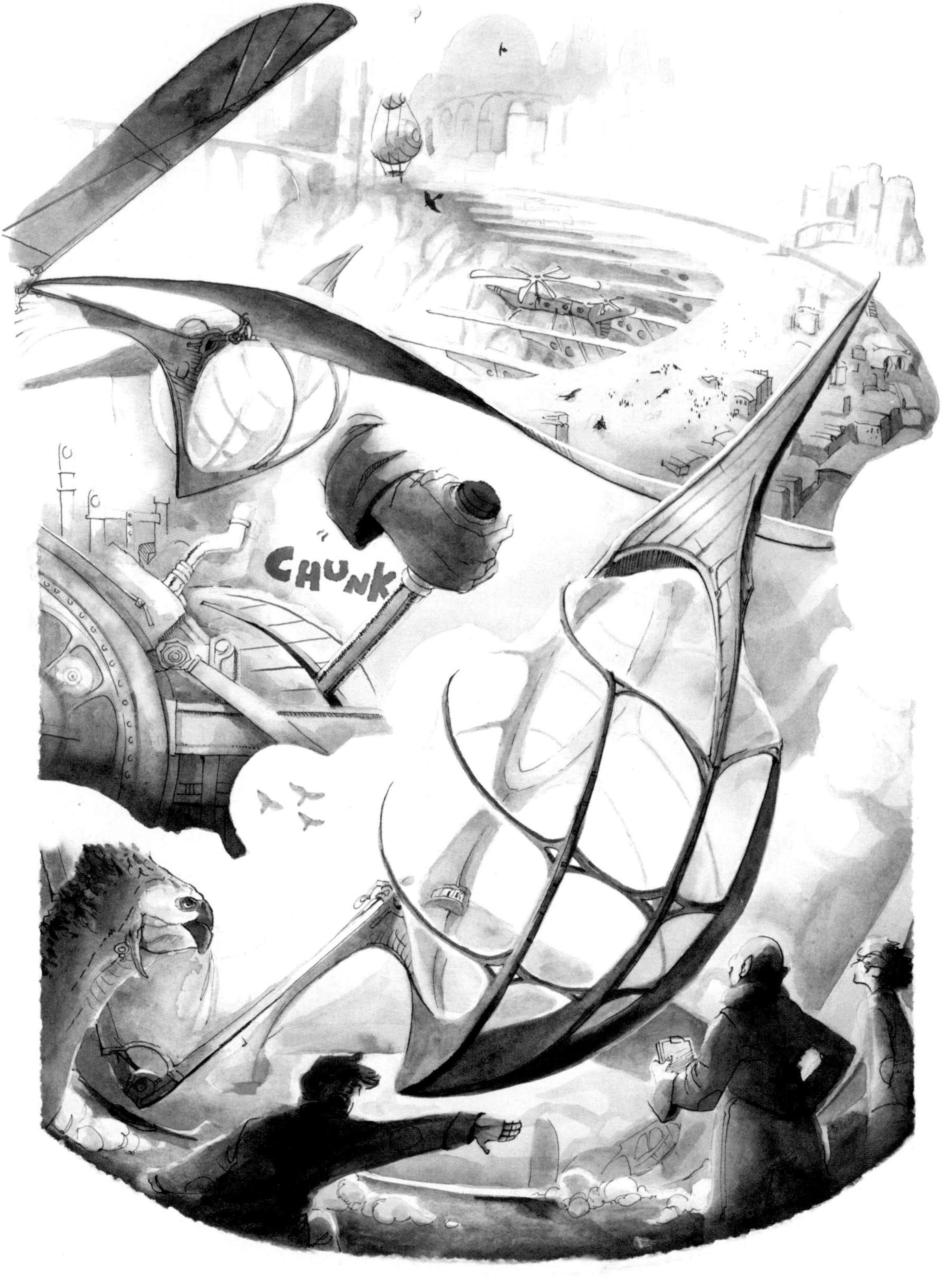
CHUNK

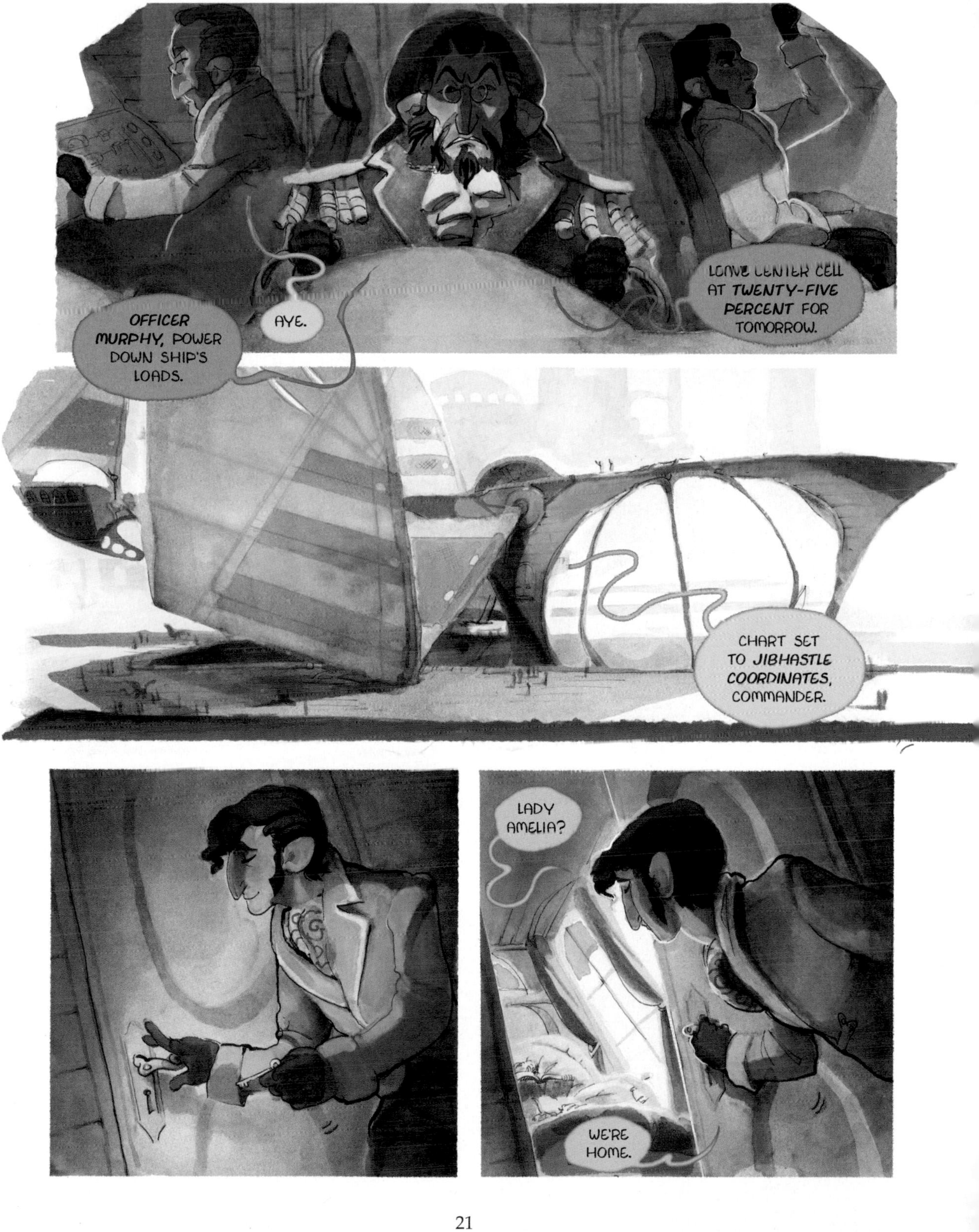
OFFICER MURPHY, POWER DOWN SHIP'S LOADS.
AYE.
LEAVE CENTER CELL AT TWENTY-FIVE PERCENT FOR TOMORROW.
CHART SET TO JIBHASTLE COORDINATES, COMMANDER.
LADY AMELIA?
WE'RE HOME.

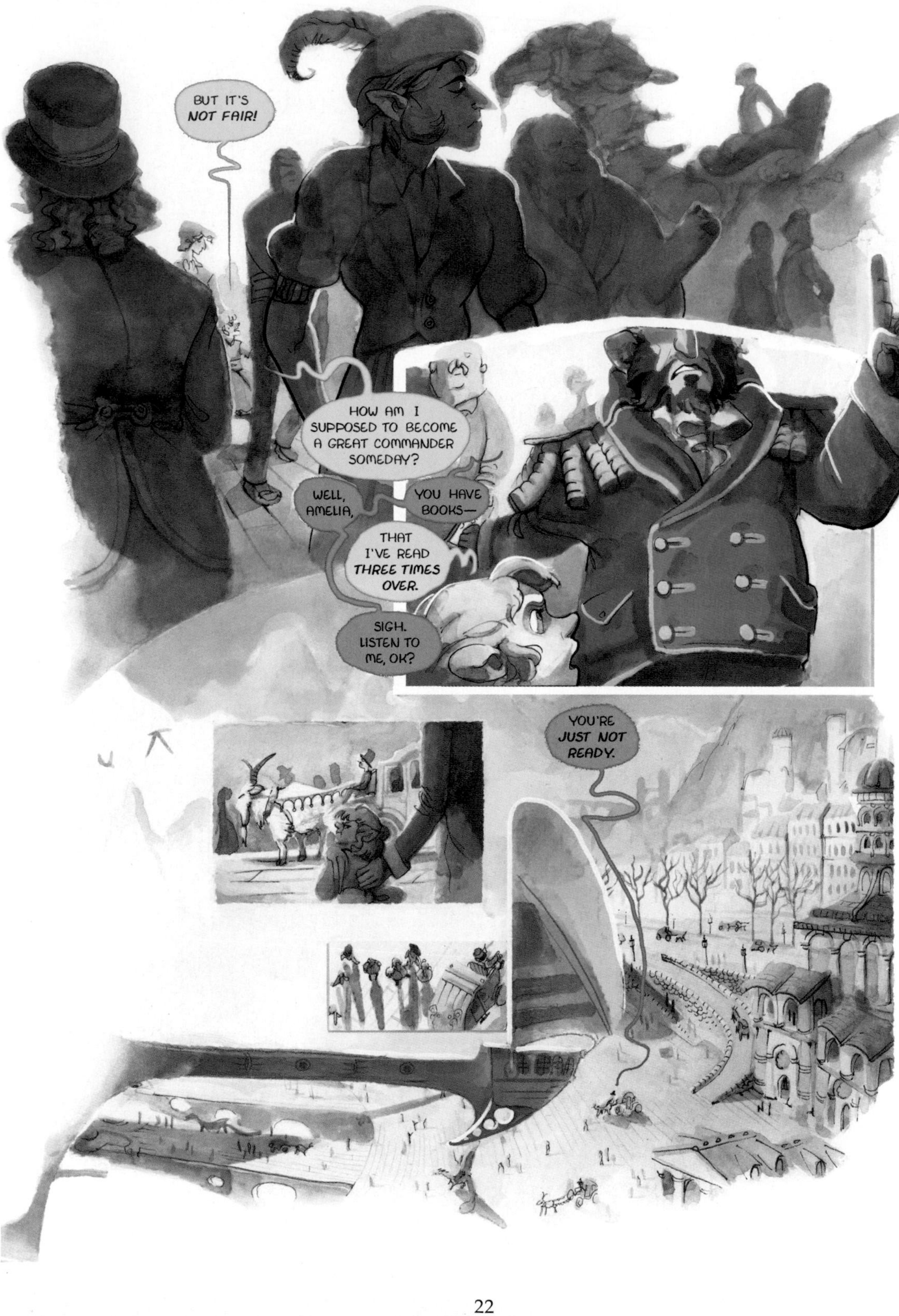
BUT IT'S NOT FAIR!
HOW AM I SUPPOSED TO BECOME A GREAT COMMANDER SOMEDAY?
WELL, AMELIA,
YOU HAVE BOOKS—
THAT I'VE READ THREE TIMES OVER.
SIGH. LISTEN TO ME, OK?
YOU'RE JUST NOT READY.

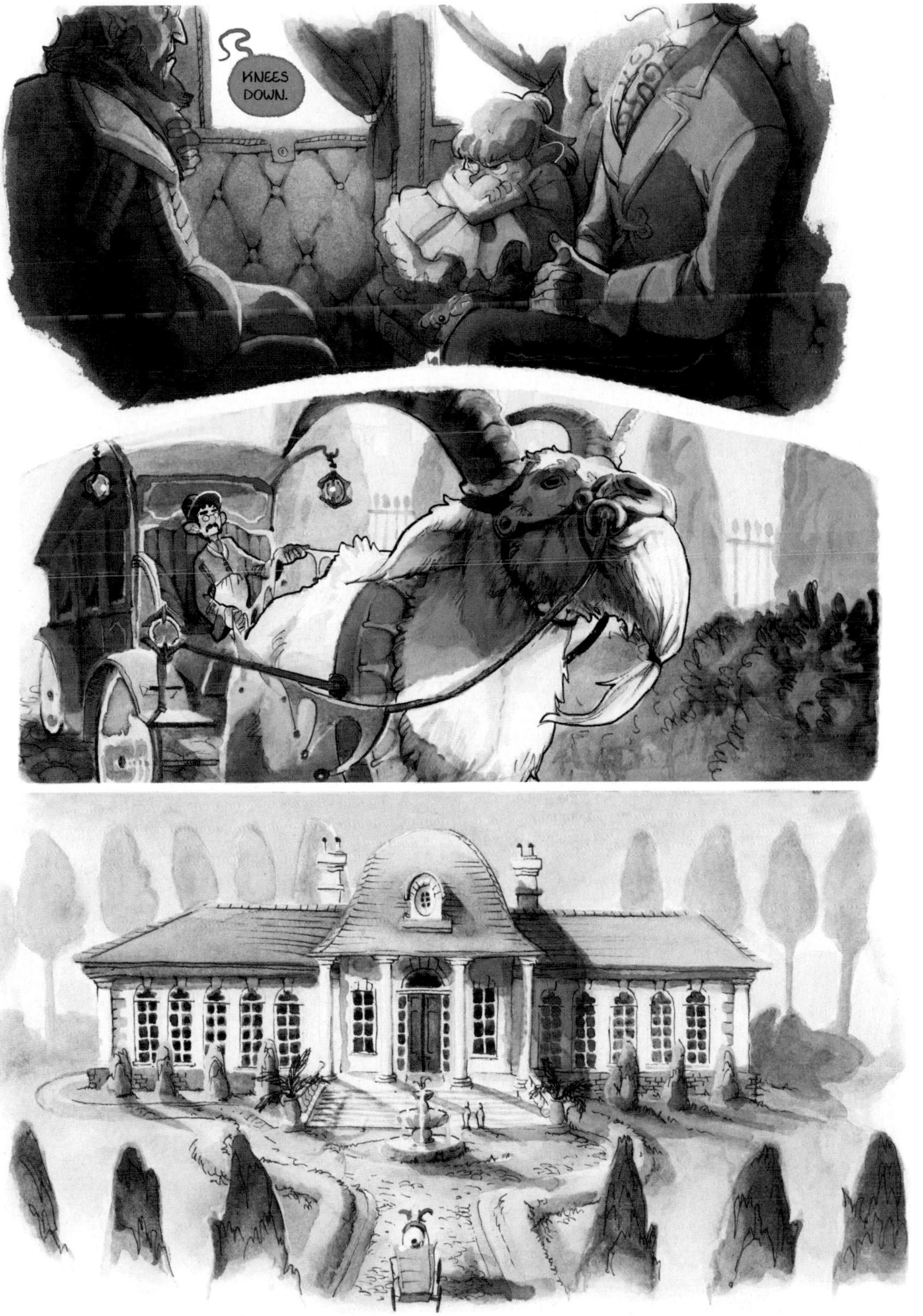
KNEES DOWN.

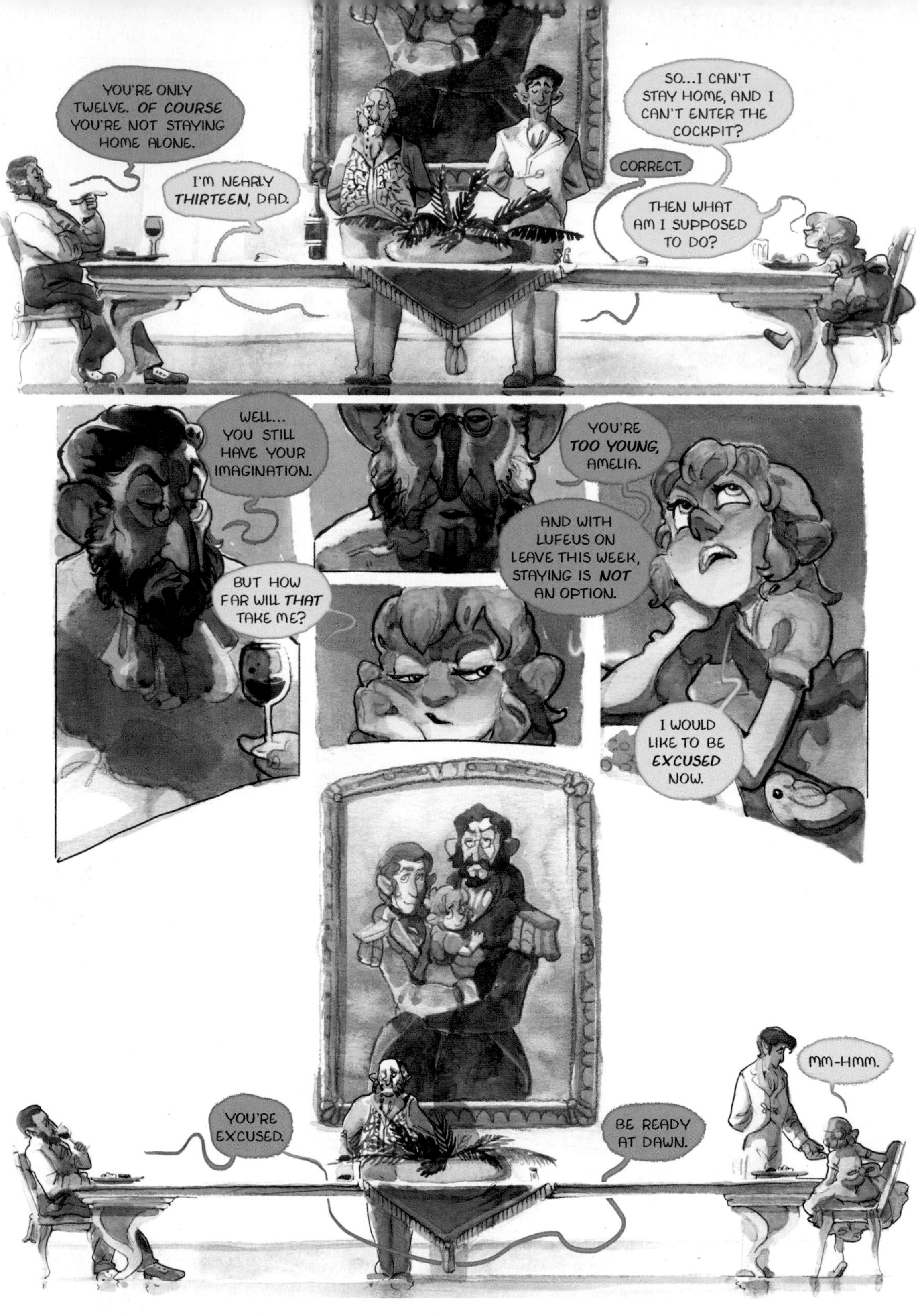

YOU'RE ONLY TWELVE. OF COURSE YOU'RE NOT STAYING HOME ALONE.
I'M NEARLY THIRTEEN, DAD.
SO...I CAN'T STAY HOME, AND I CAN'T ENTER THE COCKPIT?
CORRECT.
THEN WHAT AM I SUPPOSED TO DO?
WELL... YOU STILL HAVE YOUR IMAGINATION.
YOU'RE TOO YOUNG, AMELIA.
AND WITH LUFEUS ON LEAVE THIS WEEK, STAYING IS NOT AN OPTION.
BUT HOW FAR WILL THAT TAKE ME?
I WOULD LIKE TO BE EXCUSED NOW.
YOU'RE EXCUSED.
BE READY AT DAWN.
MM-HMM.

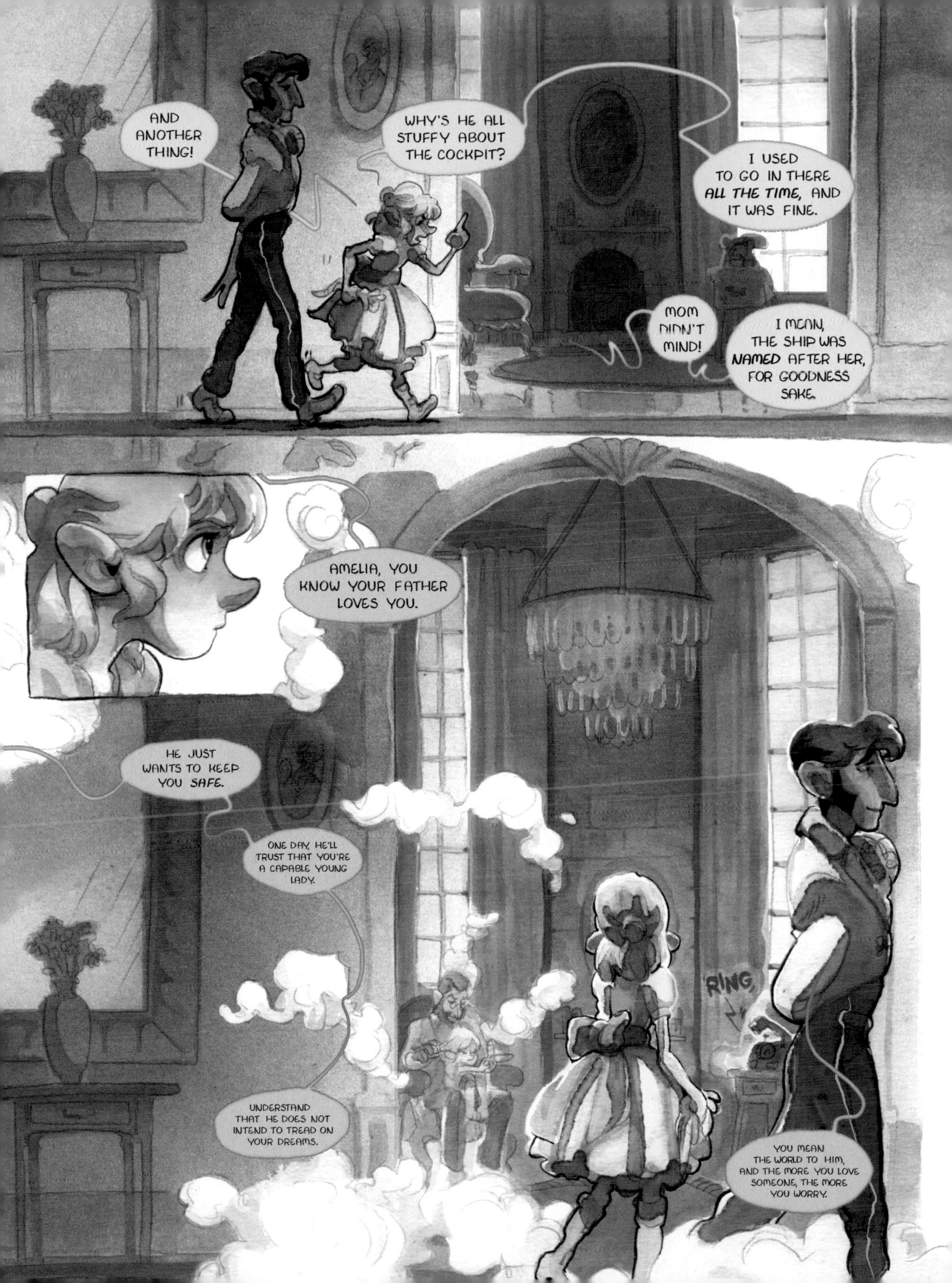
AND ANOTHER THING!
WHY'S HE ALL STUFFY ABOUT THE COCKPIT?
I USED TO GO IN THERE ALL THE TIME, AND IT WAS FINE.
MOM DIDN'T MIND!
I MEAN, THE SHIP WAS NAMED AFTER HER, FOR GOODNESS SAKE.
AMELIA, YOU KNOW YOUR FATHER LOVES YOU.
HE JUST WANTS TO KEEP YOU SAFE.
ONE DAY, HE'LL TRUST THAT YOU'RE A CAPABLE YOUNG LADY.
UNDERSTAND THAT HE DOES NOT INTEND TO TREAD ON YOUR DREAMS.
RING,
YOU MEAN THE WORLD TO HIM, AND THE MORE YOU LOVE SOMEONE, THE MORE YOU WORRY.

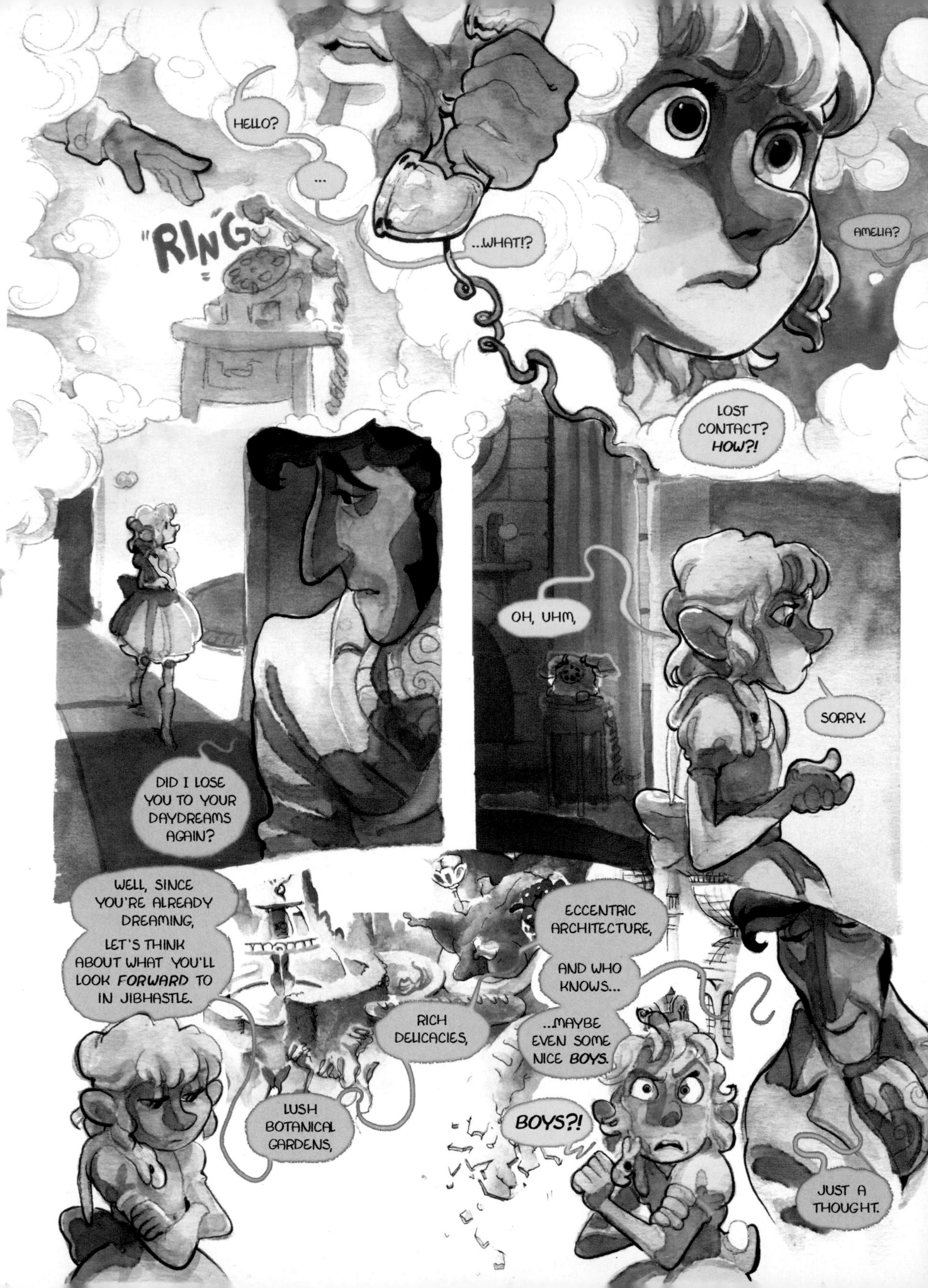
RING
HELLO?
...
...WHAT!?
AMELIA?
LOST CONTACT? HOW?!
DID I LOSE YOU TO YOUR DAYDREAMS AGAIN?
OH, UHM,
SORRY.
WELL, SINCE YOU'RE ALREADY DREAMING,
LET'S THINK ABOUT WHAT YOU'LL LOOK FORWARD TO IN JIBHASTLE.
LUSH BOTANICAL GARDENS,
RICH DELICACIES,
ECCENTRIC ARCHITECTURE,
AND WHO KNOWS...
...MAYBE EVEN SOME NICE BOYS.
BOYS?!
JUST A THOUGHT.

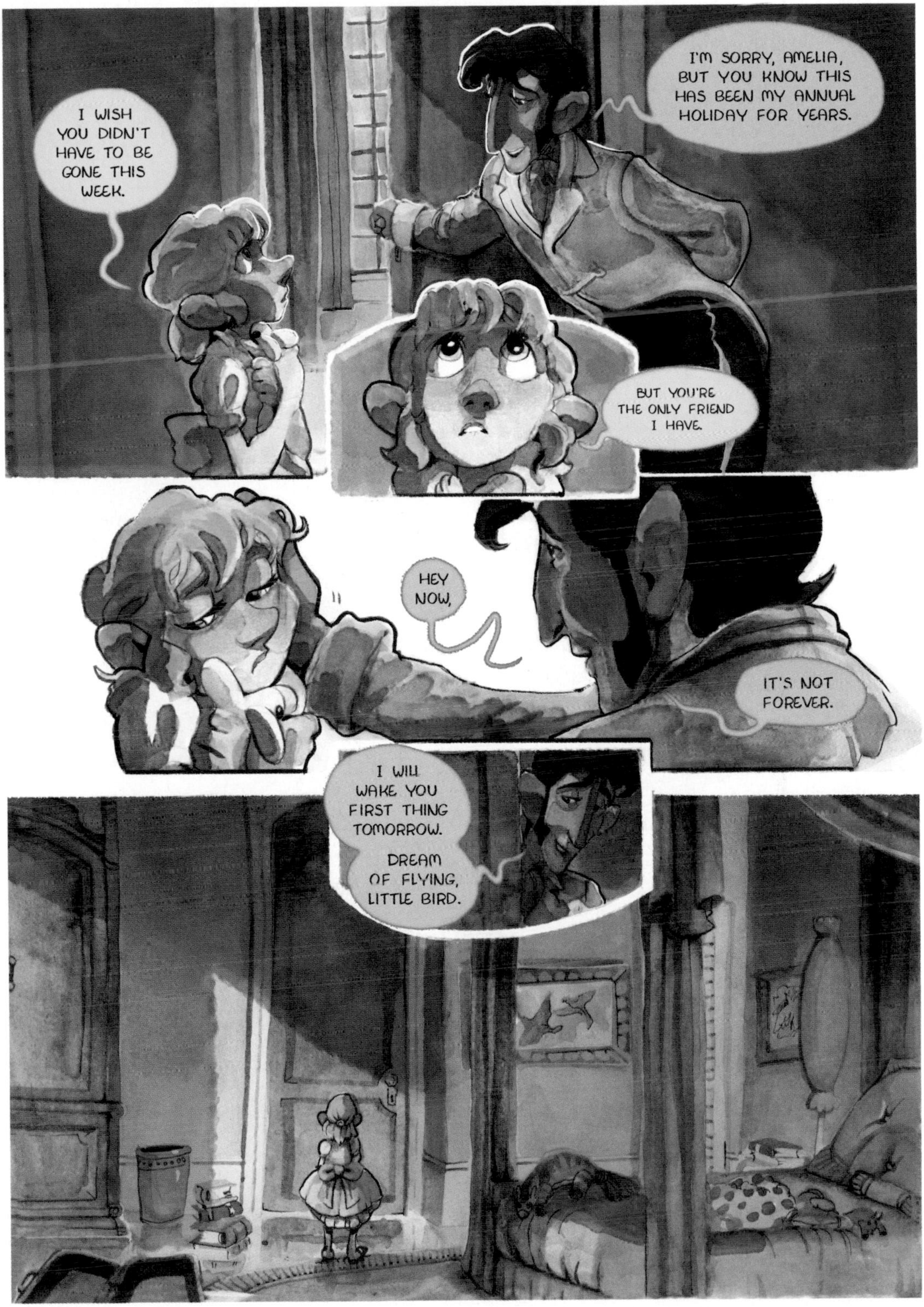
I WISH YOU DIDN'T HAVE TO BE GONE THIS WEEK.
I'M SORRY, AMELIA, BUT YOU KNOW THIS HAS BEEN MY ANNUAL HOLIDAY FOR YEARS.
BUT YOU'RE THE ONLY FRIEND I HAVE.
HEY NOW,
IT'S NOT FOREVER.
I WILL WAKE YOU FIRST THING TOMORROW.
DREAM OF FLYING, LITTLE BIRD.

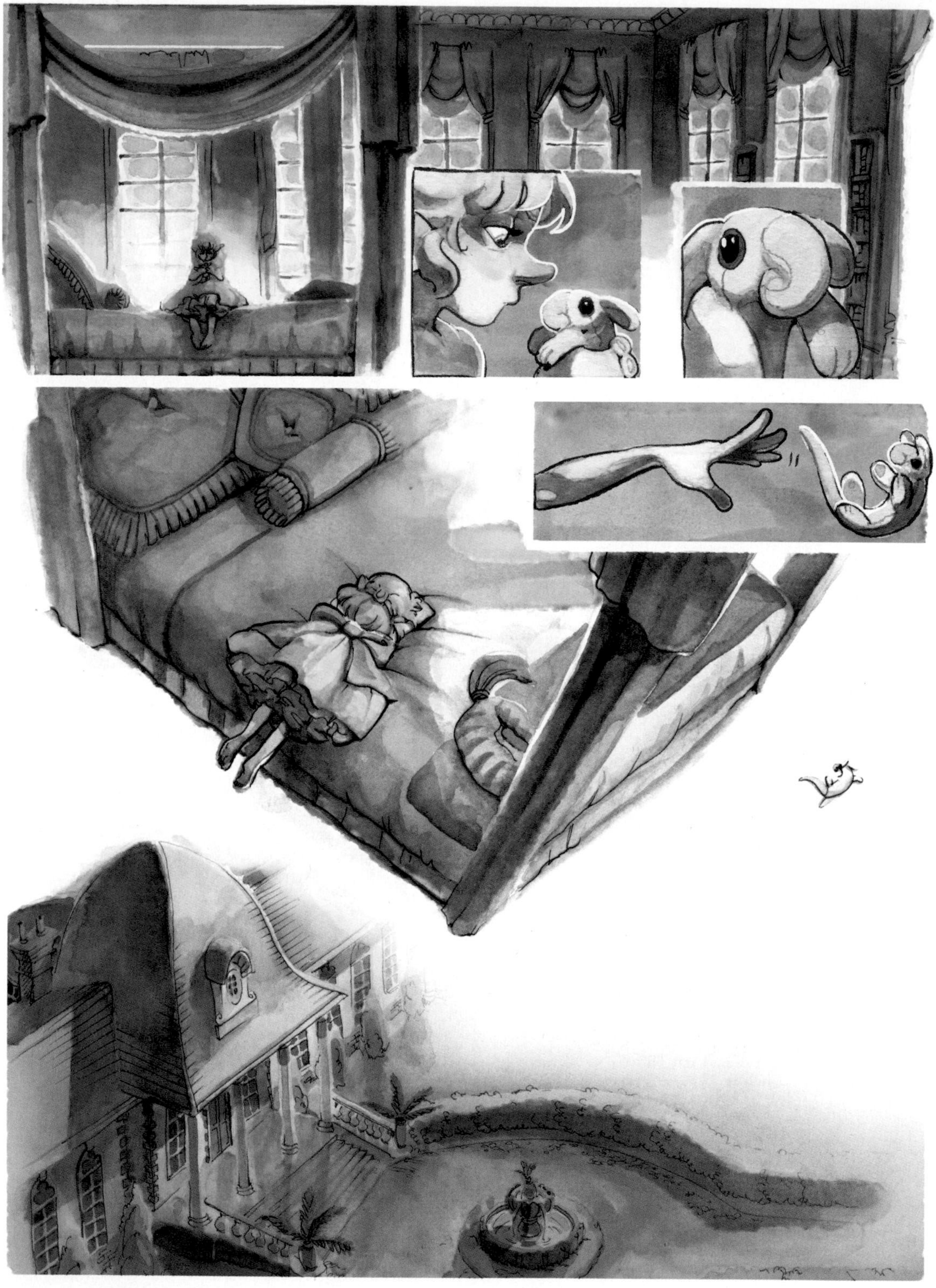

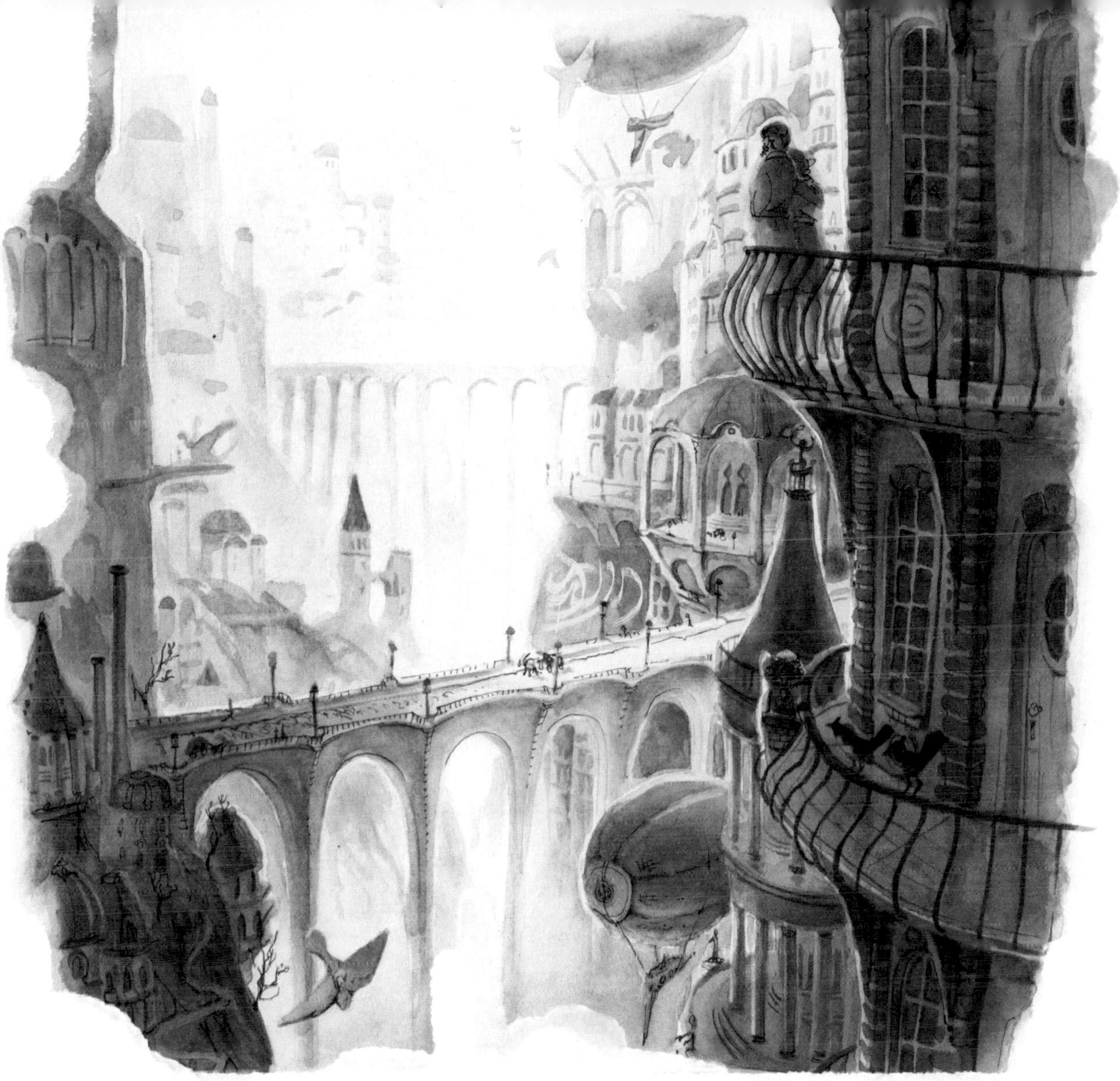

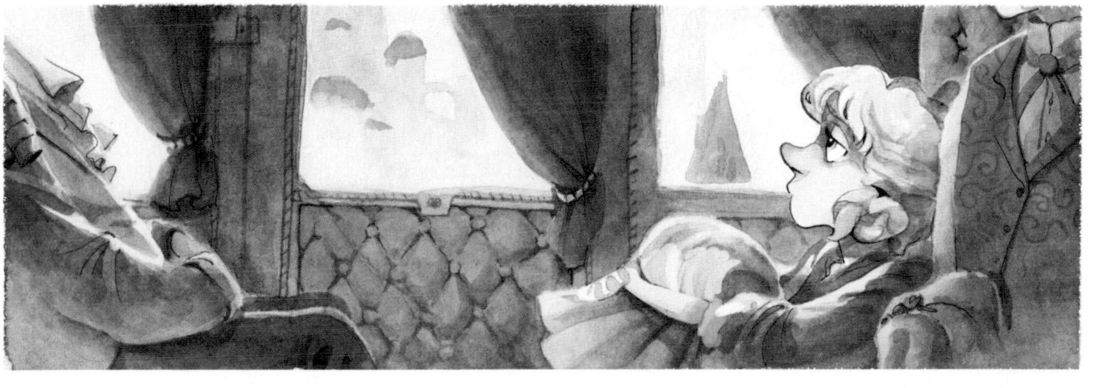

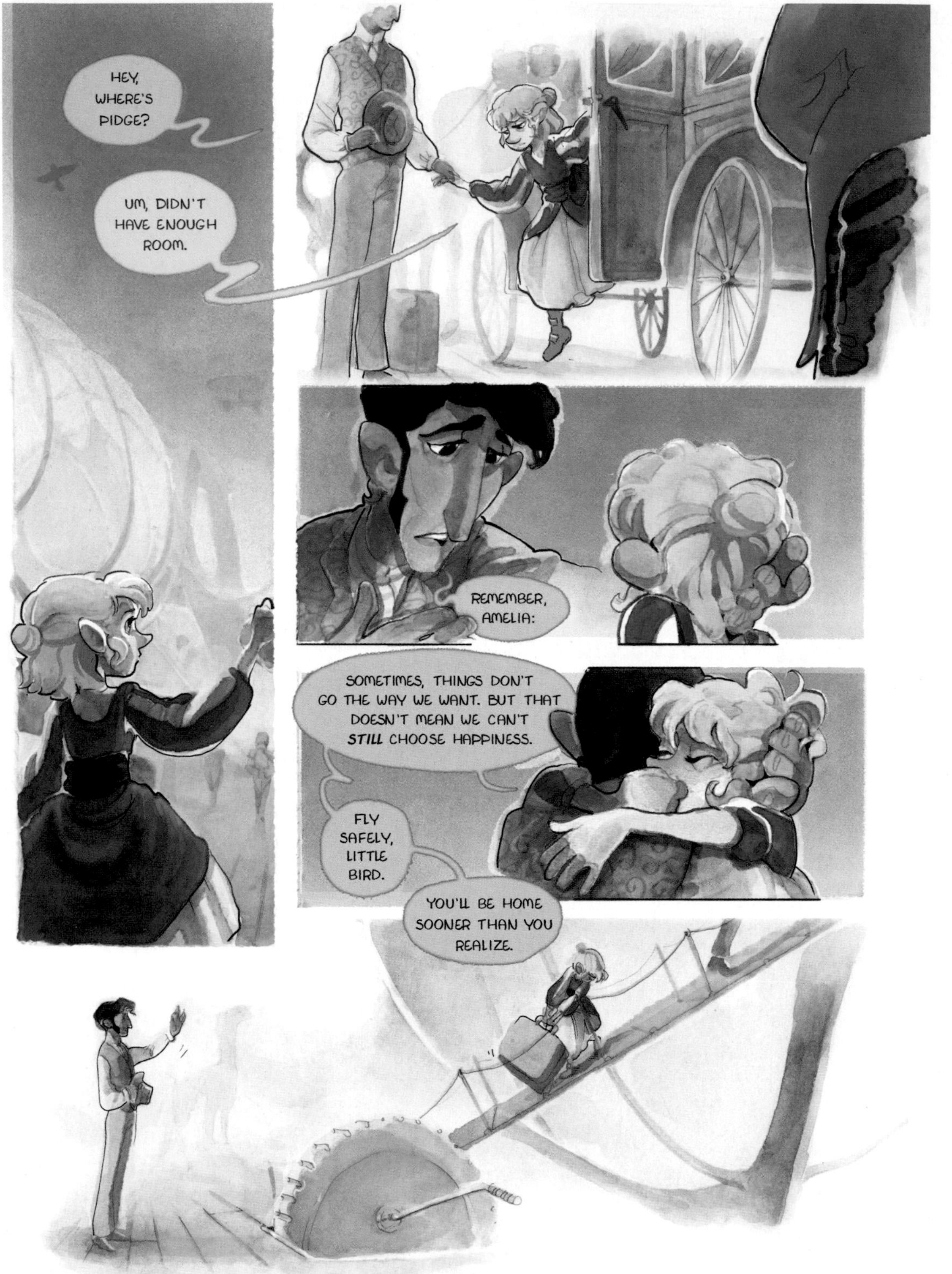
HEY, WHERE'S PIDGE?
UM, DIDN'T HAVE ENOUGH ROOM.
REMEMBER, AMELIA:
SOMETIMES, THINGS DON'T GO THE WAY WE WANT. BUT THAT DOESN'T MEAN WE CAN'T **STILL** CHOOSE HAPPINESS.
FLY SAFELY, LITTLE BIRD.
YOU'LL BE HOME SOONER THAN YOU REALIZE.

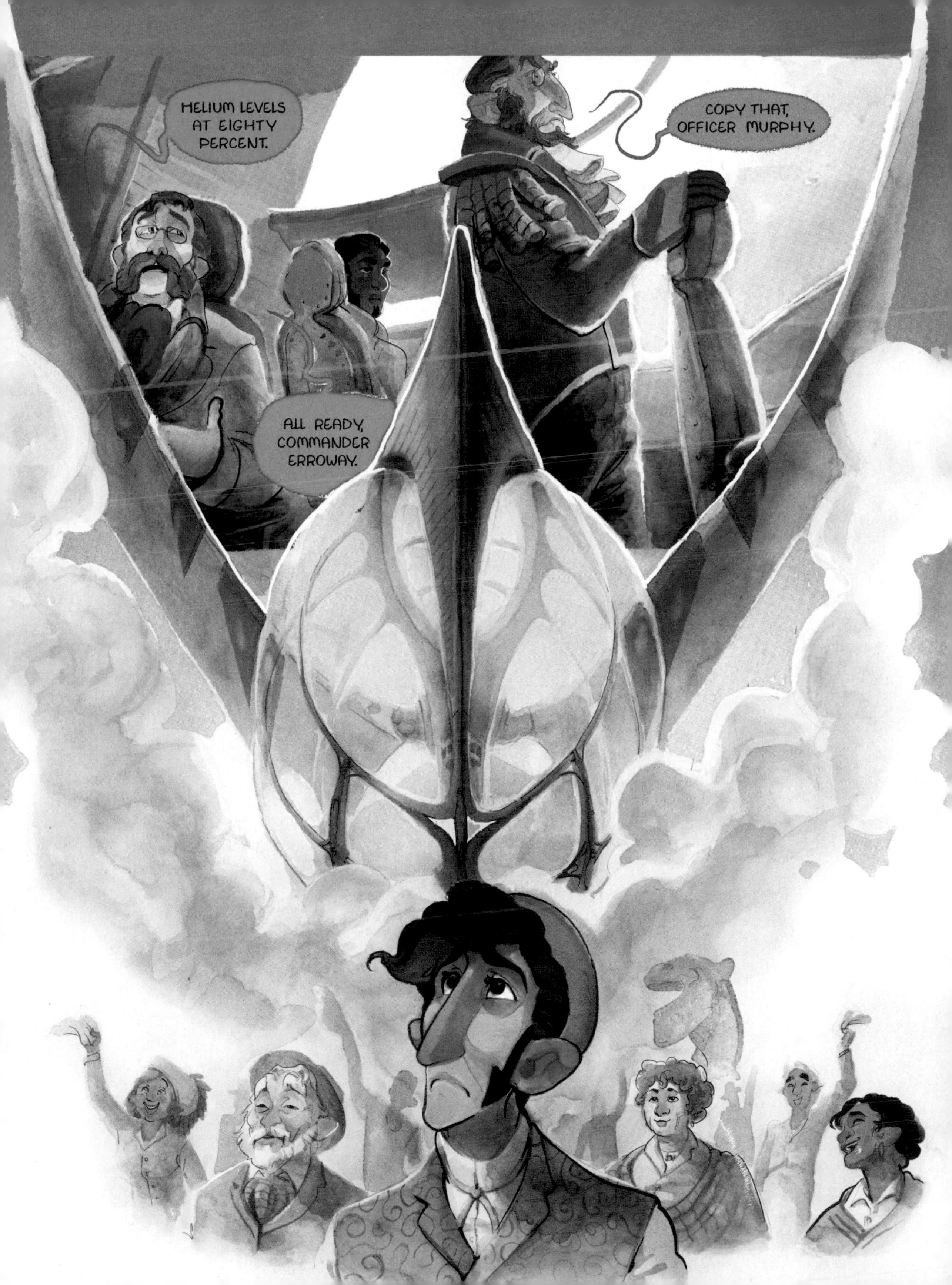
HELIUM LEVELS AT EIGHTY PERCENT.
COPY THAT, OFFICER MURPHY.
ALL READY, COMMANDER ERROWAY.

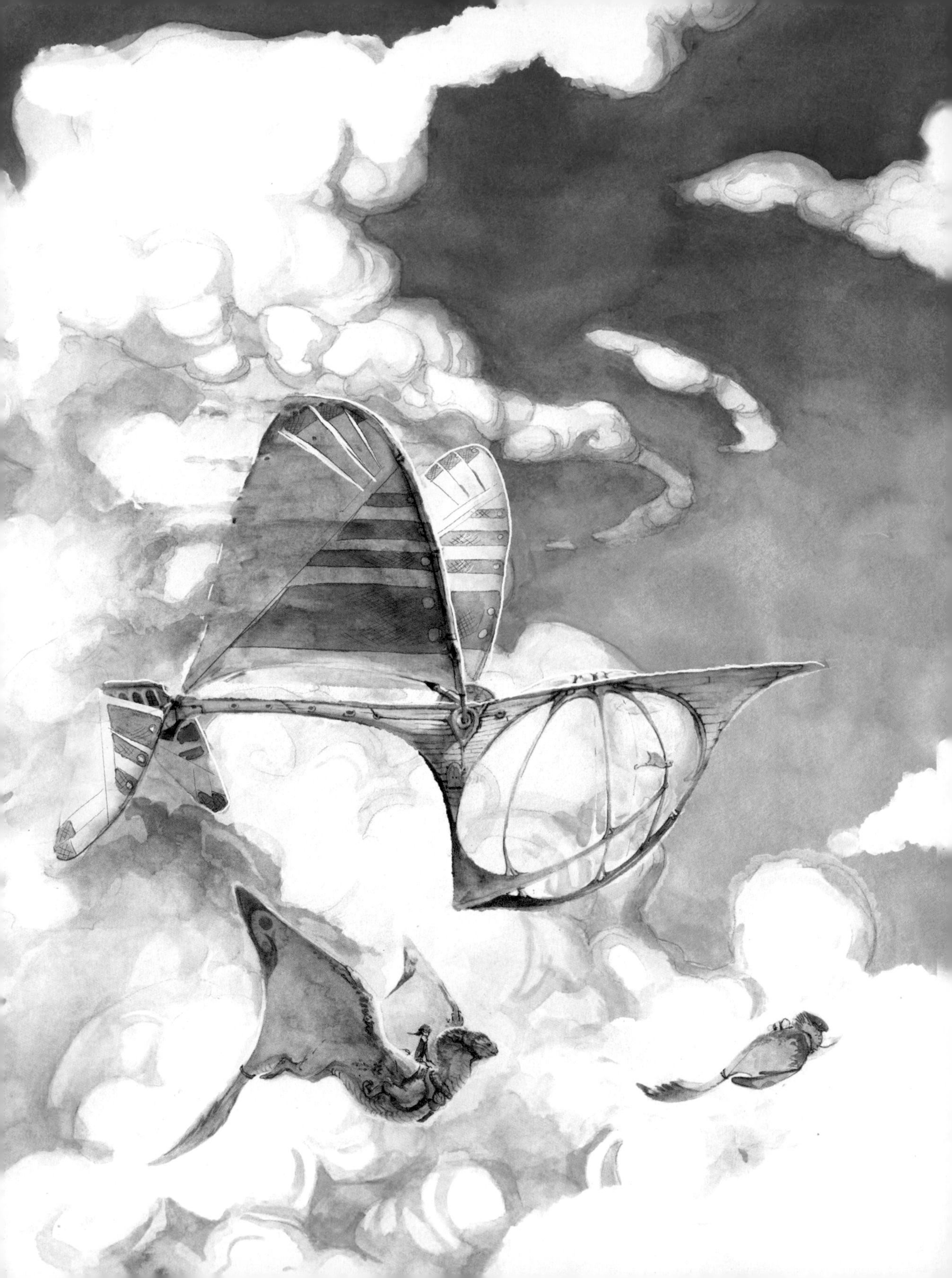

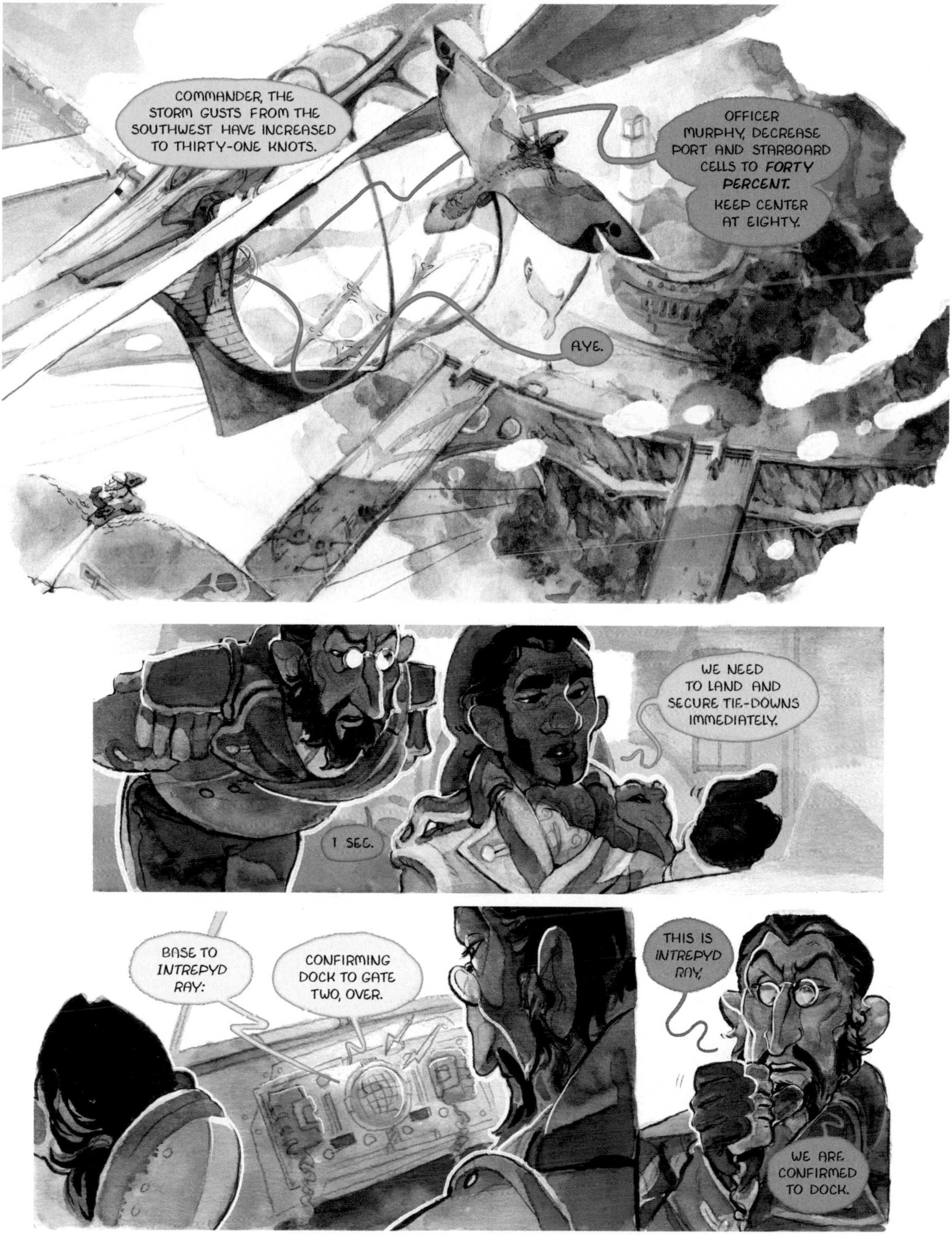
COMMANDER, THE STORM GUSTS FROM THE SOUTHWEST HAVE INCREASED TO THIRTY-ONE KNOTS.
OFFICER MURPHY, DECREASE PORT AND STARBOARD CELLS TO *FORTY PERCENT.*
KEEP CENTER AT EIGHTY.
AYE.
WE NEED TO LAND AND SECURE TIE-DOWNS IMMEDIATELY.
I SEE.
BASE TO *INTREPYD RAY:*
CONFIRMING DOCK TO GATE TWO, OVER.
THIS IS *INTREPYD RAY,*
WE ARE CONFIRMED TO DOCK.

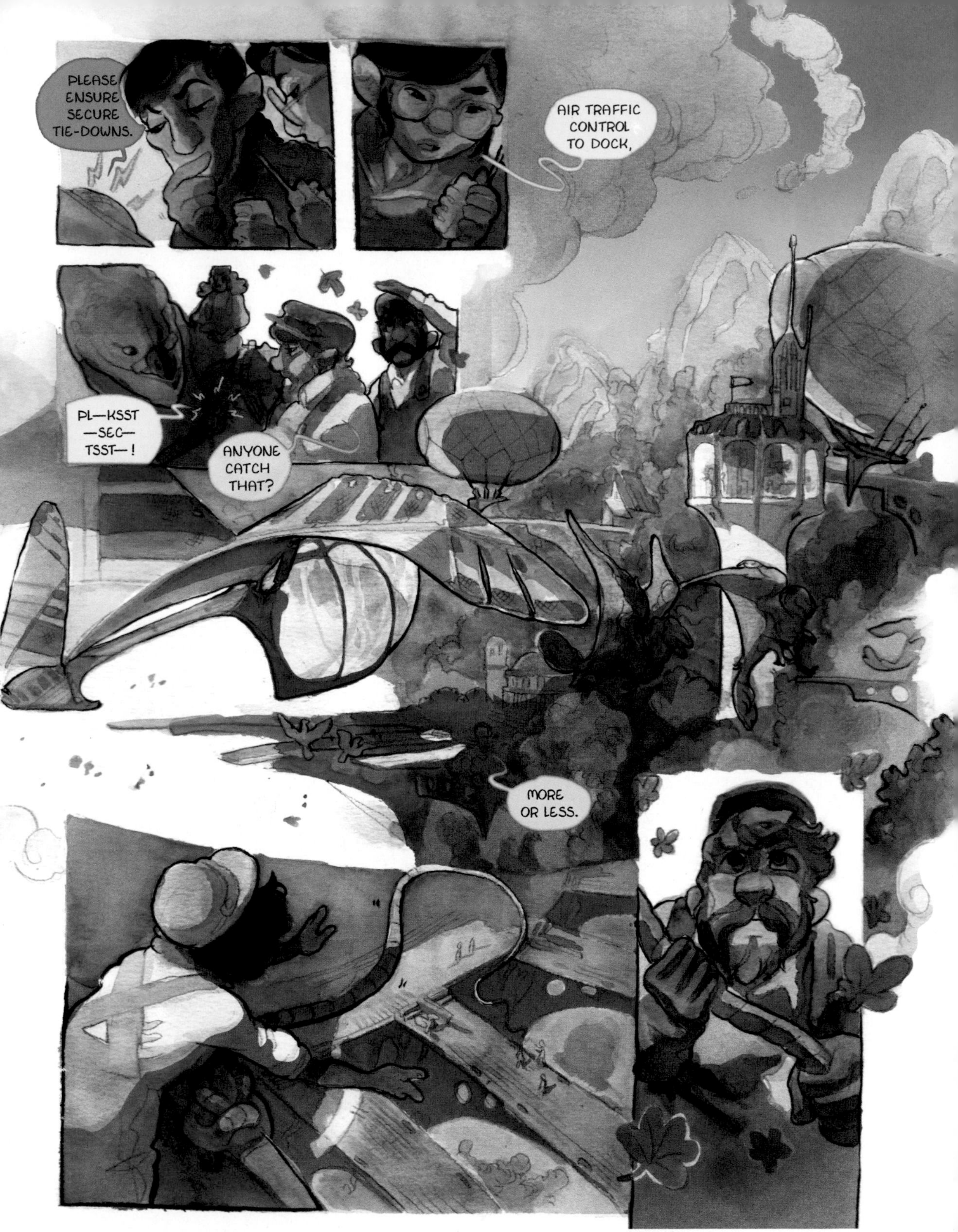

PLEASE ENSURE SECURE TIE-DOWNS.
AIR TRAFFIC CONTROL TO DOCK,
PL—KSST —SEC— TSST—!
ANYONE CATCH THAT?
MORE OR LESS.

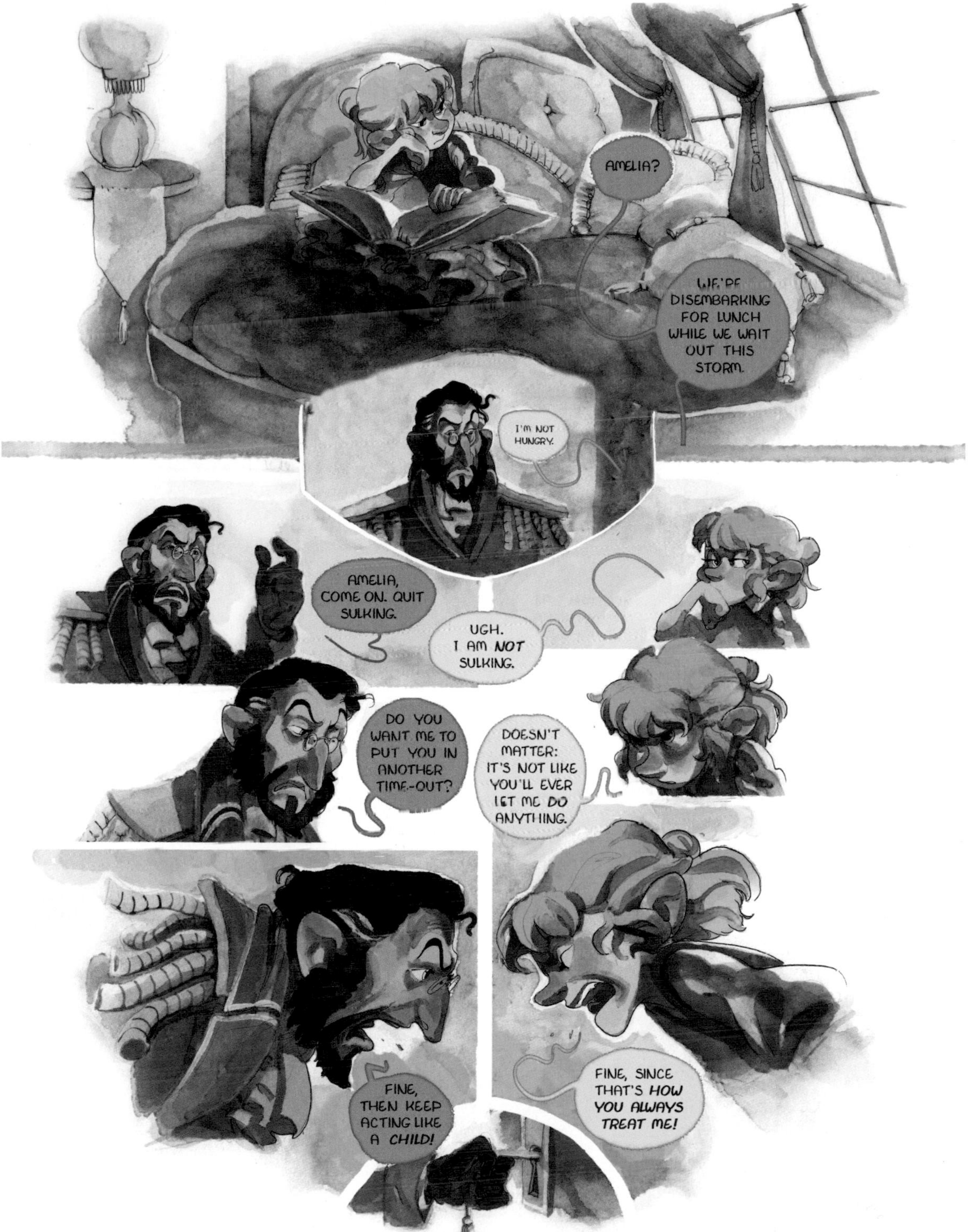
AMELIA?
WE'RE DISEMBARKING FOR LUNCH WHILE WE WAIT OUT THIS STORM.
I'M NOT HUNGRY.
AMELIA, COME ON. QUIT SULKING.
UGH. I AM *NOT* SULKING.
DO YOU WANT ME TO PUT YOU IN ANOTHER TIME-OUT?
DOESN'T MATTER: IT'S NOT LIKE YOU'LL EVER LET ME *DO* ANYTHING.
FINE, THEN KEEP ACTING LIKE A *CHILD!*
FINE, SINCE THAT'S *HOW YOU ALWAYS TREAT ME!*

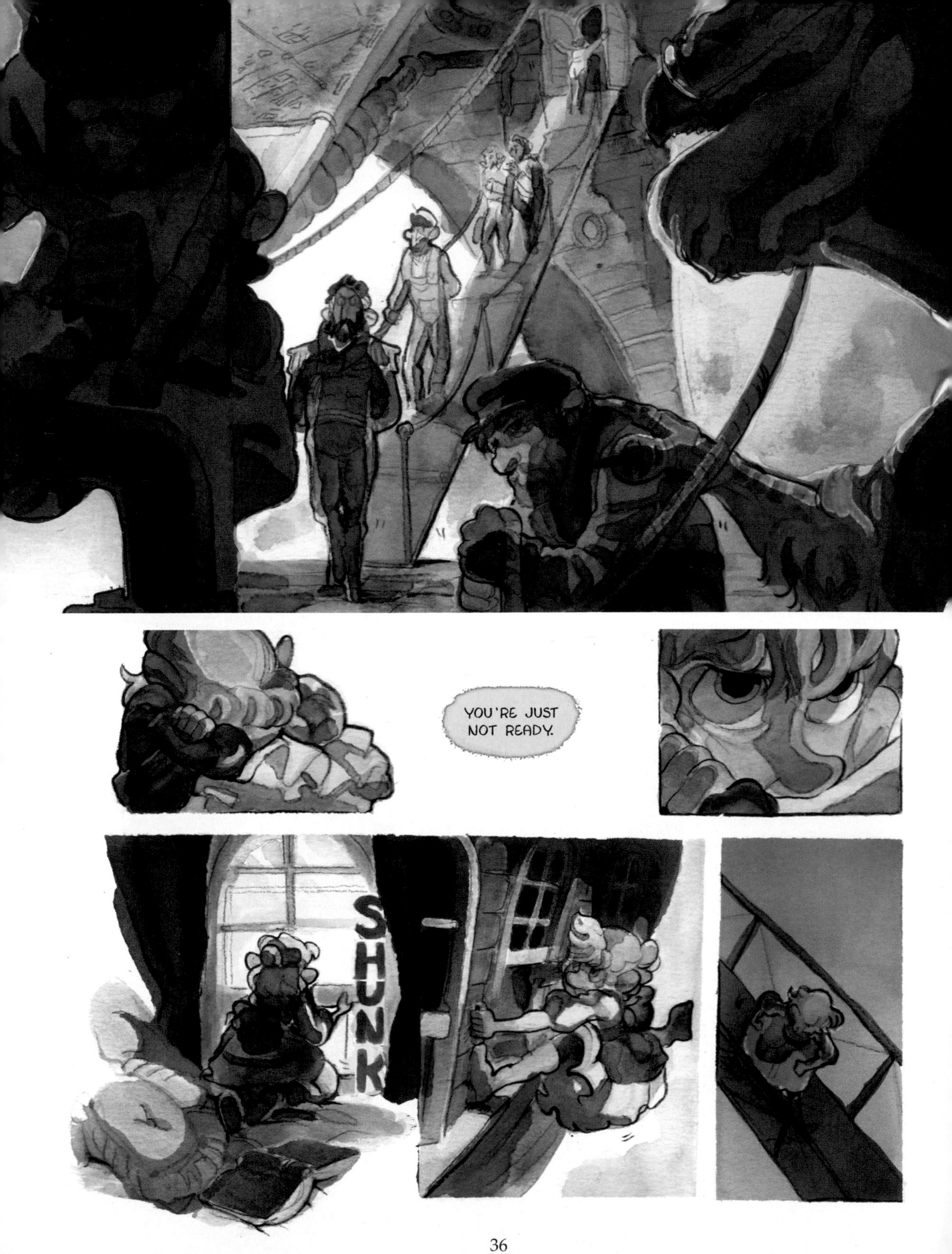
YOU'RE JUST NOT READY.
SHUNK

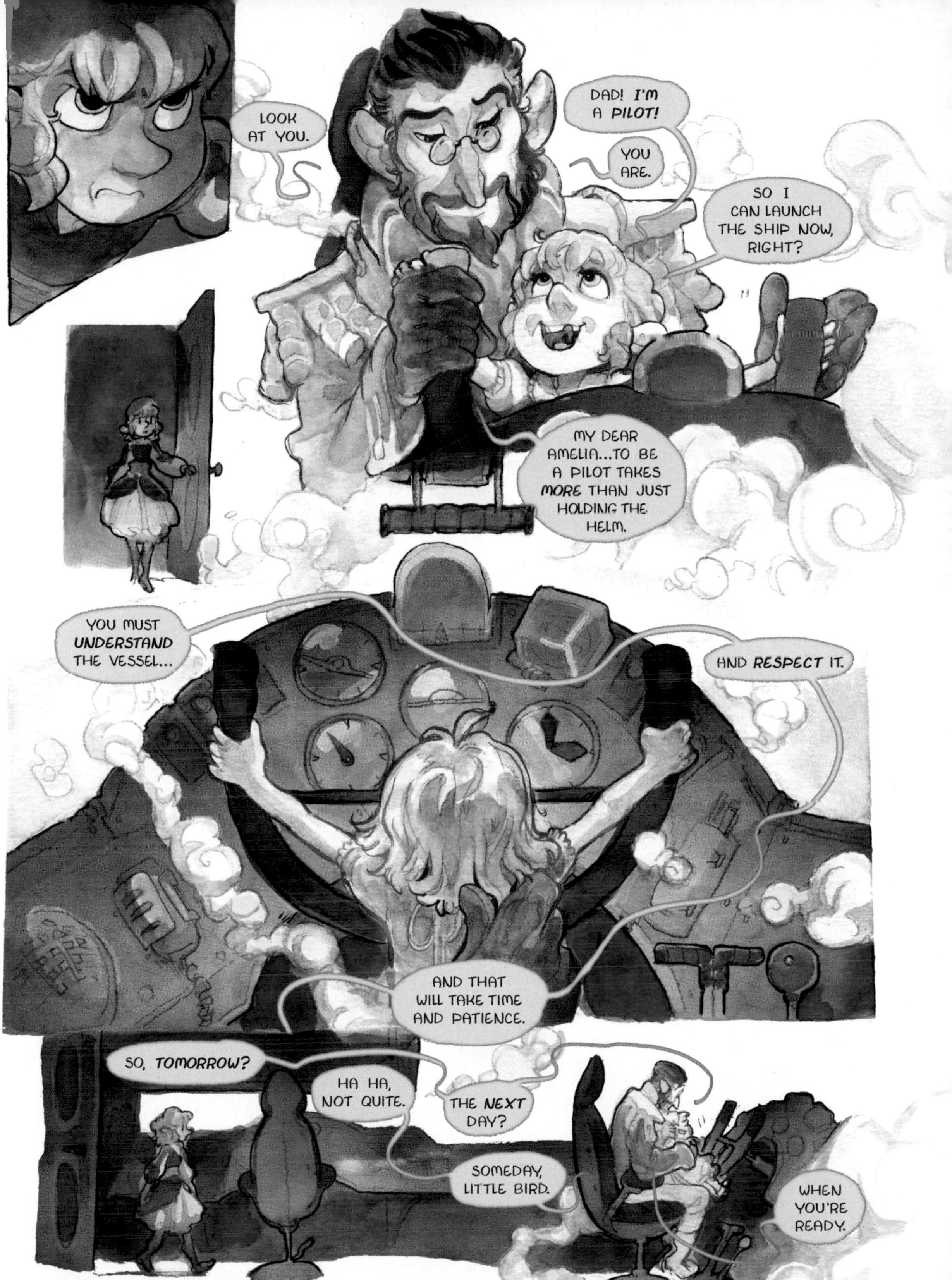
LOOK AT YOU.
DAD! I'M A PILOT!
YOU ARE.
SO I CAN LAUNCH THE SHIP NOW, RIGHT?
MY DEAR AMELIA...TO BE A PILOT TAKES MORE THAN JUST HOLDING THE HELM.
YOU MUST UNDERSTAND THE VESSEL...
AND RESPECT IT.
AND THAT WILL TAKE TIME AND PATIENCE.
SO, TOMORROW?
HA HA, NOT QUITE.
THE NEXT DAY?
SOMEDAY, LITTLE BIRD.
WHEN YOU'RE READY.

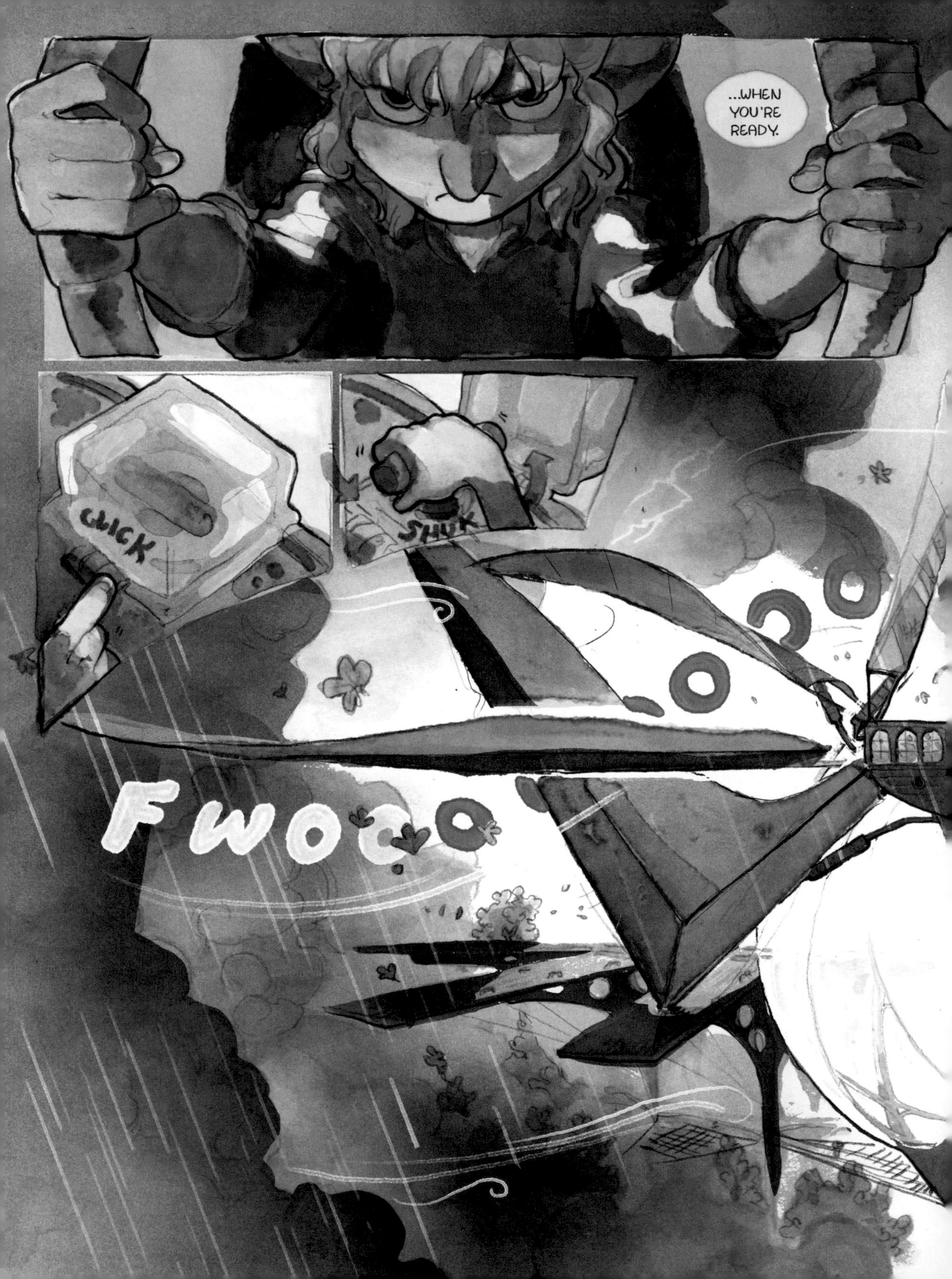
...WHEN YOU'RE READY.
CLICK
SHUK
FWOO

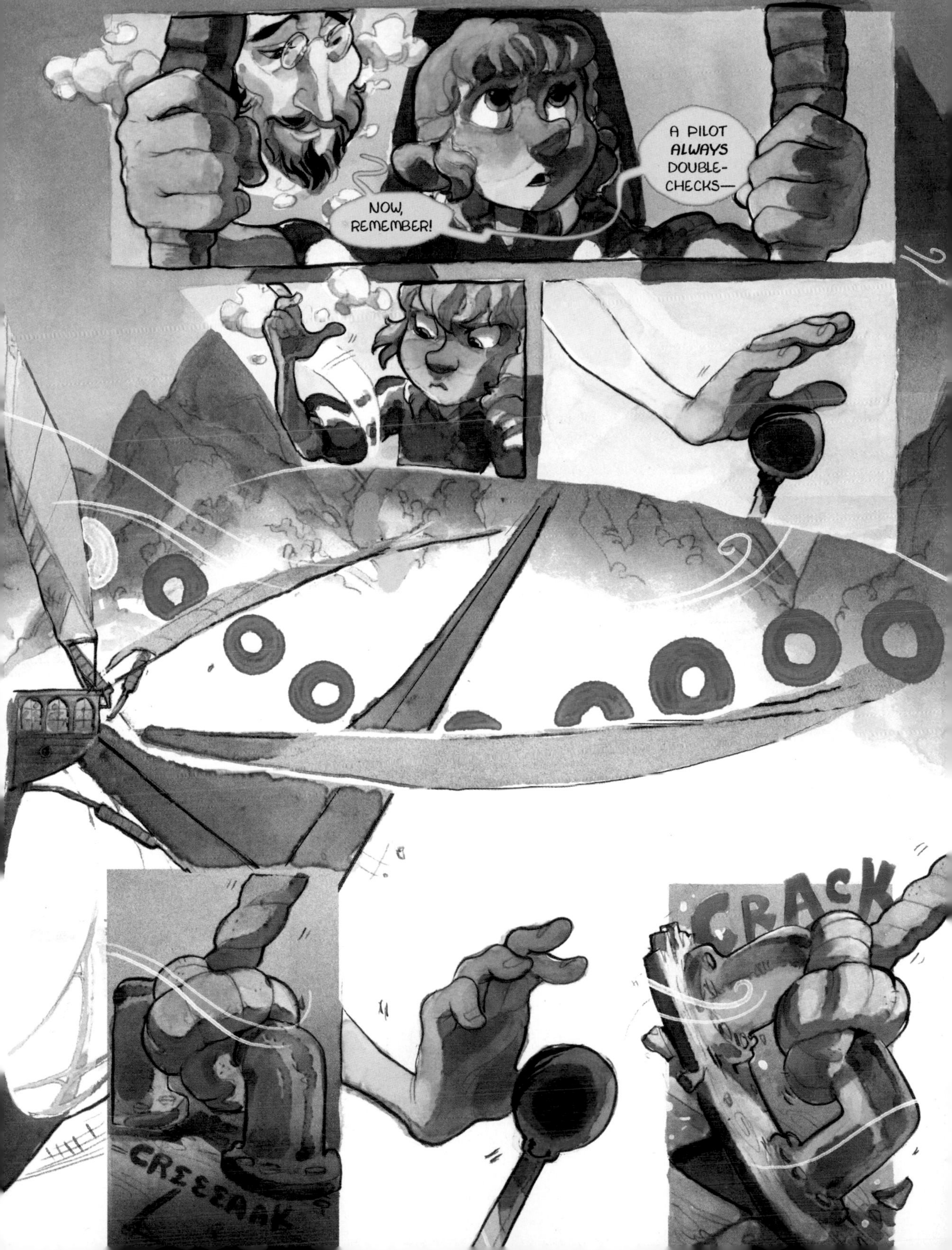
NOW, REMEMBER!
A PILOT ALWAYS DOUBLE-CHECKS—
CREEEAAK
CRACK

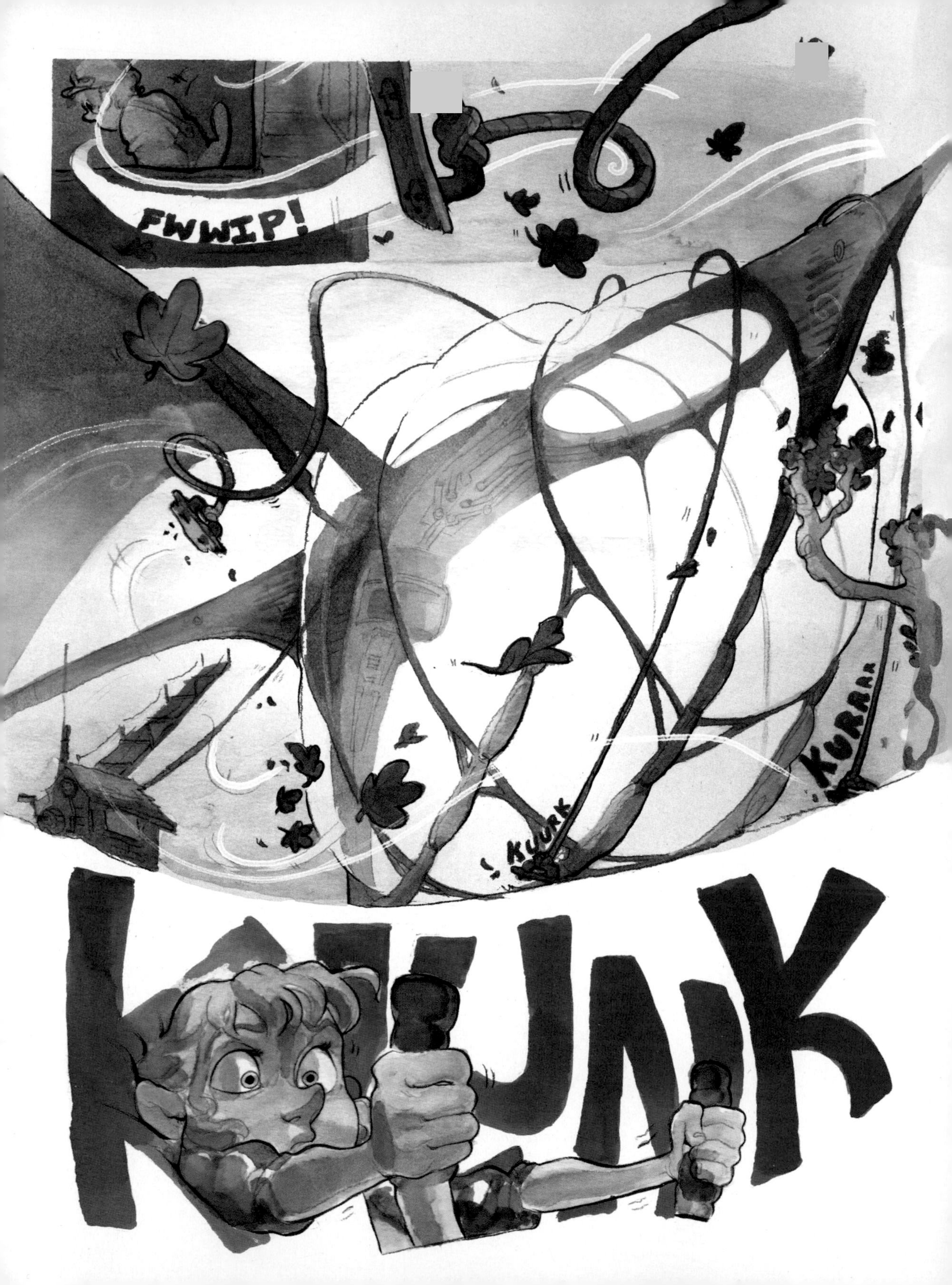
FWWIP!
KURRRR
KUURK

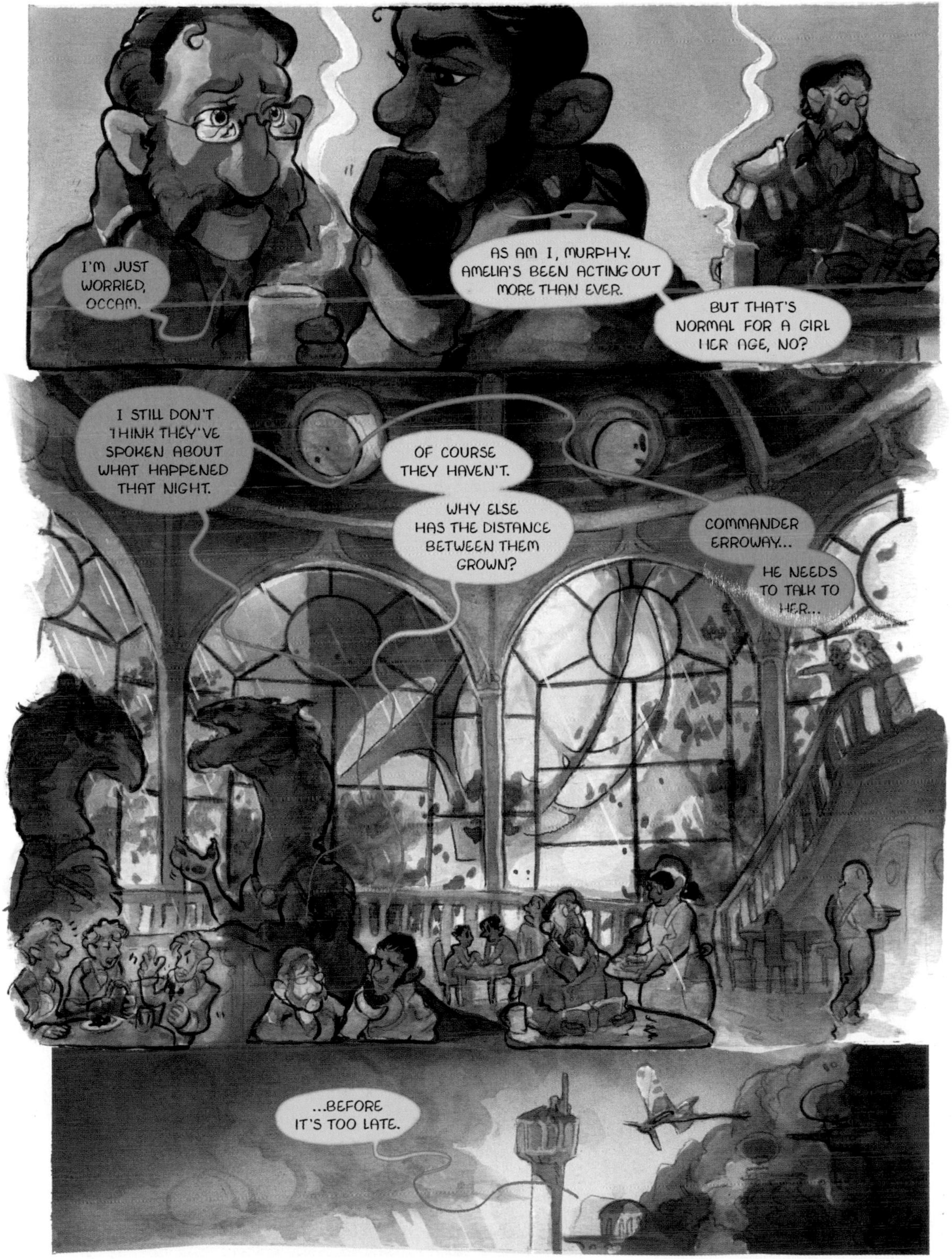
I'M JUST WORRIED, OCCAM.
AS AM I, MURPHY. AMELIA'S BEEN ACTING OUT MORE THAN EVER.
BUT THAT'S NORMAL FOR A GIRL HER AGE, NO?
I STILL DON'T THINK THEY'VE SPOKEN ABOUT WHAT HAPPENED THAT NIGHT.
OF COURSE THEY HAVEN'T.
WHY ELSE HAS THE DISTANCE BETWEEN THEM GROWN?
COMMANDER ERROWAY...
HE NEEDS TO TALK TO HER...
...BEFORE IT'S TOO LATE.

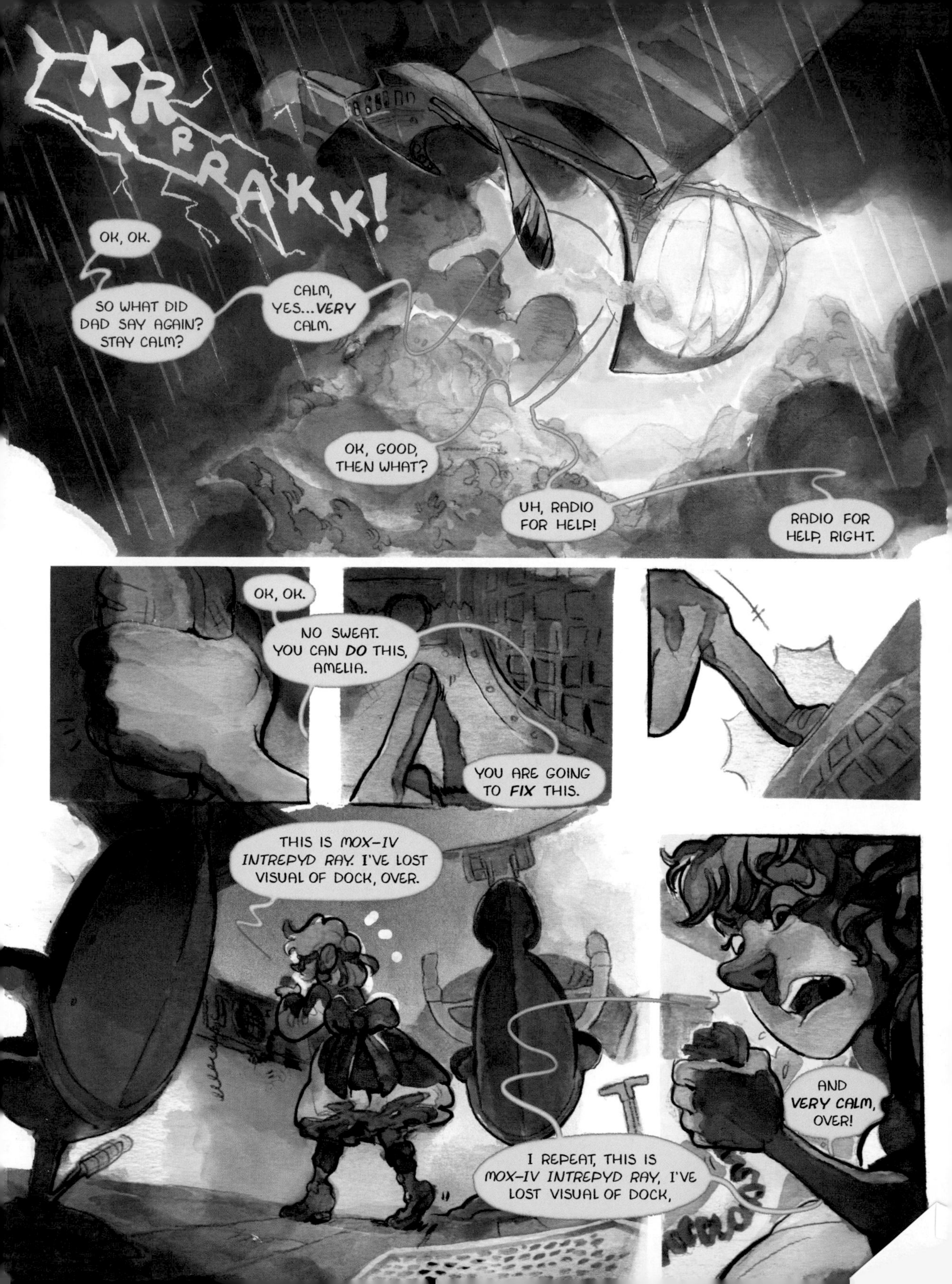
KRRRAKK!
OK, OK.
SO WHAT DID DAD SAY AGAIN? STAY CALM?
CALM, YES...VERY CALM.
OK, GOOD, THEN WHAT?
UH, RADIO FOR HELP!
RADIO FOR HELP, RIGHT.
OK, OK.
NO SWEAT. YOU CAN DO THIS, AMELIA.
YOU ARE GOING TO FIX THIS.
THIS IS MOX-IV INTREPYD RAY. I'VE LOST VISUAL OF DOCK, OVER.
AND VERY CALM, OVER!
I REPEAT, THIS IS MOX-IV INTREPYD RAY, I'VE LOST VISUAL OF DOCK,

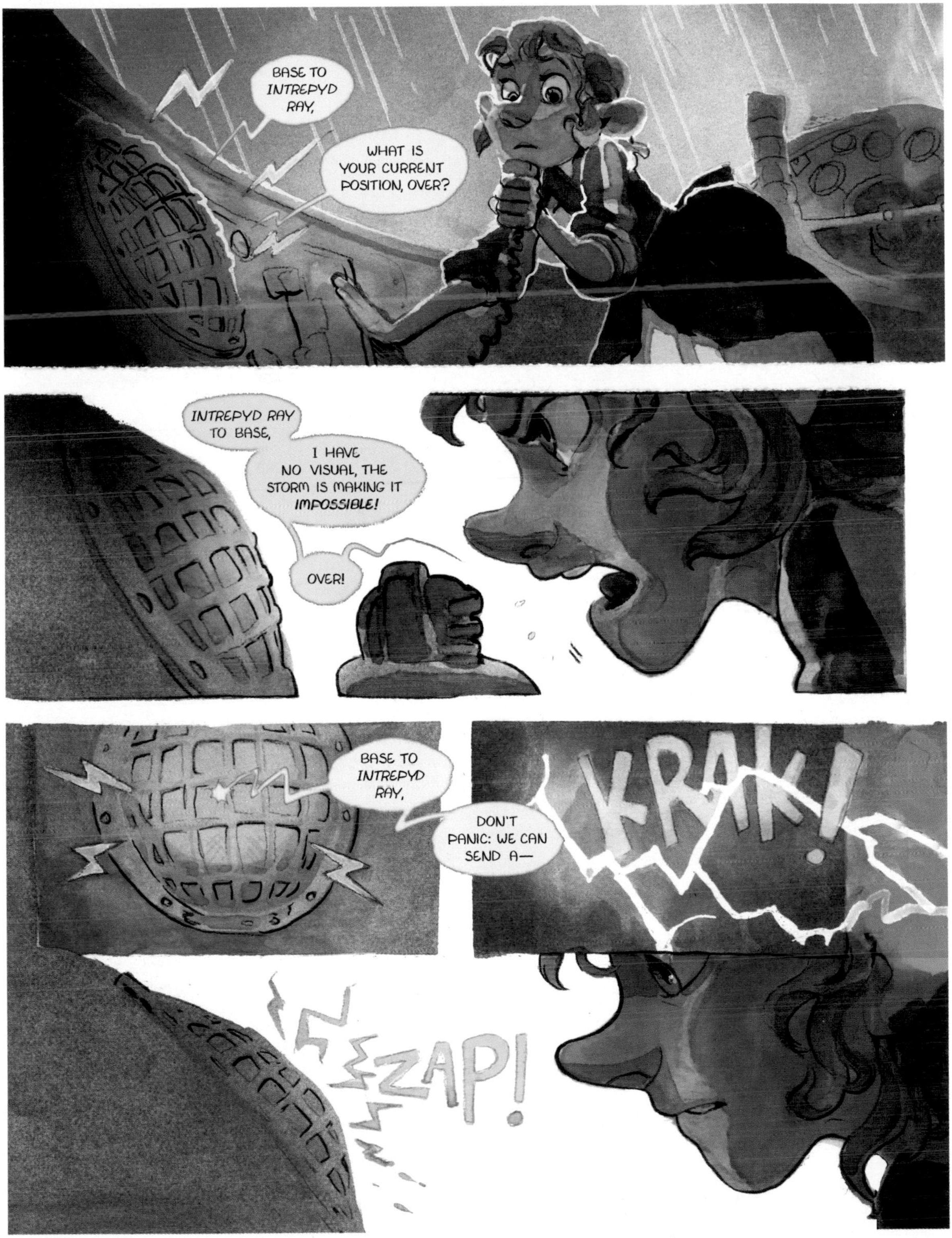
BASE TO INTREPYD RAY,
WHAT IS YOUR CURRENT POSITION, OVER?
INTREPYD RAY TO BASE,
I HAVE NO VISUAL, THE STORM IS MAKING IT *IMPOSSIBLE!*
OVER!
BASE TO INTREPYD RAY,
DON'T PANIC: WE CAN SEND A—
KRAK!
ZAP!

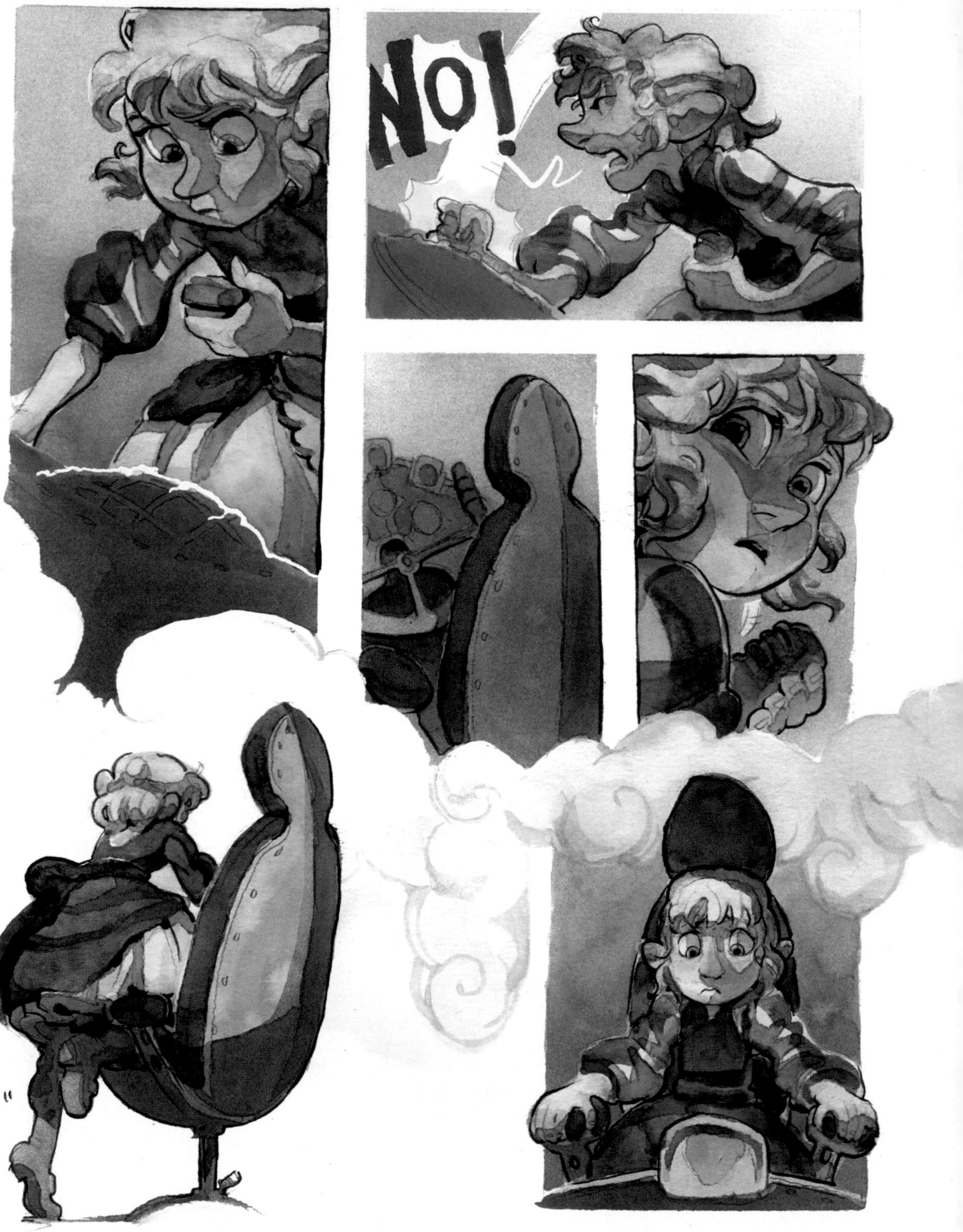
NO!

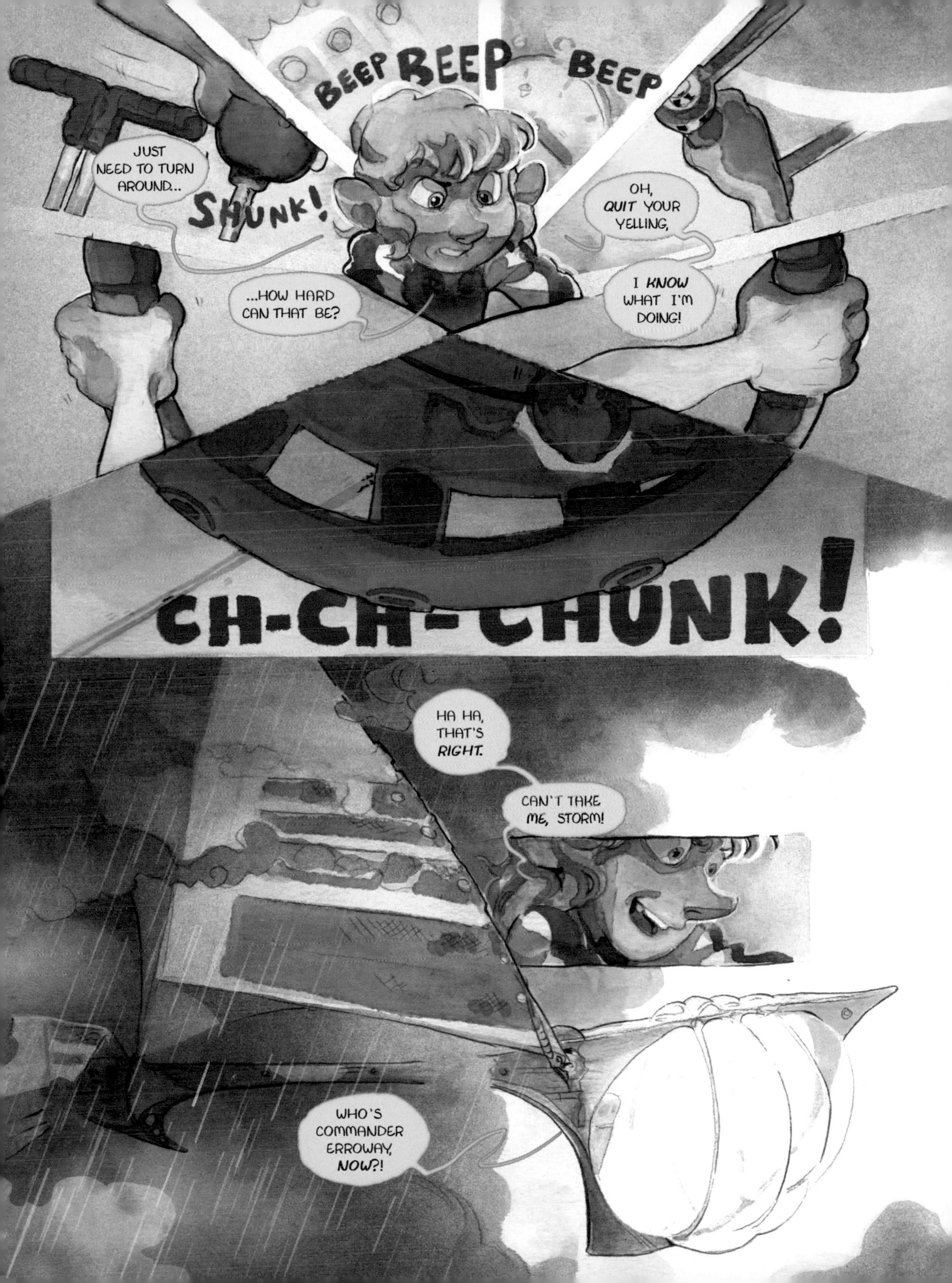
BEEP BEEP BEEP
JUST NEED TO TURN AROUND...
SHUNK!
OH, QUIT YOUR YELLING,
...HOW HARD CAN THAT BE?
I KNOW WHAT I'M DOING!
CH-CH-CHUNK!
HA HA, THAT'S RIGHT.
CAN'T TAKE ME, STORM!
WHO'S COMMANDER ERROWAY, NOW?!

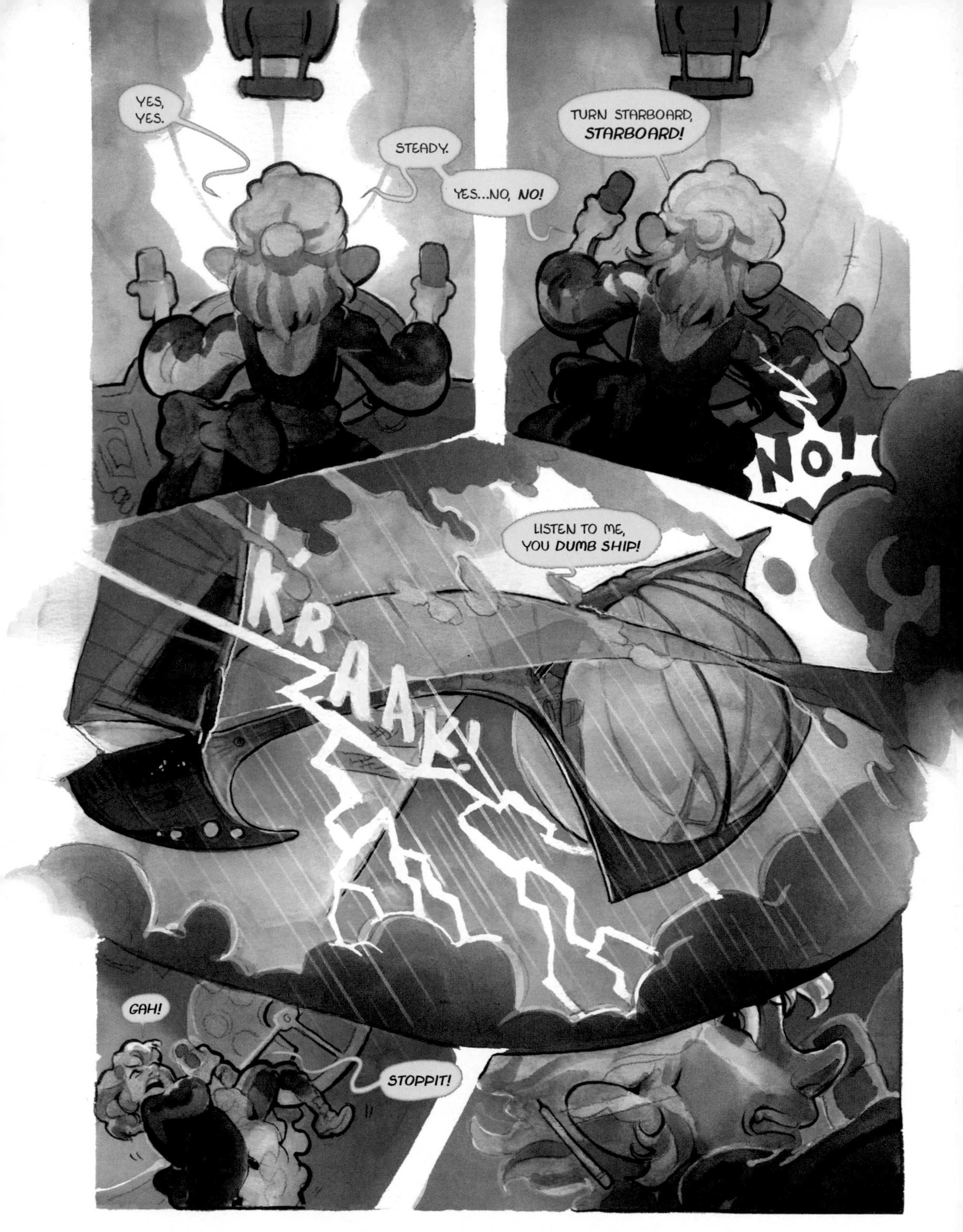
YES,
YES.
STEADY.
YES...NO, NO!
TURN STARBOARD,
STARBOARD!
NO!
LISTEN TO ME,
YOU DUMB SHIP!
KRAAK!
GAH!
STOPPIT!

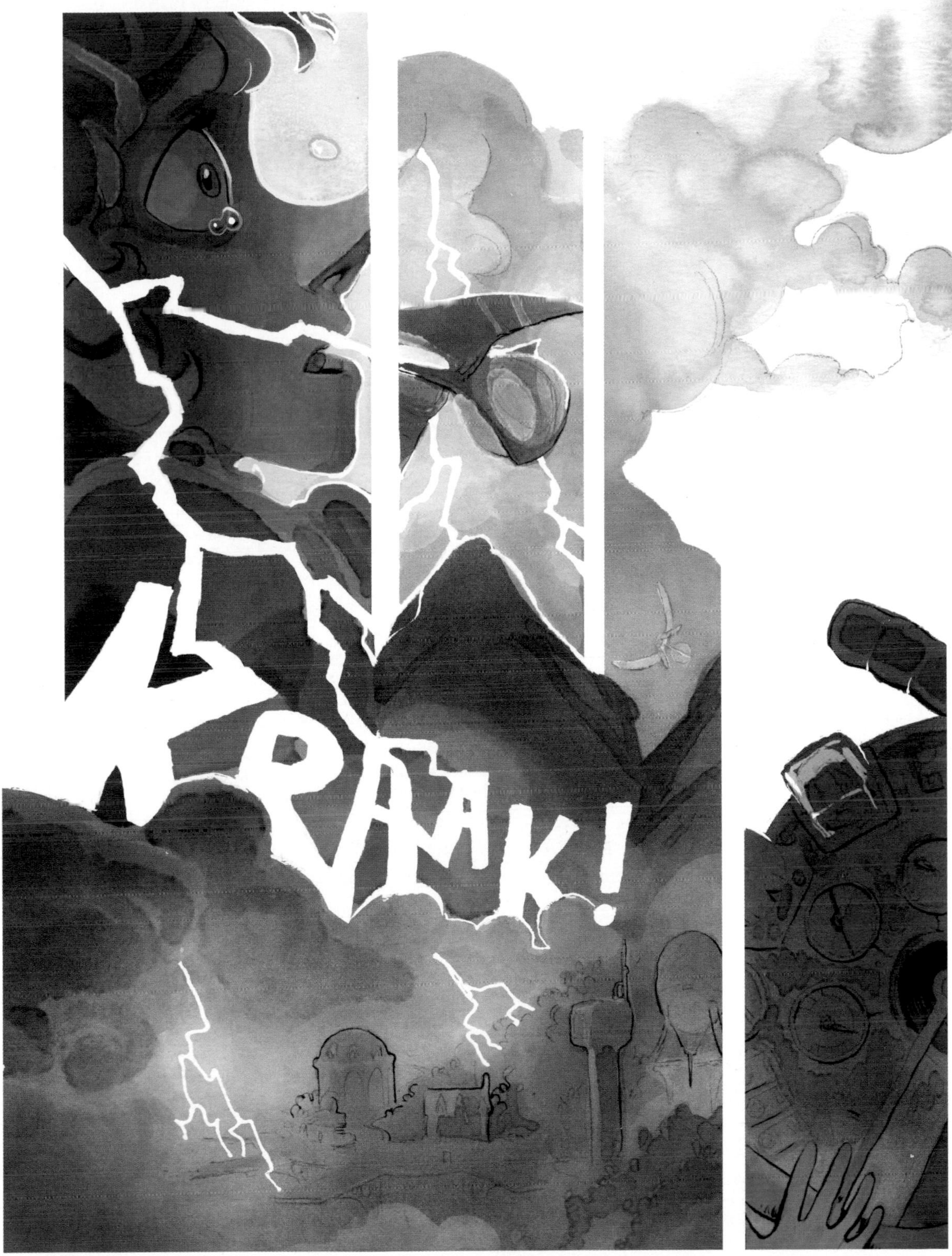
KRAAAK!

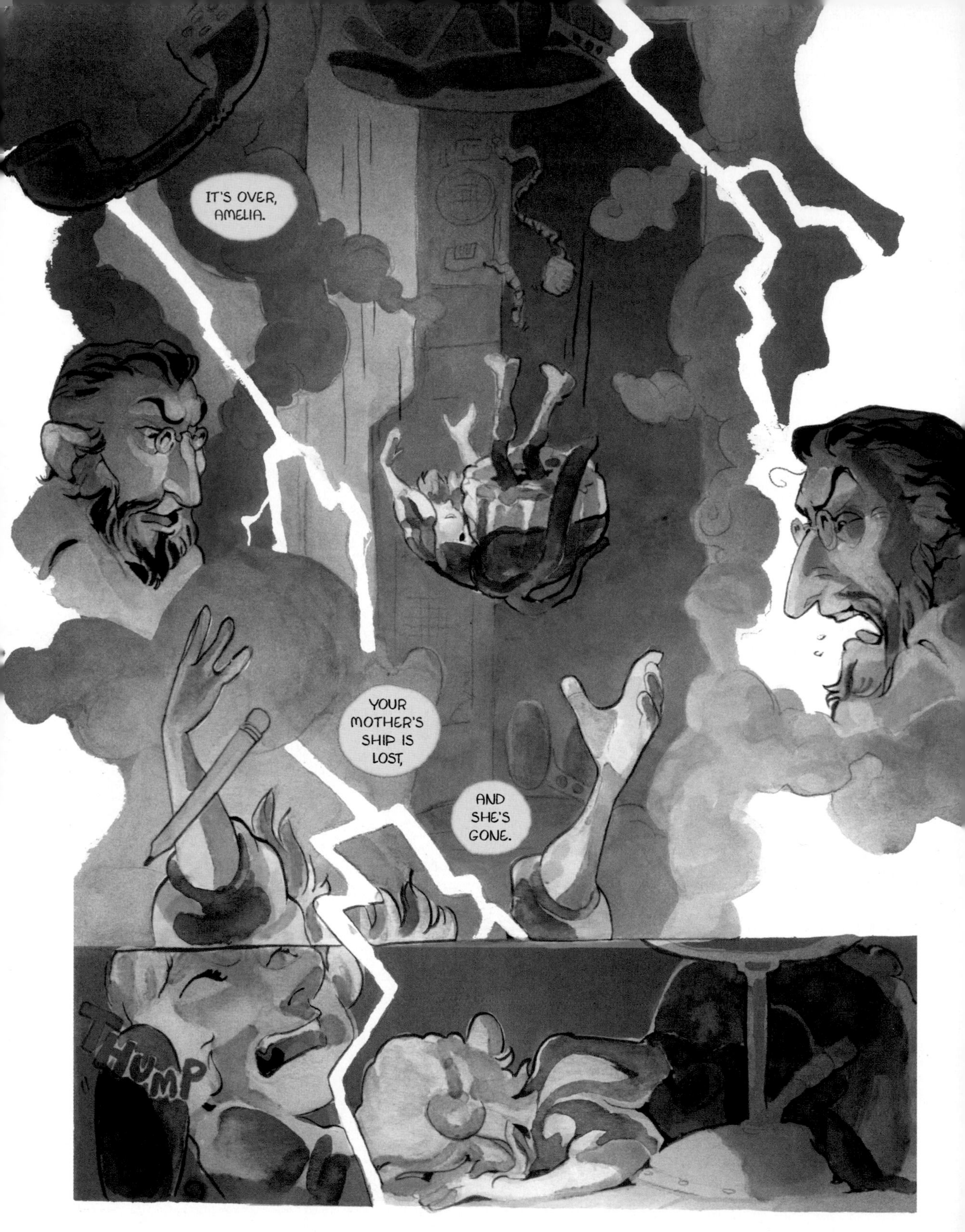
IT'S OVER, AMELIA.
YOUR MOTHER'S SHIP IS LOST,
AND SHE'S GONE.
THUMP

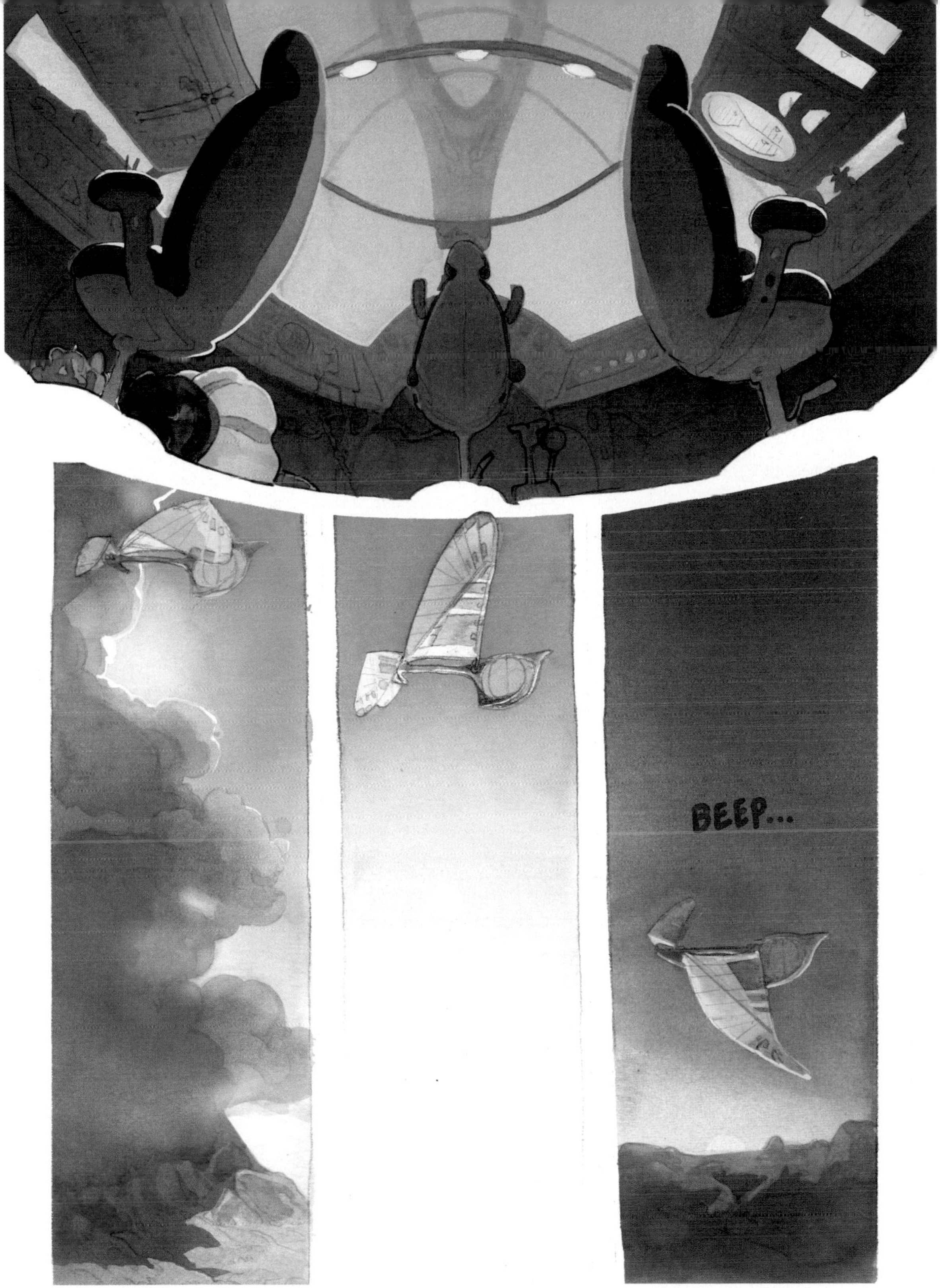
BEEP...

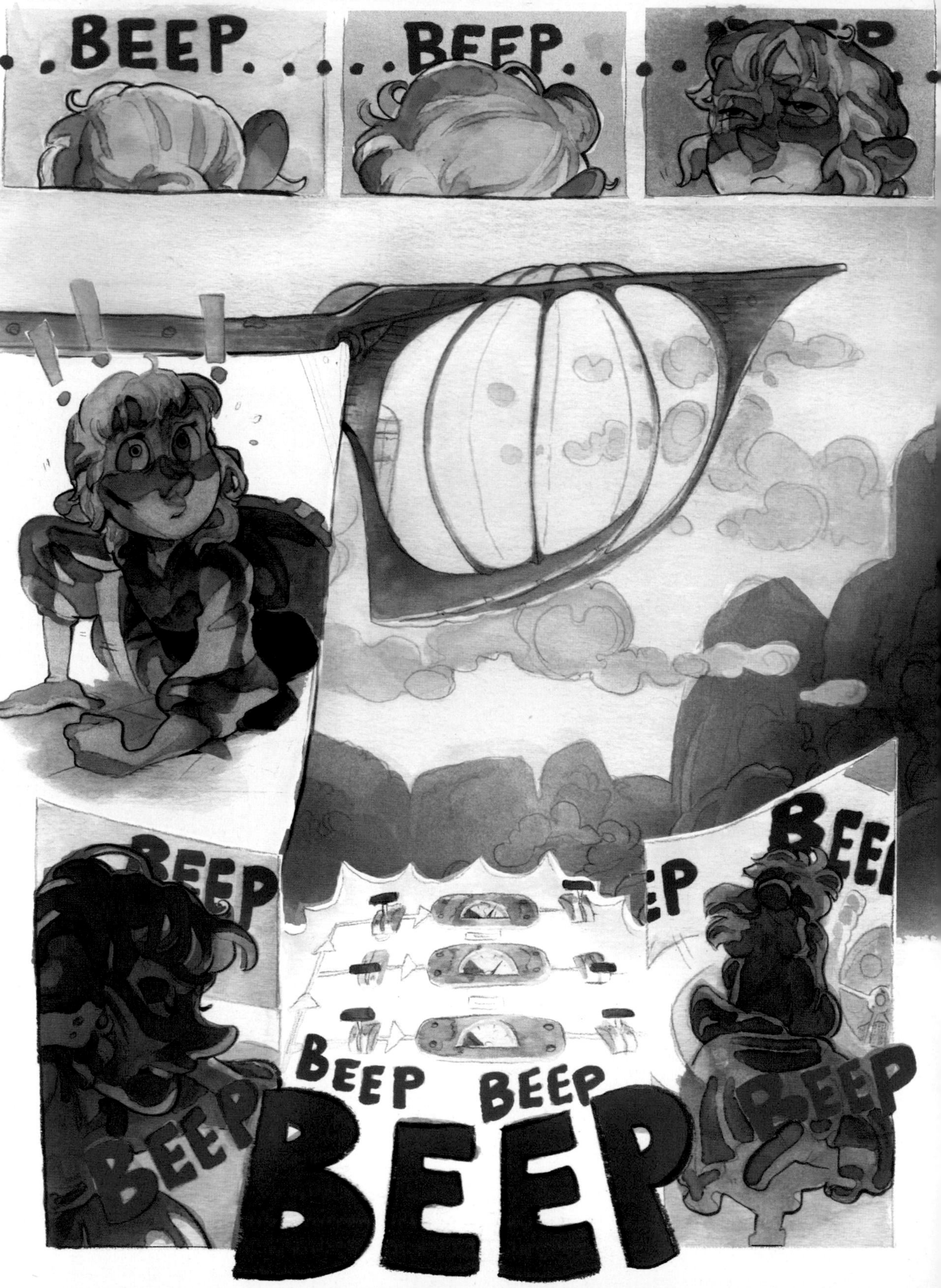
. BEEP.
BEEP.
BEEP BEEP
BEEP

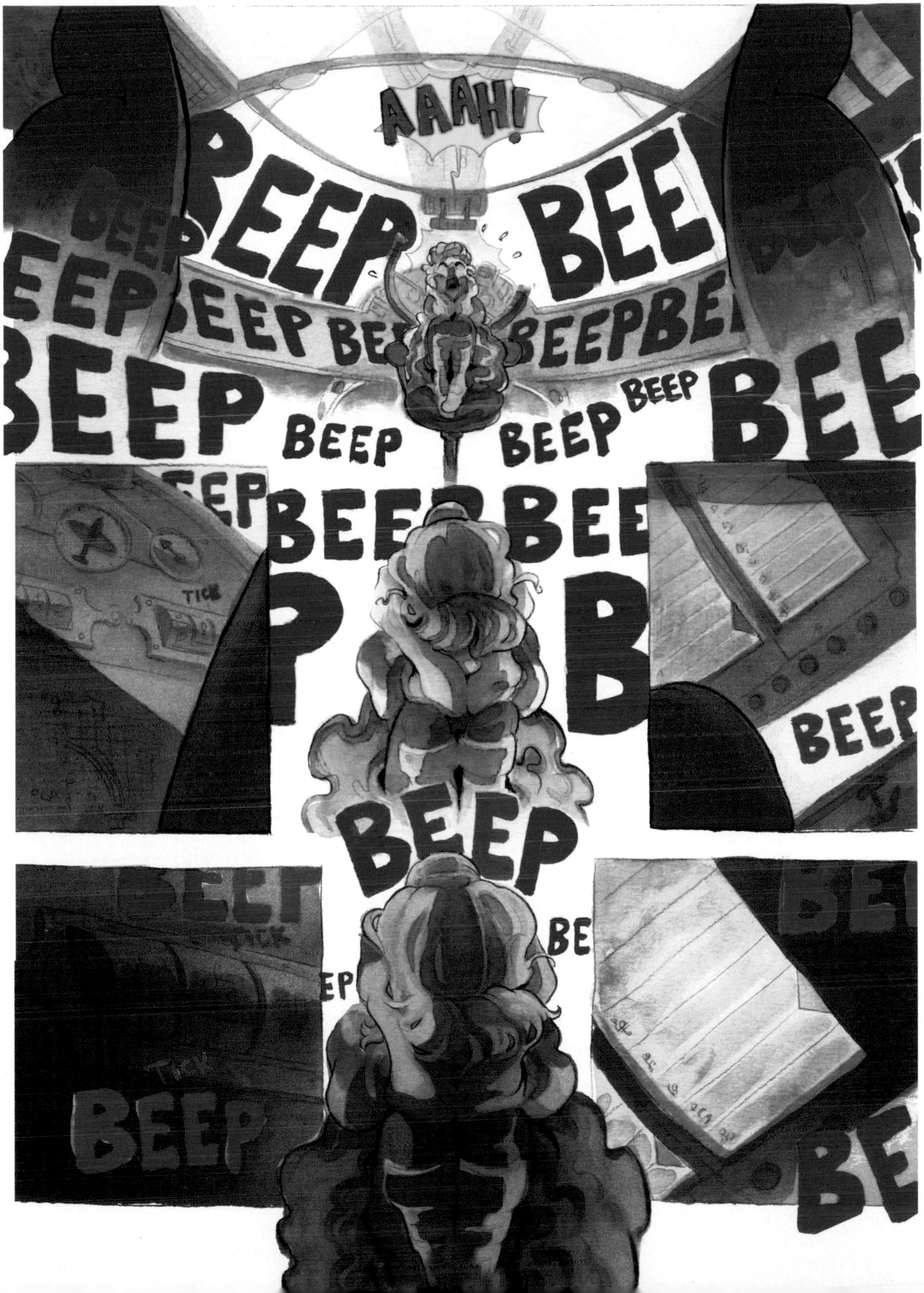
AAAH!
BEEP
BEEP
BEEP
BEEP
BEEP
BEEP
BEEP
TICK
BEEP
BEEP
TICK
BEEP

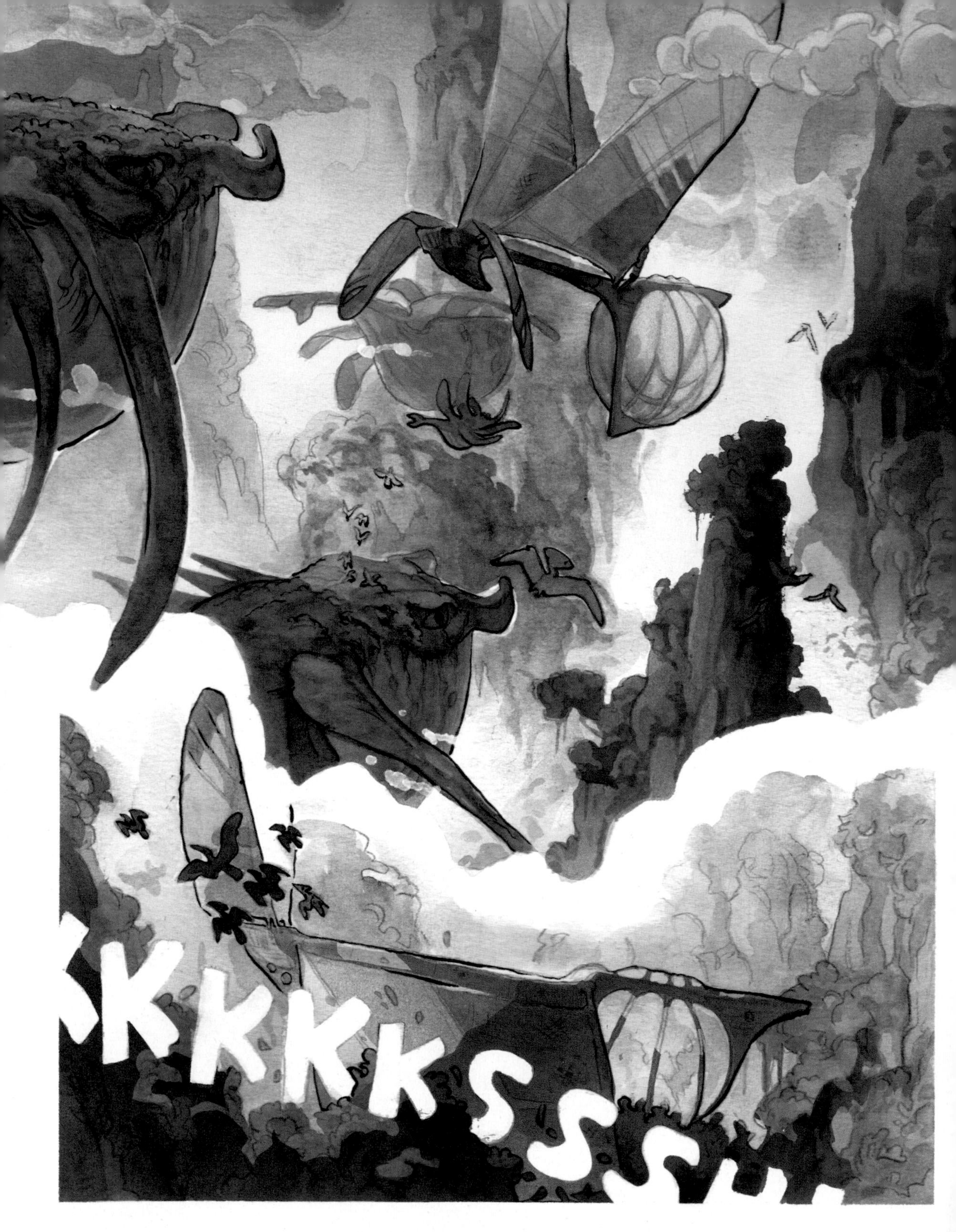
KKKKSSSH

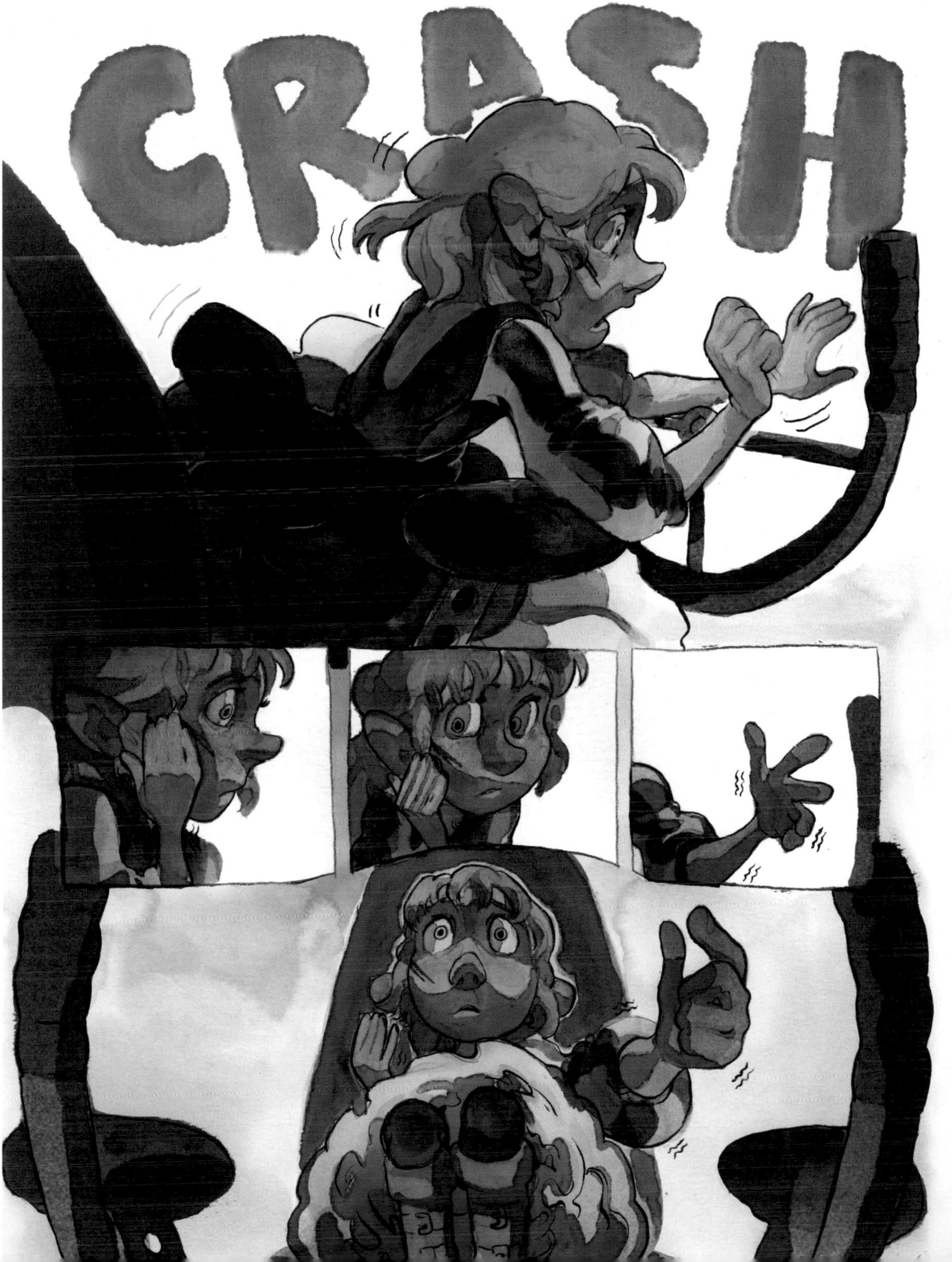
CRASH

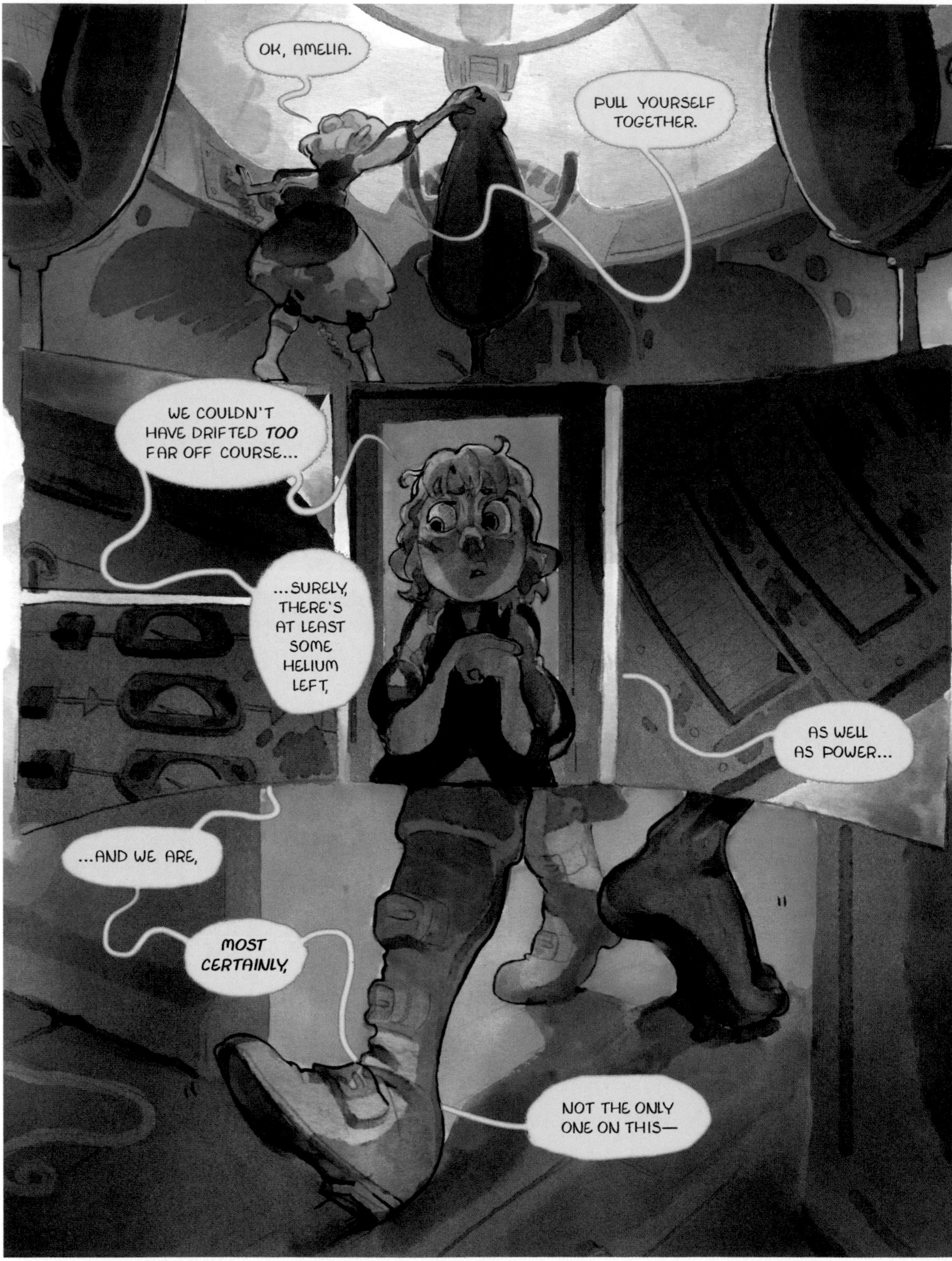
OK, AMELIA.
PULL YOURSELF TOGETHER.
WE COULDN'T HAVE DRIFTED *TOO* FAR OFF COURSE...
...SURELY, THERE'S AT LEAST SOME HELIUM LEFT,
AS WELL AS POWER...
...AND WE ARE,
MOST CERTAINLY,
NOT THE ONLY ONE ON THIS—

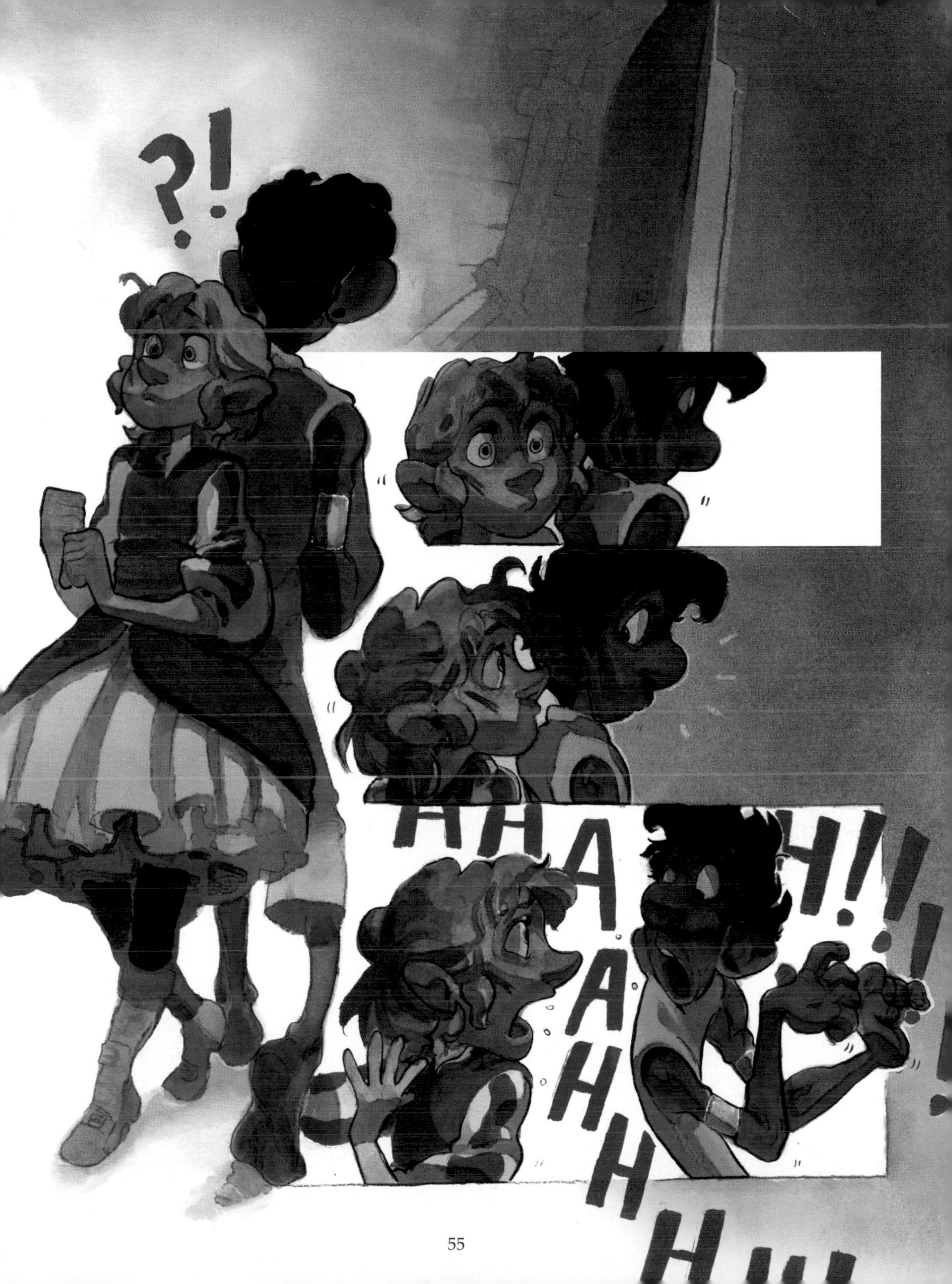
?!
AHAAAAHHHH!!!
AHHH!!!

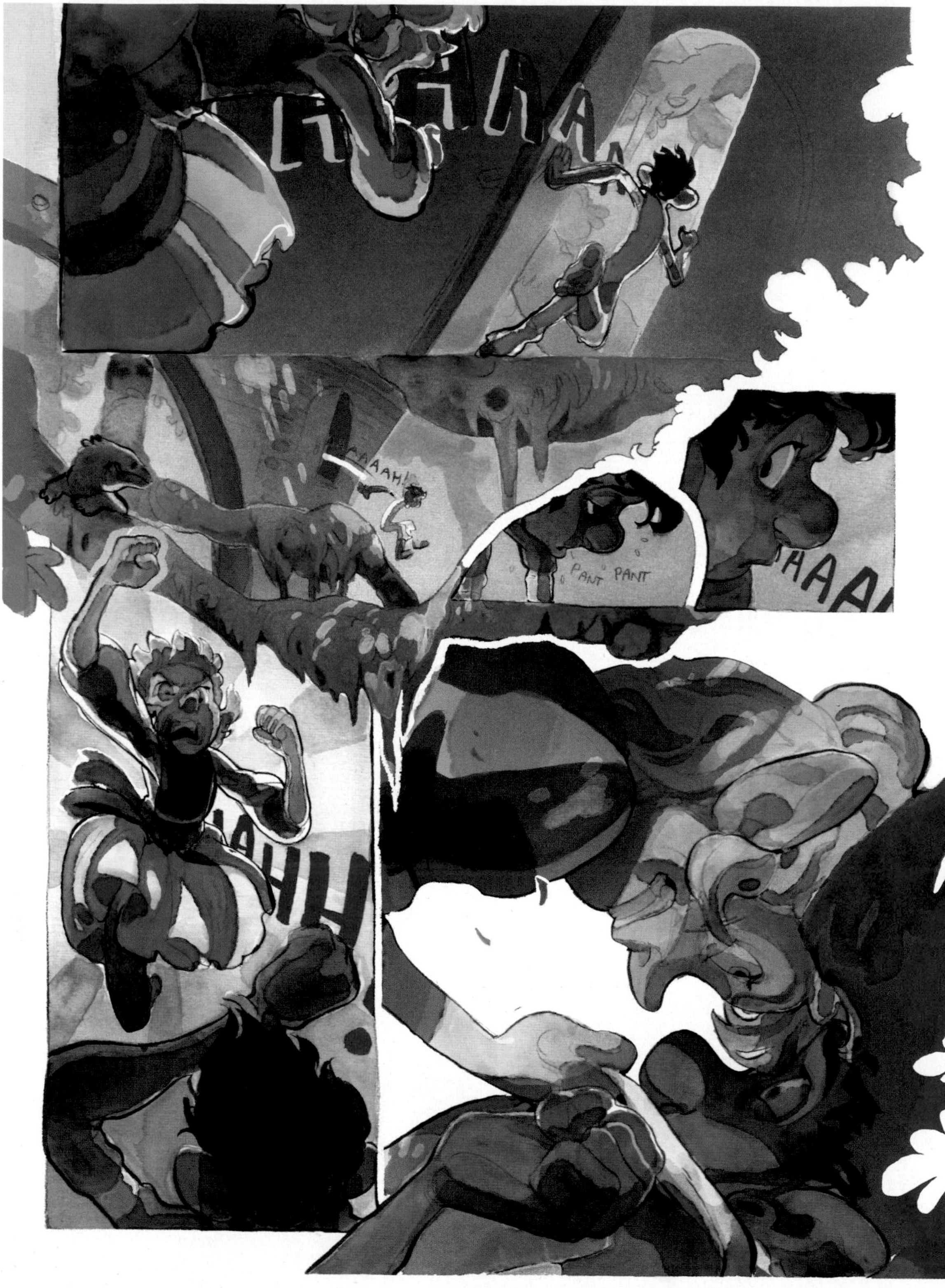
AAAH!
PANT PANT

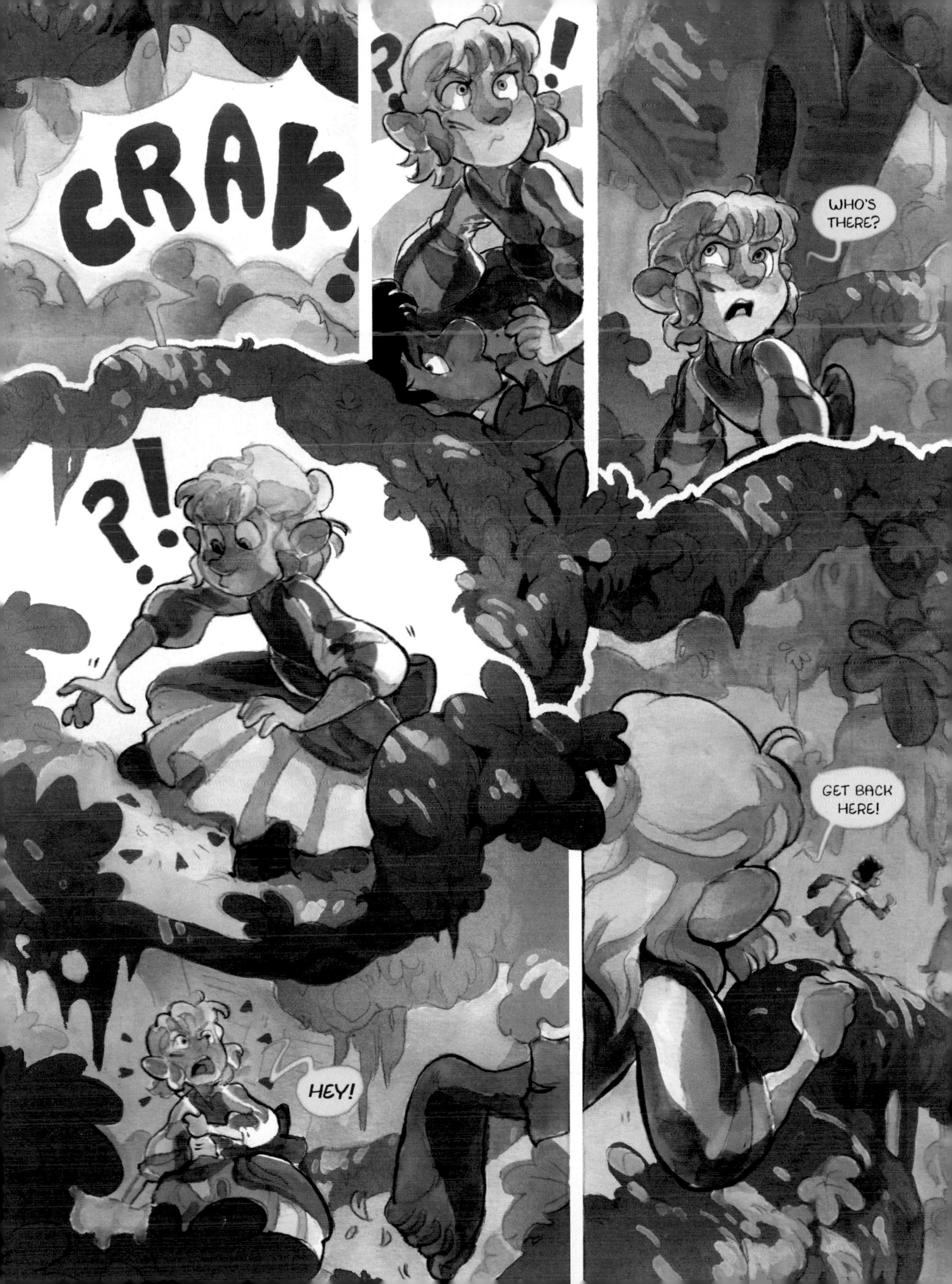
CRAK!
?!
WHO'S THERE?
?!
HEY!
GET BACK HERE!

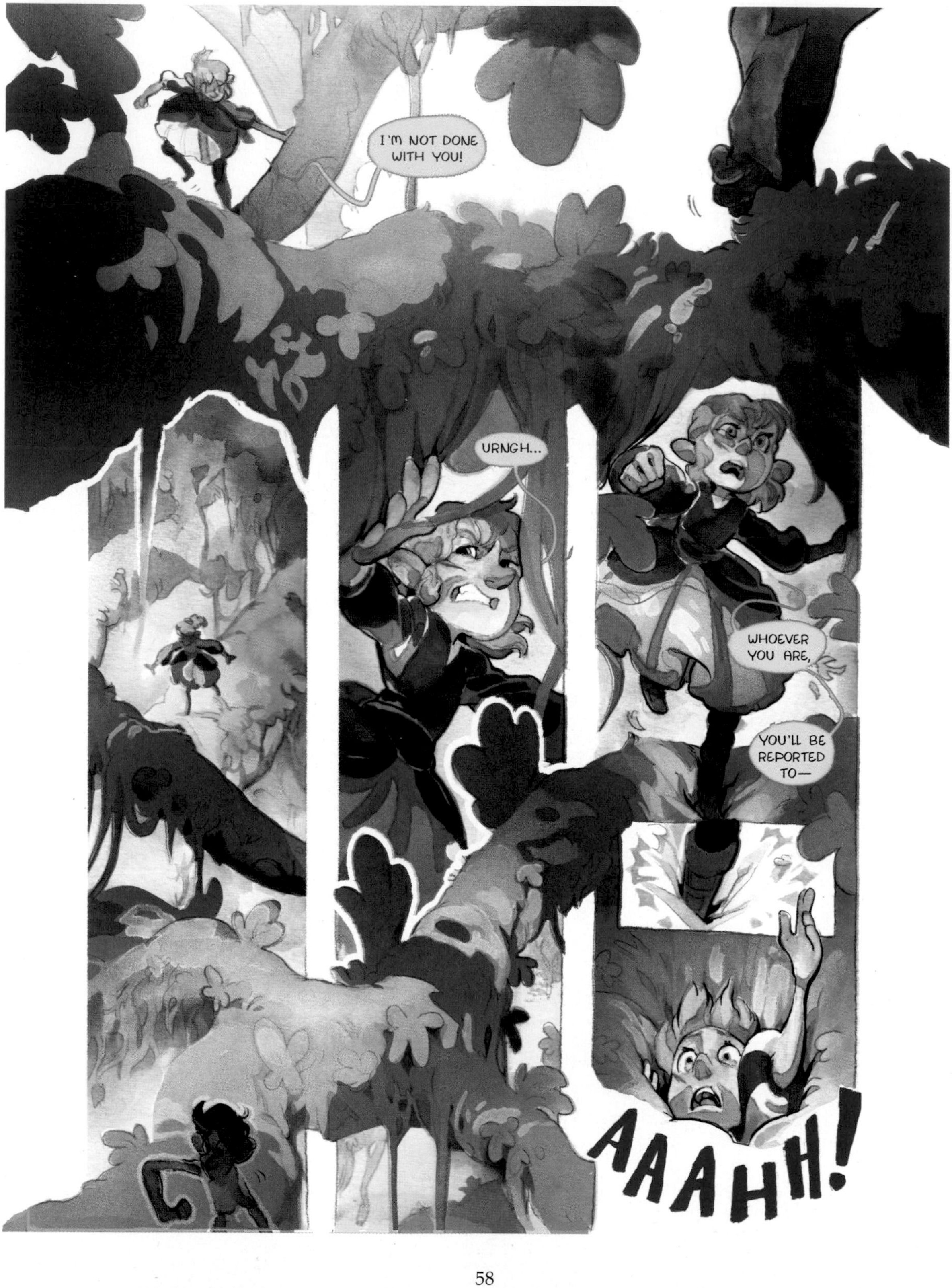
I'M NOT DONE WITH YOU!
URNGH...
WHOEVER YOU ARE,
YOU'LL BE REPORTED TO—
AAAHH!

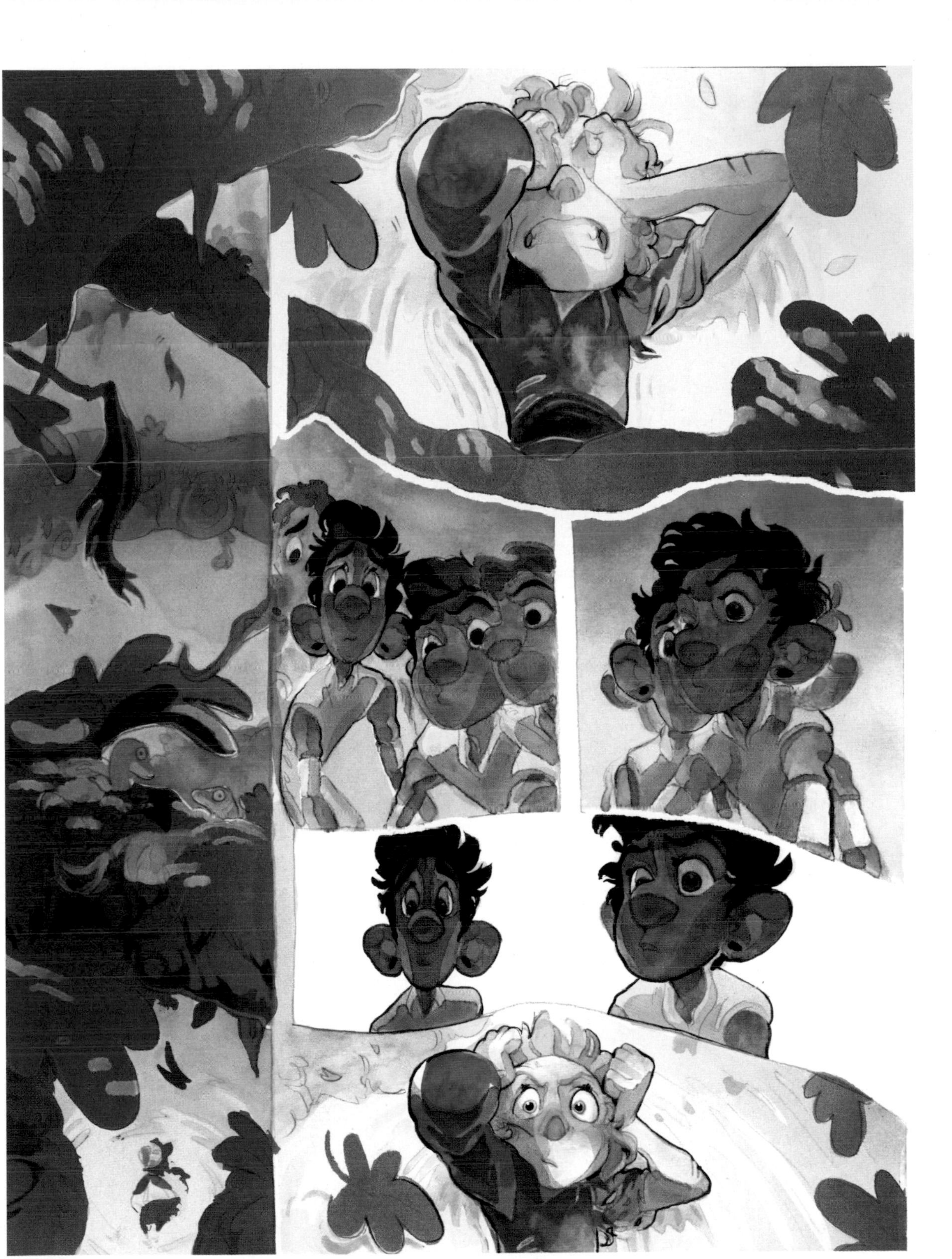

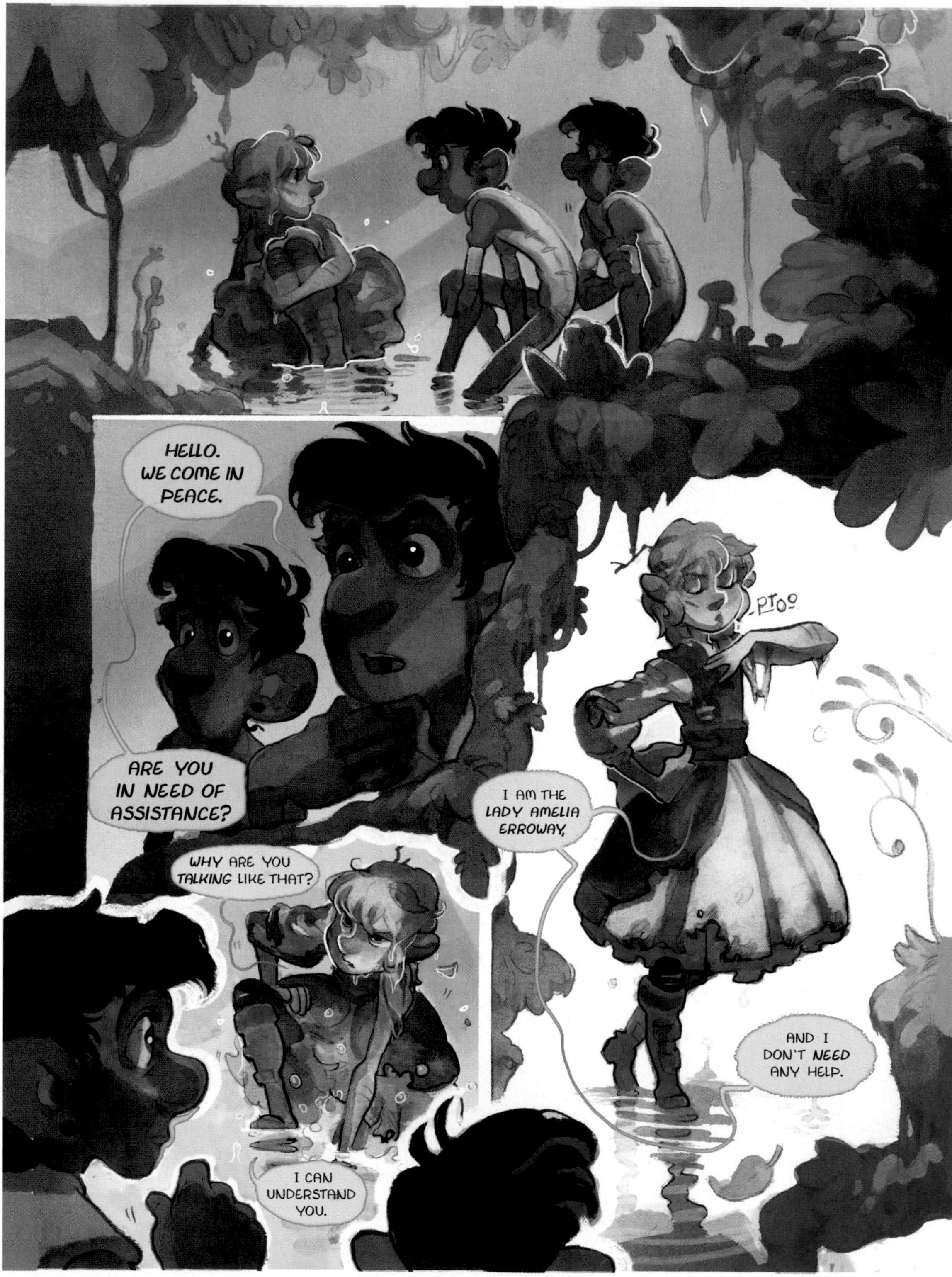
HELLO. WE COME IN PEACE.
ARE YOU IN NEED OF ASSISTANCE?
-PTOO
I AM THE LADY AMELIA ERROWAY,
AND I DON'T NEED ANY HELP.
WHY ARE YOU TALKING LIKE THAT?
I CAN UNDERSTAND YOU.

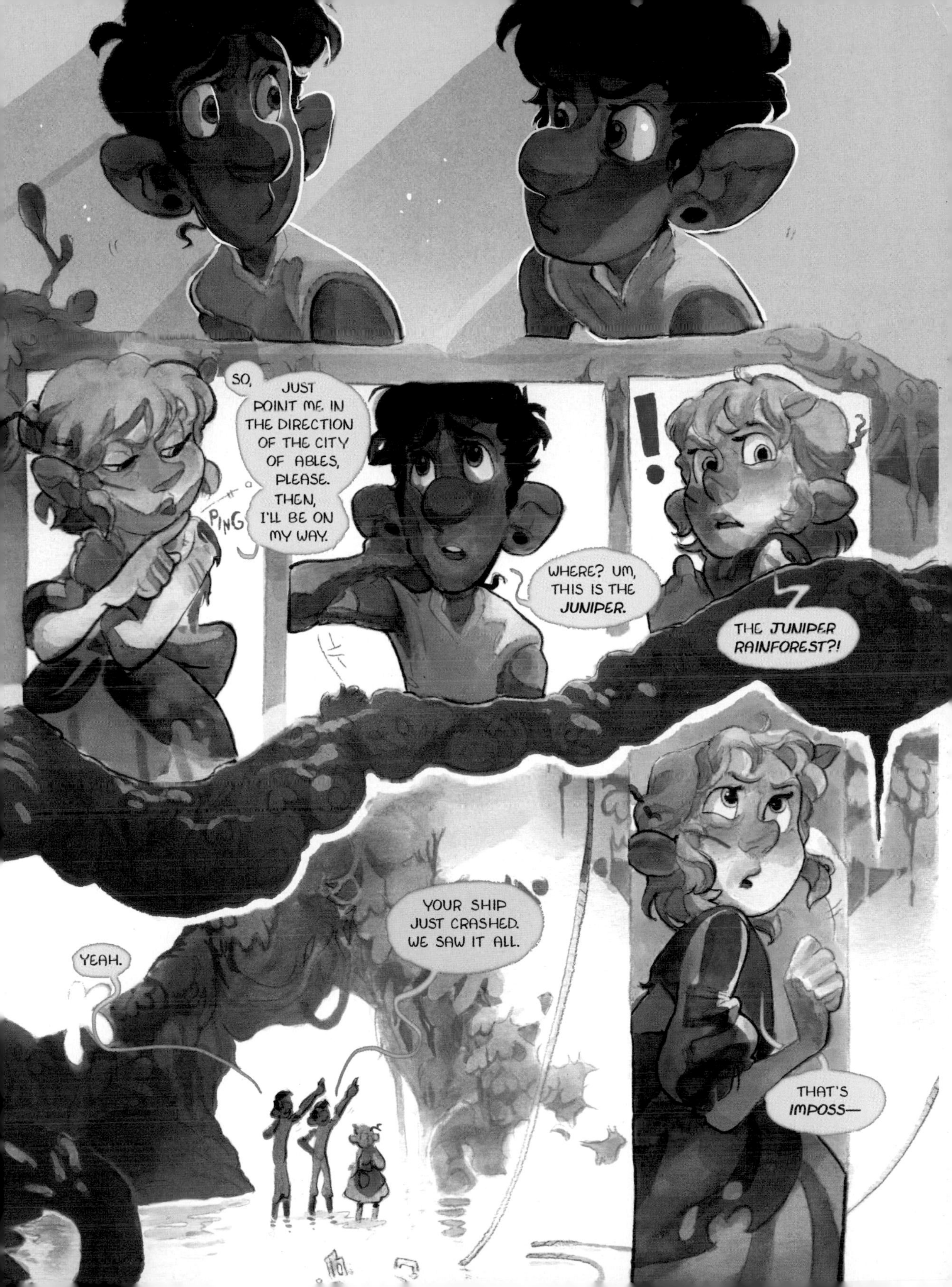
SO,
JUST POINT ME IN THE DIRECTION OF THE CITY OF ABLES, PLEASE. THEN, I'LL BE ON MY WAY.
PING
WHERE? UM, THIS IS THE JUNIPER.
!
THE JUNIPER RAINFOREST?!
YOUR SHIP JUST CRASHED. WE SAW IT ALL.
YEAH.
THAT'S IMPOSS—

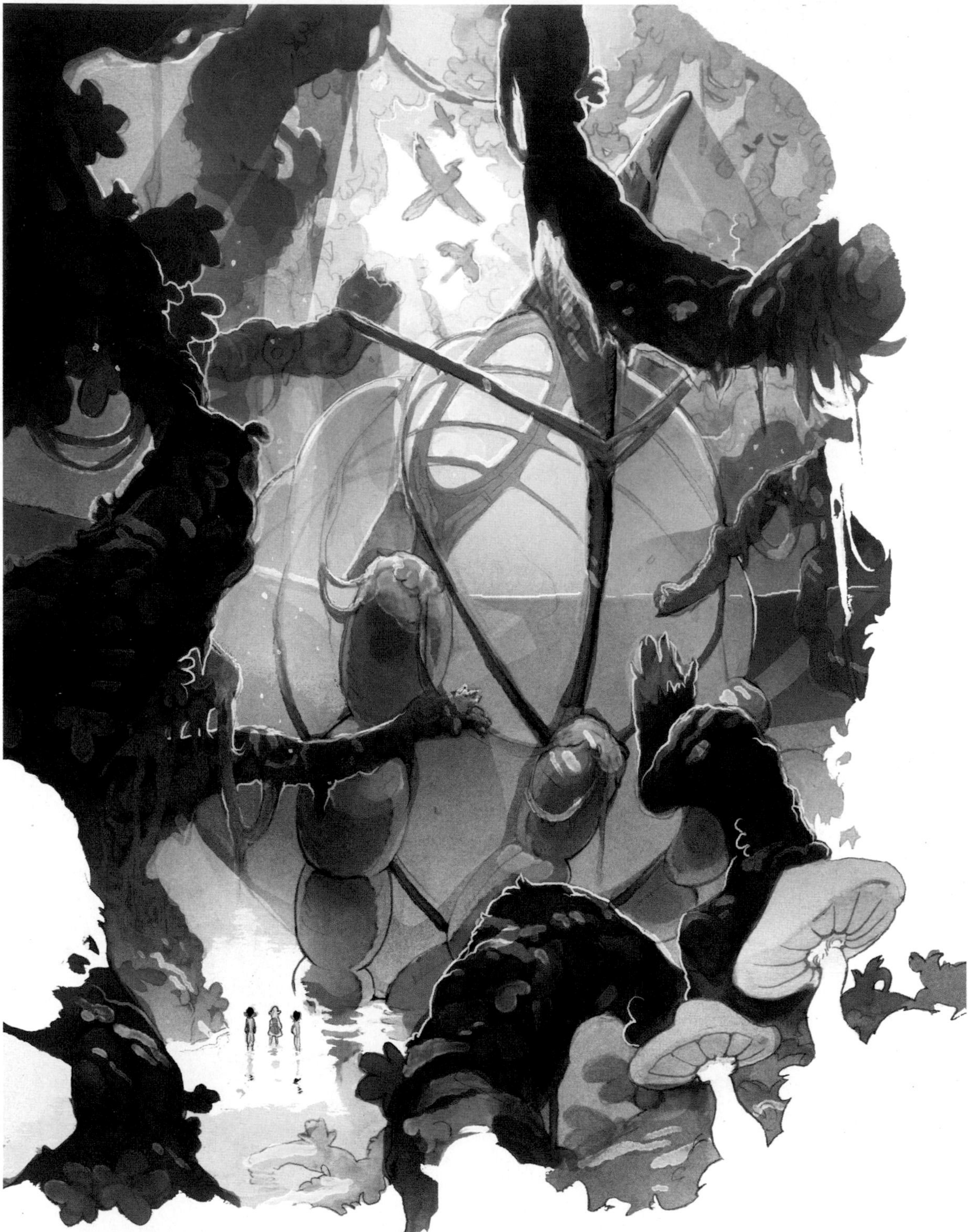

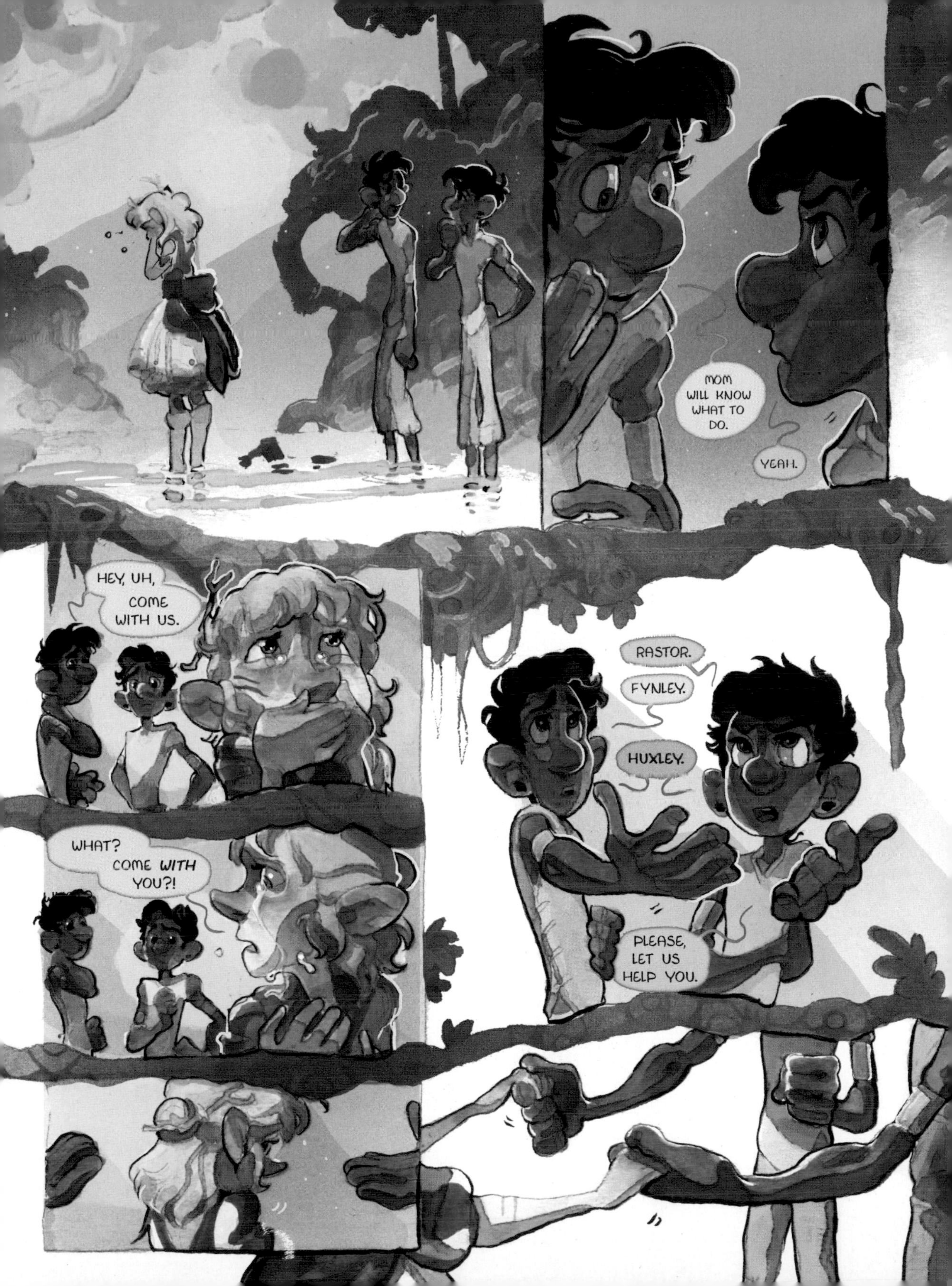
MOM WILL KNOW WHAT TO DO.
YEAH.
HEY, UH, COME WITH US.
WHAT? COME WITH YOU?!
RASTOR.
FYNLEY.
HUXLEY.
PLEASE, LET US HELP YOU.

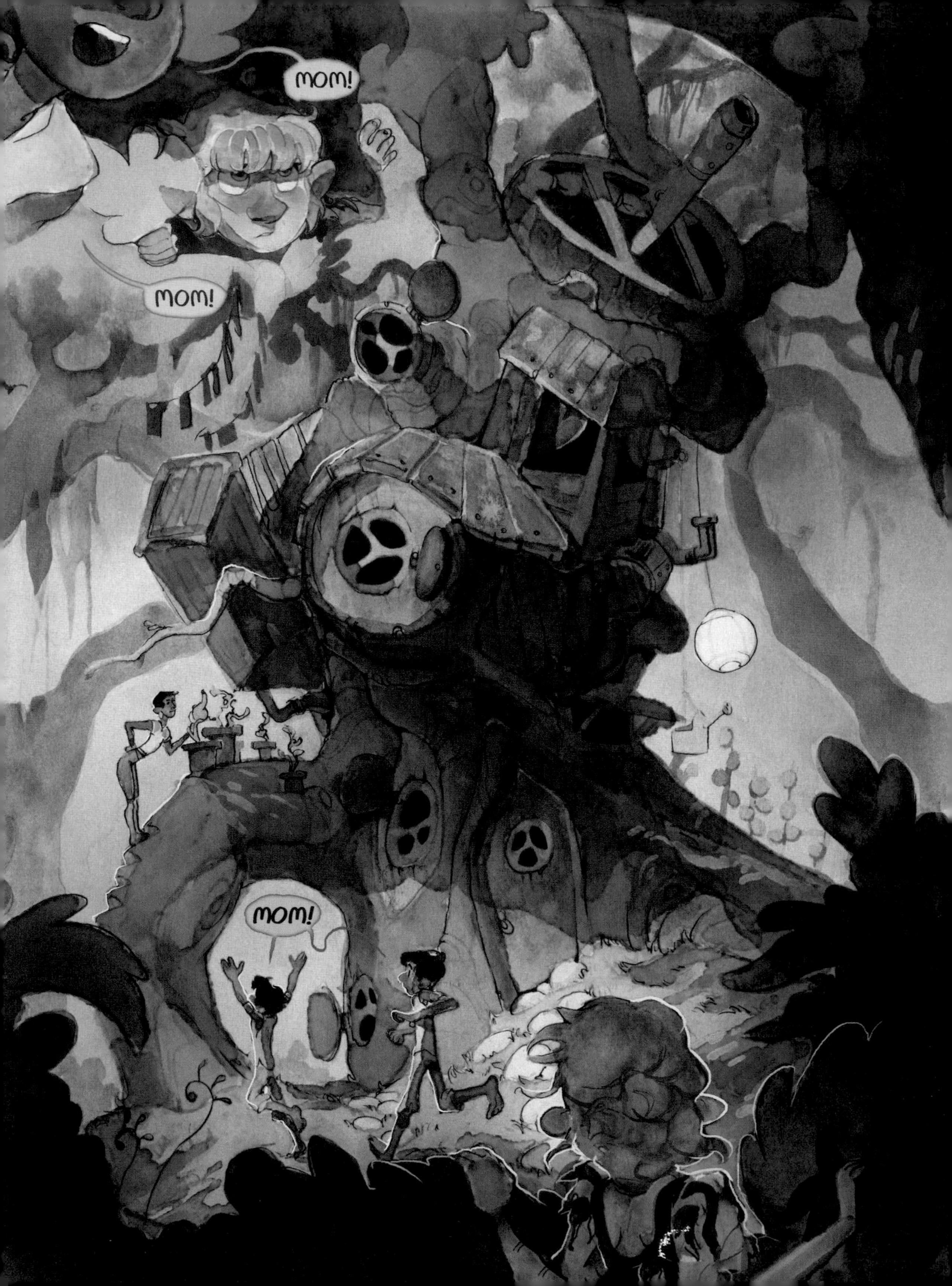
MOM!
MOM!
MOM!

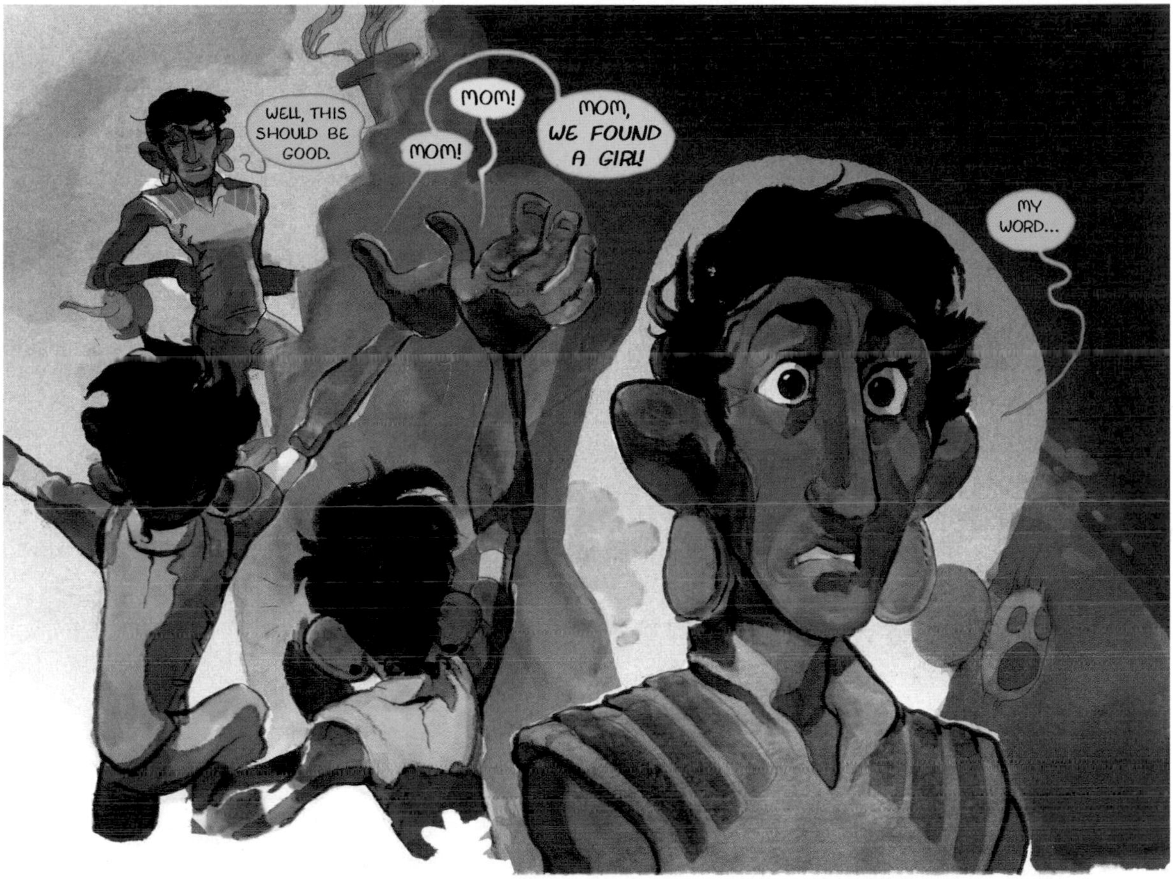
WELL, THIS SHOULD BE GOOD.
MOM!
MOM!
MOM, WE FOUND A GIRL!
MY WORD...

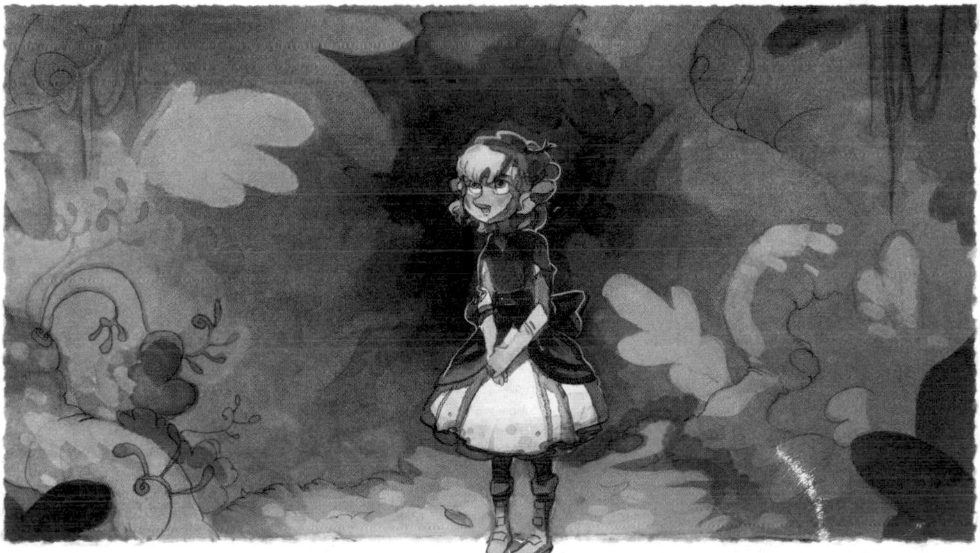

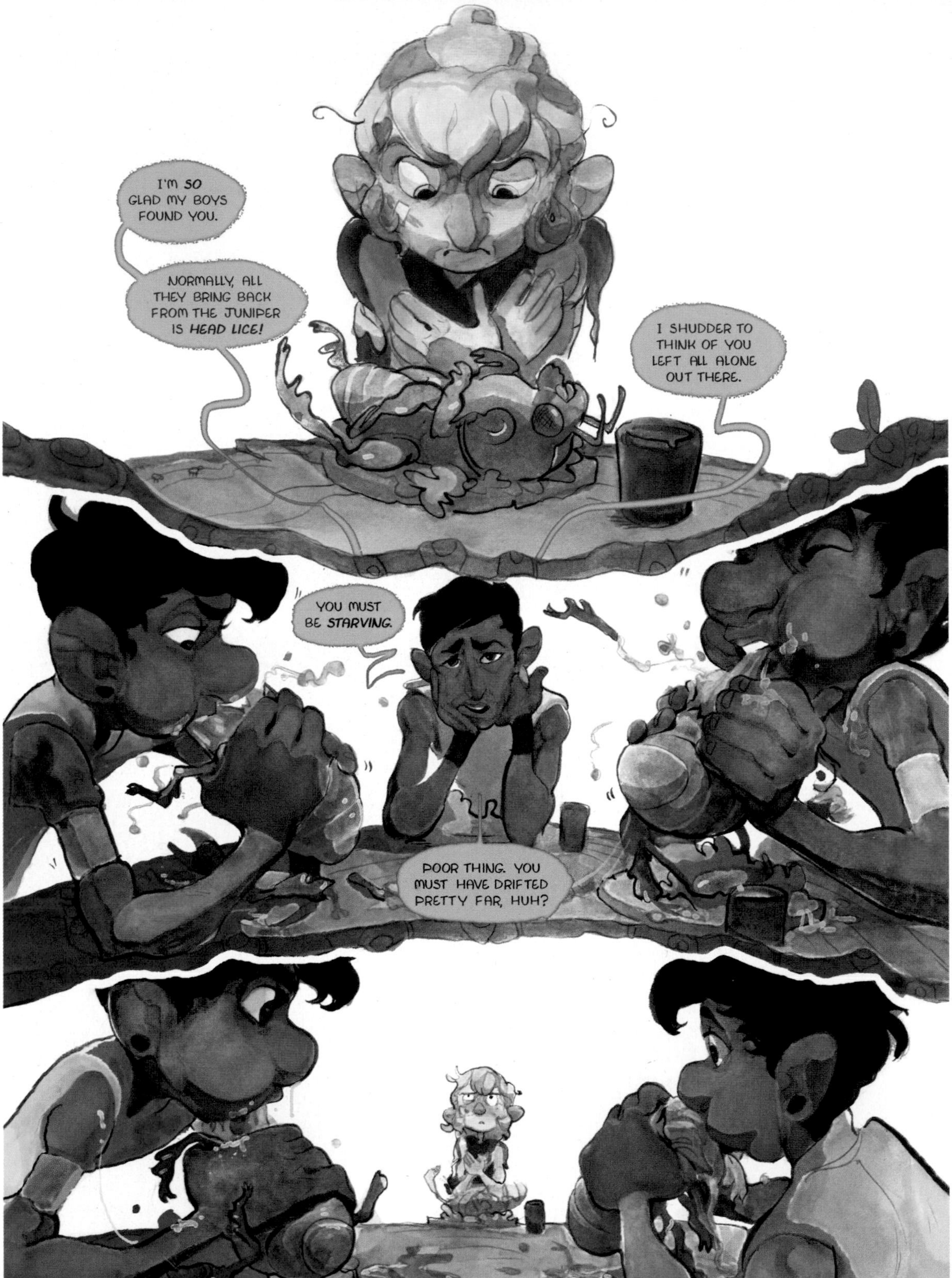
I'M SO GLAD MY BOYS FOUND YOU.
NORMALLY, ALL THEY BRING BACK FROM THE JUNIPER IS HEAD LICE!
I SHUDDER TO THINK OF YOU LEFT ALL ALONE OUT THERE.
YOU MUST BE STARVING.
POOR THING. YOU MUST HAVE DRIFTED PRETTY FAR, HUH?

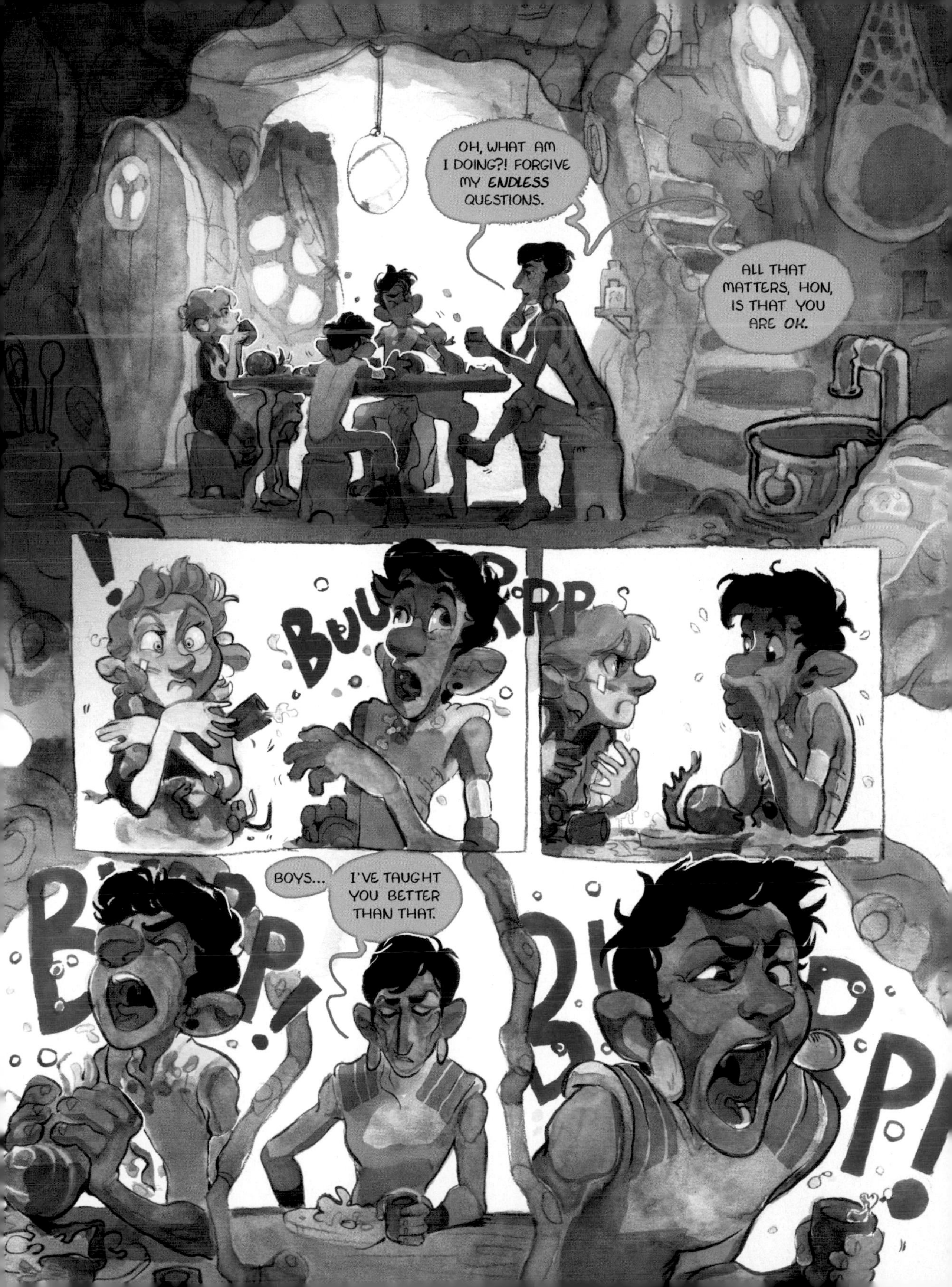
OH, WHAT AM I DOING?! FORGIVE MY *ENDLESS* QUESTIONS.
ALL THAT MATTERS, HON, IS THAT YOU ARE *OK*.
!
BUURRPP
BOYS...
I'VE TAUGHT YOU BETTER THAN THAT.

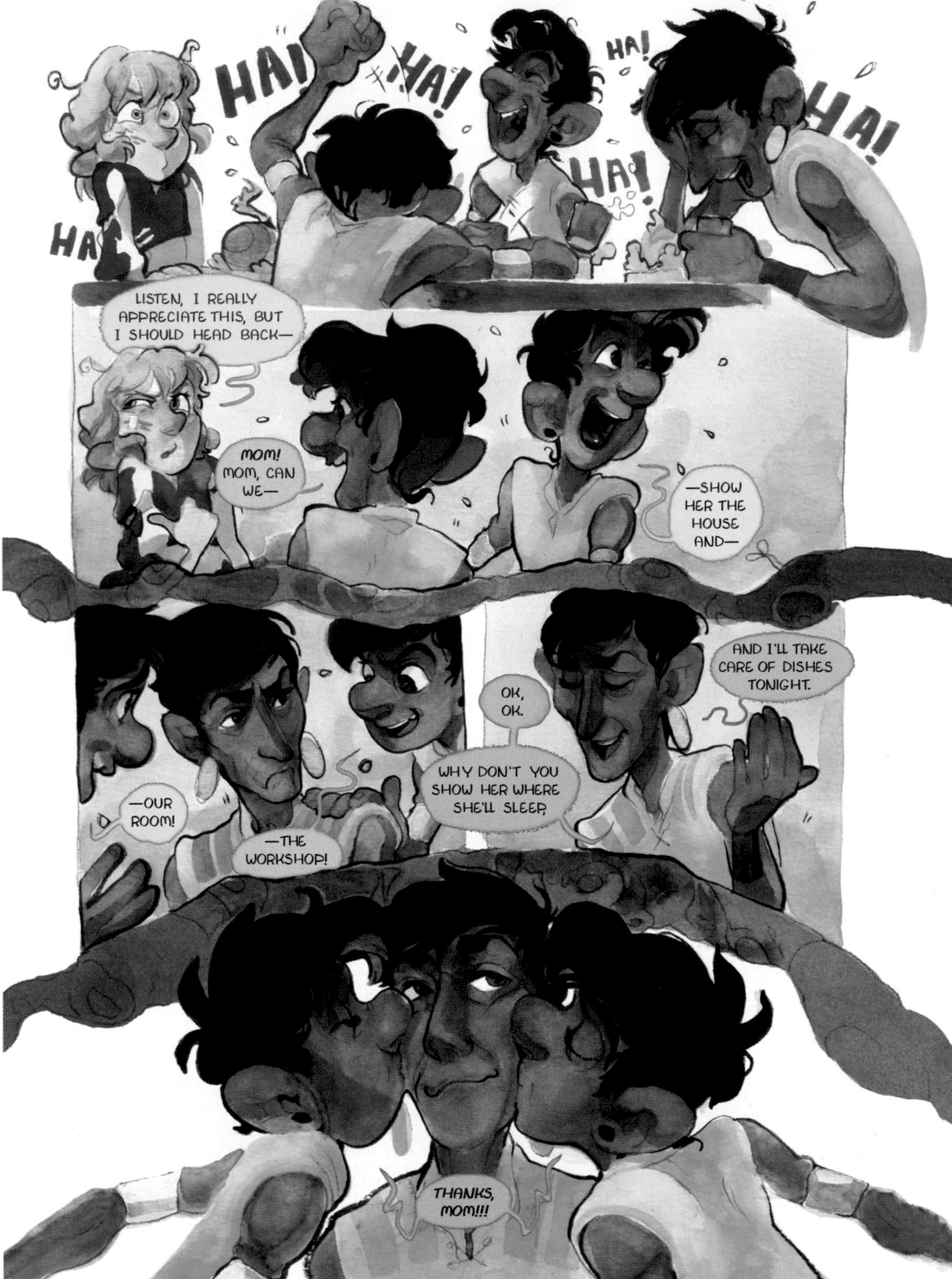
HA
HA!
HA!
HA!
HA!
HA!
LISTEN, I REALLY APPRECIATE THIS, BUT I SHOULD HEAD BACK—
MOM! MOM, CAN WE—
—SHOW HER THE HOUSE AND—
—OUR ROOM!
—THE WORKSHOP!
OK, OK.
WHY DON'T YOU SHOW HER WHERE SHE'LL SLEEP,
AND I'LL TAKE CARE OF DISHES TONIGHT.
THANKS, MOM!!!

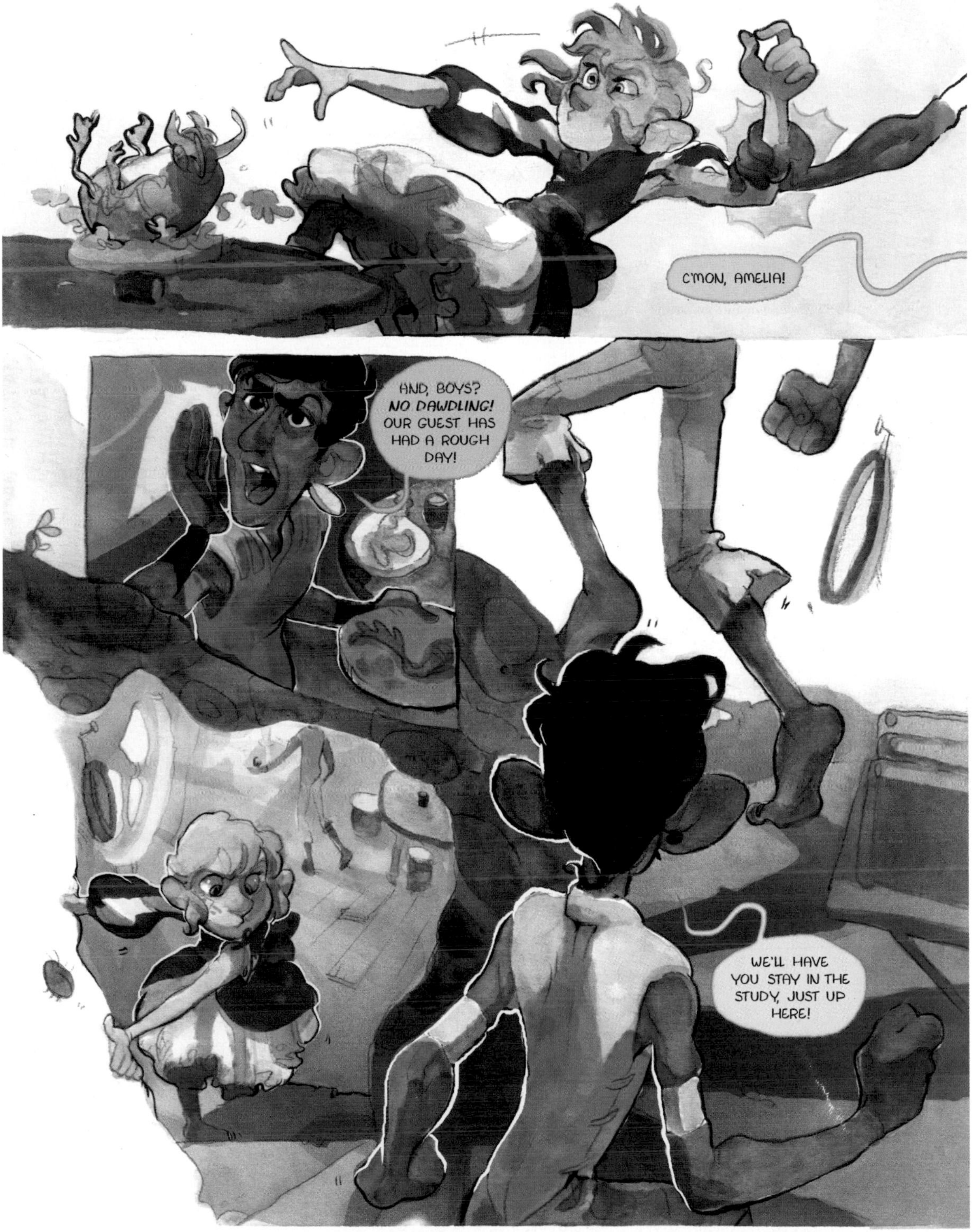
C'MON, AMELIA!
AND, BOYS? ***NO DAWDLING!*** OUR GUEST HAS HAD A ROUGH DAY!
WE'LL HAVE YOU STAY IN THE STUDY, JUST UP HERE!

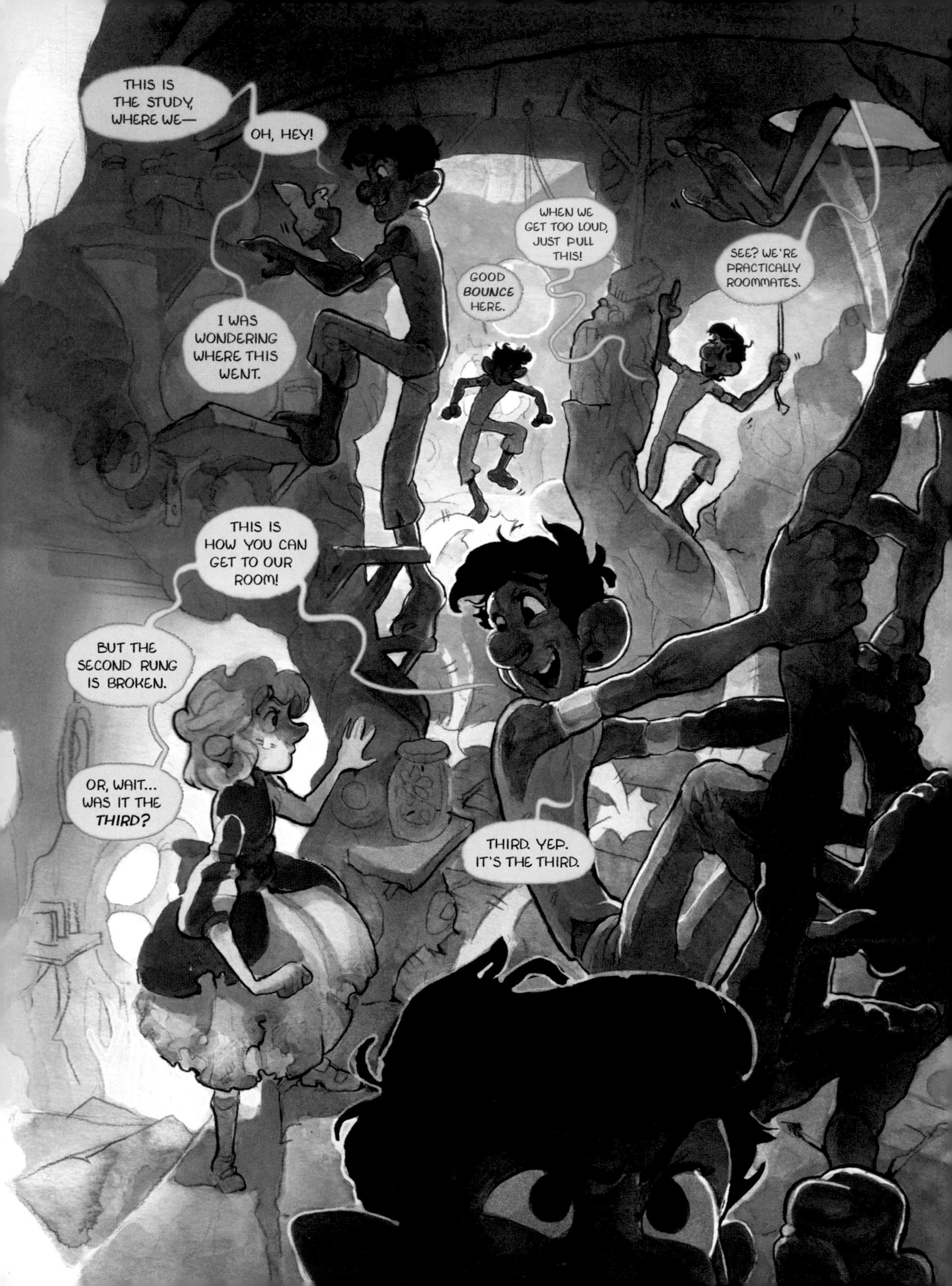
THIS IS THE STUDY, WHERE WE—
OH, HEY!
I WAS WONDERING WHERE THIS WENT.
GOOD BOUNCE HERE.
WHEN WE GET TOO LOUD, JUST PULL THIS!
SEE? WE'RE PRACTICALLY ROOMMATES.
THIS IS HOW YOU CAN GET TO OUR ROOM!
BUT THE SECOND RUNG IS BROKEN.
OR, WAIT... WAS IT THE *THIRD*?
THIRD. YEP. IT'S THE THIRD.

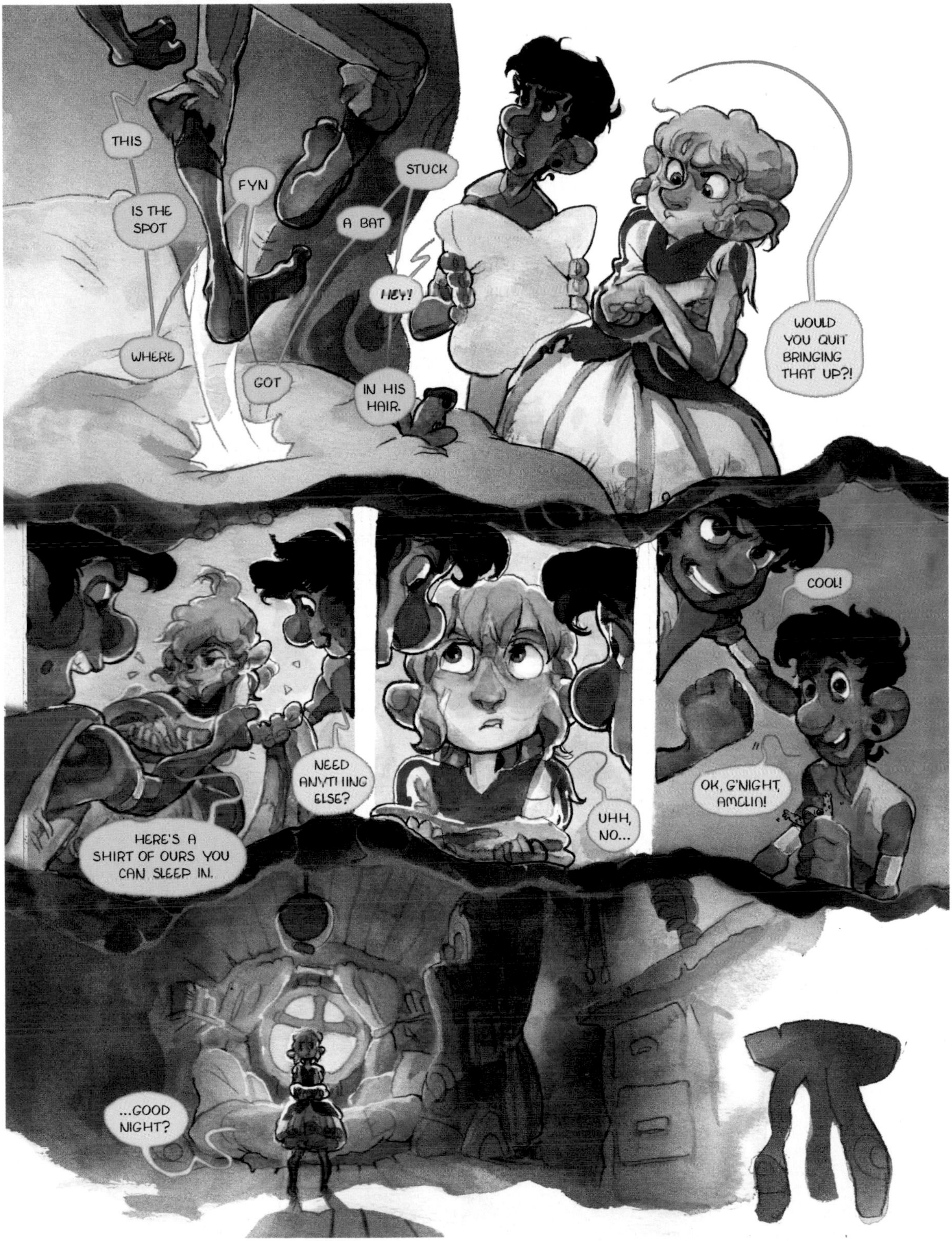
THIS
IS THE SPOT
WHERE
FYN
GOT
A BAT
STUCK
HEY!
IN HIS HAIR.
WOULD YOU QUIT BRINGING THAT UP?!
HERE'S A SHIRT OF OURS YOU CAN SLEEP IN.
NEED ANYTHING ELSE?
UHH, NO...
COOL!
OK, G'NIGHT, AMCLIN!
...GOOD NIGHT?

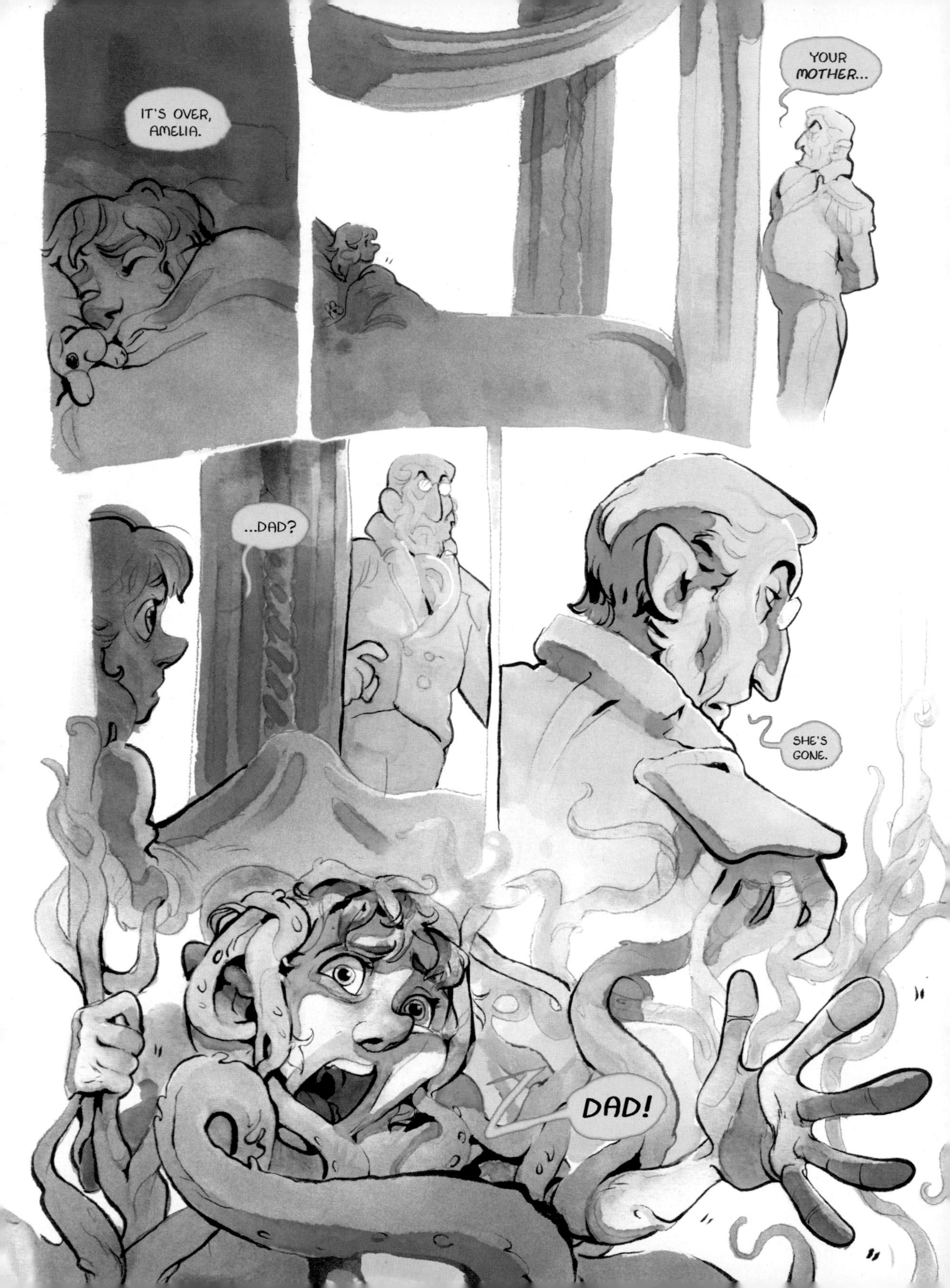
IT'S OVER, AMELIA.
YOUR MOTHER...
...DAD?
SHE'S GONE.
DAD!

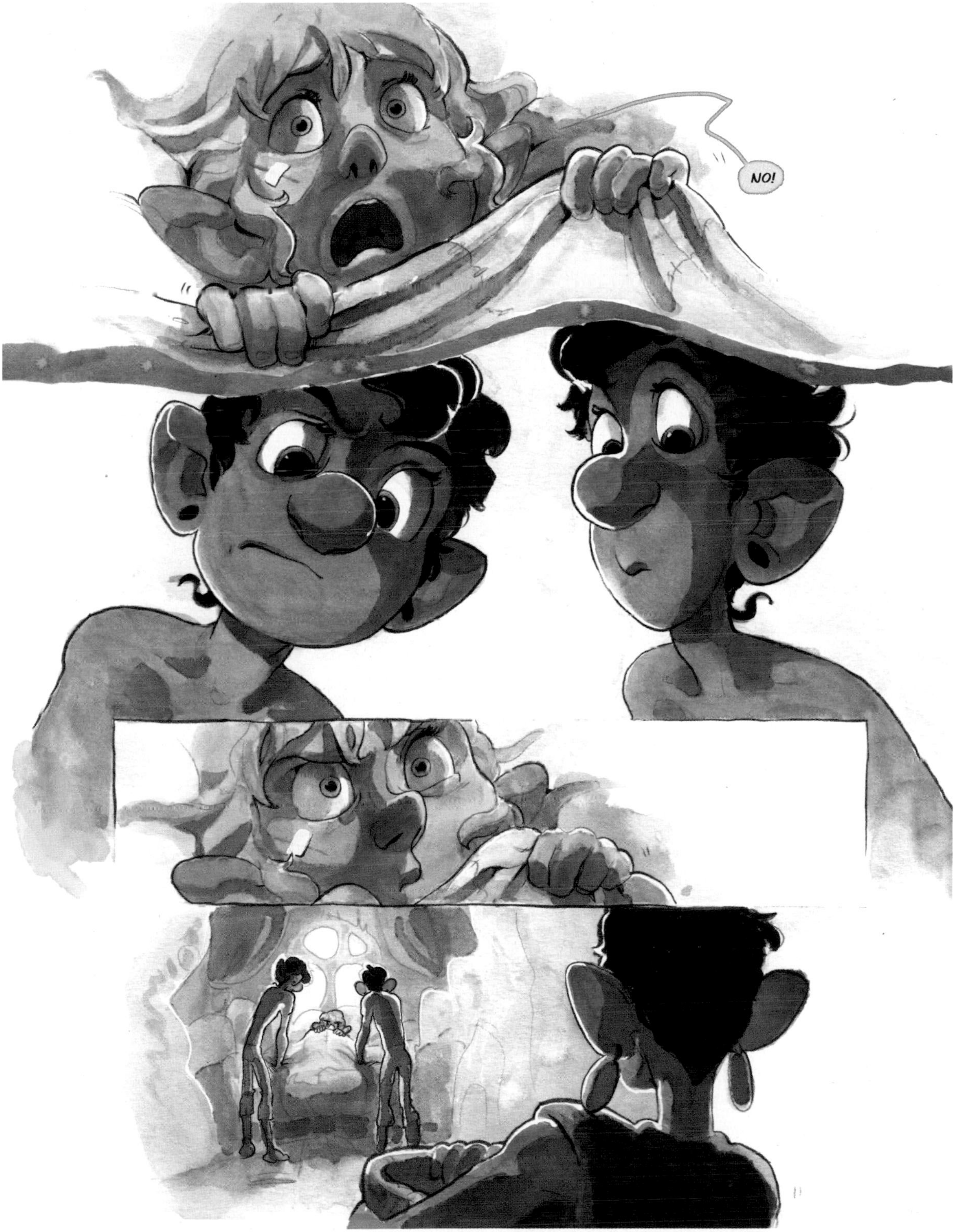
NO!

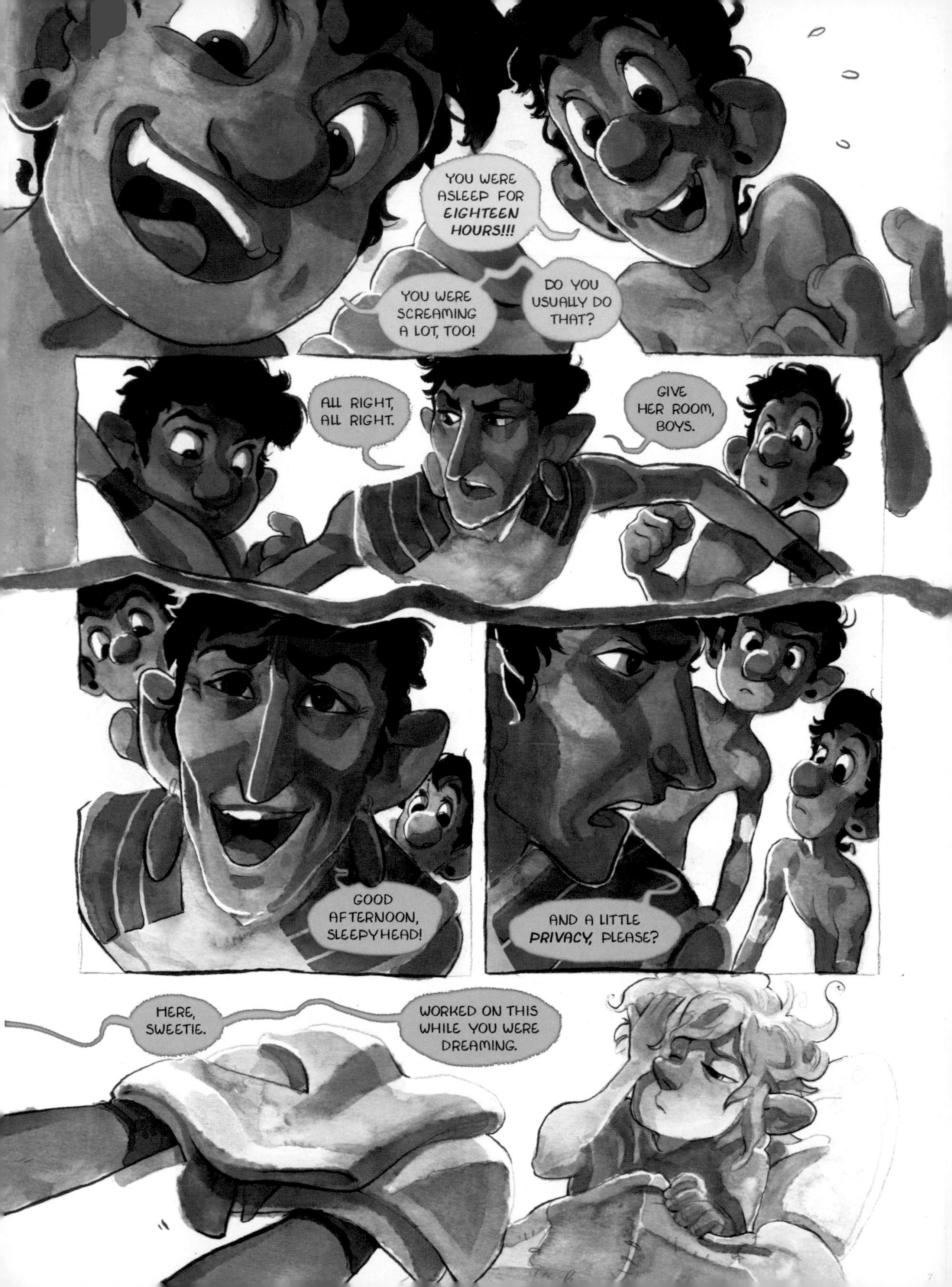
YOU WERE ASLEEP FOR EIGHTEEN HOURS!!!
YOU WERE SCREAMING A LOT, TOO!
DO YOU USUALLY DO THAT?
ALL RIGHT, ALL RIGHT.
GIVE HER ROOM, BOYS.
GOOD AFTERNOON, SLEEPYHEAD!
AND A LITTLE PRIVACY, PLEASE?
HERE, SWEETIE.
WORKED ON THIS WHILE YOU WERE DREAMING.

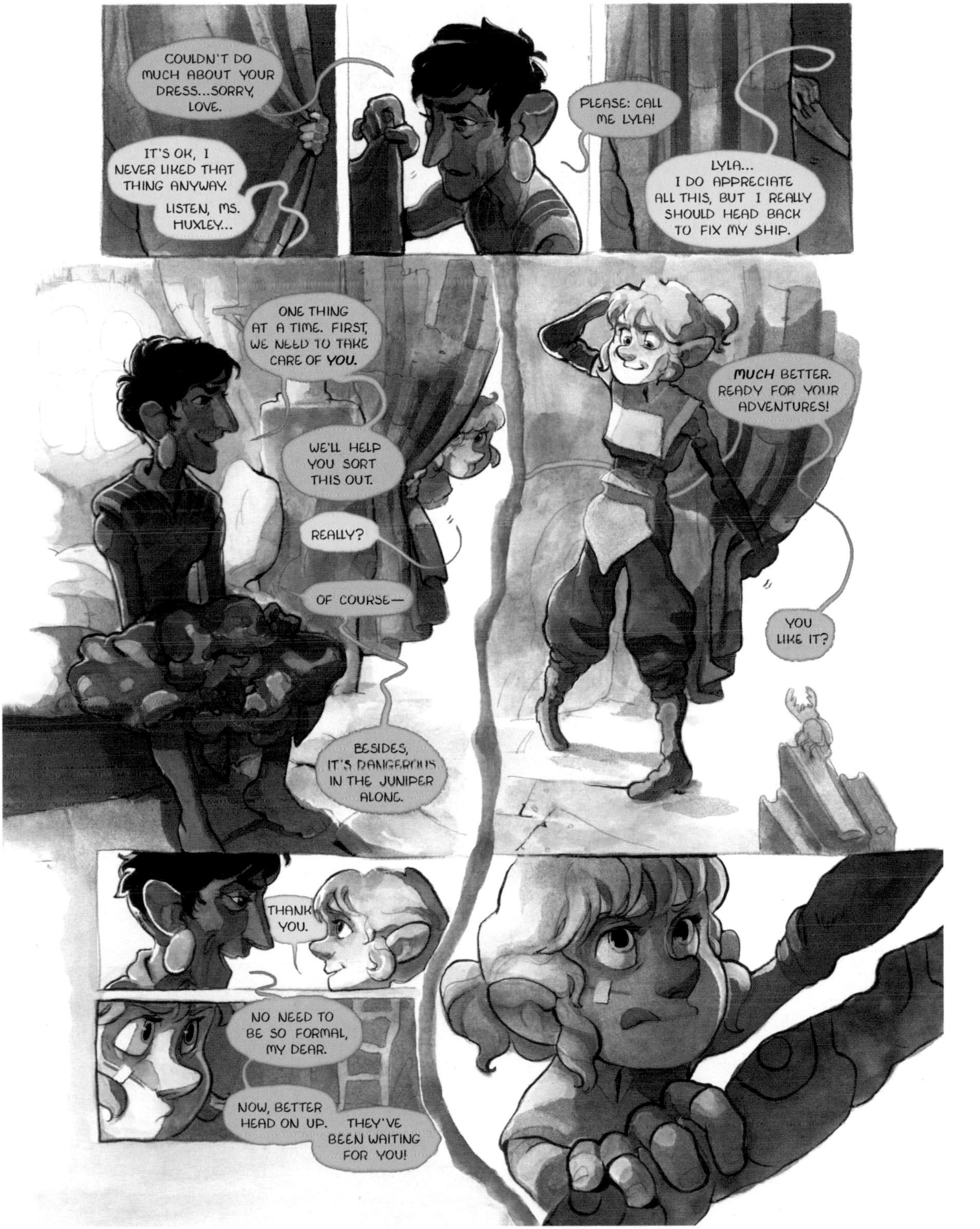
COULDN'T DO MUCH ABOUT YOUR DRESS...SORRY, LOVE.
IT'S OK, I NEVER LIKED THAT THING ANYWAY.
LISTEN, MS. HUXLEY...
PLEASE: CALL ME LYLA!
LYLA... I DO APPRECIATE ALL THIS, BUT I REALLY SHOULD HEAD BACK TO FIX MY SHIP.
ONE THING AT A TIME. FIRST, WE NEED TO TAKE CARE OF YOU.
WE'LL HELP YOU SORT THIS OUT.
REALLY?
OF COURSE—
BESIDES, IT'S DANGEROUS IN THE JUNIPER ALONE.
MUCH BETTER. READY FOR YOUR ADVENTURES!
YOU LIKE IT?
THANK YOU.
NO NEED TO BE SO FORMAL, MY DEAR.
NOW, BETTER HEAD ON UP. THEY'VE BEEN WAITING FOR YOU!

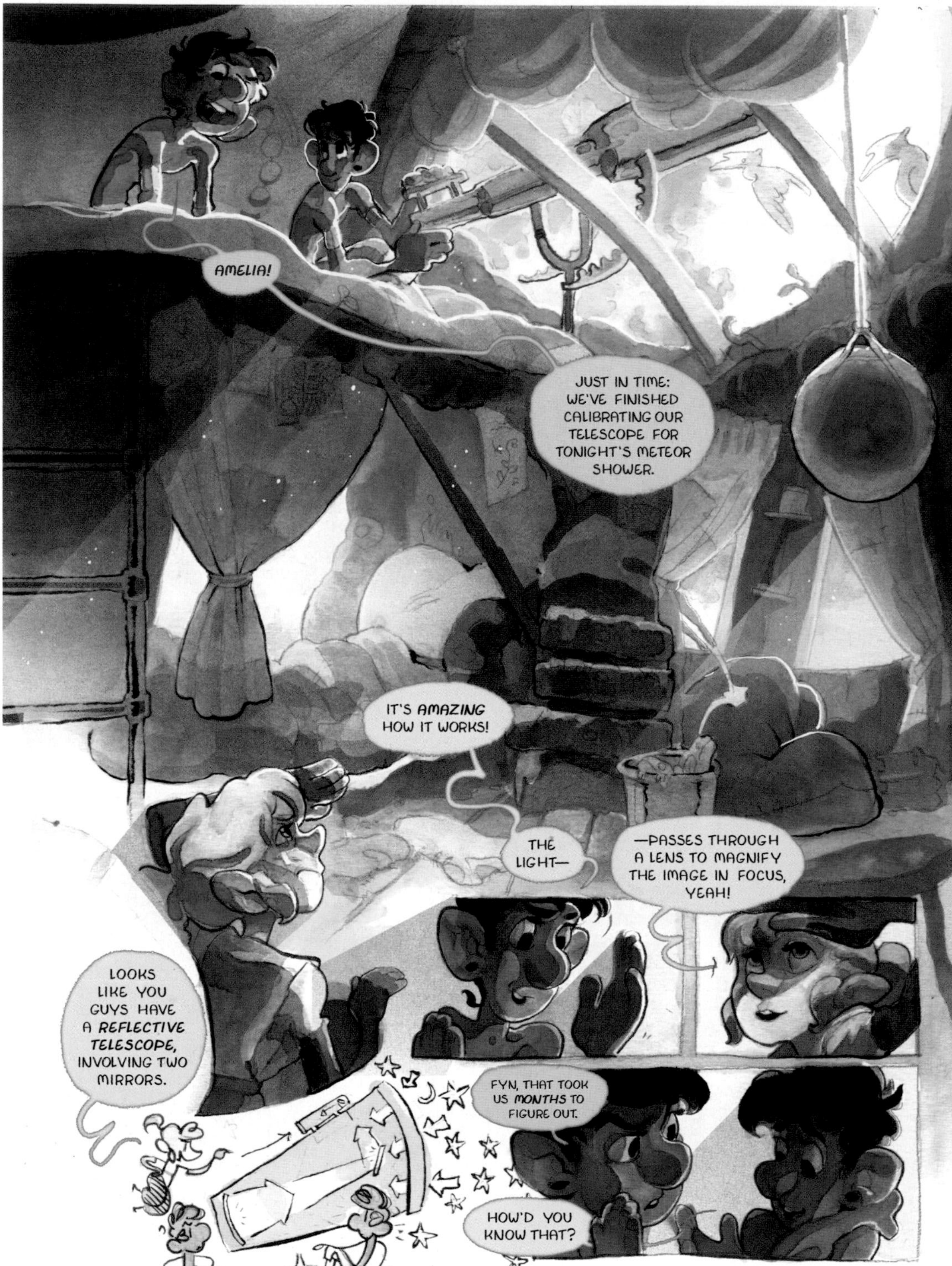
AMELIA!
JUST IN TIME: WE'VE FINISHED CALIBRATING OUR TELESCOPE FOR TONIGHT'S METEOR SHOWER.
IT'S AMAZING HOW IT WORKS!
THE LIGHT—
—PASSES THROUGH A LENS TO MAGNIFY THE IMAGE IN FOCUS, YEAH!
LOOKS LIKE YOU GUYS HAVE A REFLECTIVE TELESCOPE, INVOLVING TWO MIRRORS.
FYN, THAT TOOK US MONTHS TO FIGURE OUT.
HOW'D YOU KNOW THAT?

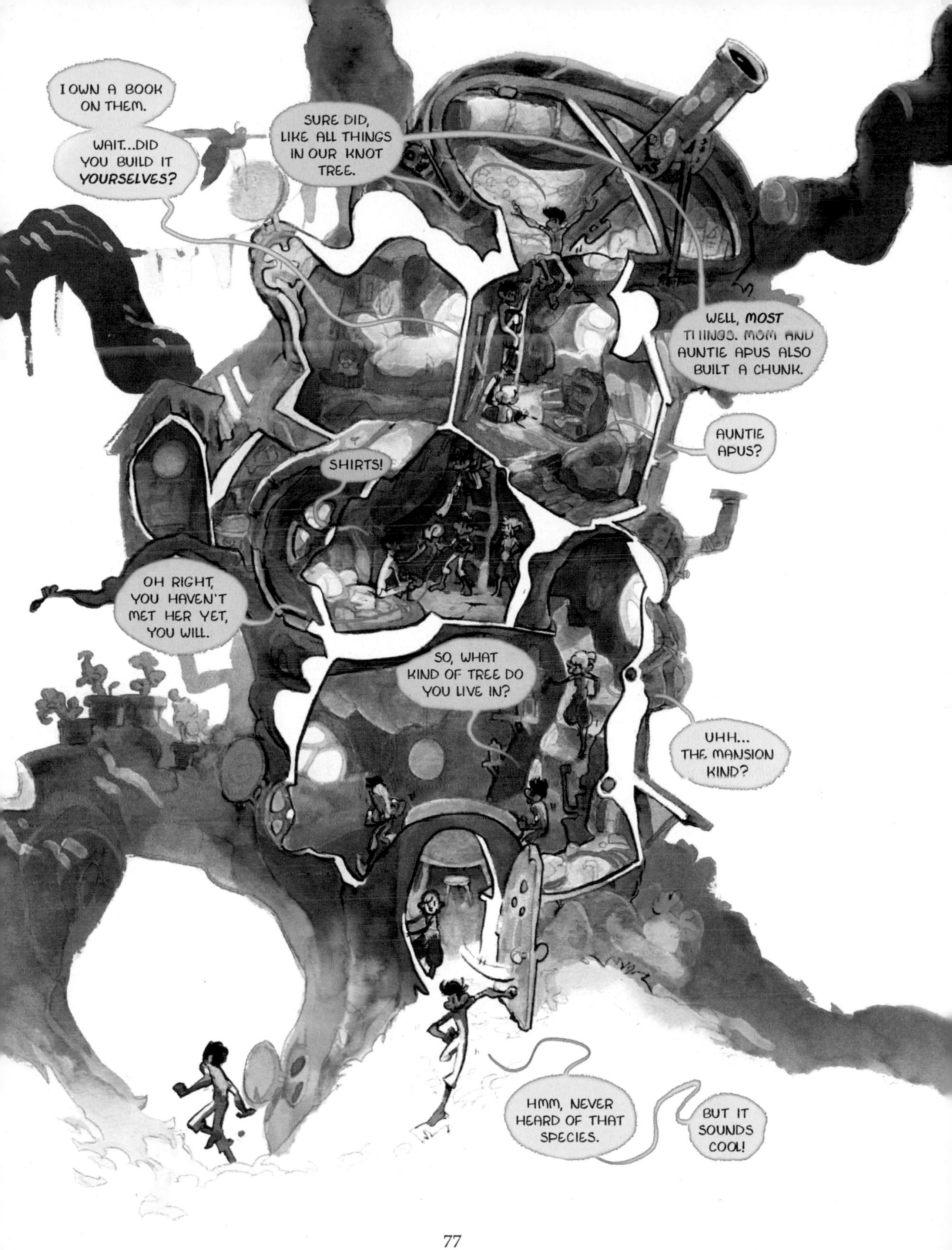
I OWN A BOOK ON THEM.
WAIT...DID YOU BUILD IT YOURSELVES?
SURE DID, LIKE ALL THINGS IN OUR KNOT TREE.
WELL, MOST THINGS. MOM AND AUNTIE APUS ALSO BUILT A CHUNK.
AUNTIE APUS?
SHIRTS!
OH RIGHT, YOU HAVEN'T MET HER YET, YOU WILL.
SO, WHAT KIND OF TREE DO YOU LIVE IN?
UHH... THE MANSION KIND?
HMM, NEVER HEARD OF THAT SPECIES.
BUT IT SOUNDS COOL!

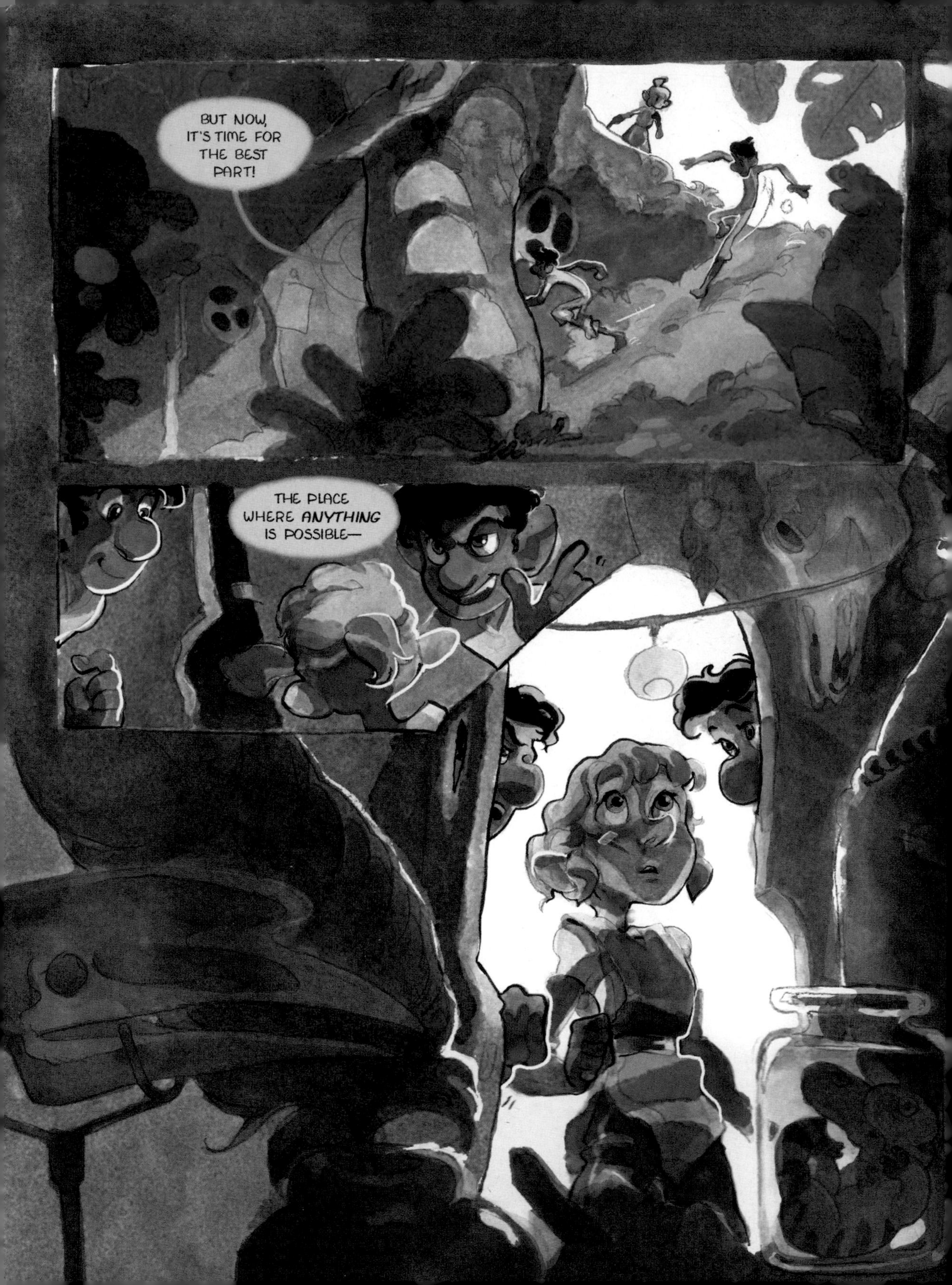
BUT NOW, IT'S TIME FOR THE BEST PART!
THE PLACE WHERE *ANYTHING* IS POSSIBLE—

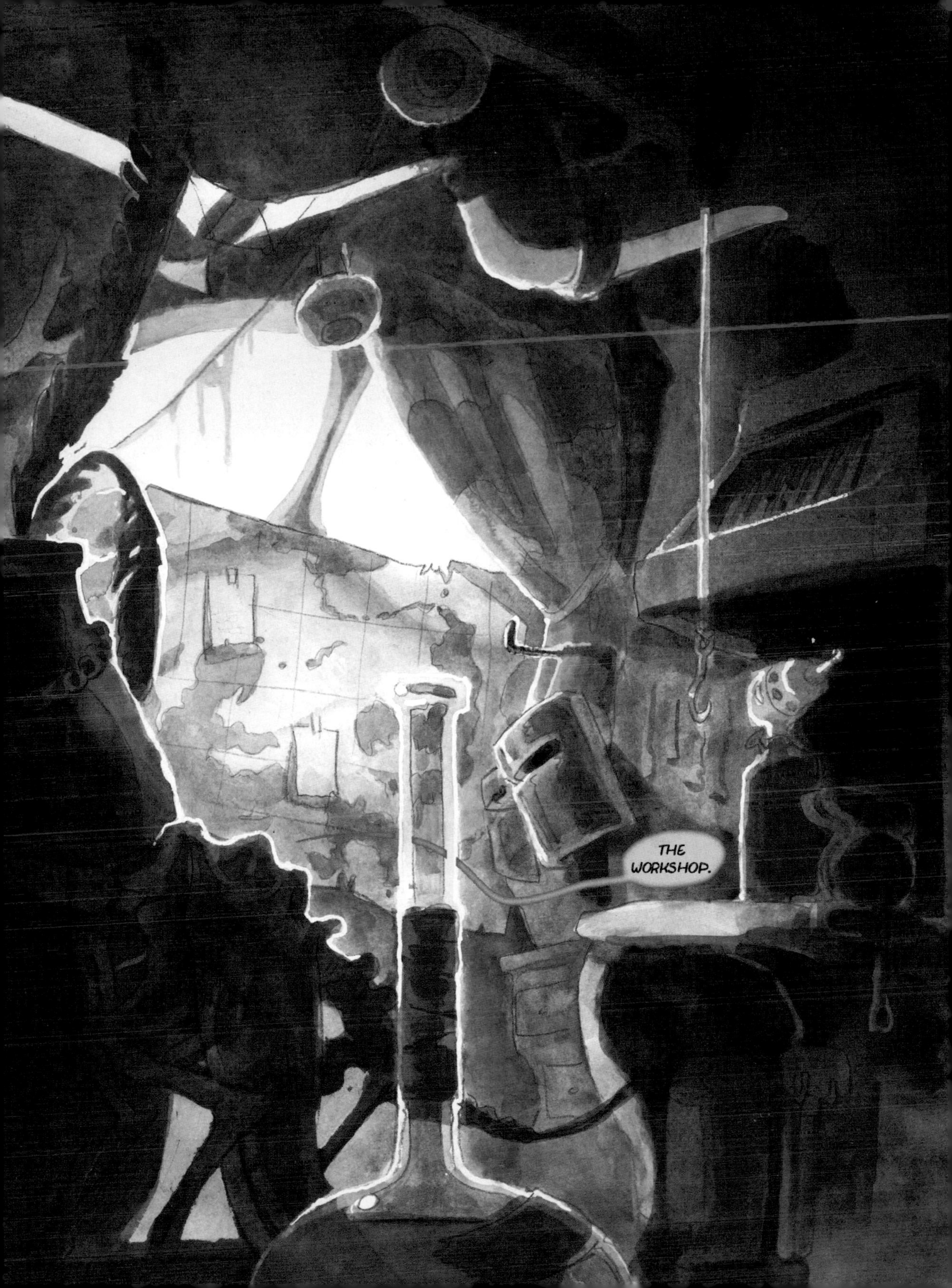
THE WORKSHOP.

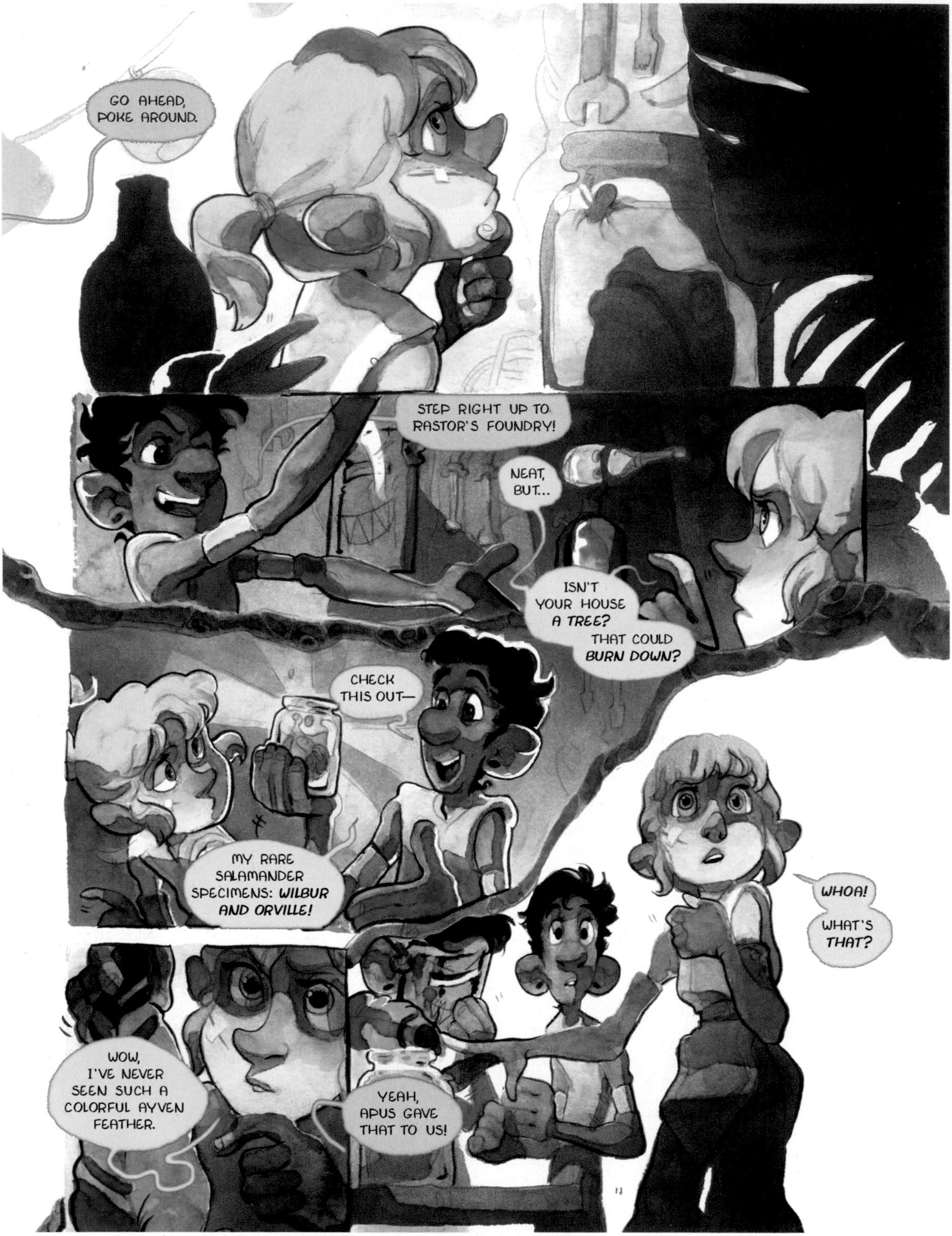
GO AHEAD, POKE AROUND.
STEP RIGHT UP TO RASTOR'S FOUNDRY!
NEAT, BUT...
ISN'T YOUR HOUSE *A TREE?*
THAT COULD *BURN DOWN?*
CHECK THIS OUT—
MY RARE SALAMANDER SPECIMENS: ***WILBUR AND ORVILLE!***
WHOA!
WHAT'S *THAT?*
WOW, I'VE NEVER SEEN SUCH A COLORFUL AYVEN FEATHER.
YEAH, APUS GAVE THAT TO US!

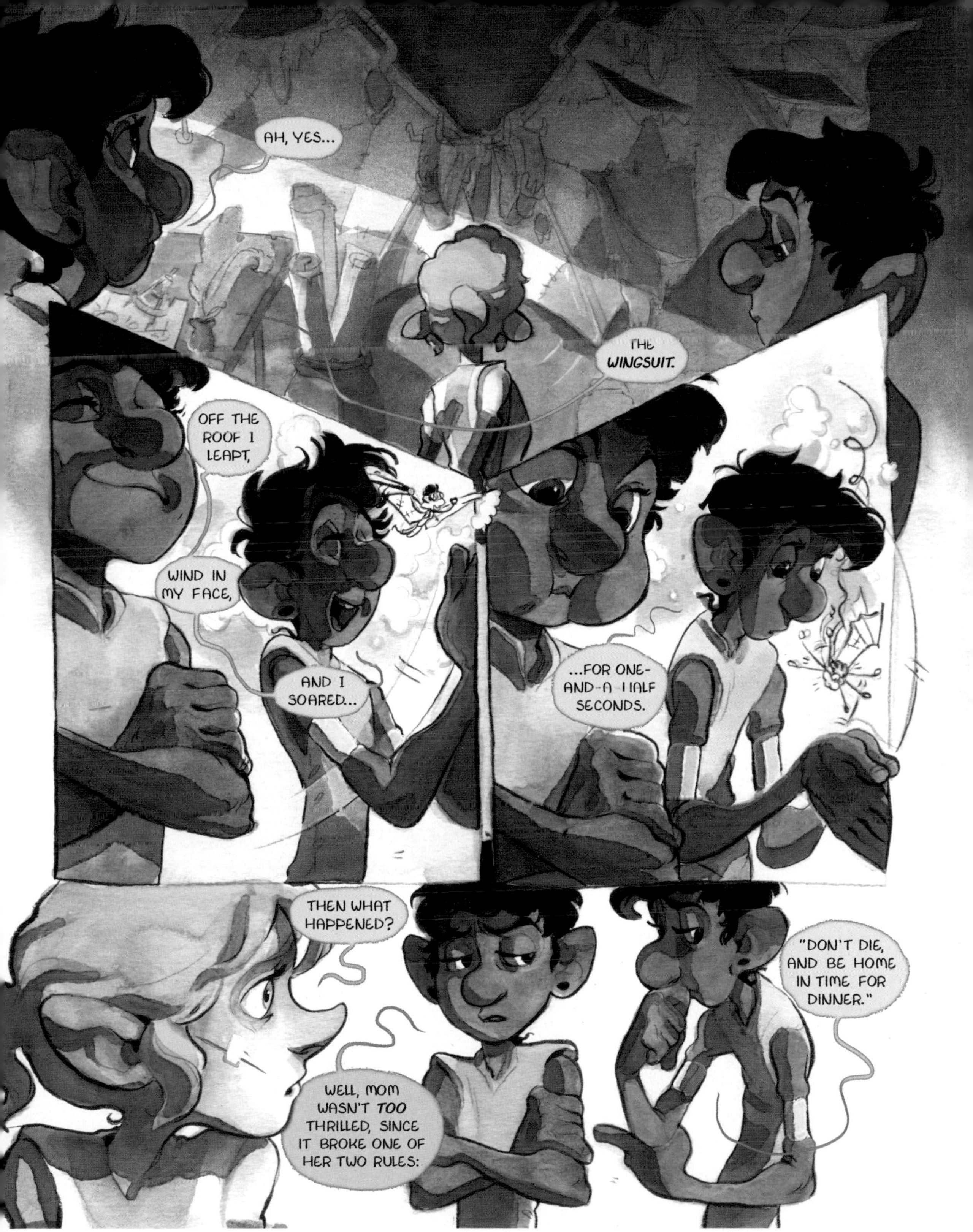
AH, YES...
THE WINGSUIT.
OFF THE ROOF I LEAPT,
WIND IN MY FACE,
AND I SOARED...
...FOR ONE-AND-A-HALF SECONDS.
THEN WHAT HAPPENED?
WELL, MOM WASN'T *TOO* THRILLED, SINCE IT BROKE ONE OF HER TWO RULES:
"DON'T DIE, AND BE HOME IN TIME FOR DINNER."

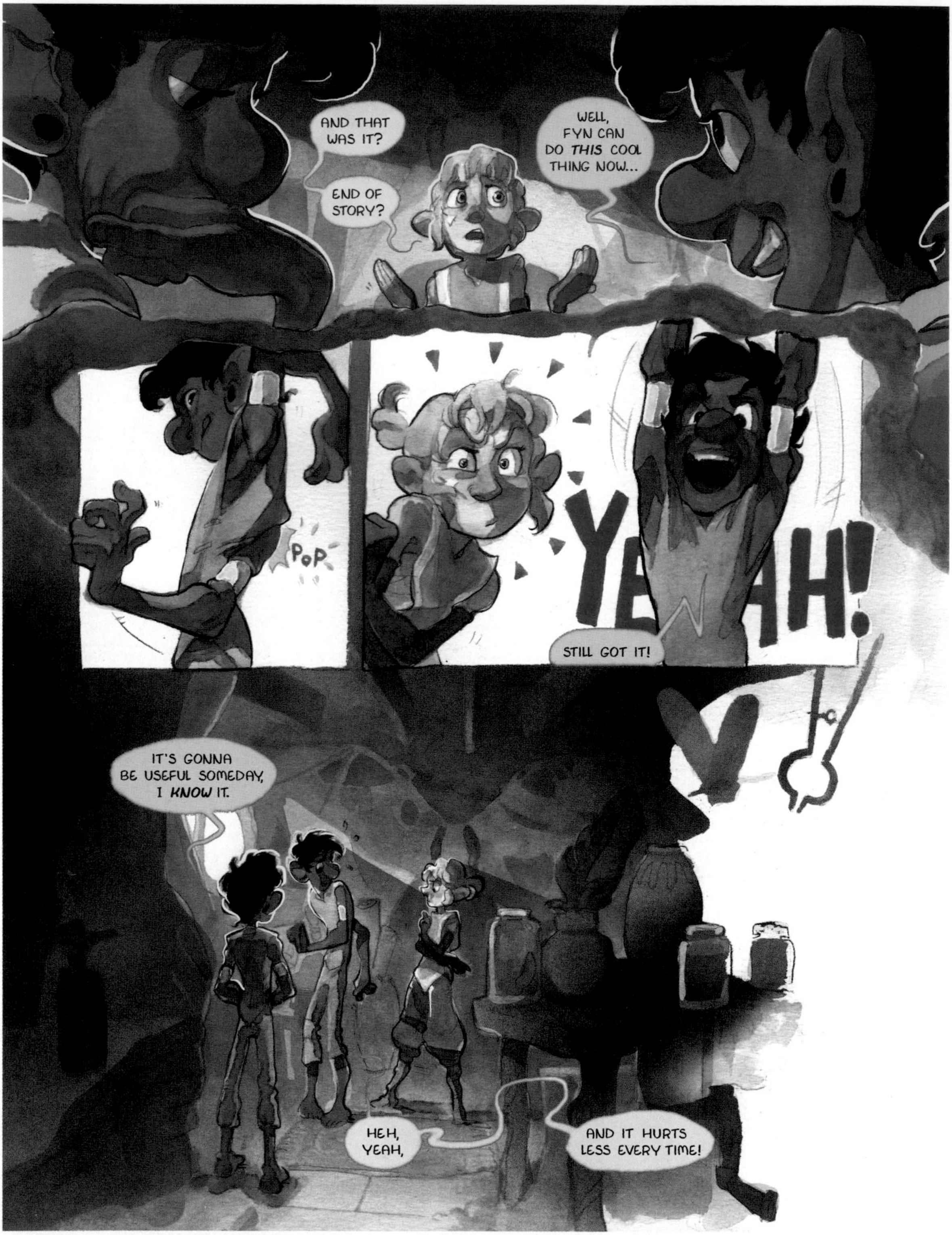
AND THAT WAS IT?
END OF STORY?
WELL, FYN CAN DO THIS COOL THING NOW...
POP
YEAH!
STILL GOT IT!
IT'S GONNA BE USEFUL SOMEDAY, I KNOW IT.
HEH, YEAH,
AND IT HURTS LESS EVERY TIME!

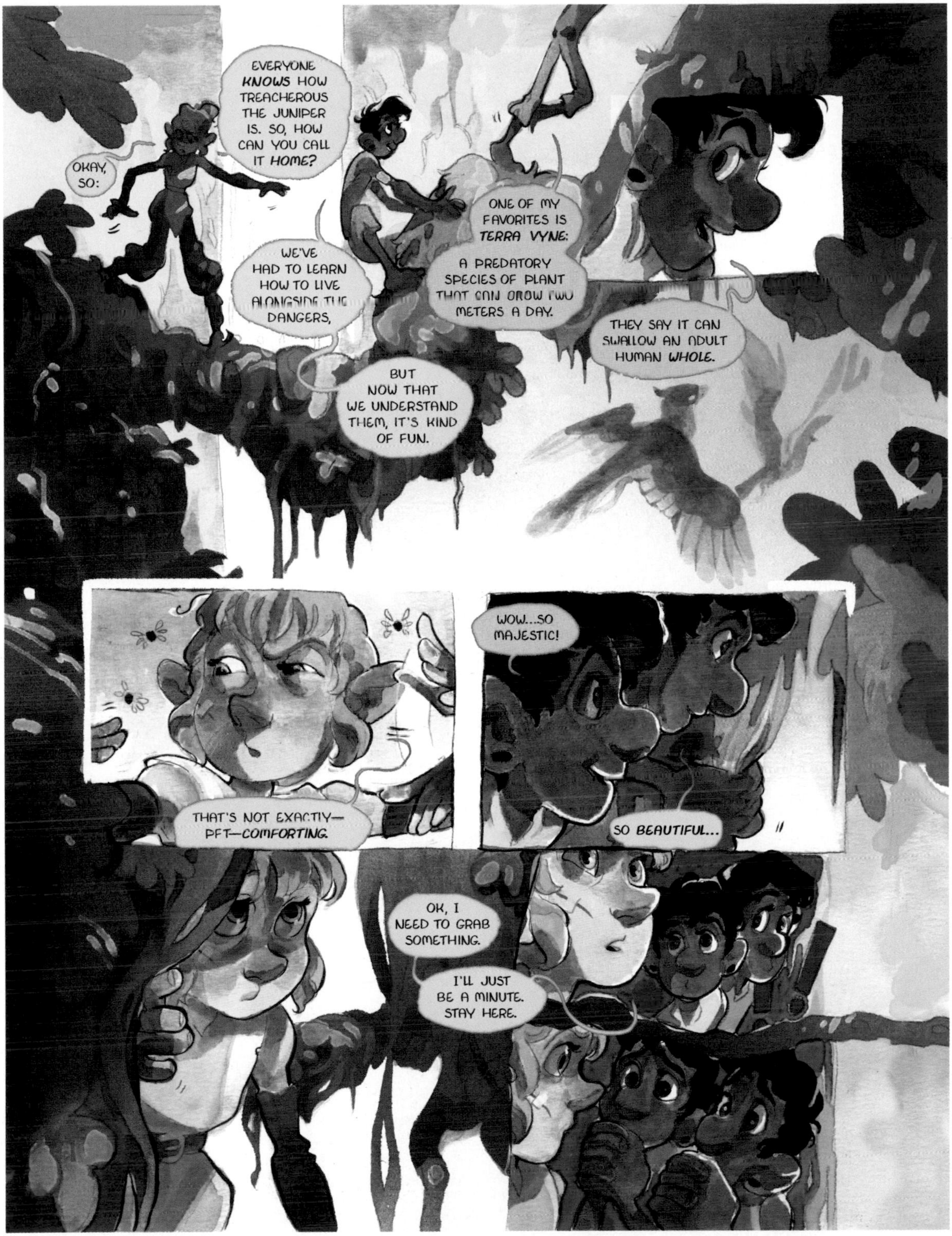
OKAY, SO:
EVERYONE KNOWS HOW TREACHEROUS THE JUNIPER IS. SO, HOW CAN YOU CALL IT HOME?
WE'VE HAD TO LEARN HOW TO LIVE ALONGSIDE THE DANGERS,
BUT NOW THAT WE UNDERSTAND THEM, IT'S KIND OF FUN.
ONE OF MY FAVORITES IS TERRA VYNE:
A PREDATORY SPECIES OF PLANT THAT CAN GROW TWO METERS A DAY.
THEY SAY IT CAN SWALLOW AN ADULT HUMAN WHOLE.
THAT'S NOT EXACTLY— PFT—COMFORTING.
WOW...SO MAJESTIC!
SO BEAUTIFUL...
OK, I NEED TO GRAB SOMETHING.
I'LL JUST BE A MINUTE. STAY HERE.

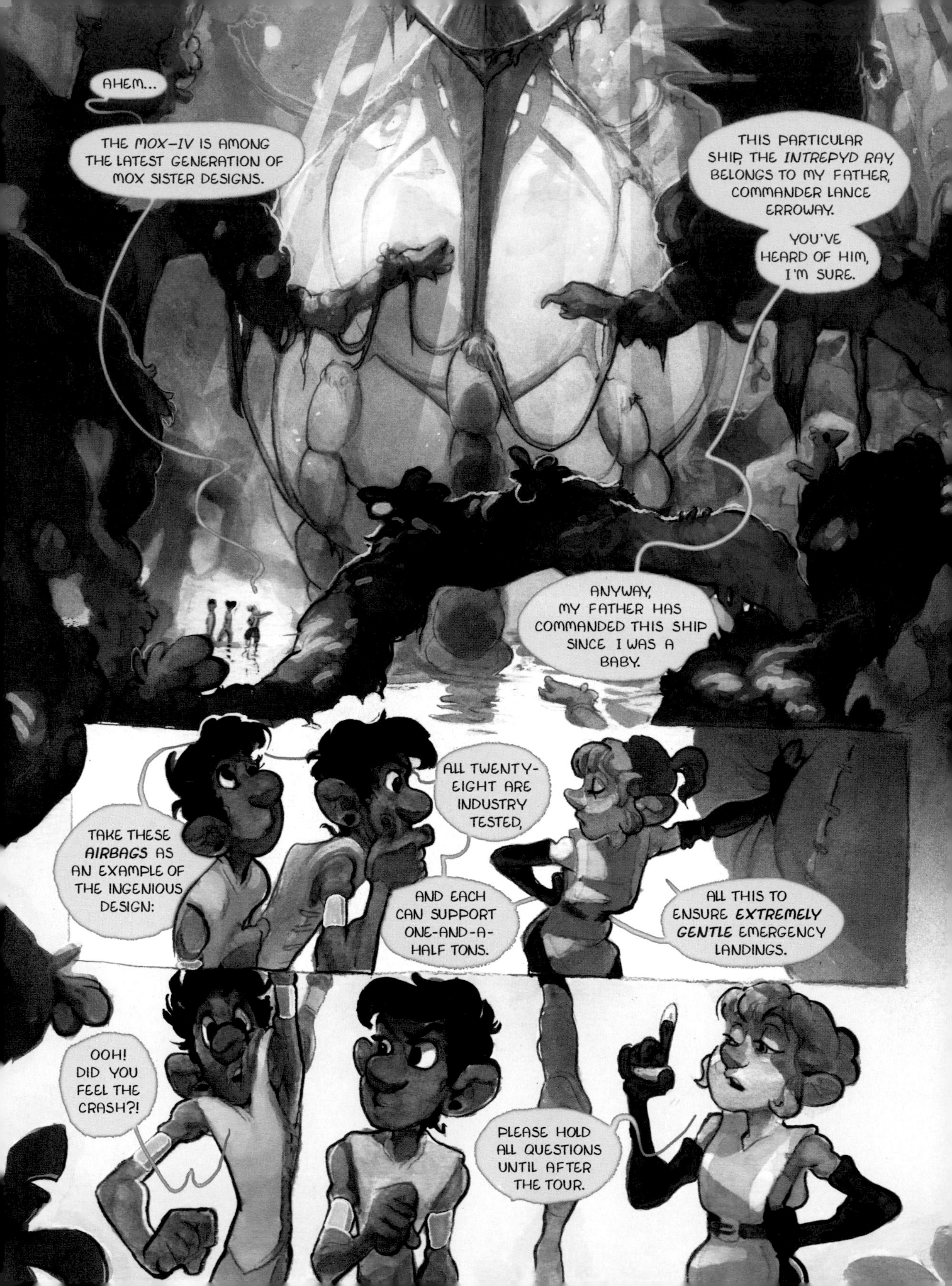
AHEM...
THE MOX-IV IS AMONG THE LATEST GENERATION OF MOX SISTER DESIGNS.
THIS PARTICULAR SHIP, THE INTREPYD RAY, BELONGS TO MY FATHER, COMMANDER LANCE ERROWAY.
YOU'VE HEARD OF HIM, I'M SURE.
ANYWAY, MY FATHER HAS COMMANDED THIS SHIP SINCE I WAS A BABY.
TAKE THESE AIRBAGS AS AN EXAMPLE OF THE INGENIOUS DESIGN:
ALL TWENTY-EIGHT ARE INDUSTRY TESTED,
AND EACH CAN SUPPORT ONE-AND-A-HALF TONS.
ALL THIS TO ENSURE EXTREMELY GENTLE EMERGENCY LANDINGS.
OOH! DID YOU FEEL THE CRASH?!
PLEASE HOLD ALL QUESTIONS UNTIL AFTER THE TOUR.

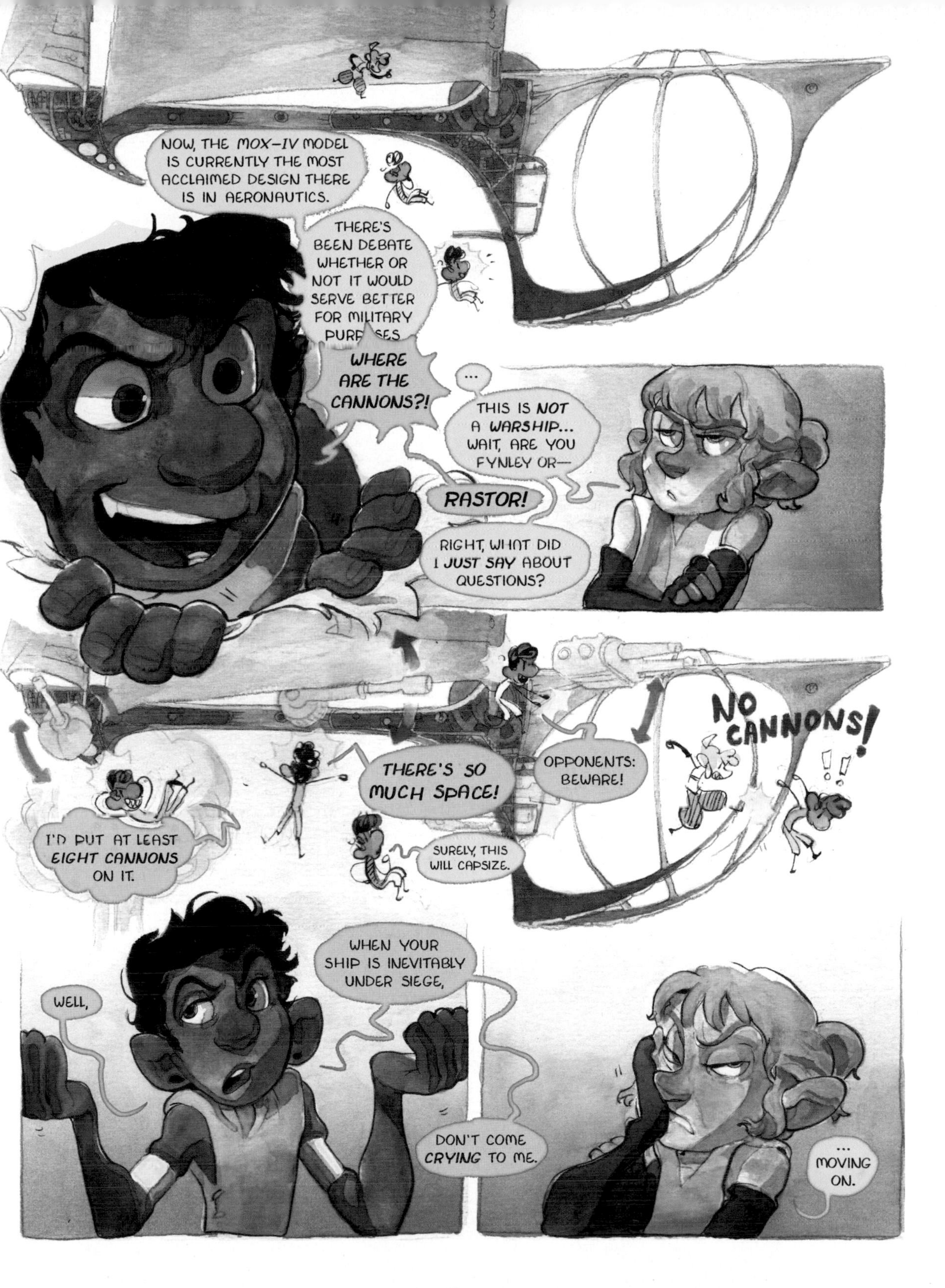
NOW, THE MOX-IV MODEL IS CURRENTLY THE MOST ACCLAIMED DESIGN THERE IS IN AERONAUTICS.
THERE'S BEEN DEBATE WHETHER OR NOT IT WOULD SERVE BETTER FOR MILITARY PURPOSES
WHERE ARE THE CANNONS?!
...
THIS IS NOT A WARSHIP... WAIT, ARE YOU FYNLEY OR—
RASTOR!
RIGHT, WHAT DID I JUST SAY ABOUT QUESTIONS?
NO CANNONS!
THERE'S SO MUCH SPACE!
OPPONENTS: BEWARE!
I'D PUT AT LEAST EIGHT CANNONS ON IT.
SURELY, THIS WILL CAPSIZE.
WELL,
WHEN YOUR SHIP IS INEVITABLY UNDER SIEGE,
DON'T COME CRYING TO ME.
... MOVING ON.

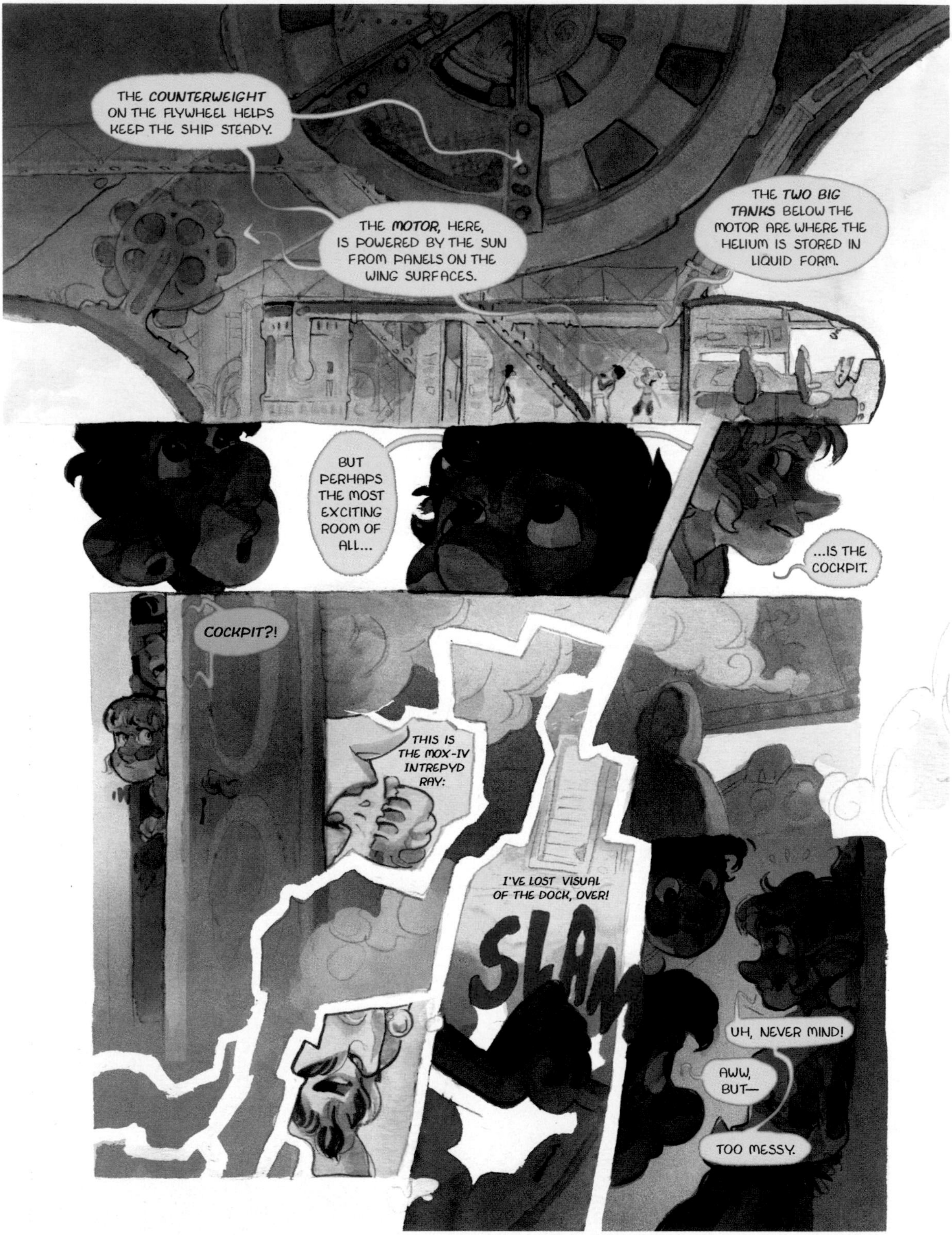
THE COUNTERWEIGHT ON THE FLYWHEEL HELPS KEEP THE SHIP STEADY.
THE MOTOR, HERE, IS POWERED BY THE SUN FROM PANELS ON THE WING SURFACES.
THE TWO BIG TANKS BELOW THE MOTOR ARE WHERE THE HELIUM IS STORED IN LIQUID FORM.
BUT PERHAPS THE MOST EXCITING ROOM OF ALL...
...IS THE COCKPIT.
COCKPIT?!
THIS IS THE MOX-IV INTREPYD RAY:
I'VE LOST VISUAL OF THE DOCK, OVER!
SLAM
UH, NEVER MIND!
AWW, BUT—
TOO MESSY.

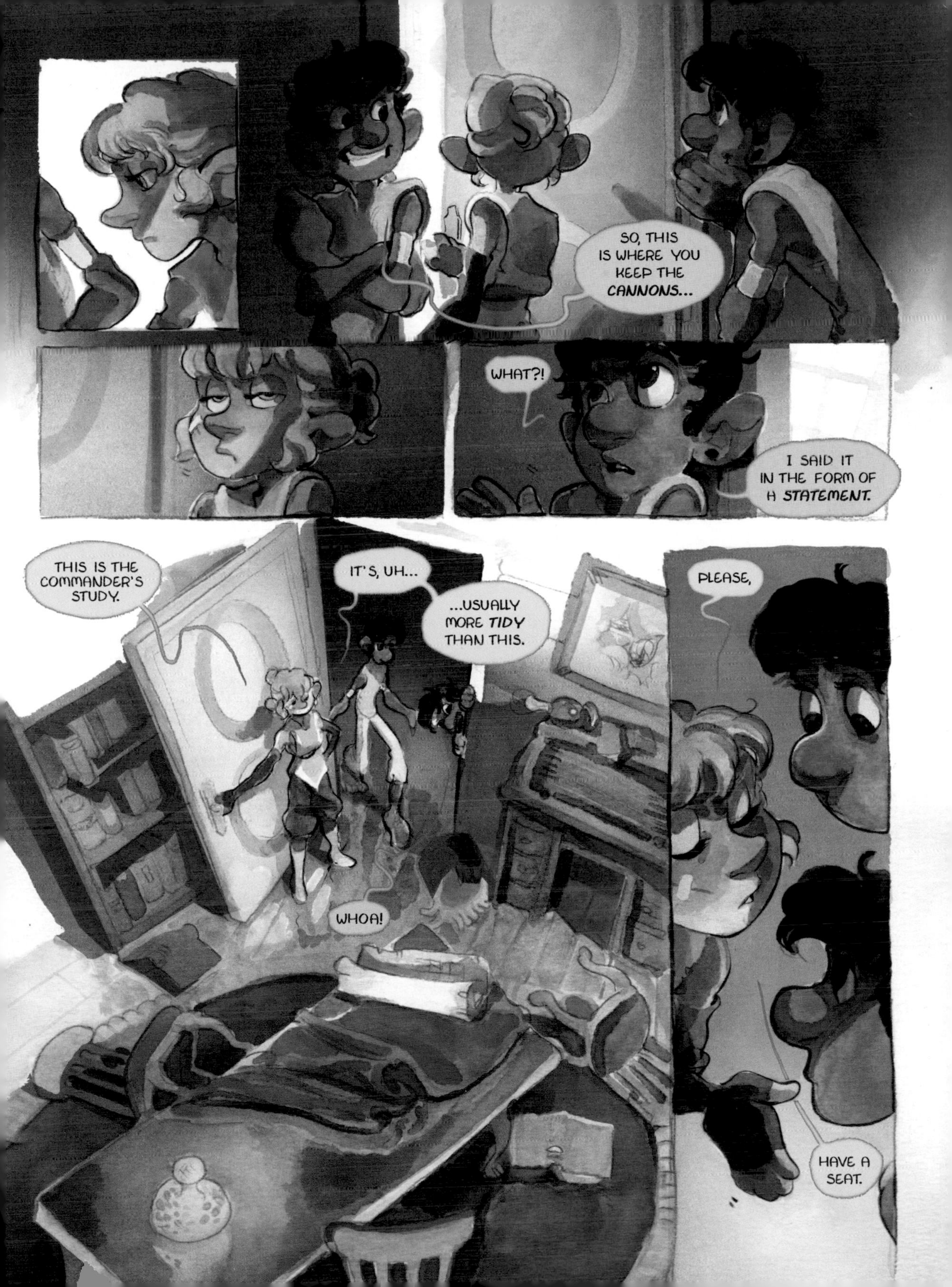
SO, THIS IS WHERE YOU KEEP THE CANNONS...
WHAT?!
I SAID IT IN THE FORM OF A STATEMENT.
THIS IS THE COMMANDER'S STUDY.
IT'S, UH...
...USUALLY MORE TIDY THAN THIS.
WHOA!
PLEASE,
HAVE A SEAT.

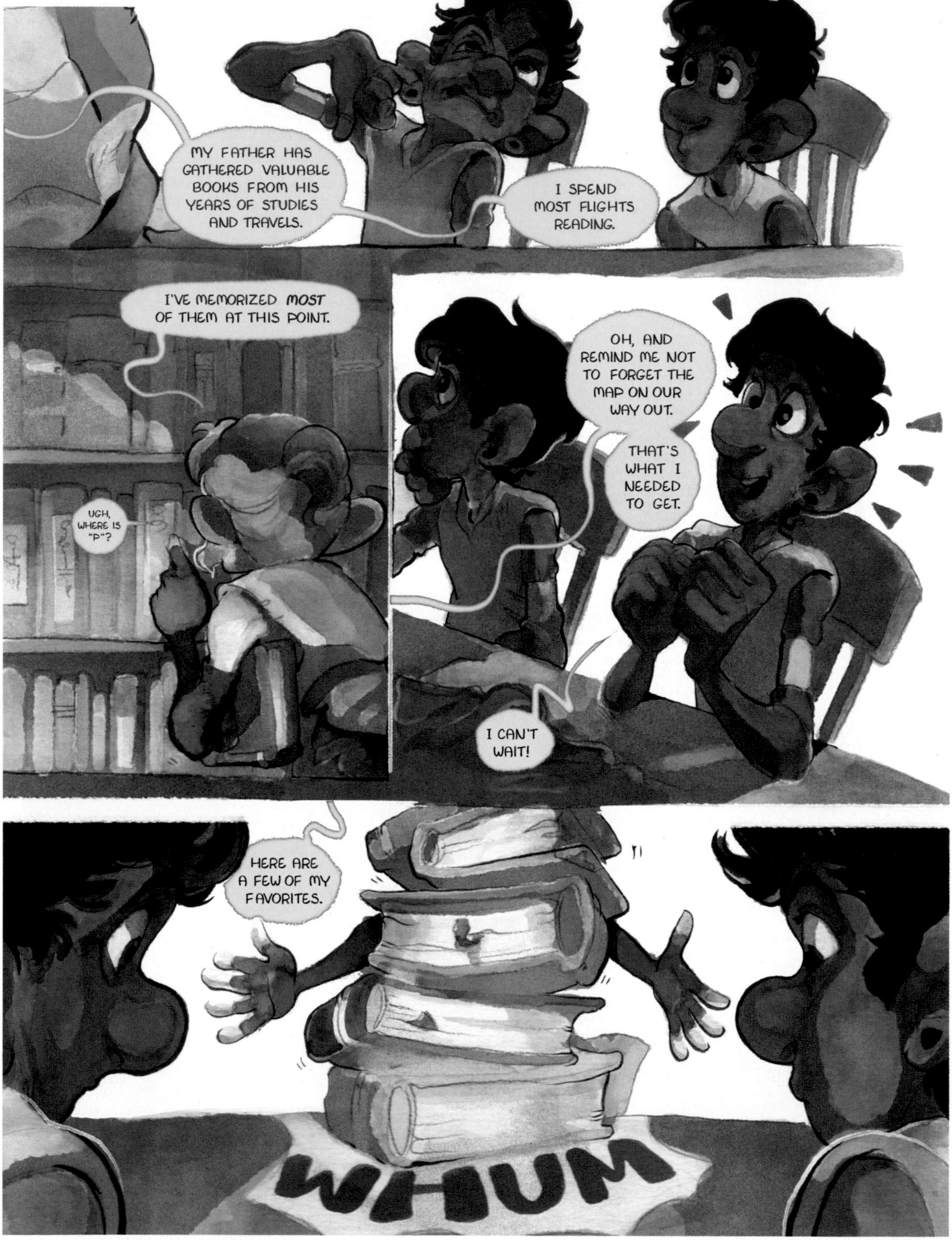
MY FATHER HAS GATHERED VALUABLE BOOKS FROM HIS YEARS OF STUDIES AND TRAVELS.
I SPEND MOST FLIGHTS READING.
I'VE MEMORIZED *MOST* OF THEM AT THIS POINT.
UGH, WHERE IS "P"?
OH, AND REMIND ME NOT TO FORGET THE MAP ON OUR WAY OUT.
THAT'S WHAT I NEEDED TO GET.
I CAN'T WAIT!
HERE ARE A FEW OF MY FAVORITES.
WHUM

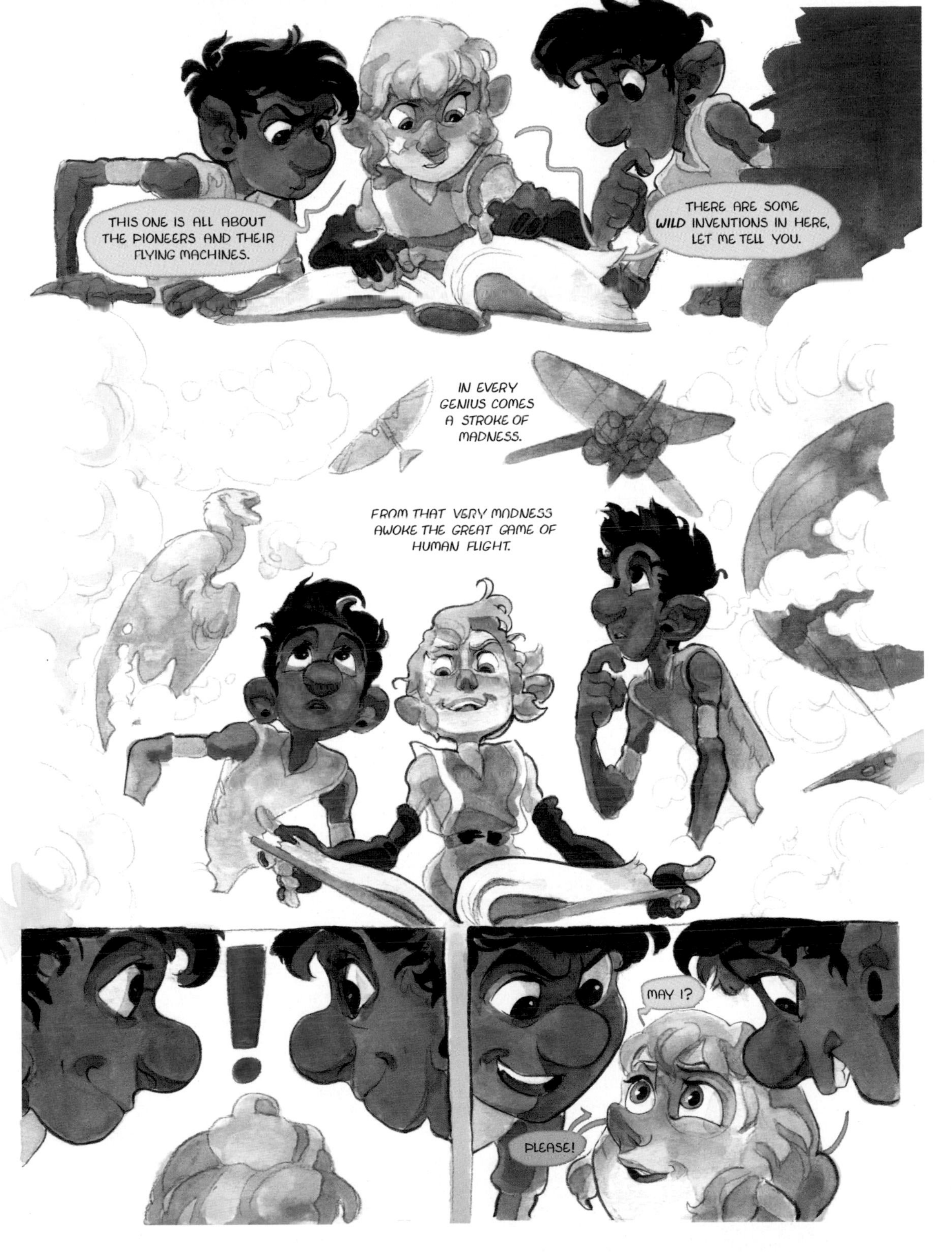
THIS ONE IS ALL ABOUT THE PIONEERS AND THEIR FLYING MACHINES.
THERE ARE SOME WILD INVENTIONS IN HERE, LET ME TELL YOU.
IN EVERY GENIUS COMES A STROKE OF MADNESS.
FROM THAT VERY MADNESS AWOKE THE GREAT GAME OF HUMAN FLIGHT.
!
MAY I?
PLEASE!

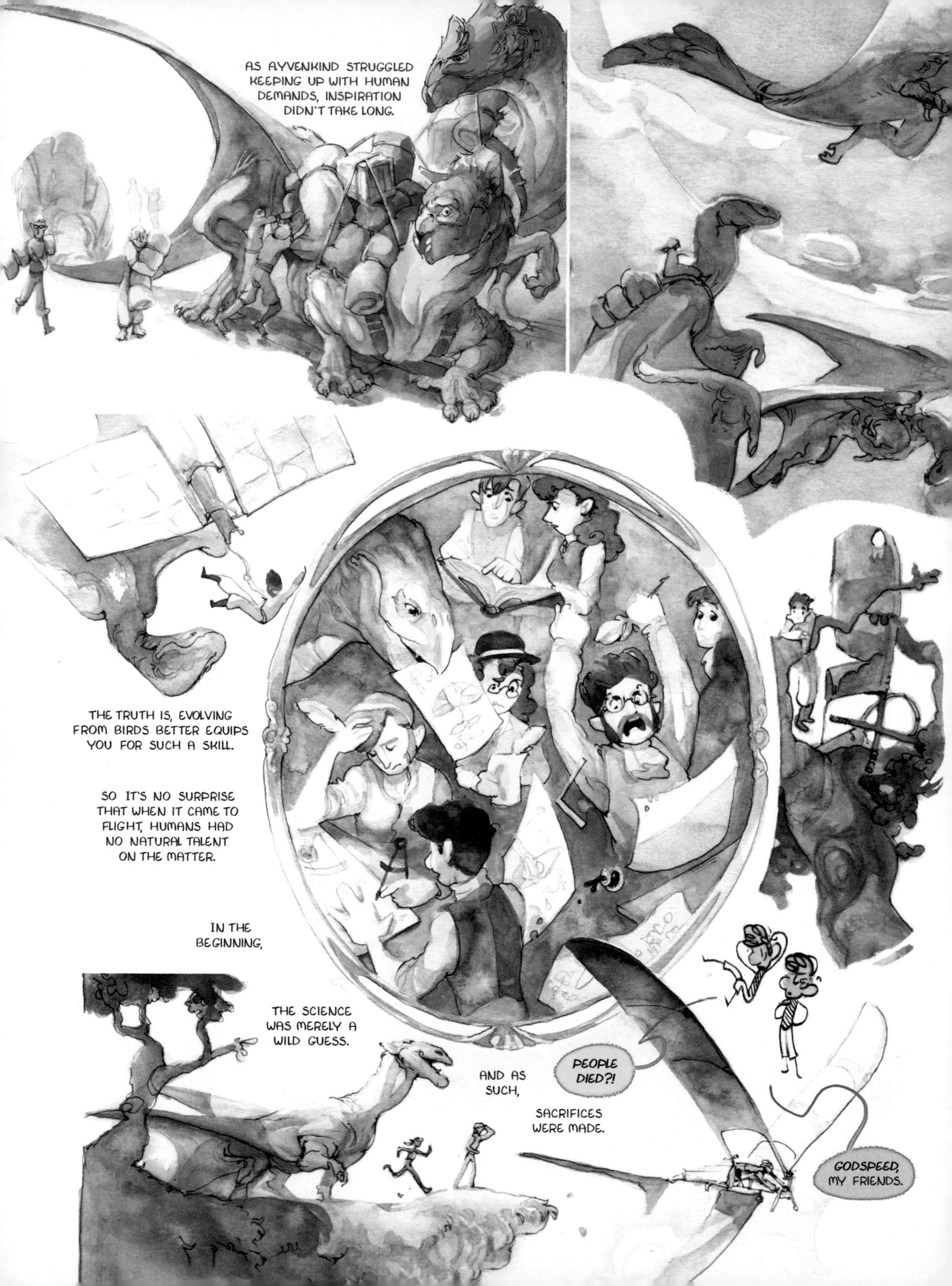
AS AYVENKIND STRUGGLED KEEPING UP WITH HUMAN DEMANDS, INSPIRATION DIDN'T TAKE LONG.
THE TRUTH IS, EVOLVING FROM BIRDS BETTER EQUIPS YOU FOR SUCH A SKILL.
SO IT'S NO SURPRISE THAT WHEN IT CAME TO FLIGHT, HUMANS HAD NO NATURAL TALENT ON THE MATTER.
IN THE BEGINNING,
THE SCIENCE WAS MERELY A WILD GUESS.
AND AS SUCH,
SACRIFICES WERE MADE.
PEOPLE DIED?!
GODSPEED, MY FRIENDS.

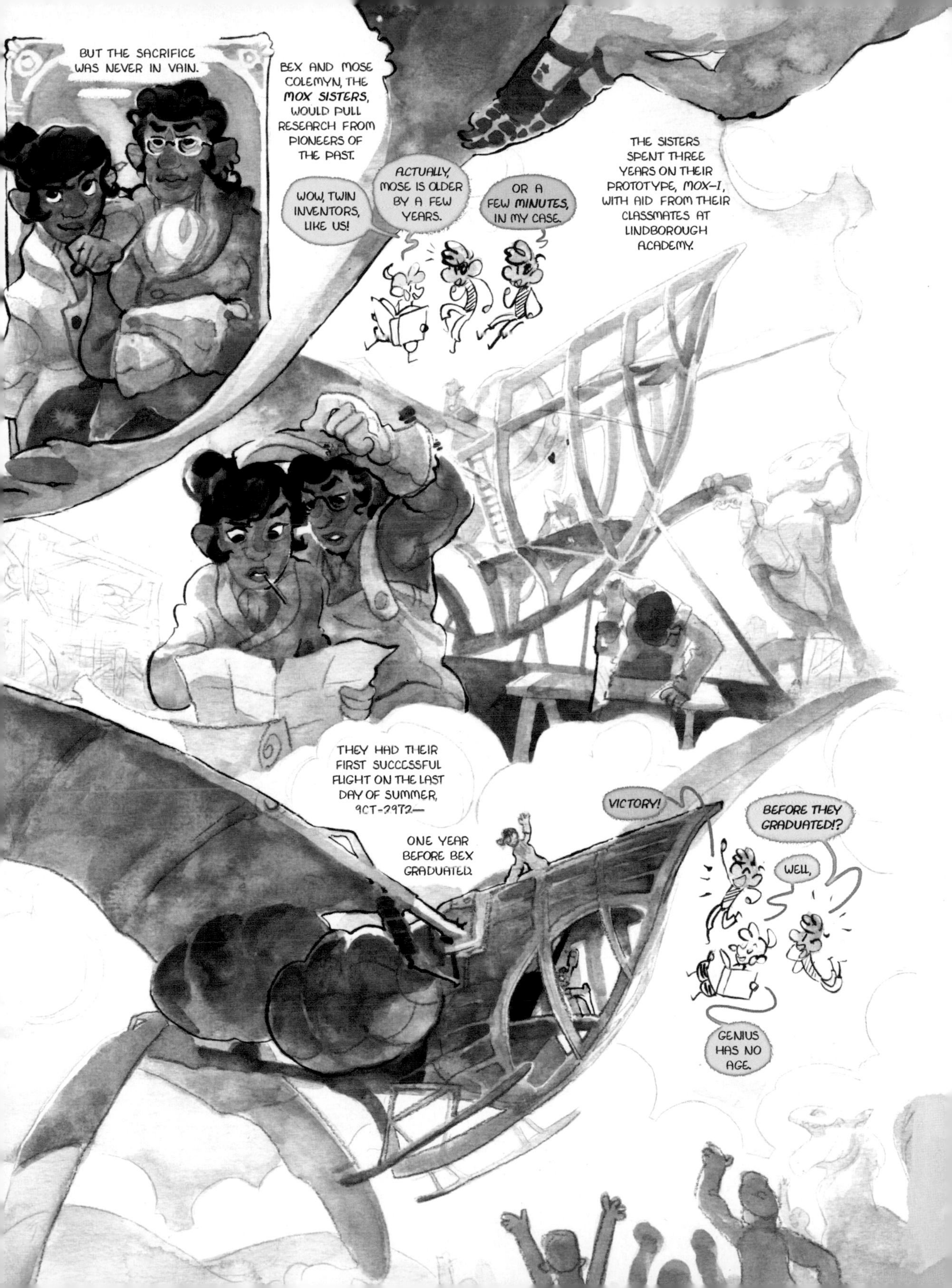
BUT THE SACRIFICE WAS NEVER IN VAIN.
BEX AND MOSE COLEMYN, THE **MOX SISTERS**, WOULD PULL RESEARCH FROM PIONEERS OF THE PAST.
WOW, TWIN INVENTORS, LIKE US!
ACTUALLY, MOSE IS OLDER BY A FEW YEARS.
OR A FEW **MINUTES**, IN MY CASE.
THE SISTERS SPENT THREE YEARS ON THEIR PROTOTYPE, *MOX-I*, WITH AID FROM THEIR CLASSMATES AT LINDBOROUGH ACADEMY.
THEY HAD THEIR FIRST SUCCESSFUL FLIGHT ON THE LAST DAY OF SUMMER, 9CT-2972—
ONE YEAR BEFORE BEX GRADUATED.
VICTORY!
BEFORE THEY GRADUATED!?
WELL,
GENIUS HAS NO AGE.

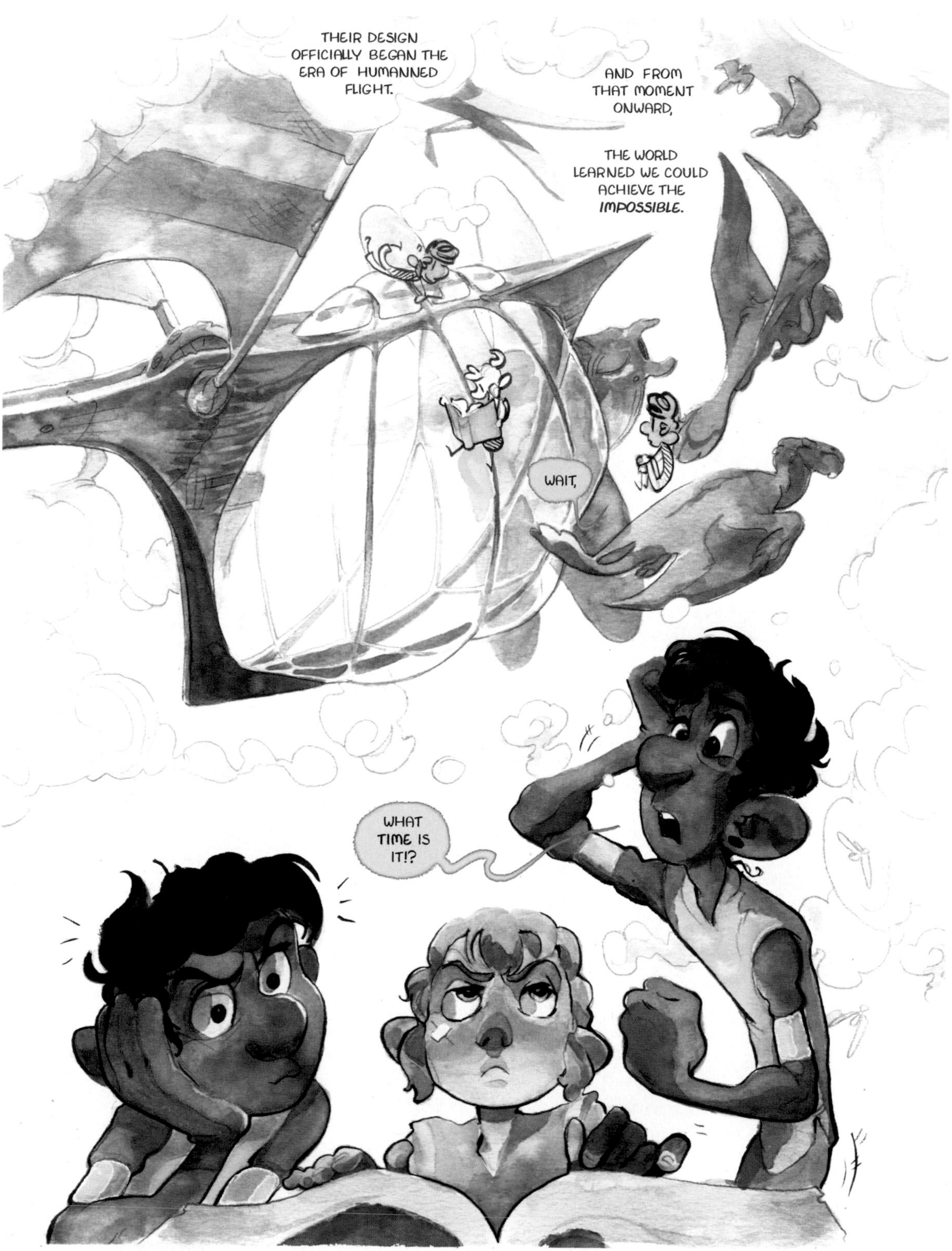
THEIR DESIGN OFFICIALLY BEGAN THE ERA OF HUMANNED FLIGHT.
AND FROM THAT MOMENT ONWARD,
THE WORLD LEARNED WE COULD ACHIEVE THE *IMPOSSIBLE.*
WAIT,
WHAT TIME IS IT!?

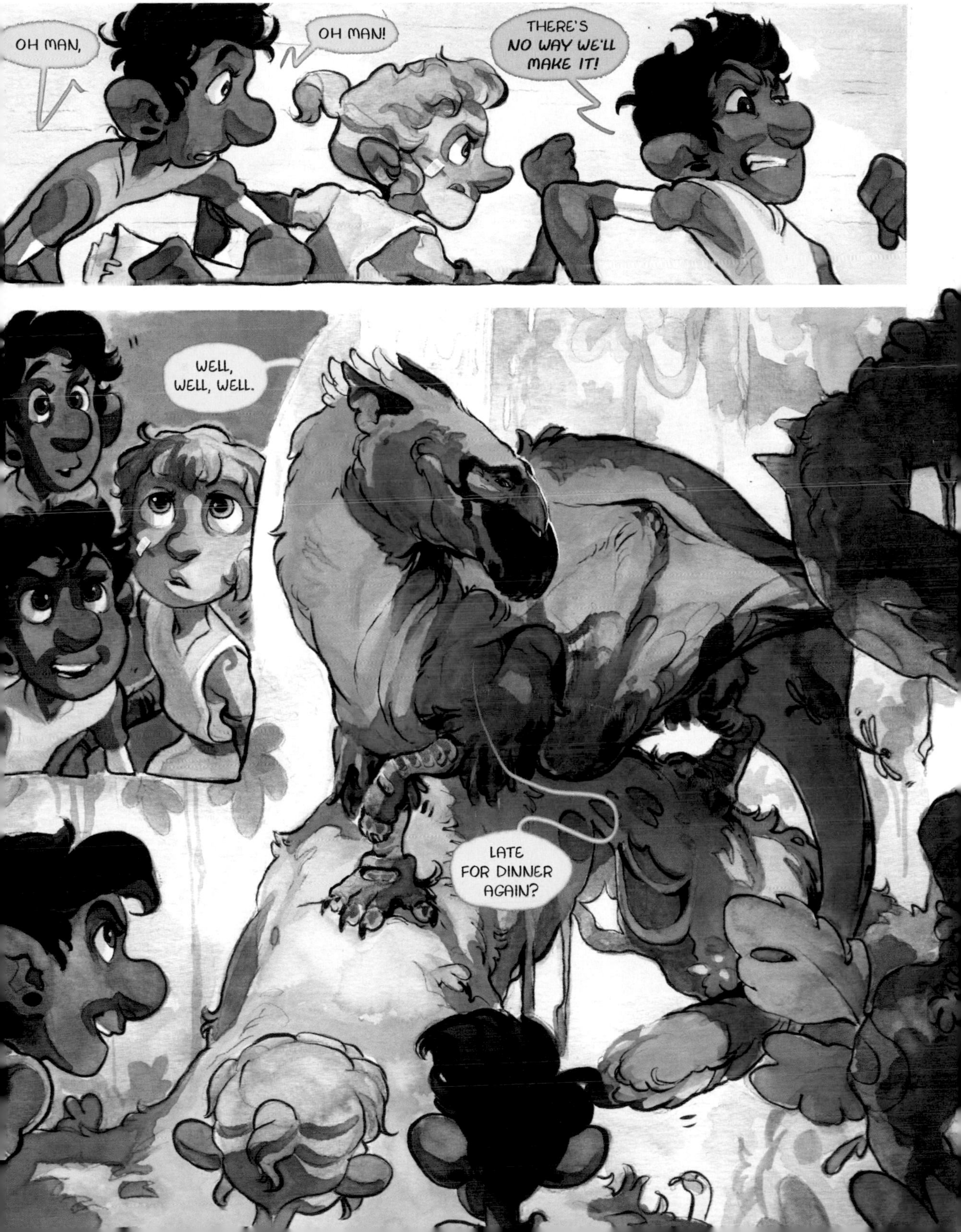
OH MAN,
OH MAN!
THERE'S NO WAY WE'LL MAKE IT!
WELL, WELL, WELL.
LATE FOR DINNER AGAIN?

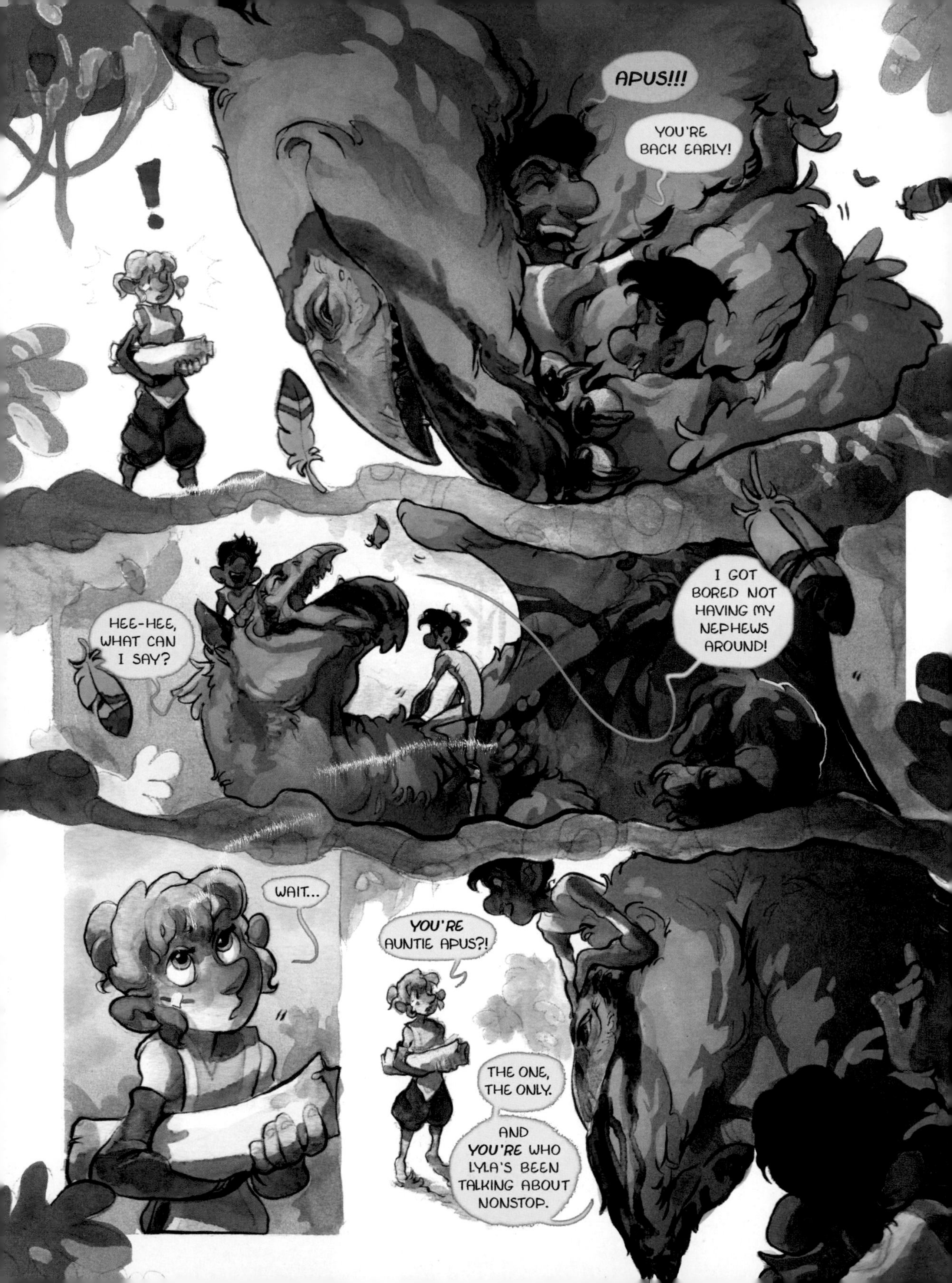
!
APUS!!!
YOU'RE BACK EARLY!
HEE-HEE, WHAT CAN I SAY?
I GOT BORED NOT HAVING MY NEPHEWS AROUND!
WAIT...
YOU'RE AUNTIE APUS?!
THE ONE, THE ONLY.
AND YOU'RE WHO LYLA'S BEEN TALKING ABOUT NONSTOP.

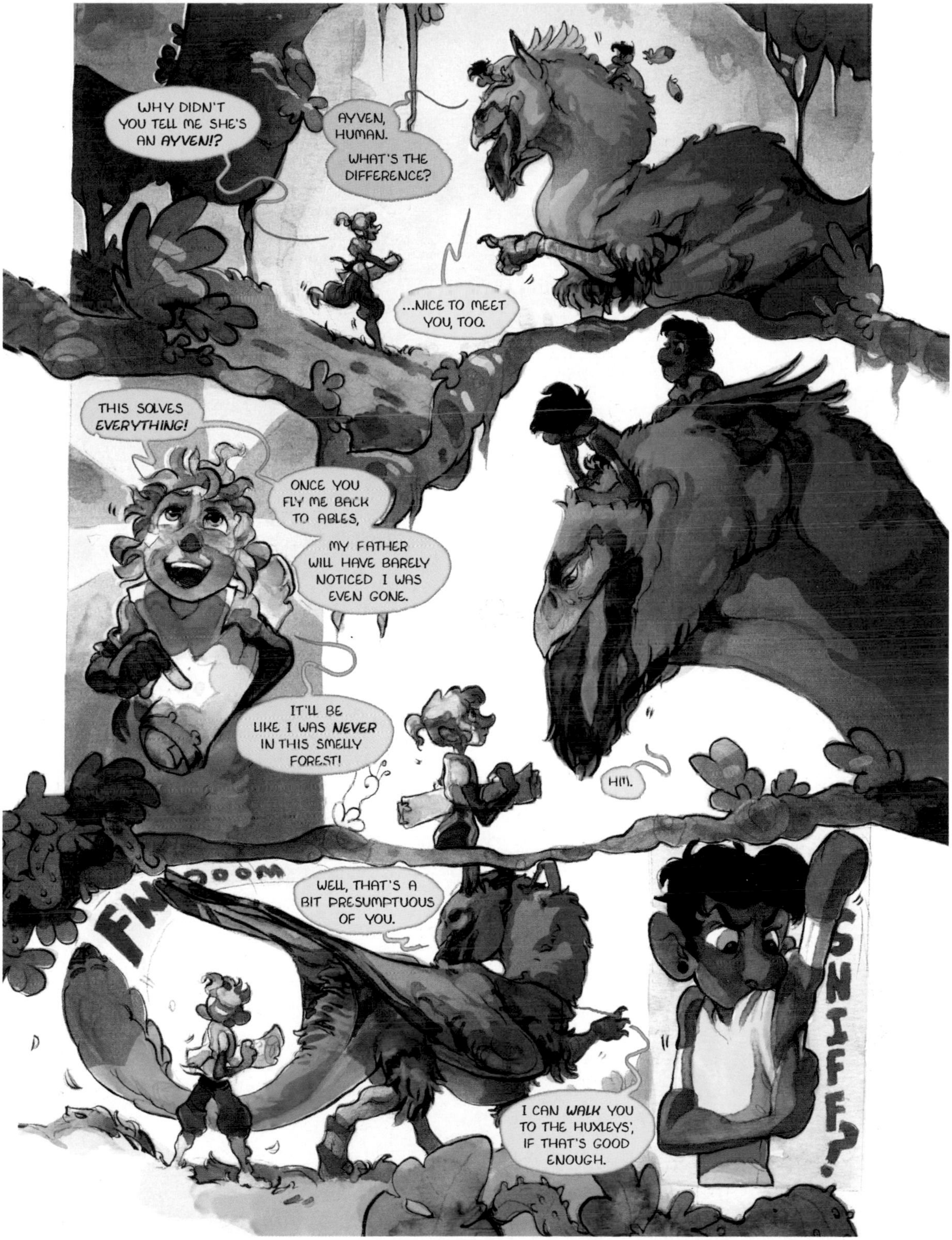
WHY DIDN'T YOU TELL ME SHE'S AN AYVEN!?
AYVEN, HUMAN.
WHAT'S THE DIFFERENCE?
...NICE TO MEET YOU, TOO.
THIS SOLVES EVERYTHING!
ONCE YOU FLY ME BACK TO ABLES,
MY FATHER WILL HAVE BARELY NOTICED I WAS EVEN GONE.
IT'LL BE LIKE I WAS NEVER IN THIS SMELLY FOREST!
HM.
FWOOOM
WELL, THAT'S A BIT PRESUMPTUOUS OF YOU.
I CAN WALK YOU TO THE HUXLEYS', IF THAT'S GOOD ENOUGH.
SNIFF?

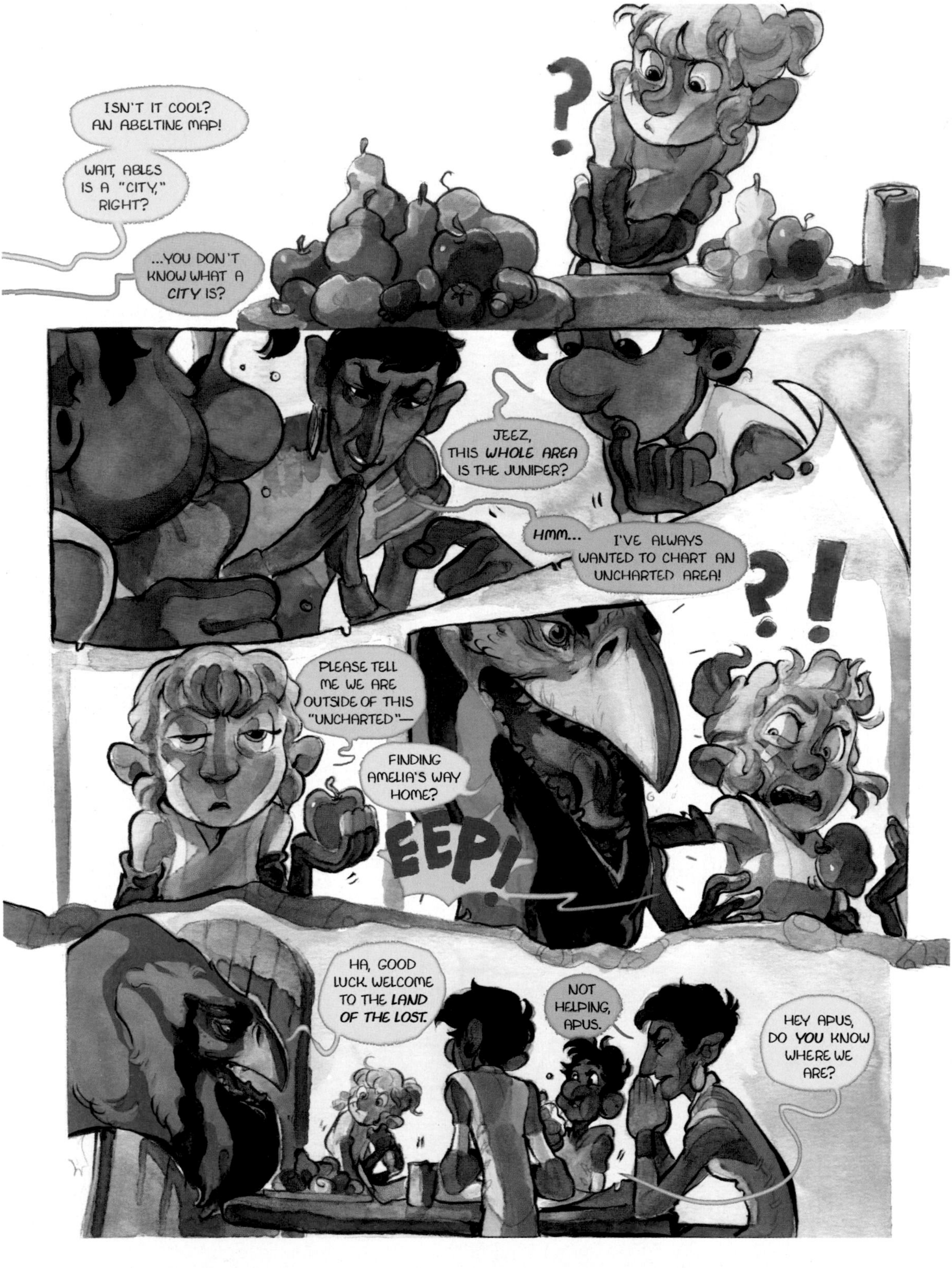
ISN'T IT COOL? AN ABELTINE MAP!
WAIT, ABLES IS A "CITY," RIGHT?
...YOU DON'T KNOW WHAT A CITY IS?
?
JEEZ, THIS WHOLE AREA IS THE JUNIPER?
HMM...
I'VE ALWAYS WANTED TO CHART AN UNCHARTED AREA!
?!
PLEASE TELL ME WE ARE OUTSIDE OF THIS "UNCHARTED"—
FINDING AMELIA'S WAY HOME?
EEP!
HA, GOOD LUCK. WELCOME TO THE LAND OF THE LOST.
NOT HELPING, APUS.
HEY APUS, DO YOU KNOW WHERE WE ARE?

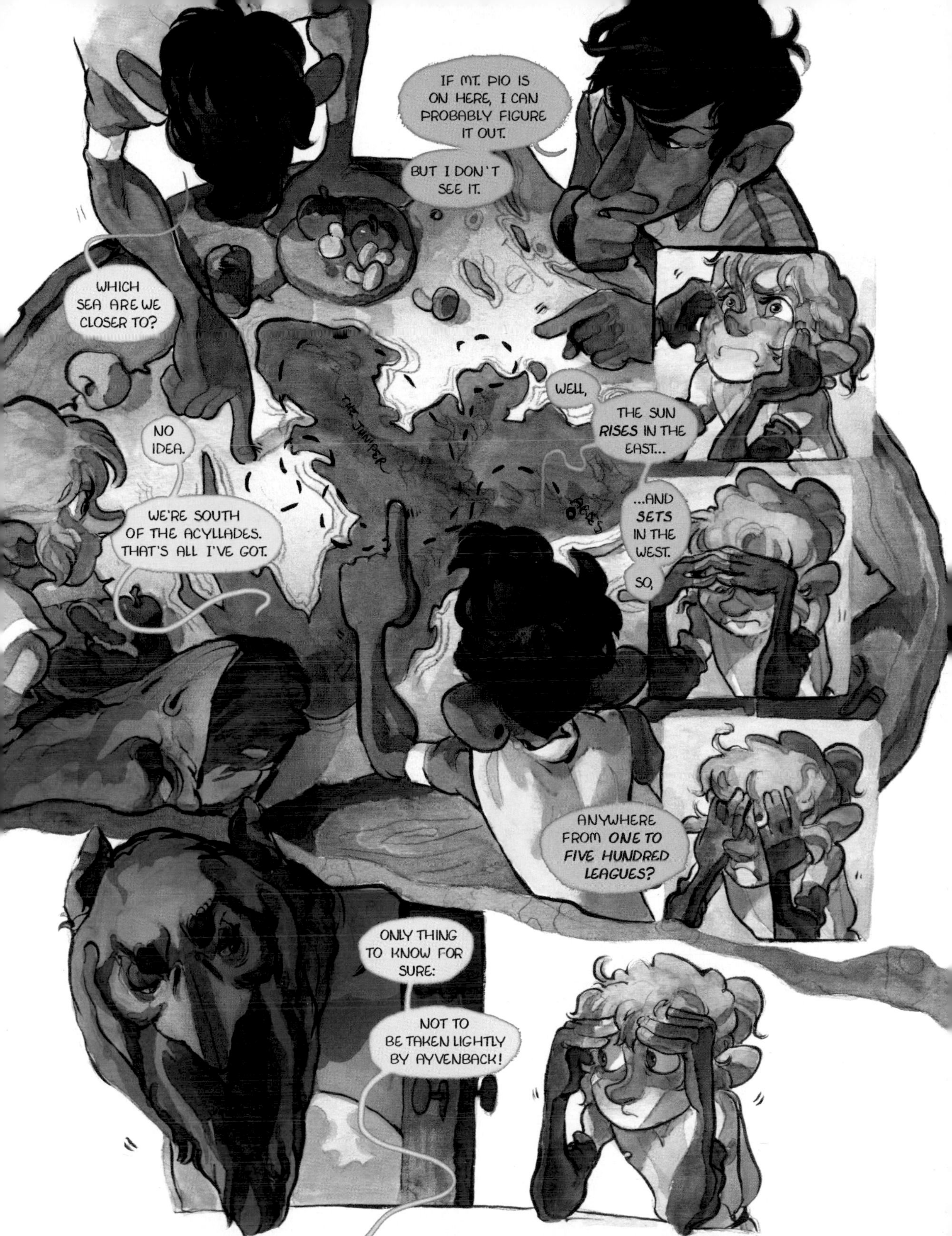
IF MT. PIO IS ON HERE, I CAN PROBABLY FIGURE IT OUT.
BUT I DON'T SEE IT.
WHICH SEA ARE WE CLOSER TO?
NO IDEA.
WE'RE SOUTH OF THE ACYLLADES. THAT'S ALL I'VE GOT.
THE JUNIPER
WELL,
THE SUN RISES IN THE EAST...
...AND SETS IN THE WEST.
SO,
ANYWHERE FROM ONE TO FIVE HUNDRED LEAGUES?
ONLY THING TO KNOW FOR SURE:
NOT TO BE TAKEN LIGHTLY BY AYVENBACK!

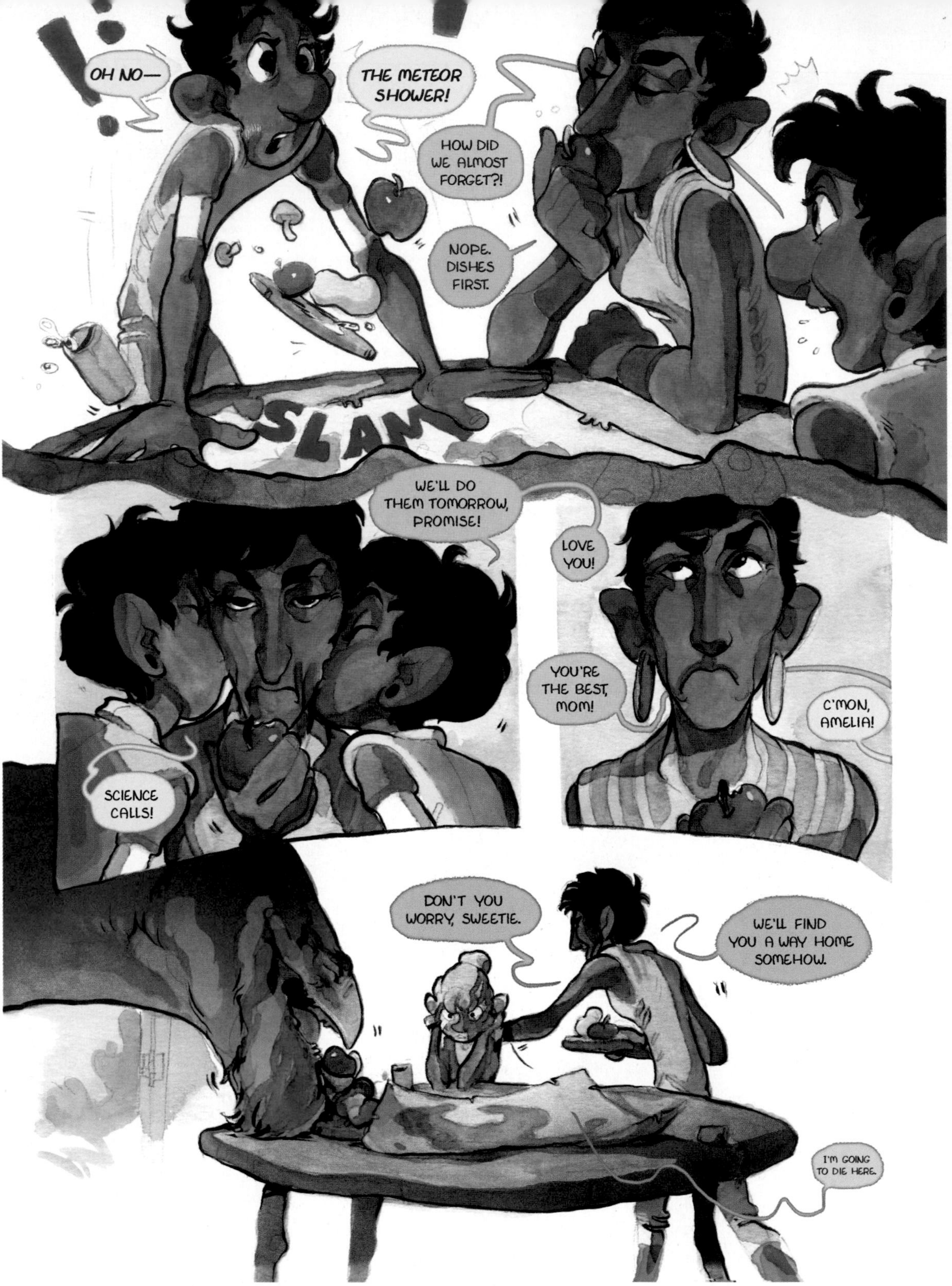
OH NO—
THE METEOR SHOWER!
HOW DID WE ALMOST FORGET?!
NOPE. DISHES FIRST.
SLAM
WE'LL DO THEM TOMORROW, PROMISE!
LOVE YOU!
SCIENCE CALLS!
YOU'RE THE BEST, MOM!
C'MON, AMELIA!
DON'T YOU WORRY, SWEETIE.
WE'LL FIND YOU A WAY HOME SOMEHOW.
I'M GOING TO DIE HERE.

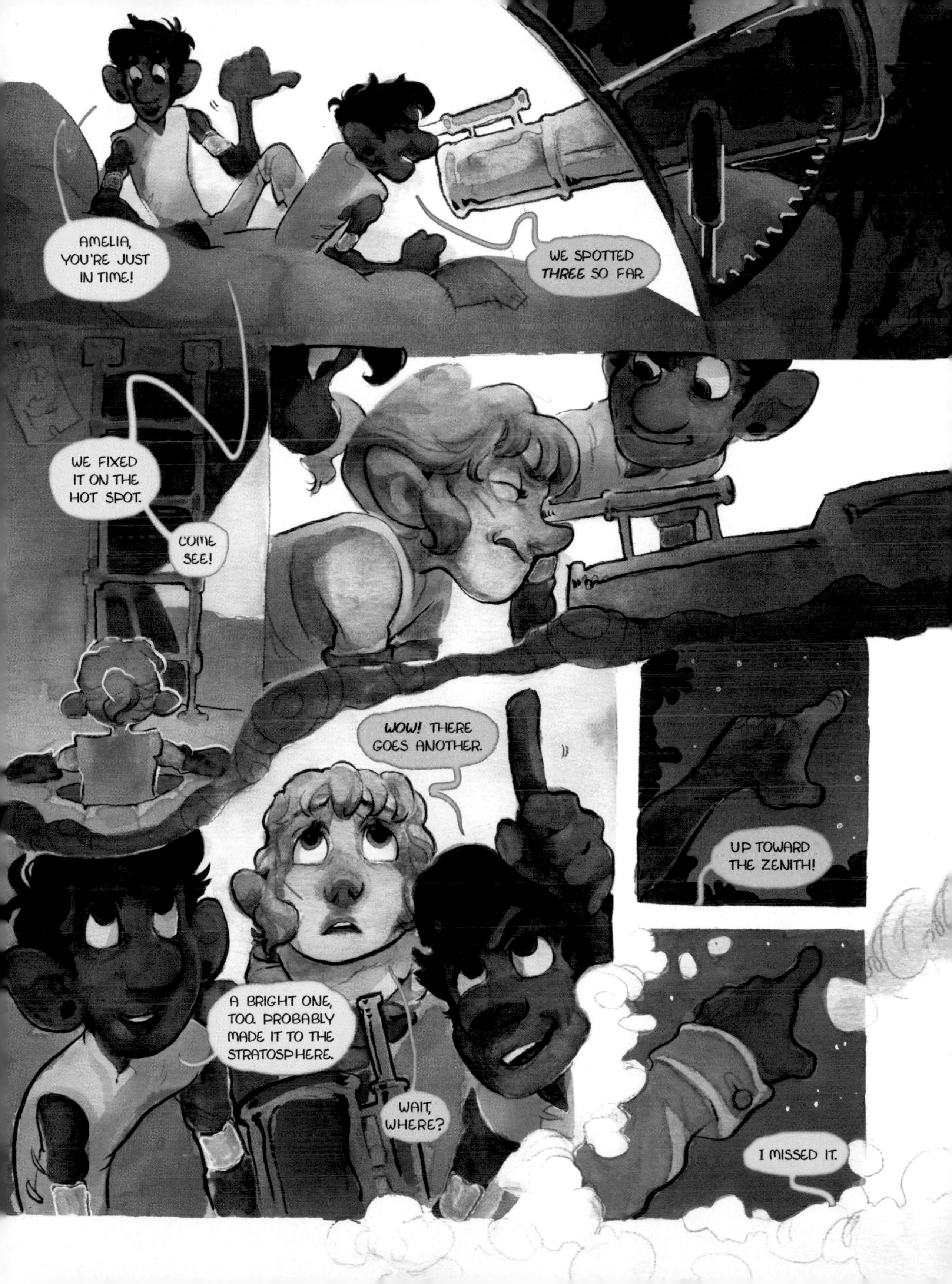
AMELIA, YOU'RE JUST IN TIME!
WE SPOTTED THREE SO FAR.
WE FIXED IT ON THE HOT SPOT.
COME SEE!
WOW! THERE GOES ANOTHER.
UP TOWARD THE ZENITH!
A BRIGHT ONE, TOO. PROBABLY MADE IT TO THE STRATOSPHERE.
WAIT, WHERE?
I MISSED IT.

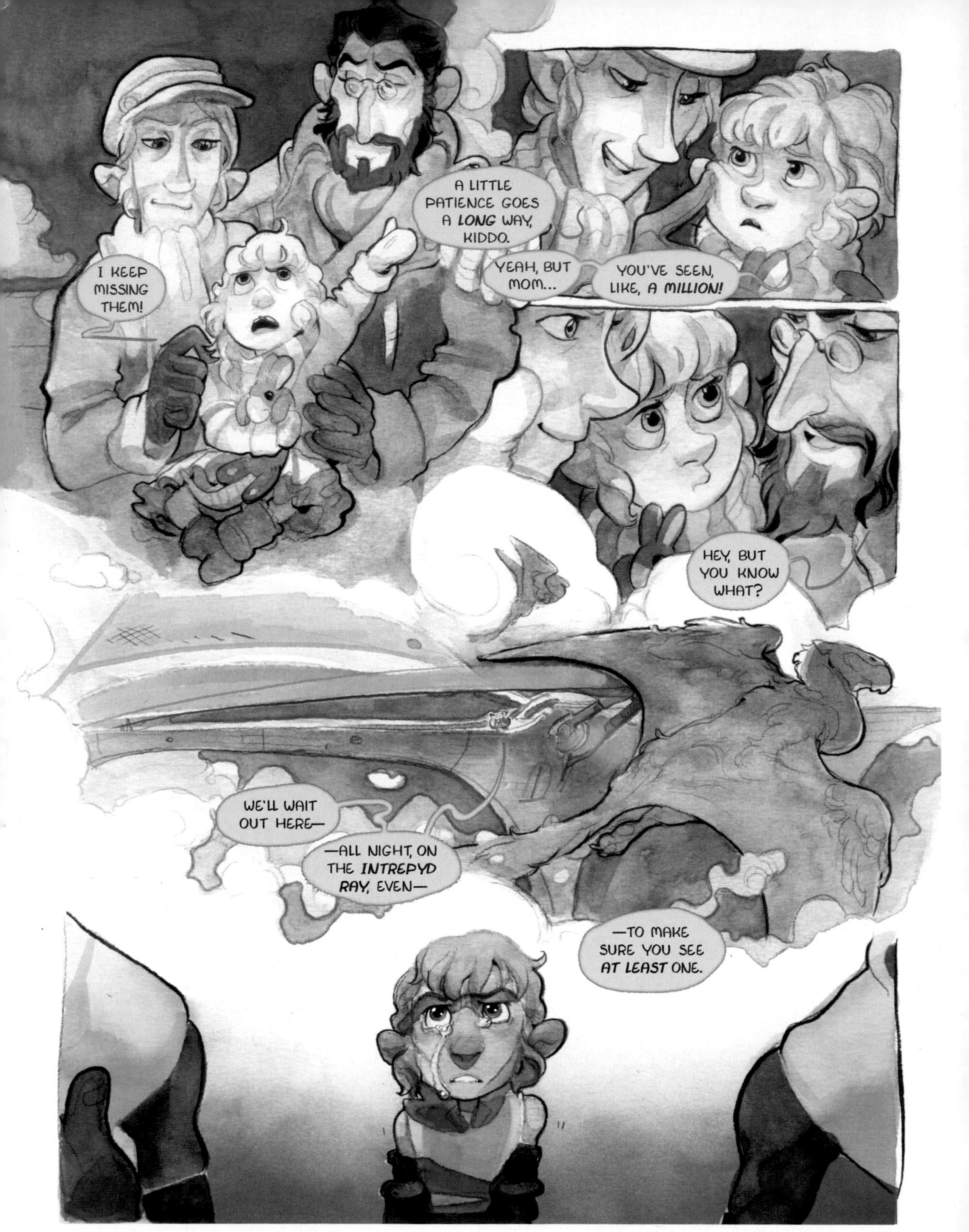
I KEEP MISSING THEM!
A LITTLE PATIENCE GOES A LONG WAY, KIDDO.
YEAH, BUT MOM...
YOU'VE SEEN, LIKE, A MILLION!
HEY, BUT YOU KNOW WHAT?
WE'LL WAIT OUT HERE—
—ALL NIGHT, ON THE INTREPYD RAY, EVEN—
—TO MAKE SURE YOU SEE AT LEAST ONE.

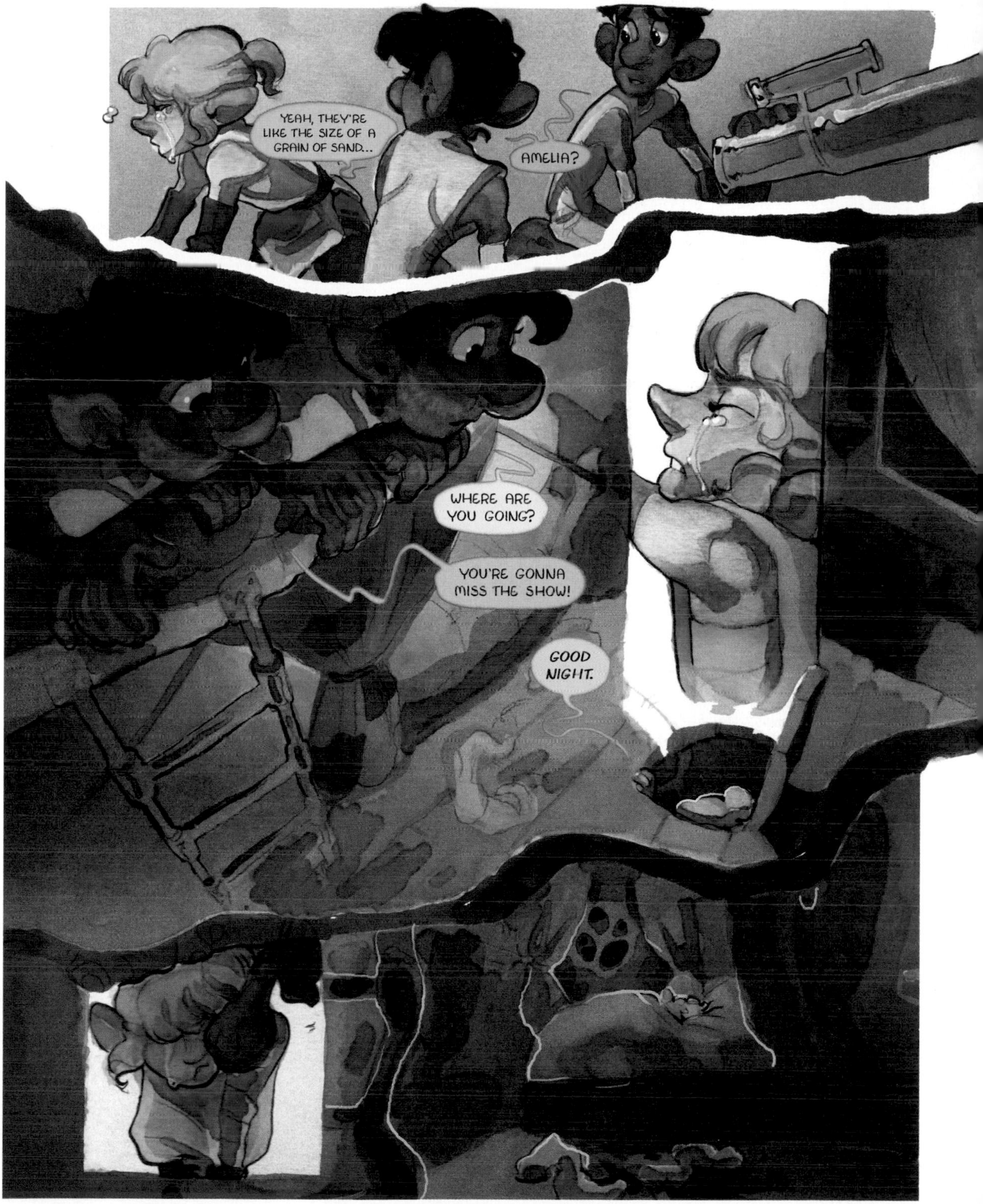
YEAH, THEY'RE LIKE THE SIZE OF A GRAIN OF SAND...
AMELIA?
WHERE ARE YOU GOING?
YOU'RE GONNA MISS THE SHOW!
GOOD NIGHT.

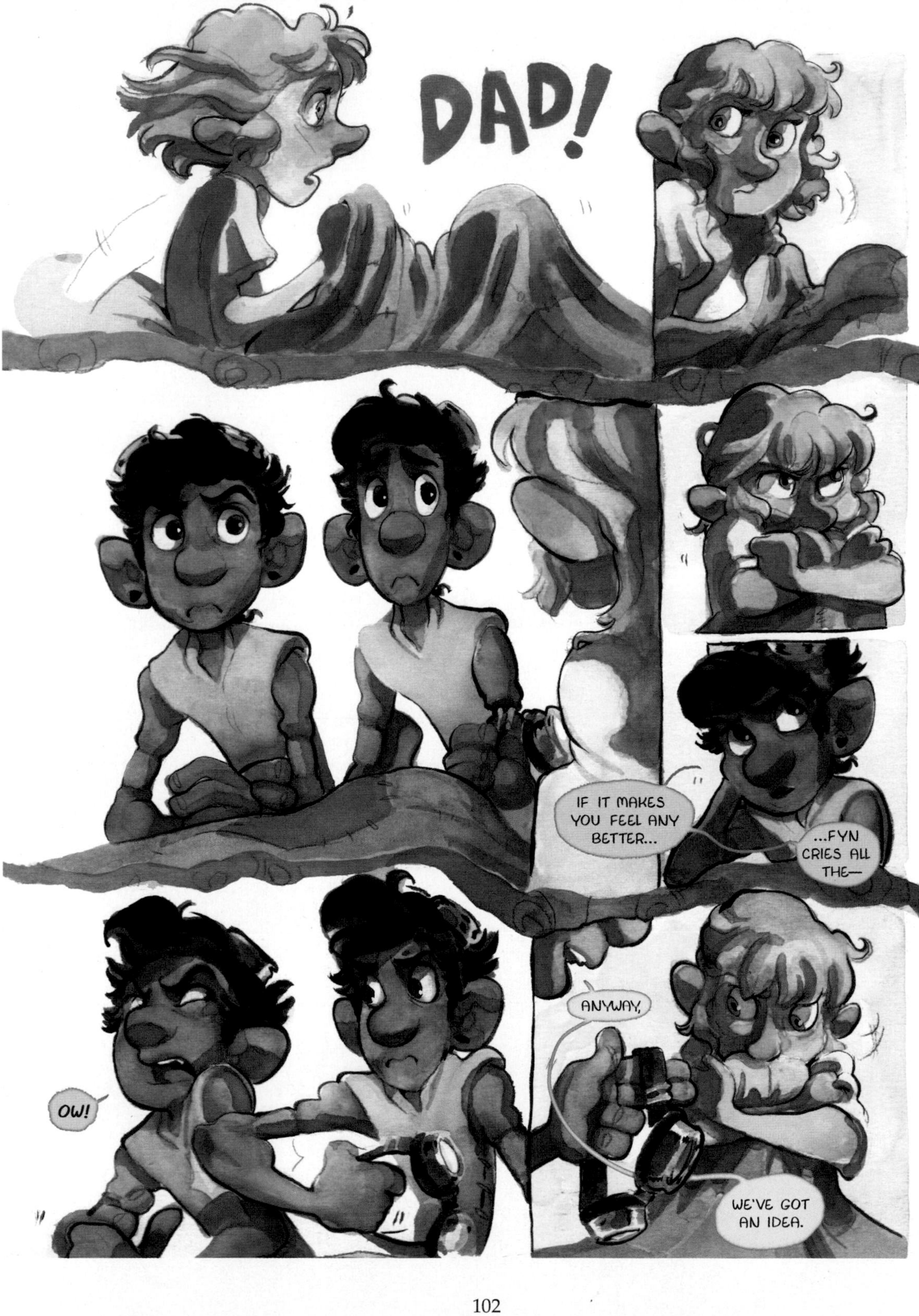
DAD!
IF IT MAKES YOU FEEL ANY BETTER...
...FYN CRIES ALL THE—
OW!
ANYWAY,
WE'VE GOT AN IDEA.

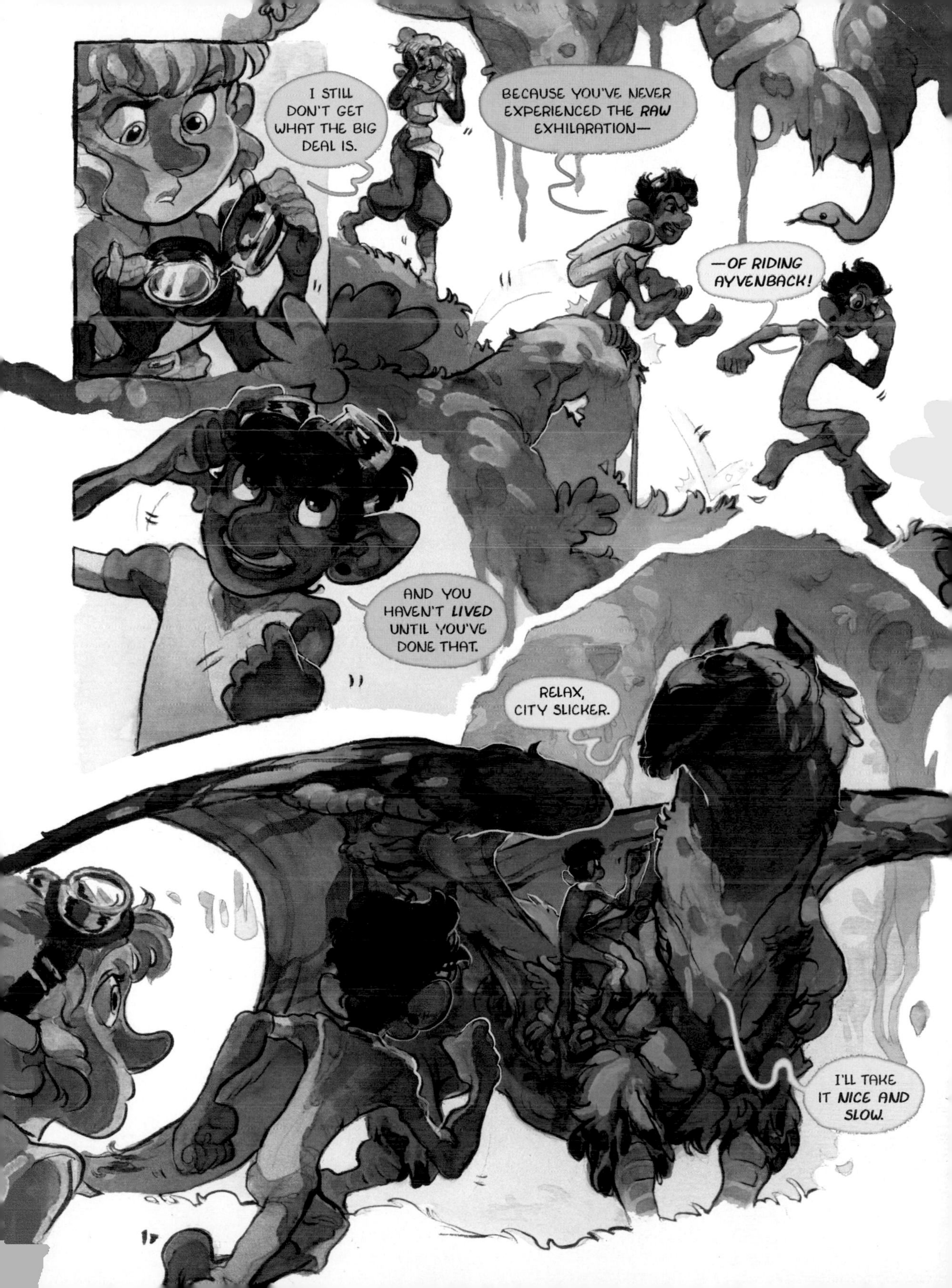
I STILL DON'T GET WHAT THE BIG DEAL IS.
BECAUSE YOU'VE NEVER EXPERIENCED THE **RAW** EXHILARATION—
—OF RIDING AYVENBACK!
AND YOU HAVEN'T **LIVED** UNTIL YOU'VE DONE THAT.
RELAX, CITY SLICKER.
I'LL TAKE IT **NICE AND SLOW.**

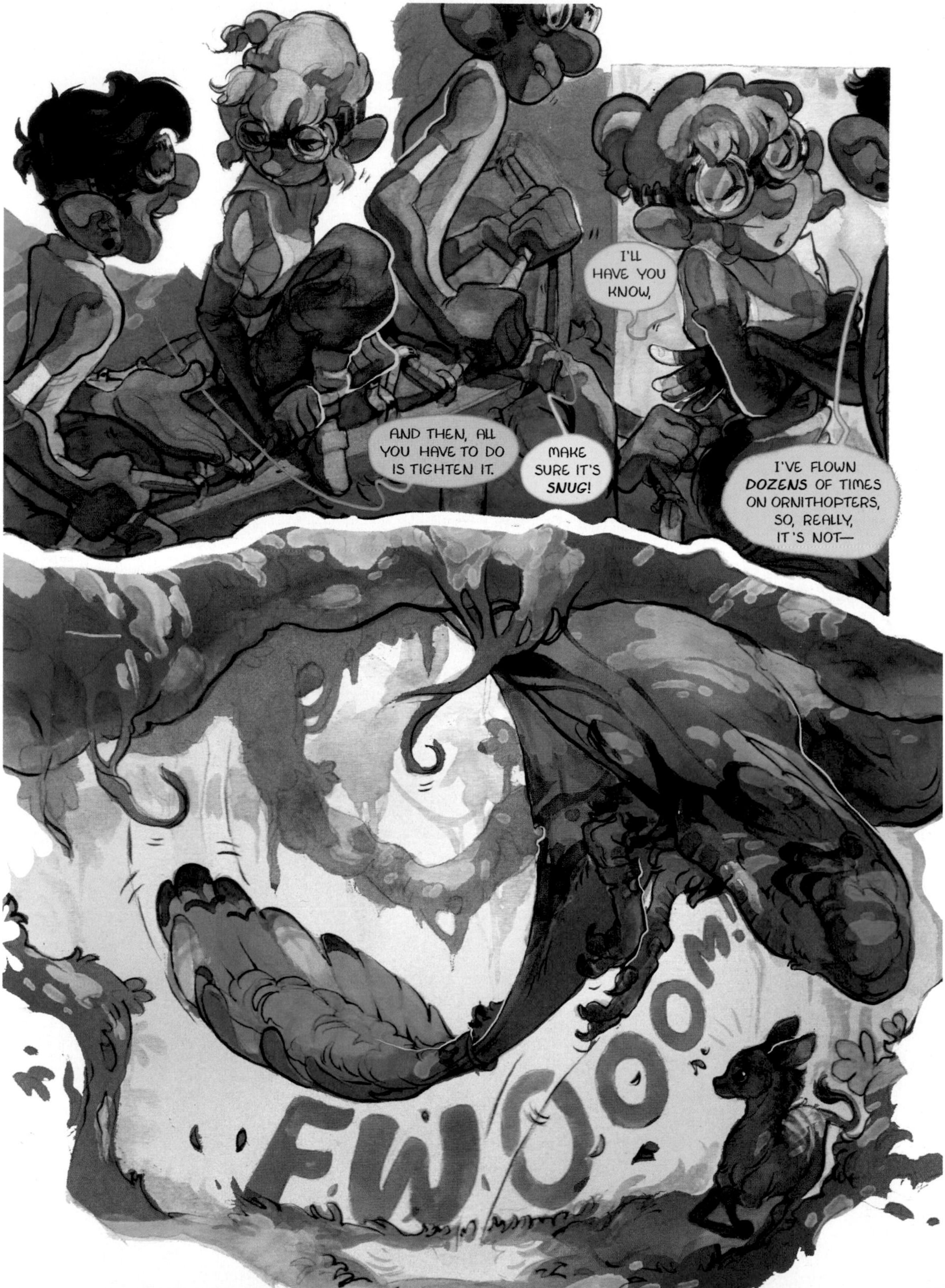
AND THEN, ALL YOU HAVE TO DO IS TIGHTEN IT.
MAKE SURE IT'S **SNUG**!
I'LL HAVE YOU KNOW,
I'VE FLOWN **DOZENS** OF TIMES ON ORNITHOPTERS, SO, REALLY, IT'S NOT—
FWOOOM!

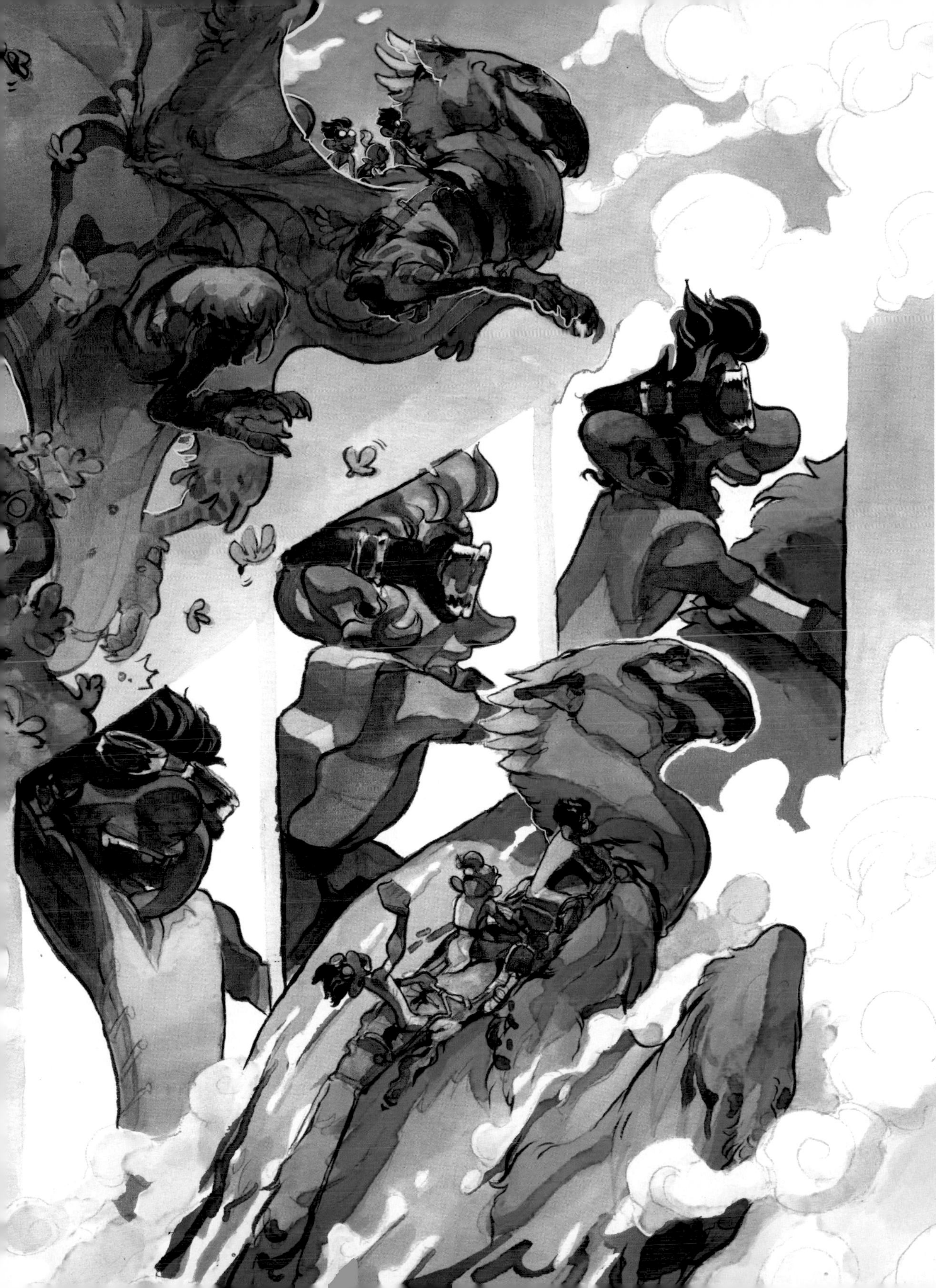

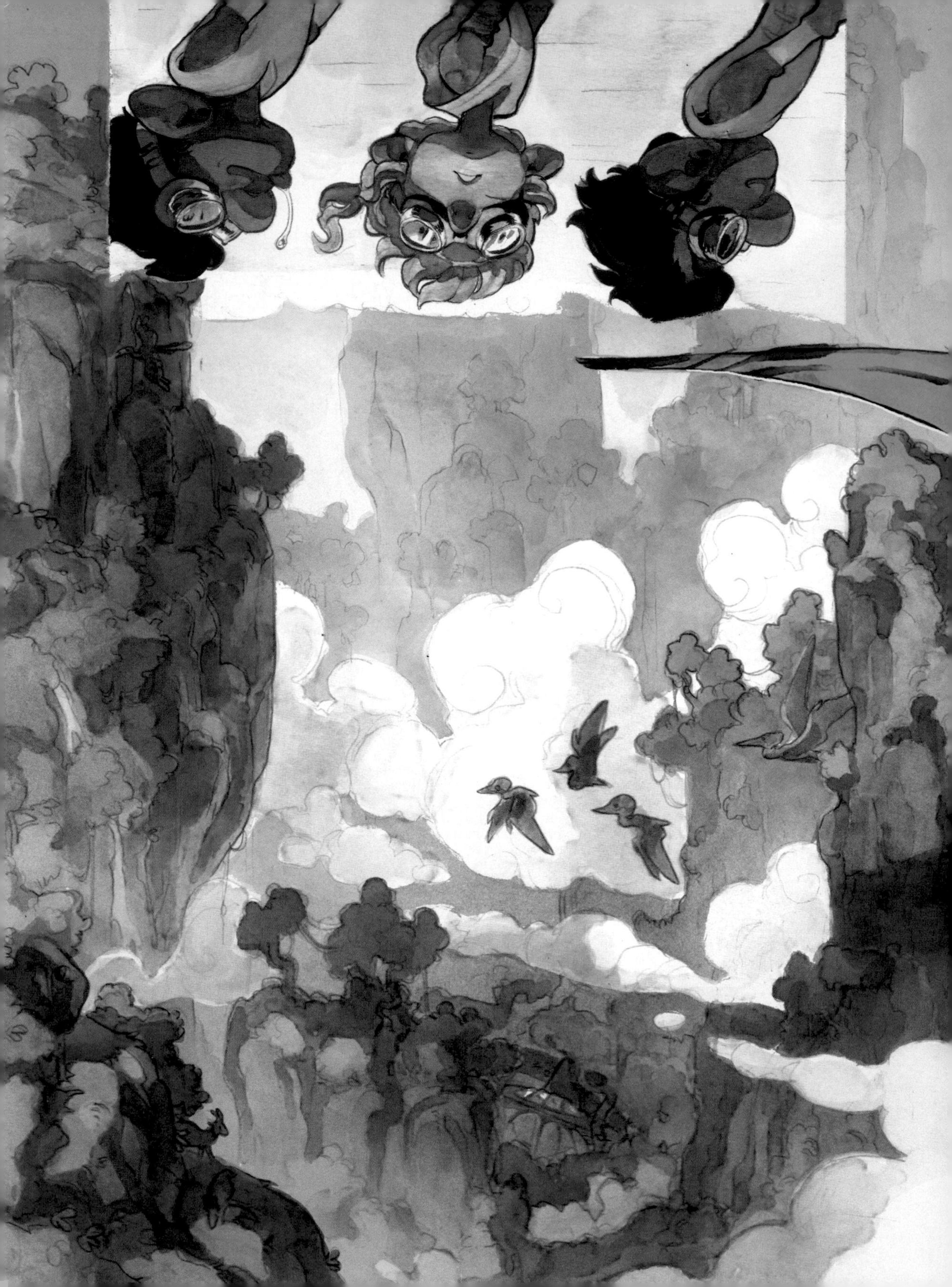

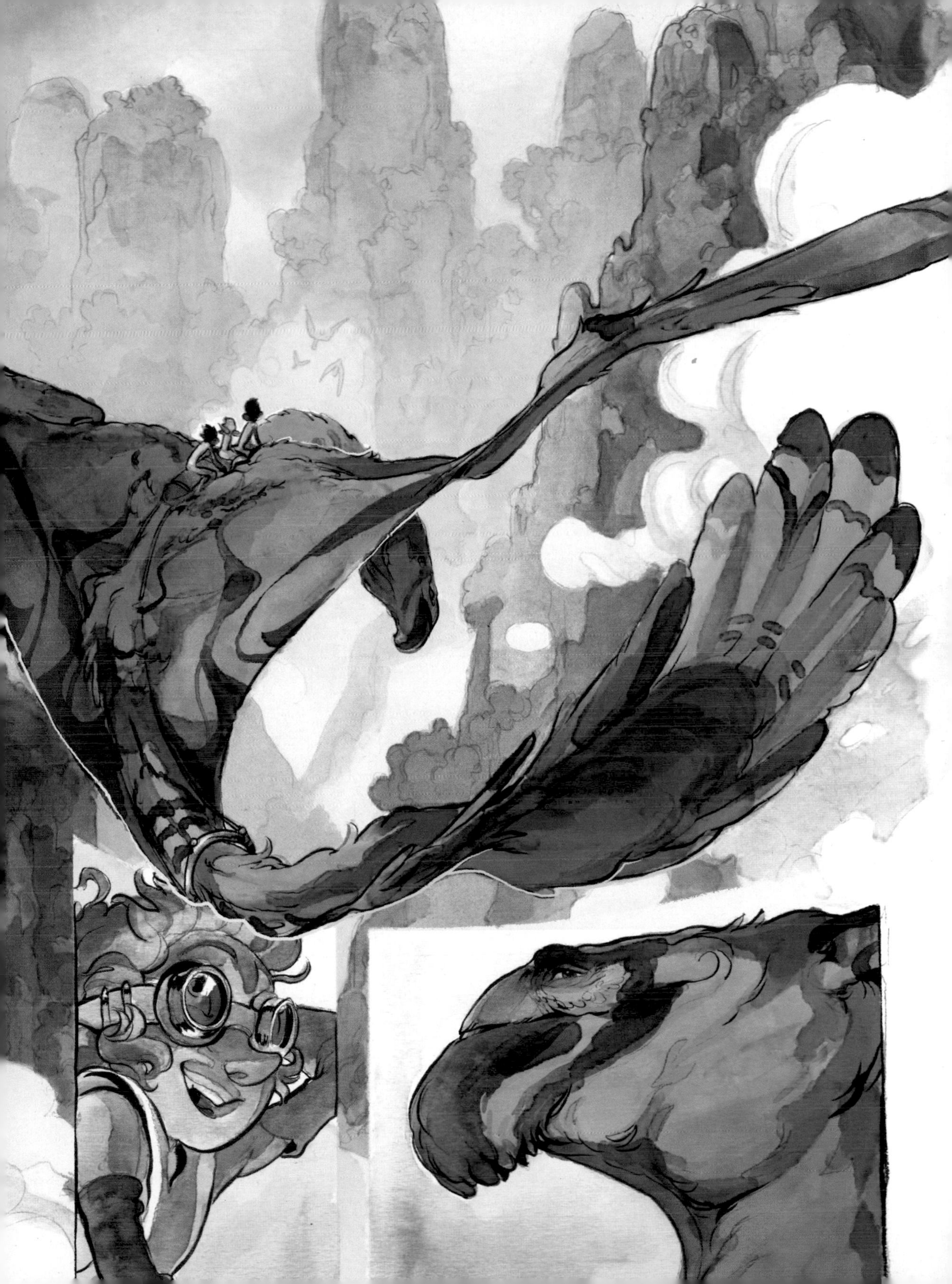

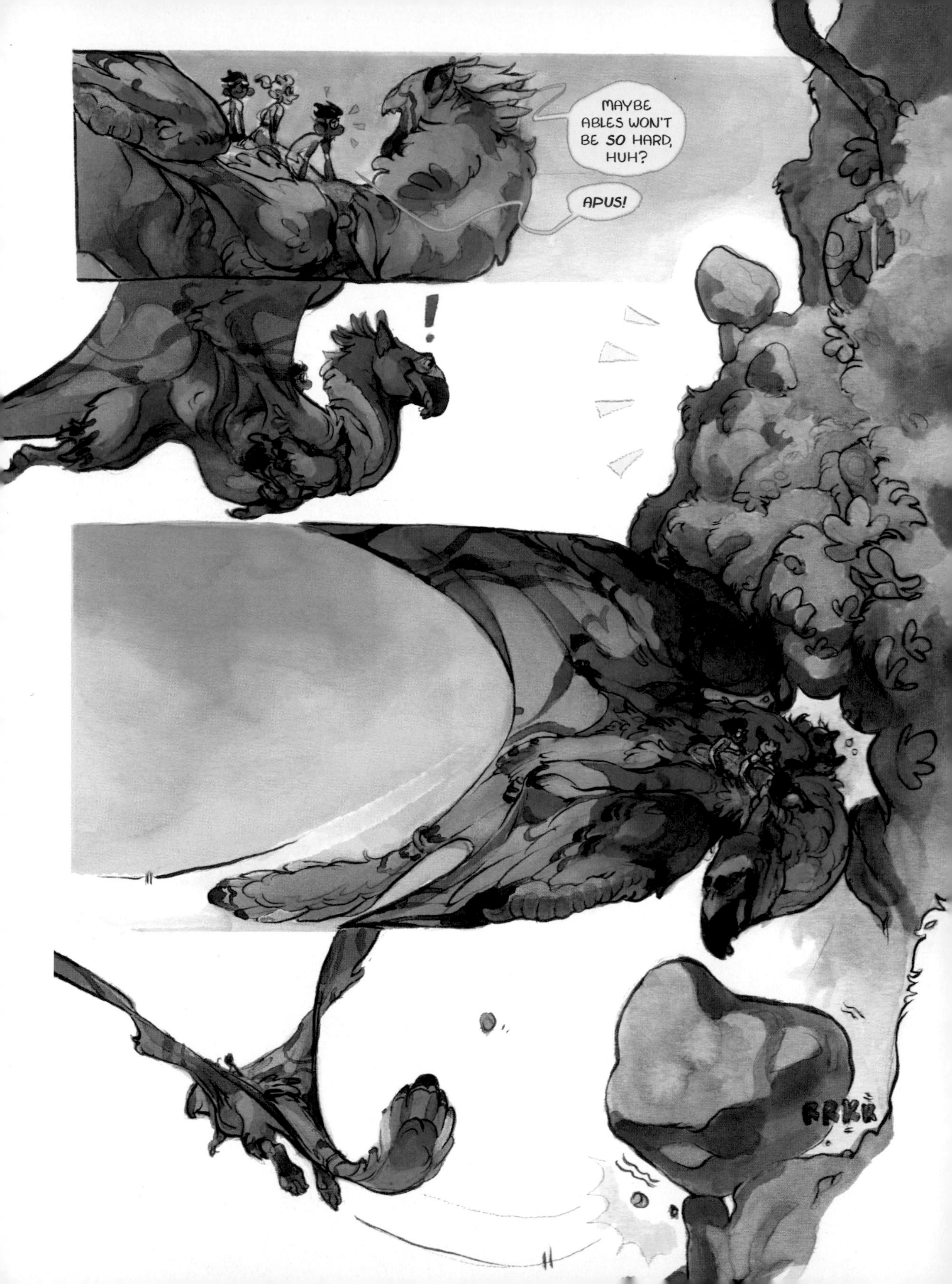
MAYBE ABLES WON'T BE SO HARD, HUH?
APUS!
!
RRKK

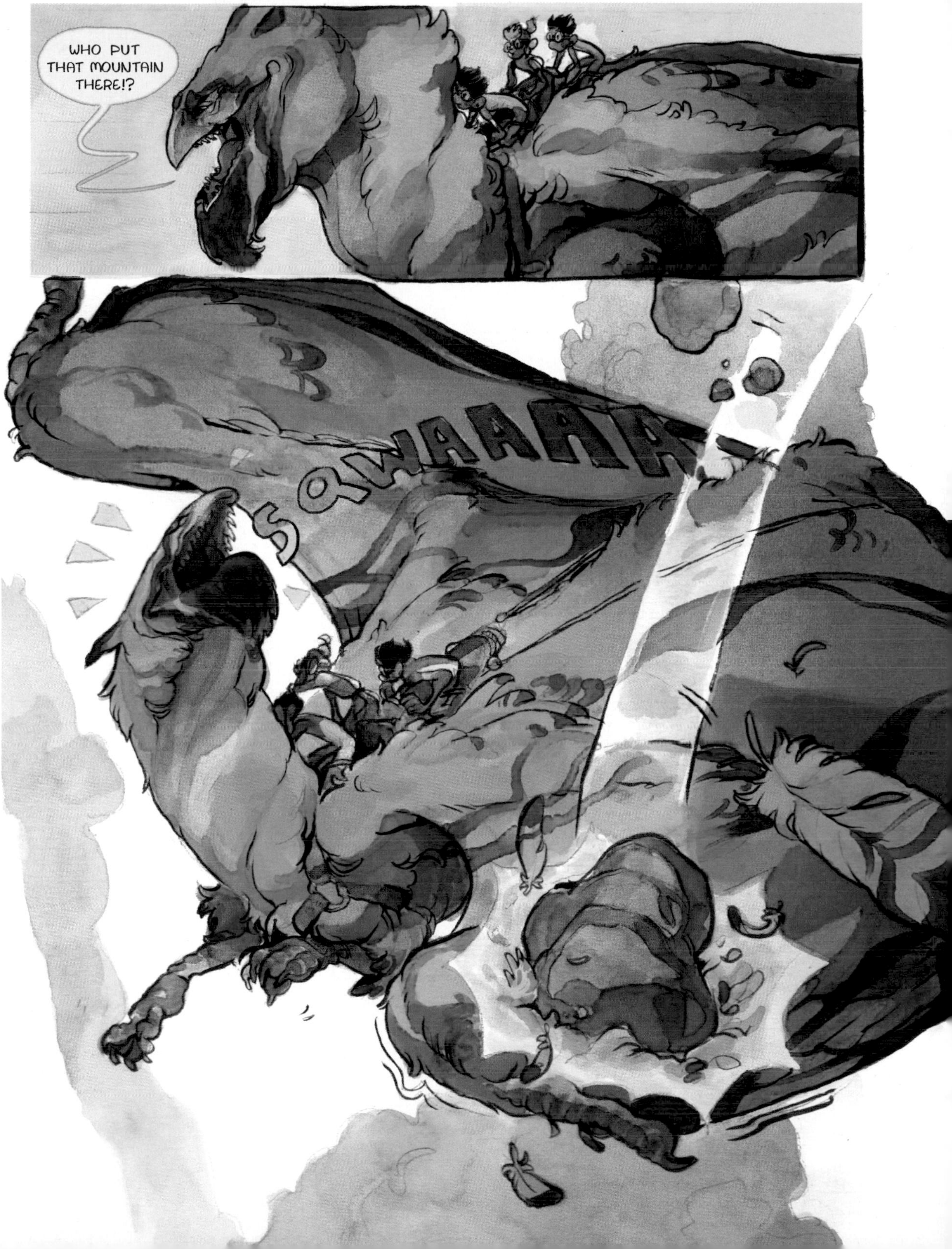
WHO PUT THAT MOUNTAIN THERE!?
SQWAAAA!

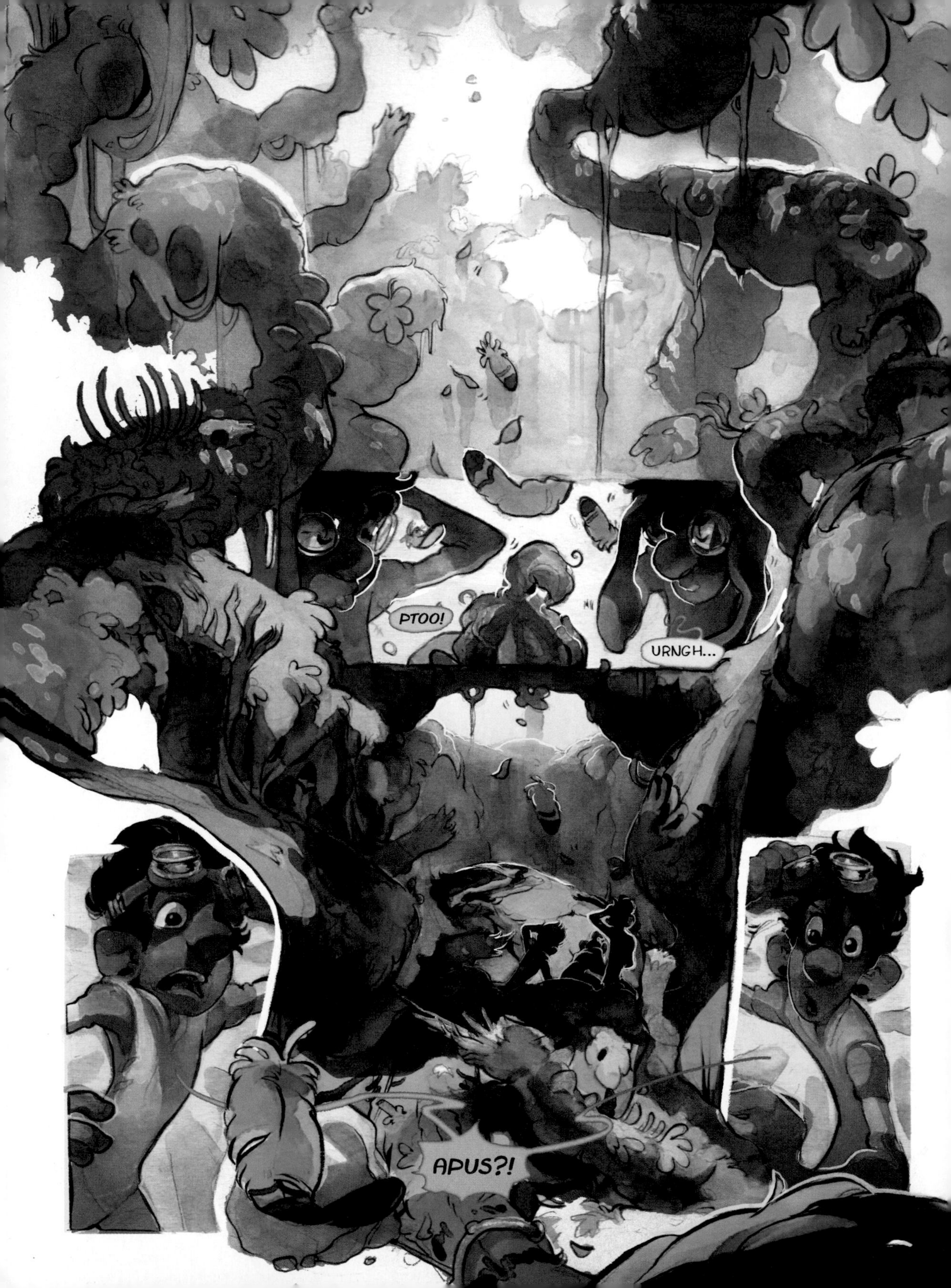
PTOO!
URNGH...
APUS?!

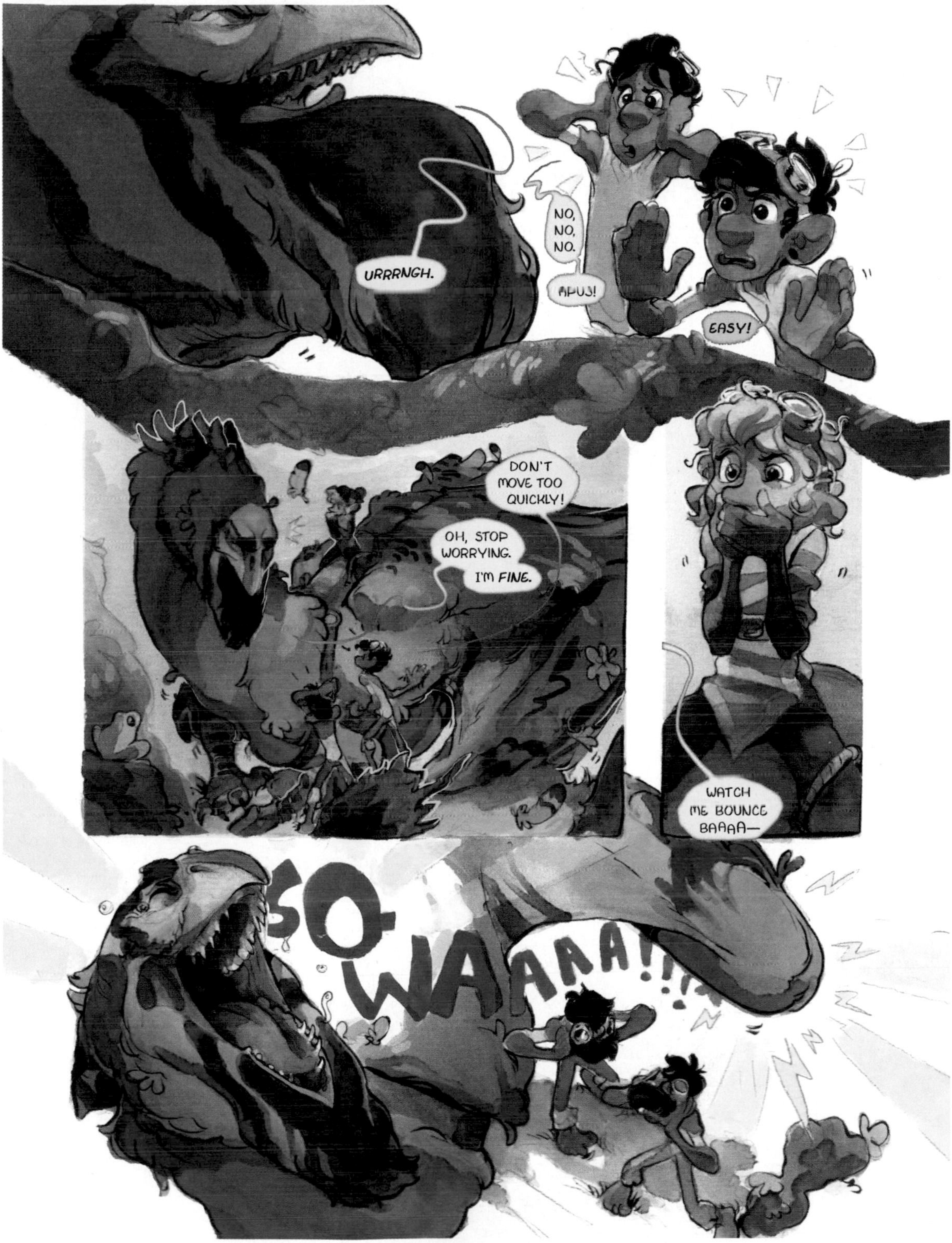
URRRNGH.
NO, NO, NO.
APUS!
EASY!
DON'T MOVE TOO QUICKLY!
OH, STOP WORRYING.
I'M *FINE.*
WATCH ME BOUNCE BAAAA—
SQ
WAAAA!!!

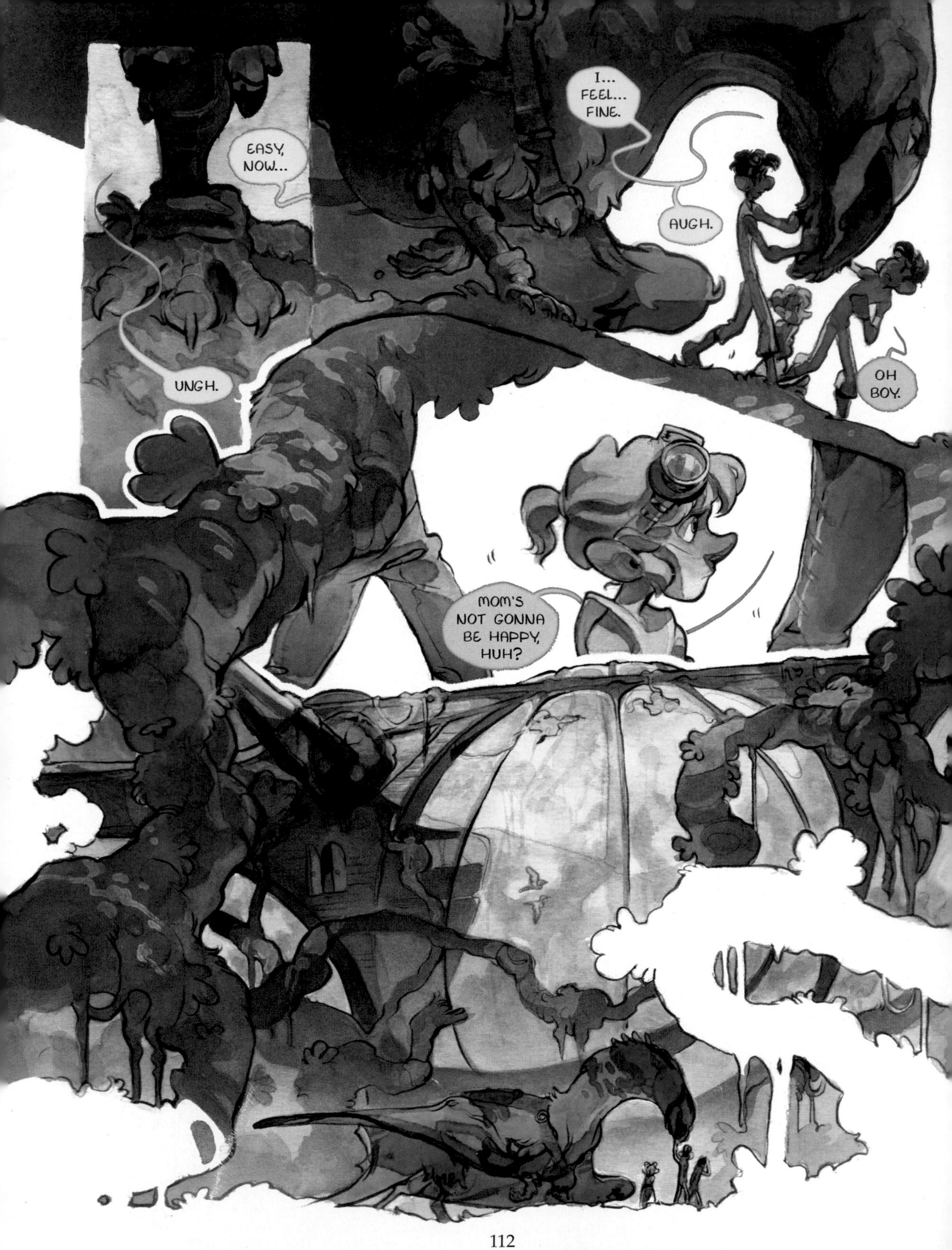
EASY, NOW...
UNGH.
I... FEEL... FINE.
AUGH.
OH BOY.
MOM'S NOT GONNA BE HAPPY, HUH?

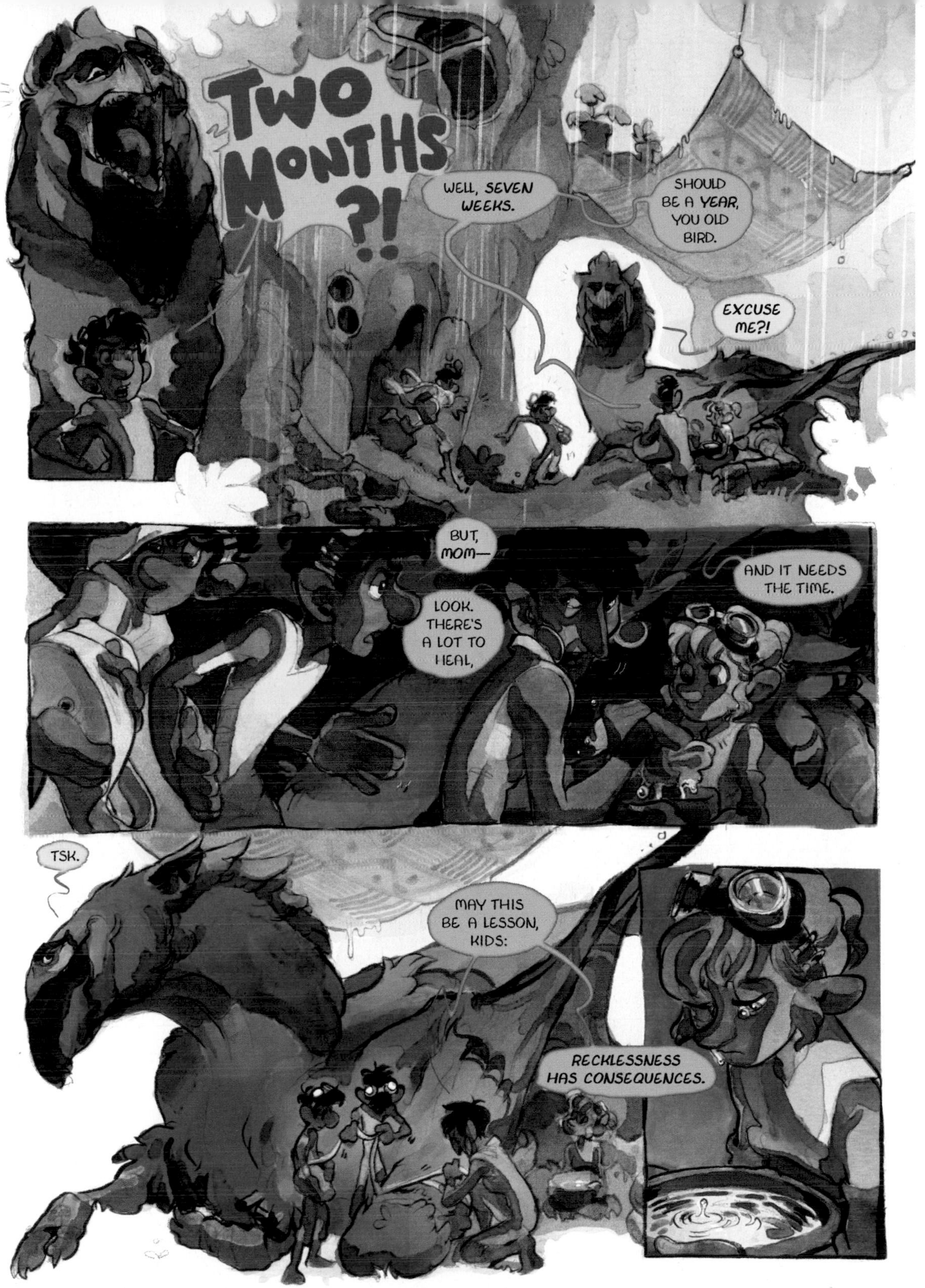
TWO MONTHS?!
WELL, SEVEN WEEKS.
SHOULD BE A YEAR, YOU OLD BIRD.
EXCUSE ME?!
BUT, MOM—
LOOK. THERE'S A LOT TO HEAL,
AND IT NEEDS THE TIME.
TSK.
MAY THIS BE A LESSON, KIDS:
RECKLESSNESS HAS CONSEQUENCES.

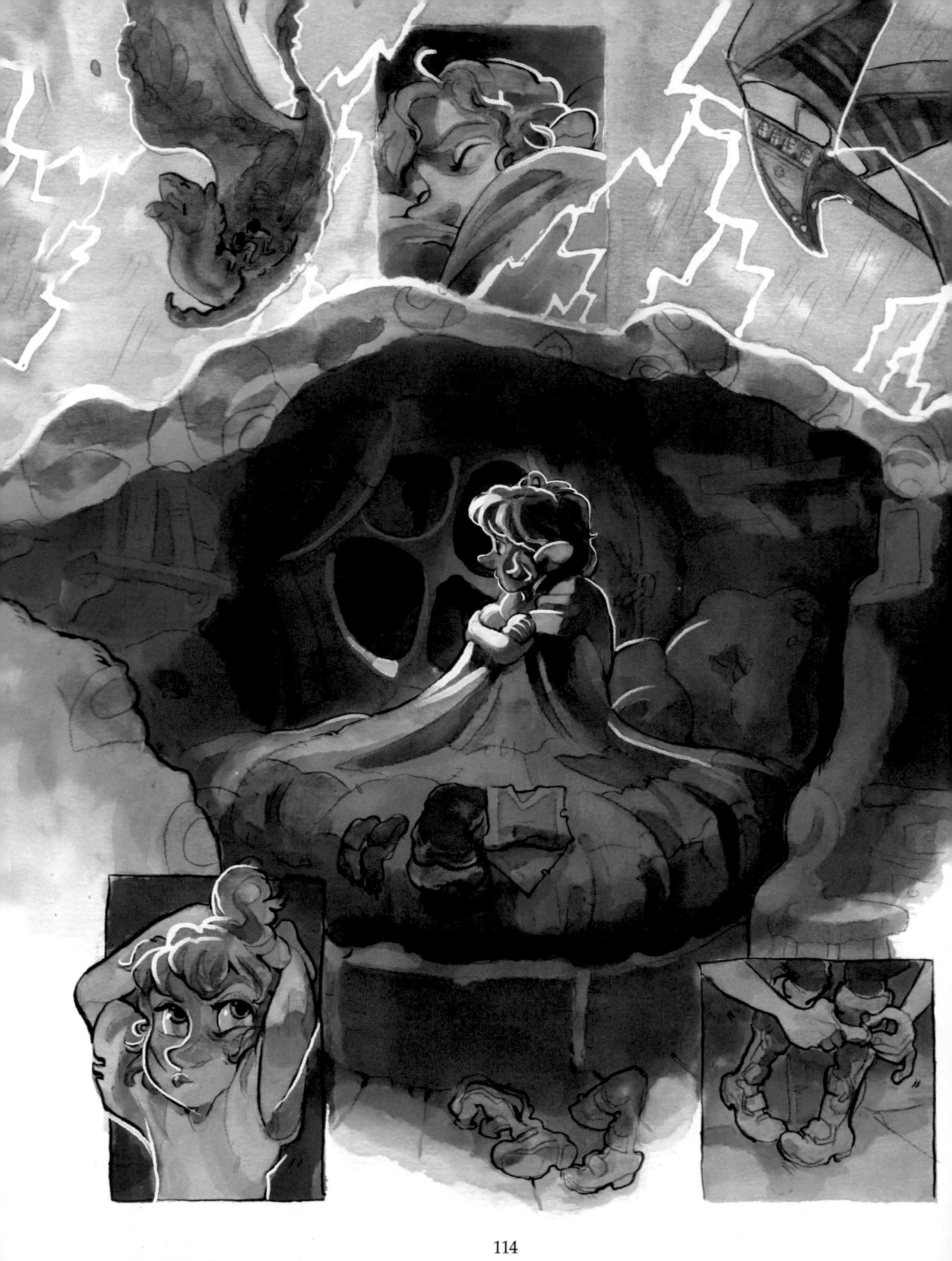

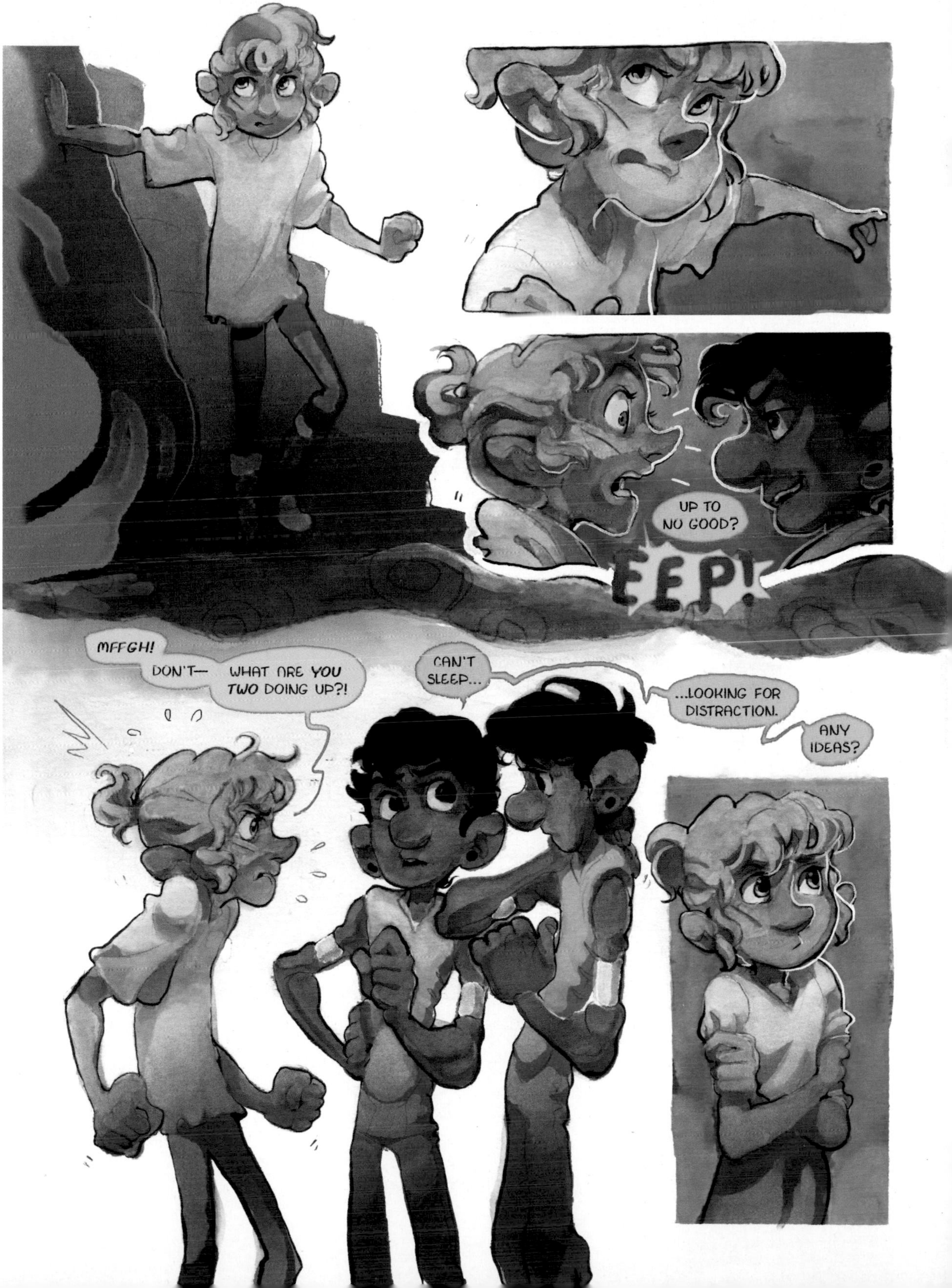
UP TO NO GOOD?
EEP!
MFFGH!
DON'T—
WHAT ARE *YOU TWO* DOING UP?!
CAN'T SLEEP...
...LOOKING FOR DISTRACTION.
ANY IDEAS?

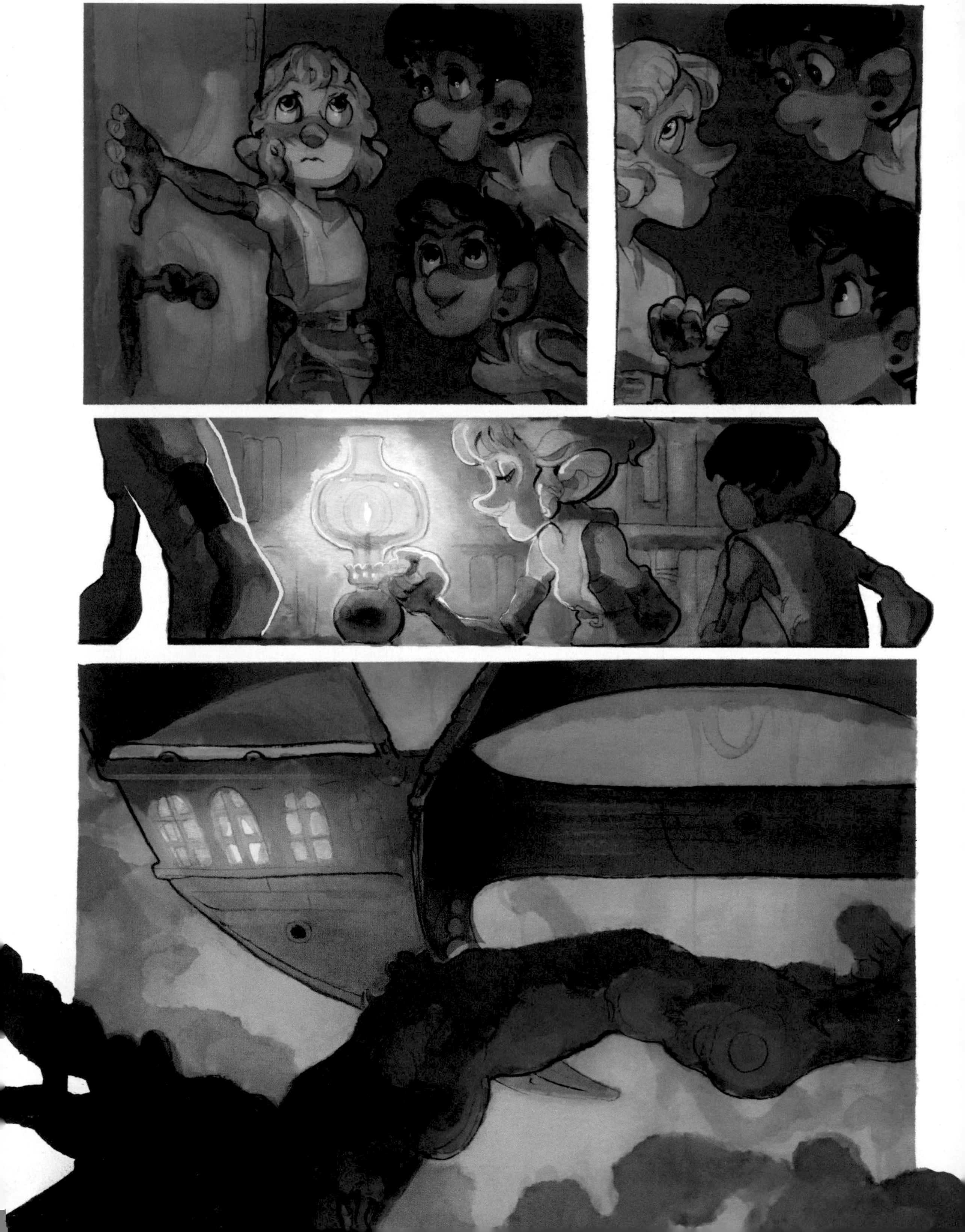

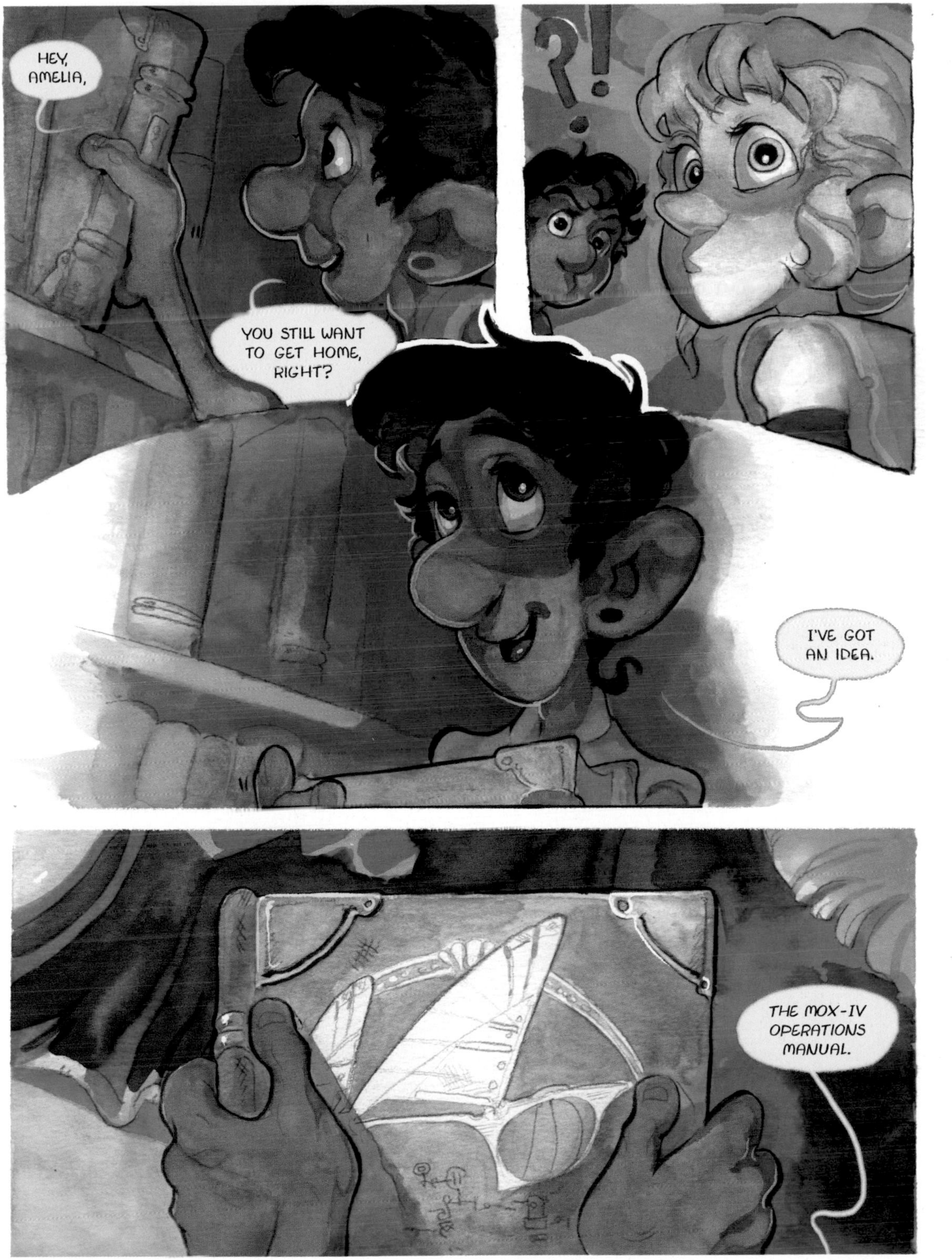
HEY, AMELIA,
YOU STILL WANT TO GET HOME, RIGHT?
?!
I'VE GOT AN IDEA.
THE MOX-IV OPERATIONS MANUAL.

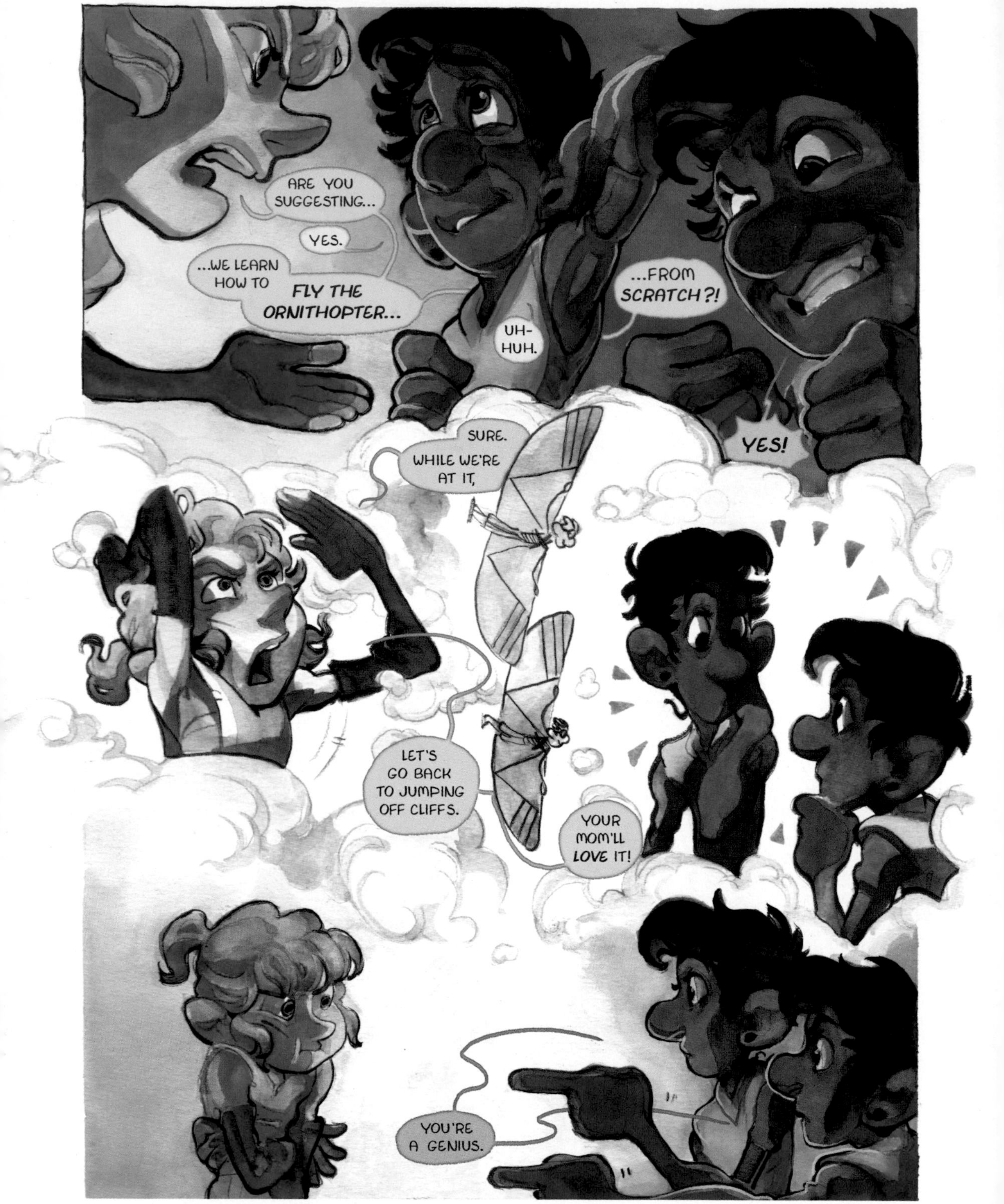
ARE YOU SUGGESTING...
YES.
...WE LEARN HOW TO FLY THE ORNITHOPTER...
UH-HUH.
...FROM SCRATCH?!
YES!
SURE. WHILE WE'RE AT IT,
LET'S GO BACK TO JUMPING OFF CLIFFS.
YOUR MOM'LL LOVE IT!
YOU'RE A GENIUS.

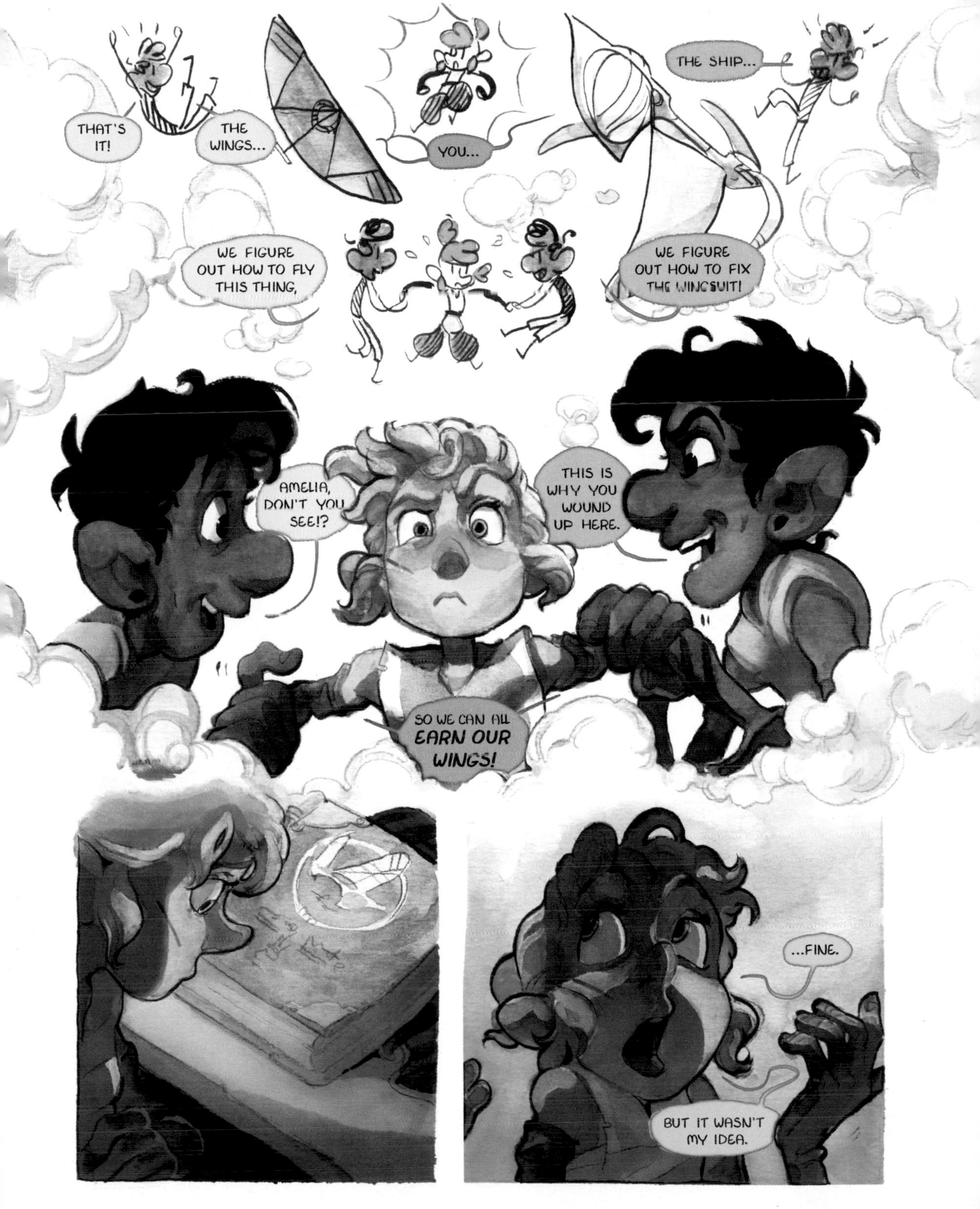
THAT'S IT!
THE WINGS...
YOU...
THE SHIP...
WE FIGURE OUT HOW TO FLY THIS THING,
WE FIGURE OUT HOW TO FIX THE WINGSUIT!
AMELIA, DON'T YOU SEE!?
THIS IS WHY YOU WOUND UP HERE.
SO WE CAN ALL EARN OUR WINGS!
...FINE.
BUT IT WASN'T MY IDEA.

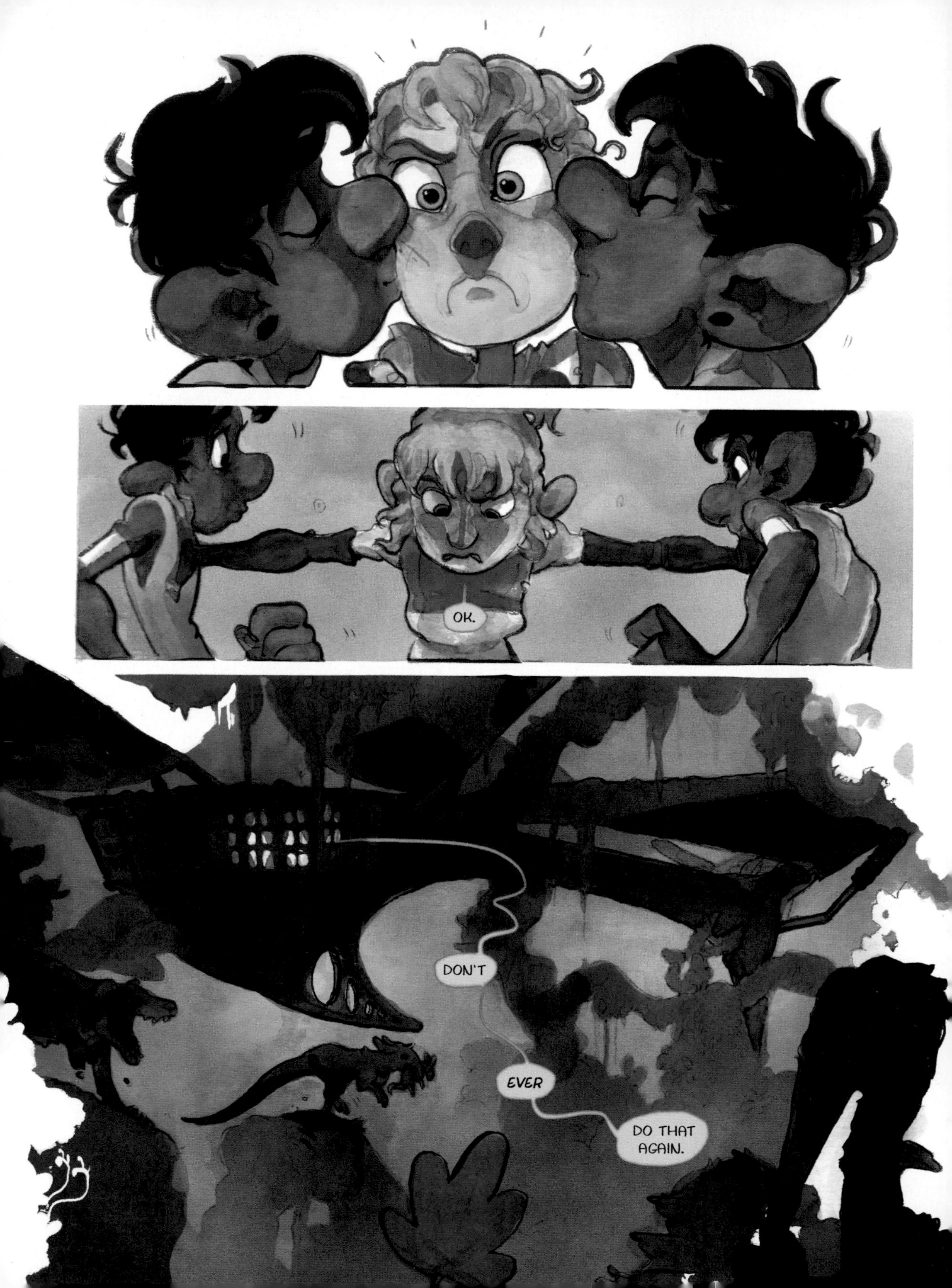
OK.
DON'T
EVER
DO THAT AGAIN.

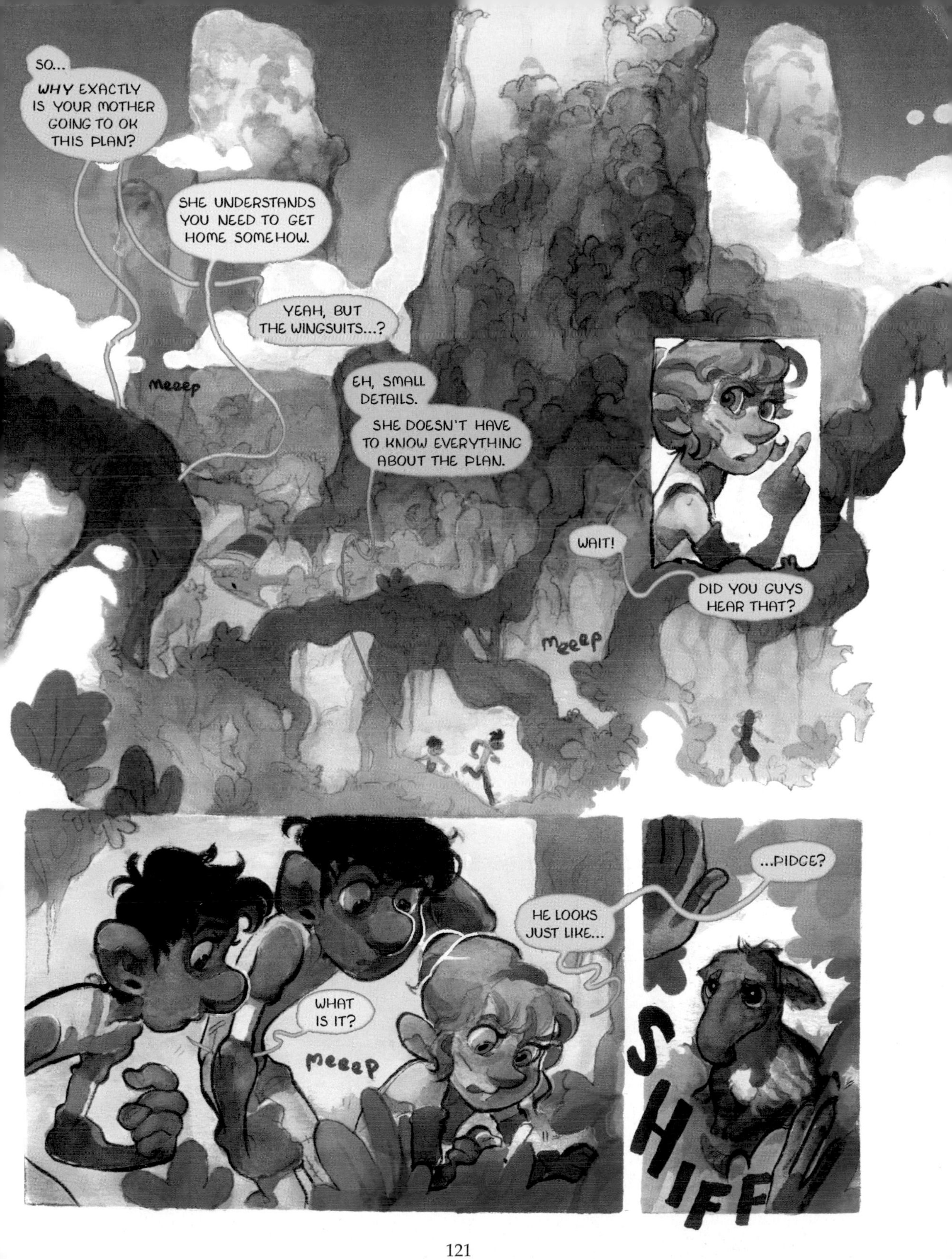
SO...
WHY EXACTLY IS YOUR MOTHER GOING TO OK THIS PLAN?
SHE UNDERSTANDS YOU NEED TO GET HOME SOMEHOW.
YEAH, BUT THE WINGSUITS...?
meeep
EH, SMALL DETAILS.
SHE DOESN'T HAVE TO KNOW EVERYTHING ABOUT THE PLAN.
WAIT!
DID YOU GUYS HEAR THAT?
meeep
...PIDGE?
HE LOOKS JUST LIKE...
WHAT IS IT?
meeep
SHIFF

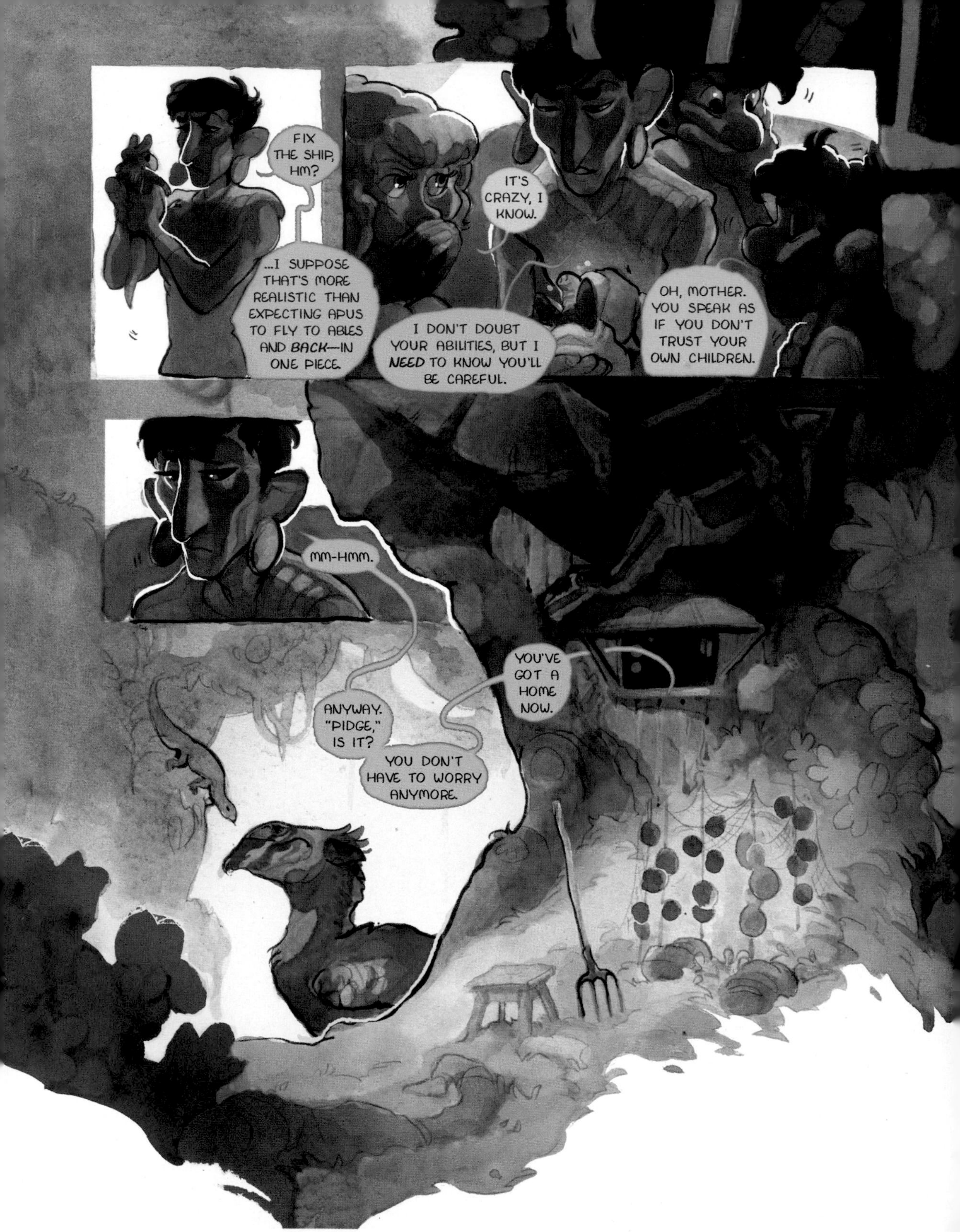
FIX THE SHIP, HM?
...I SUPPOSE THAT'S MORE REALISTIC THAN EXPECTING APUS TO FLY TO ABLES AND *BACK*—IN ONE PIECE.
IT'S CRAZY, I KNOW.
I DON'T DOUBT YOUR ABILITIES, BUT I *NEED* TO KNOW YOU'LL BE CAREFUL.
OH, MOTHER. YOU SPEAK AS IF YOU DON'T TRUST YOUR OWN CHILDREN.
MM-HMM.
ANYWAY. "PIDGE," IS IT?
YOU'VE GOT A HOME NOW.
YOU DON'T HAVE TO WORRY ANYMORE.

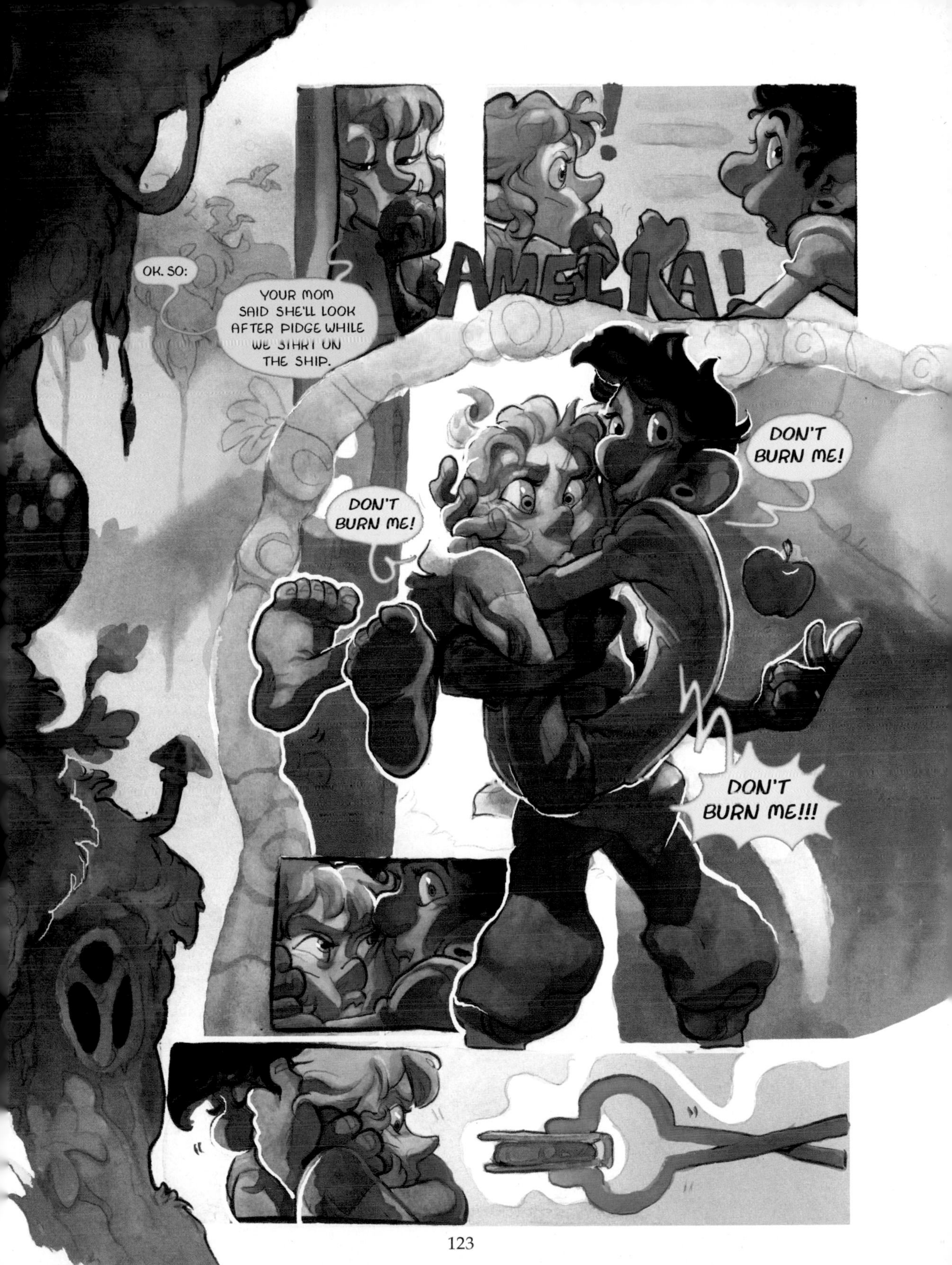

OK. SO:
YOUR MOM SAID SHE'LL LOOK AFTER PIDGE WHILE WE START ON THE SHIP.
AMELIKA!
DON'T BURN ME!
DON'T BURN ME!
DON'T BURN ME!!!

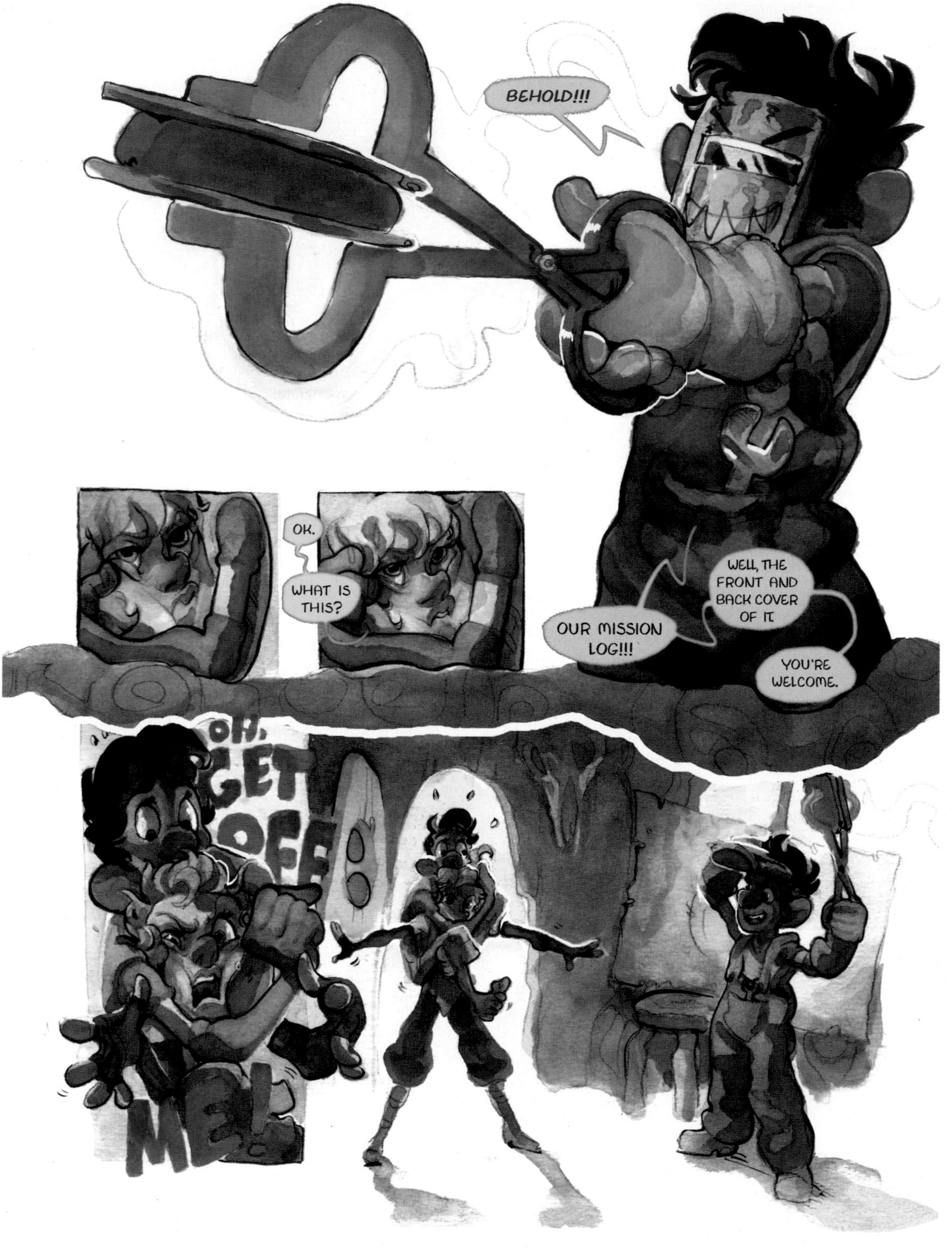
BEHOLD!!!
OK.
WHAT IS THIS?
OUR MISSION LOG!!!
WELL, THE FRONT AND BACK COVER OF IT.
YOU'RE WELCOME.
OH, GET OFF ME!

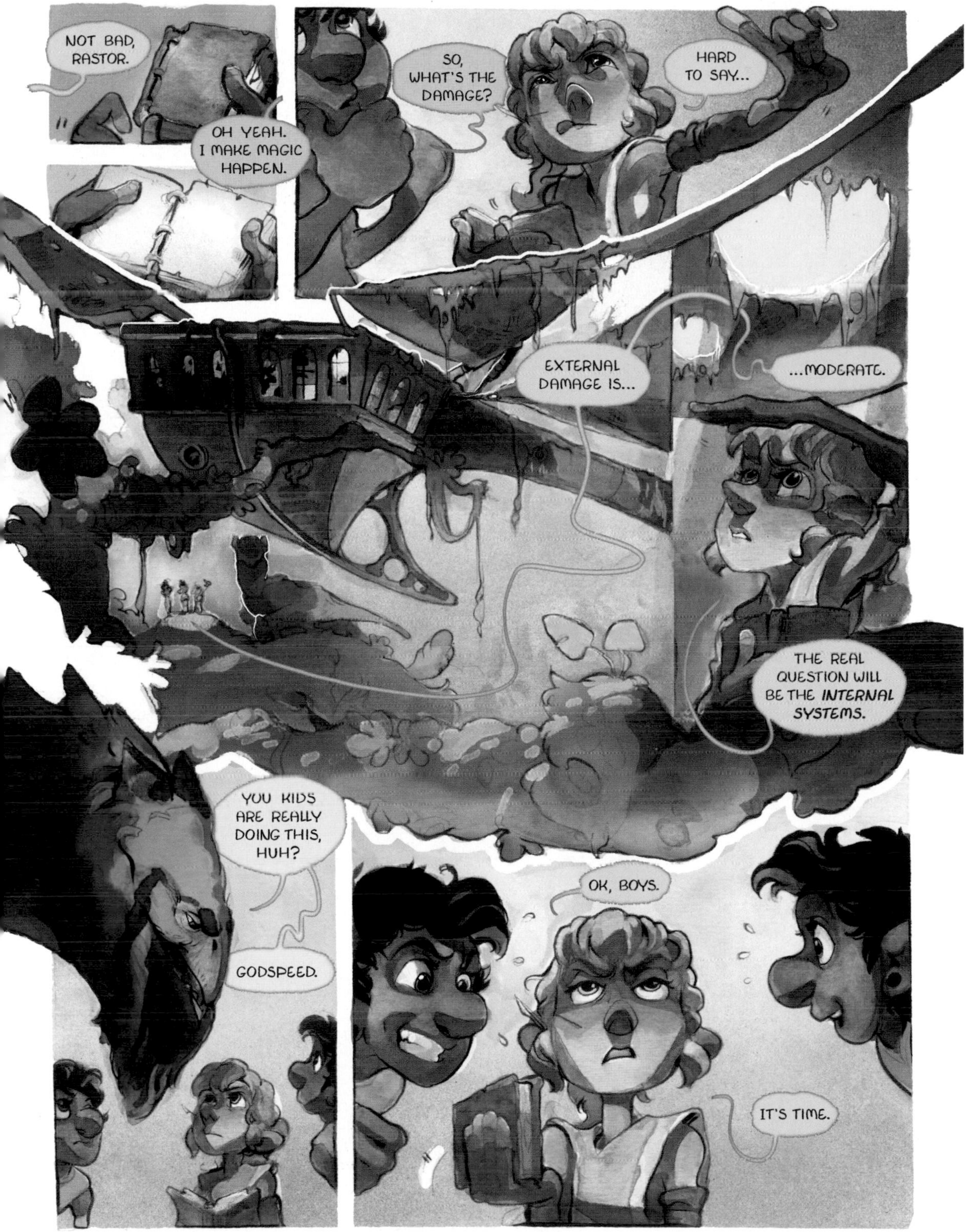
NOT BAD, RASTOR.
OH YEAH. I MAKE MAGIC HAPPEN.
SO, WHAT'S THE DAMAGE?
HARD TO SAY...
EXTERNAL DAMAGE IS...
...MODERATE.
THE REAL QUESTION WILL BE THE INTERNAL SYSTEMS.
YOU KIDS ARE REALLY DOING THIS, HUH?
GODSPEED.
OK, BOYS.
IT'S TIME.

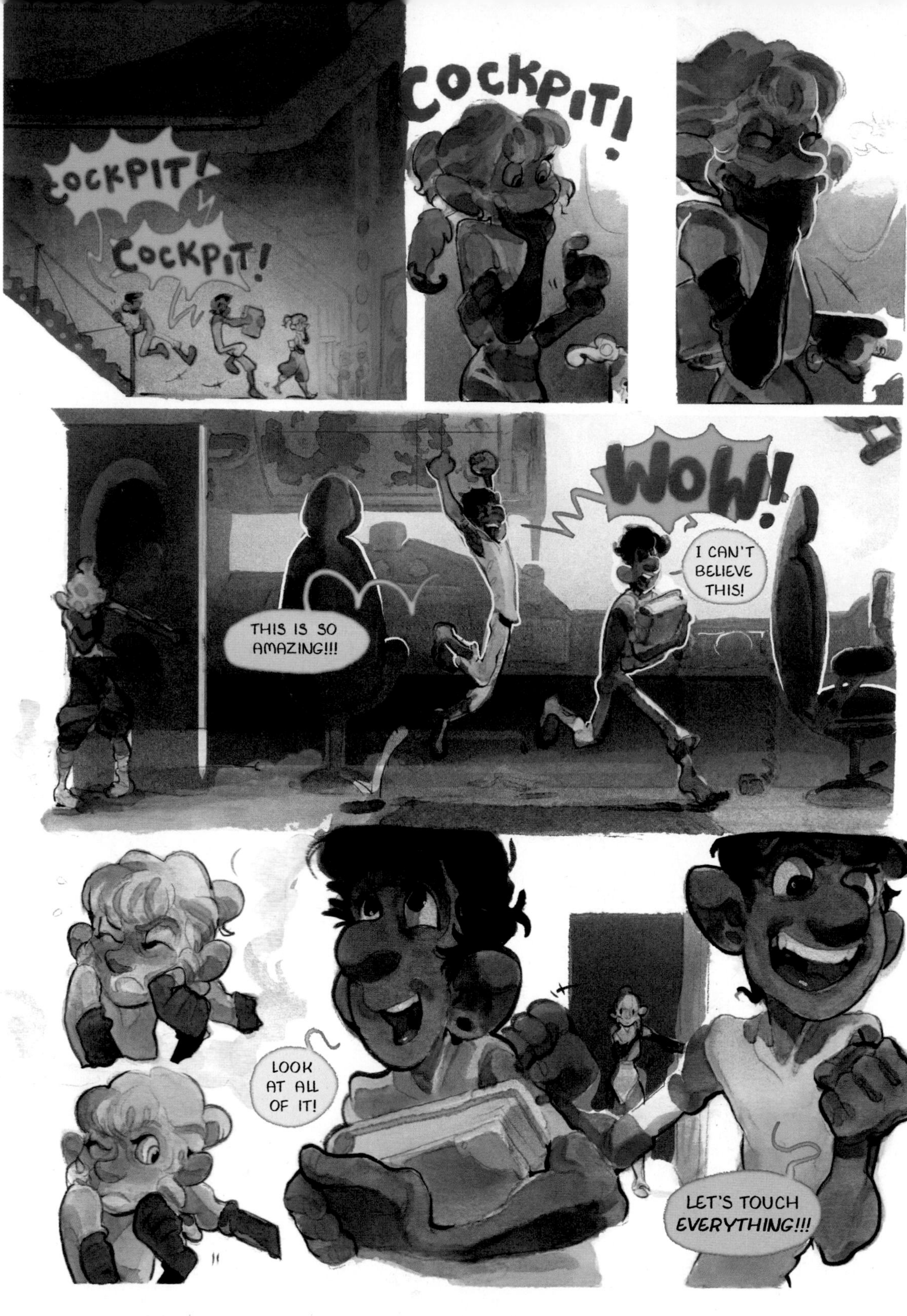
COCKPIT!
COCKPIT!
COCKPIT!
WOW!
THIS IS SO AMAZING!!!
I CAN'T BELIEVE THIS!
LOOK AT ALL OF IT!
LET'S TOUCH EVERYTHING!!!

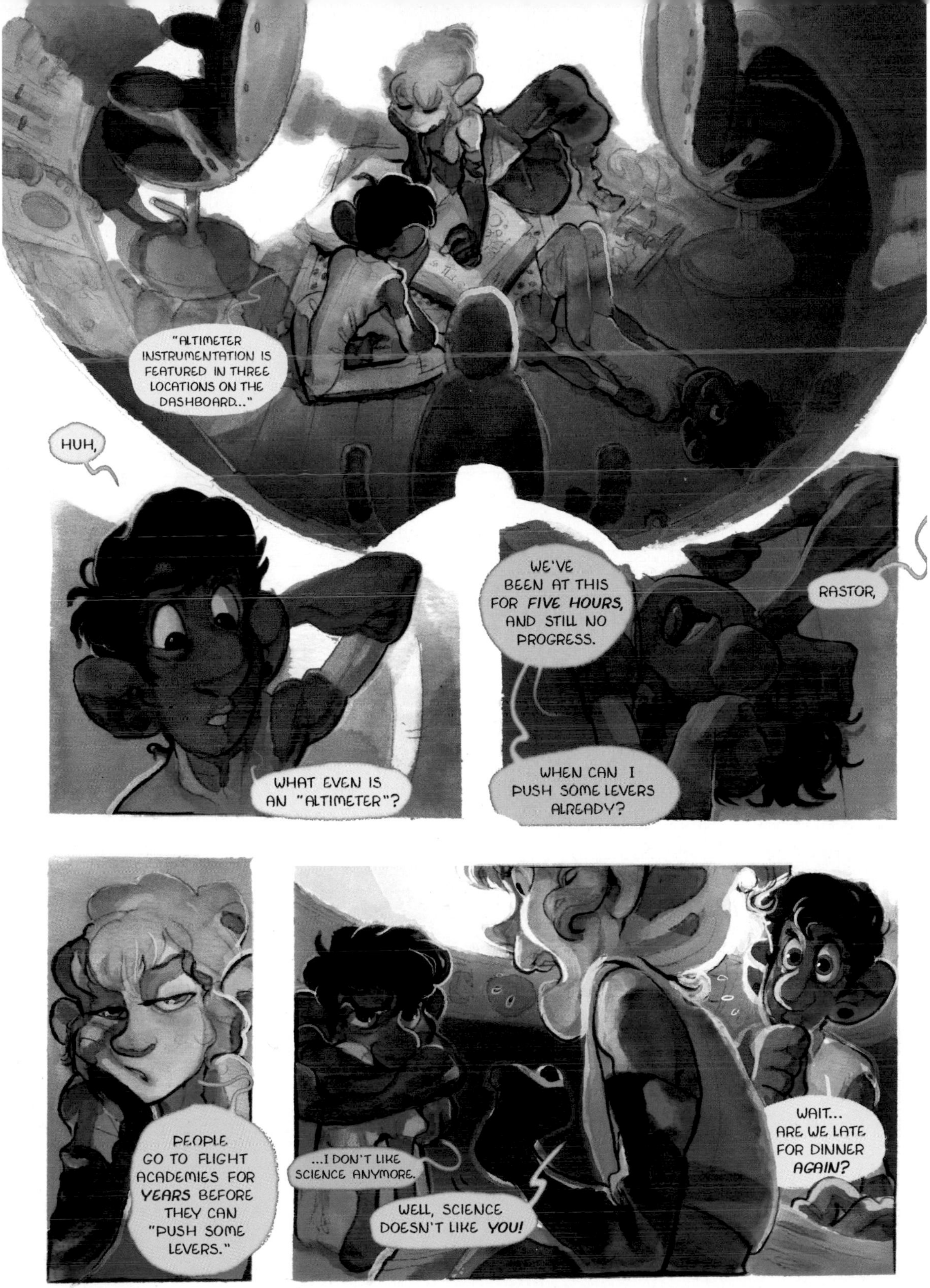
"ALTIMETER INSTRUMENTATION IS FEATURED IN THREE LOCATIONS ON THE DASHBOARD..."
HUH,
WHAT EVEN IS AN "ALTIMETER"?
RASTOR,
WE'VE BEEN AT THIS FOR *FIVE HOURS,* AND STILL NO PROGRESS.
WHEN CAN I PUSH SOME LEVERS ALREADY?
PEOPLE GO TO FLIGHT ACADEMIES FOR **YEARS** BEFORE THEY CAN "PUSH SOME LEVERS."
...I DON'T LIKE SCIENCE ANYMORE.
WELL, SCIENCE DOESN'T LIKE ***YOU!***
WAIT... ARE WE LATE FOR DINNER ***AGAIN?***

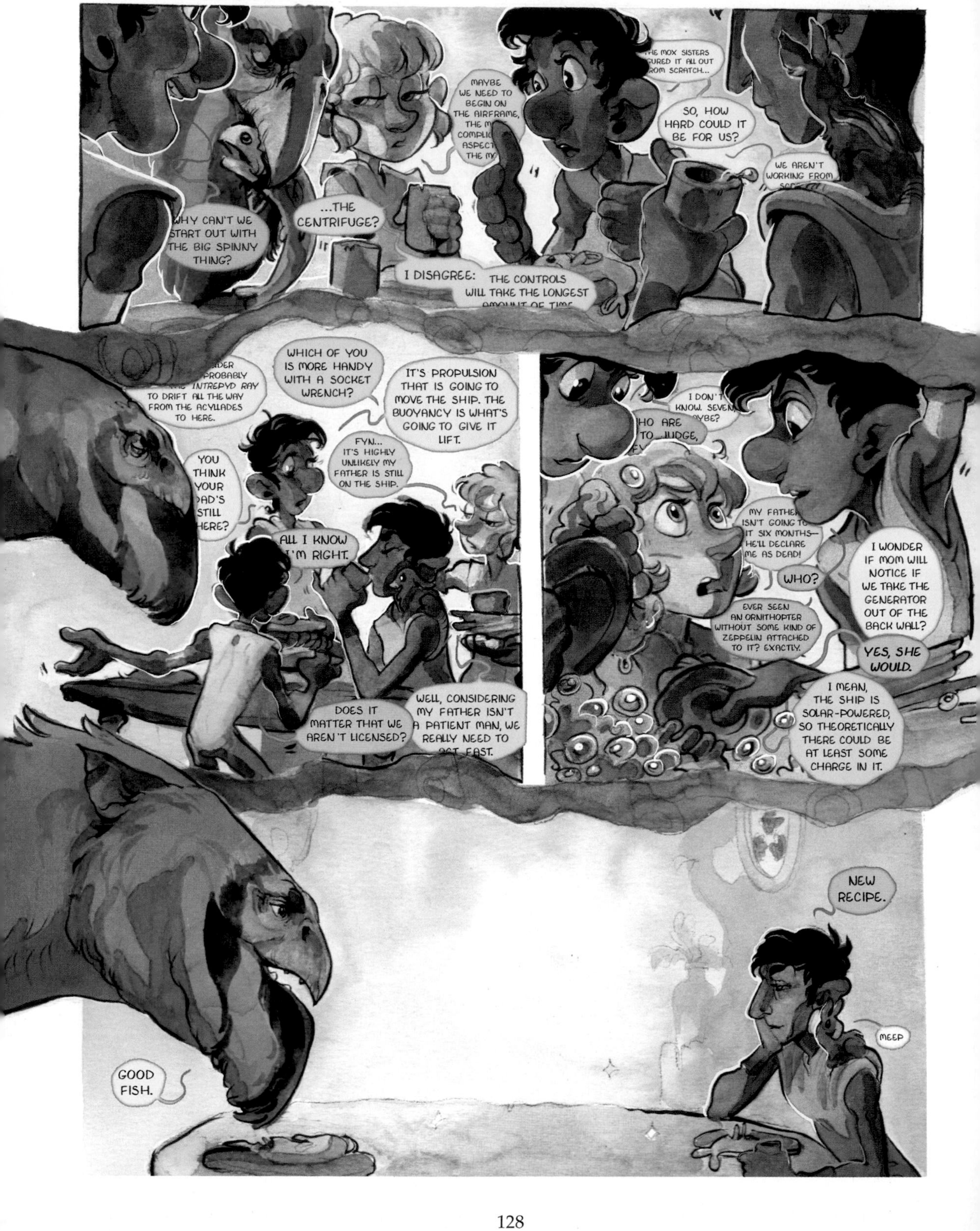
WHY CAN'T WE START OUT WITH THE BIG SPINNY THING?
...THE CENTRIFUGE?
MAYBE WE NEED TO BEGIN ON THE AIRFRAME, THE M COMPLIC ASPECT THE M
I DISAGREE: THE CONTROLS WILL TAKE THE LONGEST
THE MOX SISTERS URED IT ALL OUT ROM SCRATCH...
SO, HOW HARD COULD IT BE FOR US?
WE AREN'T WORKING FROM
PROBABLY INTREPYD RAY TO DRIFT ALL THE WAY FROM THE ACYLLADES TO HERE.
WHICH OF YOU IS MORE HANDY WITH A SOCKET WRENCH?
IT'S PROPULSION THAT IS GOING TO MOVE THE SHIP. THE BUOYANCY IS WHAT'S GOING TO GIVE IT LIFT.
YOU THINK YOUR DAD'S STILL HERE?
FYN... IT'S HIGHLY UNLIKELY MY FATHER IS STILL ON THE SHIP.
ALL I KNOW I'M RIGHT.
DOES IT MATTER THAT WE AREN'T LICENSED?
WELL, CONSIDERING MY FATHER ISN'T A PATIENT MAN, WE REALLY NEED TO
I DON'T KNOW. SEVEN MAYBE?
HO ARE TO JUDGE,
MY FATHER ISN'T GOING TO IT SIX MONTHS— HE'LL DECLARE ME AS DEAD!
WHO?
EVER SEEN AN ORNITHOPTER WITHOUT SOME KIND OF ZEPPELIN ATTACHED TO IT? EXACTLY.
I WONDER IF MOM WILL NOTICE IF WE TAKE THE GENERATOR OUT OF THE BACK WALL?
YES, SHE WOULD.
I MEAN, THE SHIP IS SOLAR-POWERED, SO THEORETICALLY THERE COULD BE AT LEAST SOME CHARGE IN IT.
NEW RECIPE.
MEEP
GOOD FISH.

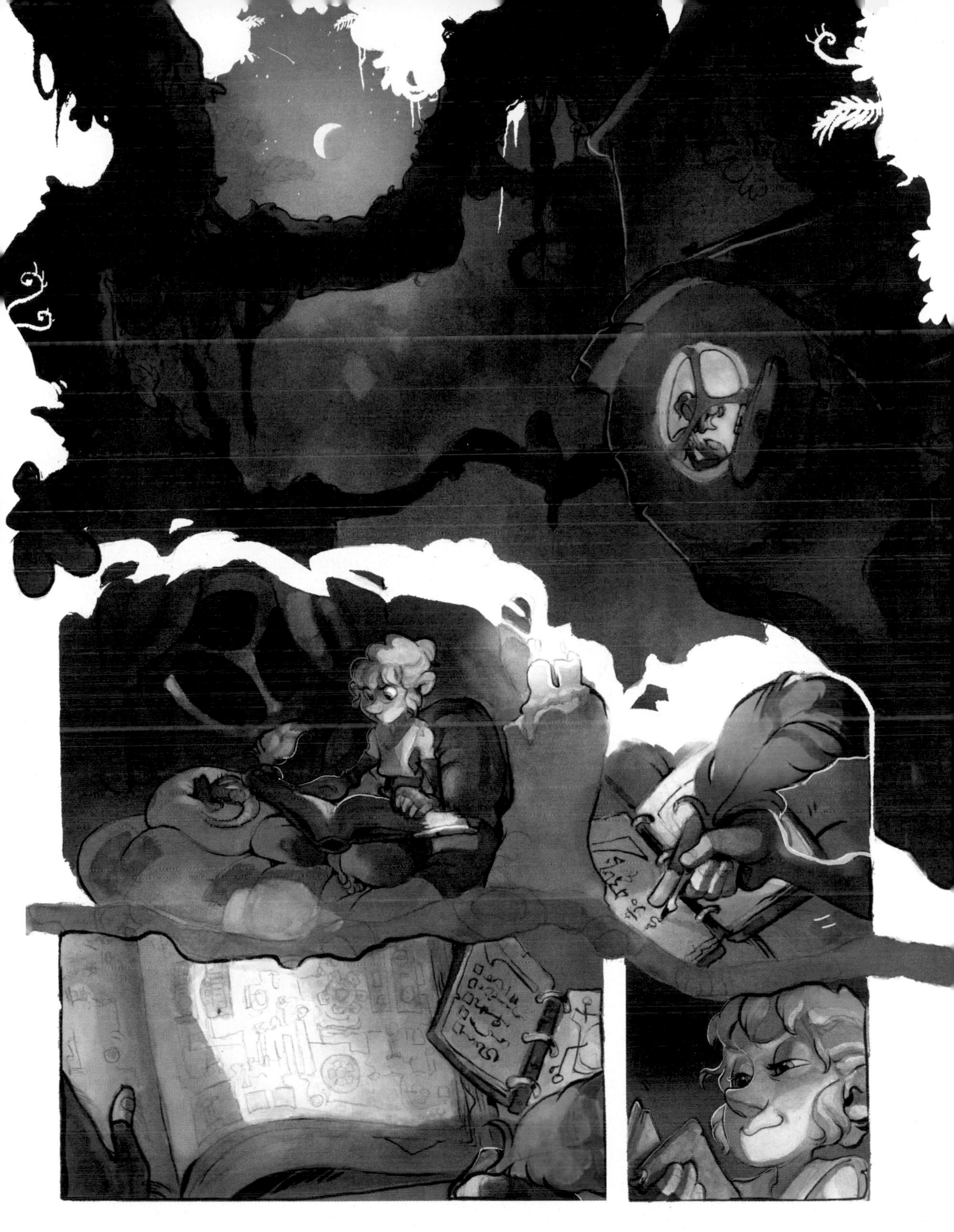

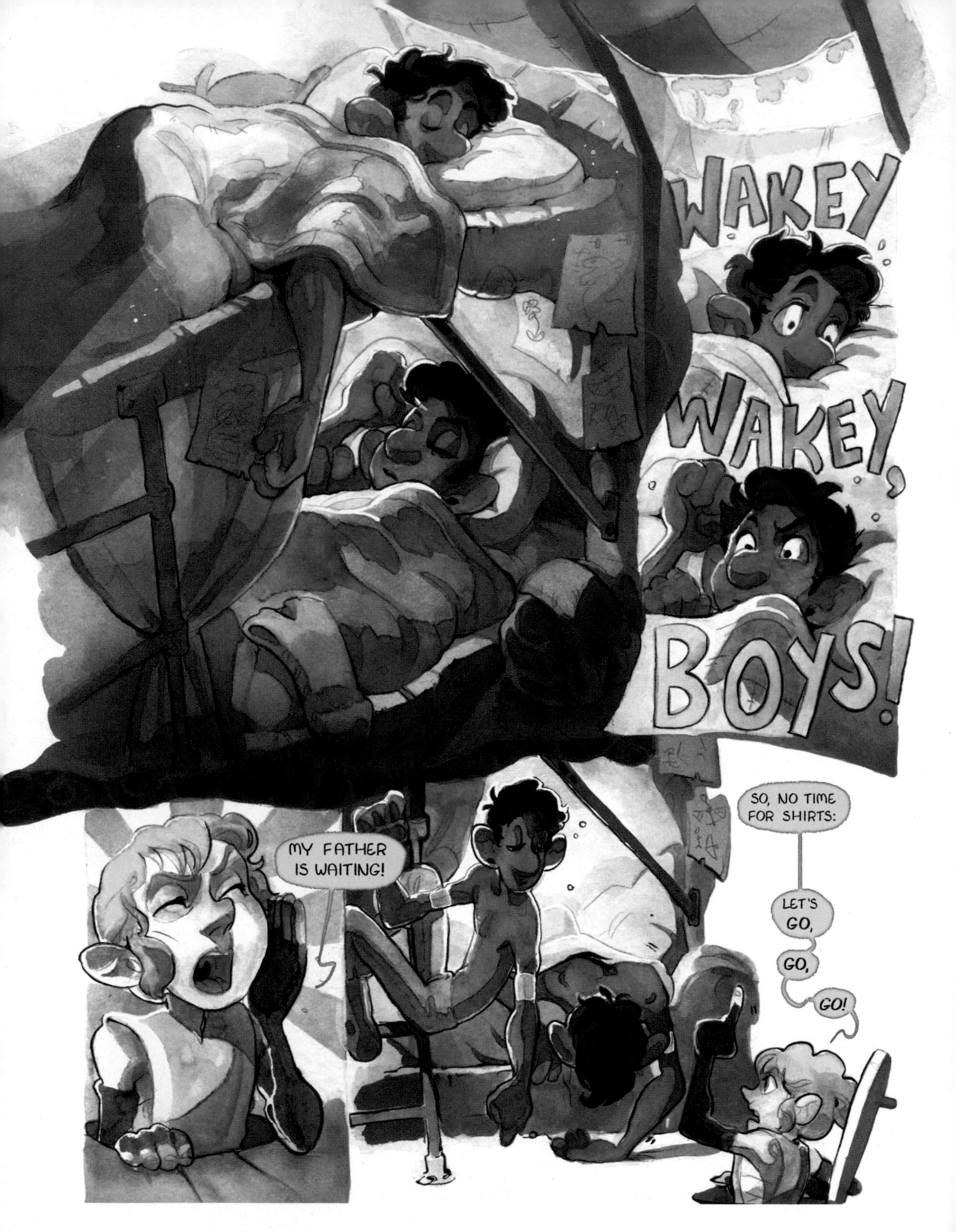
WAKEY
WAKEY,
BOYS!
MY FATHER IS WAITING!
SO, NO TIME FOR SHIRTS:
LET'S GO,
GO,
GO!

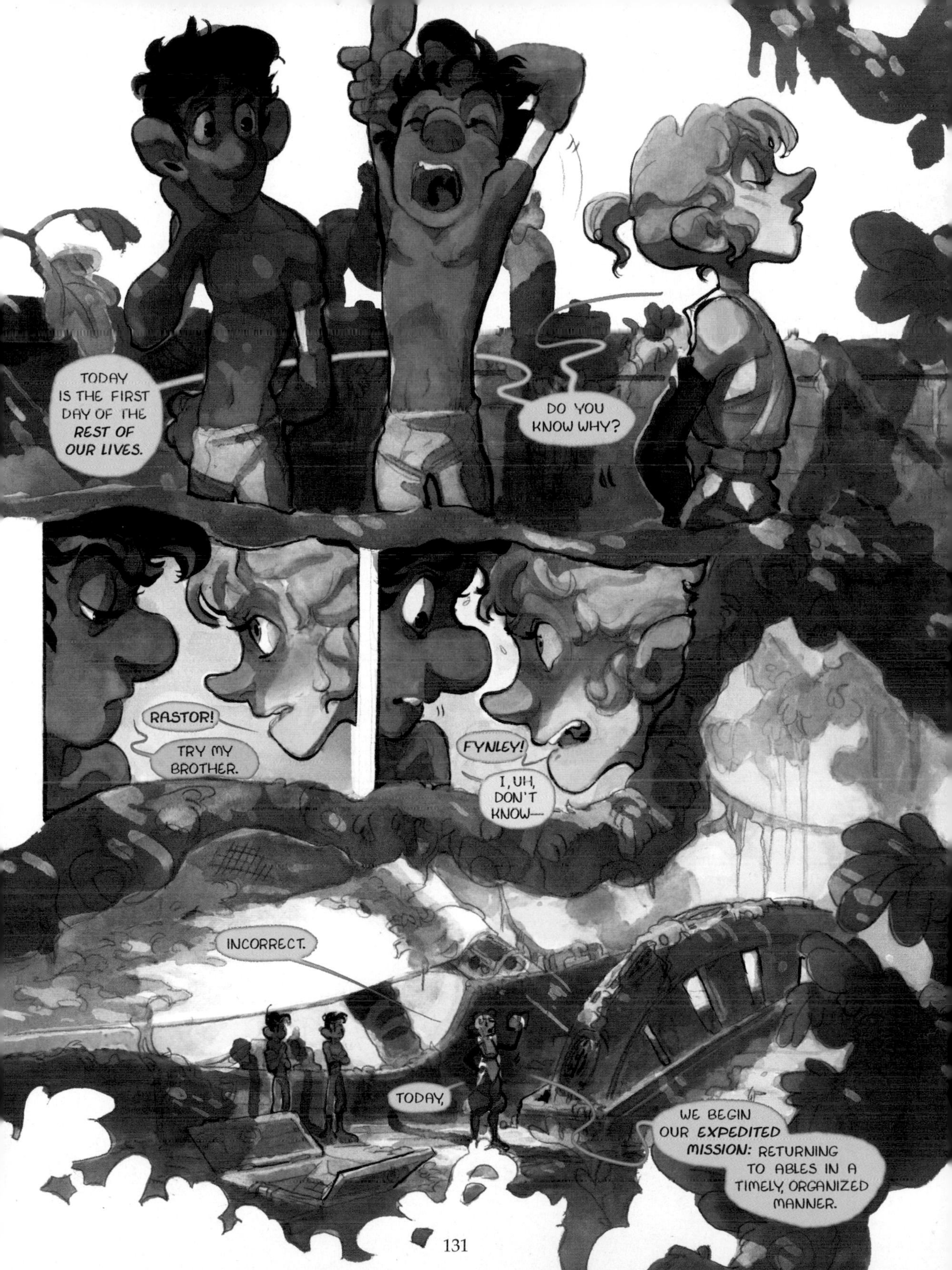
TODAY IS THE FIRST DAY OF THE REST OF OUR LIVES.
DO YOU KNOW WHY?
RASTOR!
TRY MY BROTHER.
FYNLEY!
I, UH, DON'T KNOW—
INCORRECT.
TODAY,
WE BEGIN OUR EXPEDITED MISSION: RETURNING TO ABLES IN A TIMELY, ORGANIZED MANNER.

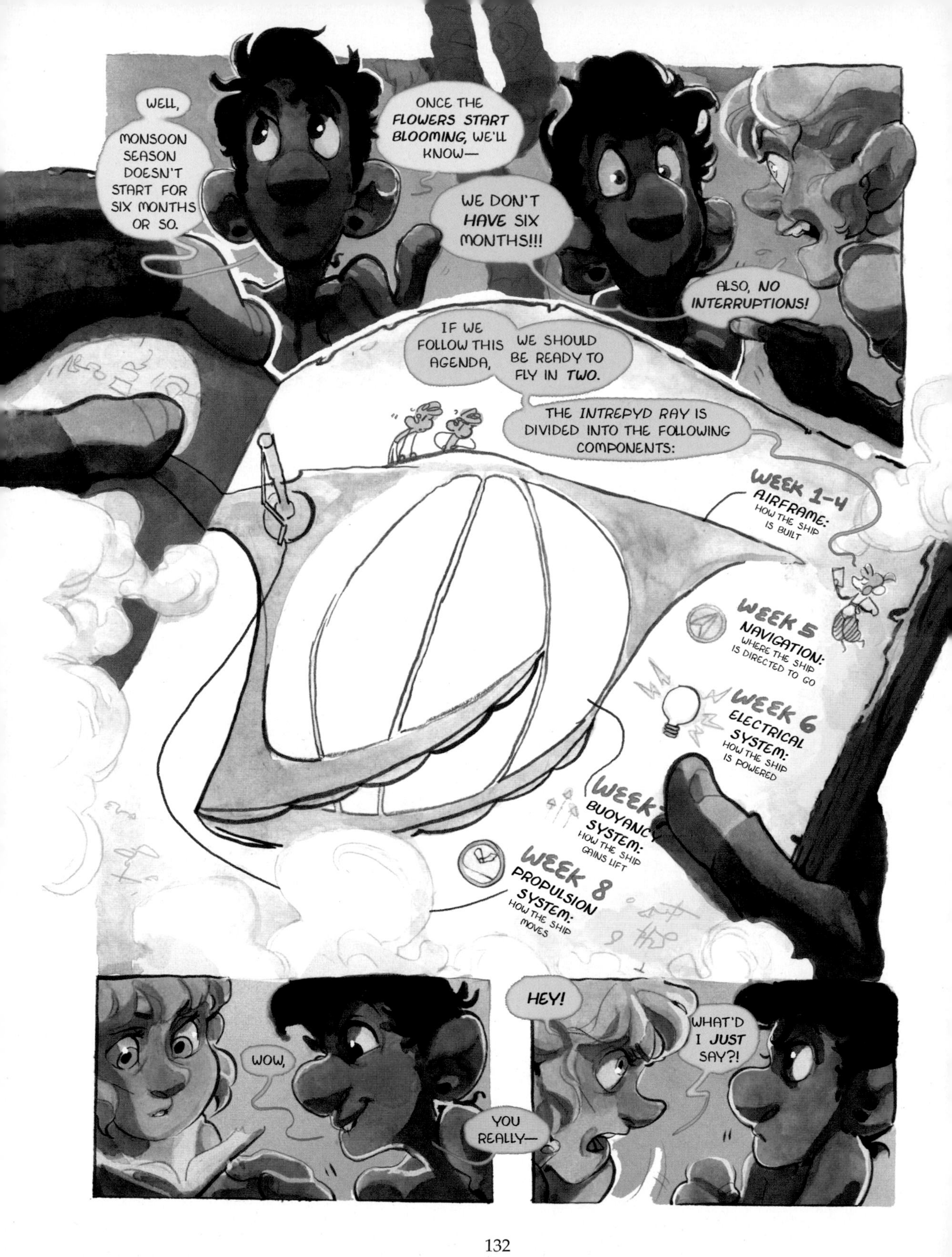
WELL,
MONSOON SEASON DOESN'T START FOR SIX MONTHS OR SO.
ONCE THE FLOWERS START BLOOMING, WE'LL KNOW—
WE DON'T HAVE SIX MONTHS!!!
ALSO, NO INTERRUPTIONS!
IF WE FOLLOW THIS AGENDA,
WE SHOULD BE READY TO FLY IN TWO.
THE INTREPYD RAY IS DIVIDED INTO THE FOLLOWING COMPONENTS:
WEEK 1–4 AIRFRAME: HOW THE SHIP IS BUILT
WEEK 5 NAVIGATION: WHERE THE SHIP IS DIRECTED TO GO
WEEK 6 ELECTRICAL SYSTEM: HOW THE SHIP IS POWERED
BUOYANCY SYSTEM: HOW THE SHIP GAINS LIFT
WEEK 8 PROPULSION SYSTEM: HOW THE SHIP MOVES
WOW,
YOU REALLY—
HEY!
WHAT'D I JUST SAY?!

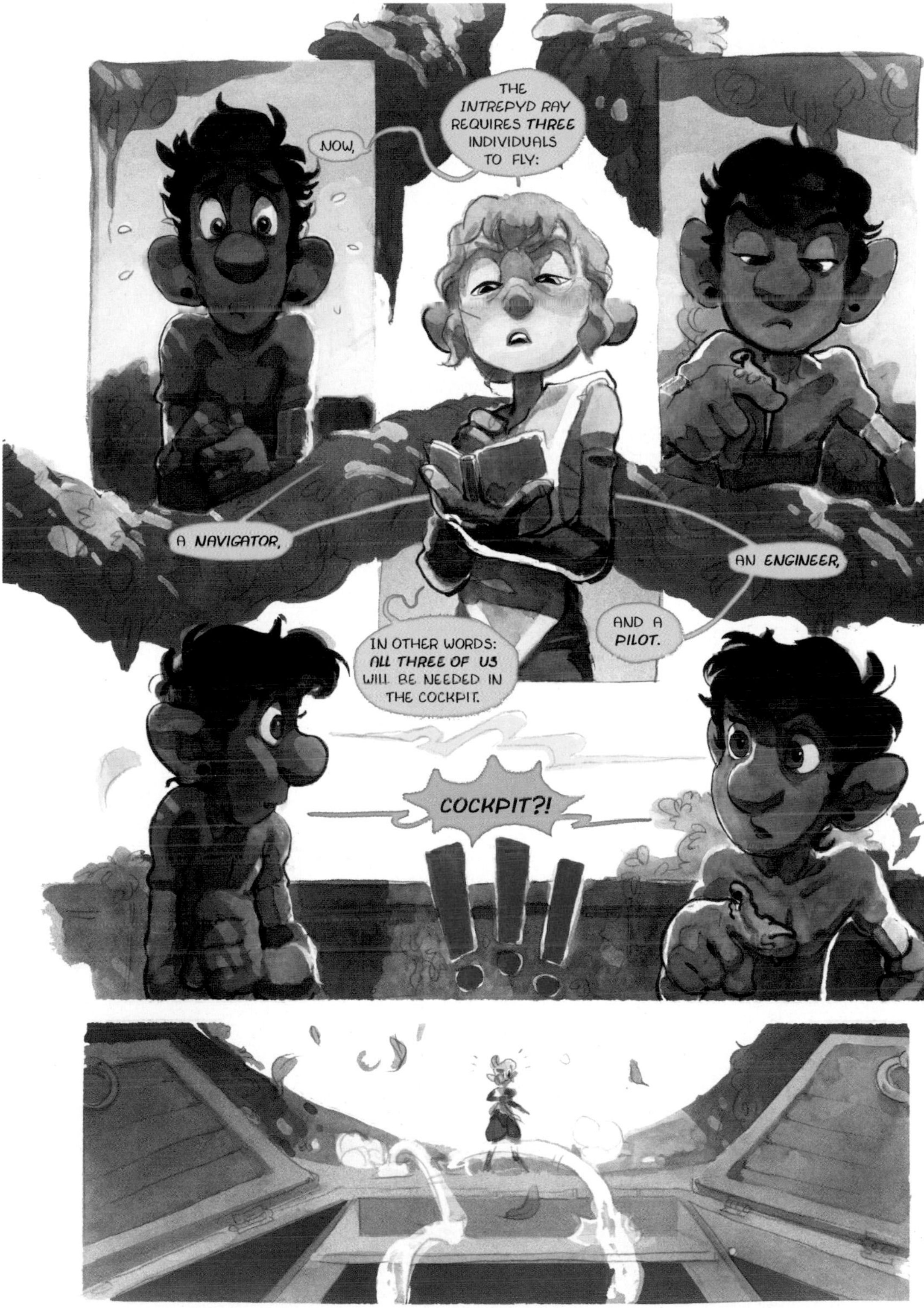

NOW,
THE INTREPYD RAY REQUIRES THREE INDIVIDUALS TO FLY:
A NAVIGATOR,
AN ENGINEER,
AND A PILOT.
IN OTHER WORDS: ALL THREE OF US WILL BE NEEDED IN THE COCKPIT.
COCKPIT?!

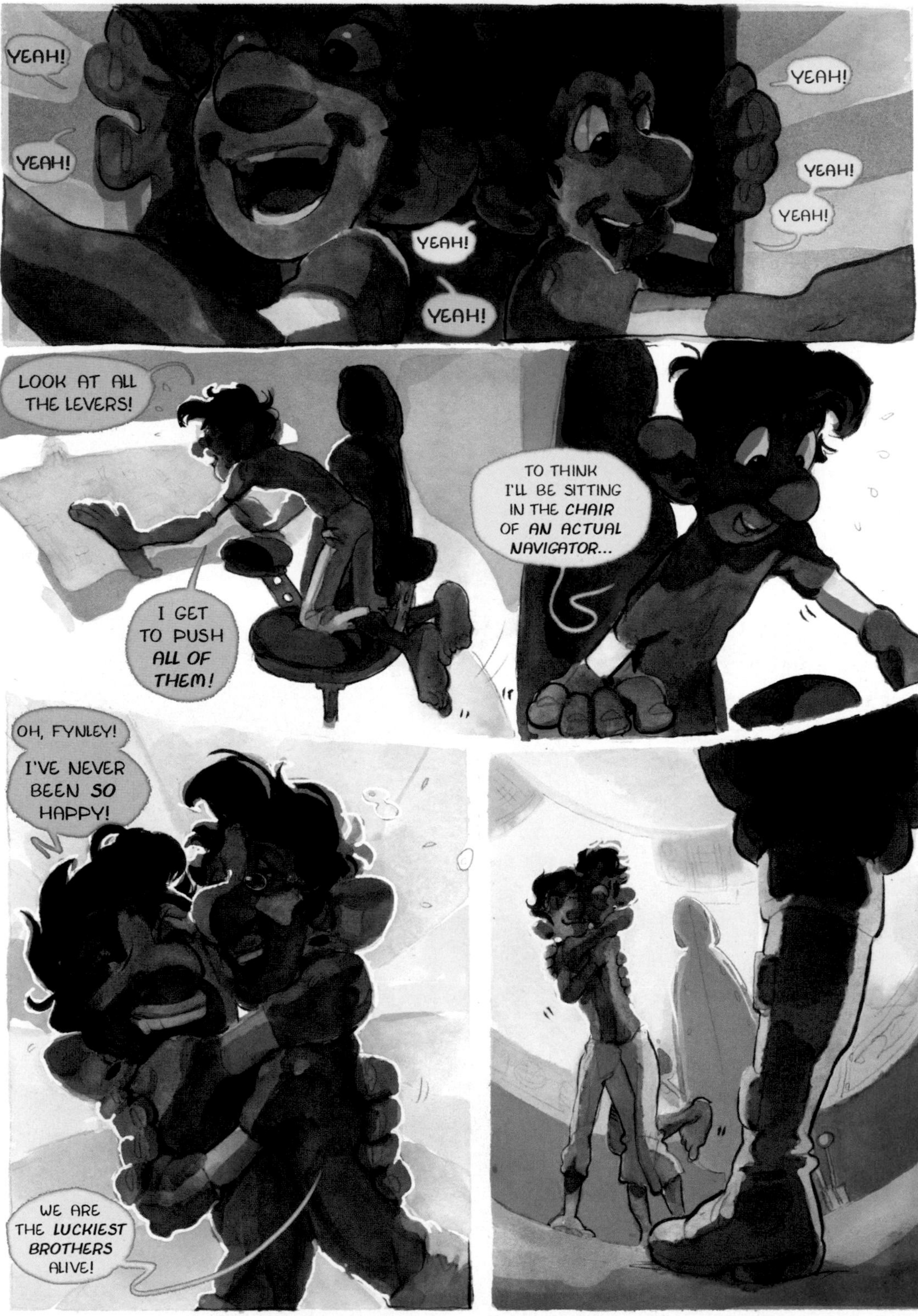
YEAH!
YEAH!
YEAH!
YEAH!
YEAH!
YEAH!
YEAH!
LOOK AT ALL THE LEVERS!
I GET TO PUSH ALL OF THEM!
TO THINK I'LL BE SITTING IN THE CHAIR OF AN ACTUAL NAVIGATOR...
OH, FYNLEY!
I'VE NEVER BEEN SO HAPPY!
WE ARE THE LUCKIEST BROTHERS ALIVE!

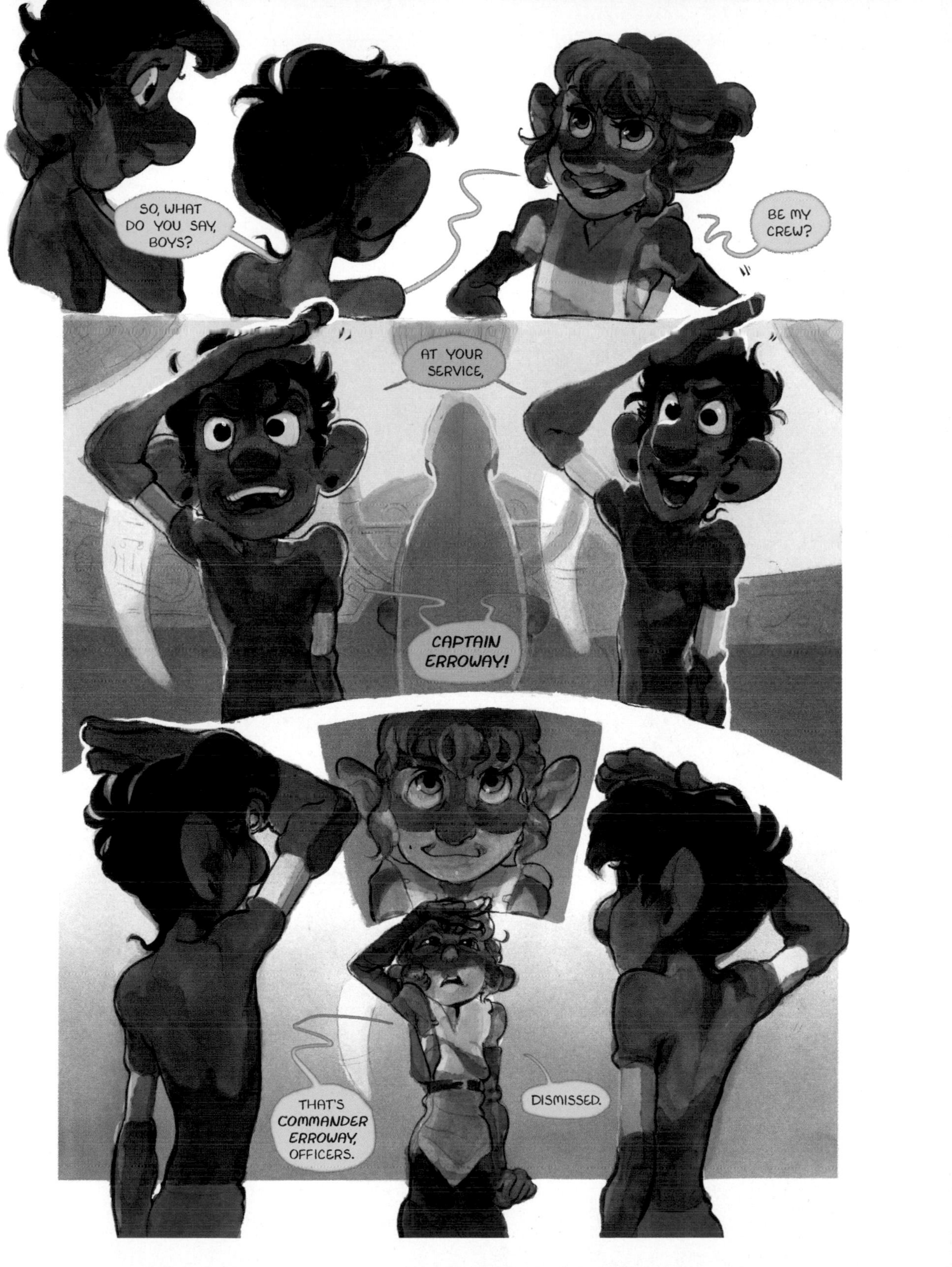
SO, WHAT DO YOU SAY, BOYS?
BE MY CREW?
AT YOUR SERVICE,
CAPTAIN ERROWAY!
THAT'S COMMANDER ERROWAY, OFFICERS.
DISMISSED.

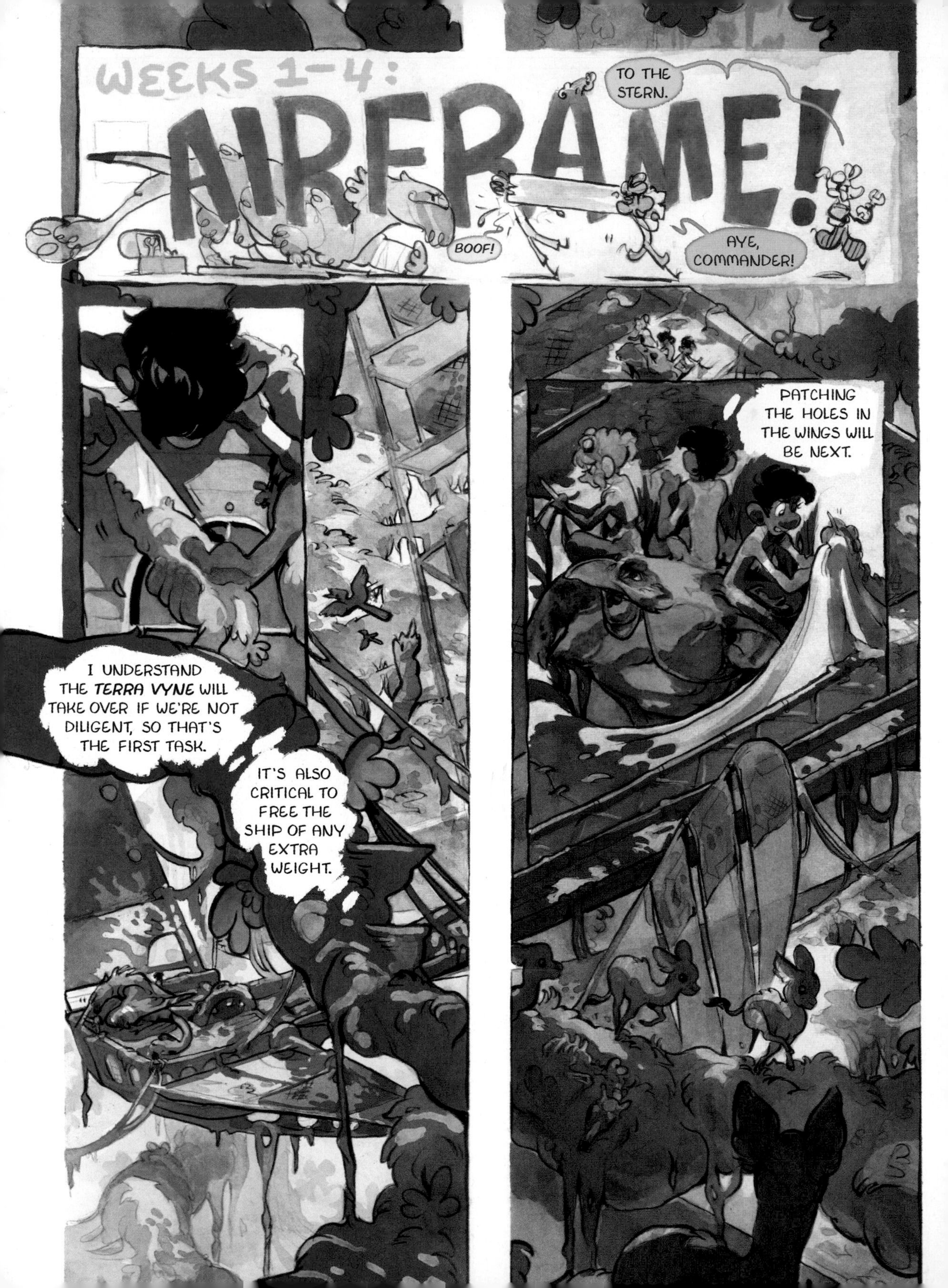
WEEKS 1–4:
AIRFRAME!
TO THE STERN.
BOOF!
AYE, COMMANDER!
I UNDERSTAND THE *TERRA VYNE* WILL TAKE OVER IF WE'RE NOT DILIGENT, SO THAT'S THE FIRST TASK.
IT'S ALSO CRITICAL TO FREE THE SHIP OF ANY EXTRA WEIGHT.
PATCHING THE HOLES IN THE WINGS WILL BE NEXT.

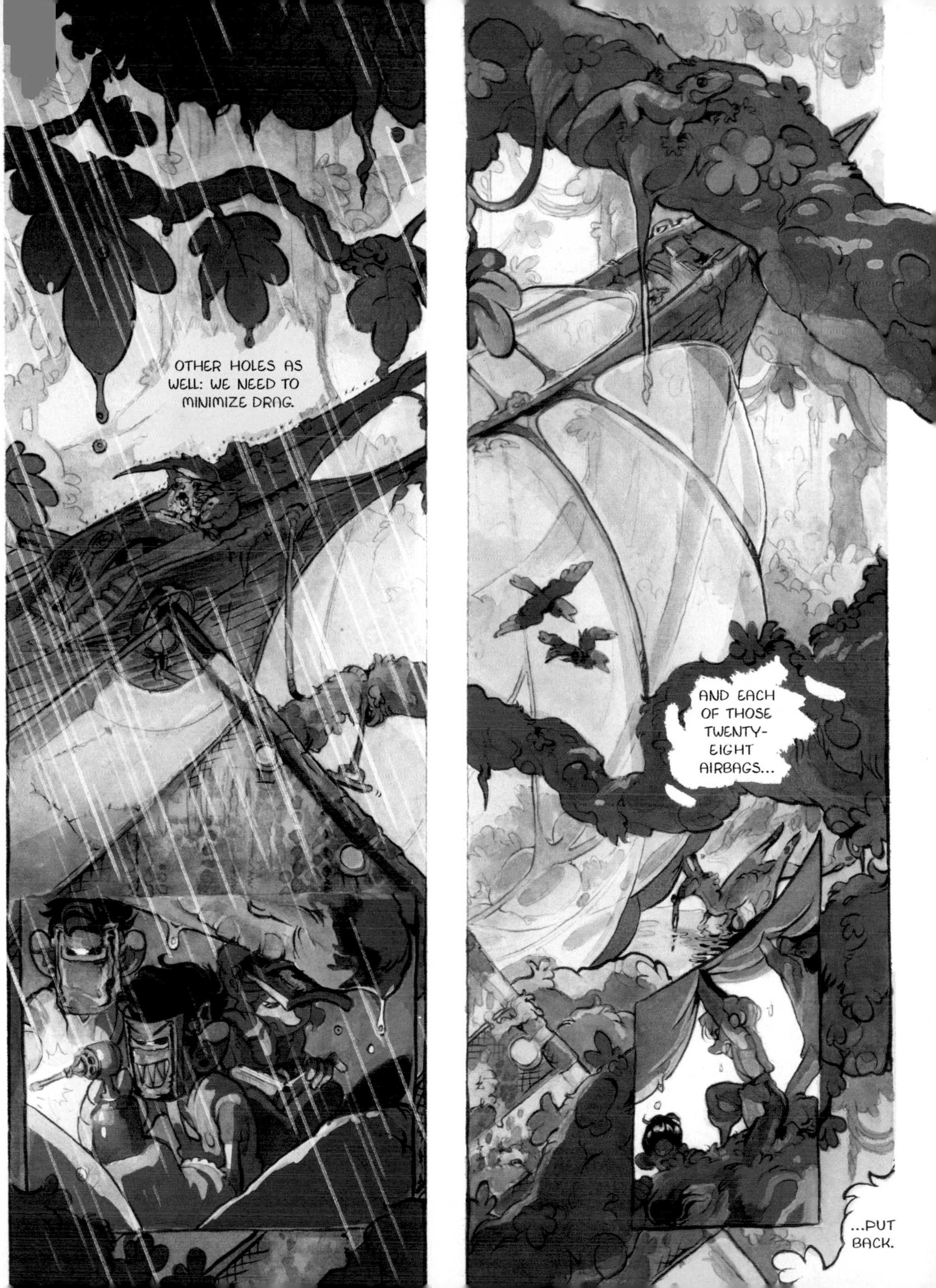
OTHER HOLES AS WELL: WE NEED TO MINIMIZE DRAG.
AND EACH OF THOSE TWENTY-EIGHT AIRBAGS...
...PUT BACK.

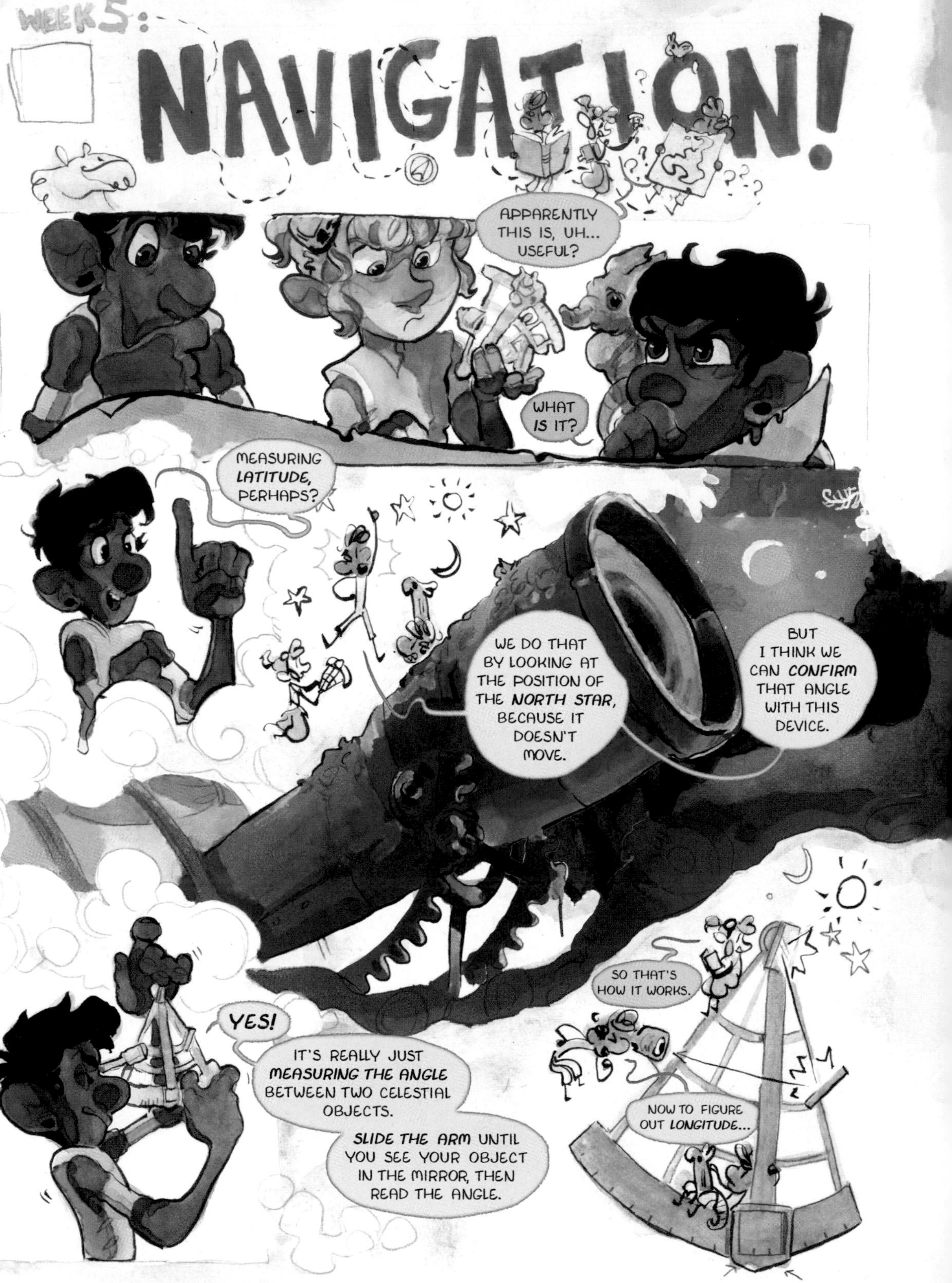
WEEK 5:
NAVIGATION!
APPARENTLY THIS IS, UH... USEFUL?
WHAT IS IT?
MEASURING LATITUDE, PERHAPS?
WE DO THAT BY LOOKING AT THE POSITION OF THE NORTH STAR, BECAUSE IT DOESN'T MOVE.
BUT I THINK WE CAN CONFIRM THAT ANGLE WITH THIS DEVICE.
YES!
IT'S REALLY JUST MEASURING THE ANGLE BETWEEN TWO CELESTIAL OBJECTS.
SLIDE THE ARM UNTIL YOU SEE YOUR OBJECT IN THE MIRROR, THEN READ THE ANGLE.
SO THAT'S HOW IT WORKS.
NOW TO FIGURE OUT LONGITUDE...

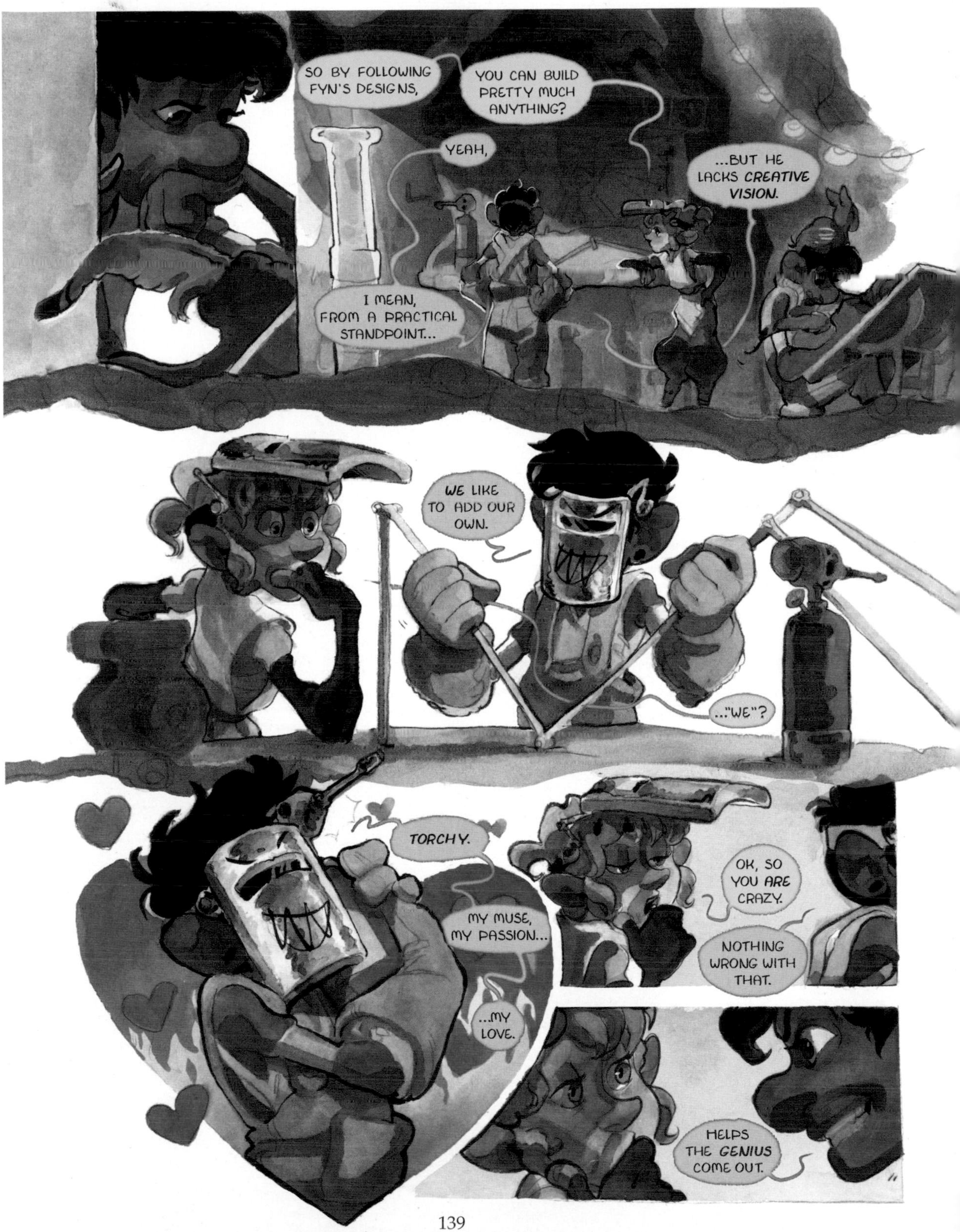
SO BY FOLLOWING FYN'S DESIGNS,
YOU CAN BUILD PRETTY MUCH ANYTHING?
YEAH,
I MEAN, FROM A PRACTICAL STANDPOINT...
...BUT HE LACKS *CREATIVE VISION*.
WE LIKE TO ADD OUR OWN.
..."WE"?
TORCHY.
MY MUSE, MY PASSION...
...MY LOVE.
OK, SO YOU *ARE* CRAZY.
NOTHING WRONG WITH THAT.
HELPS THE *GENIUS* COME OUT.

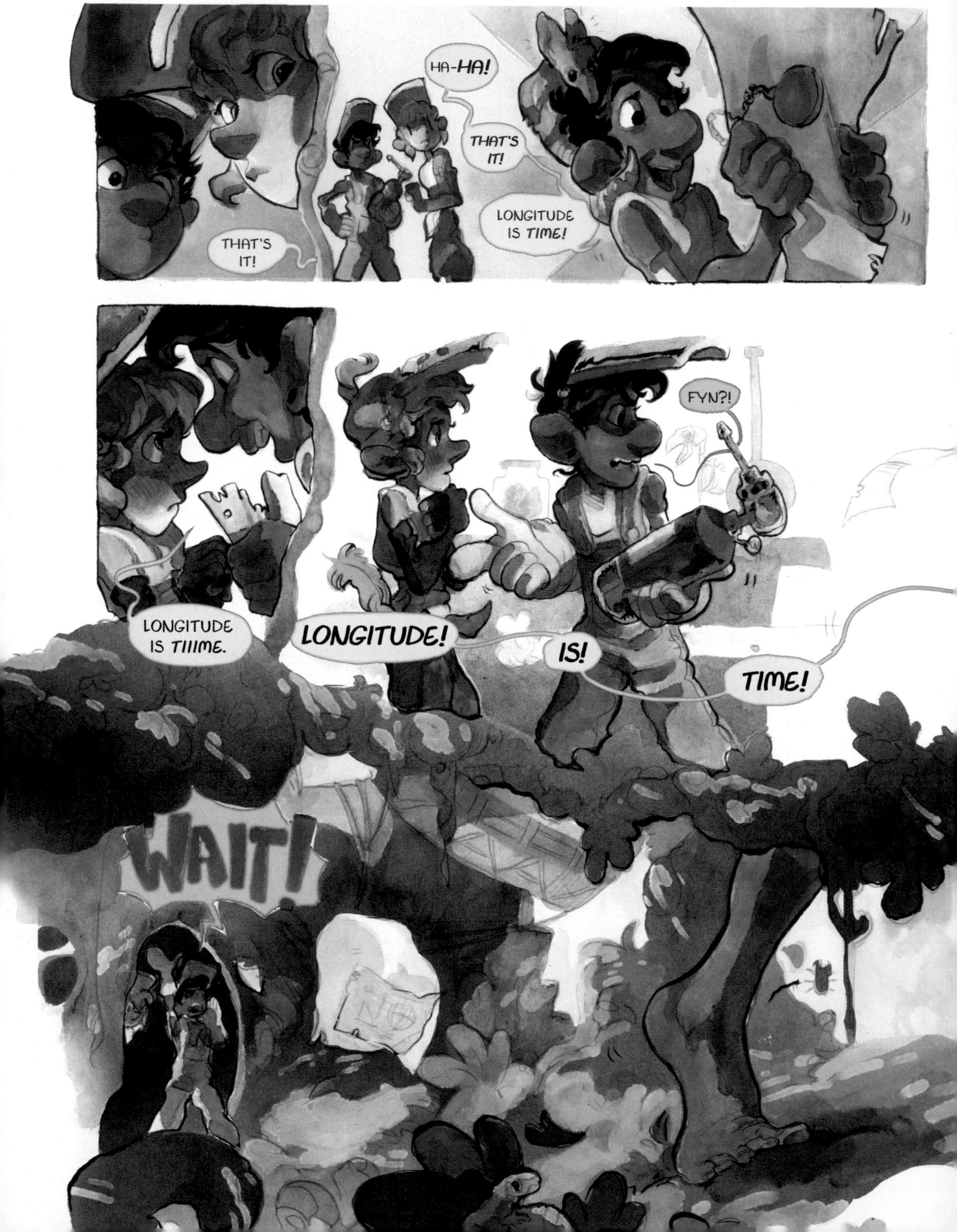
HA-HA!
THAT'S IT!
THAT'S IT!
LONGITUDE IS TIME!
FYN?!
LONGITUDE IS TIIIME.
LONGITUDE!
IS!
TIME!
WAIT!

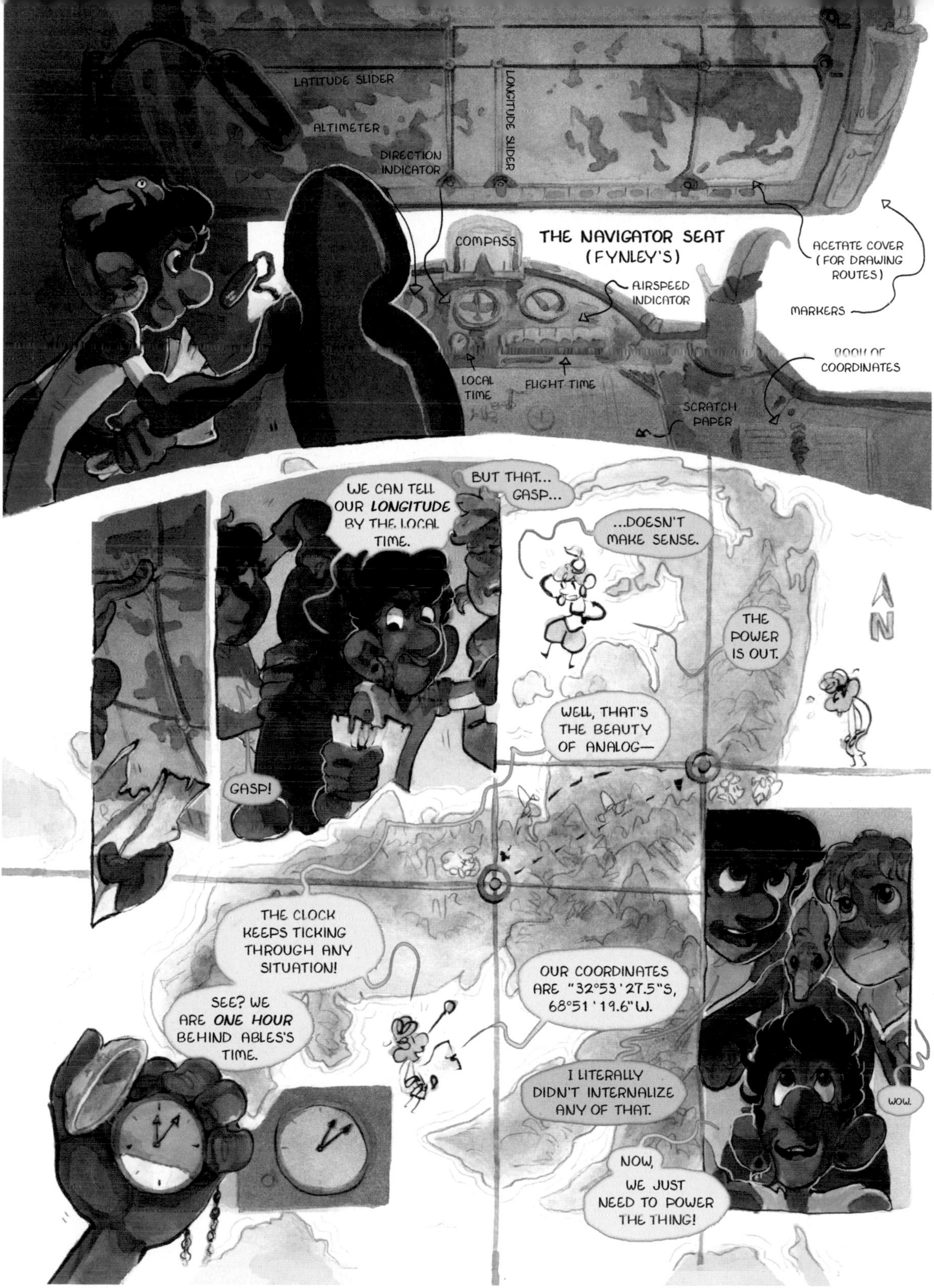
LATITUDE SLIDER
ALTIMETER
DIRECTION INDICATOR
LONGITUDE SLIDER
THE NAVIGATOR SEAT (FYNLEY'S)
COMPASS
AIRSPEED INDICATOR
ACETATE COVER (FOR DRAWING ROUTES)
MARKERS
BOOK OF COORDINATES
LOCAL TIME
FLIGHT TIME
SCRATCH PAPER
WE CAN TELL OUR **LONGITUDE** BY THE LOCAL TIME.
BUT THAT... GASP...
...DOESN'T MAKE SENSE.
THE POWER IS OUT.
WELL, THAT'S THE BEAUTY OF ANALOG—
GASP!
N
THE CLOCK KEEPS TICKING THROUGH ANY SITUATION!
SEE? WE ARE **ONE HOUR** BEHIND ABLES'S TIME.
OUR COORDINATES ARE "32°53'27.5"S, 68°51'19.6"W.
I LITERALLY DIDN'T INTERNALIZE ANY OF THAT.
WOW.
NOW, WE JUST NEED TO POWER THE THING!

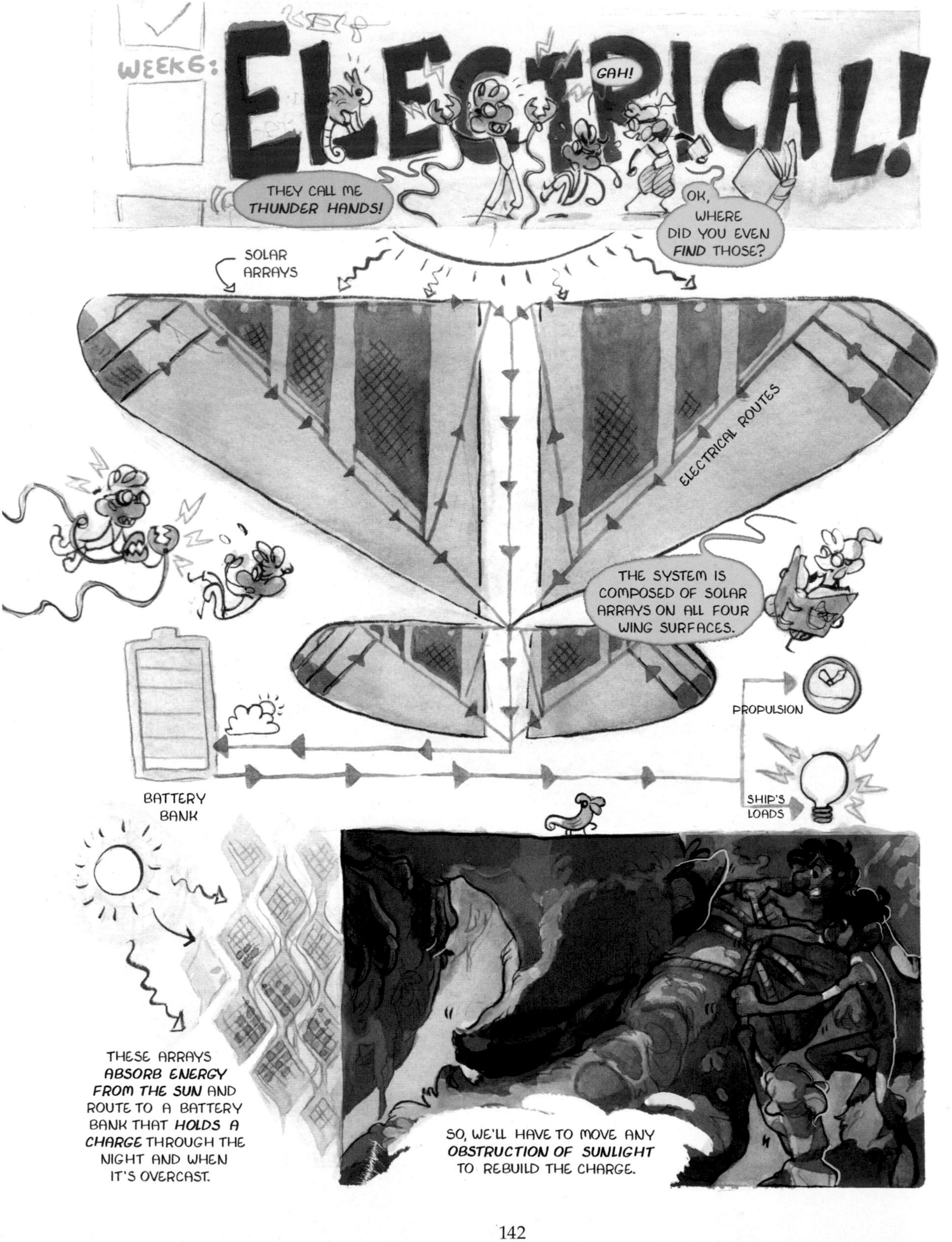
WEEK 6: ELECTRICAL!
GAH!
THEY CALL ME THUNDER HANDS!
OK, WHERE DID YOU EVEN FIND THOSE?
SOLAR ARRAYS
ELECTRICAL ROUTES
THE SYSTEM IS COMPOSED OF SOLAR ARRAYS ON ALL FOUR WING SURFACES.
PROPULSION
BATTERY BANK
SHIP'S LOADS
THESE ARRAYS ABSORB ENERGY FROM THE SUN AND ROUTE TO A BATTERY BANK THAT HOLDS A CHARGE THROUGH THE NIGHT AND WHEN IT'S OVERCAST.
SO, WE'LL HAVE TO MOVE ANY OBSTRUCTION OF SUNLIGHT TO REBUILD THE CHARGE.

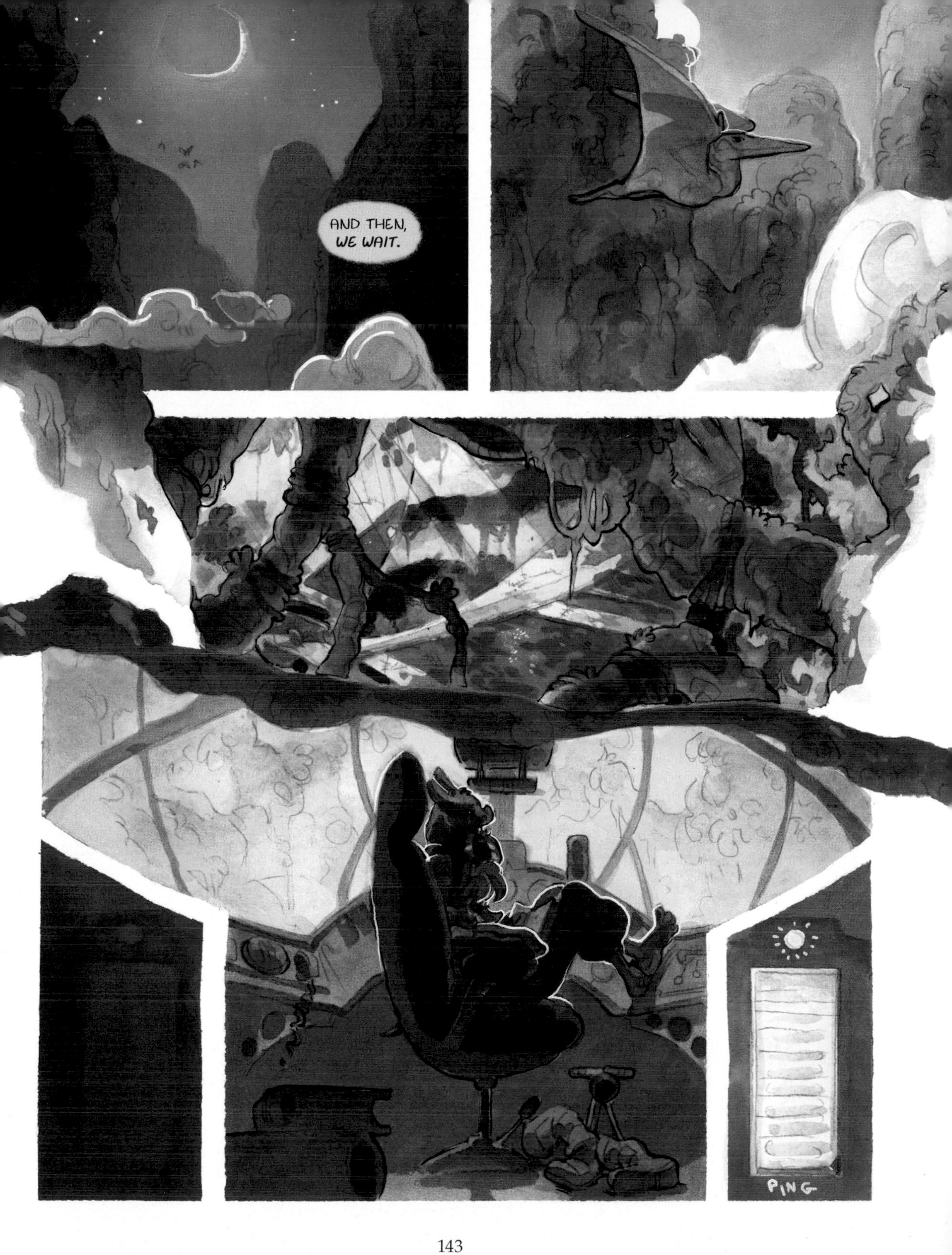
AND THEN, WE WAIT.
PING

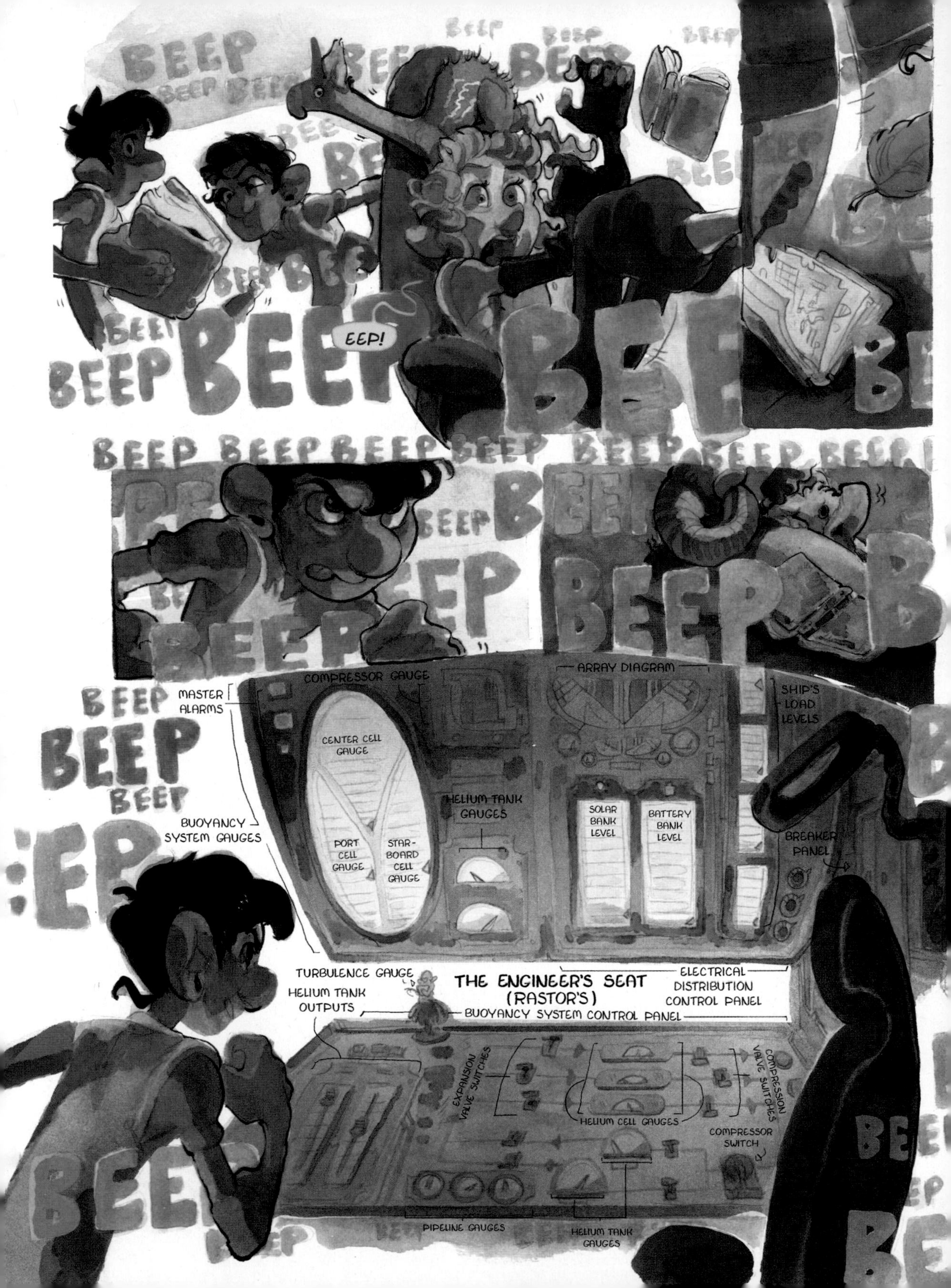
EEP!
BEEP BEEP BEEP
MASTER ALARMS
COMPRESSOR GAUGE
ARRAY DIAGRAM
SHIP'S LOAD LEVELS
CENTER CELL GAUGE
HELIUM TANK GAUGES
SOLAR BANK LEVEL
BATTERY BANK LEVEL
BUOYANCY SYSTEM GAUGES
PORT CELL GAUGE
STARBOARD CELL GAUGE
BREAKER PANEL
TURBULENCE GAUGE
THE ENGINEER'S SEAT (RASTOR'S)
ELECTRICAL DISTRIBUTION CONTROL PANEL
HELIUM TANK OUTPUTS
BUOYANCY SYSTEM CONTROL PANEL
EXPANSION VALVE SWITCHES
COMPRESSION VALVE SWITCHES
HELIUM CELL GAUGES
COMPRESSOR SWITCH
PIPELINE GAUGES
HELIUM TANK GAUGES

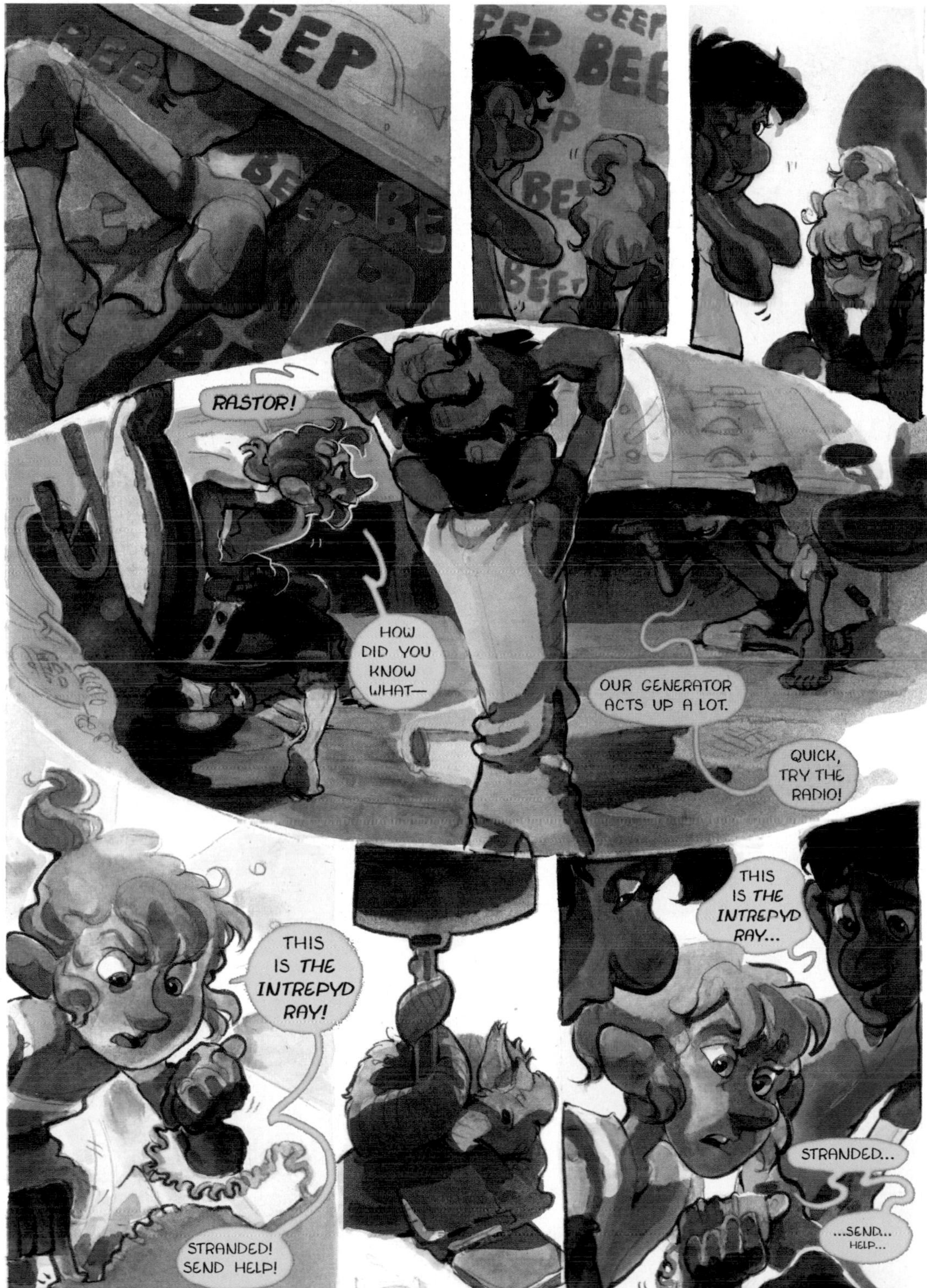
BEEP
BEEP
BEEP
BEEP
RASTOR!
HOW DID YOU KNOW WHAT—
OUR GENERATOR ACTS UP A LOT.
QUICK, TRY THE RADIO!
THIS IS THE INTREPYD RAY!
STRANDED! SEND HELP!
THIS IS THE INTREPYD RAY...
STRANDED...
...SEND... HELP...

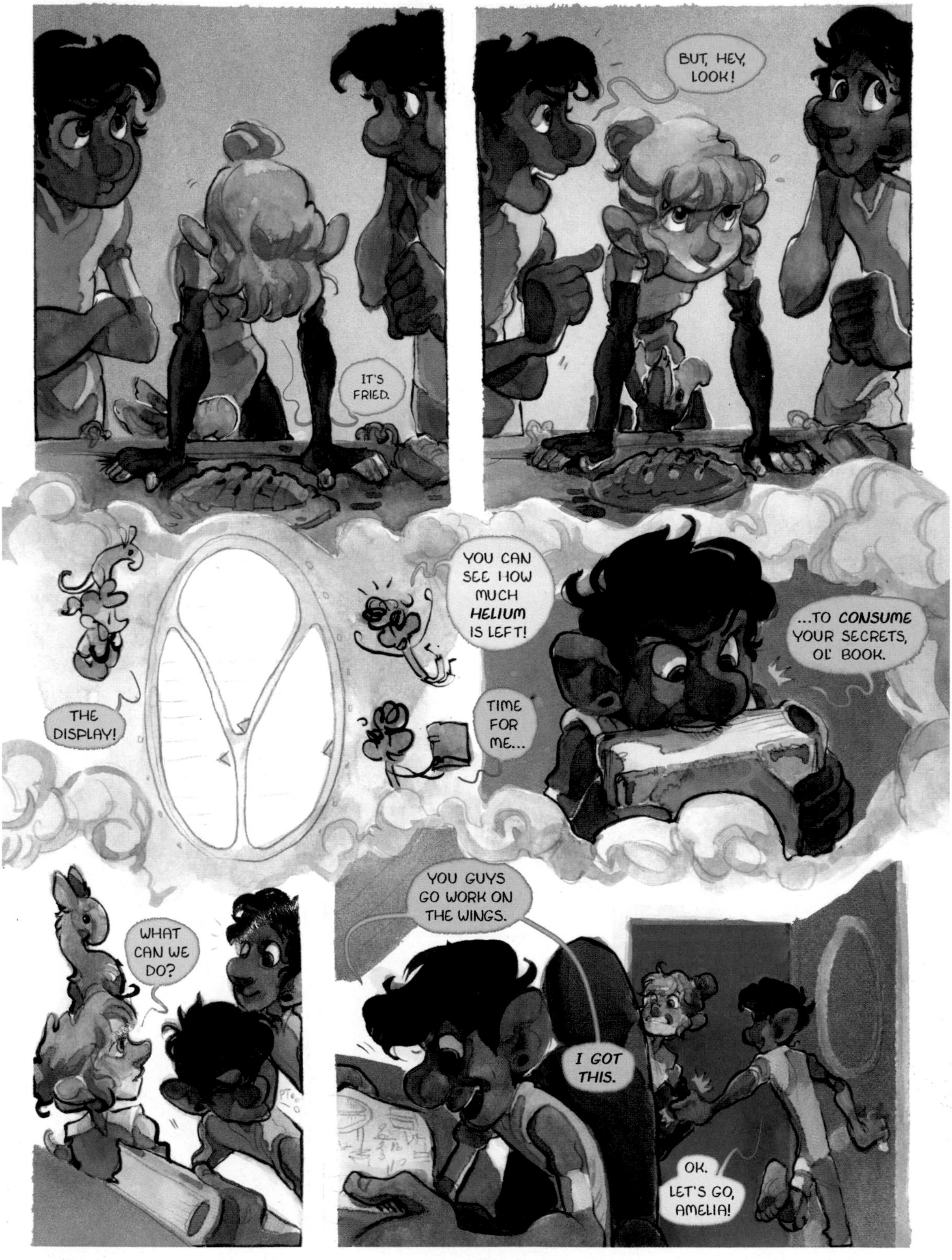
IT'S FRIED.
BUT, HEY, LOOK!
THE DISPLAY!
YOU CAN SEE HOW MUCH HELIUM IS LEFT!
TIME FOR ME...
...TO CONSUME YOUR SECRETS, OL' BOOK.
WHAT CAN WE DO?
YOU GUYS GO WORK ON THE WINGS.
I GOT THIS.
OK. LET'S GO, AMELIA!

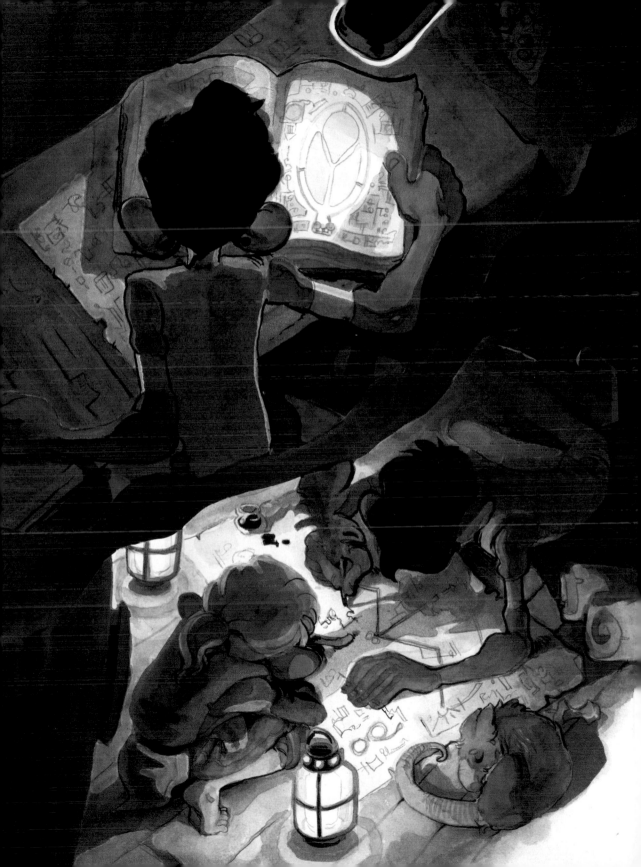

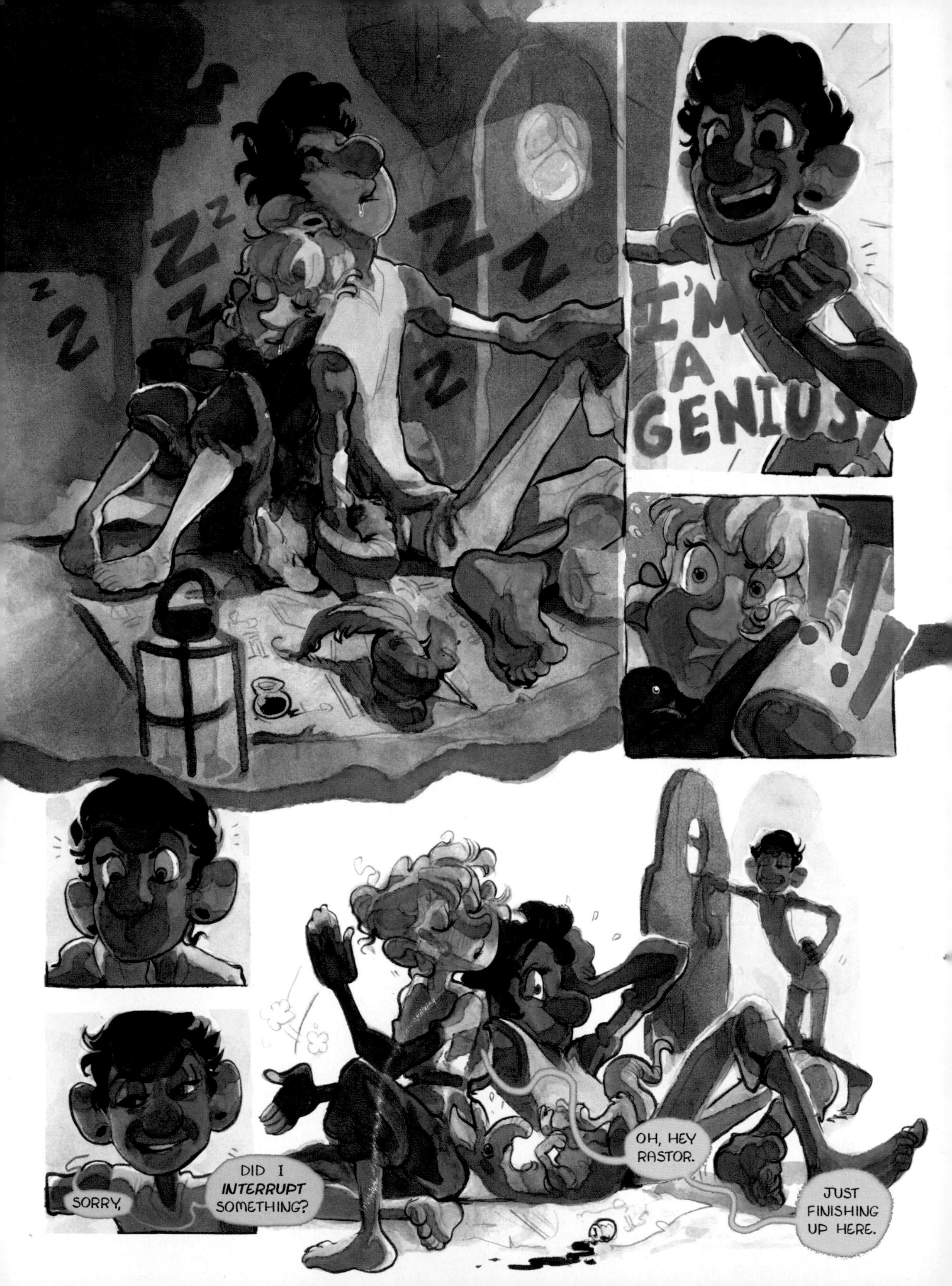
Z
Z
Z
Z
Z
Z
Z
Z
I'M A GENIUS!
SORRY,
DID I INTERRUPT SOMETHING?
OH, HEY RASTOR.
JUST FINISHING UP HERE.

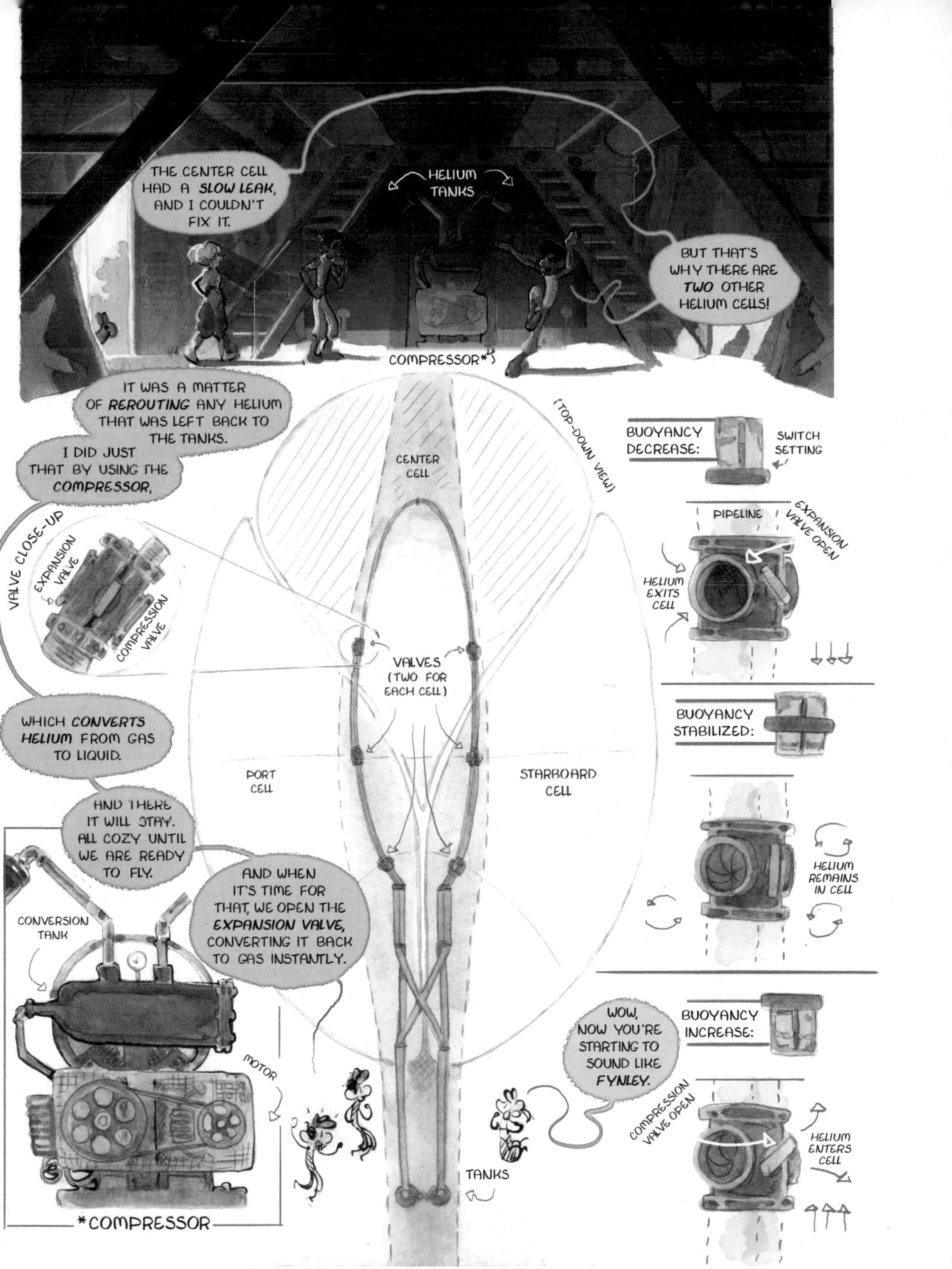
THE CENTER CELL HAD A SLOW LEAK, AND I COULDN'T FIX IT.
HELIUM TANKS
BUT THAT'S WHY THERE ARE TWO OTHER HELIUM CELLS!
COMPRESSOR*
IT WAS A MATTER OF REROUTING ANY HELIUM THAT WAS LEFT BACK TO THE TANKS.
I DID JUST THAT BY USING THE COMPRESSOR,
(TOP-DOWN VIEW)
CENTER CELL
VALVE CLOSE-UP
EXPANSION VALVE
COMPRESSION VALVE
VALVES (TWO FOR EACH CELL)
WHICH CONVERTS HELIUM FROM GAS TO LIQUID.
PORT CELL
STARBOARD CELL
AND THERE IT WILL STAY. ALL COZY UNTIL WE ARE READY TO FLY.
AND WHEN IT'S TIME FOR THAT, WE OPEN THE EXPANSION VALVE, CONVERTING IT BACK TO GAS INSTANTLY.
CONVERSION TANK
MOTOR
*COMPRESSOR
TANKS
WOW, NOW YOU'RE STARTING TO SOUND LIKE FYNLEY.
BUOYANCY DECREASE:
SWITCH SETTING
PIPELINE
EXPANSION VALVE OPEN
HELIUM EXITS CELL
BUOYANCY STABILIZED:
HELIUM REMAINS IN CELL
BUOYANCY INCREASE:
COMPRESSION VALVE OPEN
HELIUM ENTERS CELL

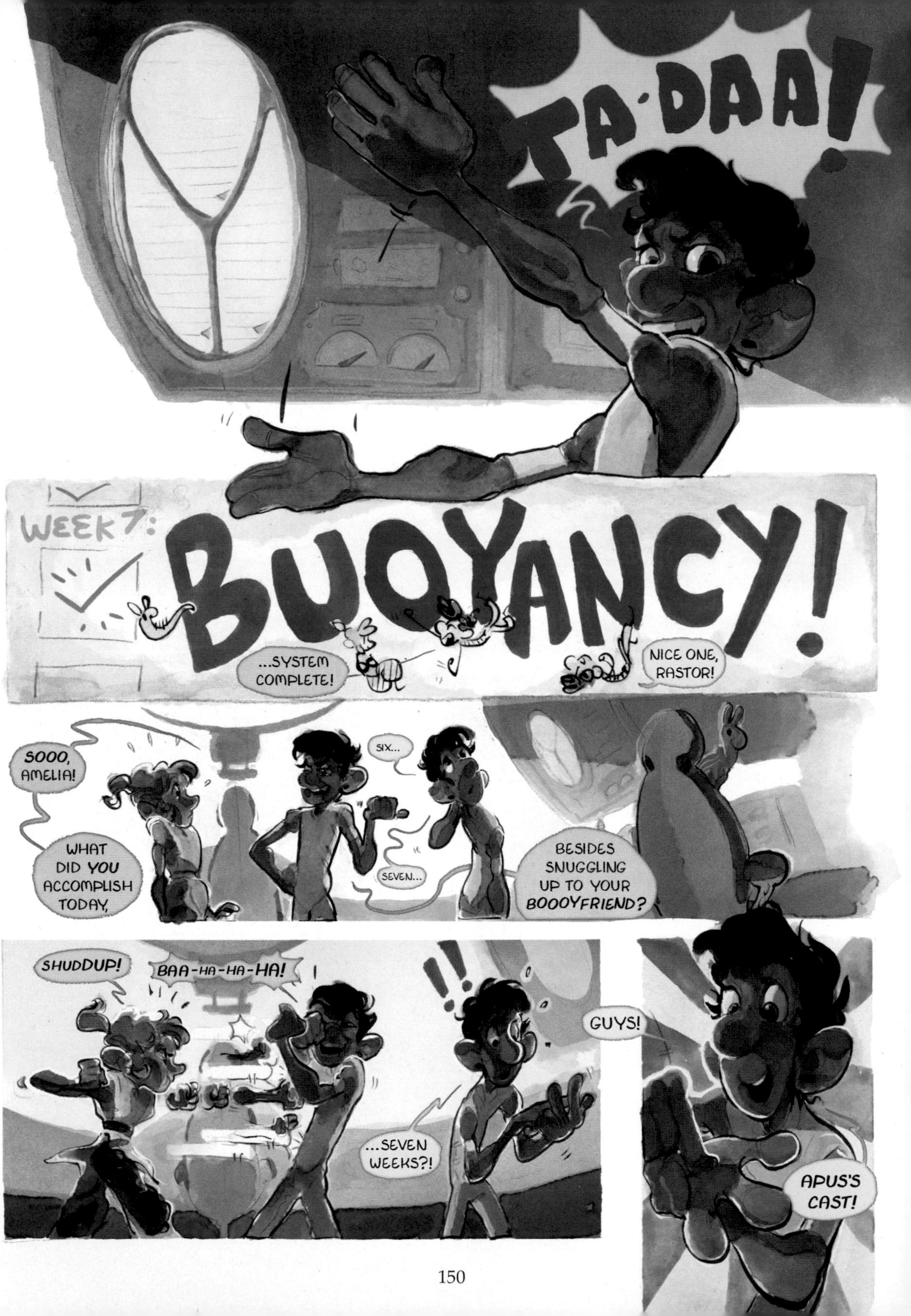
TA-DAA!
WEEK 7:
BUOYANCY!
...SYSTEM COMPLETE!
NICE ONE, RASTOR!
SOOO, AMELIA!
WHAT DID YOU ACCOMPLISH TODAY,
SIX...
SEVEN...
BESIDES SNUGGLING UP TO YOUR BOOOYFRIEND?
SHUDDUP!
BAA-HA-HA-HA!
!!
...SEVEN WEEKS?!
GUYS!
APUS'S CAST!

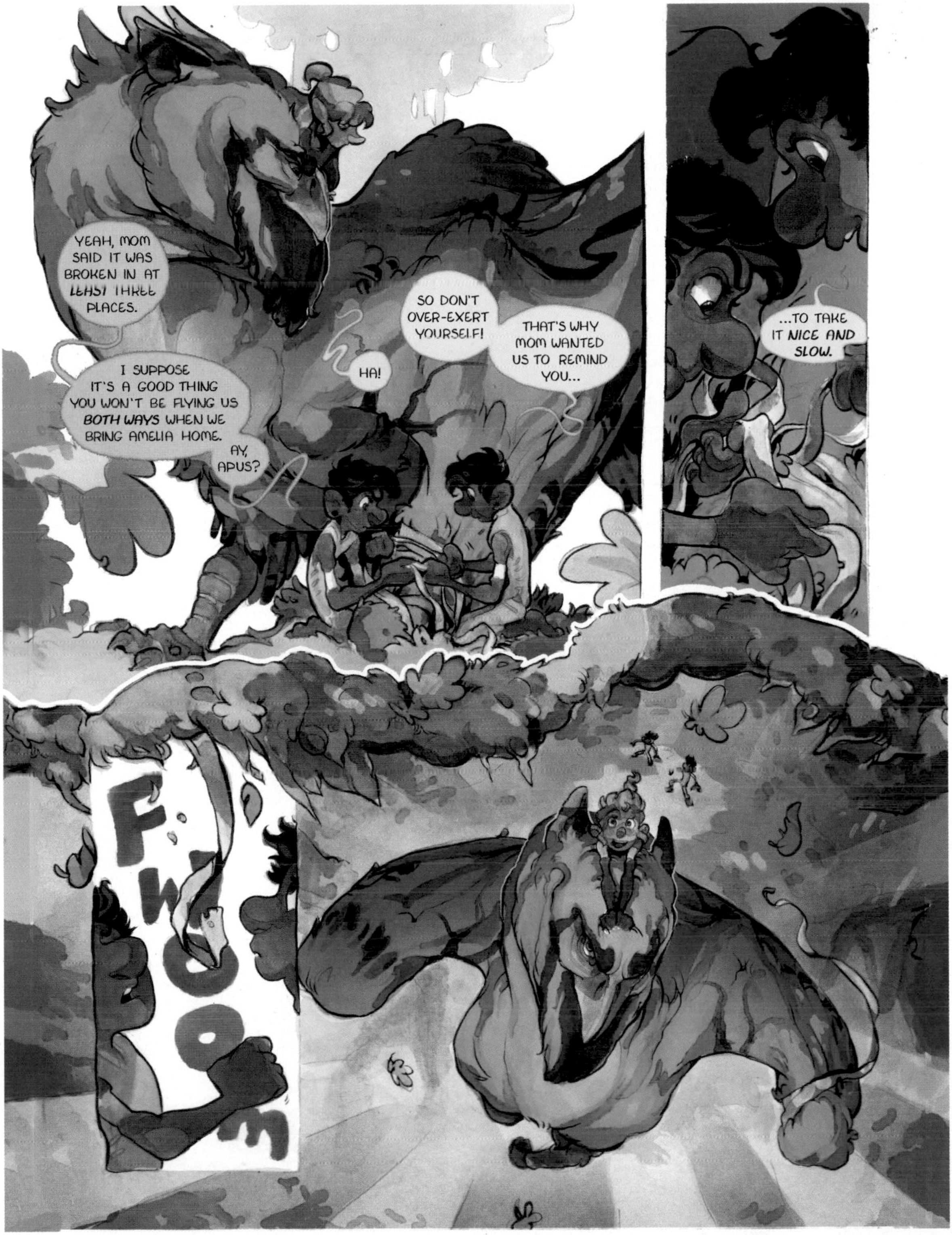
YEAH, MOM SAID IT WAS BROKEN IN AT LEAST THREE PLACES.
SO DON'T OVER-EXERT YOURSELF!
THAT'S WHY MOM WANTED US TO REMIND YOU...
HA!
I SUPPOSE IT'S A GOOD THING YOU WON'T BE FLYING US BOTH WAYS WHEN WE BRING AMELIA HOME.
AY, APUS?
...TO TAKE IT NICE AND SLOW.
FWOOM

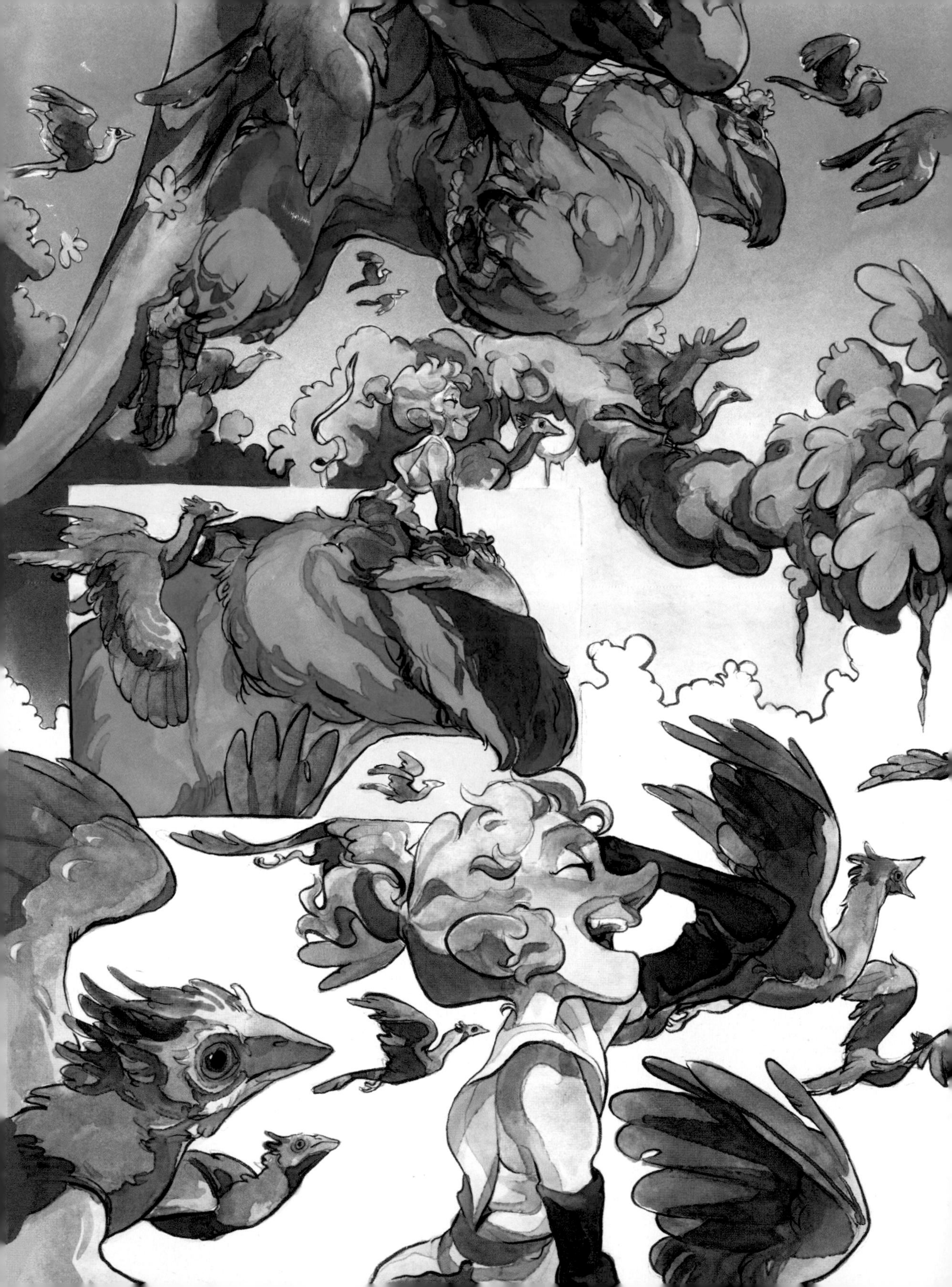

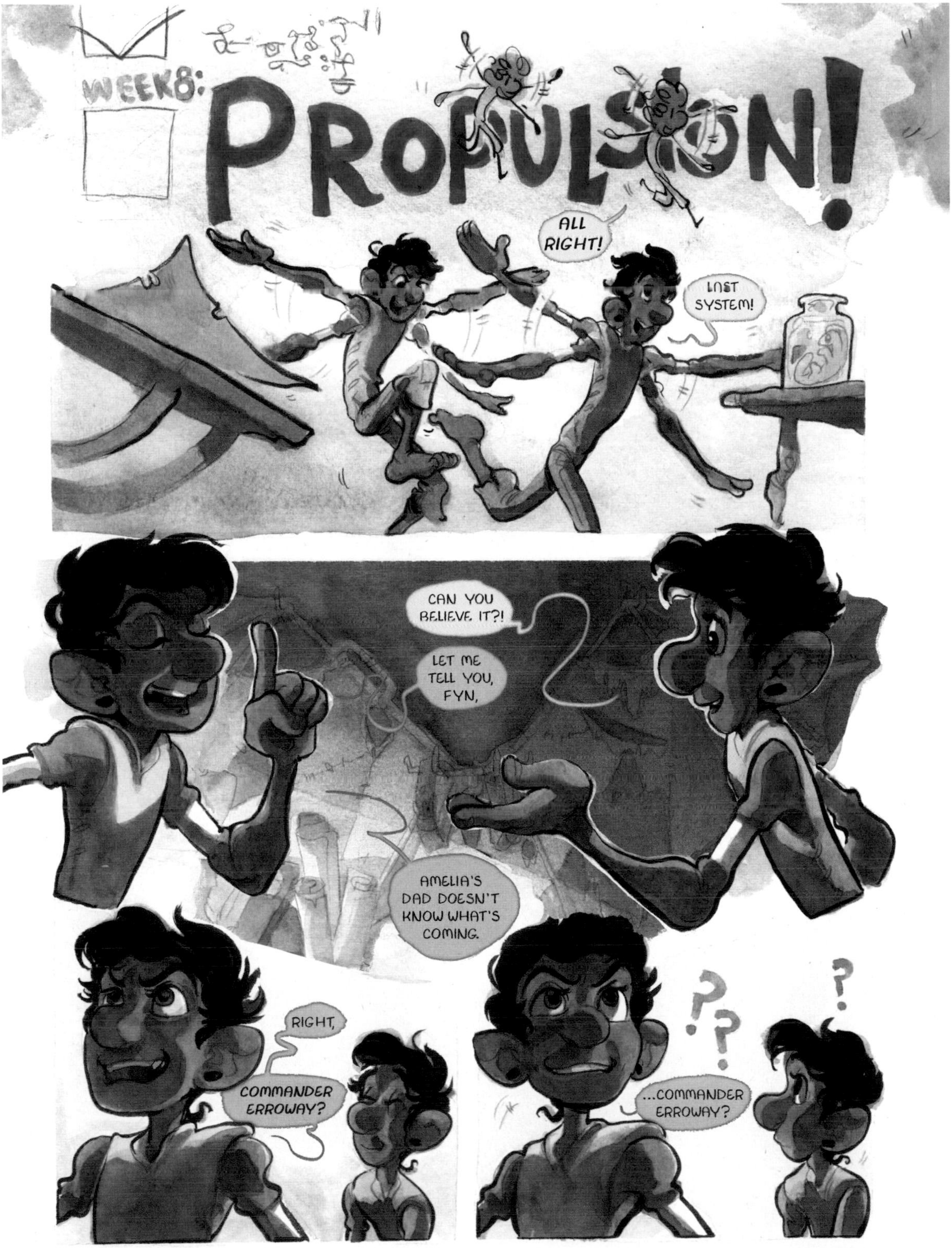
WEEK8:
PROPULSION!
ALL RIGHT!
LAST SYSTEM!
CAN YOU BELIEVE IT?!
LET ME TELL YOU, FYN,
AMELIA'S DAD DOESN'T KNOW WHAT'S COMING.
RIGHT,
COMMANDER ERROWAY?
...COMMANDER ERROWAY?

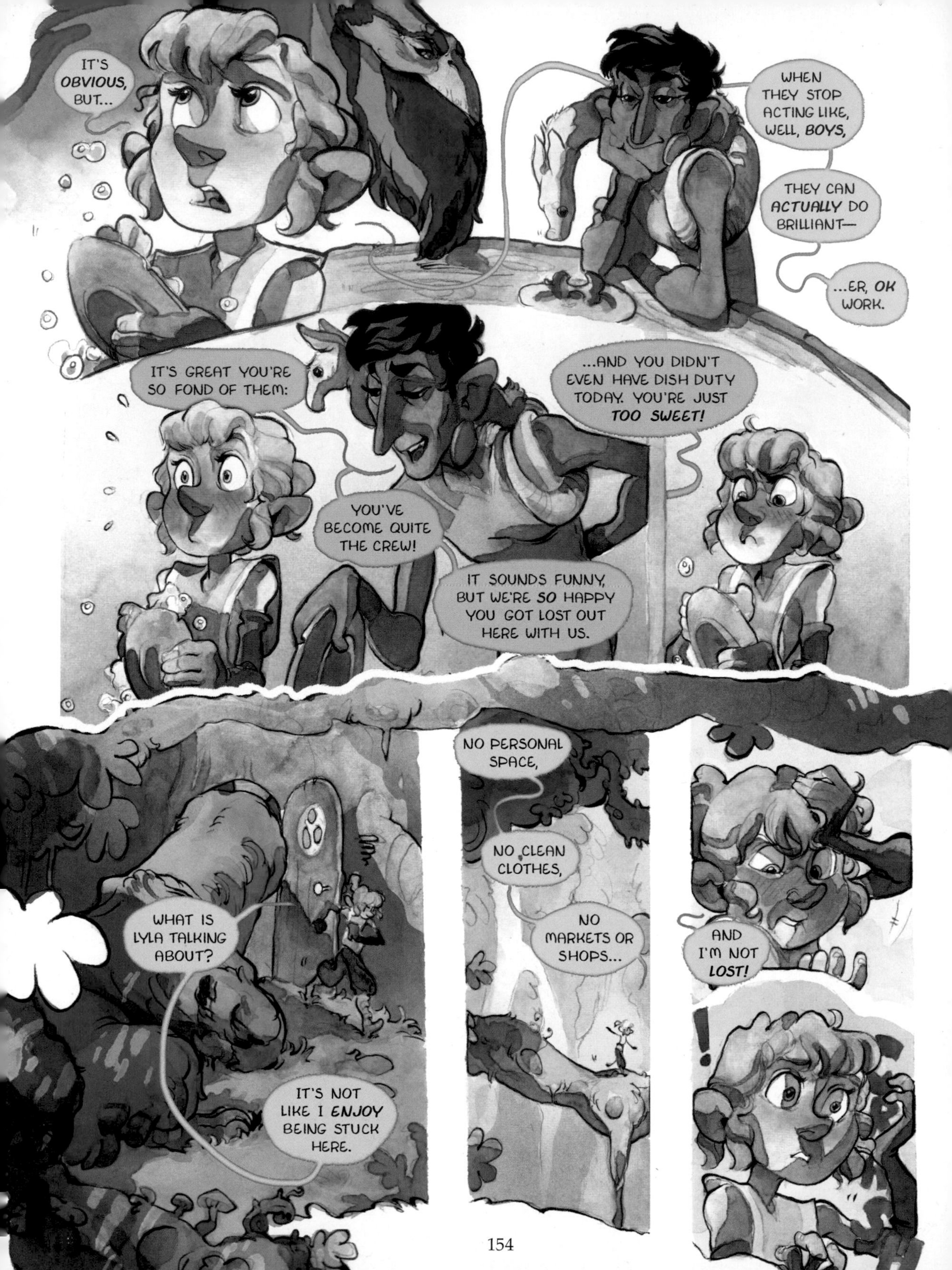
IT'S OBVIOUS, BUT...
WHEN THEY STOP ACTING LIKE, WELL, BOYS,
THEY CAN ACTUALLY DO BRILLIANT—
...ER, OK WORK.
IT'S GREAT YOU'RE SO FOND OF THEM:
YOU'VE BECOME QUITE THE CREW!
...AND YOU DIDN'T EVEN HAVE DISH DUTY TODAY. YOU'RE JUST TOO SWEET!
IT SOUNDS FUNNY, BUT WE'RE SO HAPPY YOU GOT LOST OUT HERE WITH US.
WHAT IS LYLA TALKING ABOUT?
IT'S NOT LIKE I ENJOY BEING STUCK HERE.
NO PERSONAL SPACE,
NO CLEAN CLOTHES,
NO MARKETS OR SHOPS...
AND I'M NOT LOST!
!

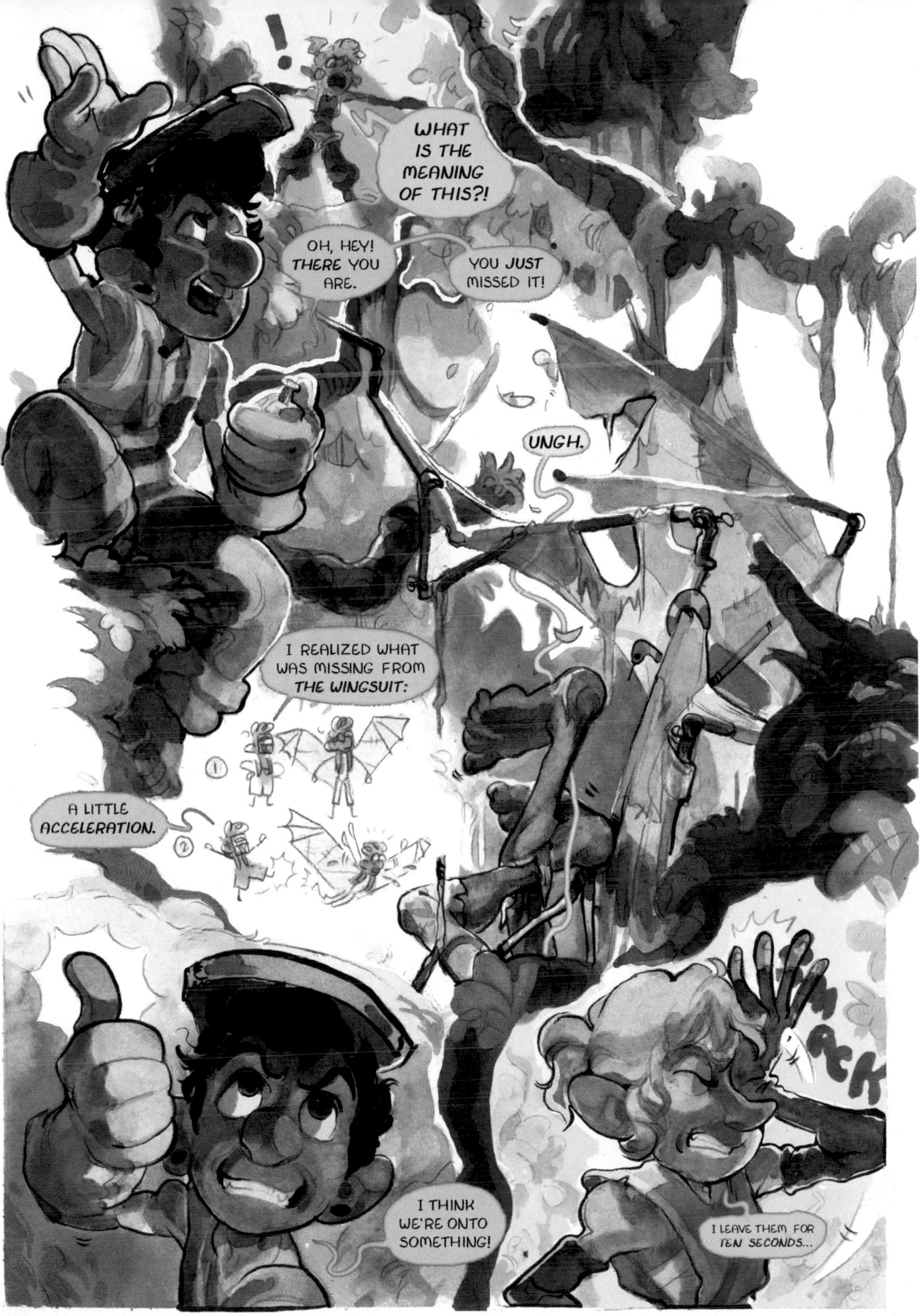
!
WHAT IS THE MEANING OF THIS?!
OH, HEY! THERE YOU ARE.
YOU JUST MISSED IT!
UNGH.
I REALIZED WHAT WAS MISSING FROM THE WINGSUIT:
A LITTLE ACCELERATION.
I THINK WE'RE ONTO SOMETHING!
I LEAVE THEM FOR TEN SECONDS...

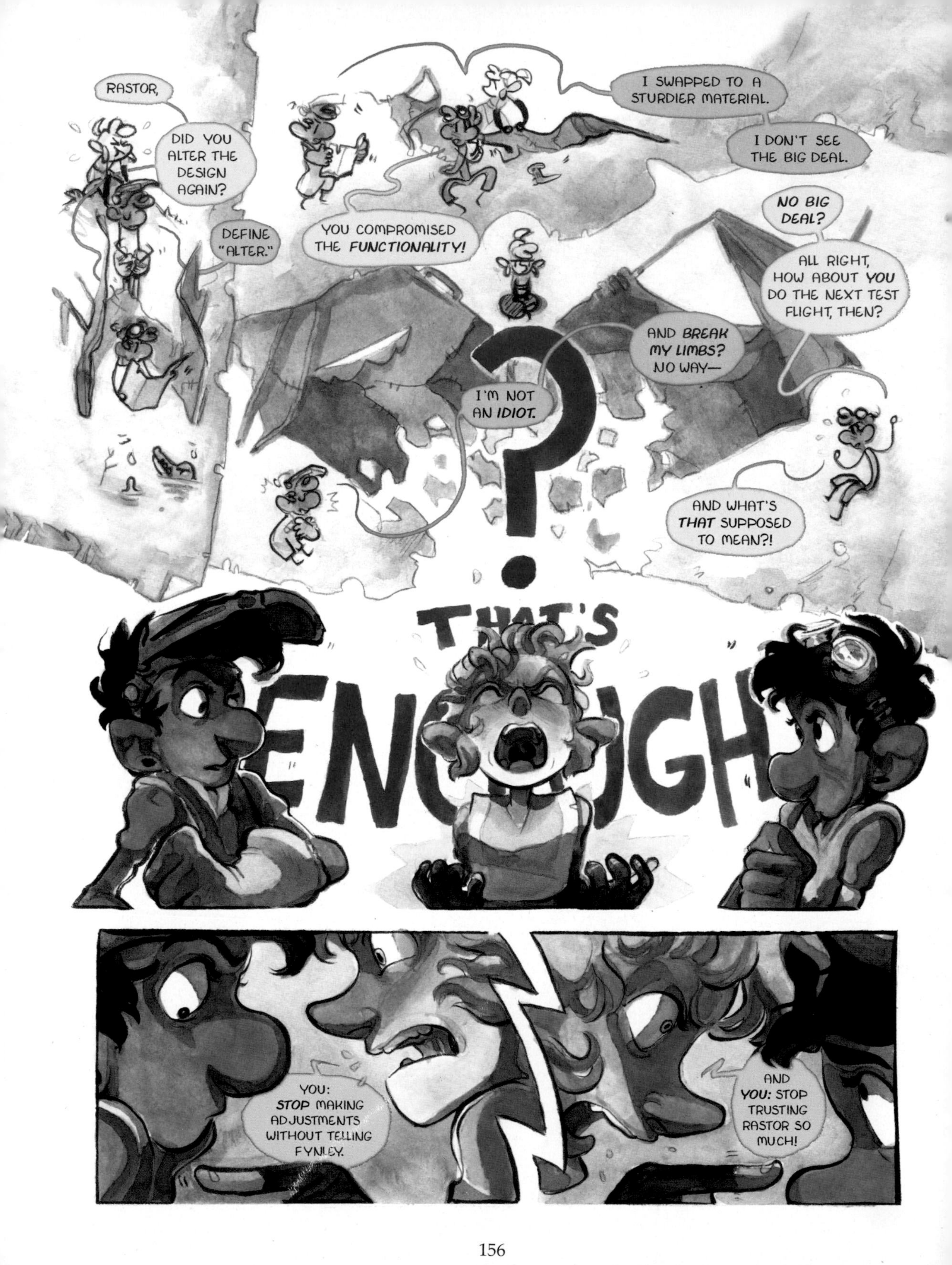
RASTOR,
DID YOU ALTER THE DESIGN AGAIN?
DEFINE "ALTER."
YOU COMPROMISED THE *FUNCTIONALITY!*
I SWAPPED TO A STURDIER MATERIAL.
I DON'T SEE THE BIG DEAL.
NO BIG DEAL?
ALL RIGHT, HOW ABOUT *YOU* DO THE NEXT TEST FLIGHT, THEN?
AND *BREAK MY LIMBS?* NO WAY—
I'M NOT AN *IDIOT.*
AND WHAT'S *THAT* SUPPOSED TO MEAN?!
?
THAT'S ENOUGH
YOU: *STOP* MAKING ADJUSTMENTS WITHOUT TELLING FYNLEY.
AND *YOU:* STOP TRUSTING RASTOR SO MUCH!

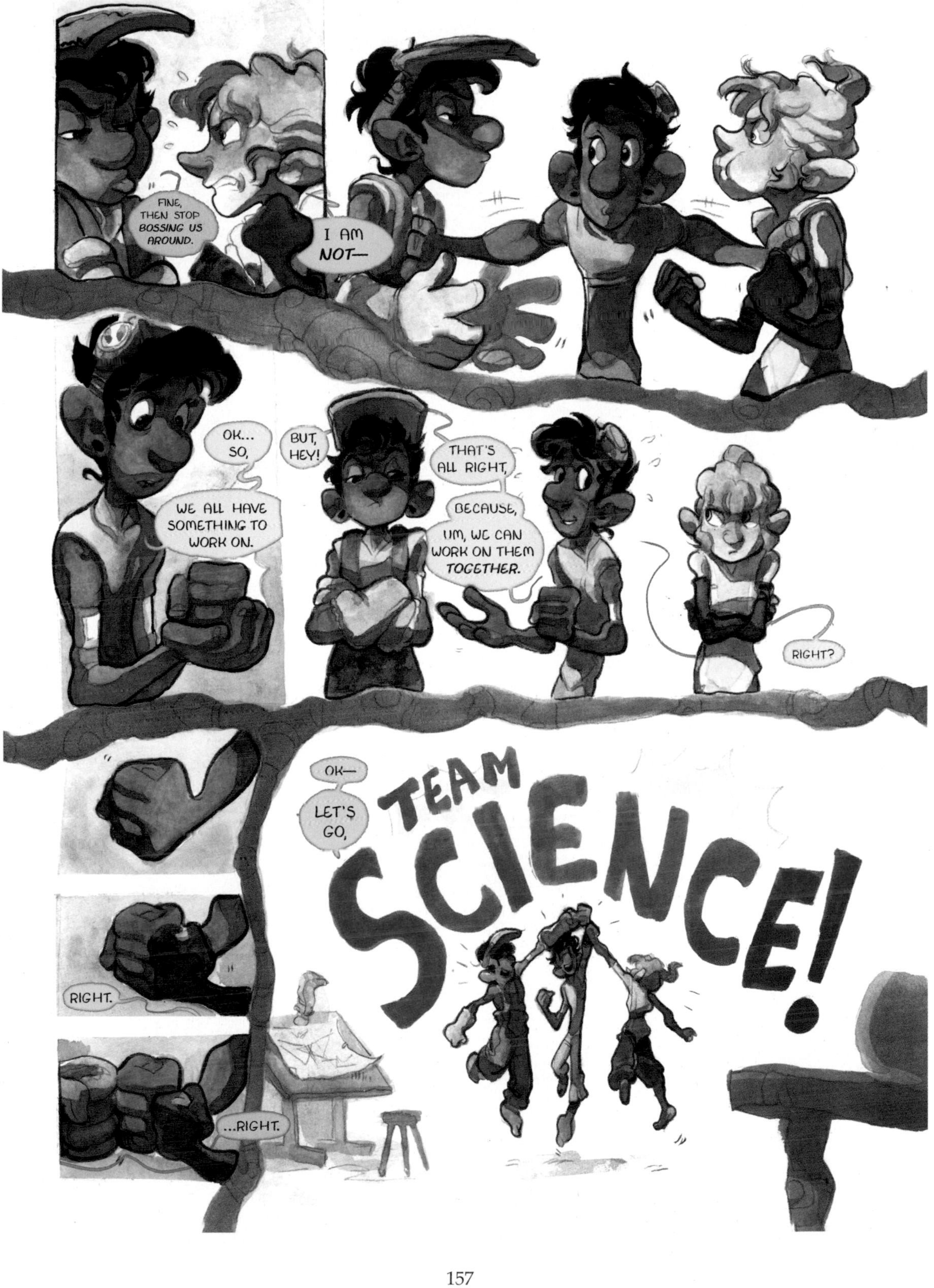
FINE, THEN STOP *BOSSING* US AROUND.
I AM ***NOT***—
OK... SO,
WE ALL HAVE SOMETHING TO WORK ON.
BUT, HEY!
THAT'S ALL RIGHT,
BECAUSE, UM, WE CAN WORK ON THEM *TOGETHER*.
RIGHT?
RIGHT.
...RIGHT.
OK—
LET'S GO,
TEAM SCIENCE!

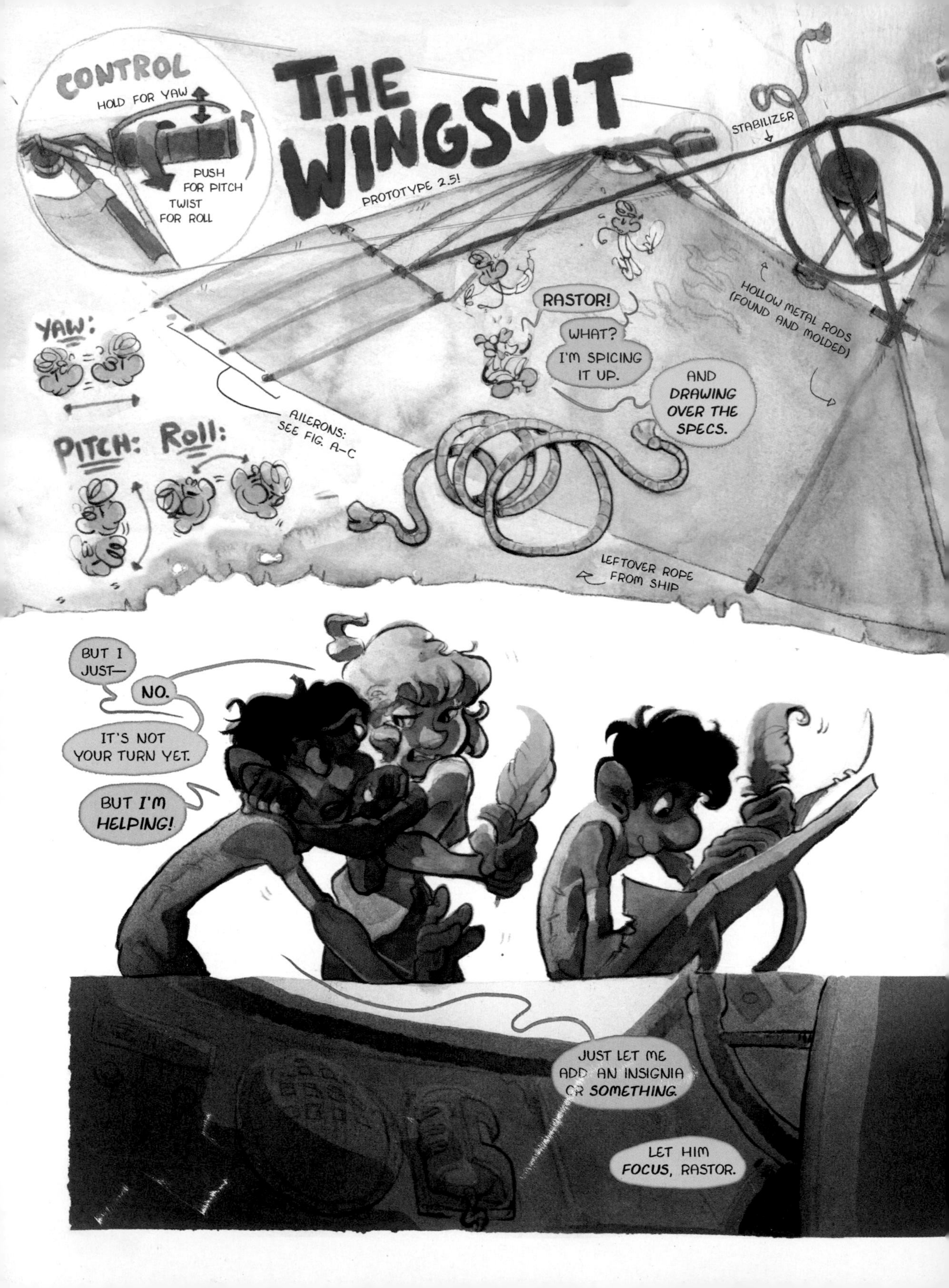
CONTROL
HOLD FOR YAW
PUSH FOR PITCH
TWIST FOR ROLL
THE WINGSUIT
PROTOTYPE 2.5!
STABILIZER
YAW:
PITCH: ROLL:
AILERONS: SEE FIG. A-C
RASTOR!
WHAT?
I'M SPICING IT UP.
AND DRAWING OVER THE SPECS.
HOLLOW METAL RODS (FOUND AND MOLDED)
LEFTOVER ROPE FROM SHIP
BUT I JUST—
NO.
IT'S NOT YOUR TURN YET.
BUT I'M HELPING!
JUST LET ME ADD AN INSIGNIA OR SOMETHING.
LET HIM FOCUS, RASTOR.

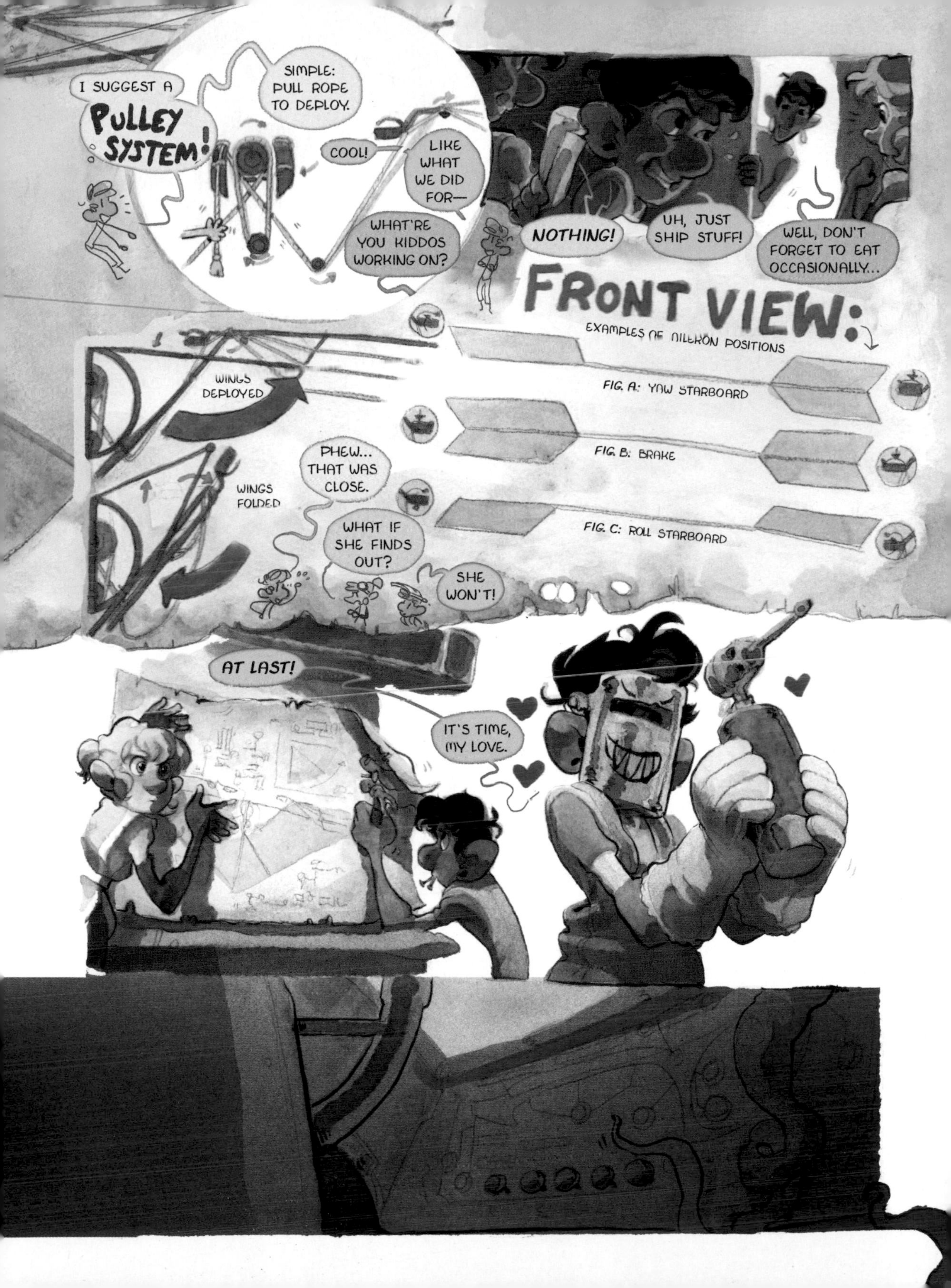
I SUGGEST A
PULLEY SYSTEM!
SIMPLE: PULL ROPE TO DEPLOY.
COOL!
LIKE WHAT WE DID FOR—
WHAT'RE YOU KIDDOS WORKING ON?
NOTHING!
UH, JUST SHIP STUFF!
WELL, DON'T FORGET TO EAT OCCASIONALLY...
FRONT VIEW:
EXAMPLES OF AILERON POSITIONS
WINGS DEPLOYED
FIG. A: YAW STARBOARD
FIG. B: BRAKE
WINGS FOLDED
FIG. C: ROLL STARBOARD
PHEW... THAT WAS CLOSE.
WHAT IF SHE FINDS OUT?
SHE WON'T!
AT LAST!
IT'S TIME, MY LOVE.

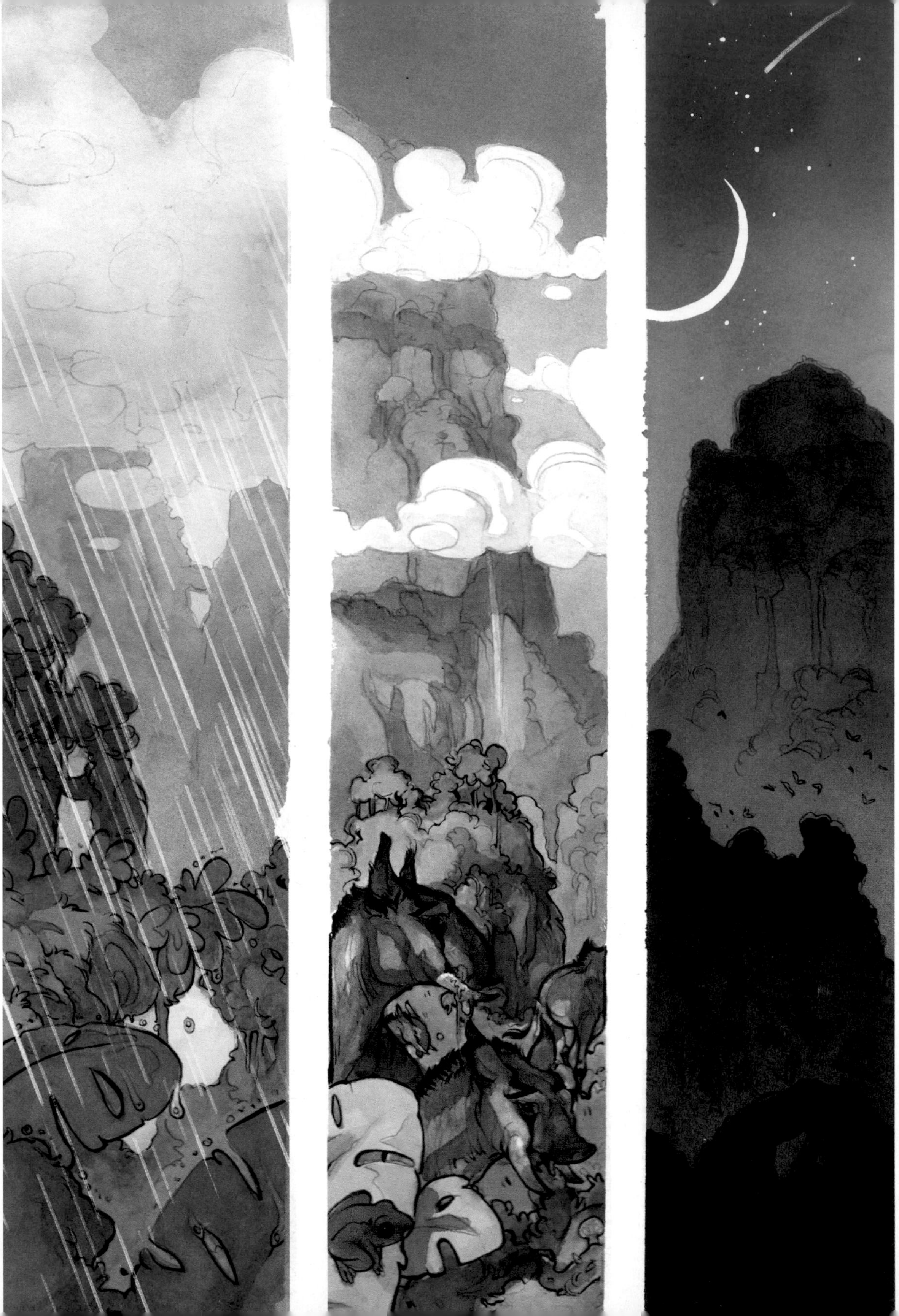

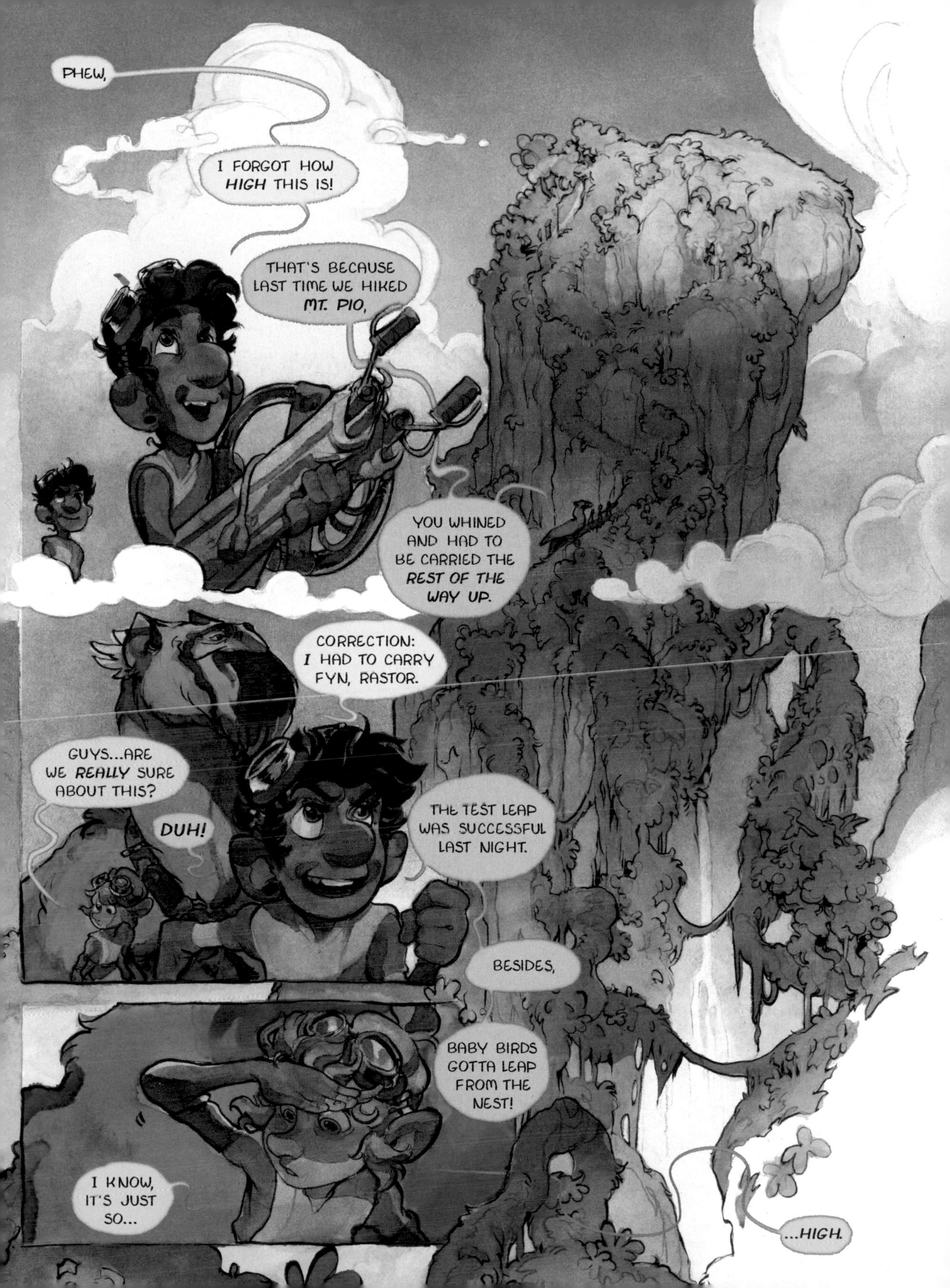

PHEW,
I FORGOT HOW *HIGH* THIS IS!
THAT'S BECAUSE LAST TIME WE HIKED *MT. PIO,*
YOU WHINED AND HAD TO BE CARRIED THE *REST OF THE WAY UP.*
CORRECTION: *I* HAD TO CARRY FYN, RASTOR.
GUYS...ARE WE *REALLY* SURE ABOUT THIS?
DUH!
THE TEST LEAP WAS SUCCESSFUL LAST NIGHT.
BESIDES,
BABY BIRDS GOTTA LEAP FROM THE NEST!
I KNOW, IT'S JUST SO...
...*HIGH.*

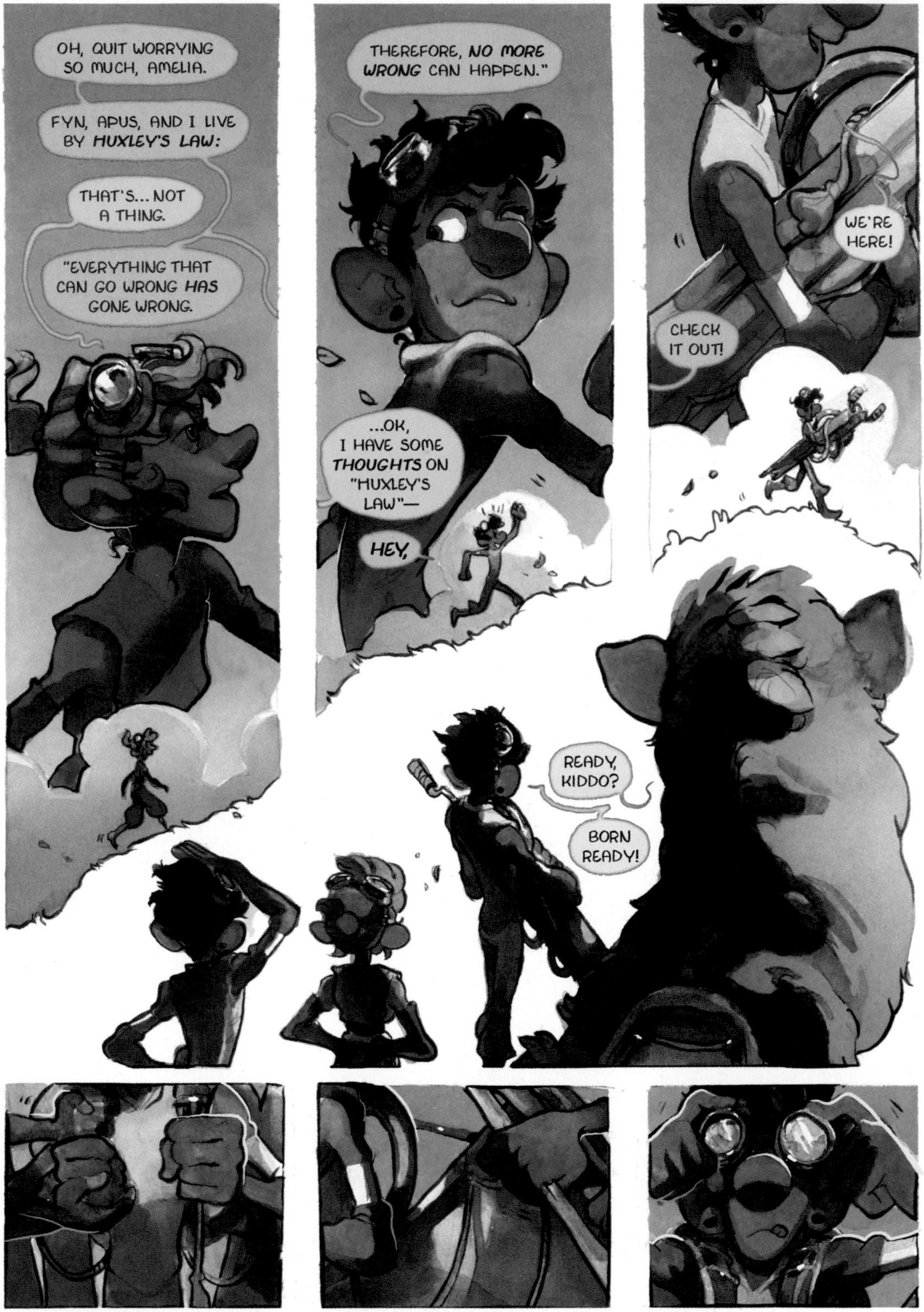
OH, QUIT WORRYING SO MUCH, AMELIA.
FYN, APUS, AND I LIVE BY HUXLEY'S LAW:
THAT'S... NOT A THING.
"EVERYTHING THAT CAN GO WRONG HAS GONE WRONG.
THEREFORE, NO MORE WRONG CAN HAPPEN."
...OK, I HAVE SOME THOUGHTS ON "HUXLEY'S LAW"—
HEY,
WE'RE HERE!
CHECK IT OUT!
READY, KIDDO?
BORN READY!

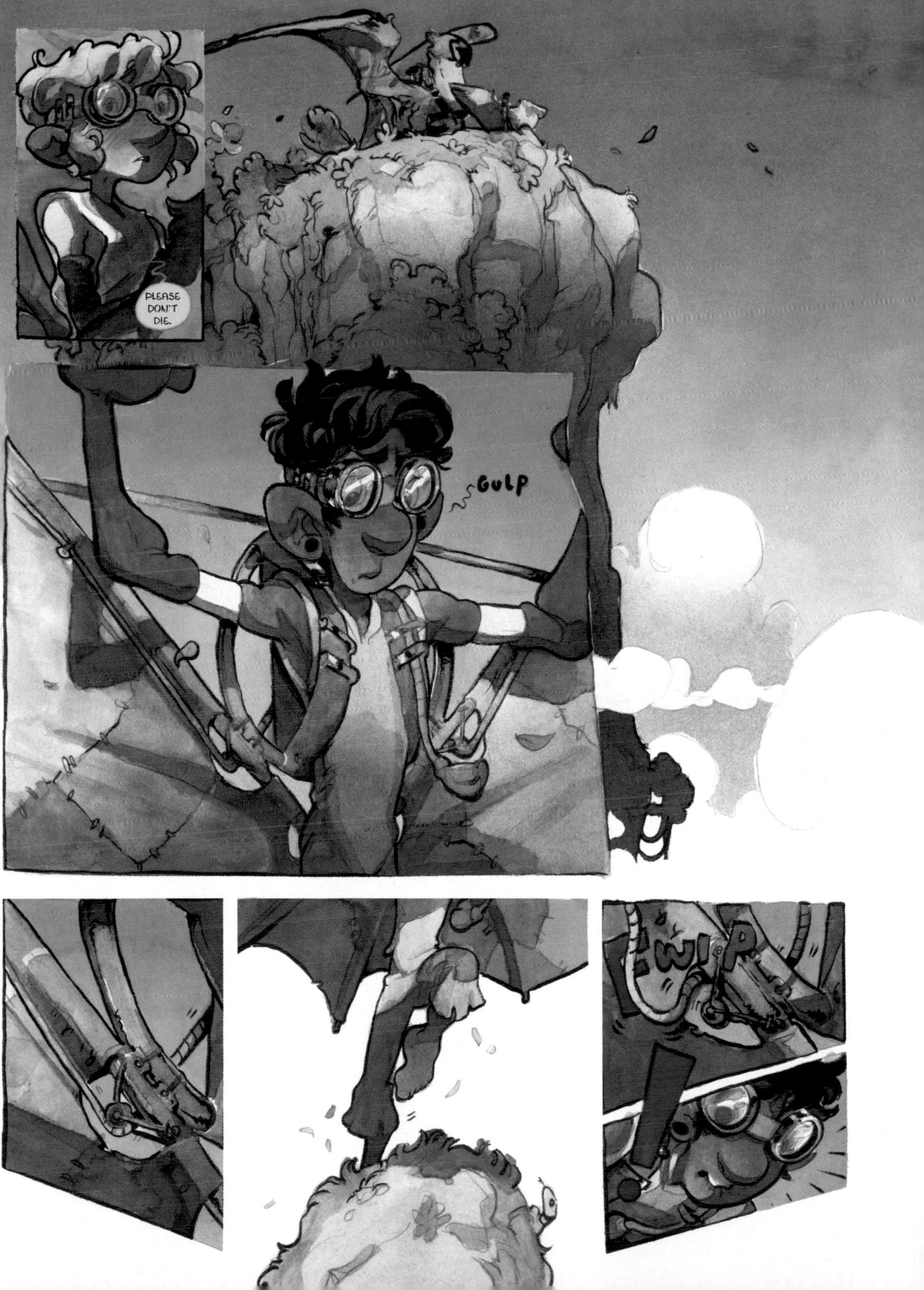
PLEASE DON'T DIE.
GULP
WIP

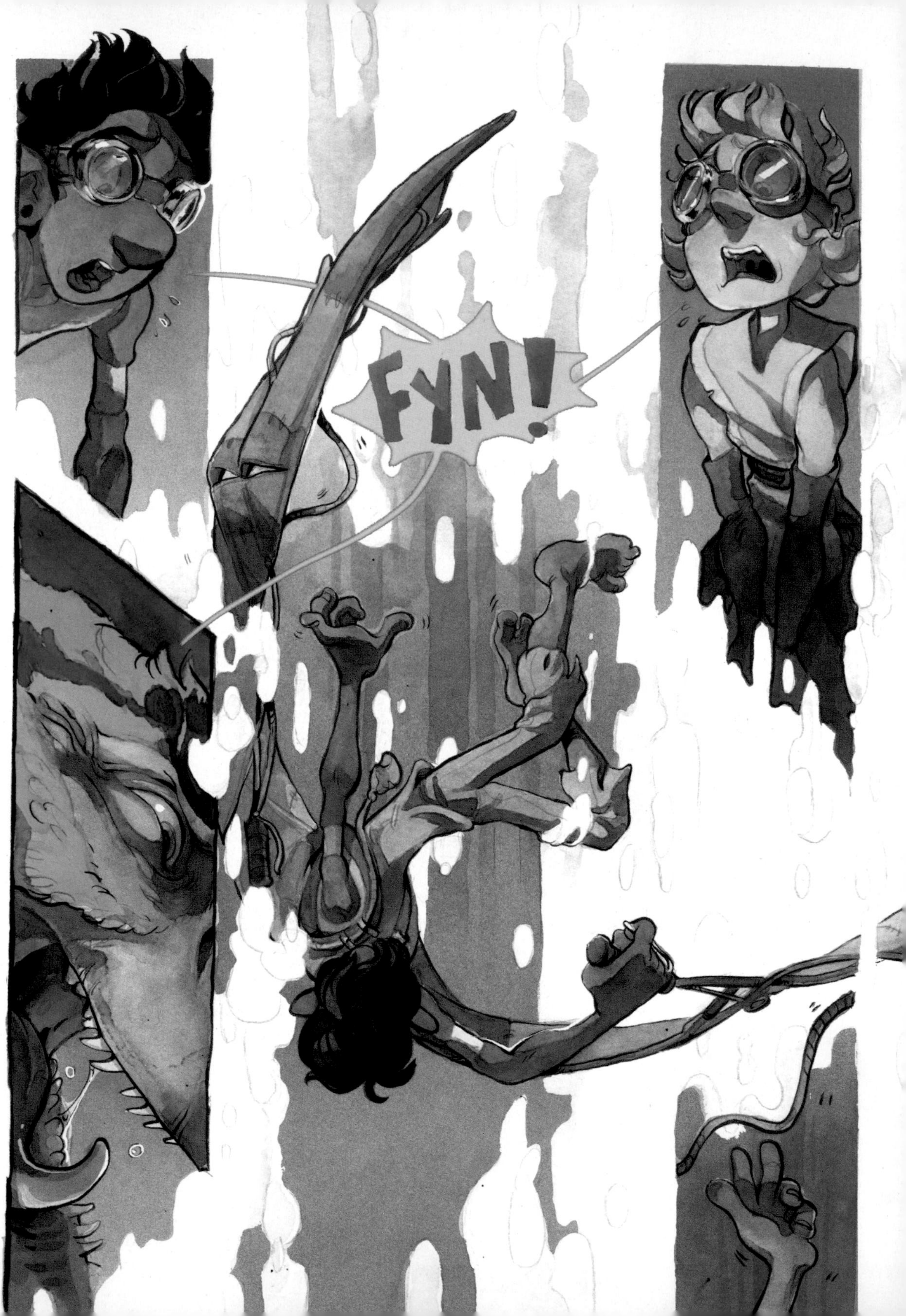
FYN!

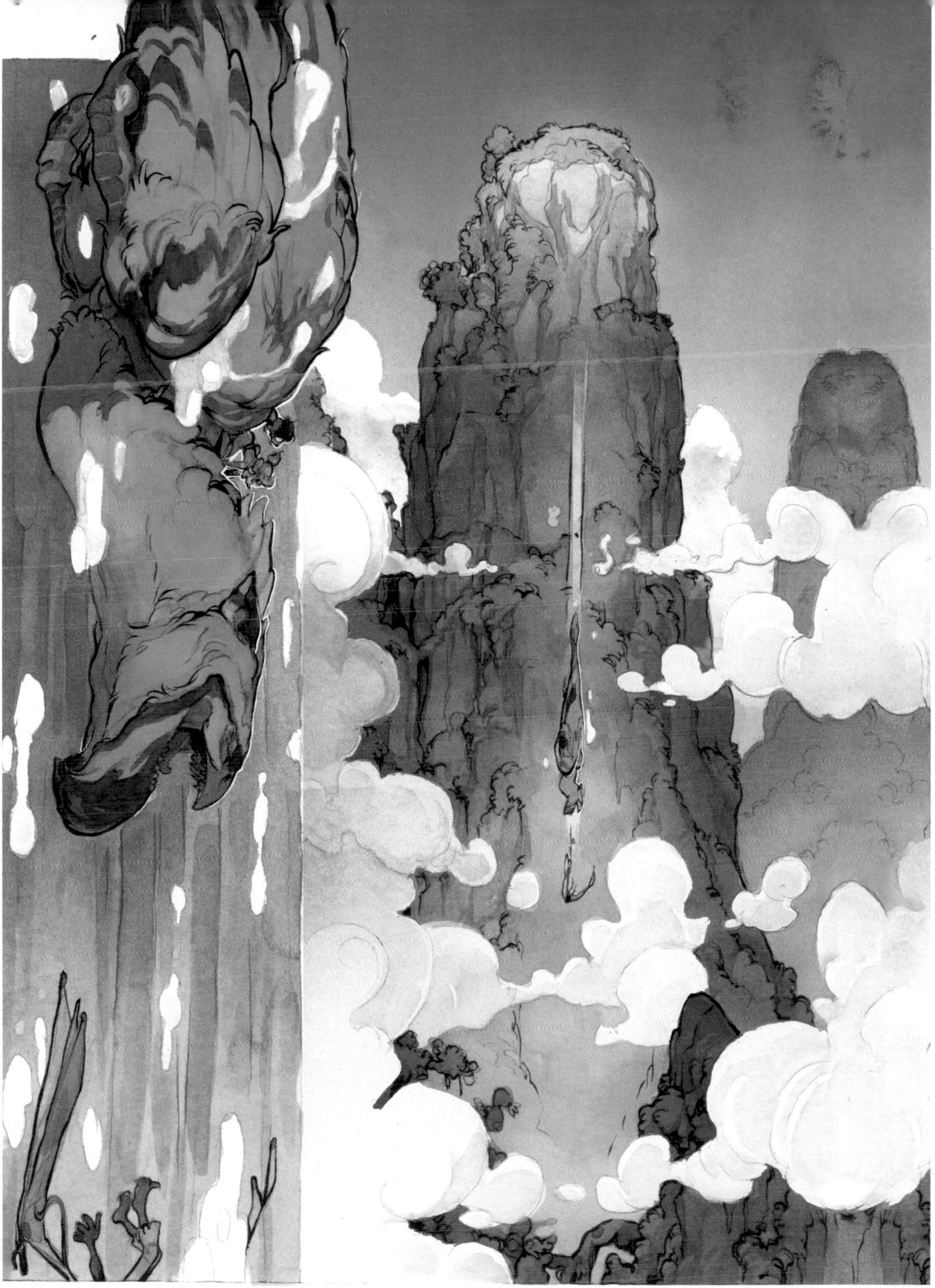

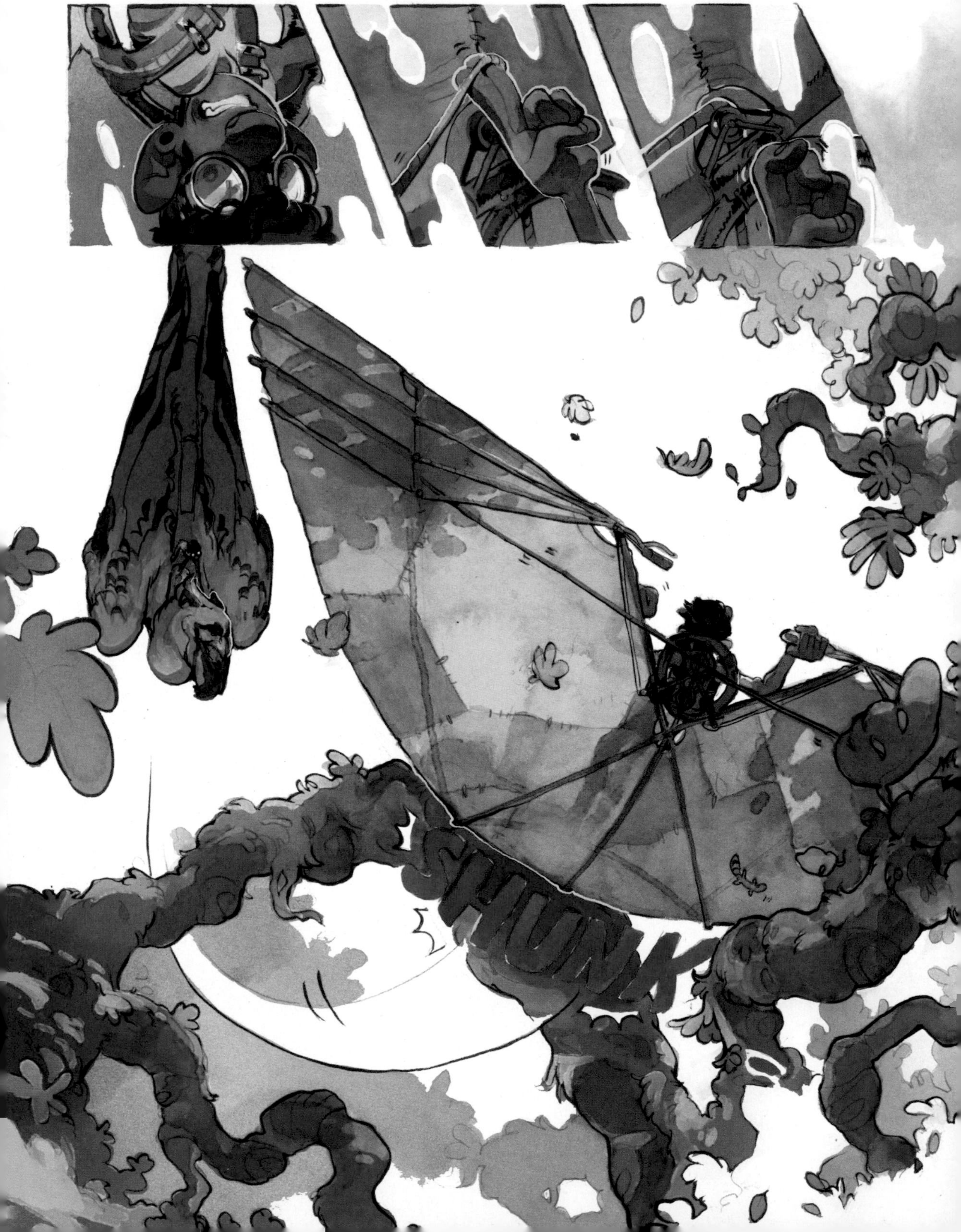
SHUNK

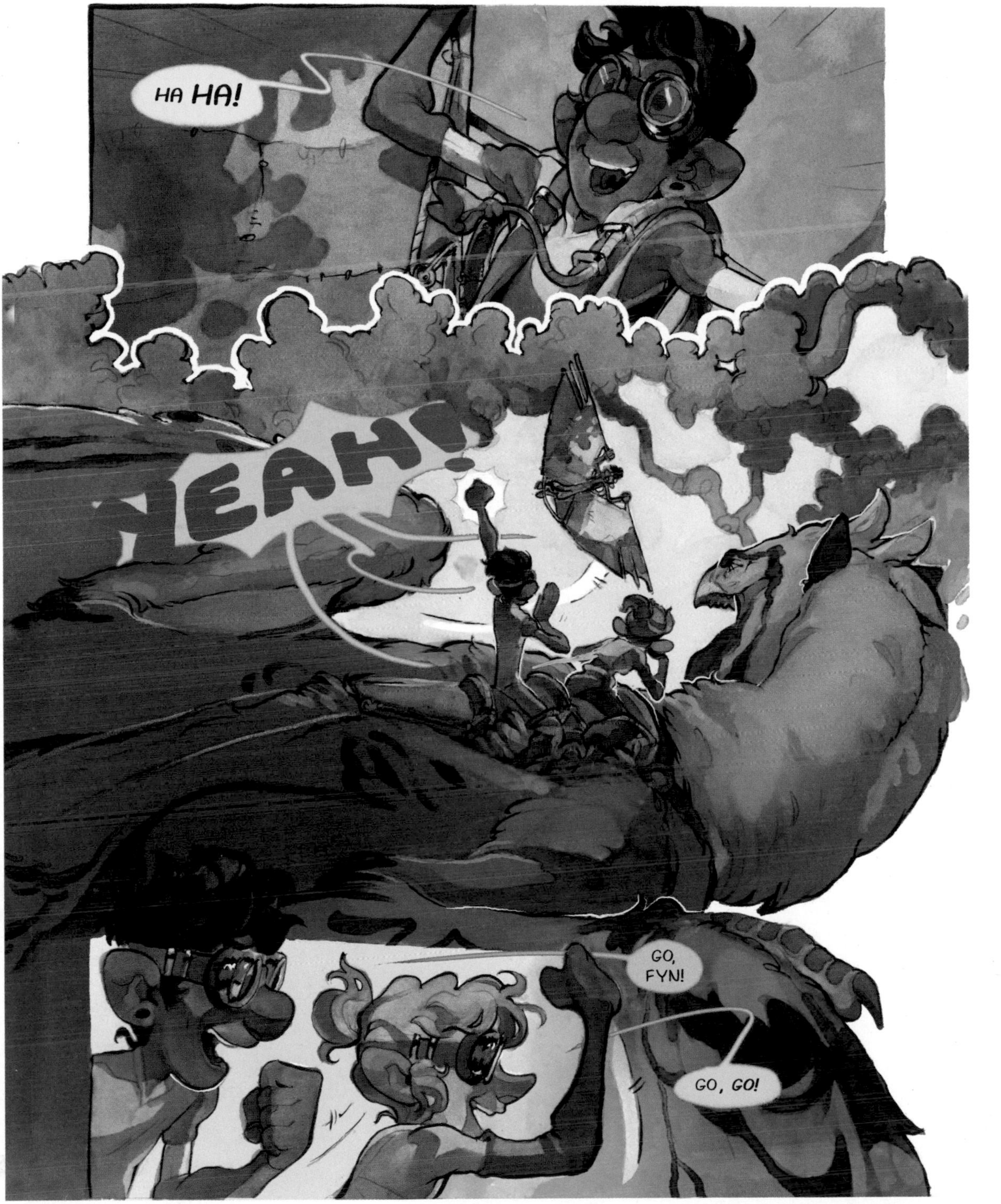
HA HA!
YEAH!
GO, FYN!
GO, GO!

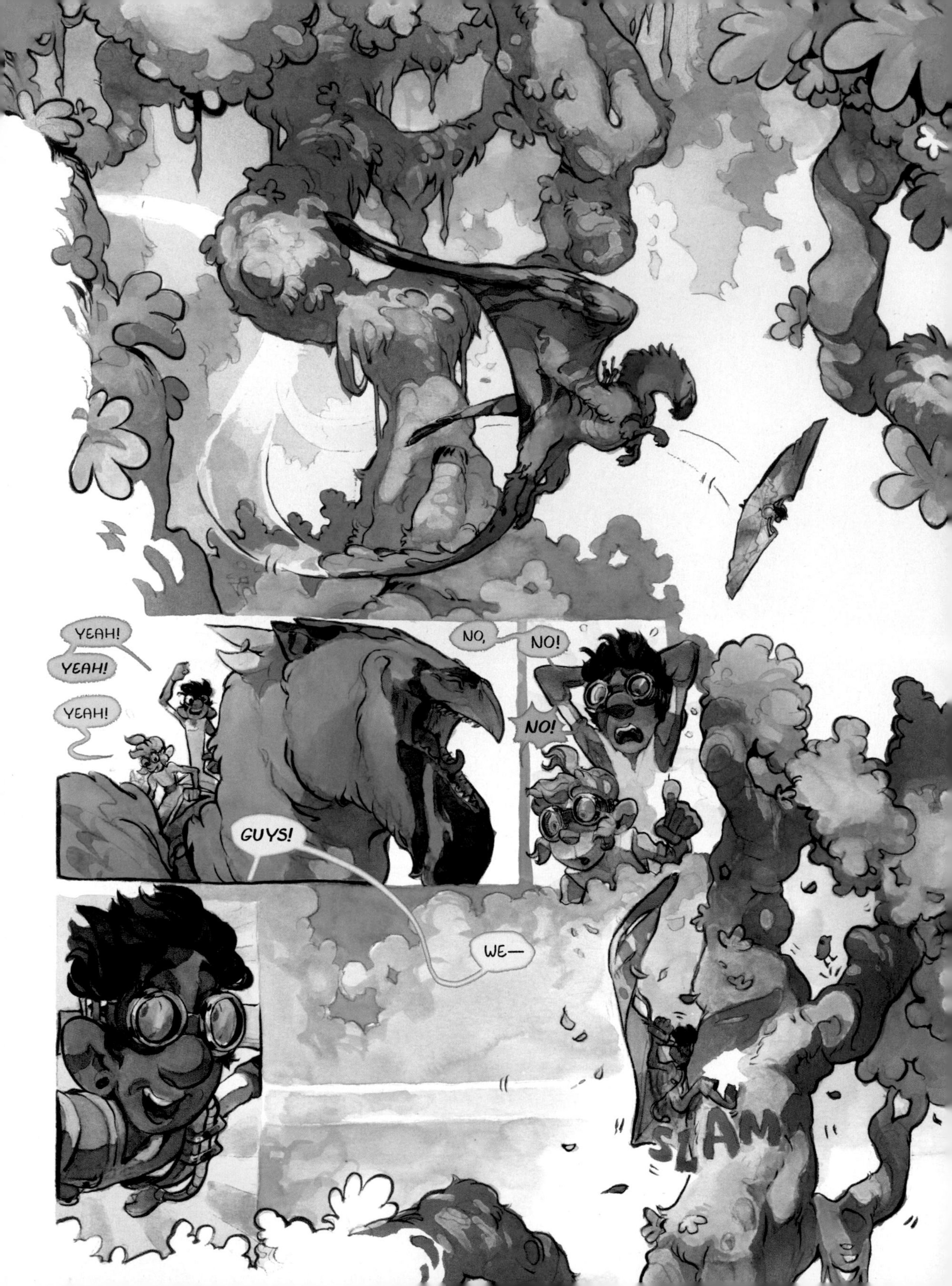
YEAH!
YEAH!
YEAH!
NO,
NO!
NO!
GUYS!
WE—
SLAM

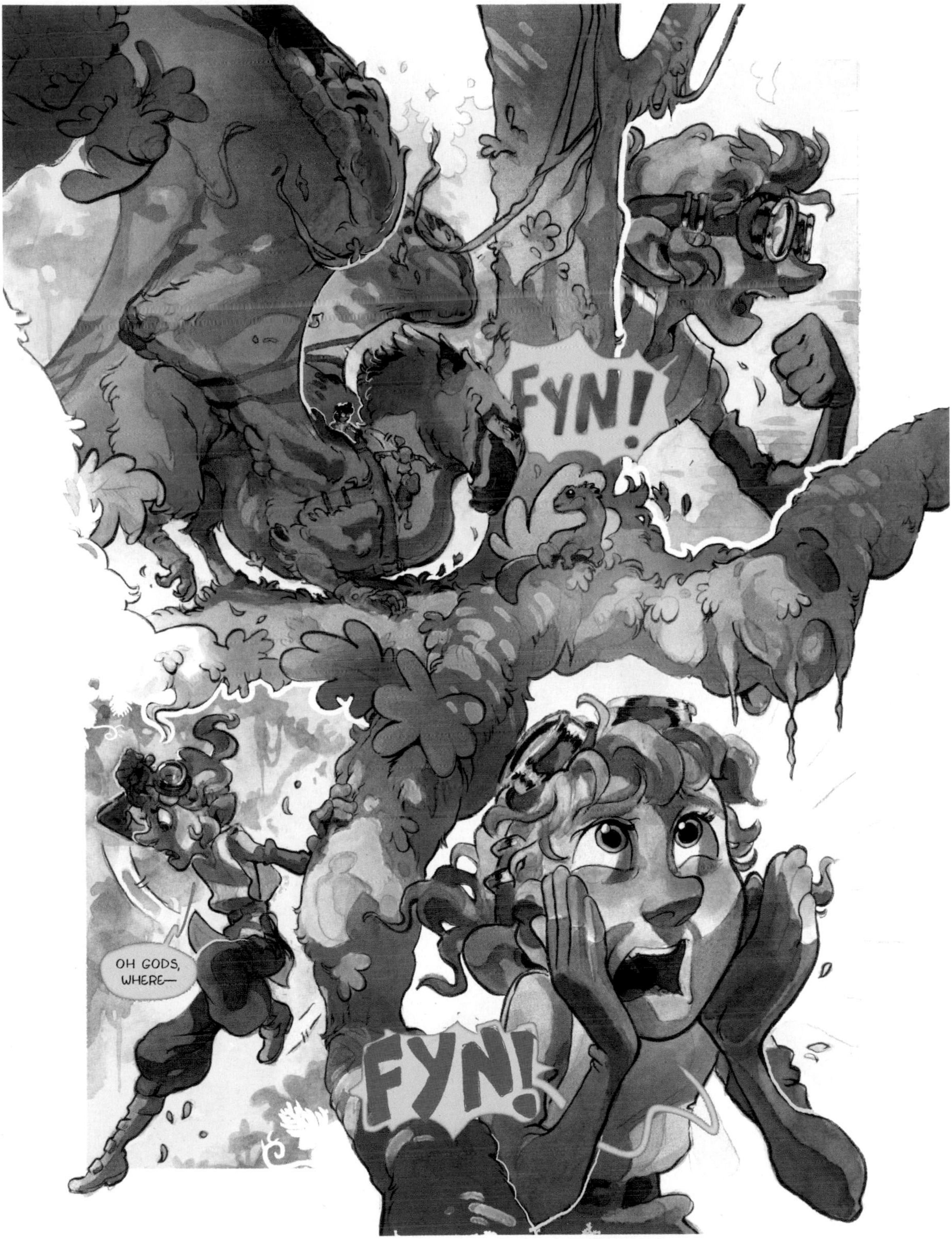
FYN!
OH GODS, WHERE—
FYN!

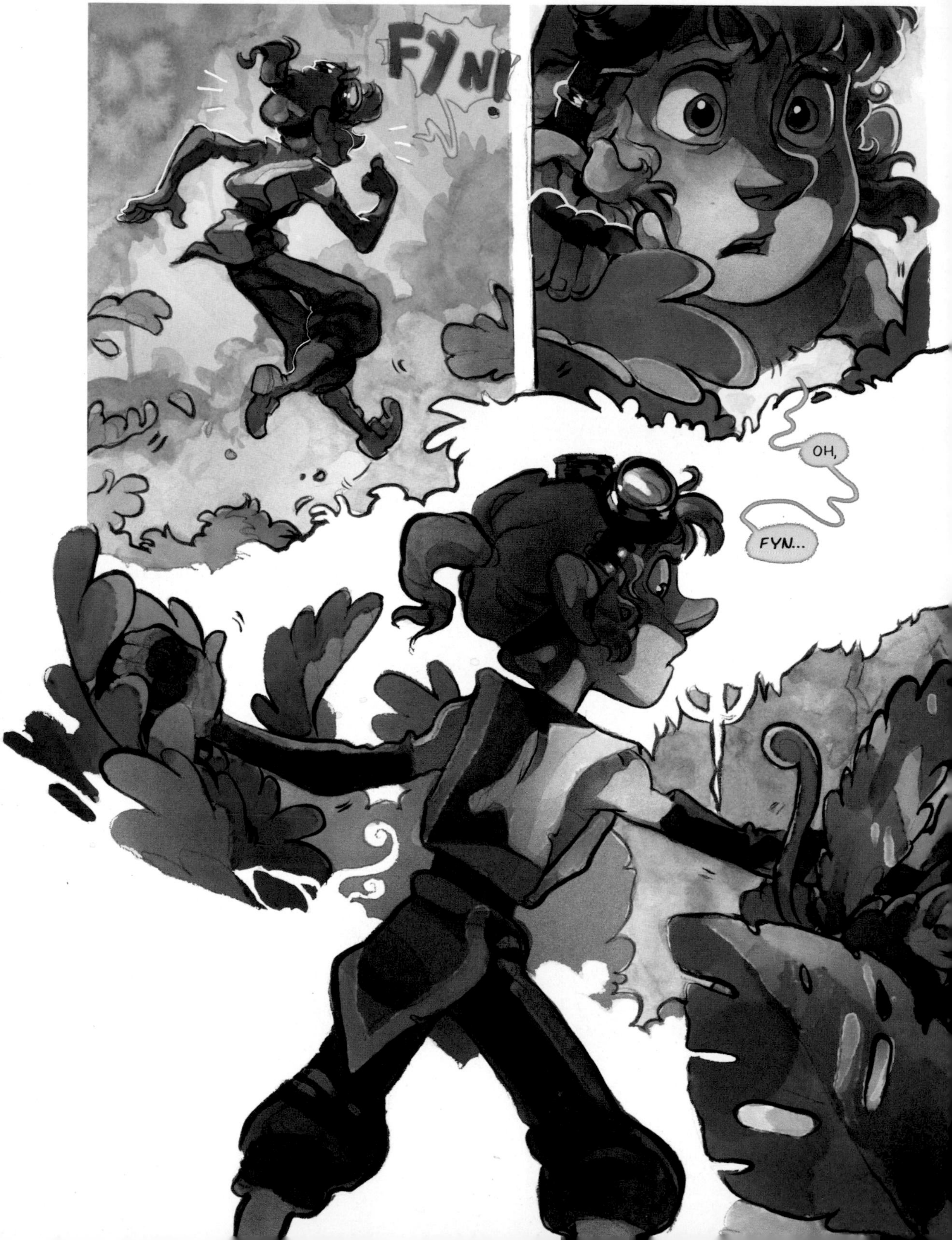
FYN!
OH,
FYN...

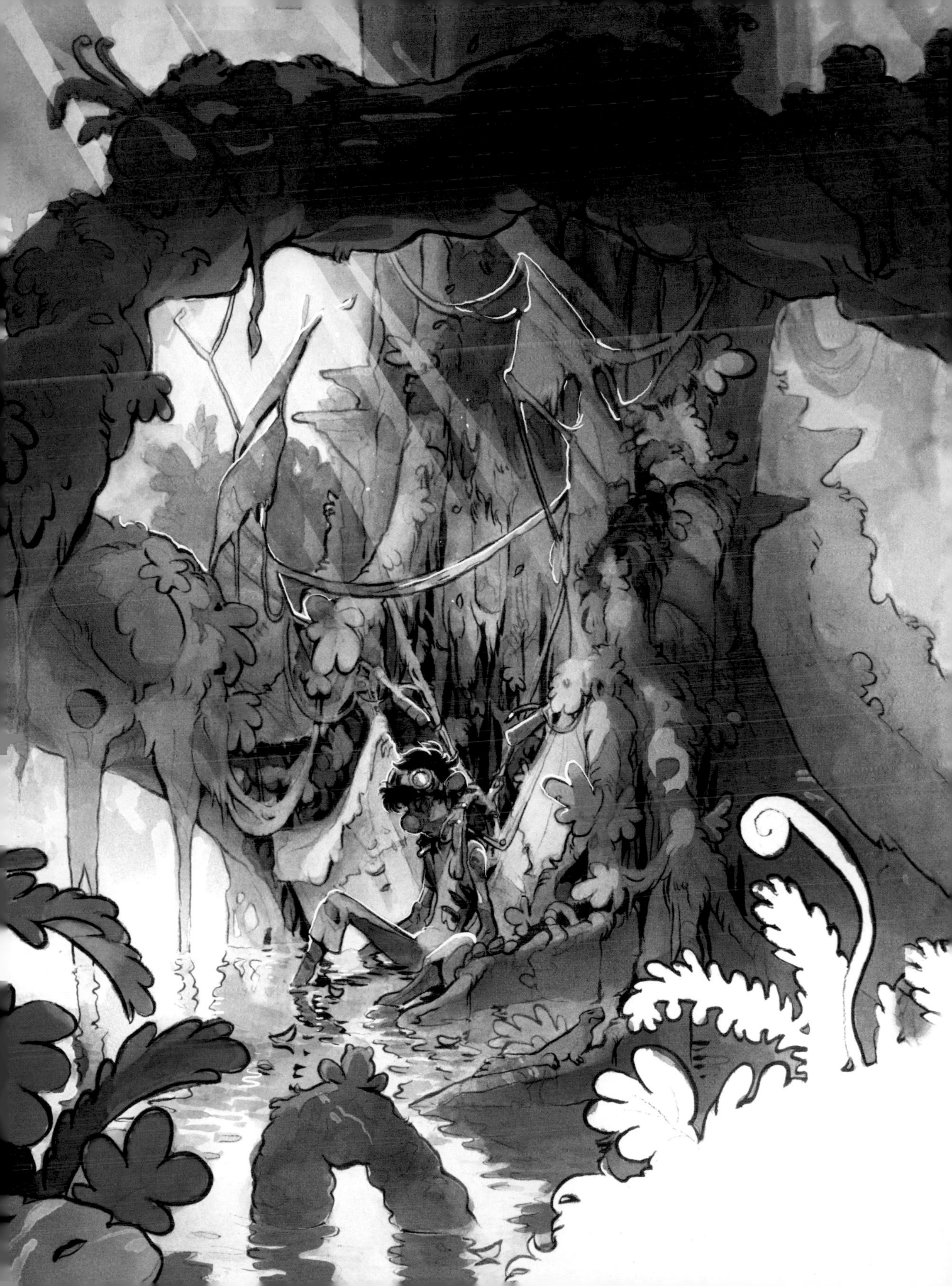

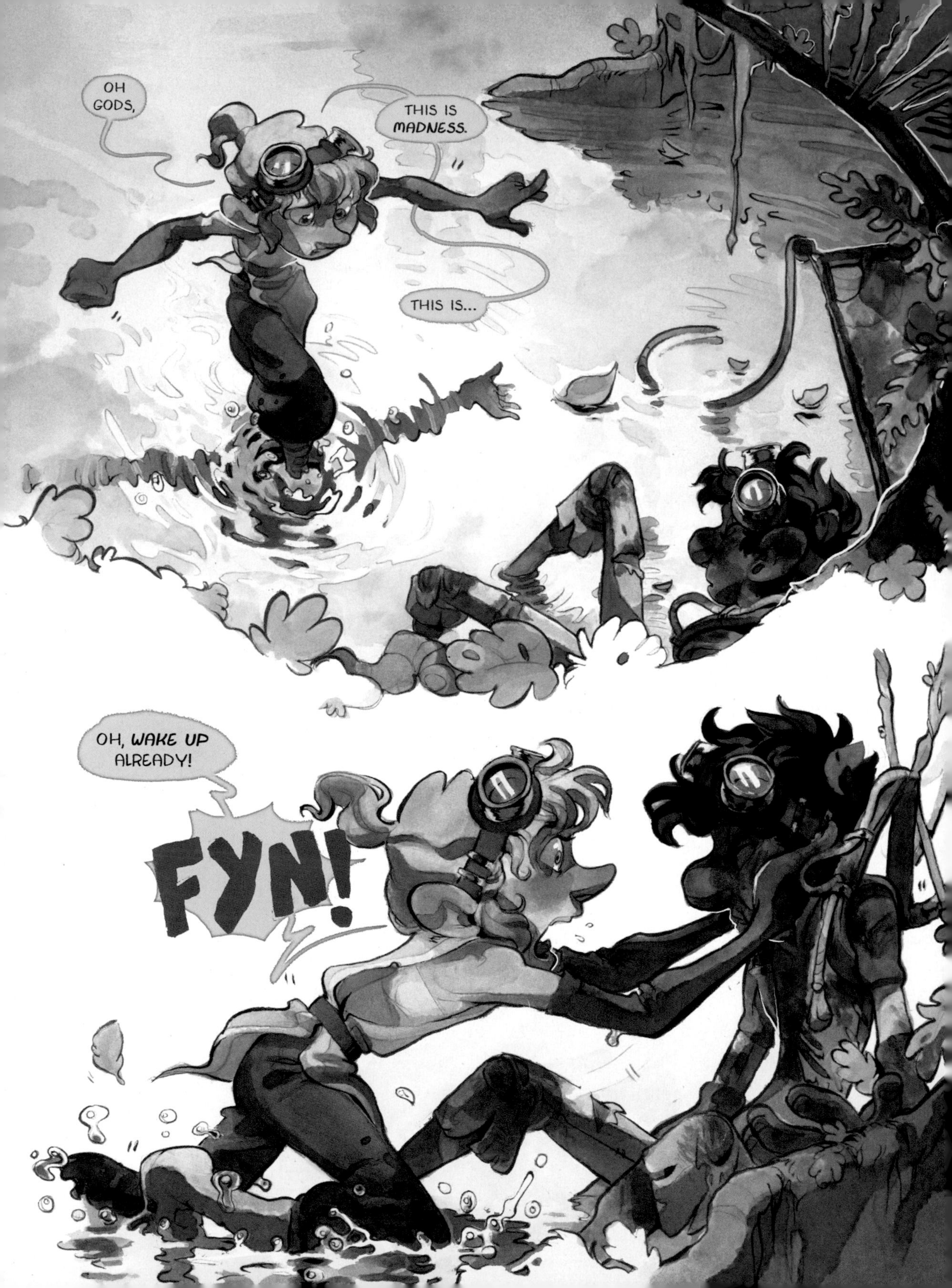
OH GODS,
THIS IS MADNESS.
THIS IS...
OH, WAKE UP ALREADY!
FYN!

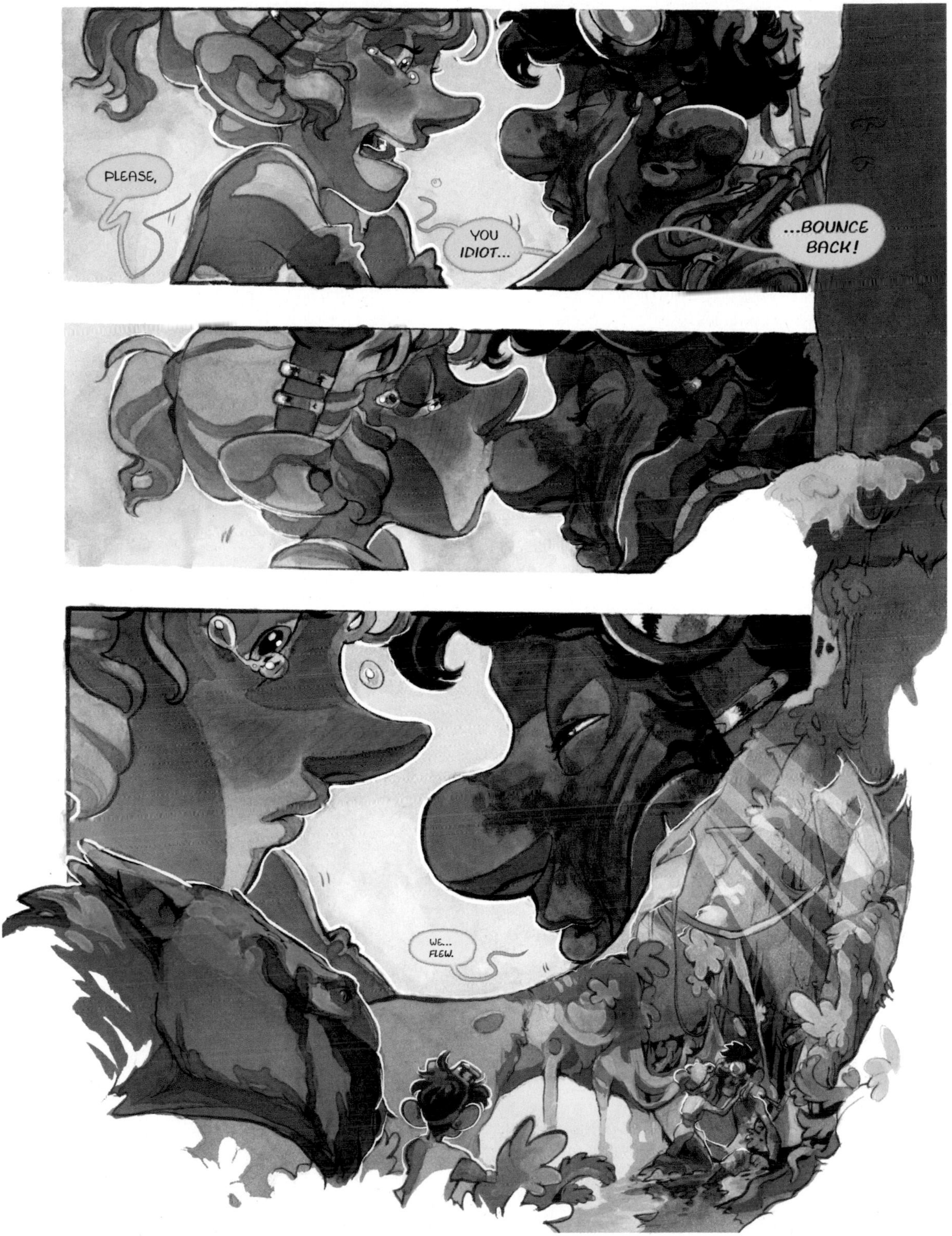
PLEASE,
YOU IDIOT...
...BOUNCE BACK!
WE... FLEW.

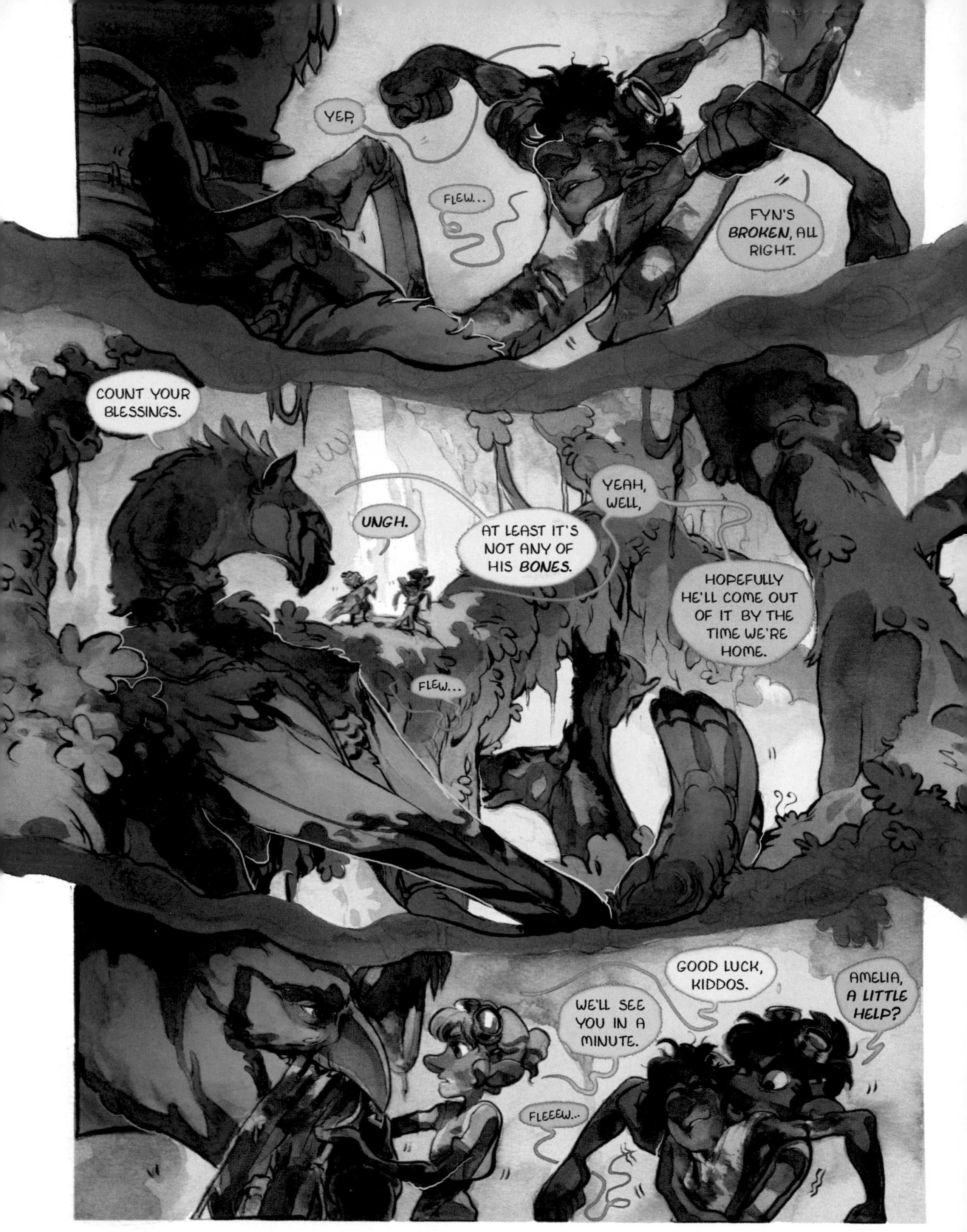
YEP,
FLEW...
FYN'S BROKEN, ALL RIGHT.
COUNT YOUR BLESSINGS.
UNGH.
AT LEAST IT'S NOT ANY OF HIS BONES.
YEAH, WELL,
HOPEFULLY HE'LL COME OUT OF IT BY THE TIME WE'RE HOME.
FLEW...
GOOD LUCK, KIDDOS.
WE'LL SEE YOU IN A MINUTE.
AMELIA, A LITTLE HELP?
FLEEEW...

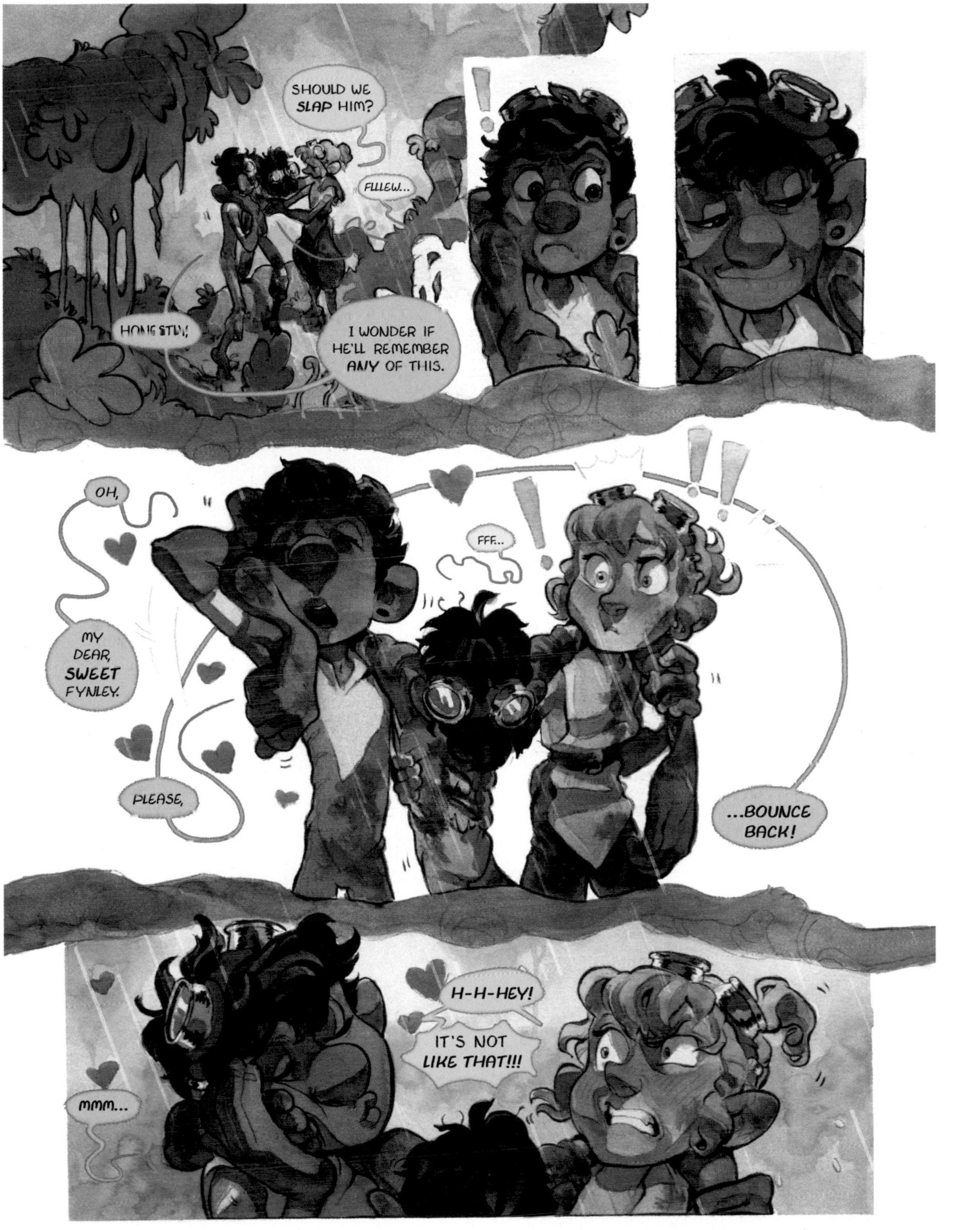
SHOULD WE SLAP HIM?
FLLLEW...
HONESTLY,
I WONDER IF HE'LL REMEMBER ANY OF THIS.
OH,
MY DEAR, SWEET FYNLEY.
PLEASE,
FFF...
...BOUNCE BACK!
H-H-HEY!
IT'S NOT LIKE THAT!!!
mmm...

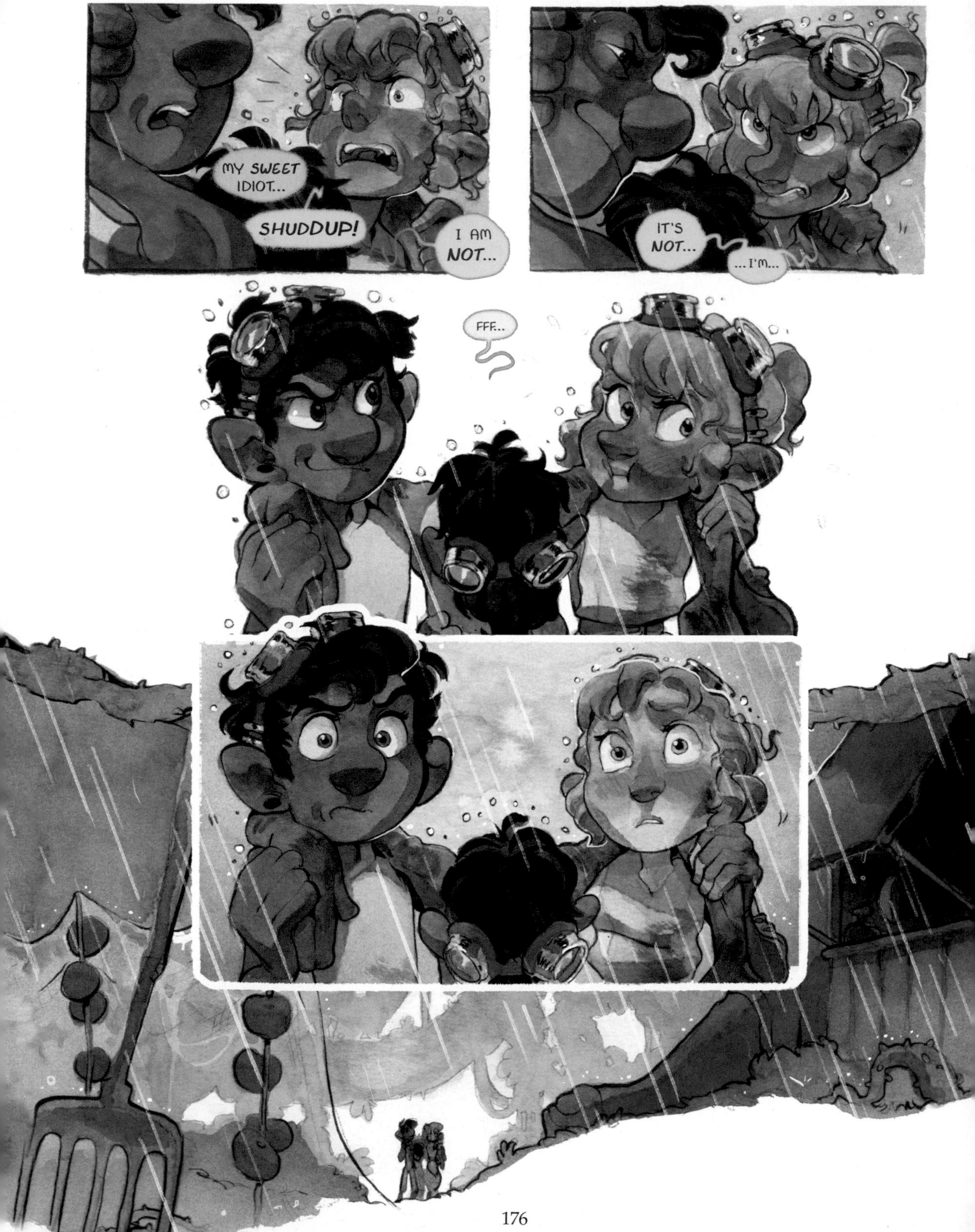
MY SWEET IDIOT...
SHUDDUP!
I AM NOT...
IT'S NOT...
...I'M...
FFF...

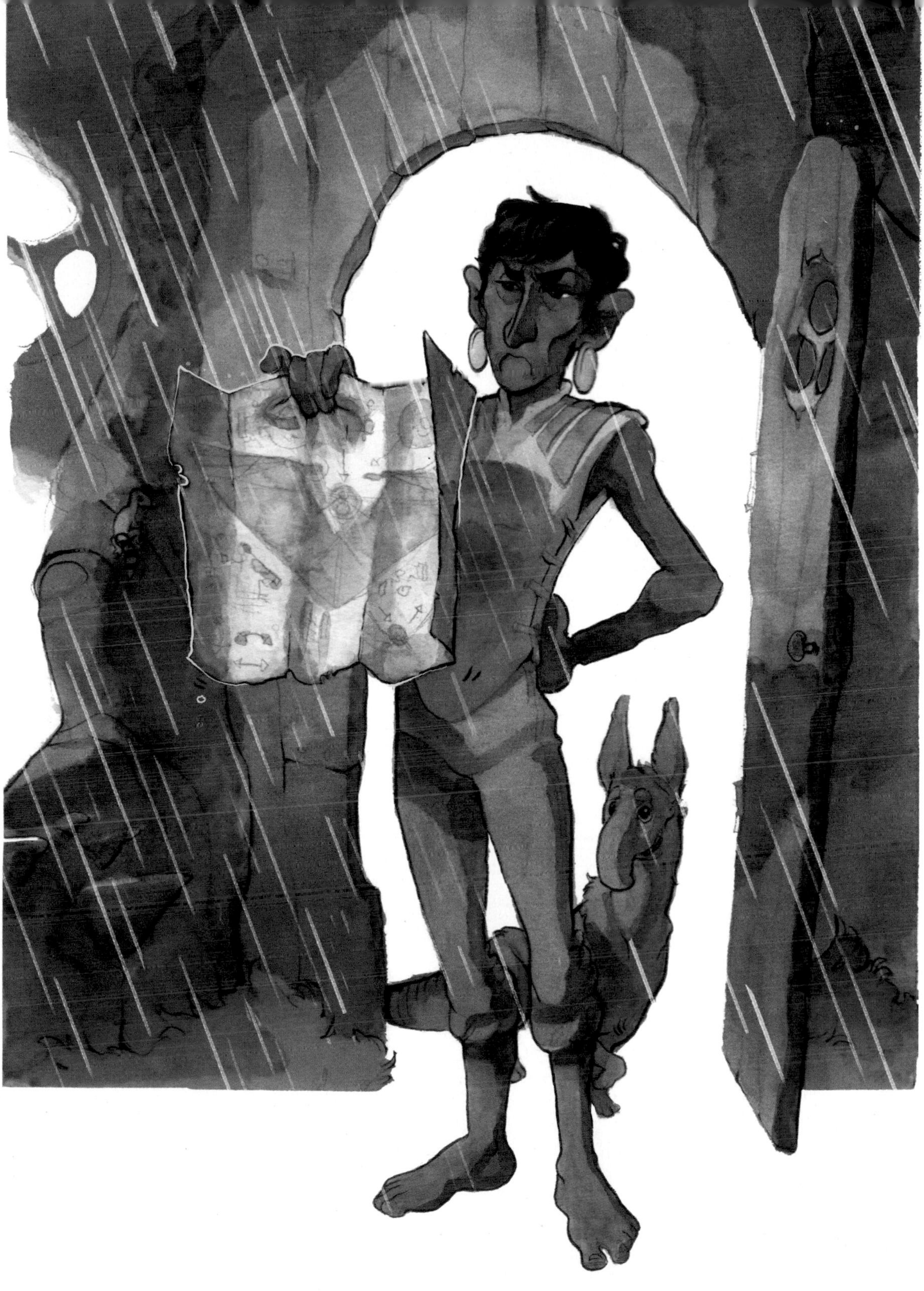

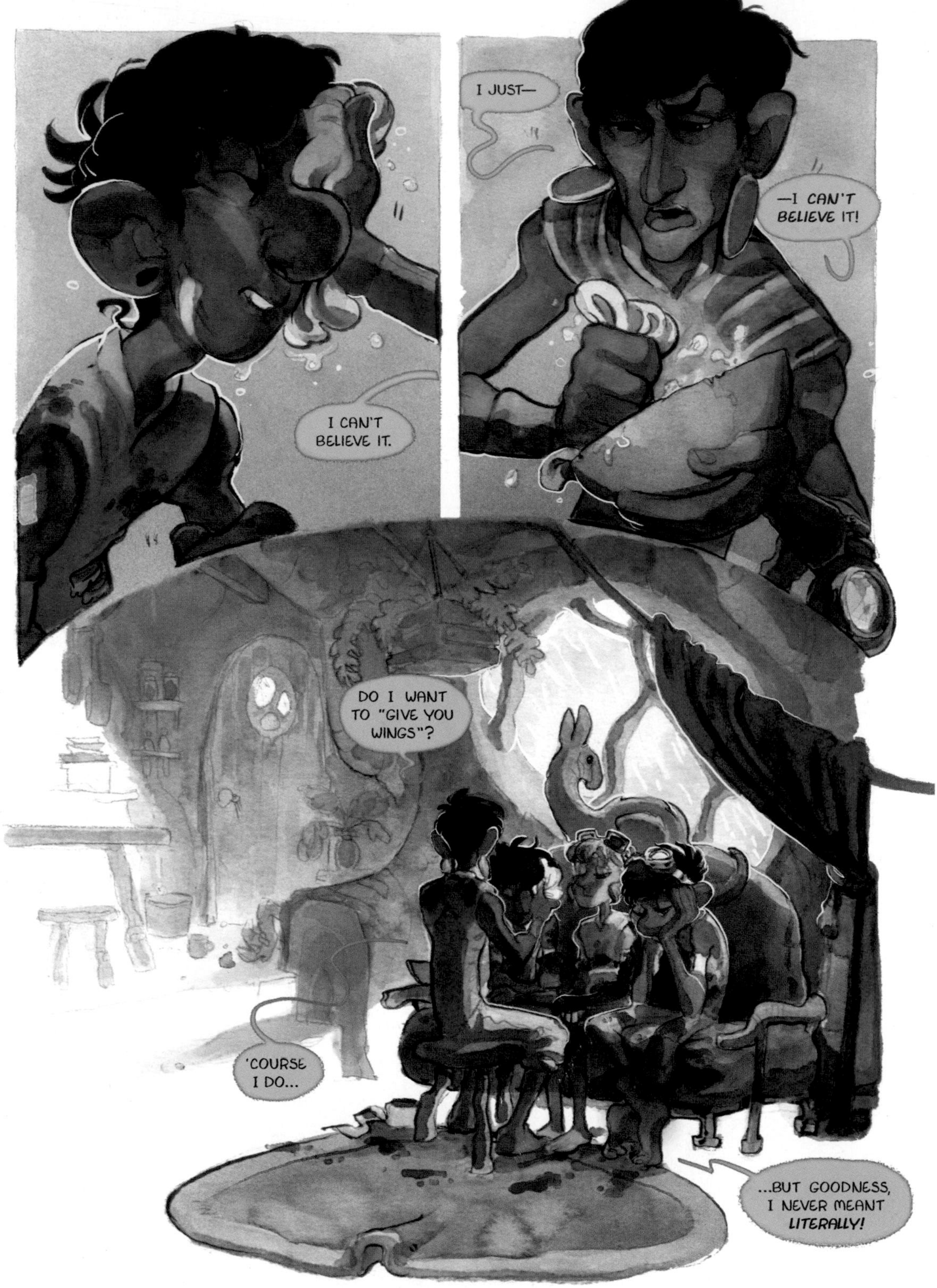
I CAN'T BELIEVE IT.
I JUST—
—I CAN'T BELIEVE IT!
DO I WANT TO "GIVE YOU WINGS"?
'COURSE I DO...
...BUT GOODNESS, I NEVER MEANT *LITERALLY!*

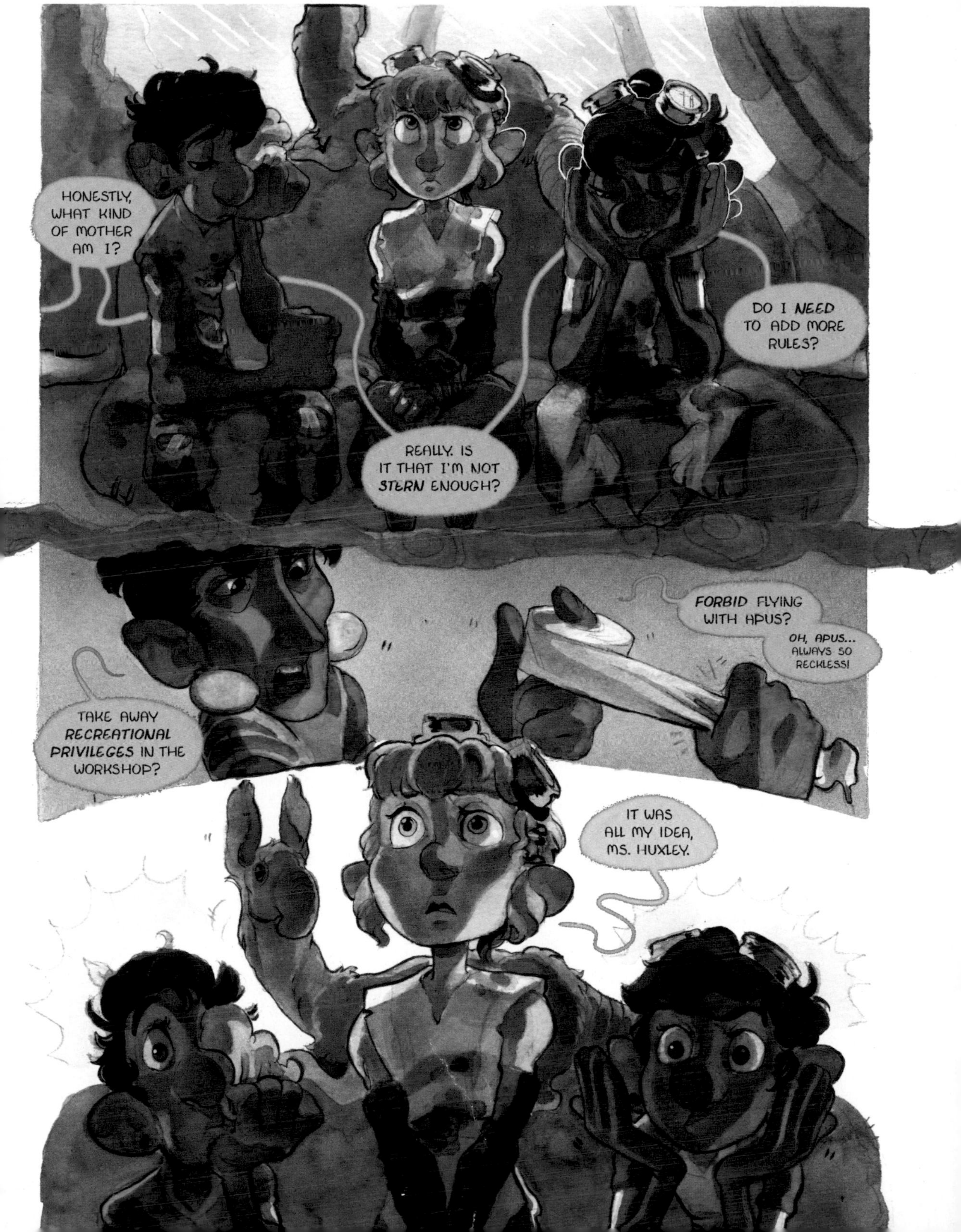
HONESTLY, WHAT KIND OF MOTHER AM I?
REALLY. IS IT THAT I'M NOT STERN ENOUGH?
DO I NEED TO ADD MORE RULES?
TAKE AWAY RECREATIONAL PRIVILEGES IN THE WORKSHOP?
FORBID FLYING WITH APUS?
OH, APUS... ALWAYS SO RECKLESS!
IT WAS ALL MY IDEA, MS. HUXLEY.

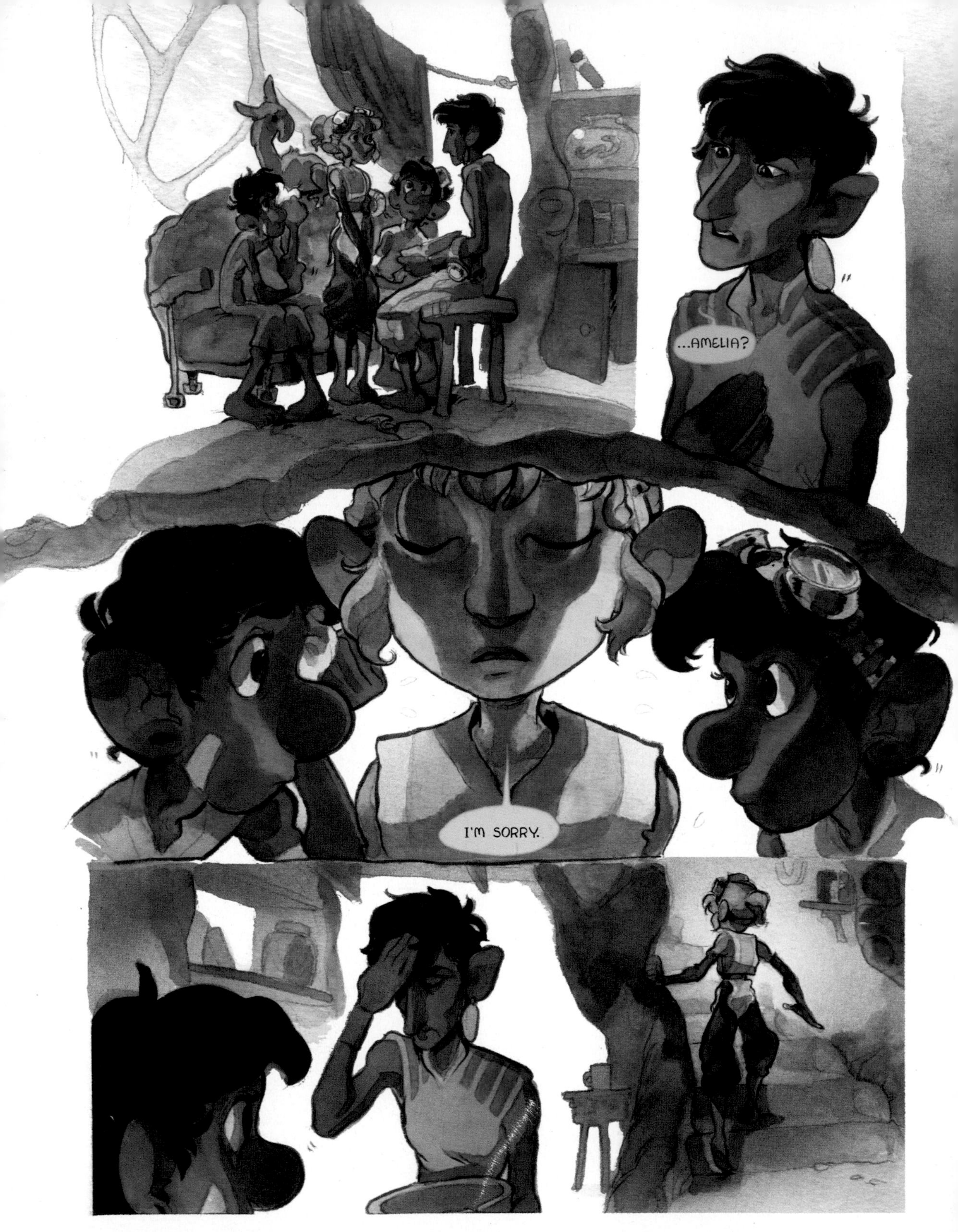
...AMELIA?
I'M SORRY.

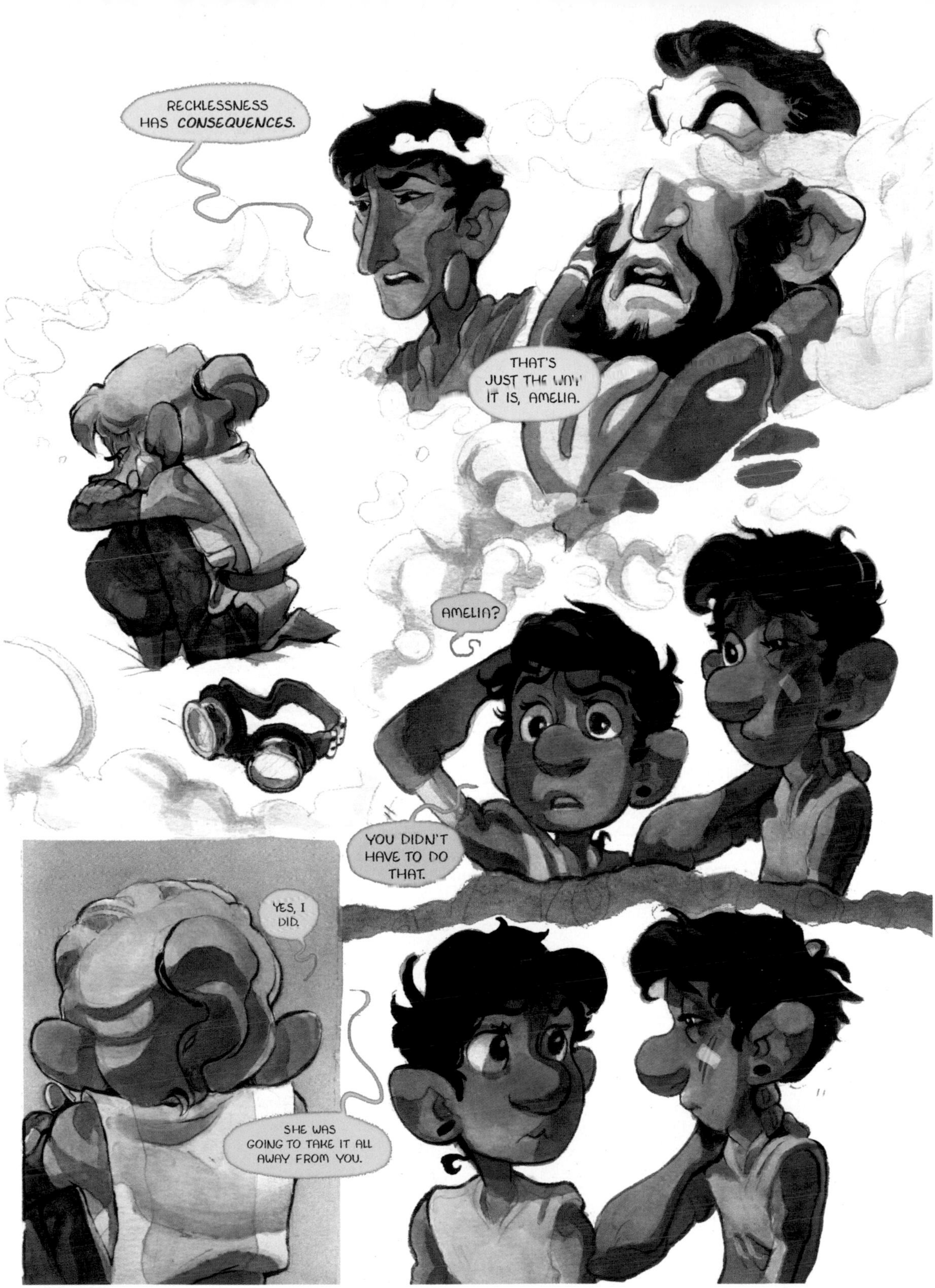
RECKLESSNESS HAS ***CONSEQUENCES.***
THAT'S JUST THE WAY IT IS, AMELIA.
AMELIA?
YOU DIDN'T HAVE TO DO THAT.
YES, I DID.
SHE WAS GOING TO TAKE IT ALL AWAY FROM YOU.

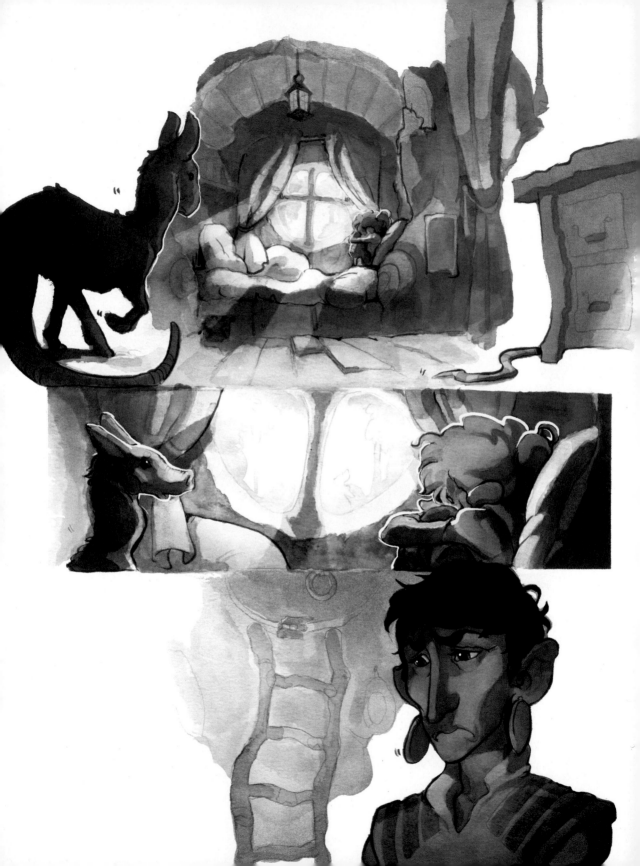

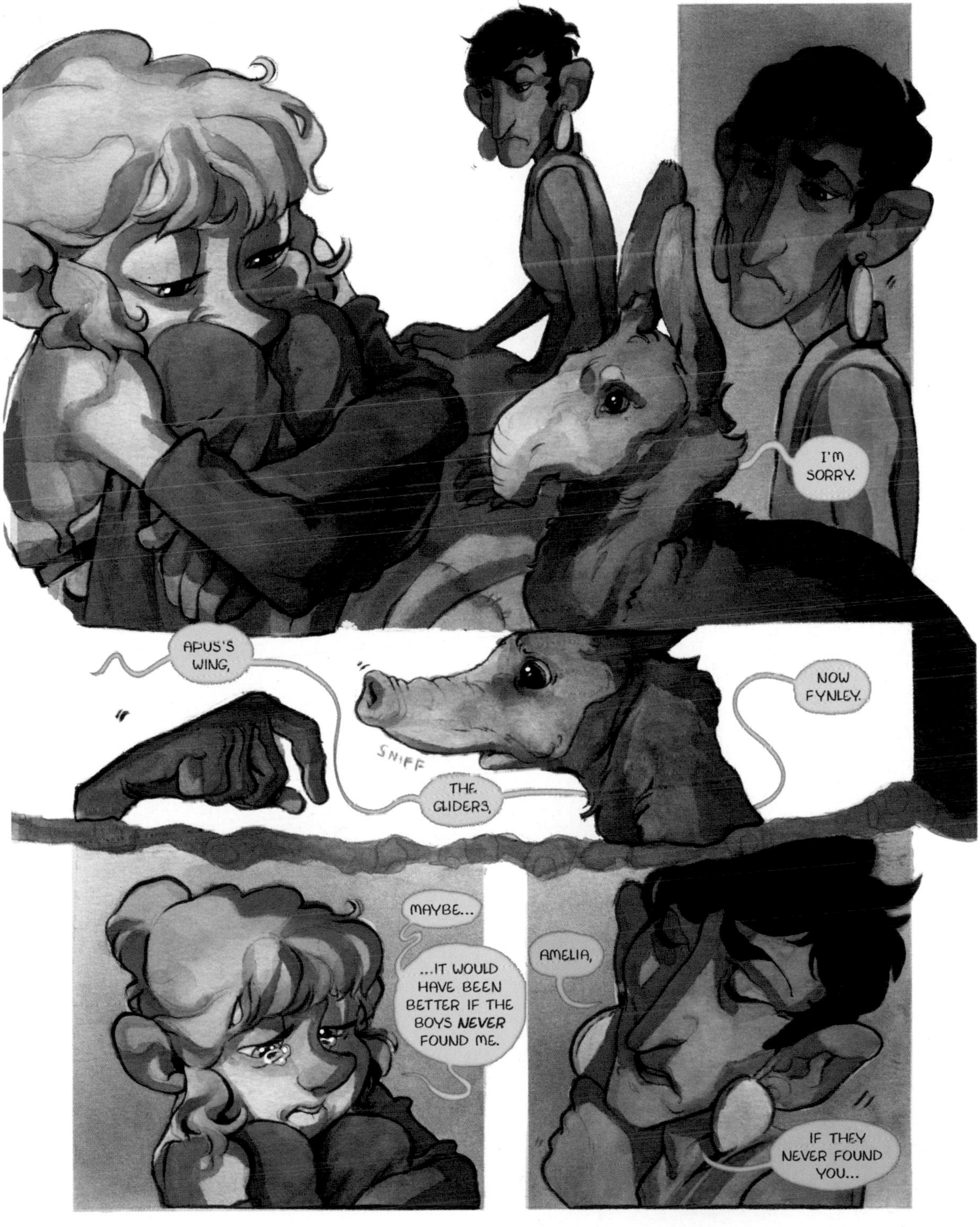
I'M SORRY.
APUS'S WING,
THE GLIDERS,
NOW FYNLEY.
SNIFF
MAYBE...
...IT WOULD HAVE BEEN BETTER IF THE BOYS NEVER FOUND ME.
AMELIA,
IF THEY NEVER FOUND YOU...

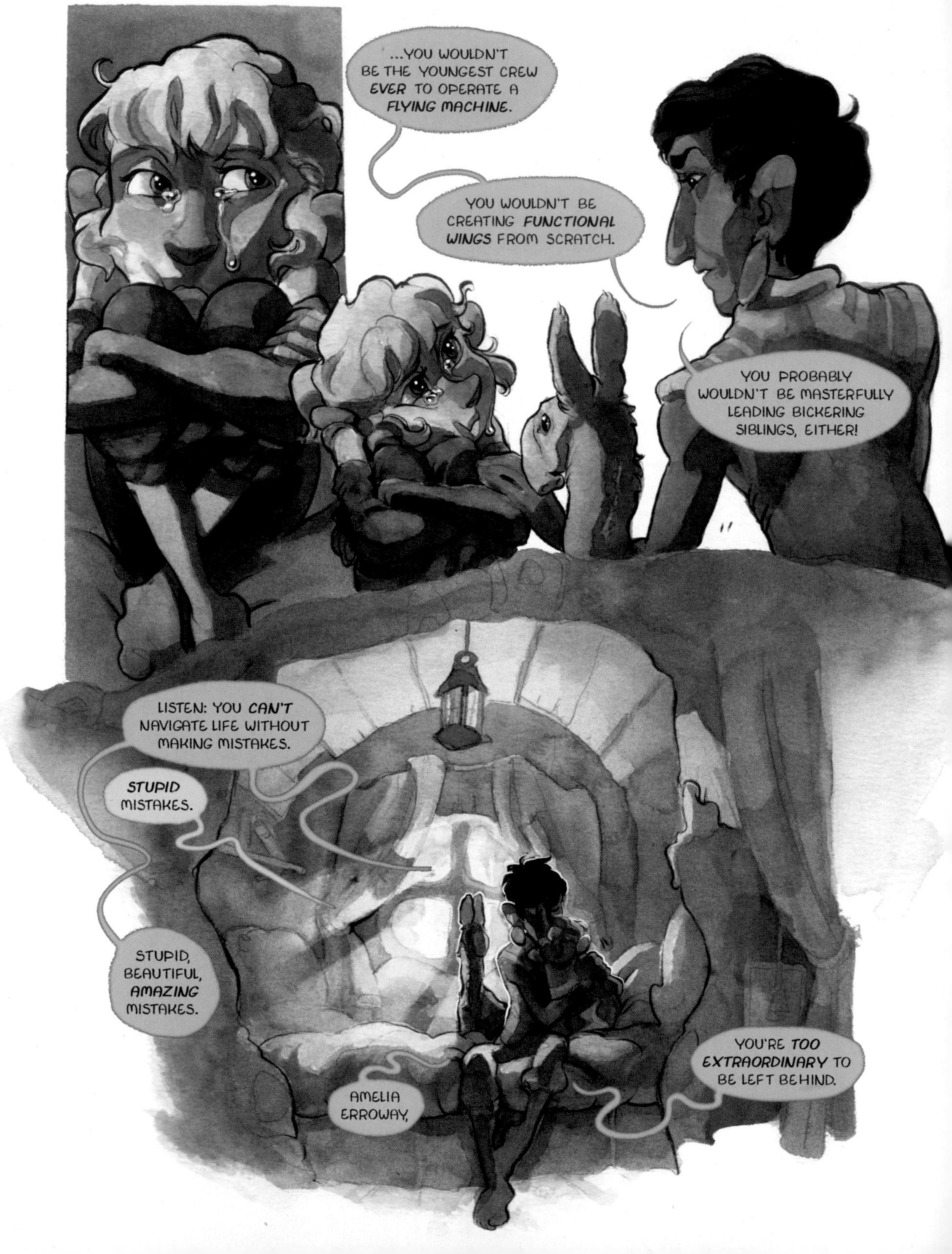
...YOU WOULDN'T BE THE YOUNGEST CREW *EVER* TO OPERATE A *FLYING MACHINE*.
YOU WOULDN'T BE CREATING *FUNCTIONAL WINGS* FROM SCRATCH.
YOU PROBABLY WOULDN'T BE MASTERFULLY LEADING BICKERING SIBLINGS, EITHER!
LISTEN: YOU *CAN'T* NAVIGATE LIFE WITHOUT MAKING MISTAKES.
STUPID MISTAKES.
STUPID, BEAUTIFUL, *AMAZING* MISTAKES.
AMELIA ERROWAY,
YOU'RE *TOO EXTRAORDINARY* TO BE LEFT BEHIND.

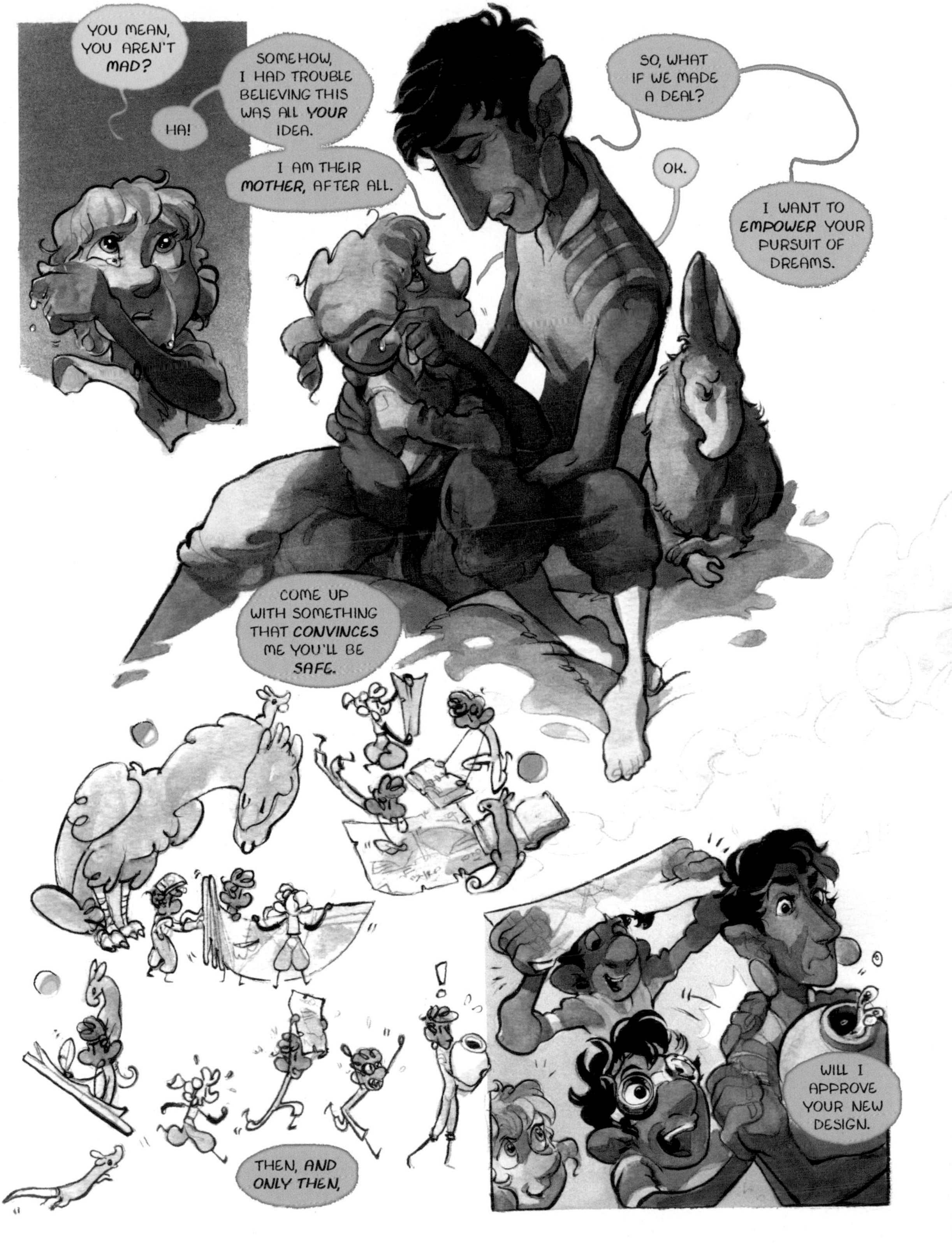

YOU MEAN, YOU AREN'T MAD?
HA!
SOMEHOW, I HAD TROUBLE BELIEVING THIS WAS ALL YOUR IDEA.
I AM THEIR MOTHER, AFTER ALL.
SO, WHAT IF WE MADE A DEAL?
OK.
I WANT TO EMPOWER YOUR PURSUIT OF DREAMS.
COME UP WITH SOMETHING THAT CONVINCES ME YOU'LL BE SAFE.
THEN, AND ONLY THEN,
WILL I APPROVE YOUR NEW DESIGN.

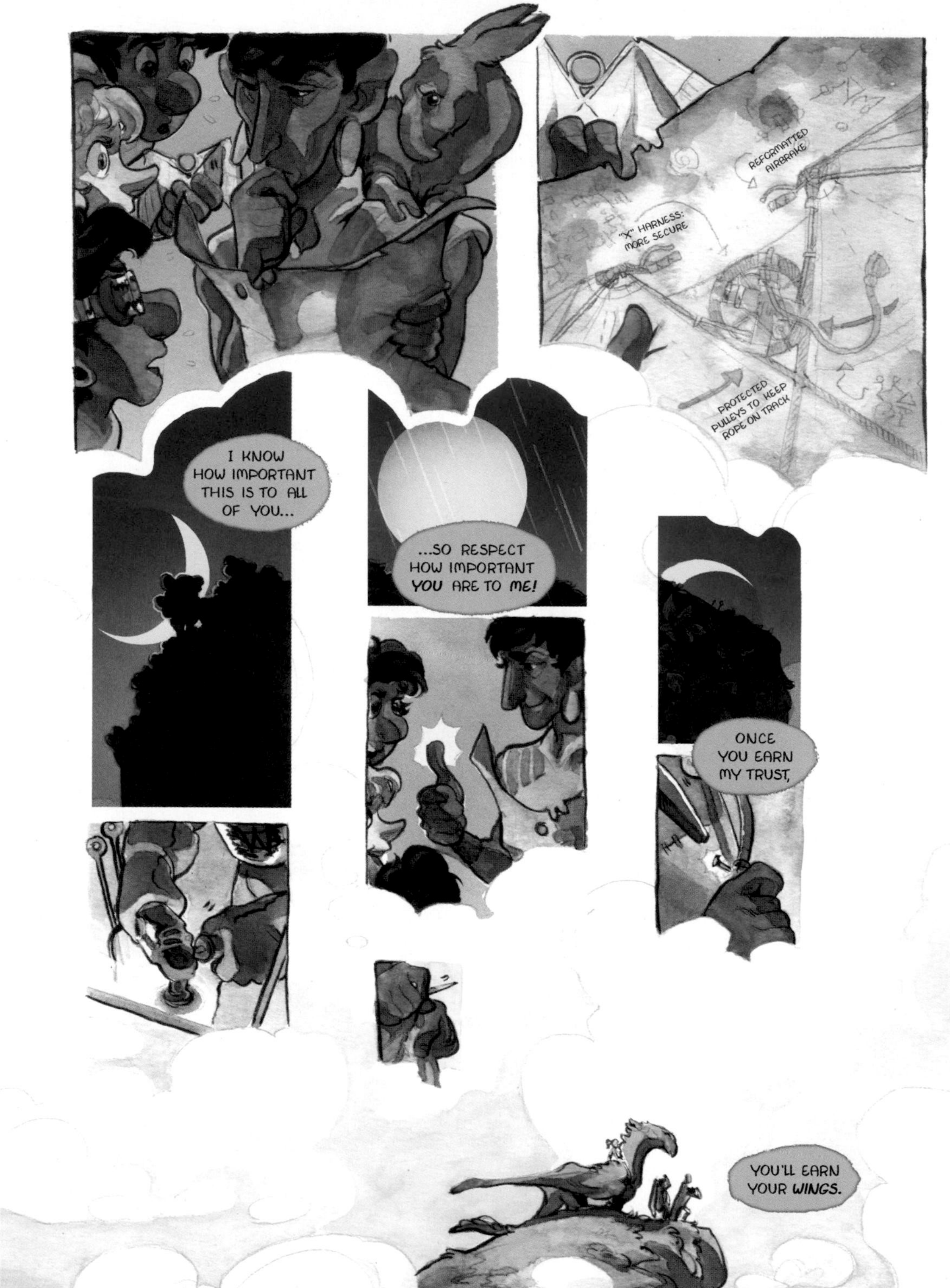
REFORMATTED AIRBRAKE
"X" HARNESS: MORE SECURE
PROTECTED PULLEYS TO KEEP ROPE ON TRACK
I KNOW HOW IMPORTANT THIS IS TO ALL OF YOU...
...SO RESPECT HOW IMPORTANT YOU ARE TO ME!
ONCE YOU EARN MY TRUST,
YOU'LL EARN YOUR WINGS.

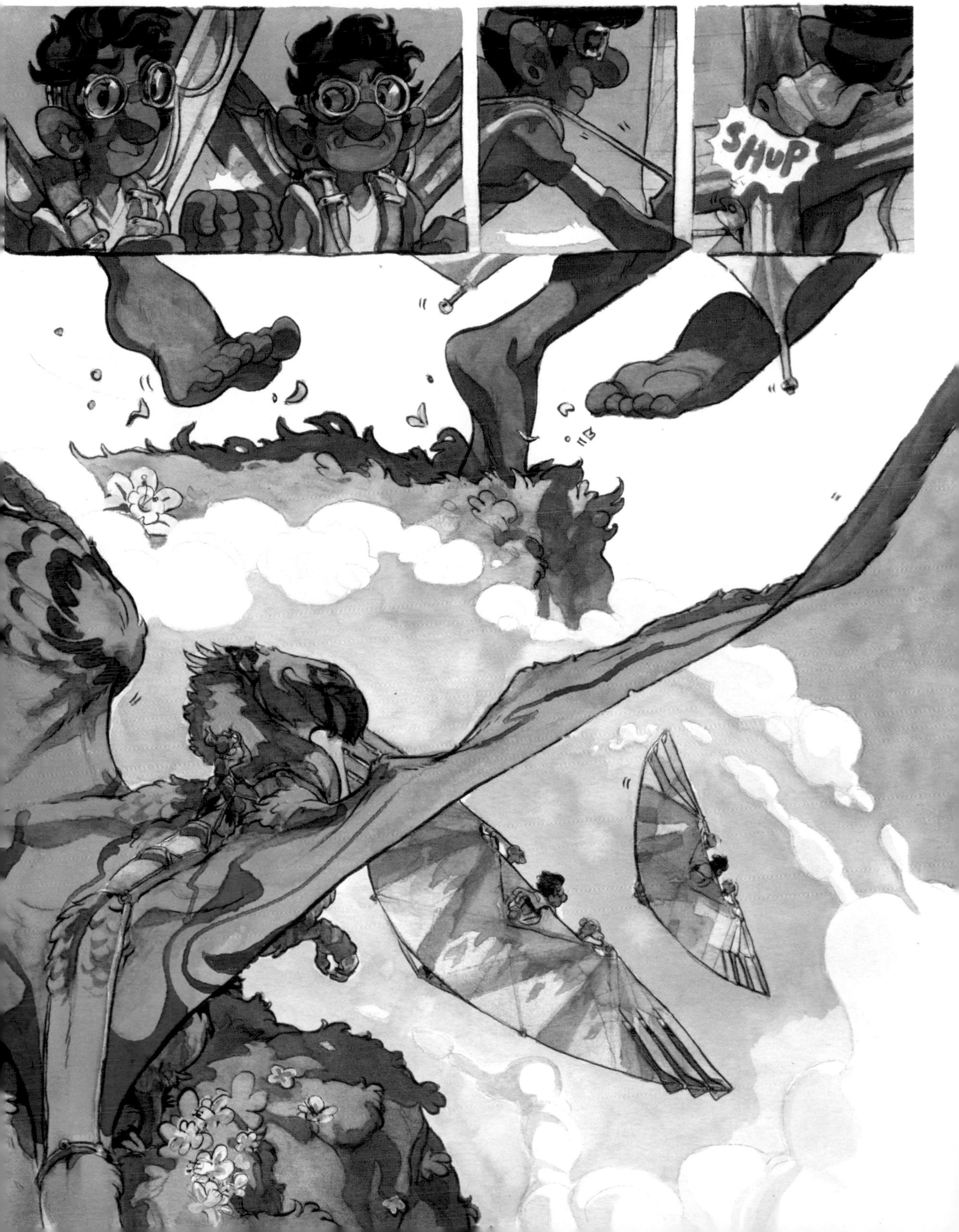
SHUP

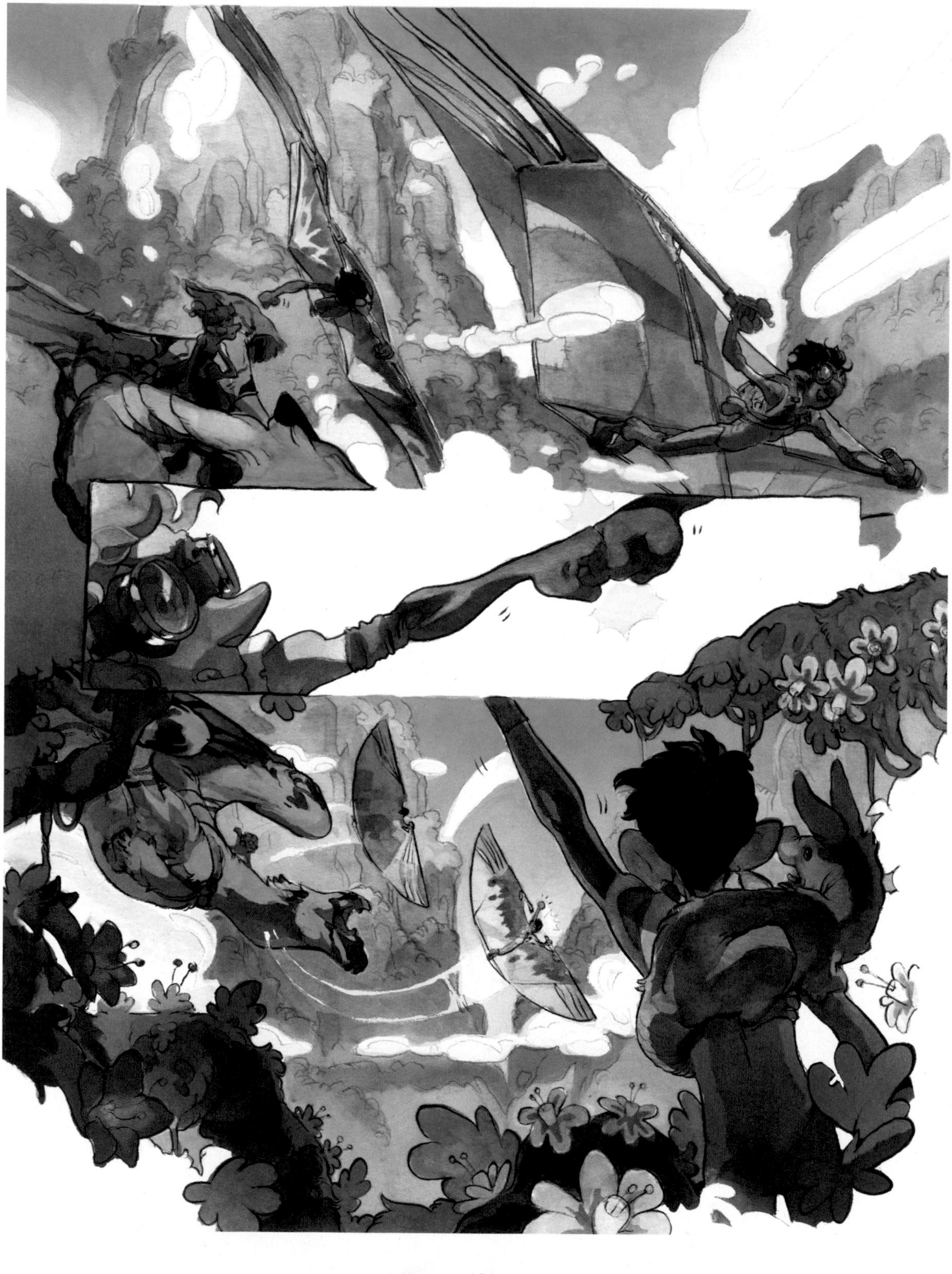

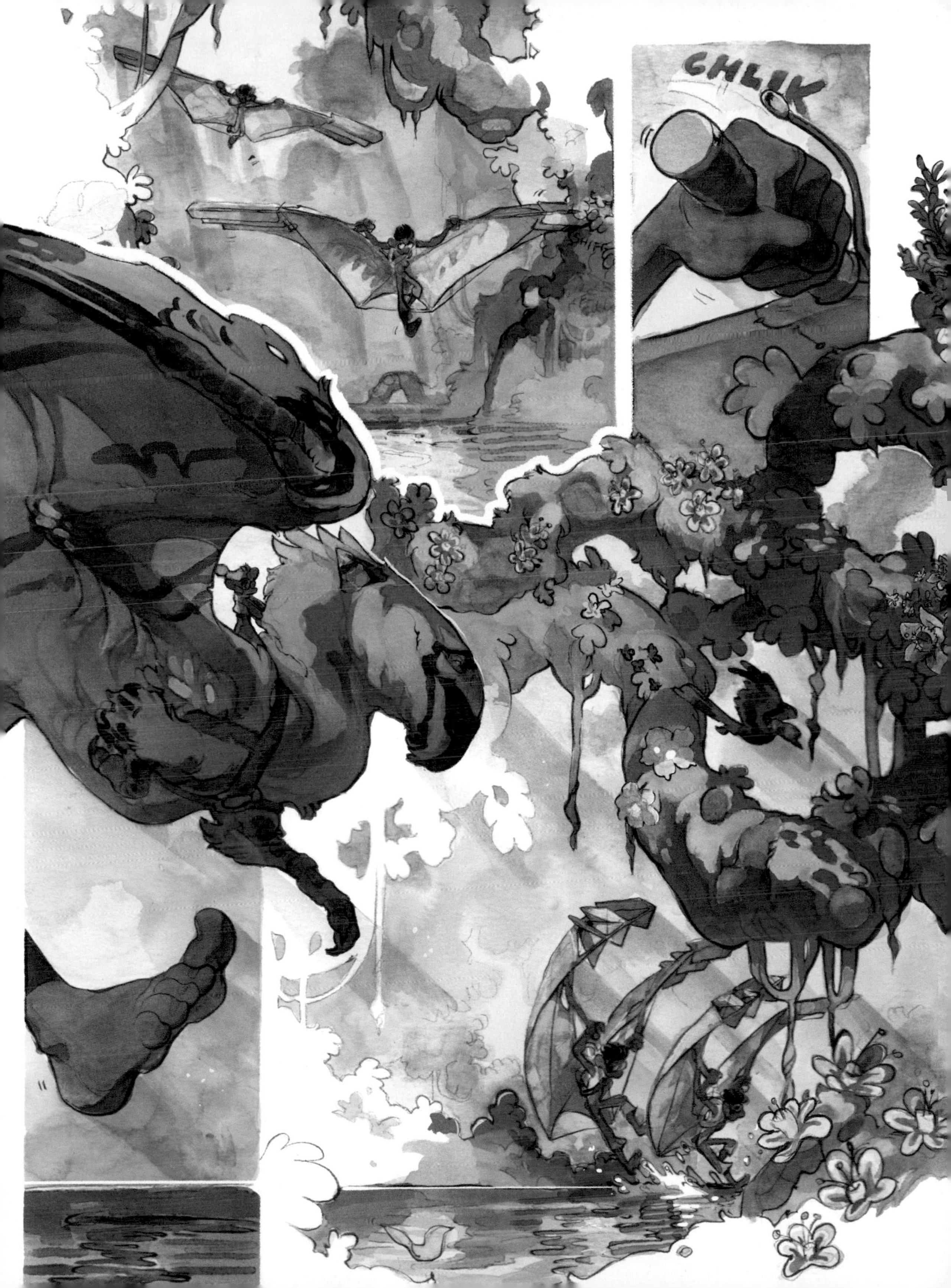
SHIFF
CHLIK

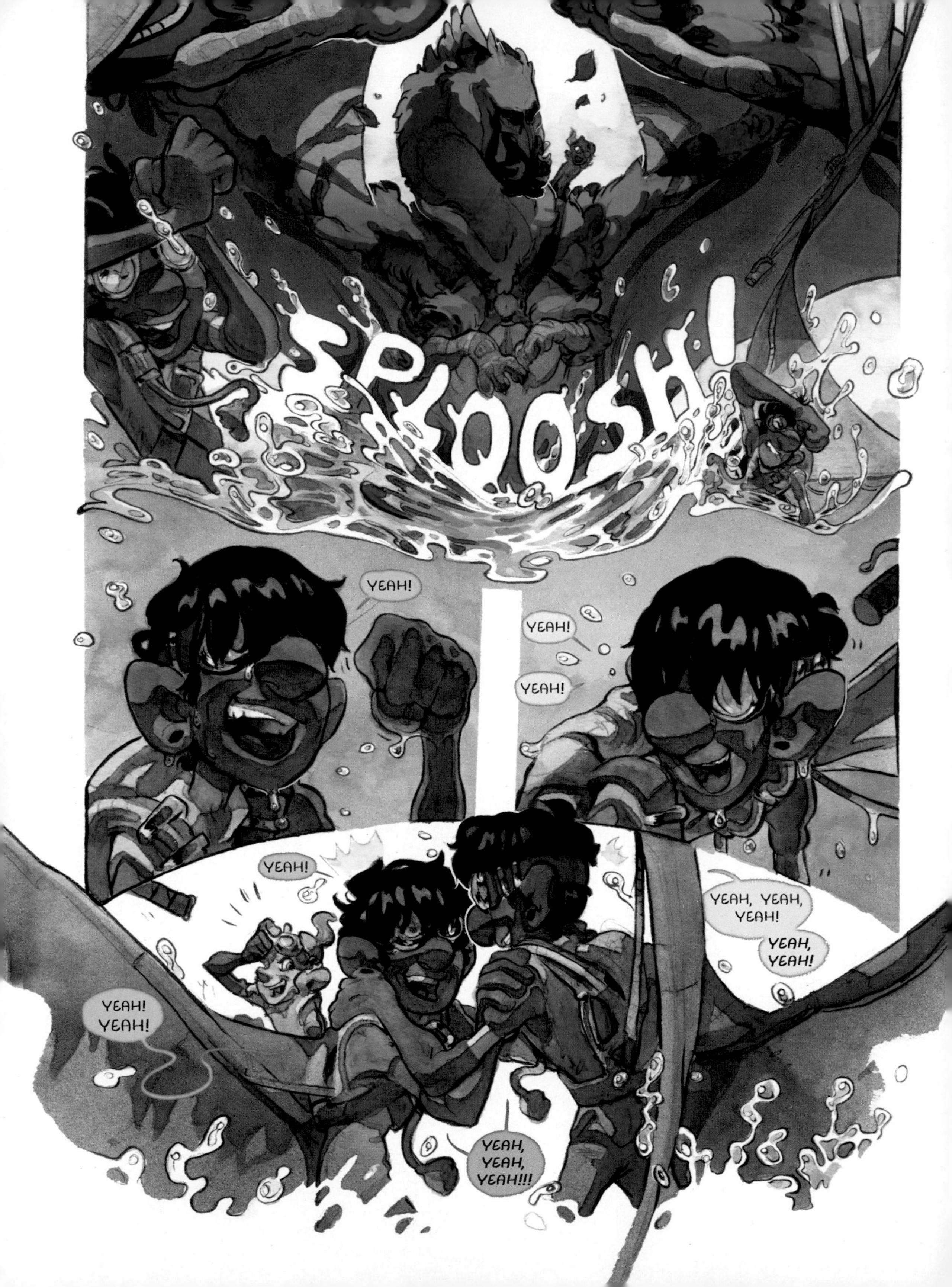
SPLOOSH!
YEAH!
YEAH!
YEAH!
YEAH!
YEAH, YEAH, YEAH!
YEAH, YEAH!
YEAH! YEAH!
YEAH, YEAH, YEAH!!!

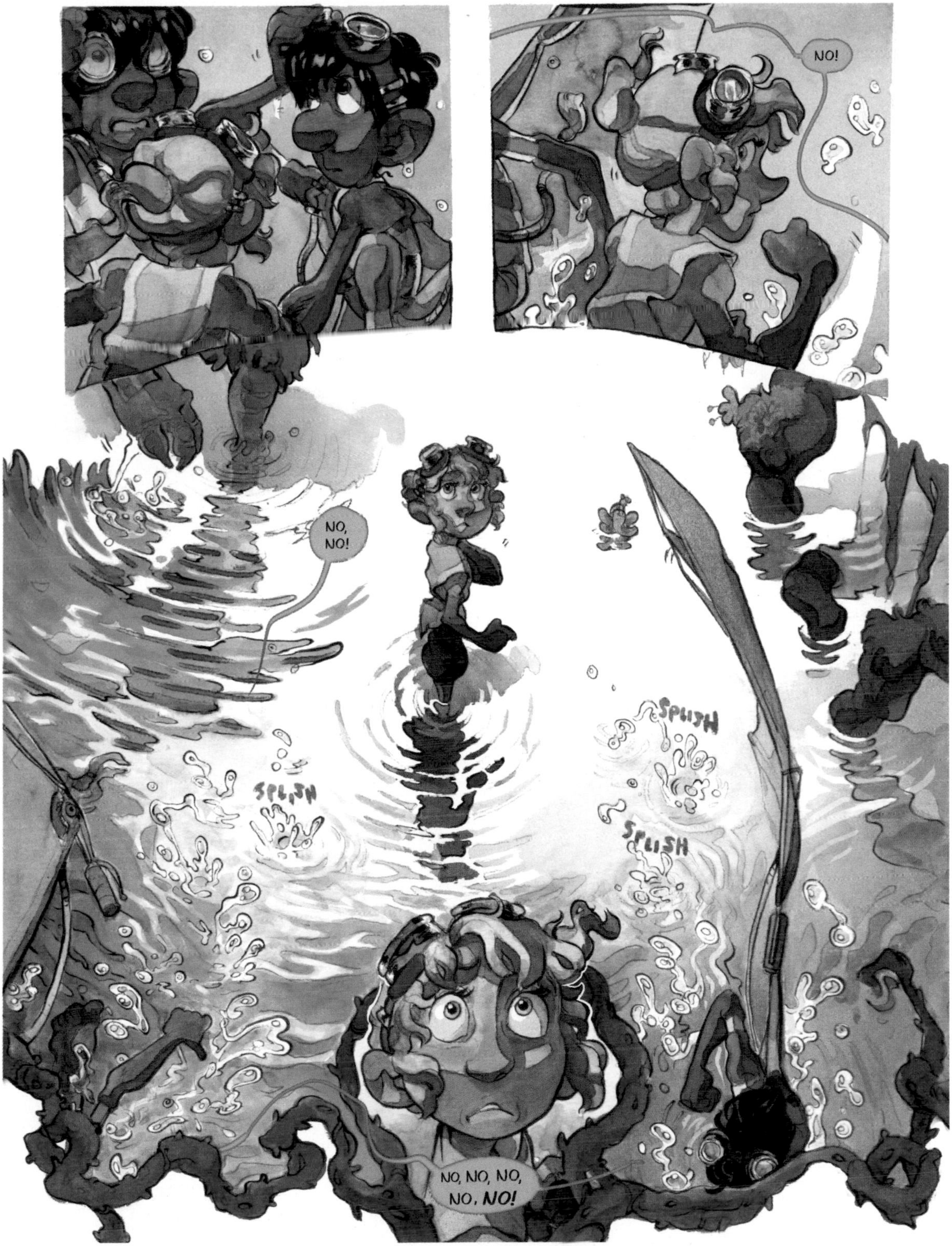

NO!
NO, NO!
SPLISH
SPLISH
SPLISH
NO, NO, NO, NO, NO!

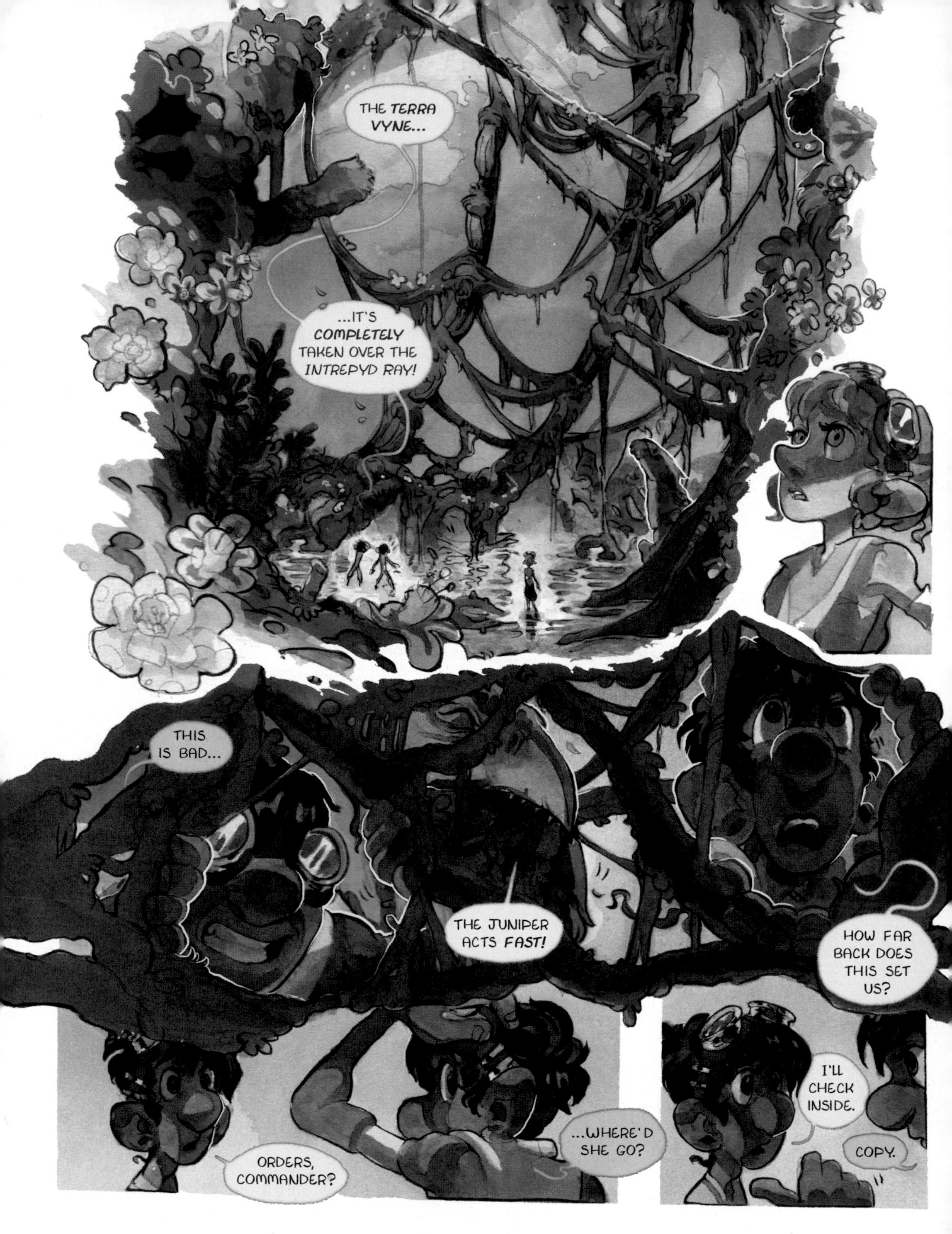
THE TERRA VYNE...
...IT'S COMPLETELY TAKEN OVER THE INTREPYD RAY!
THIS IS BAD...
THE JUNIPER ACTS FAST!
HOW FAR BACK DOES THIS SET US?
ORDERS, COMMANDER?
...WHERE'D SHE GO?
I'LL CHECK INSIDE.
COPY.

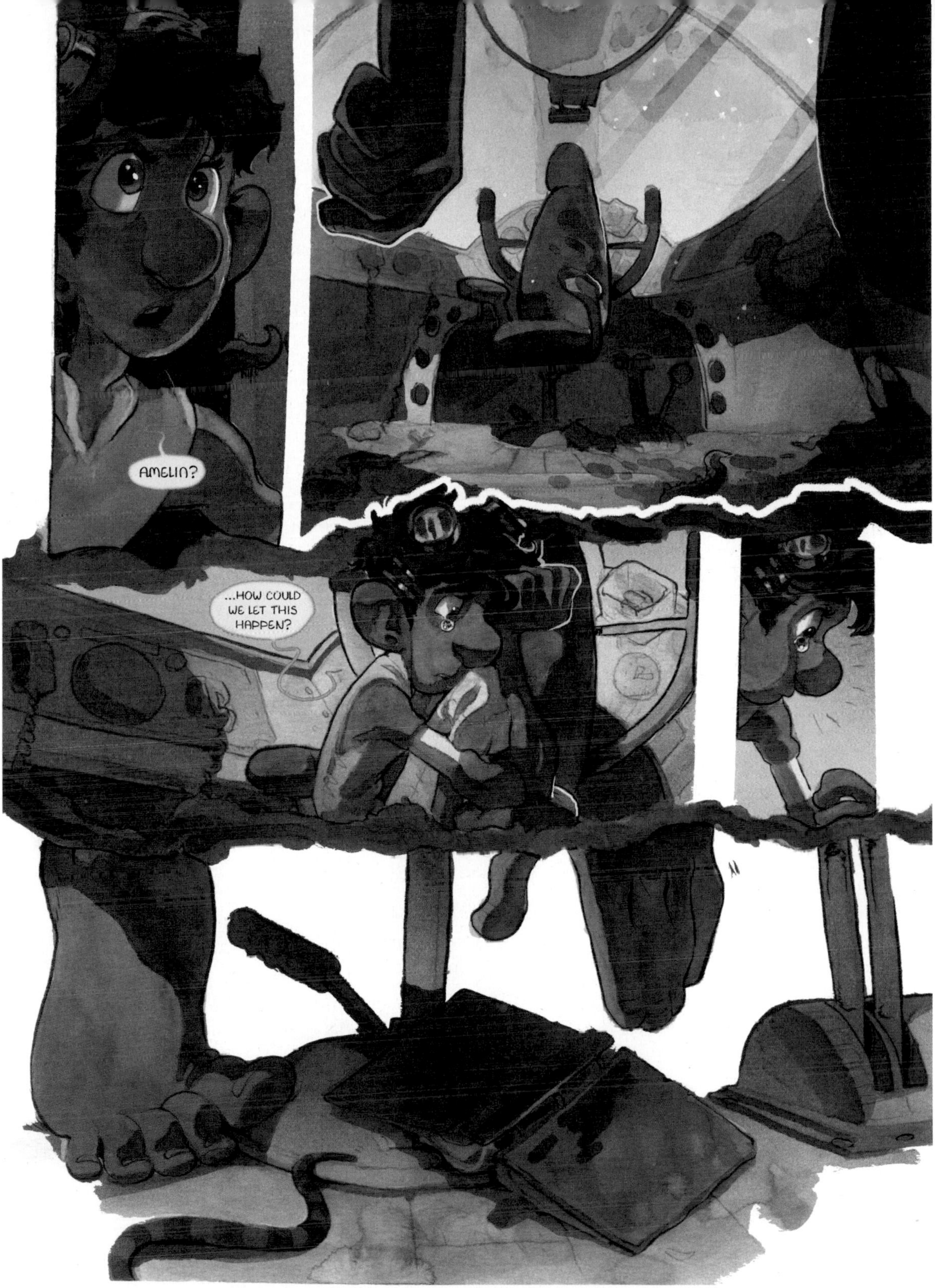
AMELIN?
...HOW COULD WE LET THIS HAPPEN?

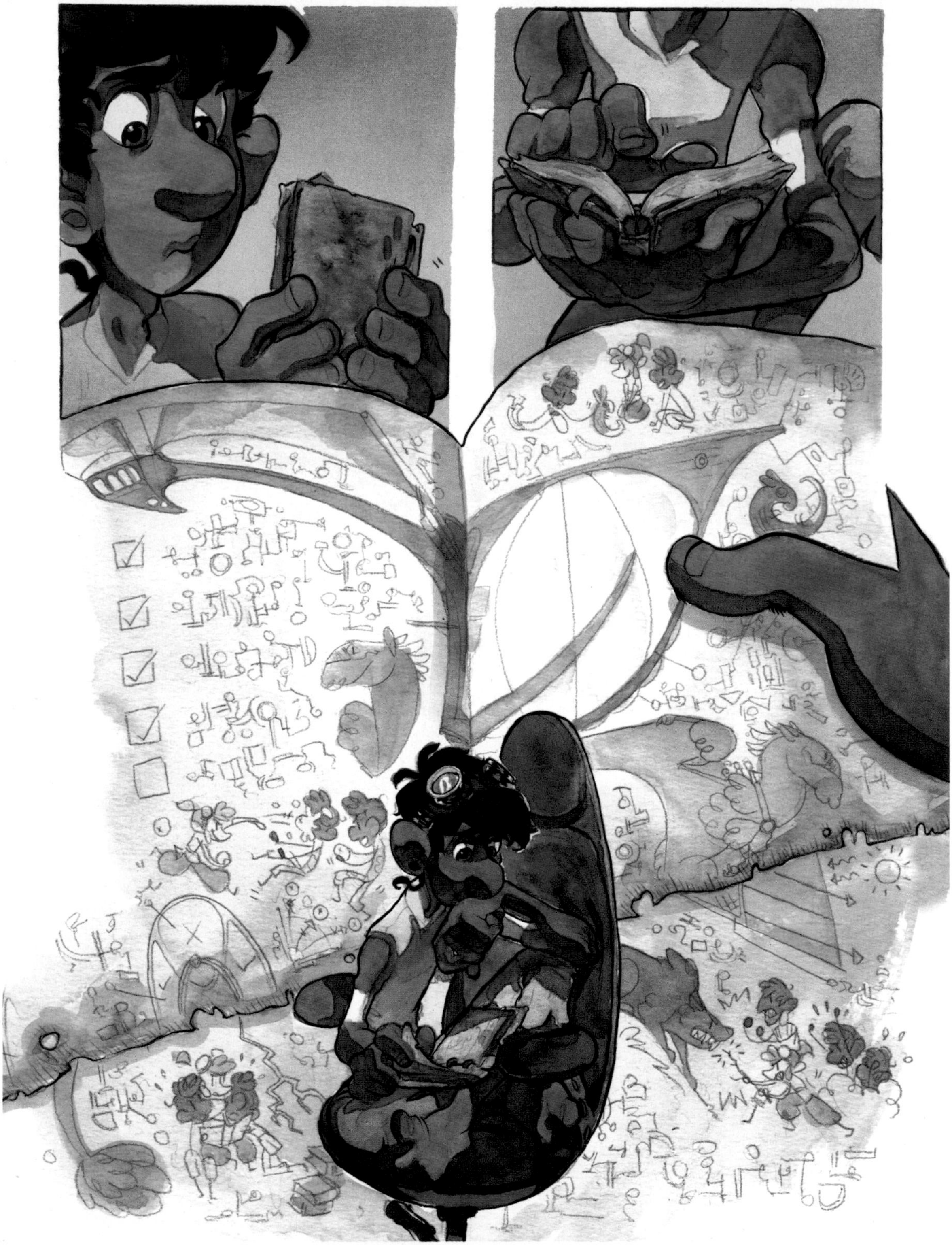

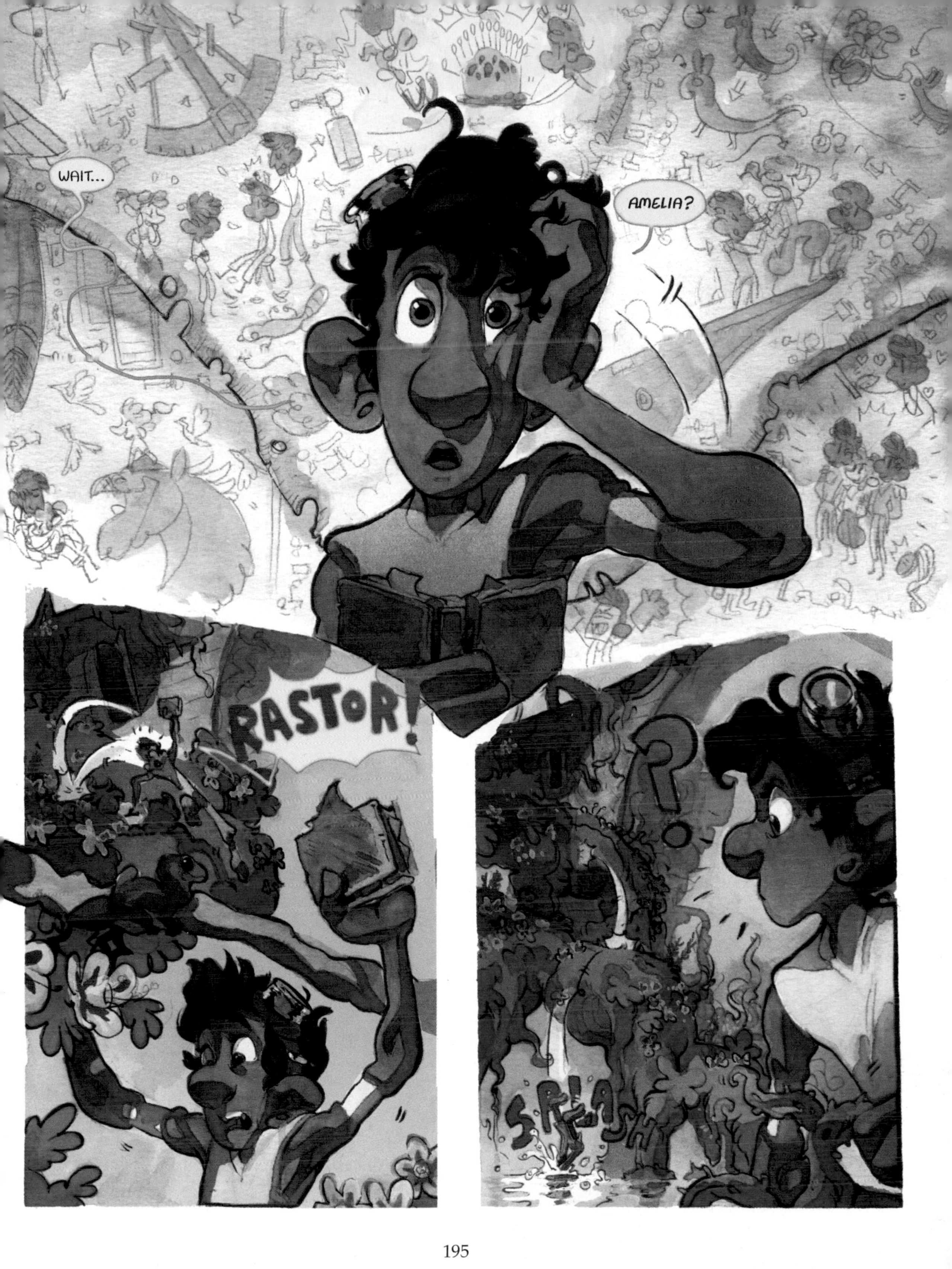
WAIT...
AMELIA?
RASTOR!
?
SPLASH

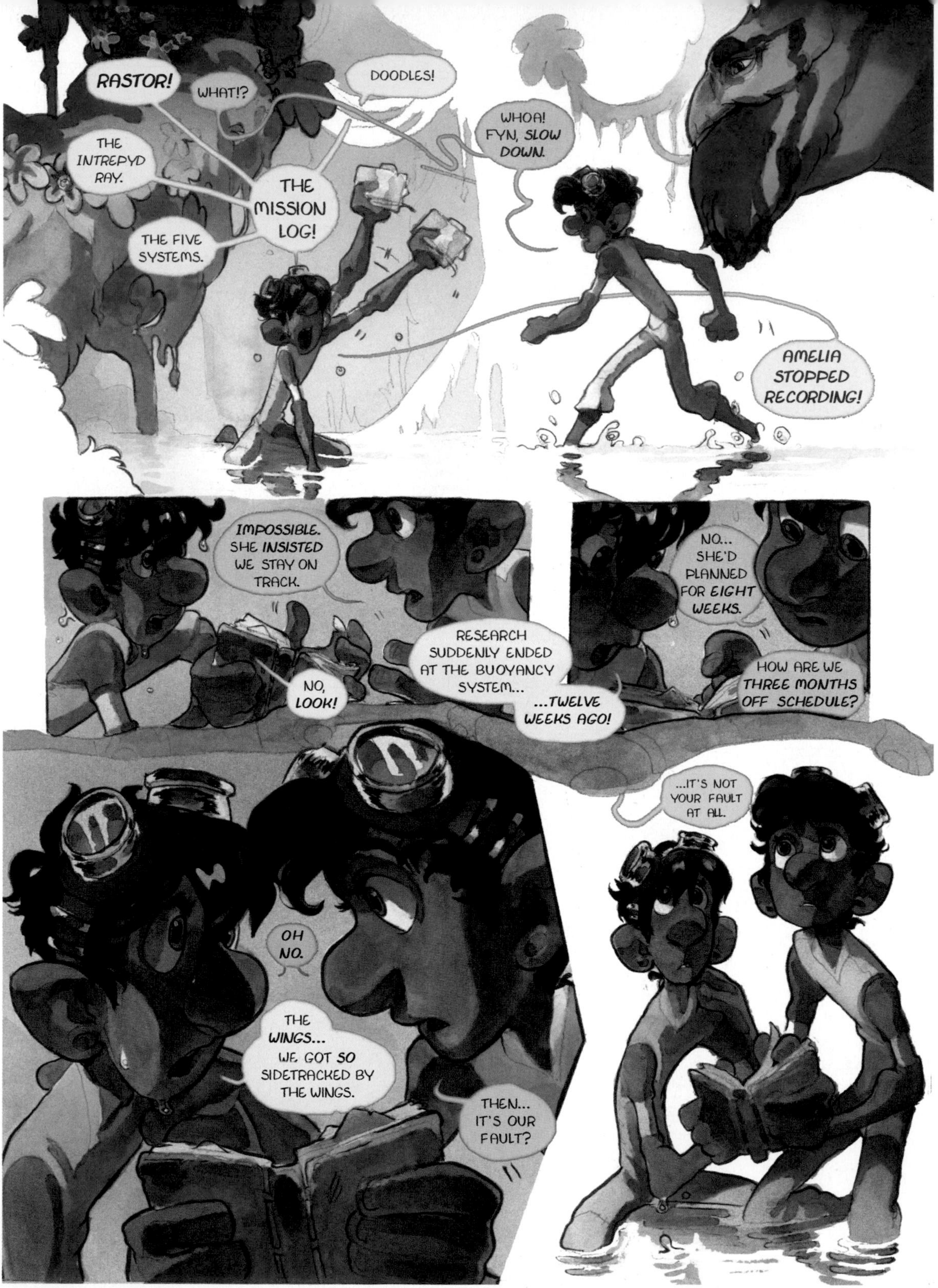
RASTOR!
WHAT!?
DOODLES!
THE INTREPYD RAY.
THE MISSION LOG!
THE FIVE SYSTEMS.
WHOA! FYN, SLOW DOWN.
AMELIA STOPPED RECORDING!
IMPOSSIBLE. SHE INSISTED WE STAY ON TRACK.
NO, LOOK!
RESEARCH SUDDENLY ENDED AT THE BUOYANCY SYSTEM...
...TWELVE WEEKS AGO!
NO... SHE'D PLANNED FOR EIGHT WEEKS.
HOW ARE WE THREE MONTHS OFF SCHEDULE?
OH NO.
THE WINGS... WE GOT SO SIDETRACKED BY THE WINGS.
THEN... IT'S OUR FAULT?
...IT'S NOT YOUR FAULT AT ALL.

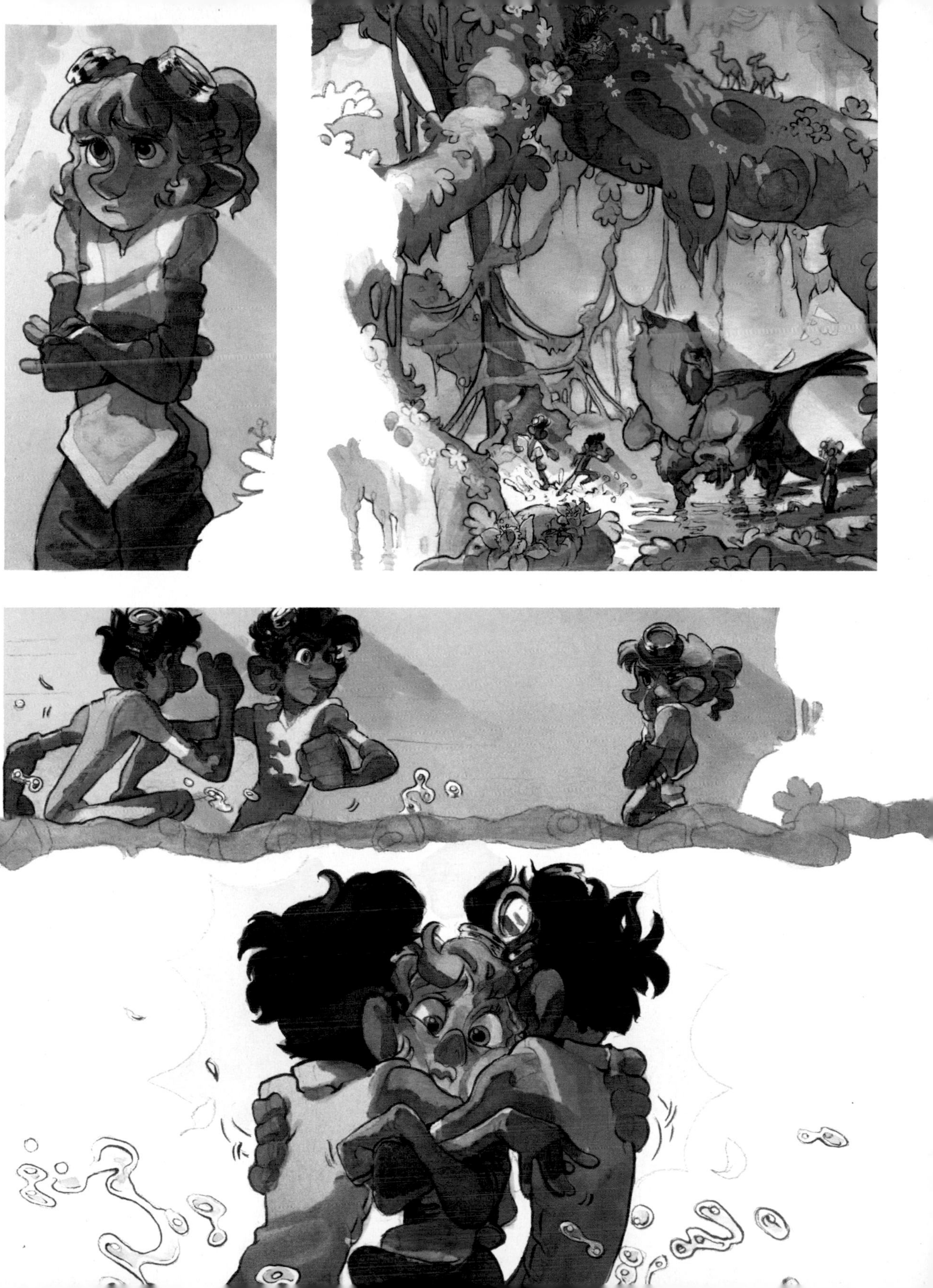

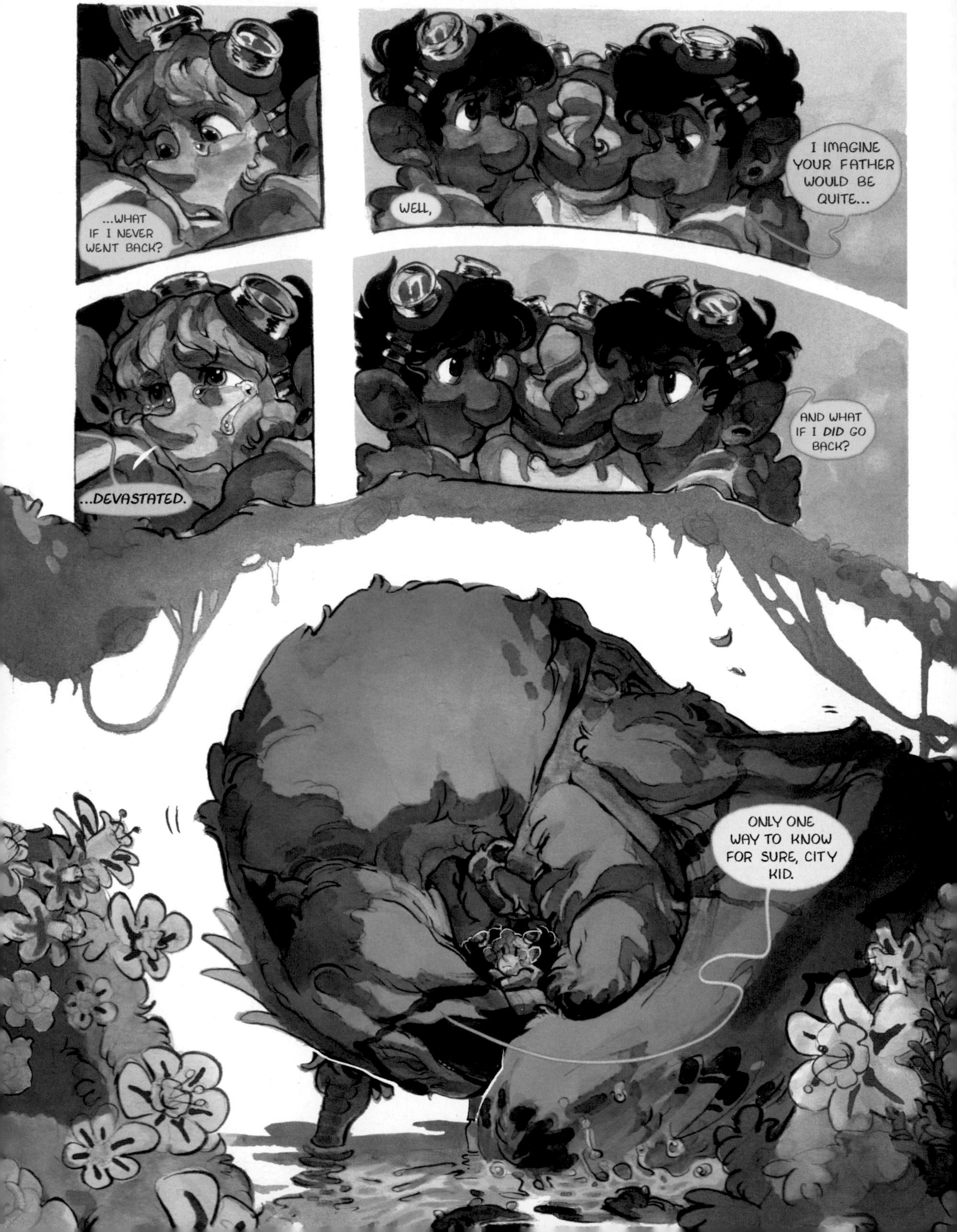
...WHAT IF I NEVER WENT BACK?
WELL,
I IMAGINE YOUR FATHER WOULD BE QUITE...
...DEVASTATED.
AND WHAT IF I *DID* GO BACK?
ONLY ONE WAY TO KNOW FOR SURE, CITY KID.

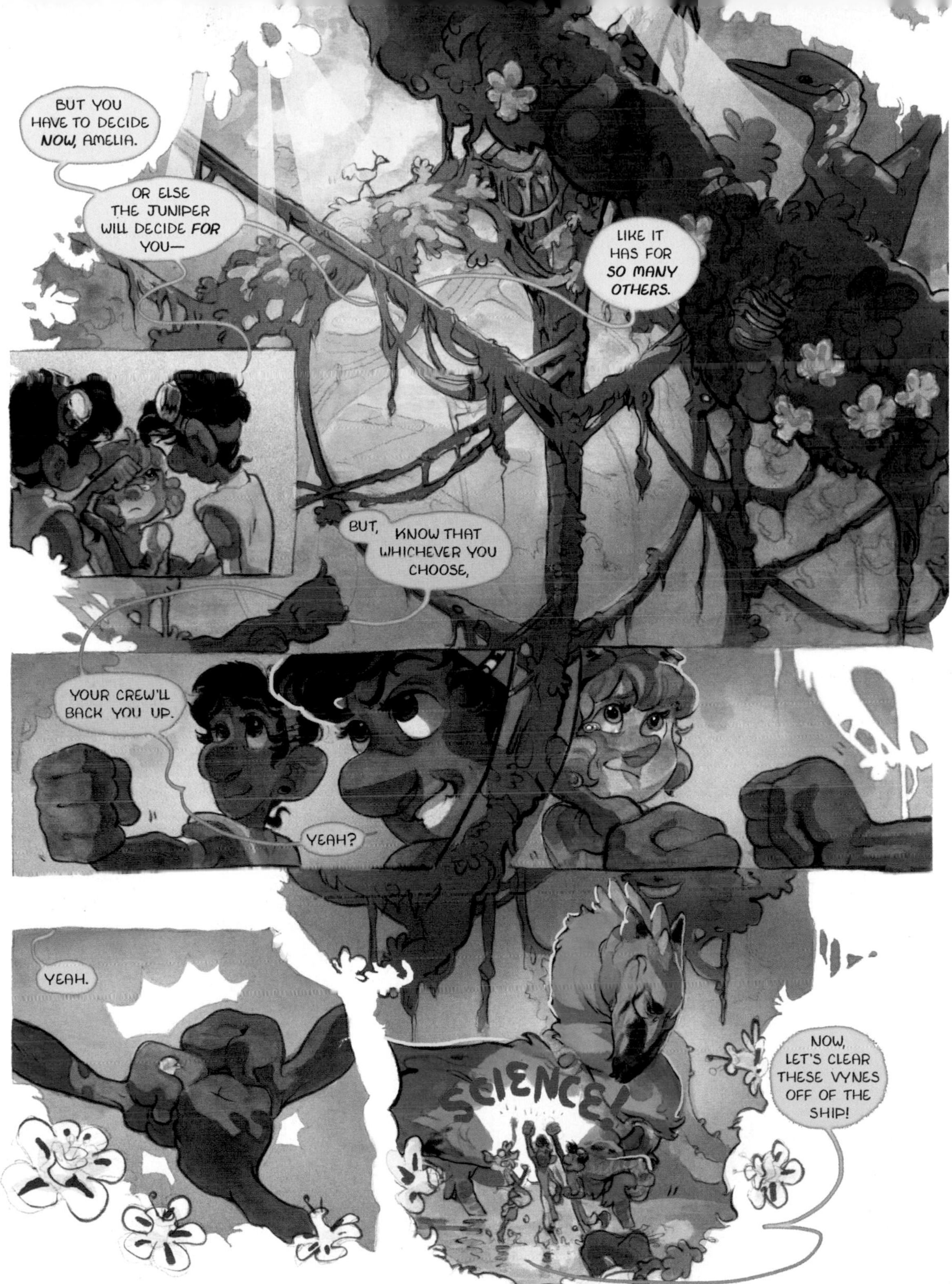

BUT YOU HAVE TO DECIDE NOW, AMELIA.
OR ELSE THE JUNIPER WILL DECIDE FOR YOU—
LIKE IT HAS FOR SO MANY OTHERS.
BUT,
KNOW THAT WHICHEVER YOU CHOOSE,
YOUR CREW'LL BACK YOU UP.
YEAH?
YEAH.
SCIENCE!
NOW, LET'S CLEAR THESE VYNES OFF OF THE SHIP!

WEEK 8 20
PROPULSION!
HEY!
GET BACK HERE, FIEND!
THAT'S MY LOGBOOK!
AILERONS (ROLL)
TURN COORDINATOR
NUISANCE
RADIO
AIRSPEED INDICATOR
FALSE HORIZON
HELIUM OUTPUT DISPLAY
THROTTLE (CONTROLS RPM³)
COMPASS
LANDING GEAR (WITH SAFETY HATCH)¹
FLYWHEEL SPEED INDICATOR (RPM)
AIR BRAKES (CONTROLS YAW)
SECONDARY WINGS
ALTIMETER
SPEED RANGE (CONTROLS OPM²)
HELM (CONTROLS ROLL)
INPUT
OUTPUT
POSITION LOCKS
STERN
THE PILOT SEAT (AMELIA'S)
SECONDARY FLYWHEEL
SHAFT (ANCHORS PRIMARY AND SECONDARY WINGS)
BRACE
ENGINE
BRACE
THE FLYWHEEL
PRIMARY WINGS
VENTS (PREVENT OVERHEATING)
COUNTERWEIGHT
CLOCKWISE ROTATION
FRONT VIEW
UPSTROKE
STARBOARD WING
PORT WING
COUNTERWEIGHT TRACK
CENTER POINT
TELESCOPING ARM
FLYWHEEL
DOWNSTROKE
(SEE FIG. A)
WING SOCKET
MAN,
TERRA VYNE IS TOUGH!
¹WORKS BY FOLDING PRIMARY WINGS
²OSCILLATIONS PER MINUTE
³REVOLUTIONS PER MINUTE

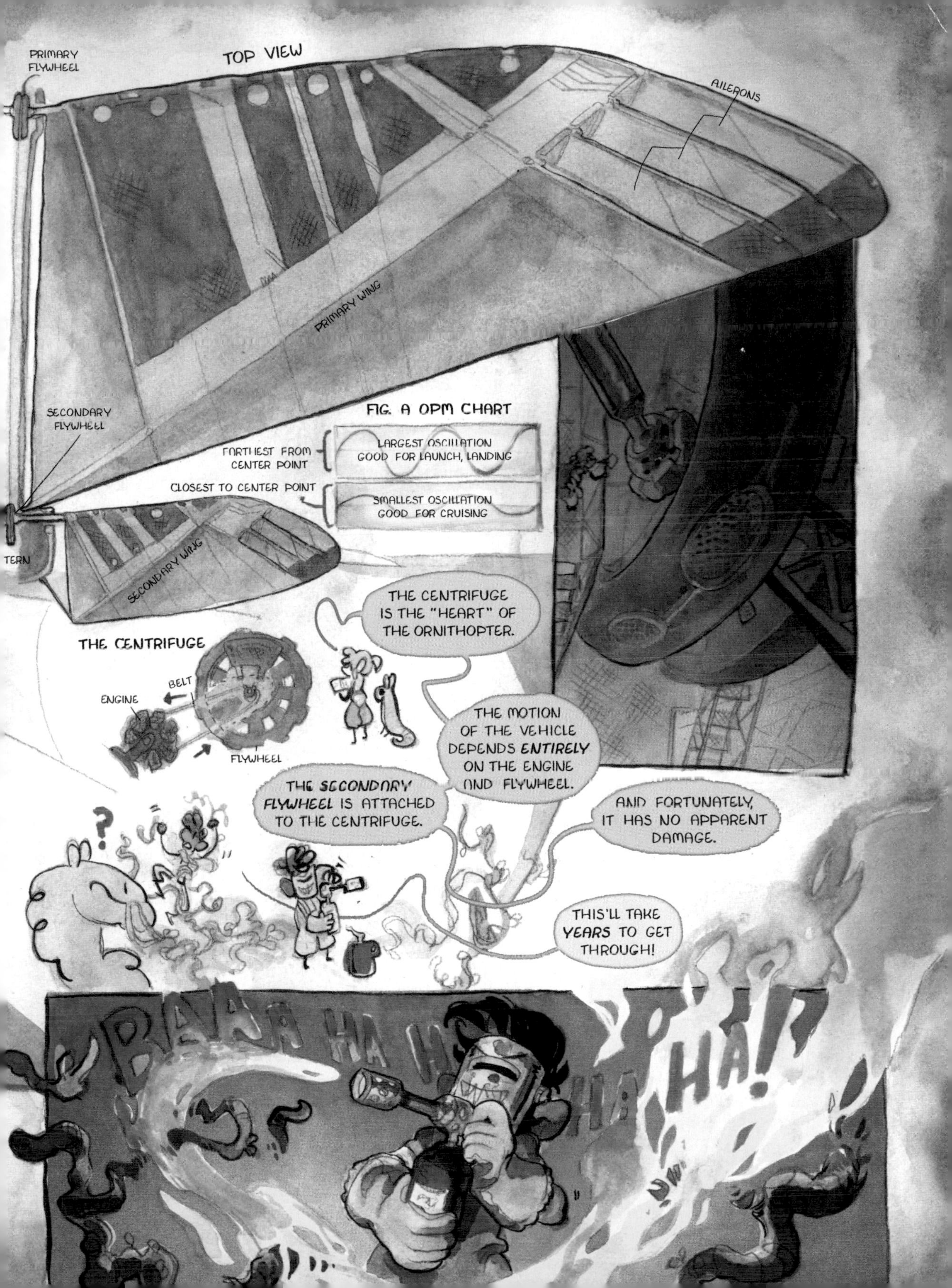
TOP VIEW
PRIMARY FLYWHEEL
AILERONS
PRIMARY WING
SECONDARY FLYWHEEL
FIG. A OPM CHART
FARTHEST FROM CENTER POINT
LARGEST OSCILLATION GOOD FOR LAUNCH, LANDING
CLOSEST TO CENTER POINT
SMALLEST OSCILLATION GOOD FOR CRUISING
TERN
SECONDARY WING
THE CENTRIFUGE IS THE "HEART" OF THE ORNITHOPTER.
THE CENTRIFUGE
BELT
ENGINE
FLYWHEEL
THE MOTION OF THE VEHICLE DEPENDS ENTIRELY ON THE ENGINE AND FLYWHEEL.
THE SECONDARY FLYWHEEL IS ATTACHED TO THE CENTRIFUGE.
AND FORTUNATELY, IT HAS NO APPARENT DAMAGE.
THIS'LL TAKE YEARS TO GET THROUGH!
BAHA HA HA HA HA!

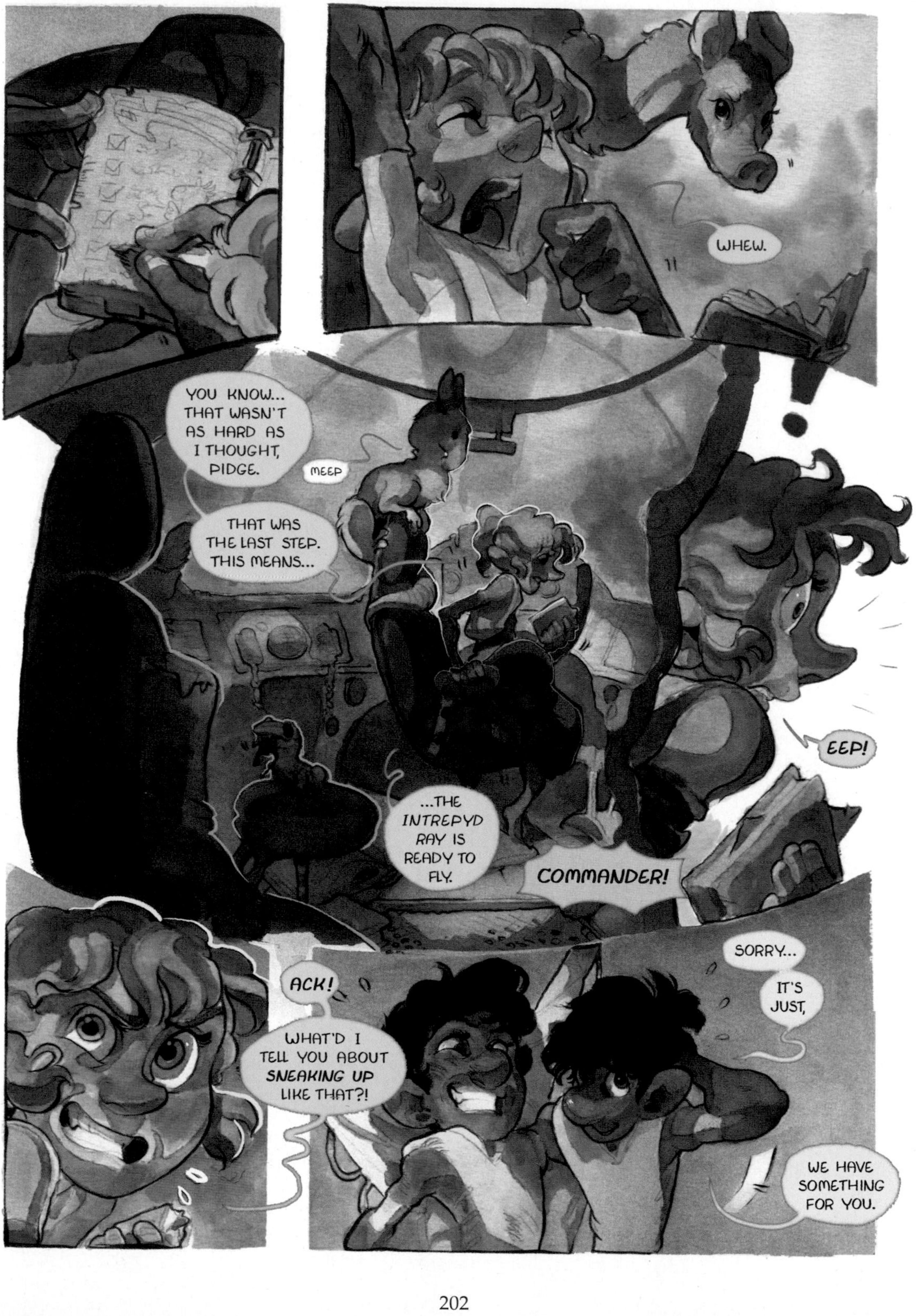
WHEW.
YOU KNOW... THAT WASN'T AS HARD AS I THOUGHT, PIDGE.
MEEP
THAT WAS THE LAST STEP. THIS MEANS...
...THE INTREPYD RAY IS READY TO FLY.
EEP!
COMMANDER!
ACK!
WHAT'D I TELL YOU ABOUT SNEAKING UP LIKE THAT?!
SORRY...
IT'S JUST,
WE HAVE SOMETHING FOR YOU.

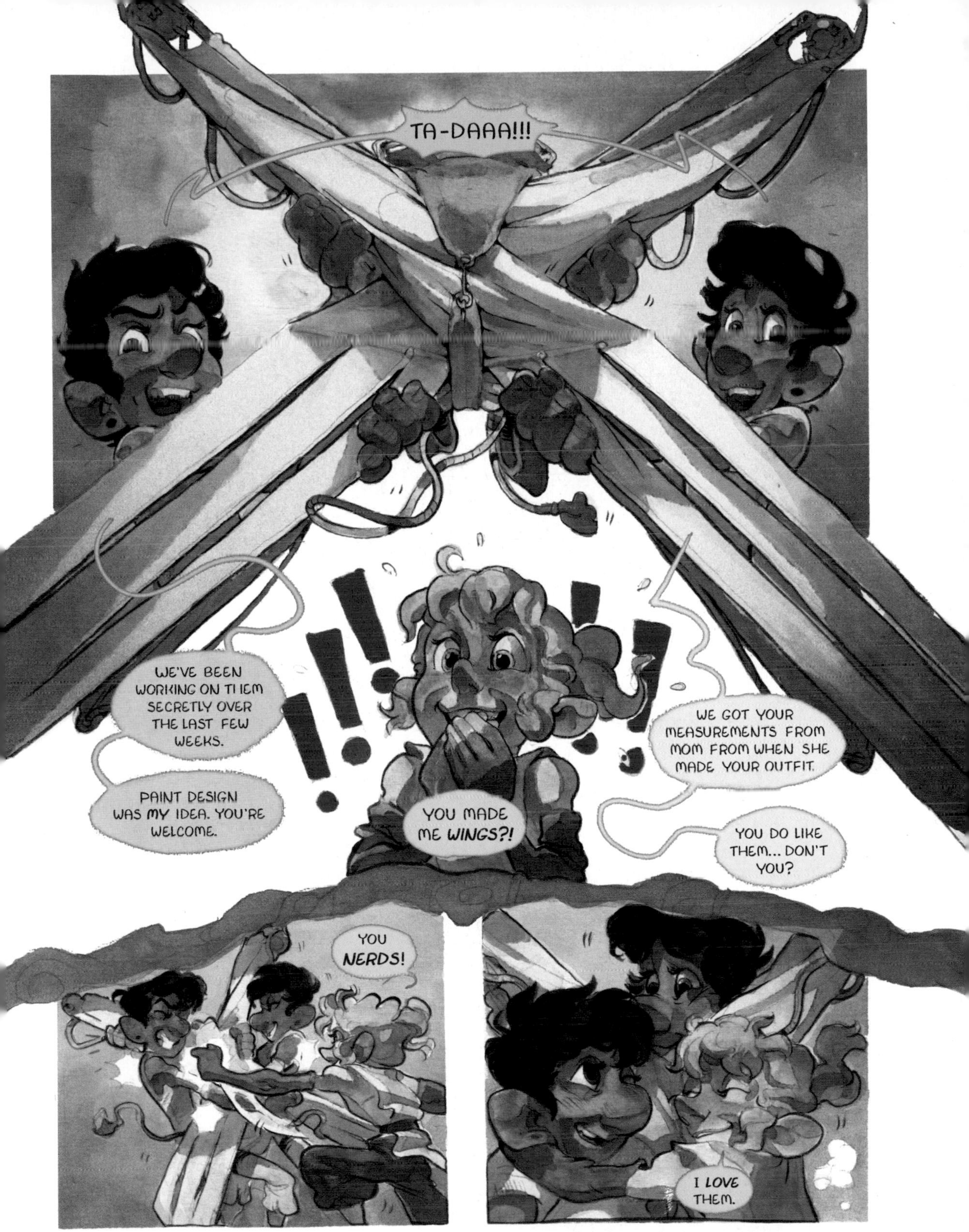
TA-DAAA!!!
WE'VE BEEN WORKING ON THEM SECRETLY OVER THE LAST FEW WEEKS.
PAINT DESIGN WAS MY IDEA. YOU'RE WELCOME.
YOU MADE ME WINGS?!
WE GOT YOUR MEASUREMENTS FROM MOM FROM WHEN SHE MADE YOUR OUTFIT.
YOU DO LIKE THEM... DON'T YOU?
YOU NERDS!
I LOVE THEM.

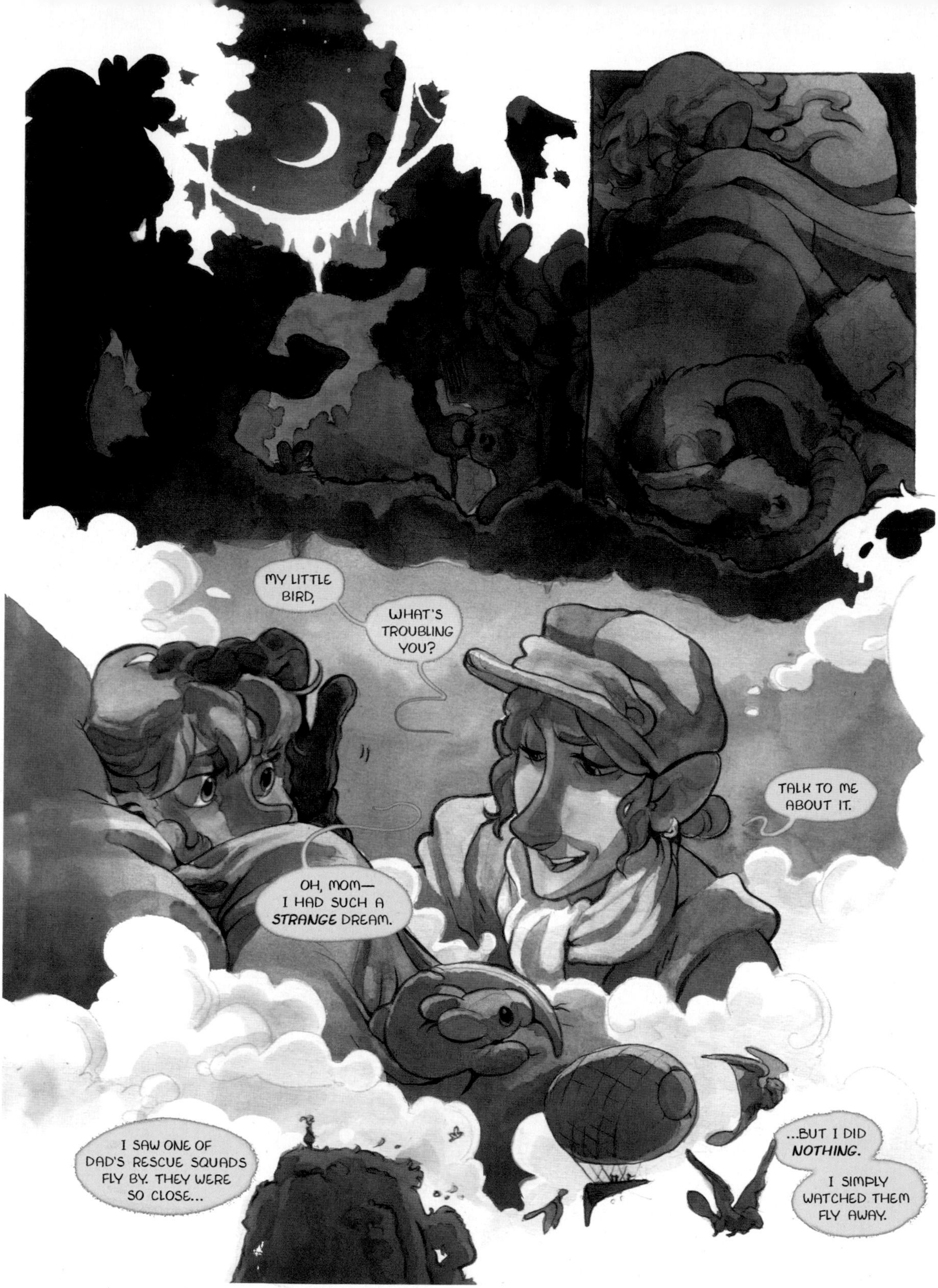
MY LITTLE BIRD,
WHAT'S TROUBLING YOU?
TALK TO ME ABOUT IT.
OH, MOM— I HAD SUCH A *STRANGE* DREAM.
I SAW ONE OF DAD'S RESCUE SQUADS FLY BY. THEY WERE SO CLOSE...
...BUT I DID *NOTHING.*
I SIMPLY WATCHED THEM FLY AWAY.

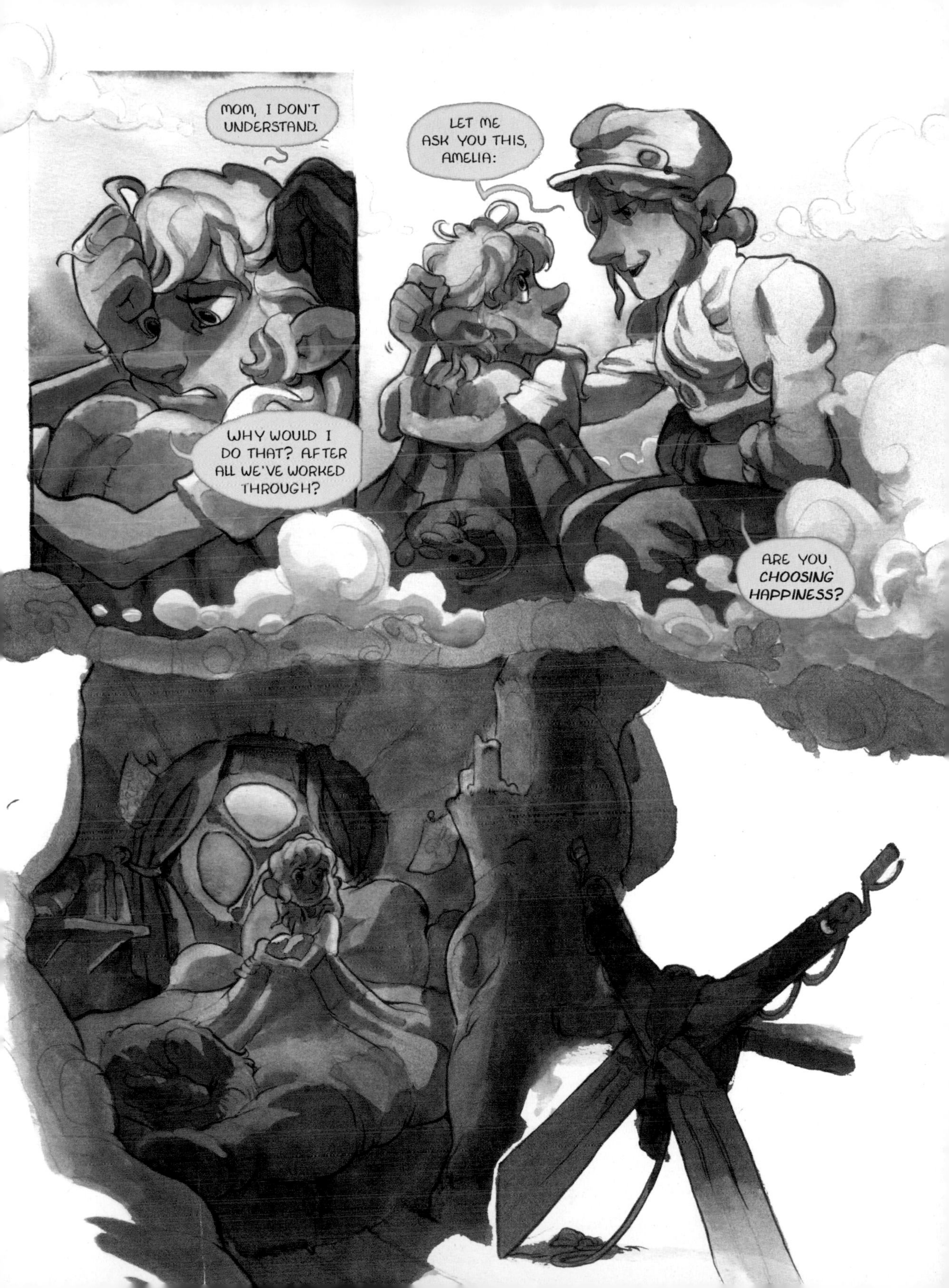
MOM, I DON'T UNDERSTAND.
LET ME ASK YOU THIS, AMELIA:
WHY WOULD I DO THAT? AFTER ALL WE'VE WORKED THROUGH?
ARE YOU CHOOSING HAPPINESS?

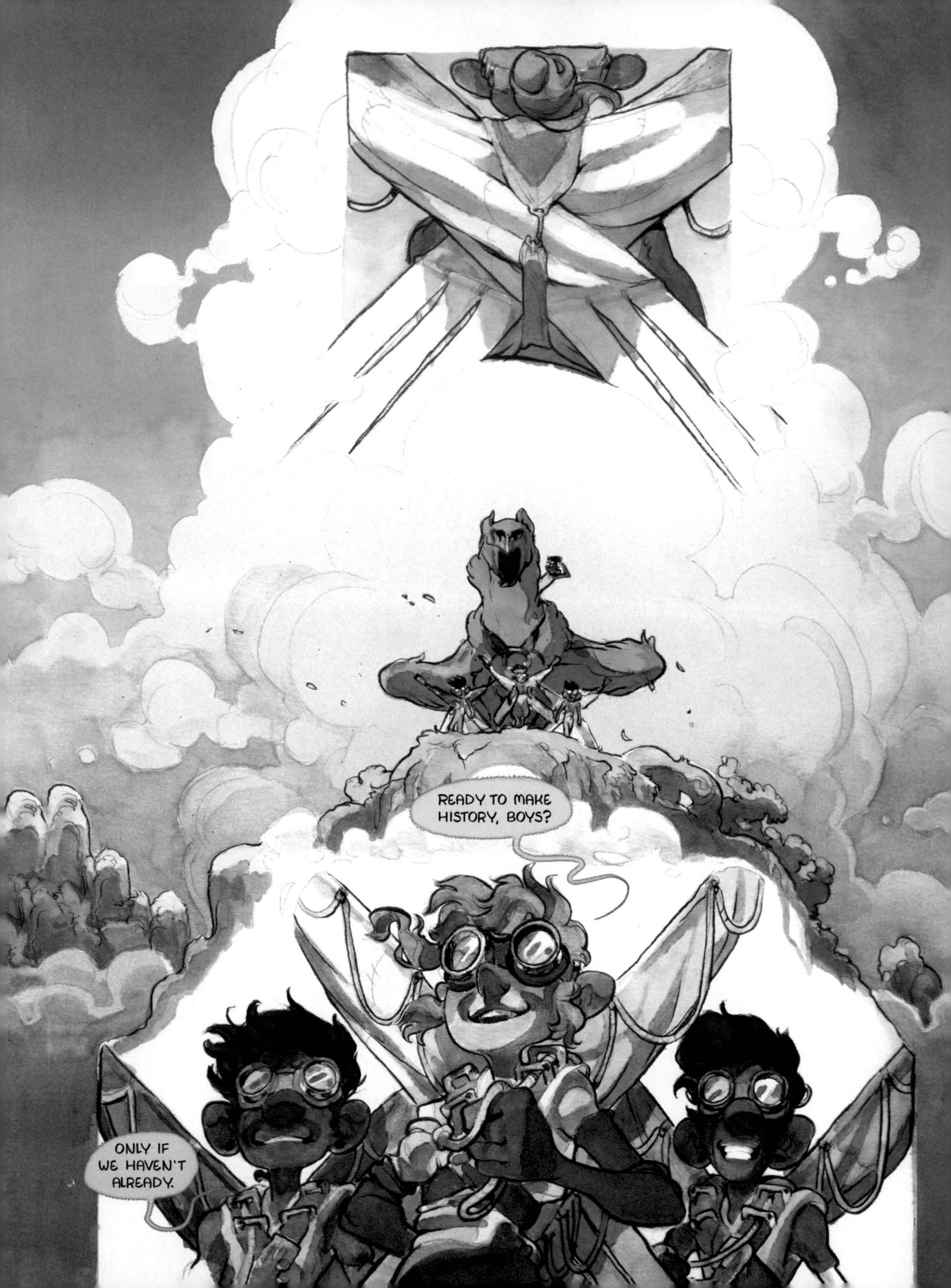
READY TO MAKE HISTORY, BOYS?
ONLY IF WE HAVEN'T ALREADY.

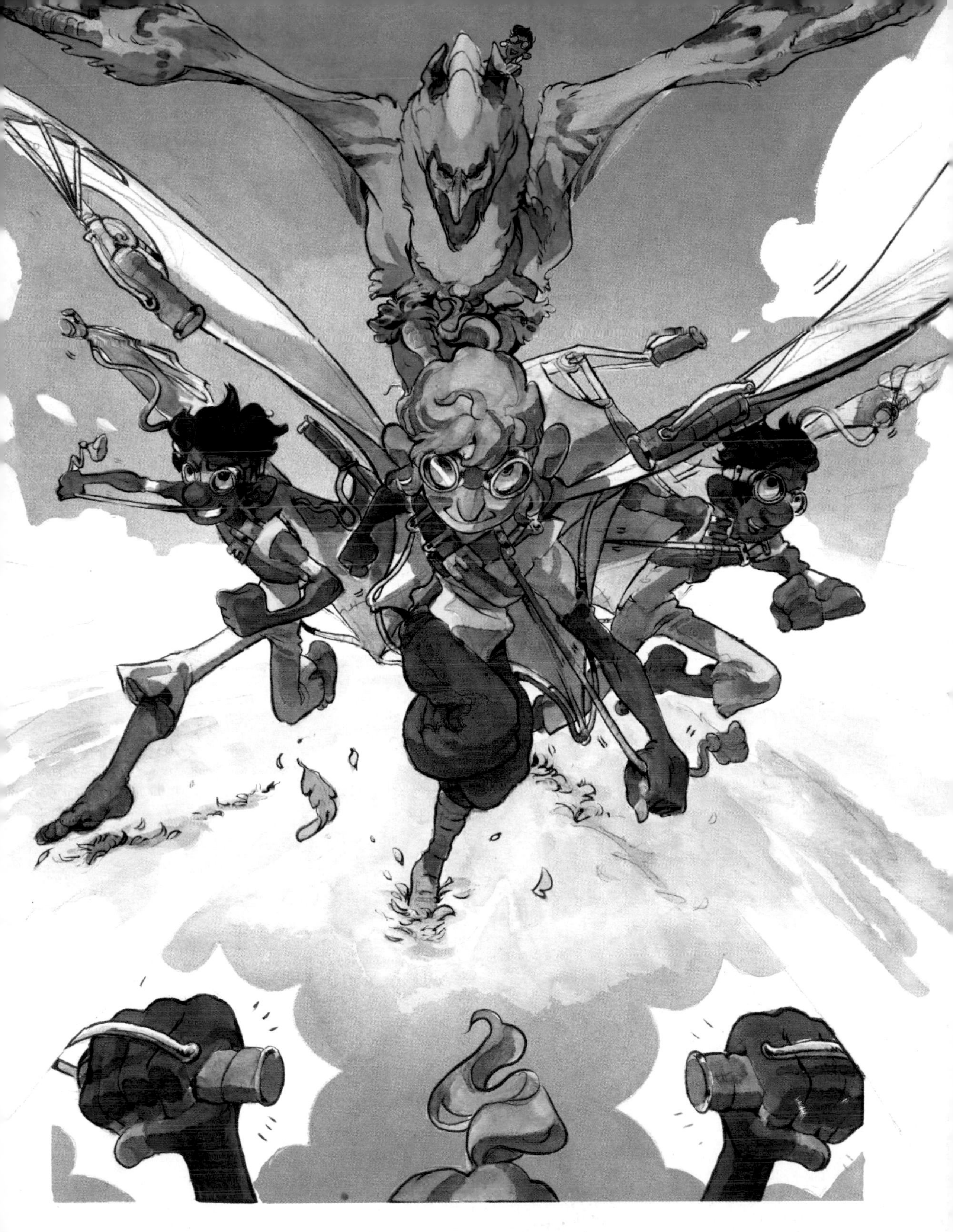

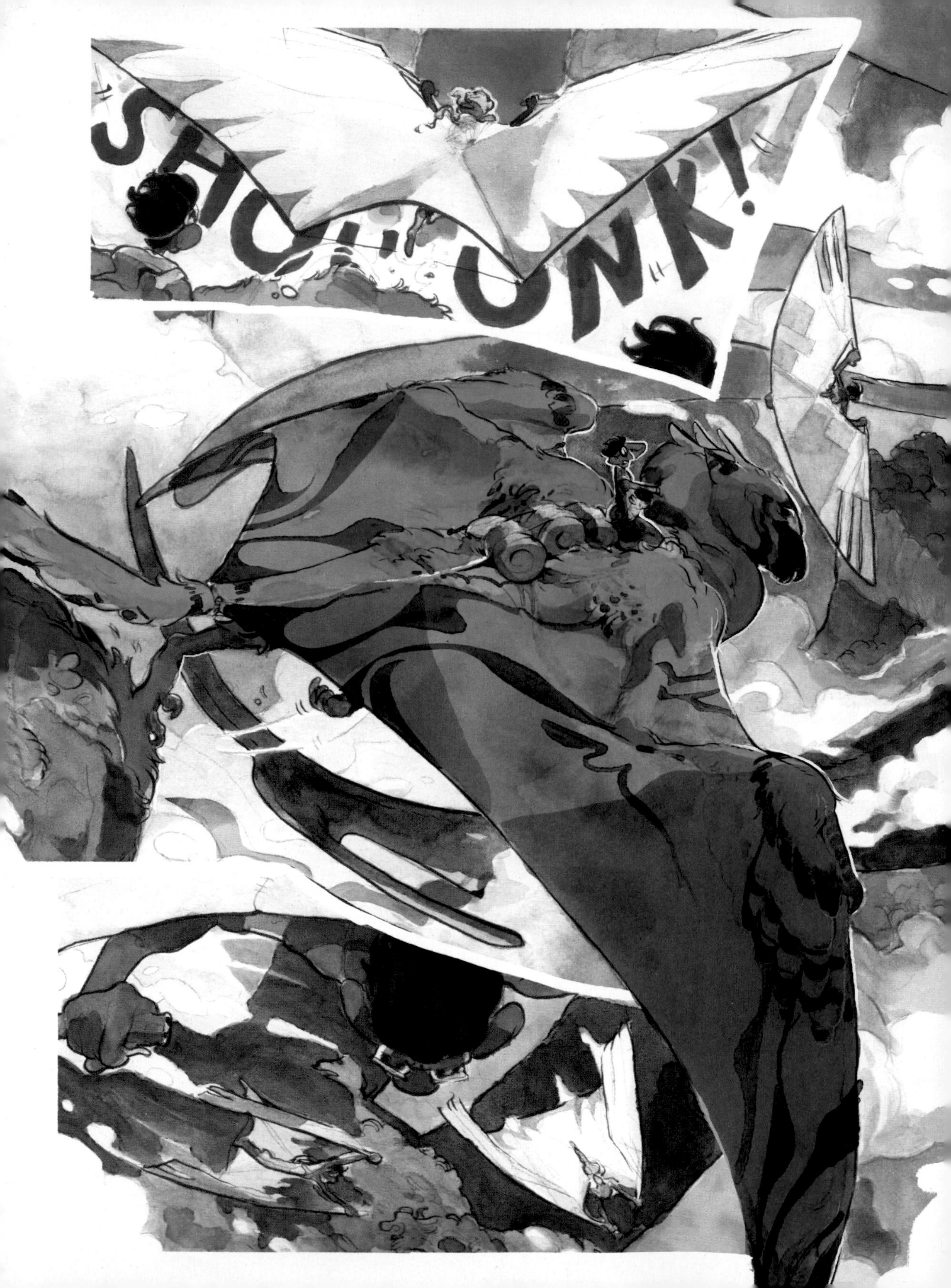
SHOOONK!

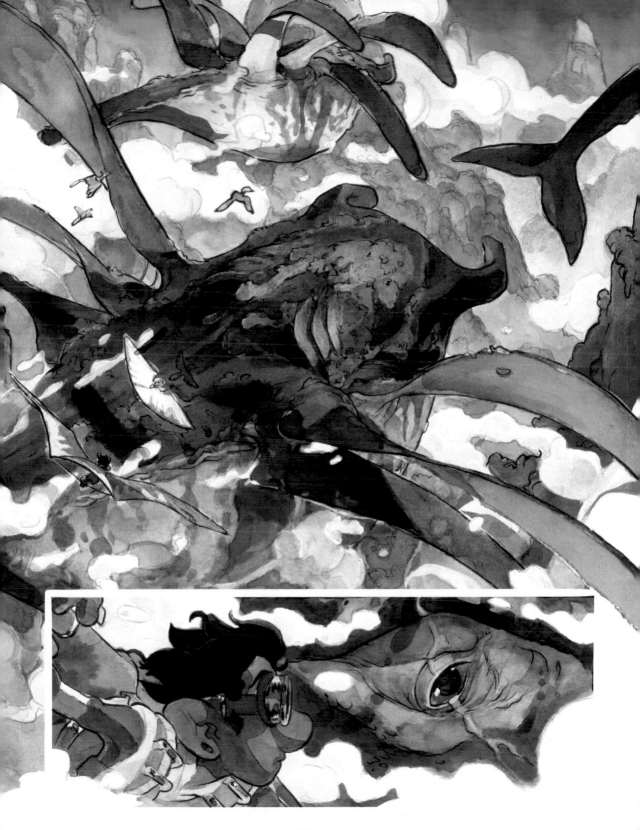

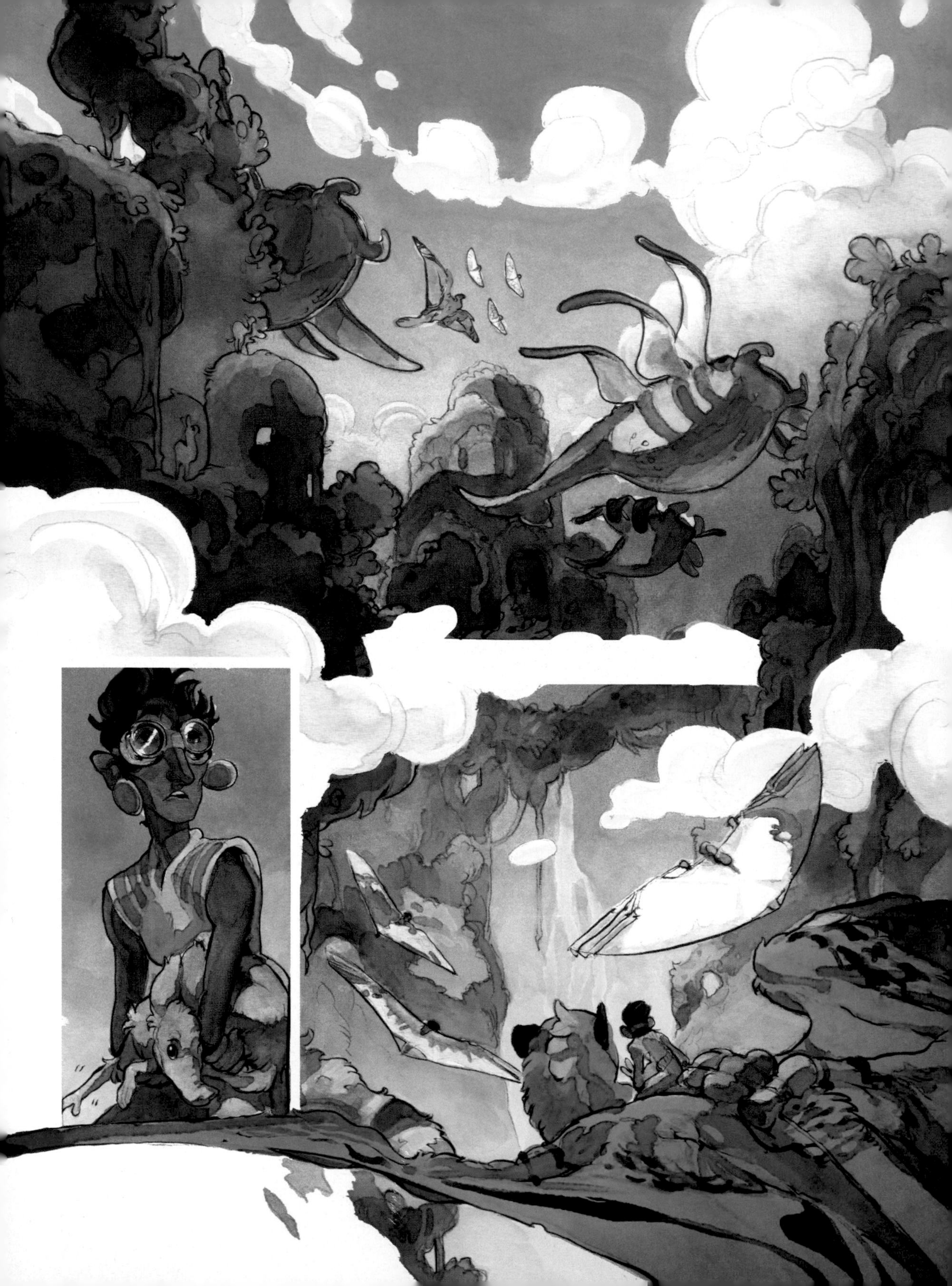

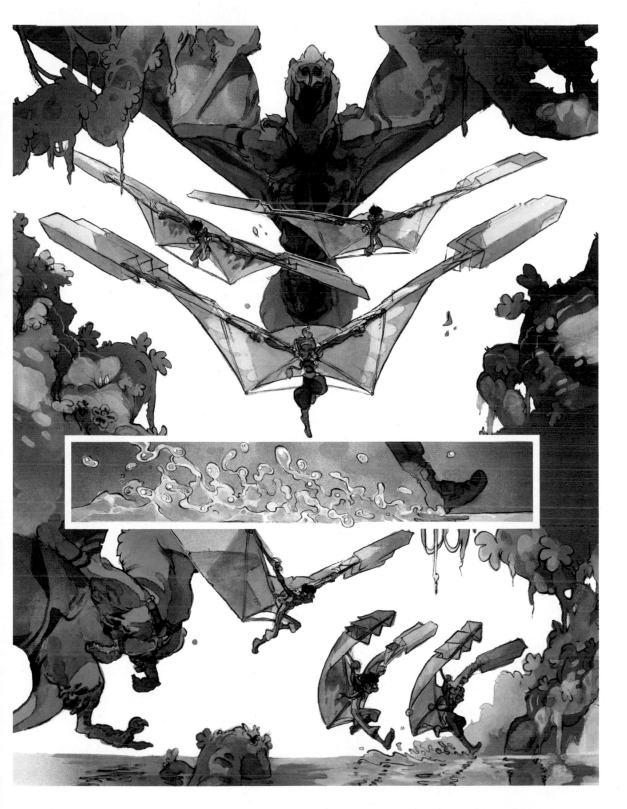

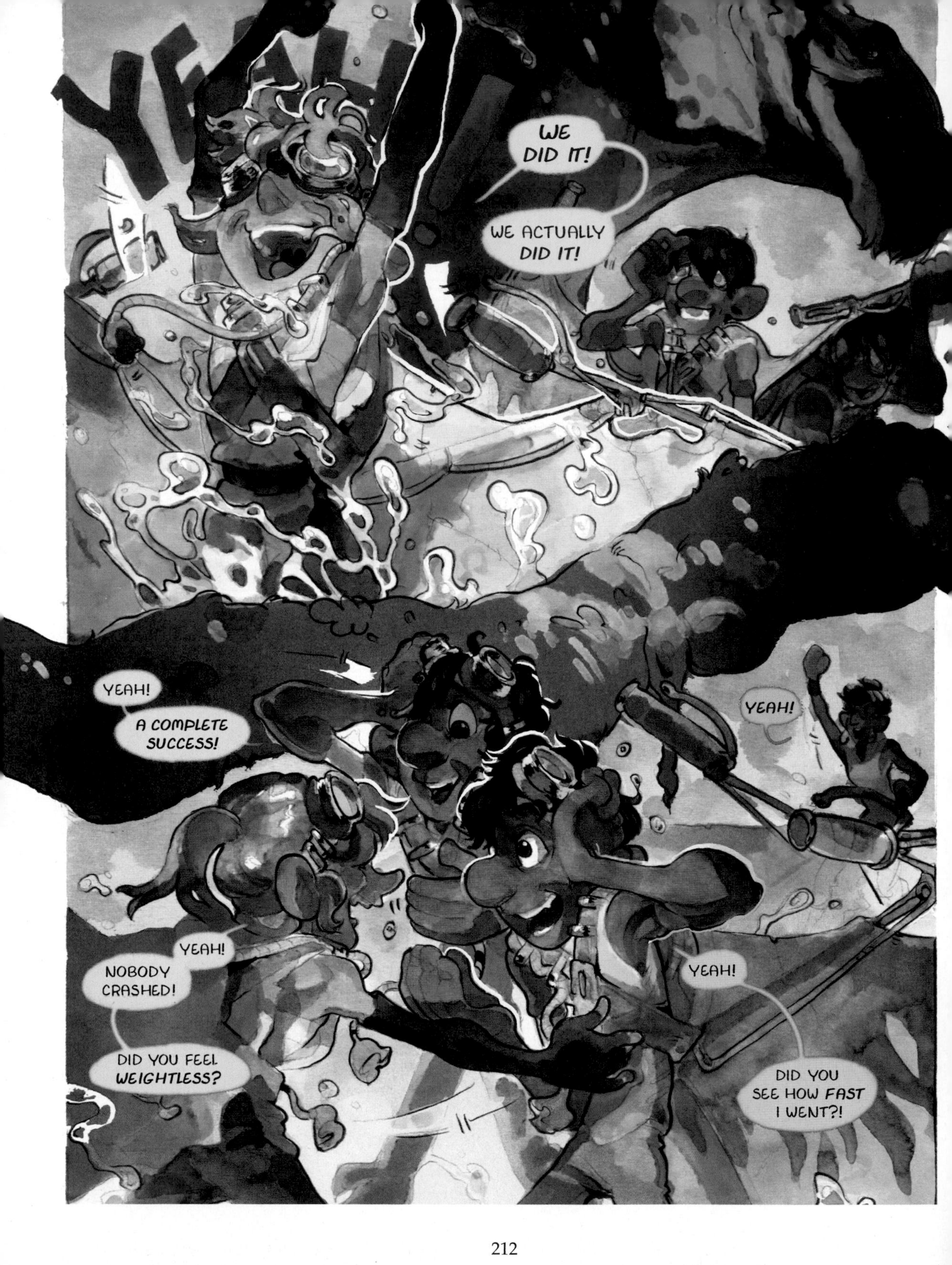
YEAH!
WE DID IT!
WE ACTUALLY DID IT!
YEAH!
A COMPLETE SUCCESS!
YEAH!
YEAH!
NOBODY CRASHED!
DID YOU FEEL WEIGHTLESS?
YEAH!
DID YOU SEE HOW FAST I WENT?!

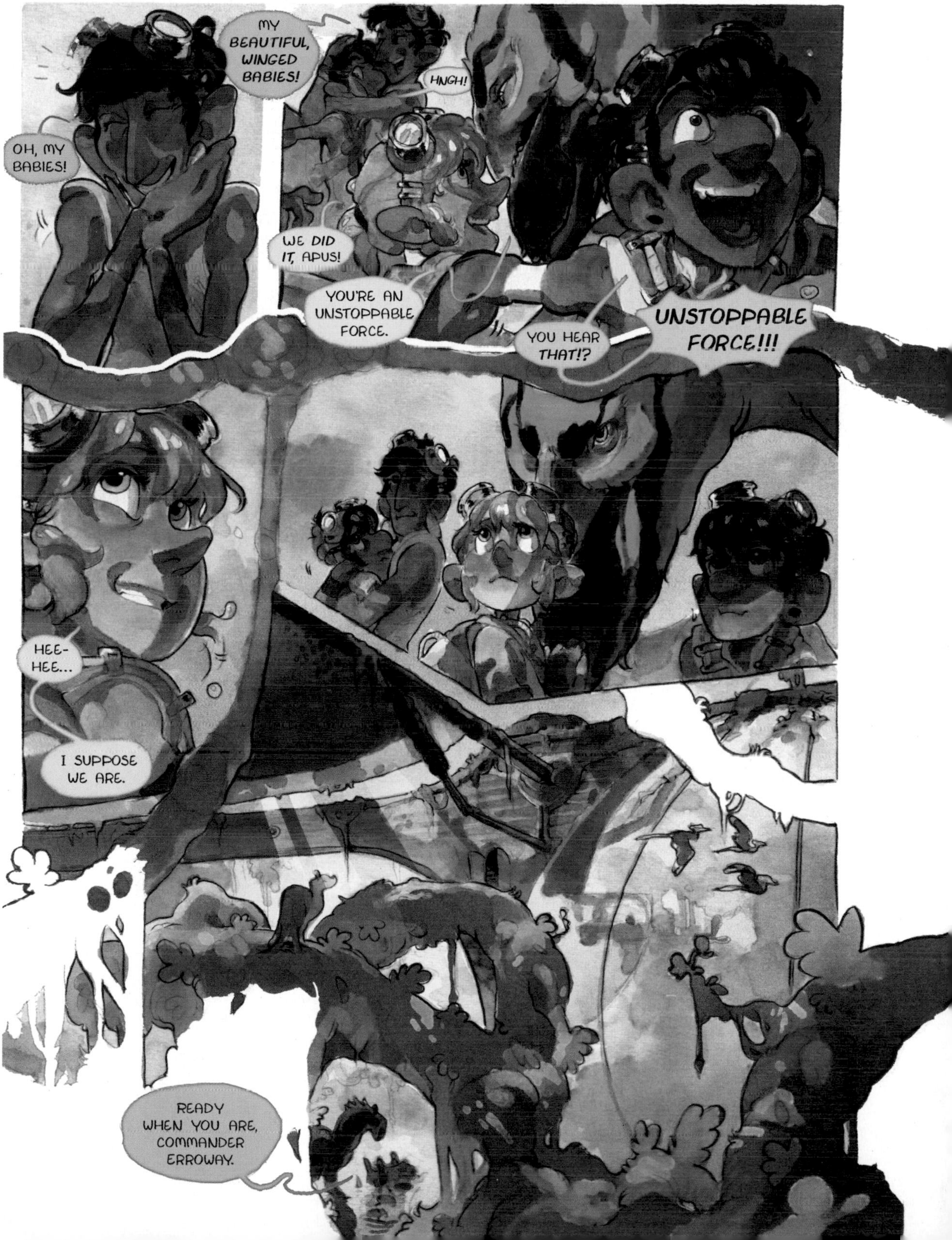
OH, MY BABIES!
MY BEAUTIFUL, WINGED BABIES!
HNGH!
WE DID IT, APUS!
YOU'RE AN UNSTOPPABLE FORCE.
YOU HEAR THAT!?
UNSTOPPABLE FORCE!!!
HEE-HEE...
I SUPPOSE WE ARE.
READY WHEN YOU ARE, COMMANDER ERROWAY.

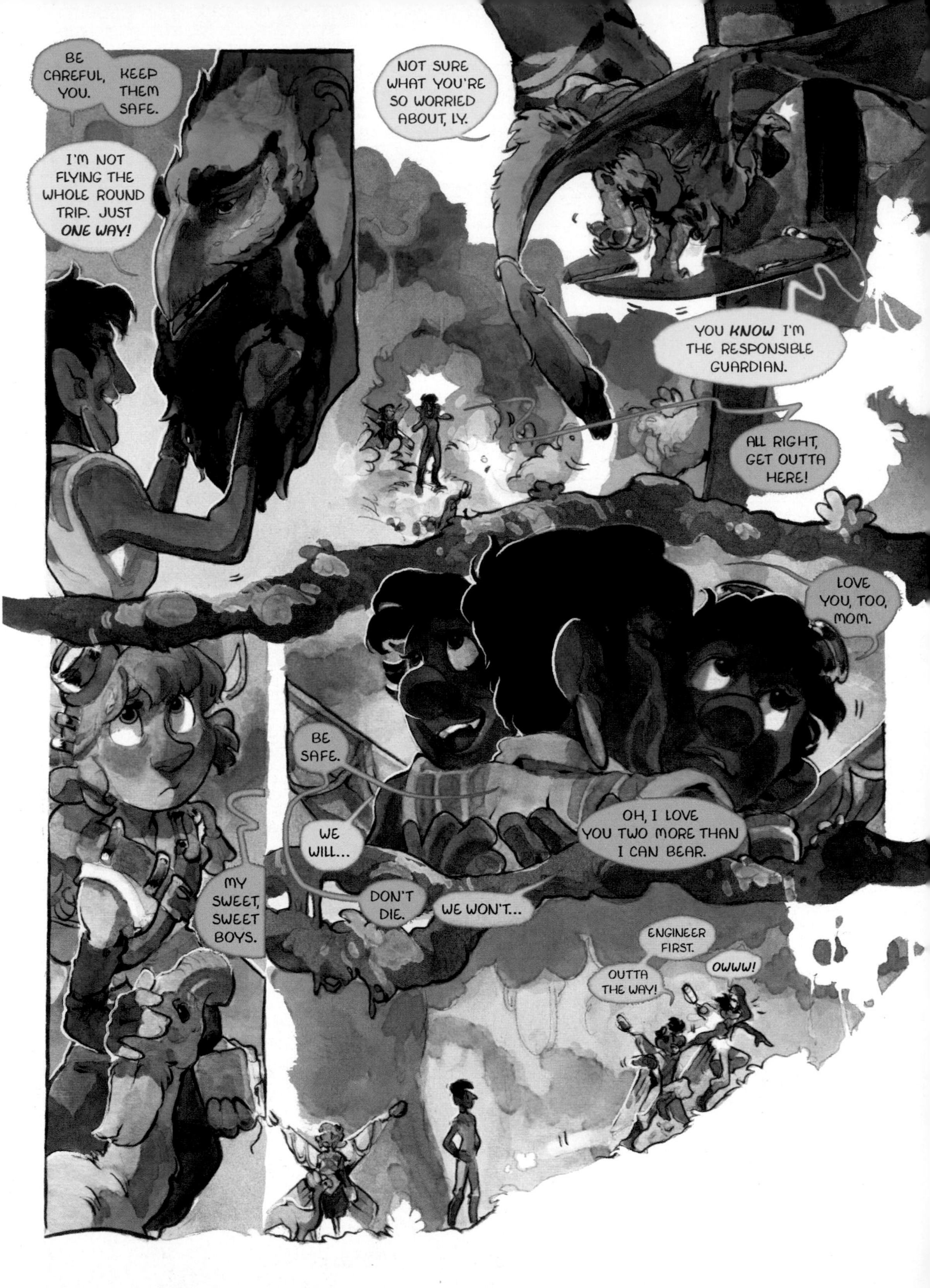
BE CAREFUL, YOU.
KEEP THEM SAFE.
I'M NOT FLYING THE WHOLE ROUND TRIP. JUST *ONE WAY!*
NOT SURE WHAT YOU'RE SO WORRIED ABOUT, LY.
YOU *KNOW* I'M THE RESPONSIBLE GUARDIAN.
ALL RIGHT, GET OUTTA HERE!
LOVE YOU, TOO, MOM.
BE SAFE.
WE WILL...
OH, I LOVE YOU TWO MORE THAN I CAN BEAR.
DON'T DIE.
WE WON'T...
MY SWEET, SWEET BOYS.
ENGINEER FIRST.
OUTTA THE WAY!
OWWW!

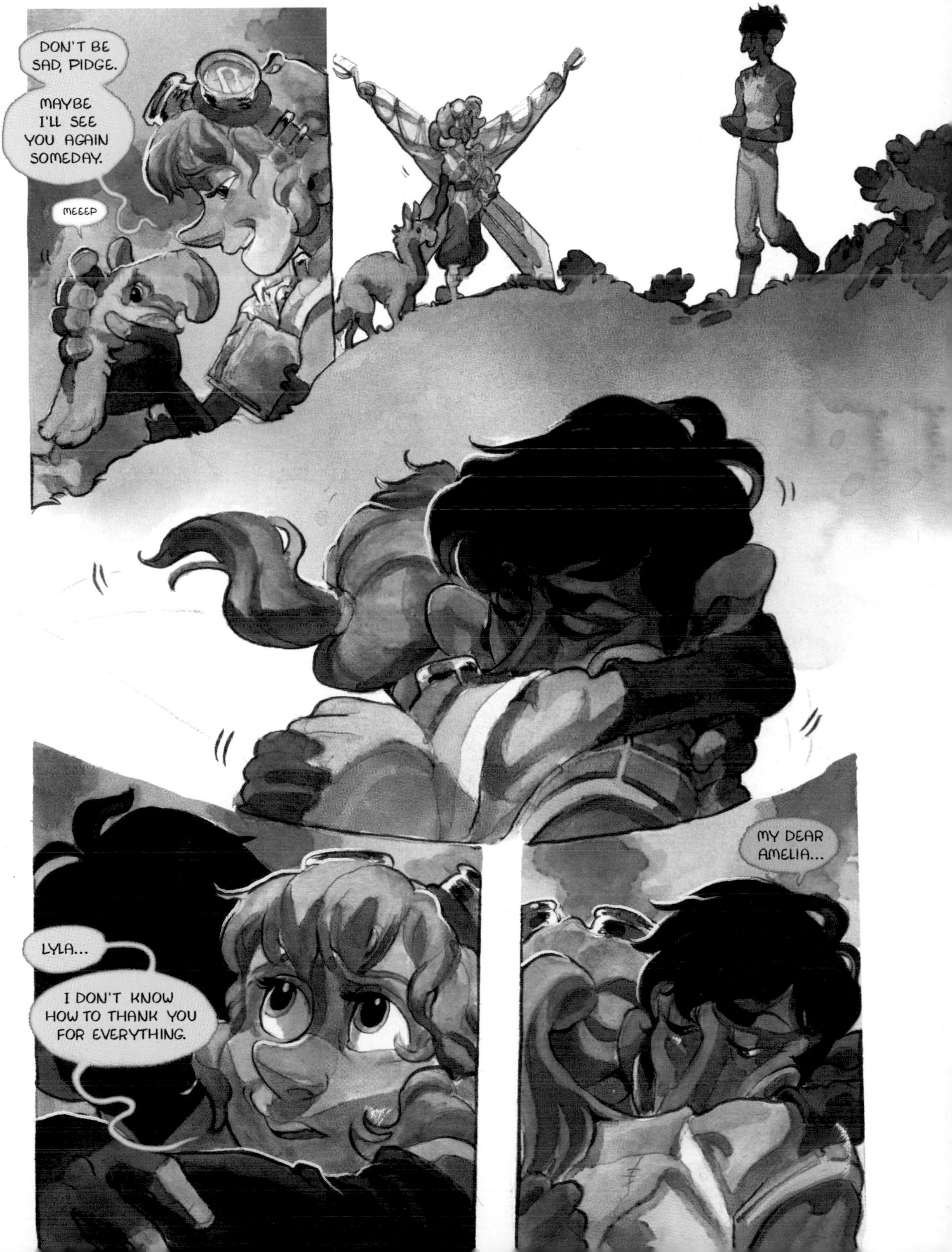
DON'T BE SAD, PIDGE.
MAYBE I'LL SEE YOU AGAIN SOMEDAY.
MEEEP
LYLA...
I DON'T KNOW HOW TO THANK YOU FOR EVERYTHING.
MY DEAR AMELIA...

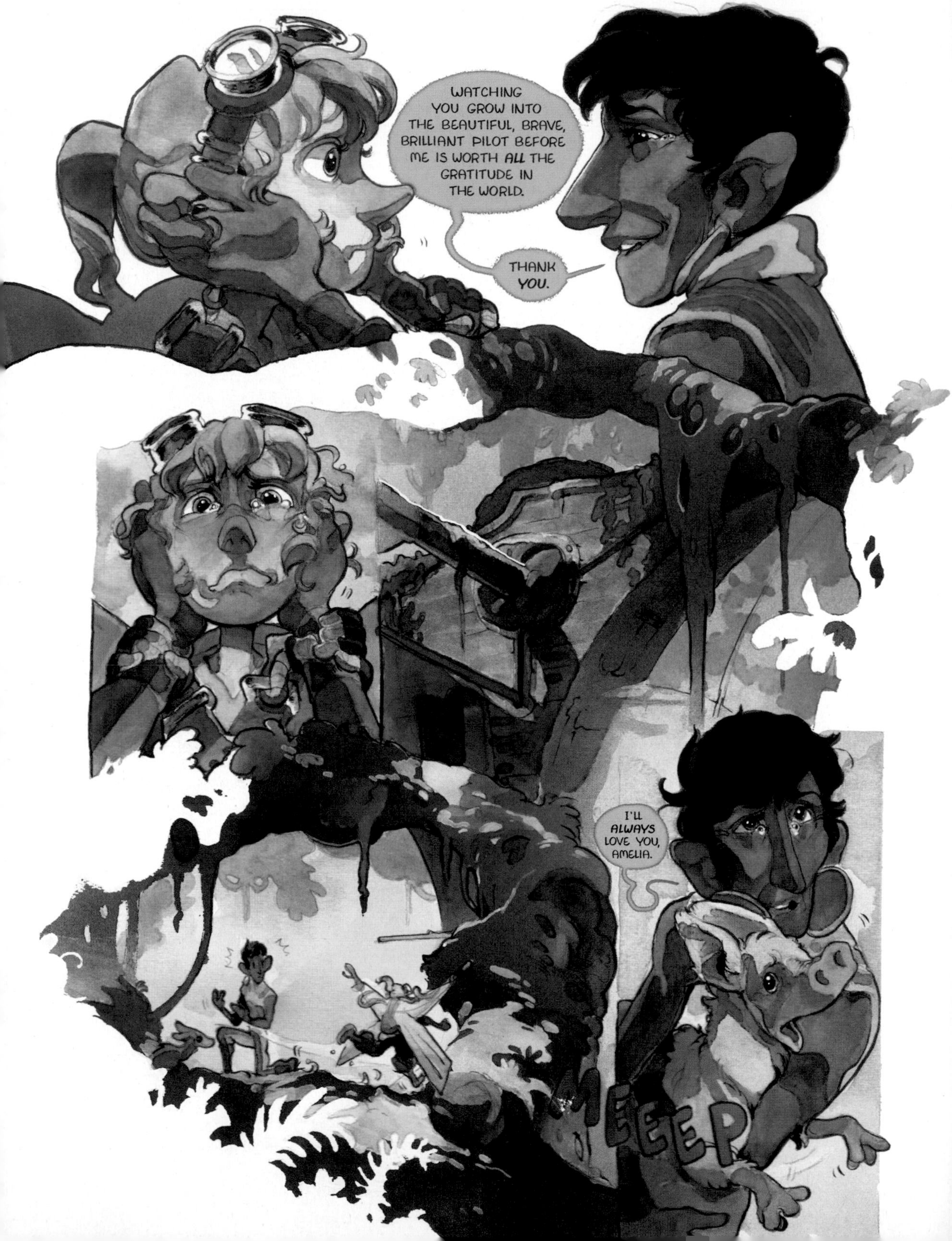
WATCHING YOU GROW INTO THE BEAUTIFUL, BRAVE, BRILLIANT PILOT BEFORE ME IS WORTH ALL THE GRATITUDE IN THE WORLD.
THANK YOU.
I'LL ALWAYS LOVE YOU, AMELIA.
MEEEP

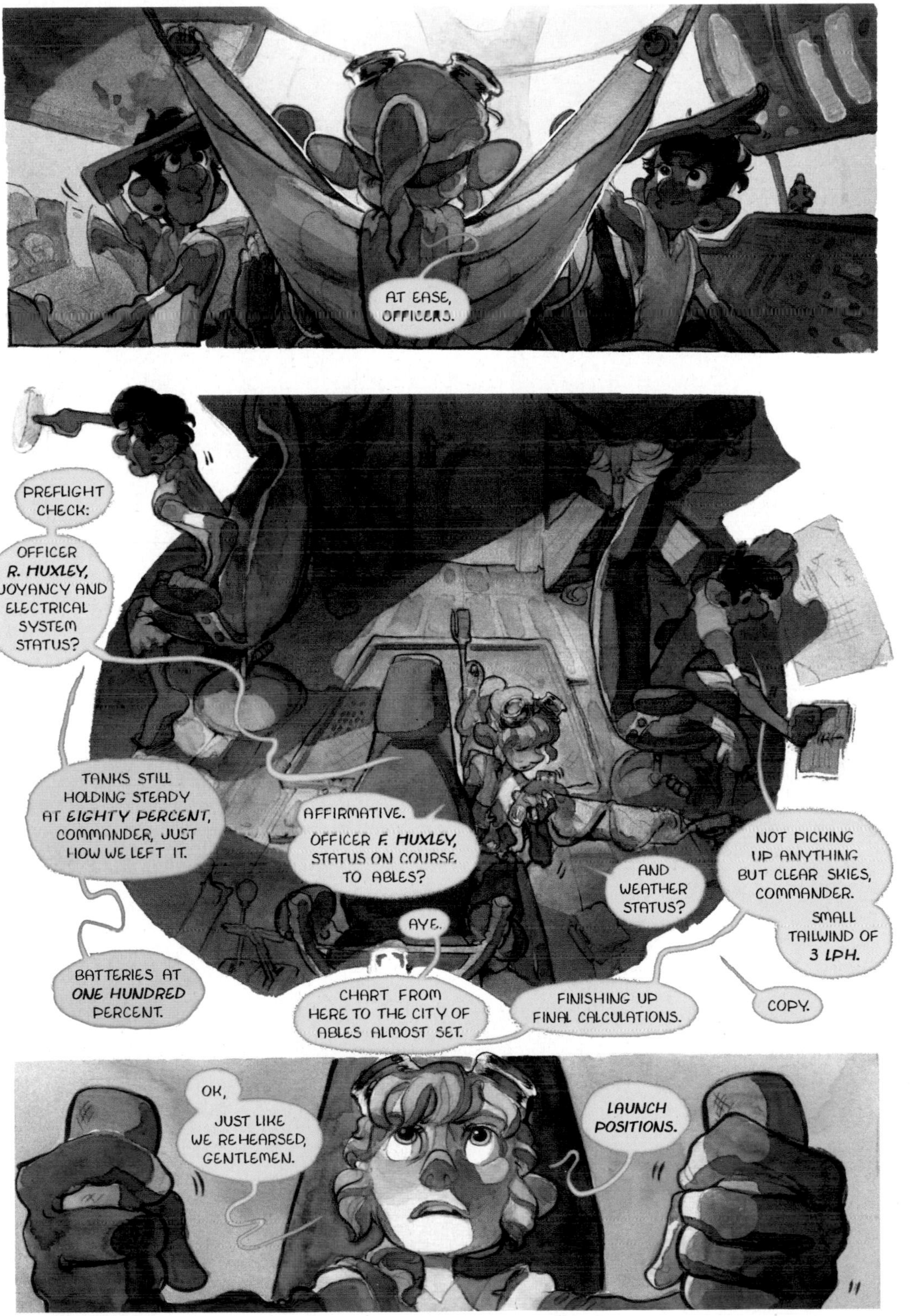
AT EASE, OFFICERS.
PREFLIGHT CHECK:
OFFICER **R. HUXLEY,** BUOYANCY AND ELECTRICAL SYSTEM STATUS?
TANKS STILL HOLDING STEADY AT ***EIGHTY PERCENT,*** COMMANDER, JUST HOW WE LEFT IT.
BATTERIES AT ***ONE HUNDRED*** PERCENT.
AFFIRMATIVE.
OFFICER F. **HUXLEY,** STATUS ON COURSE TO ABLES?
AYE.
CHART FROM HERE TO THE CITY OF ABLES ALMOST SET.
AND WEATHER STATUS?
FINISHING UP FINAL CALCULATIONS.
NOT PICKING UP ANYTHING BUT CLEAR SKIES, COMMANDER.
SMALL TAILWIND OF ***3 LPH.***
COPY.
OK,
JUST LIKE WE REHEARSED, GENTLEMEN.
LAUNCH POSITIONS.

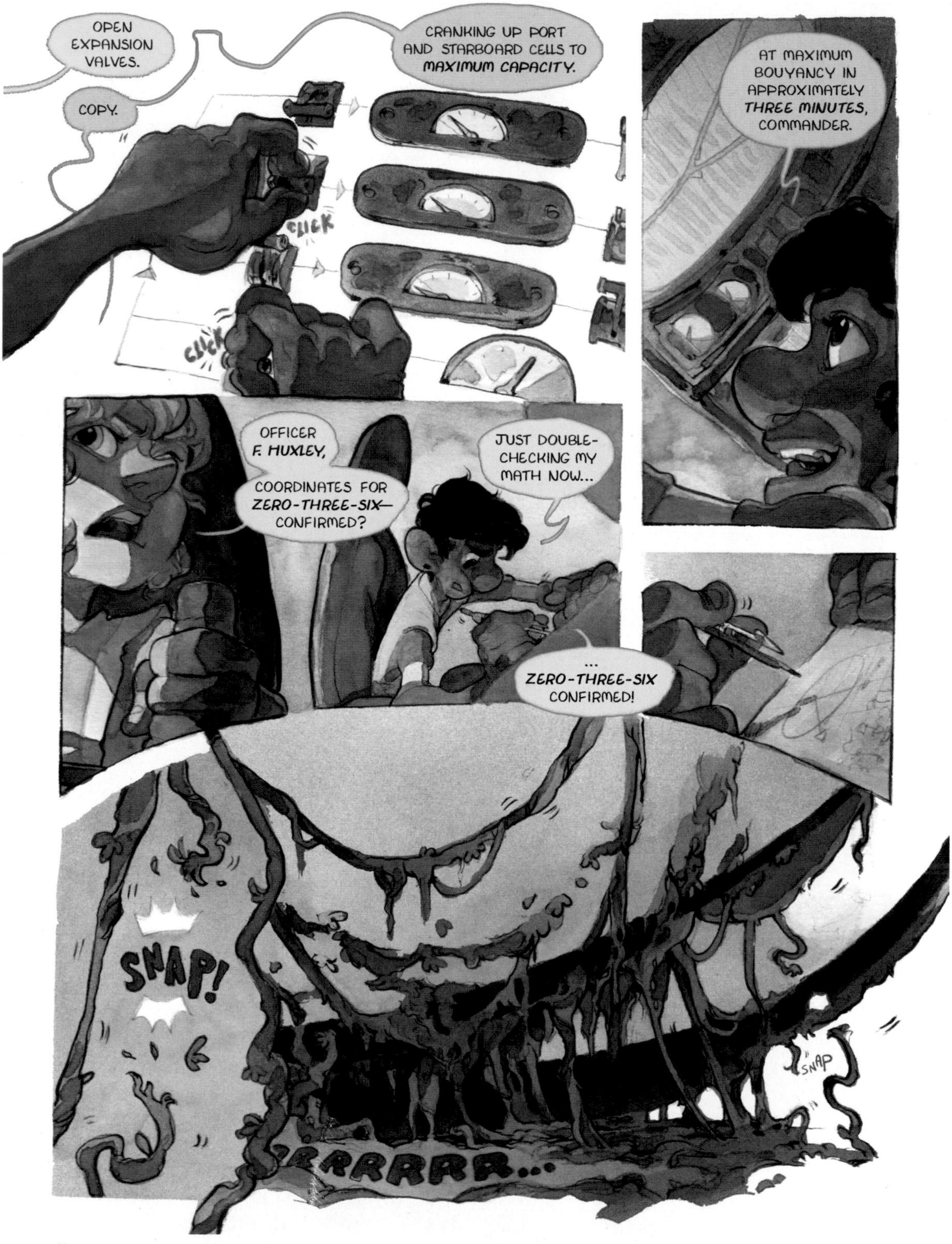
OPEN EXPANSION VALVES.
COPY.
CRANKING UP PORT AND STARBOARD CELLS TO MAXIMUM CAPACITY.
CLICK
CLICK
AT MAXIMUM BOUYANCY IN APPROXIMATELY THREE MINUTES, COMMANDER.
OFFICER F. HUXLEY,
COORDINATES FOR ZERO-THREE-SIX— CONFIRMED?
JUST DOUBLE-CHECKING MY MATH NOW...
... ZERO-THREE-SIX CONFIRMED!
SNAP!
SNAP
RRRRRRR...

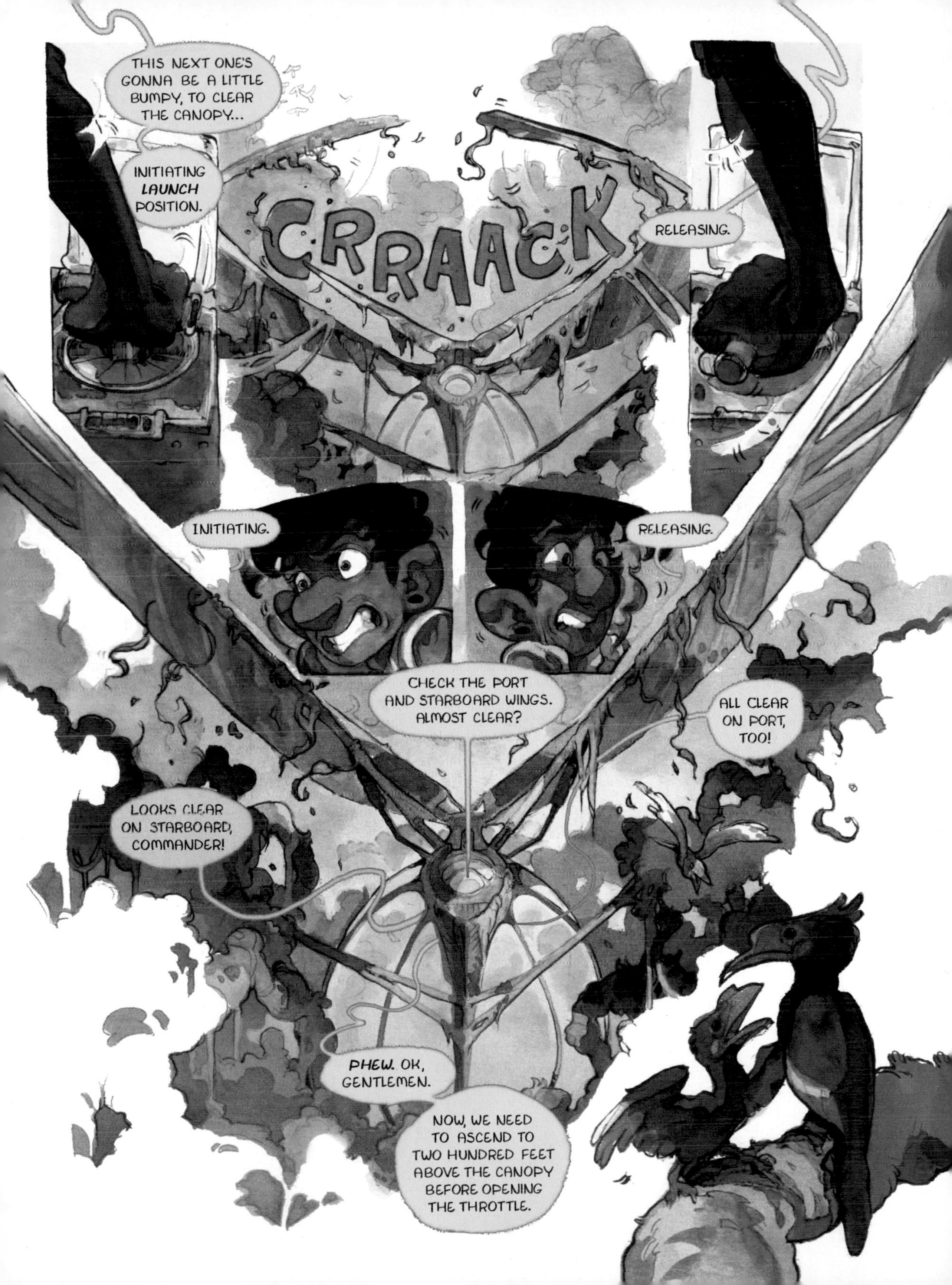
THIS NEXT ONE'S GONNA BE A LITTLE BUMPY, TO CLEAR THE CANOPY...
INITIATING ***LAUNCH*** POSITION.
CRRAACK
RELEASING.
INITIATING.
RELEASING.
CHECK THE PORT AND STARBOARD WINGS. ALMOST CLEAR?
ALL CLEAR ON PORT, TOO!
LOOKS CLEAR ON STARBOARD, COMMANDER!
PHEW. OK, GENTLEMEN.
NOW, WE NEED TO ASCEND TO TWO HUNDRED FEET ABOVE THE CANOPY BEFORE OPENING THE THROTTLE.

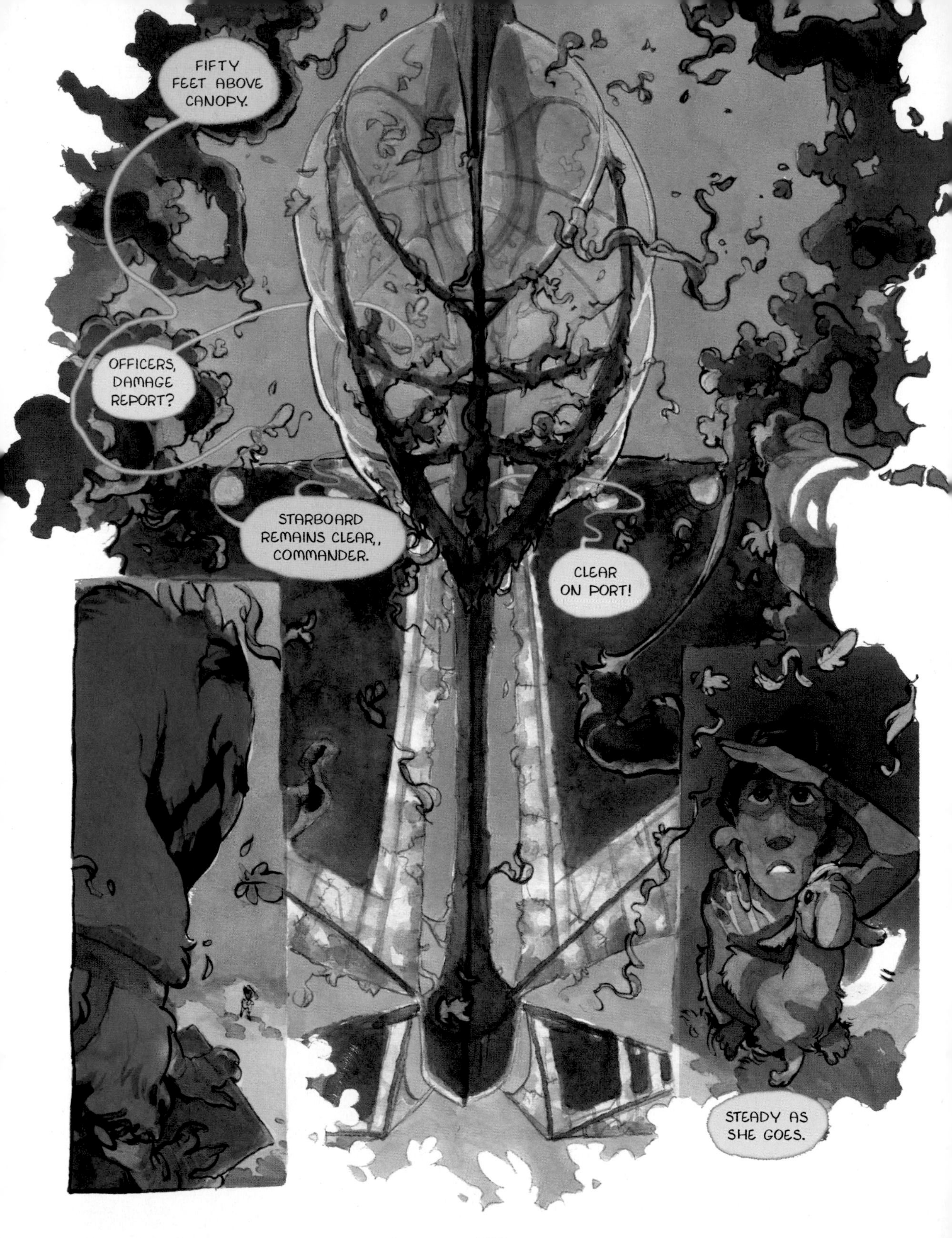
FIFTY FEET ABOVE CANOPY.
OFFICERS, DAMAGE REPORT?
STARBOARD REMAINS CLEAR,, COMMANDER.
CLEAR ON PORT!
STEADY AS SHE GOES.

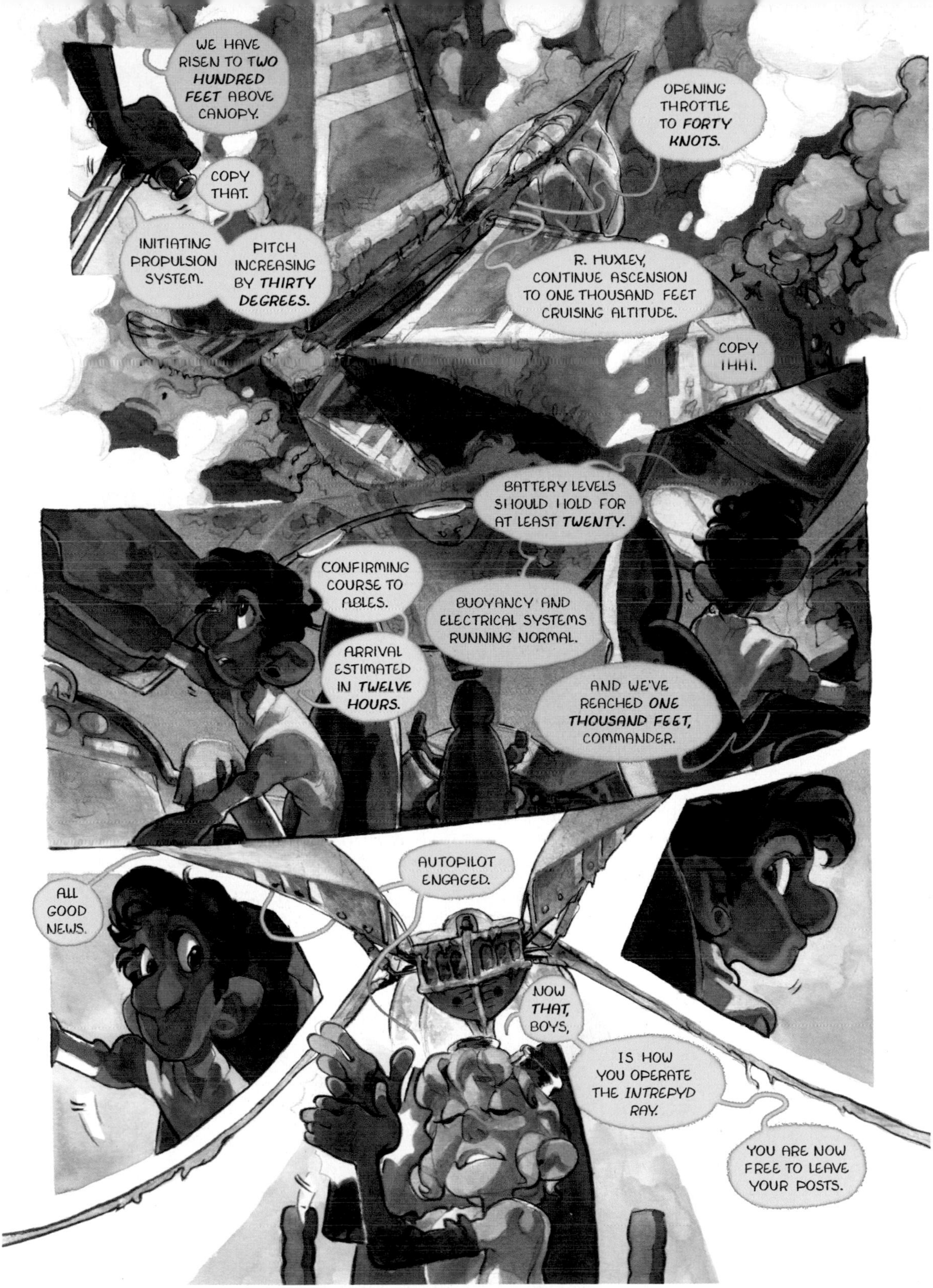
WE HAVE RISEN TO **TWO HUNDRED FEET** ABOVE CANOPY.
OPENING THROTTLE TO **FORTY KNOTS.**
COPY THAT.
INITIATING PROPULSION SYSTEM.
PITCH INCREASING BY **THIRTY DEGREES.**
R. HUXLEY, CONTINUE ASCENSION TO ONE THOUSAND FEET CRUISING ALTITUDE.
COPY THAT.
BATTERY LEVELS SHOULD HOLD FOR AT LEAST **TWENTY.**
CONFIRMING COURSE TO ABLES.
BUOYANCY AND ELECTRICAL SYSTEMS RUNNING NORMAL.
ARRIVAL ESTIMATED IN **TWELVE HOURS.**
AND WE'VE REACHED **ONE THOUSAND FEET,** COMMANDER.
ALL GOOD NEWS.
AUTOPILOT ENGAGED.
NOW **THAT,** BOYS,
IS HOW YOU OPERATE THE *INTREPYD RAY.*
YOU ARE NOW FREE TO LEAVE YOUR POSTS.

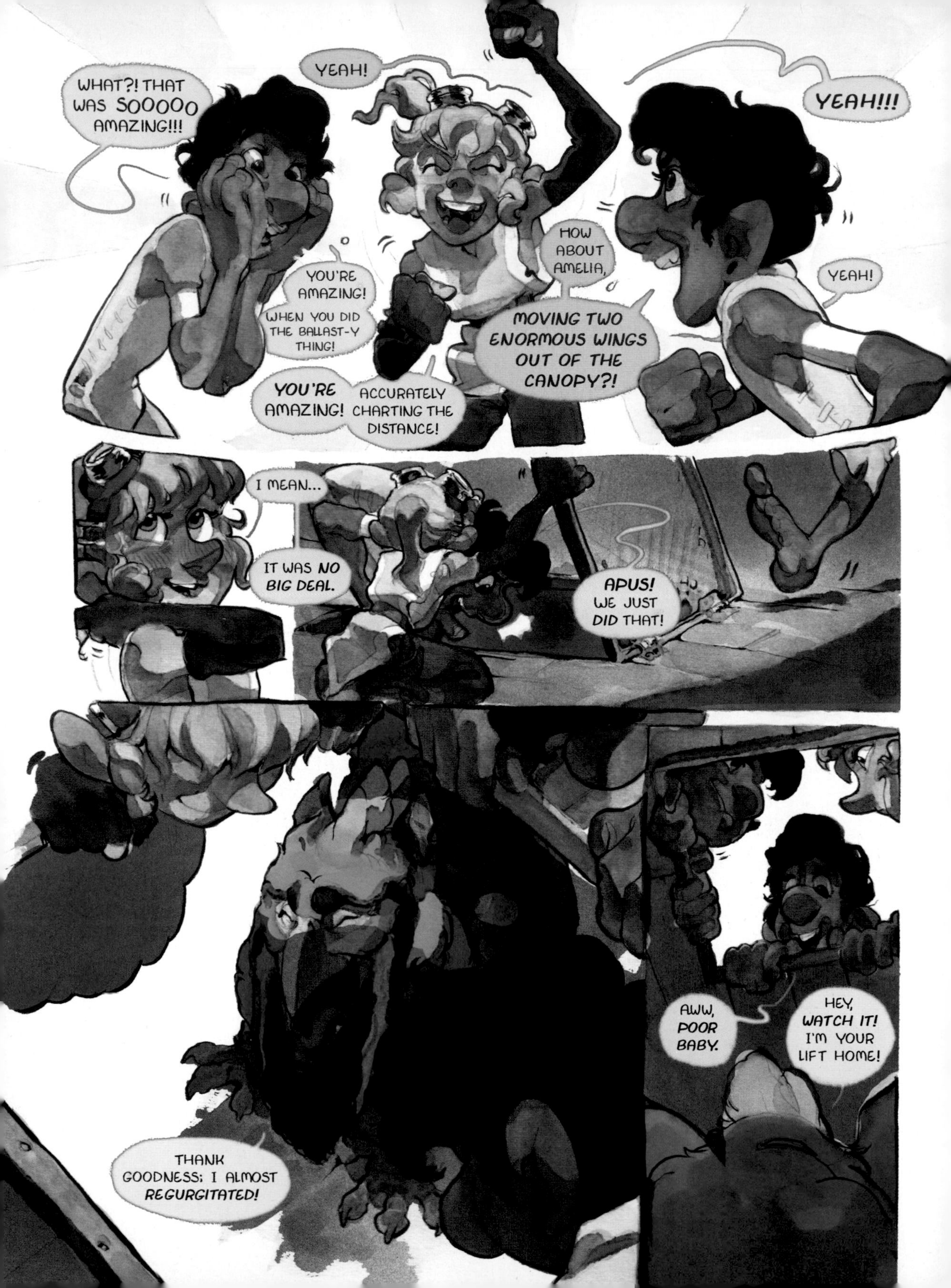

WHAT?! THAT WAS SOOOOO AMAZING!!!
YEAH!
YEAH!!!
YOU'RE AMAZING!
WHEN YOU DID THE BALLAST-Y THING!
HOW ABOUT AMELIA,
MOVING TWO ENORMOUS WINGS OUT OF THE CANOPY?!
YEAH!
YOU'RE AMAZING!
ACCURATELY CHARTING THE DISTANCE!
I MEAN...
IT WAS NO BIG DEAL.
APUS! WE JUST DID THAT!
AWW, POOR BABY.
HEY, WATCH IT! I'M YOUR LIFT HOME!
THANK GOODNESS; I ALMOST REGURGITATED!

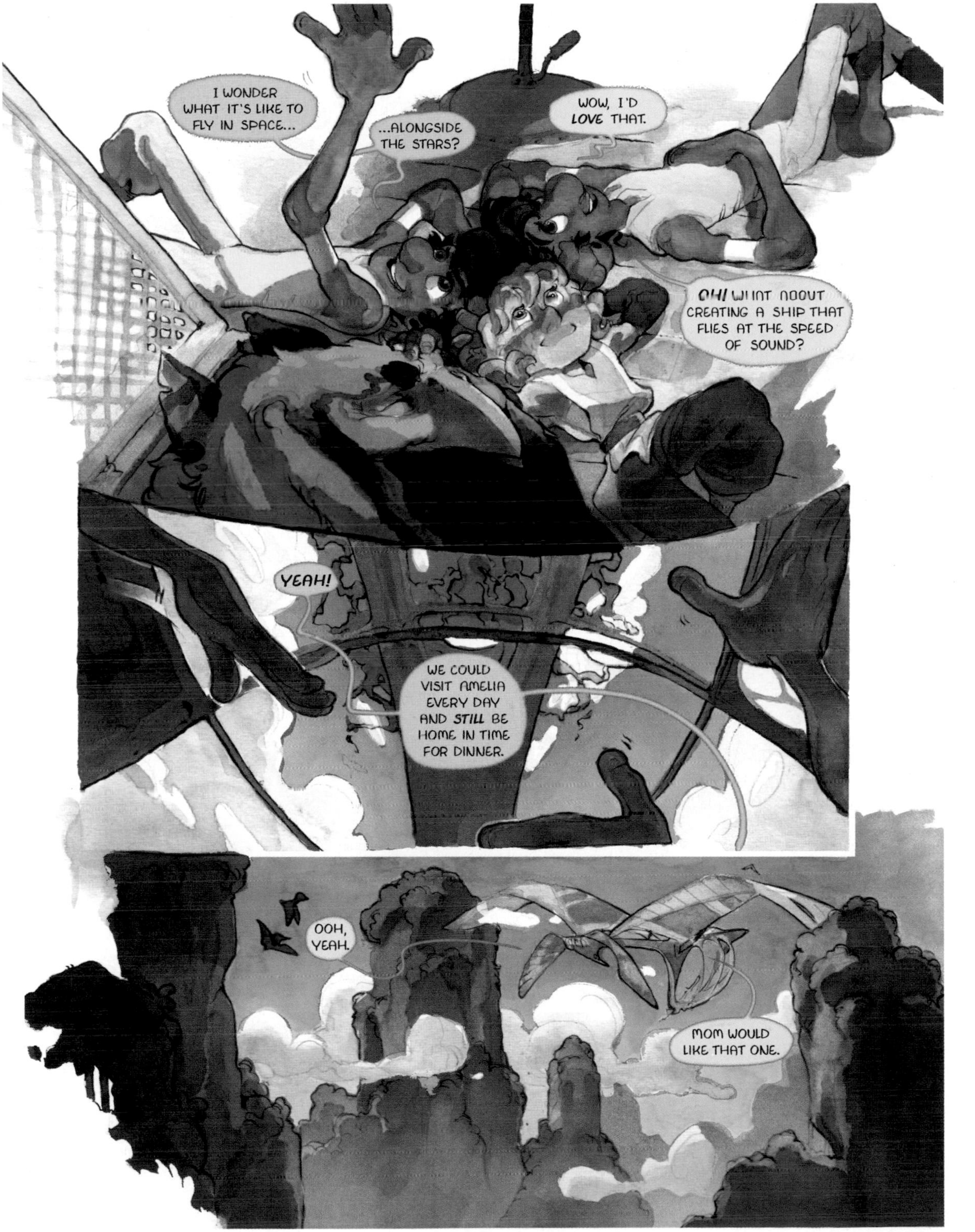
I WONDER WHAT IT'S LIKE TO FLY IN SPACE...
...ALONGSIDE THE STARS?
WOW, I'D LOVE THAT.
OH! WHAT ABOUT CREATING A SHIP THAT FLIES AT THE SPEED OF SOUND?
YEAH!
WE COULD VISIT AMELIA EVERY DAY AND STILL BE HOME IN TIME FOR DINNER.
OOH, YEAH.
MOM WOULD LIKE THAT ONE.

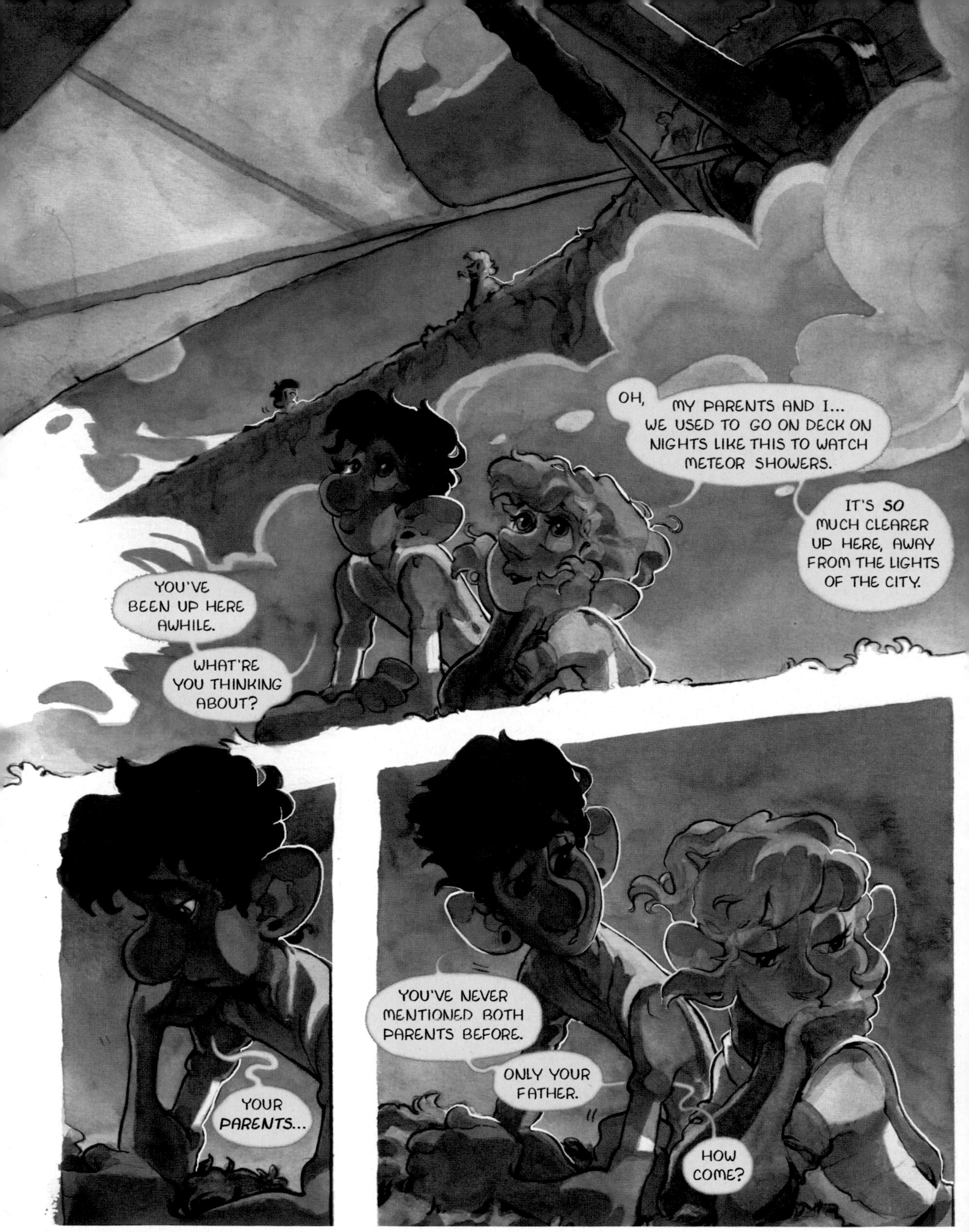
YOU'VE BEEN UP HERE AWHILE.
WHAT'RE YOU THINKING ABOUT?
OH,
MY PARENTS AND I... WE USED TO GO ON DECK ON NIGHTS LIKE THIS TO WATCH METEOR SHOWERS.
IT'S *SO* MUCH CLEARER UP HERE, AWAY FROM THE LIGHTS OF THE CITY.
YOUR *PARENTS*...
YOU'VE NEVER MENTIONED BOTH PARENTS BEFORE.
ONLY YOUR FATHER.
HOW COME?

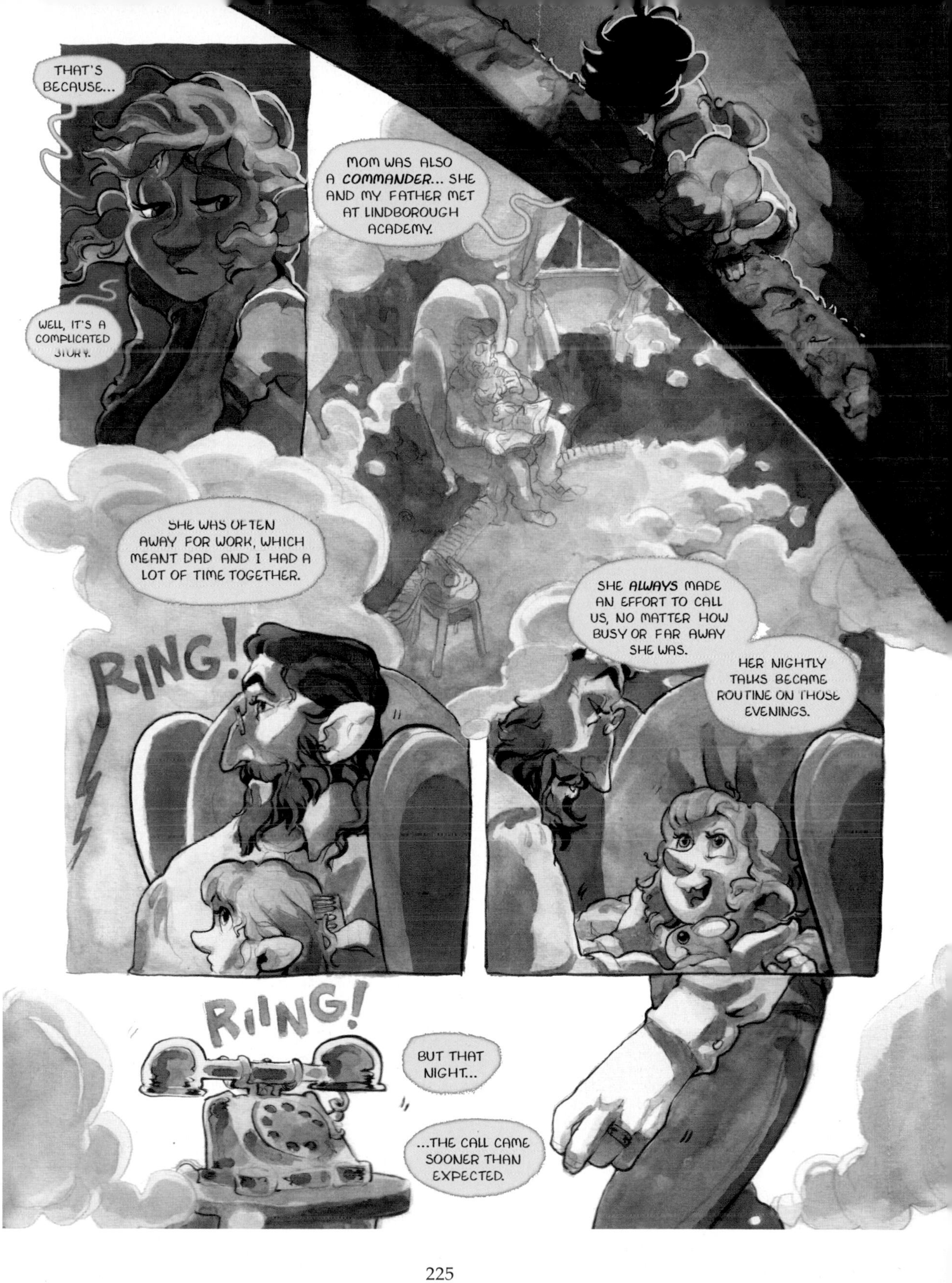
THAT'S BECAUSE...
WELL, IT'S A COMPLICATED STORY.
MOM WAS ALSO A COMMANDER... SHE AND MY FATHER MET AT LINDBOROUGH ACADEMY.
SHE WAS OFTEN AWAY FOR WORK, WHICH MEANT DAD AND I HAD A LOT OF TIME TOGETHER.
SHE ALWAYS MADE AN EFFORT TO CALL US, NO MATTER HOW BUSY OR FAR AWAY SHE WAS.
HER NIGHTLY TALKS BECAME ROUTINE ON THOSE EVENINGS.
RING!
RIING!
BUT THAT NIGHT...
...THE CALL CAME SOONER THAN EXPECTED.

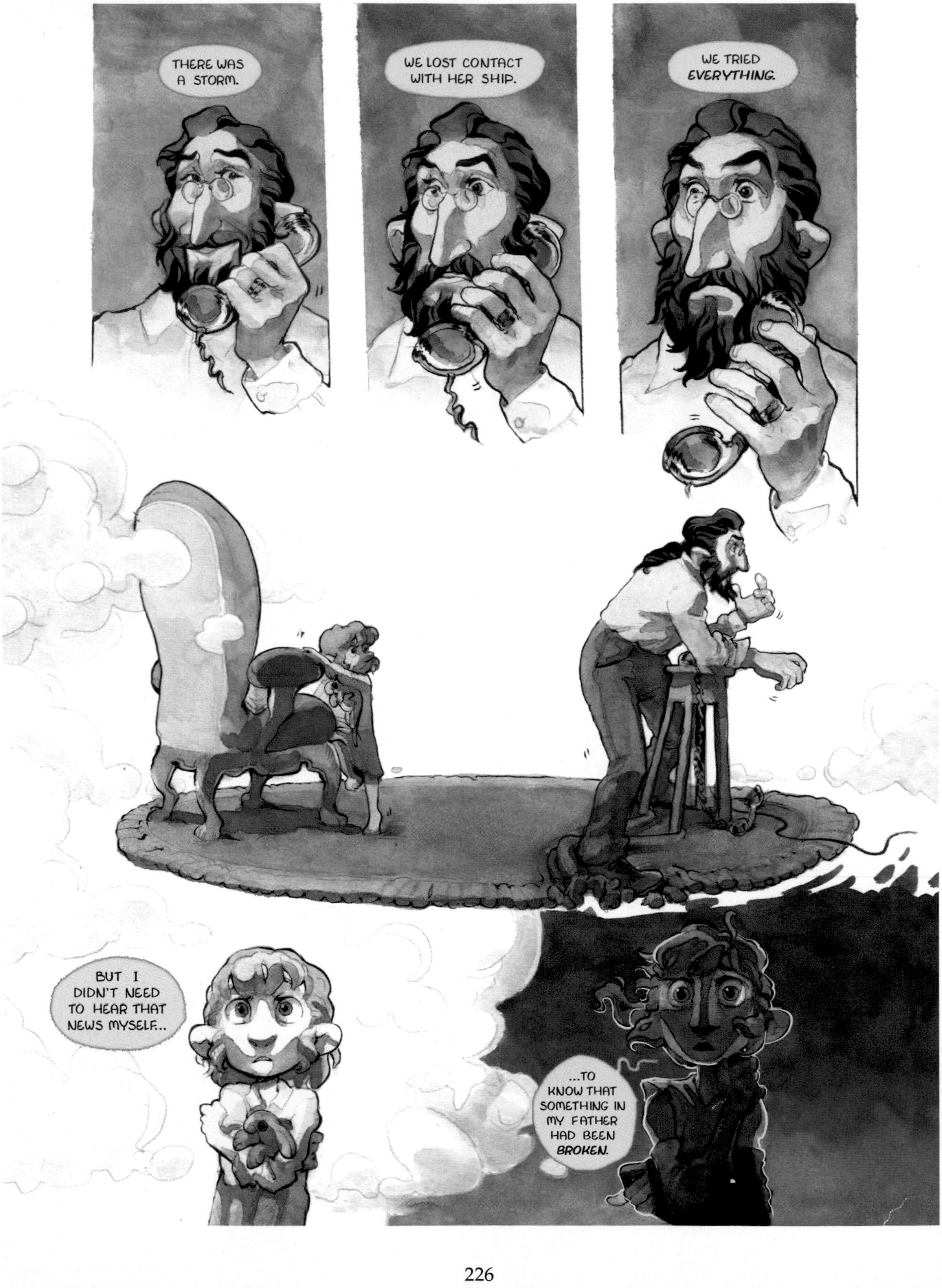
THERE WAS A STORM.
WE LOST CONTACT WITH HER SHIP.
WE TRIED EVERYTHING.
BUT I DIDN'T NEED TO HEAR THAT NEWS MYSELF...
...TO KNOW THAT SOMETHING IN MY FATHER HAD BEEN BROKEN.

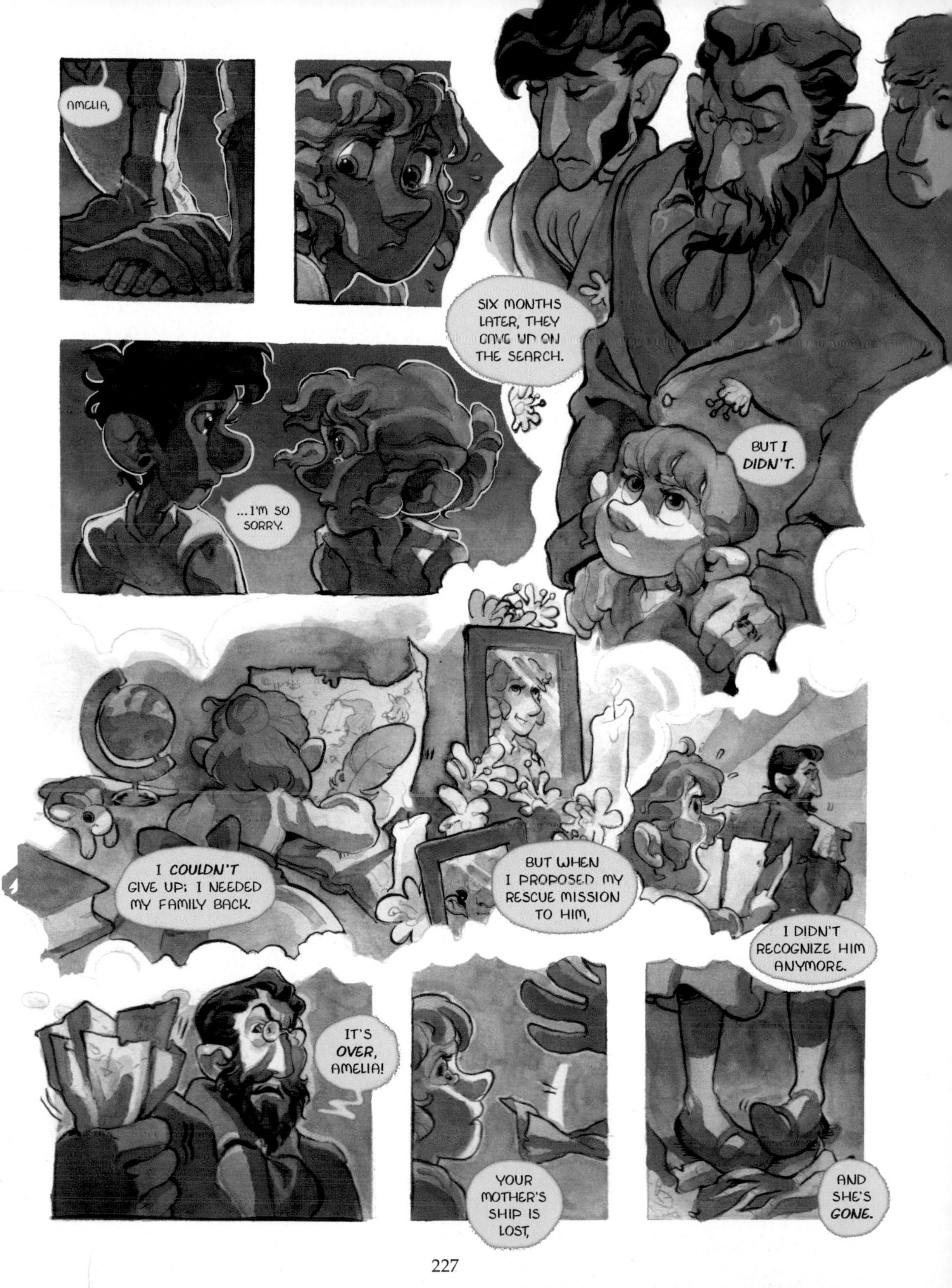
AMELIA,
SIX MONTHS LATER, THEY GAVE UP ON THE SEARCH.
...I'M SO SORRY.
BUT I DIDN'T.
I COULDN'T GIVE UP; I NEEDED MY FAMILY BACK.
BUT WHEN I PROPOSED MY RESCUE MISSION TO HIM,
I DIDN'T RECOGNIZE HIM ANYMORE.
IT'S OVER, AMELIA!
YOUR MOTHER'S SHIP IS LOST,
AND SHE'S GONE.

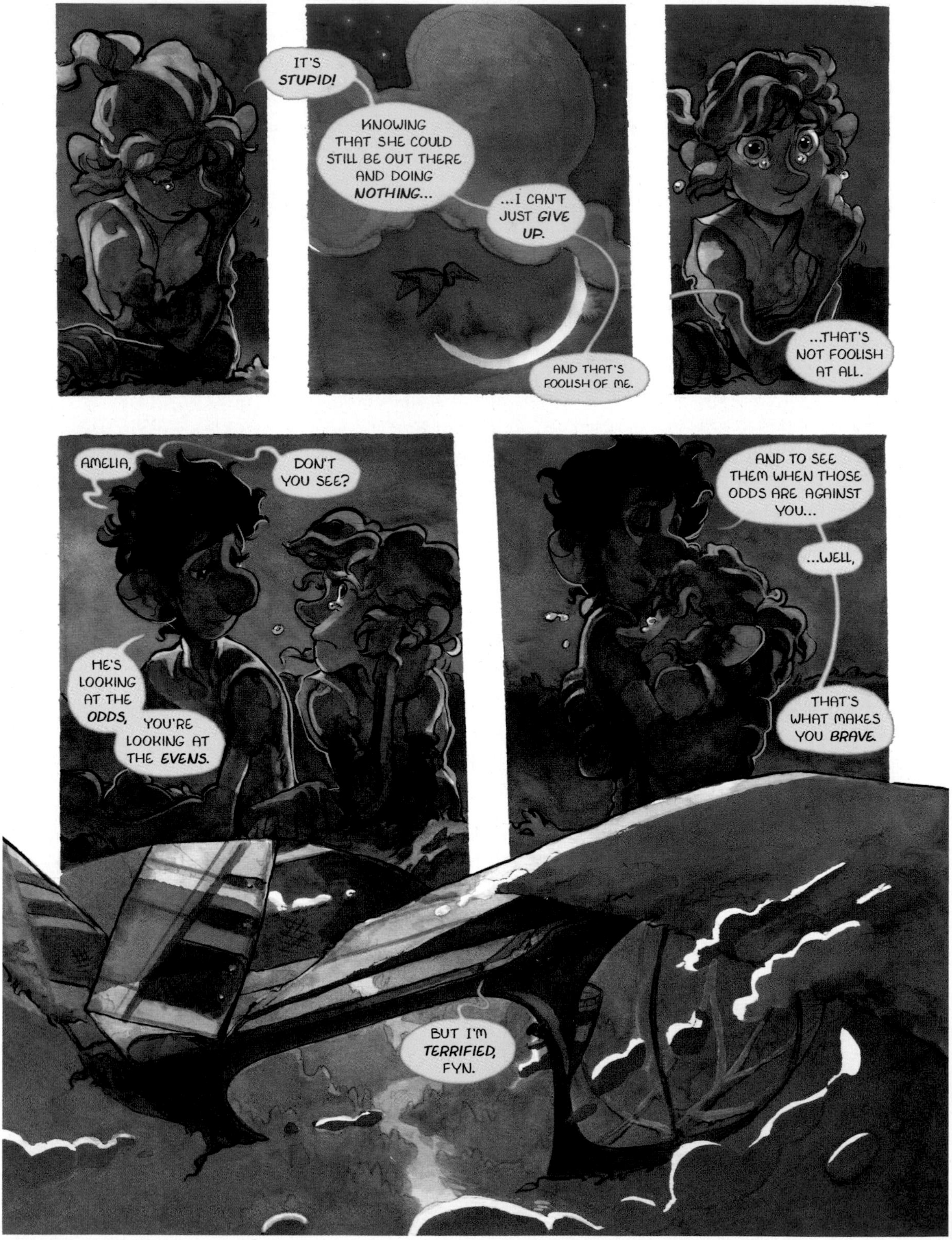
IT'S STUPID!
KNOWING THAT SHE COULD STILL BE OUT THERE AND DOING NOTHING...
...I CAN'T JUST GIVE UP.
AND THAT'S FOOLISH OF ME.
...THAT'S NOT FOOLISH AT ALL.
AMELIA,
DON'T YOU SEE?
HE'S LOOKING AT THE ODDS,
YOU'RE LOOKING AT THE EVENS.
AND TO SEE THEM WHEN THOSE ODDS ARE AGAINST YOU...
...WELL,
THAT'S WHAT MAKES YOU BRAVE.
BUT I'M TERRIFIED, FYN.

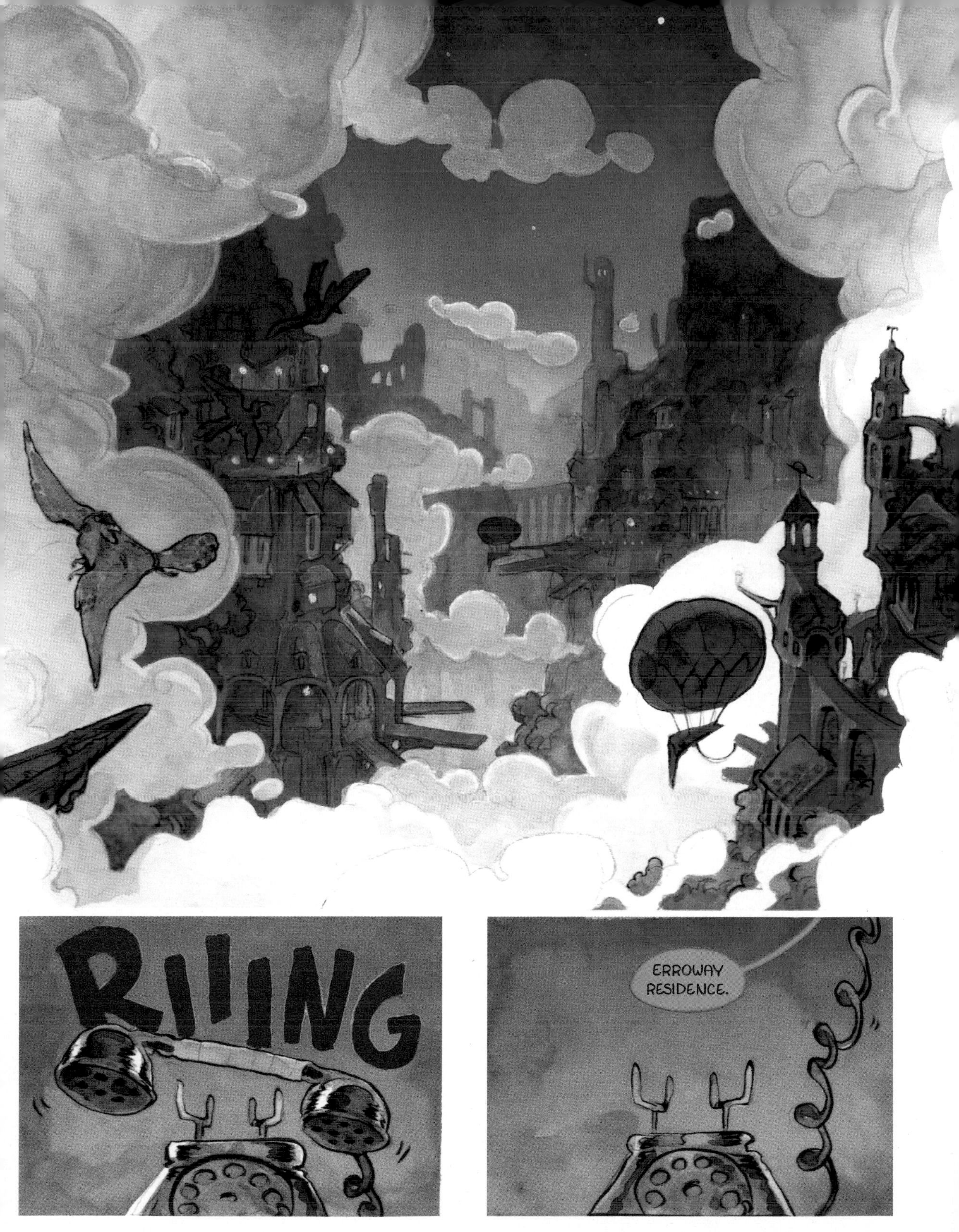
RIIING
ERROWAY RESIDENCE.

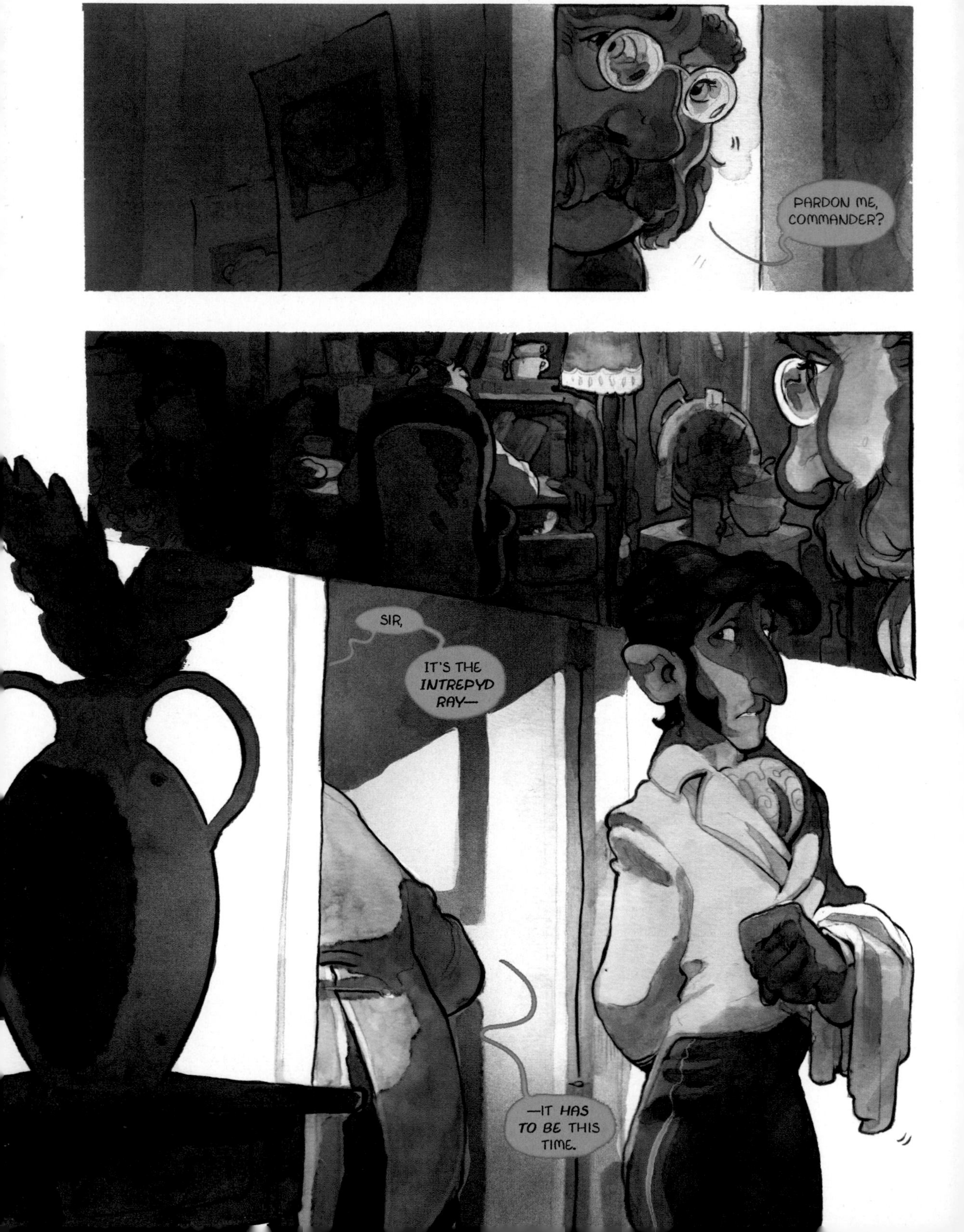
PARDON ME, COMMANDER?
SIR,
IT'S THE *INTREPYD RAY*—
—IT *HAS TO BE* THIS TIME.

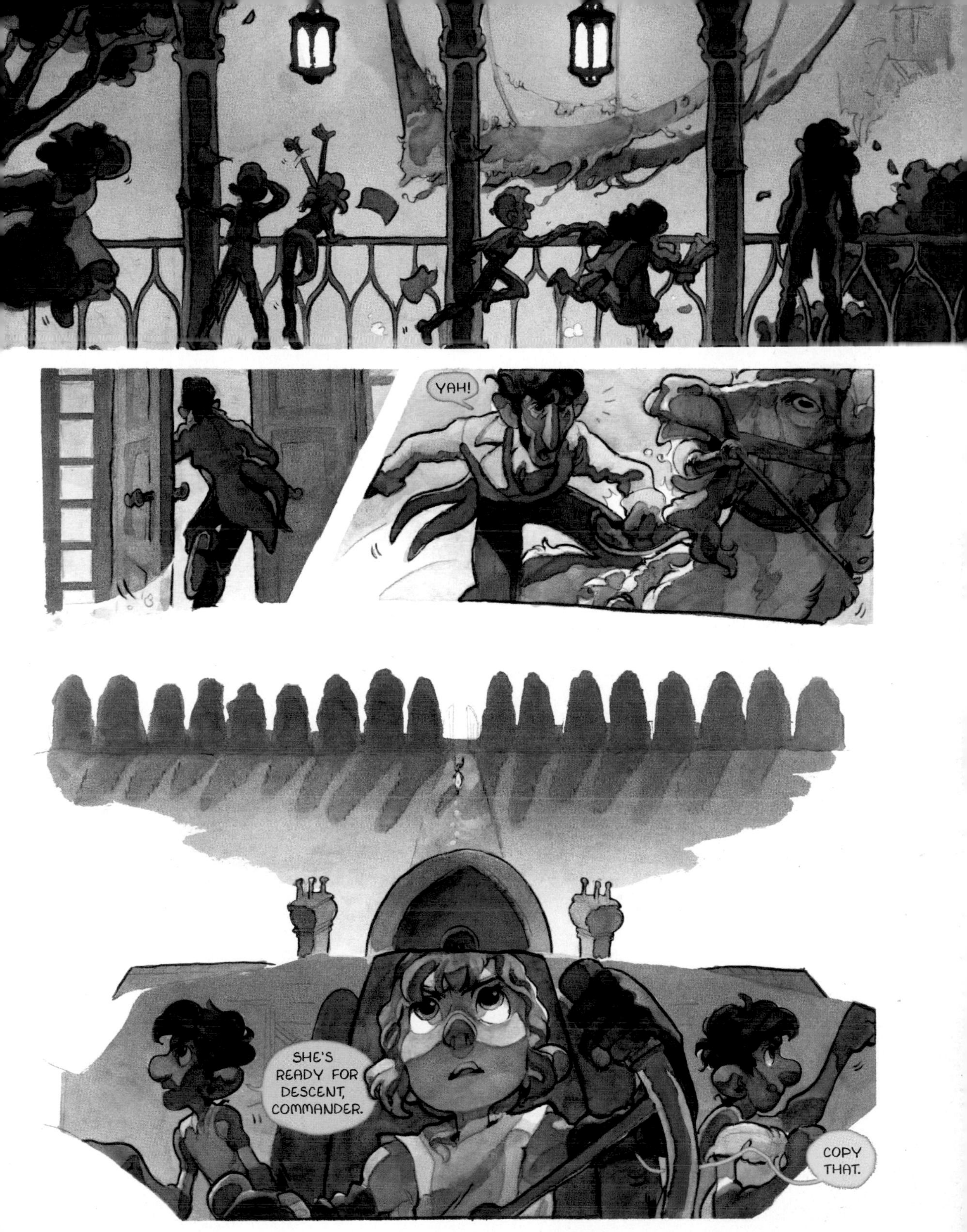
YAH!
SHE'S READY FOR DESCENT, COMMANDER.
COPY THAT.

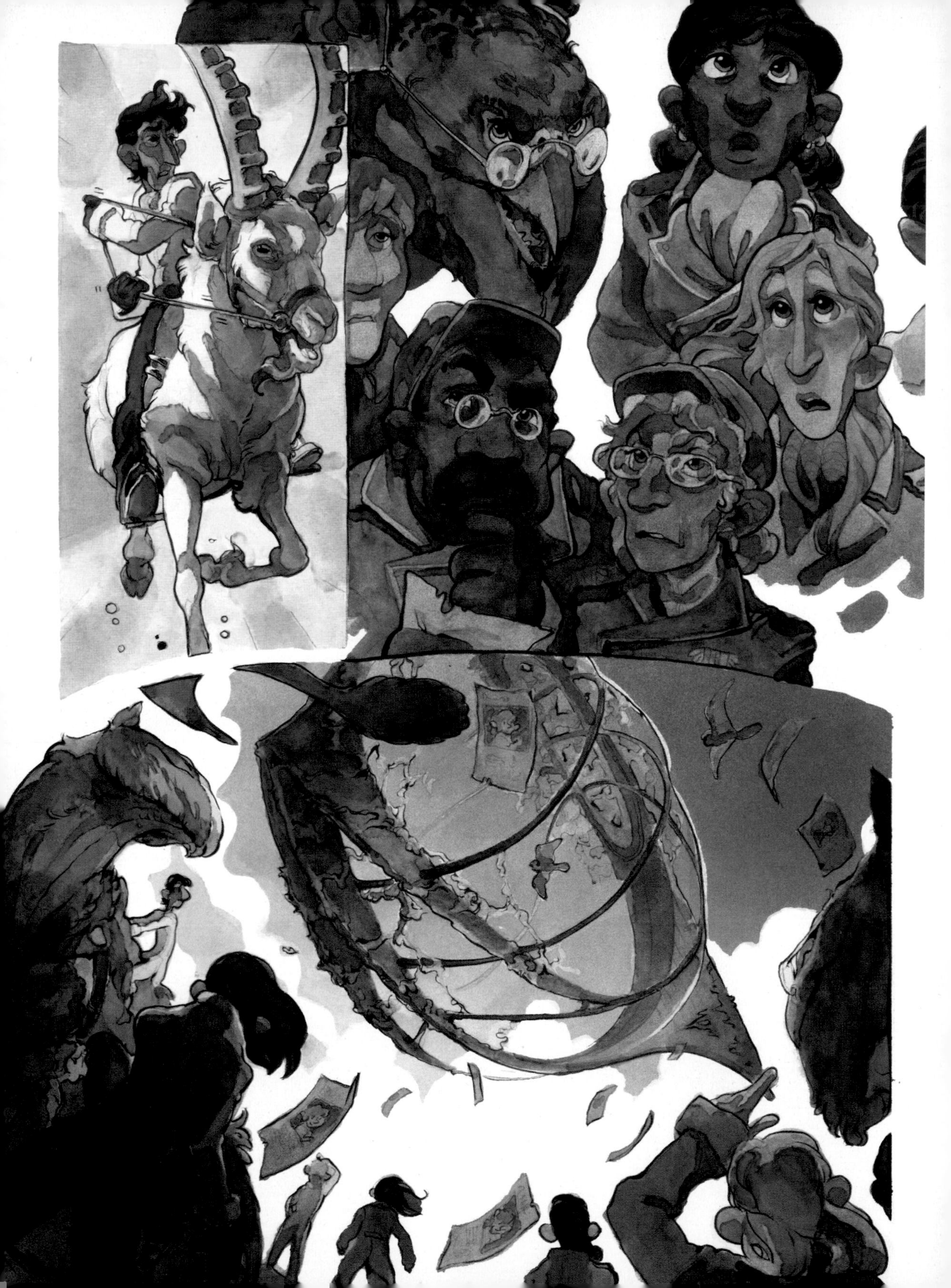

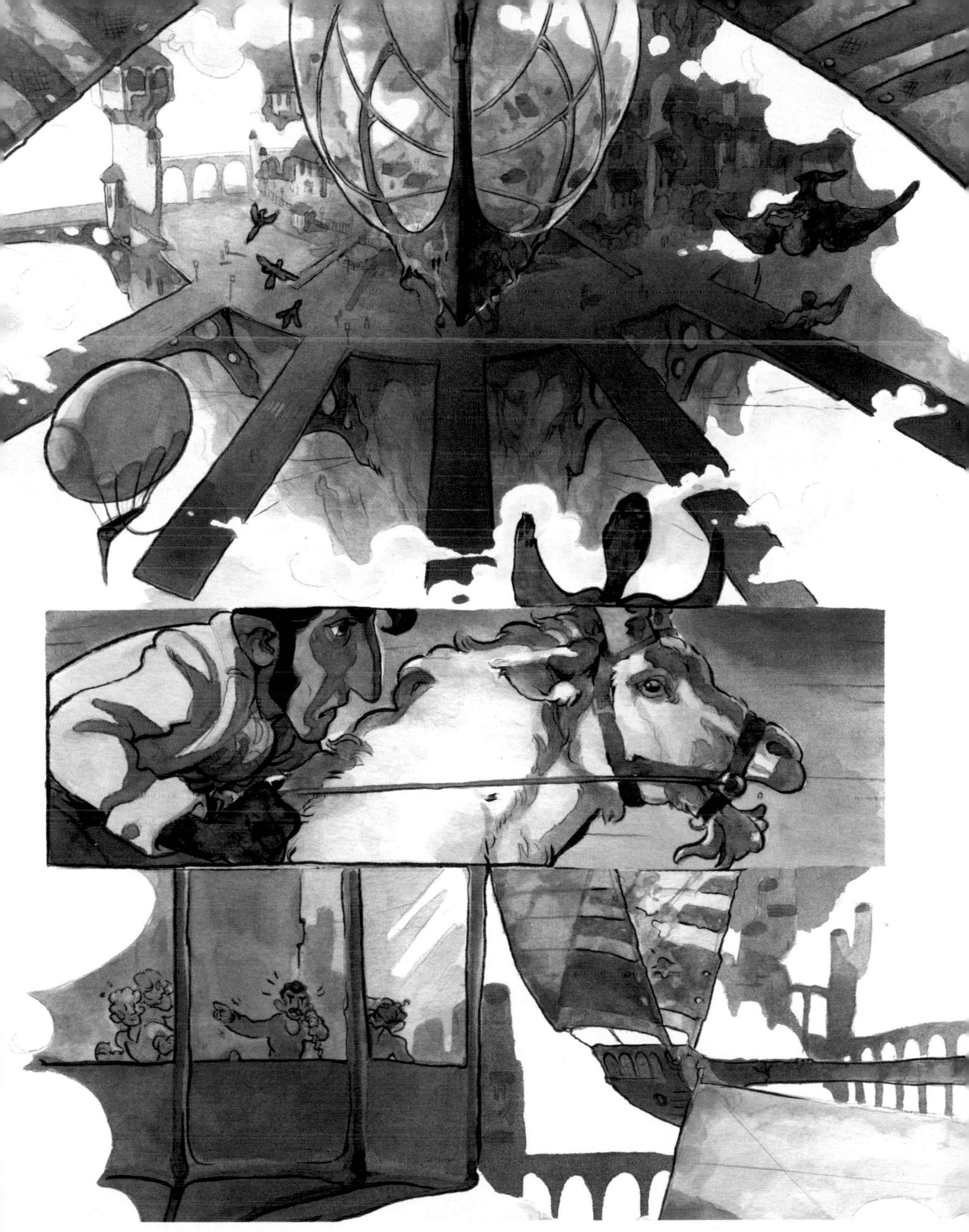

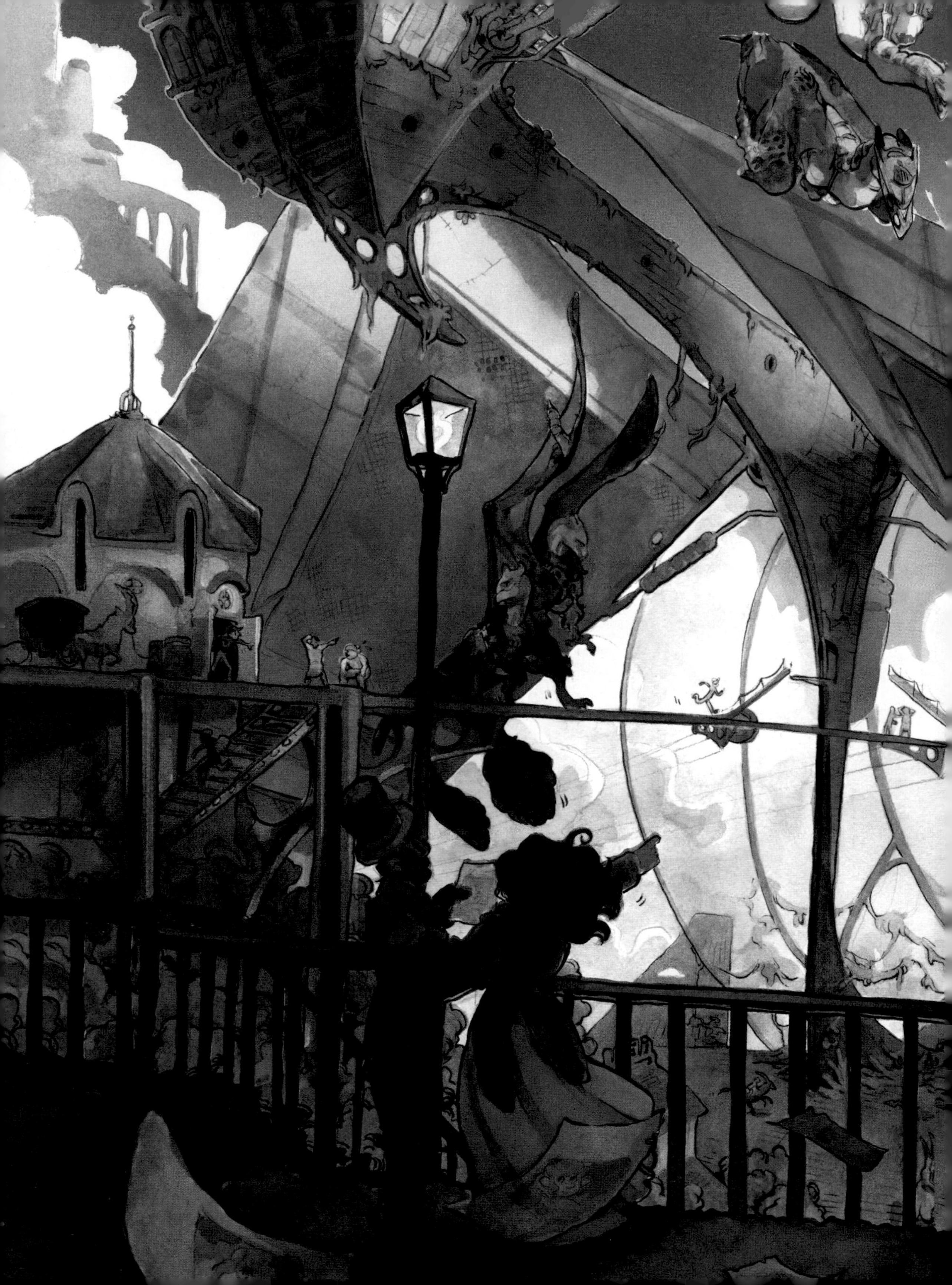

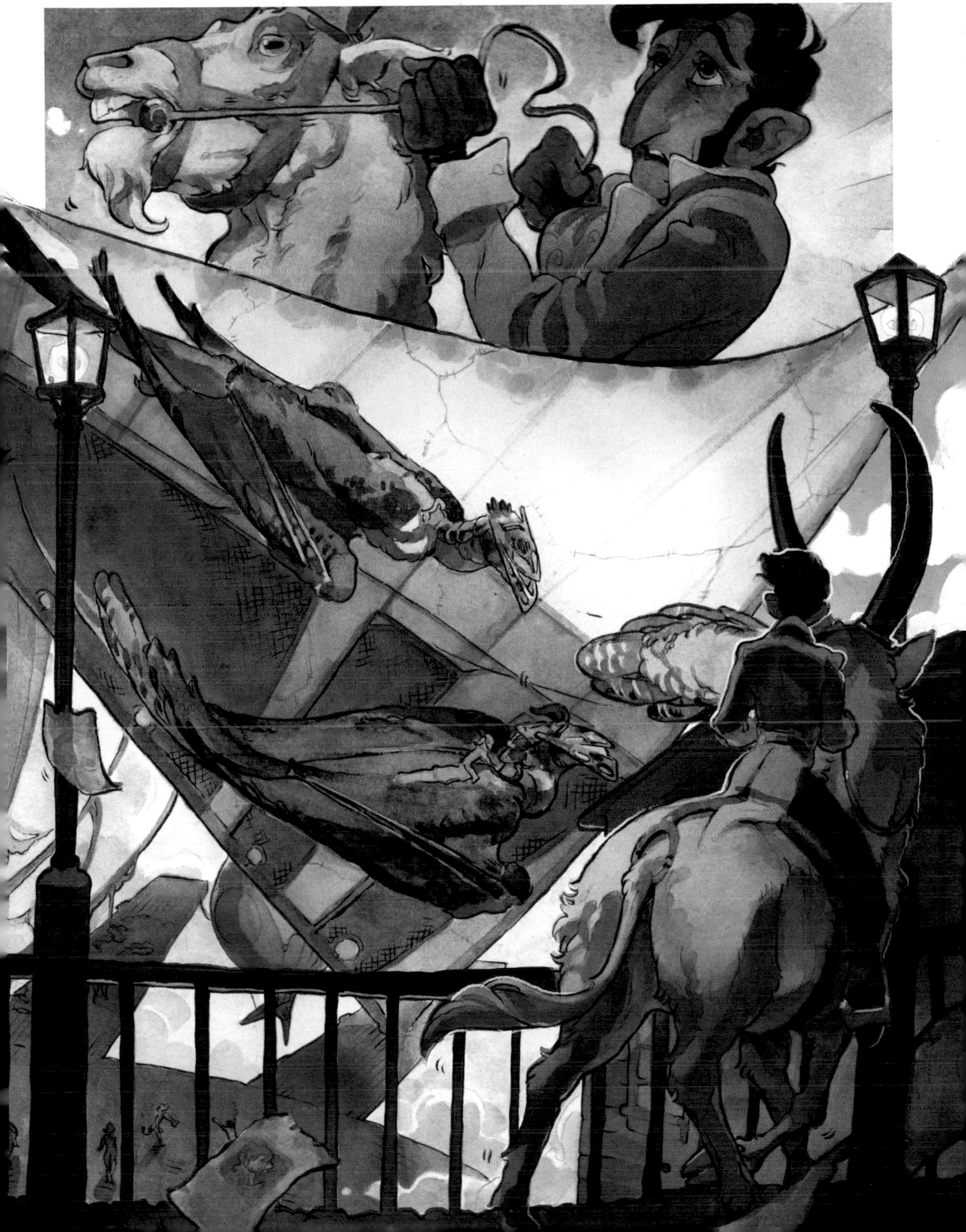

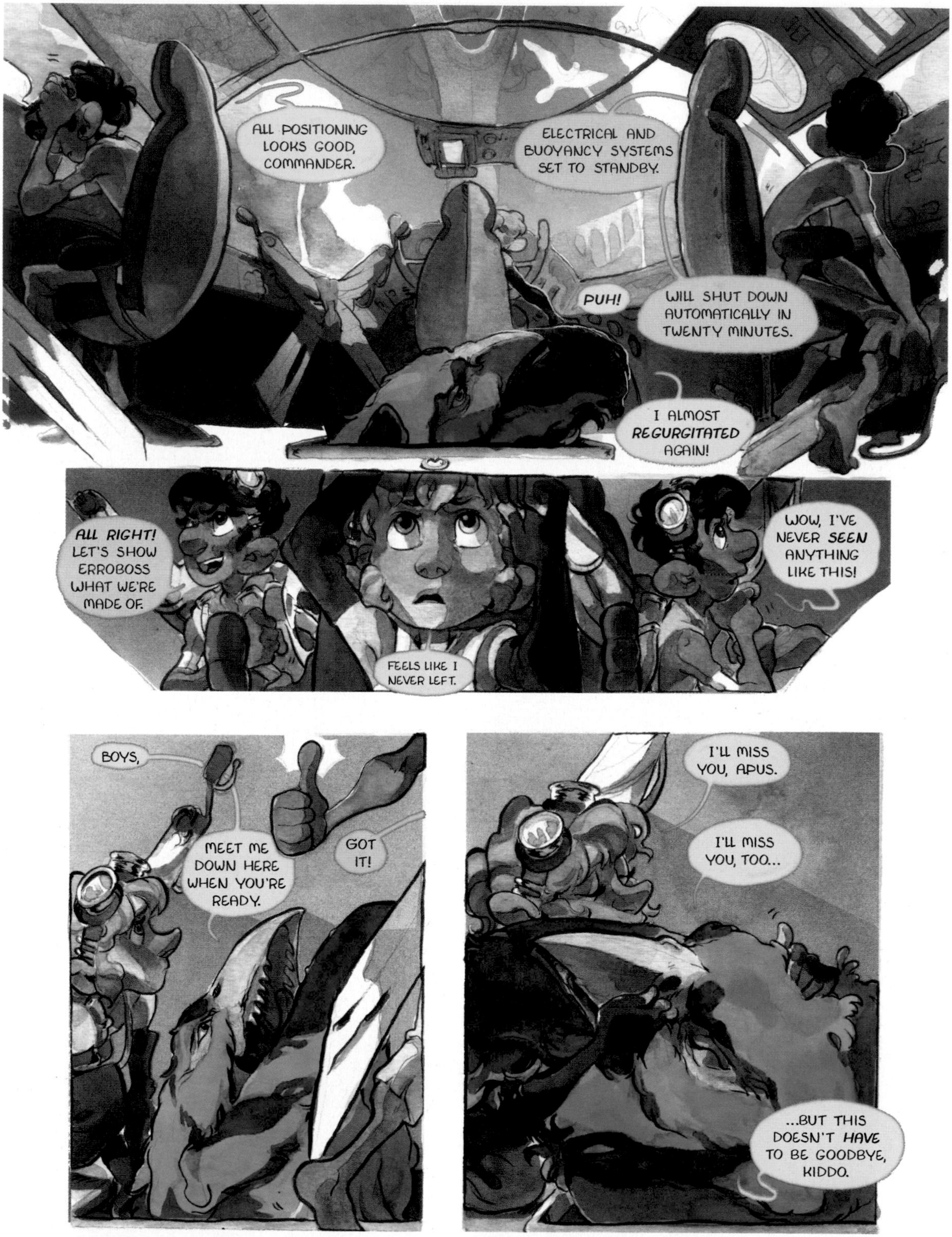
ALL POSITIONING LOOKS GOOD, COMMANDER.
ELECTRICAL AND BUOYANCY SYSTEMS SET TO STANDBY.
PUH!
WILL SHUT DOWN AUTOMATICALLY IN TWENTY MINUTES.
I ALMOST **REGURGITATED** AGAIN!
ALL RIGHT! LET'S SHOW ERROBOSS WHAT WE'RE MADE OF.
FEELS LIKE I NEVER LEFT.
WOW, I'VE NEVER ***SEEN*** ANYTHING LIKE THIS!
BOYS,
MEET ME DOWN HERE WHEN YOU'RE READY.
GOT IT!
I'LL MISS YOU, APUS.
I'LL MISS YOU, TOO...
...BUT THIS DOESN'T ***HAVE*** TO BE GOODBYE, KIDDO.

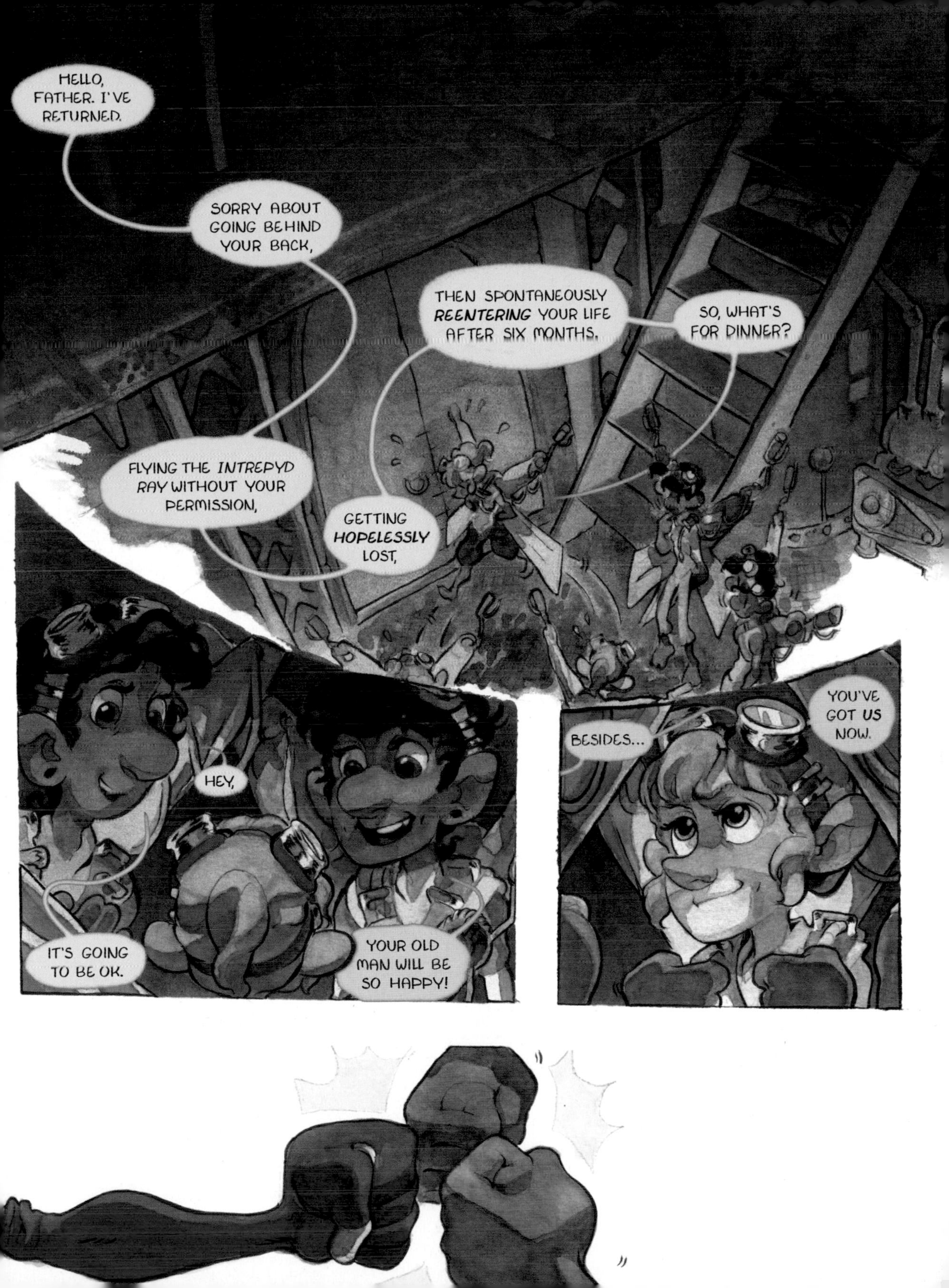
HELLO, FATHER. I'VE RETURNED.
SORRY ABOUT GOING BEHIND YOUR BACK,
FLYING THE *INTREPYD RAY* WITHOUT YOUR PERMISSION,
GETTING **HOPELESSLY** LOST,
THEN SPONTANEOUSLY **REENTERING** YOUR LIFE AFTER SIX MONTHS.
SO, WHAT'S FOR DINNER?
HEY,
IT'S GOING TO BE OK.
YOUR OLD MAN WILL BE SO HAPPY!
BESIDES...
YOU'VE GOT **US** NOW.

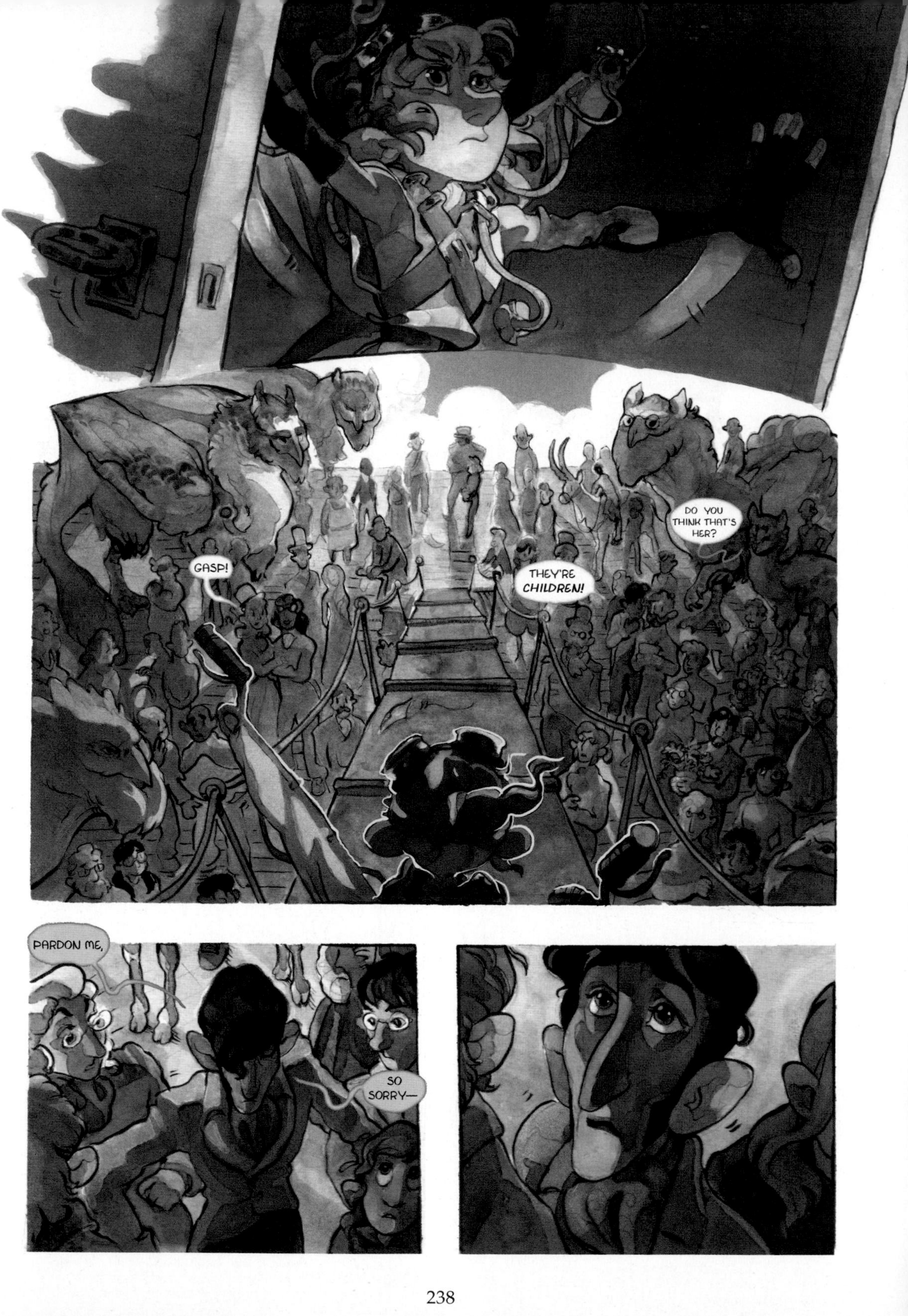
GASP!
THEY'RE CHILDREN!
DO YOU THINK THAT'S HER?
PARDON ME,
SO SORRY—

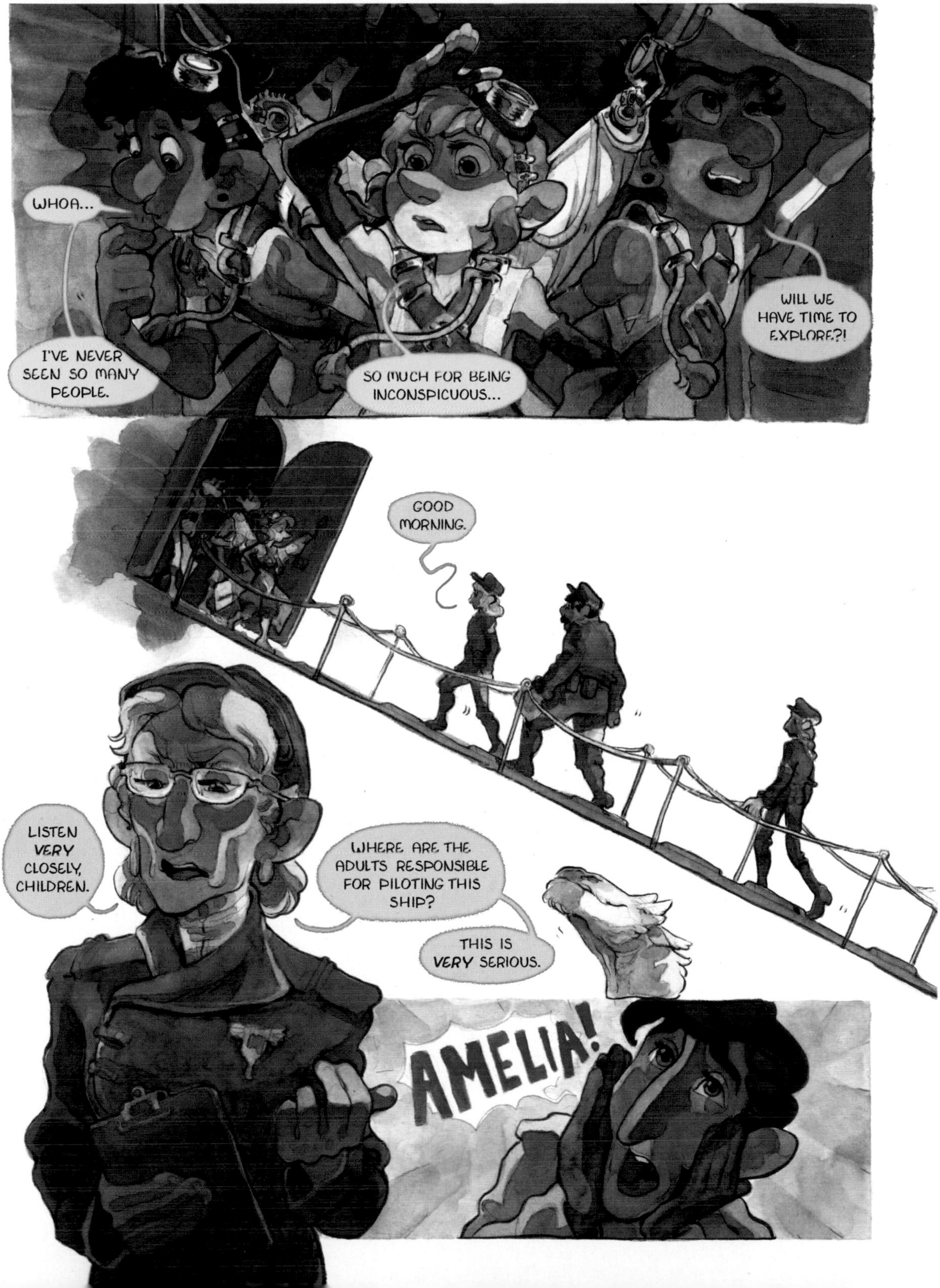
WHOA...
I'VE NEVER SEEN SO MANY PEOPLE.
SO MUCH FOR BEING INCONSPICUOUS...
WILL WE HAVE TIME TO EXPLORE?!
GOOD MORNING.
LISTEN VERY CLOSELY, CHILDREN.
WHERE ARE THE ADULTS RESPONSIBLE FOR PILOTING THIS SHIP?
THIS IS VERY SERIOUS.
AMELIA!

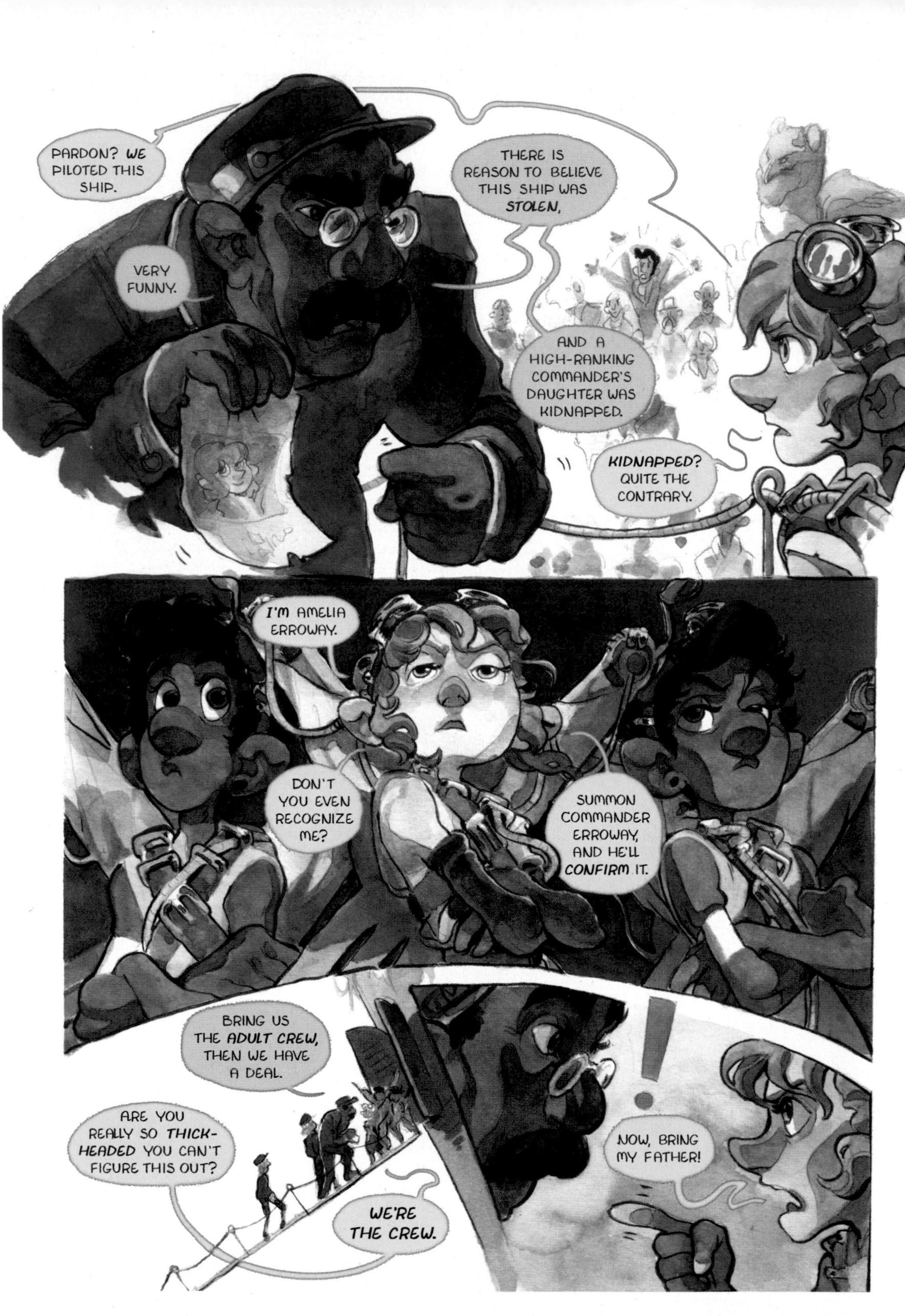
PARDON? WE PILOTED THIS SHIP.
VERY FUNNY.
THERE IS REASON TO BELIEVE THIS SHIP WAS STOLEN,
AND A HIGH-RANKING COMMANDER'S DAUGHTER WAS KIDNAPPED.
KIDNAPPED? QUITE THE CONTRARY.
I'M AMELIA ERROWAY.
DON'T YOU EVEN RECOGNIZE ME?
SUMMON COMMANDER ERROWAY, AND HE'LL CONFIRM IT.
BRING US THE ADULT CREW, THEN WE HAVE A DEAL.
ARE YOU REALLY SO THICK-HEADED YOU CAN'T FIGURE THIS OUT?
WE'RE THE CREW.
NOW, BRING MY FATHER!

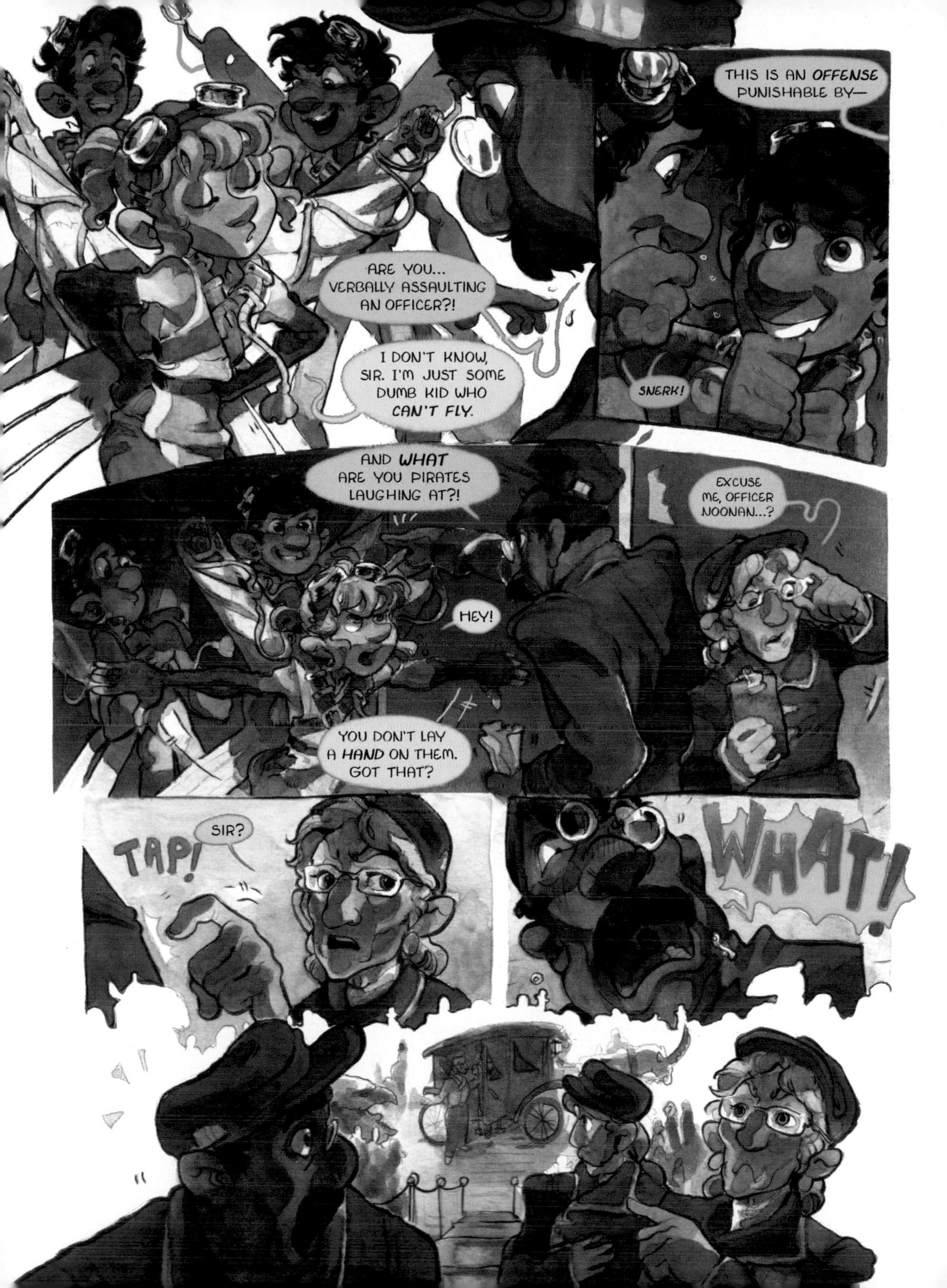
ARE YOU... VERBALLY ASSAULTING AN OFFICER?!
THIS IS AN OFFENSE PUNISHABLE BY—
SNERK!
I DON'T KNOW, SIR. I'M JUST SOME DUMB KID WHO CAN'T FLY.
AND WHAT ARE YOU PIRATES LAUGHING AT?!
EXCUSE ME, OFFICER NOONAN...?
HEY!
YOU DON'T LAY A HAND ON THEM. GOT THAT?
TAP!
SIR?
WHAT!

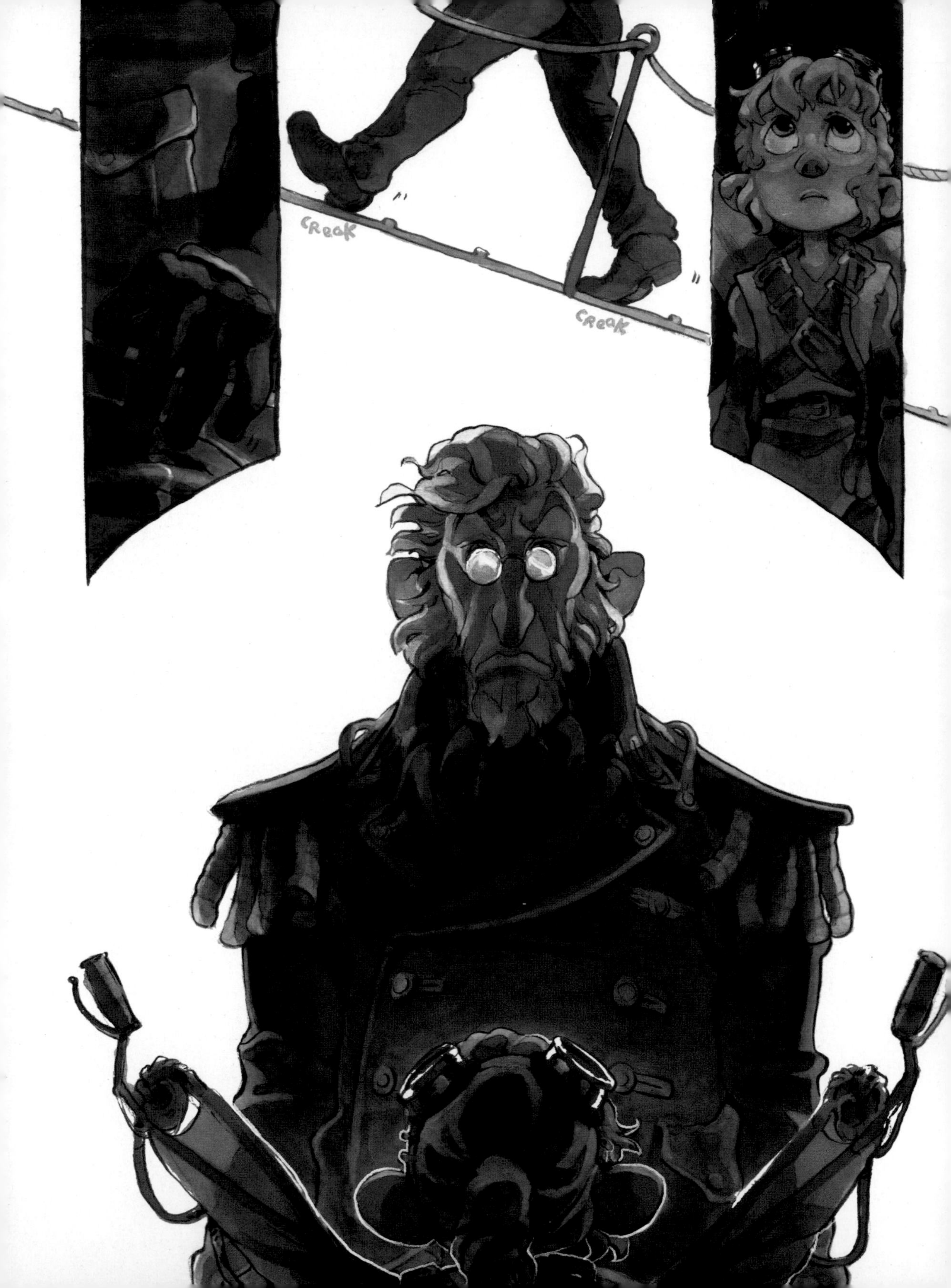
Creak
Creak

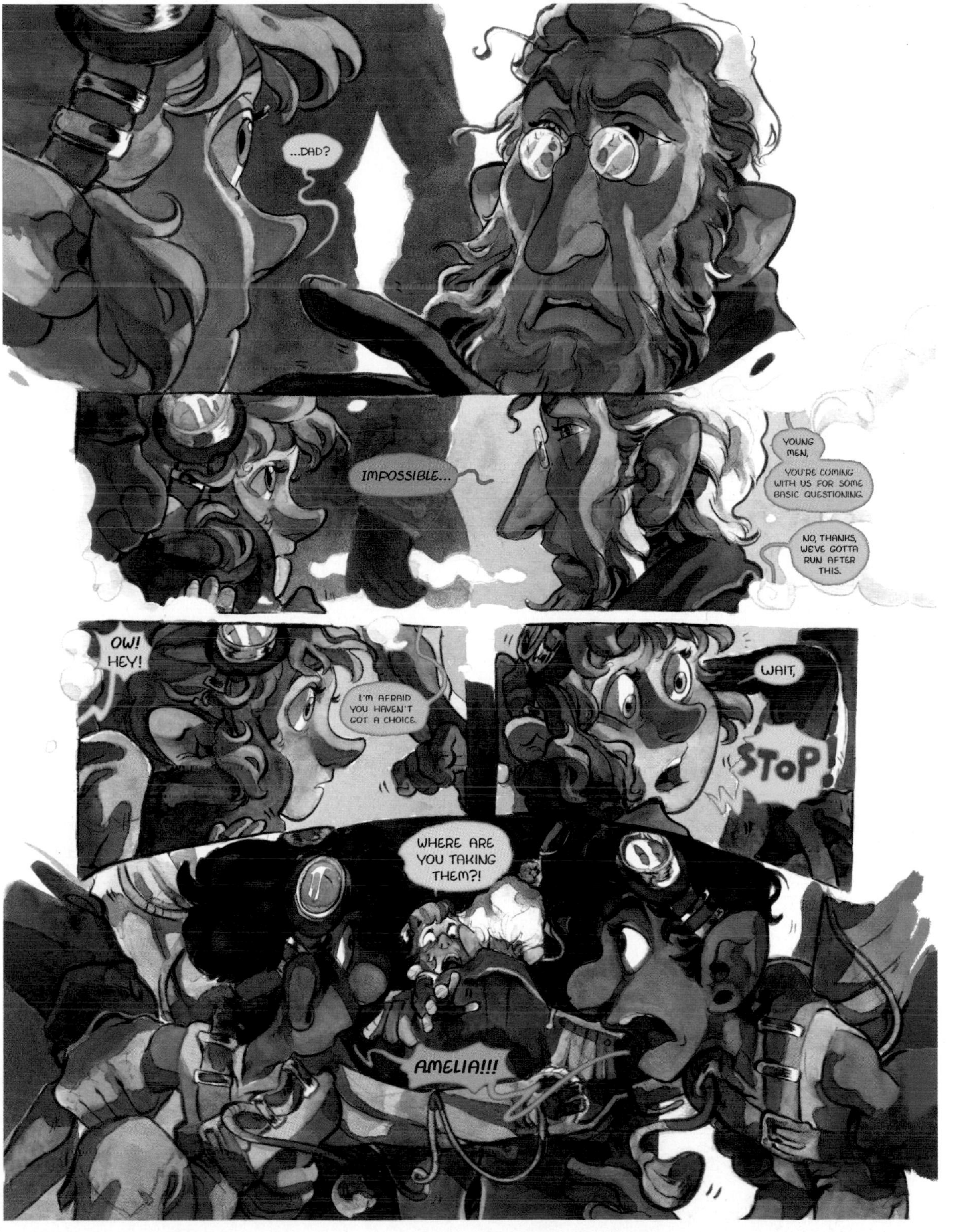
...DAD?
IMPOSSIBLE...
YOUNG MEN,
YOU'RE COMING WITH US FOR SOME BASIC QUESTIONING.
NO, THANKS, WE'VE GOTTA RUN AFTER THIS.
OW! HEY!
I'M AFRAID YOU HAVEN'T GOT A CHOICE.
WAIT,
STOP!
WHERE ARE YOU TAKING THEM?!
AMELIA!!!

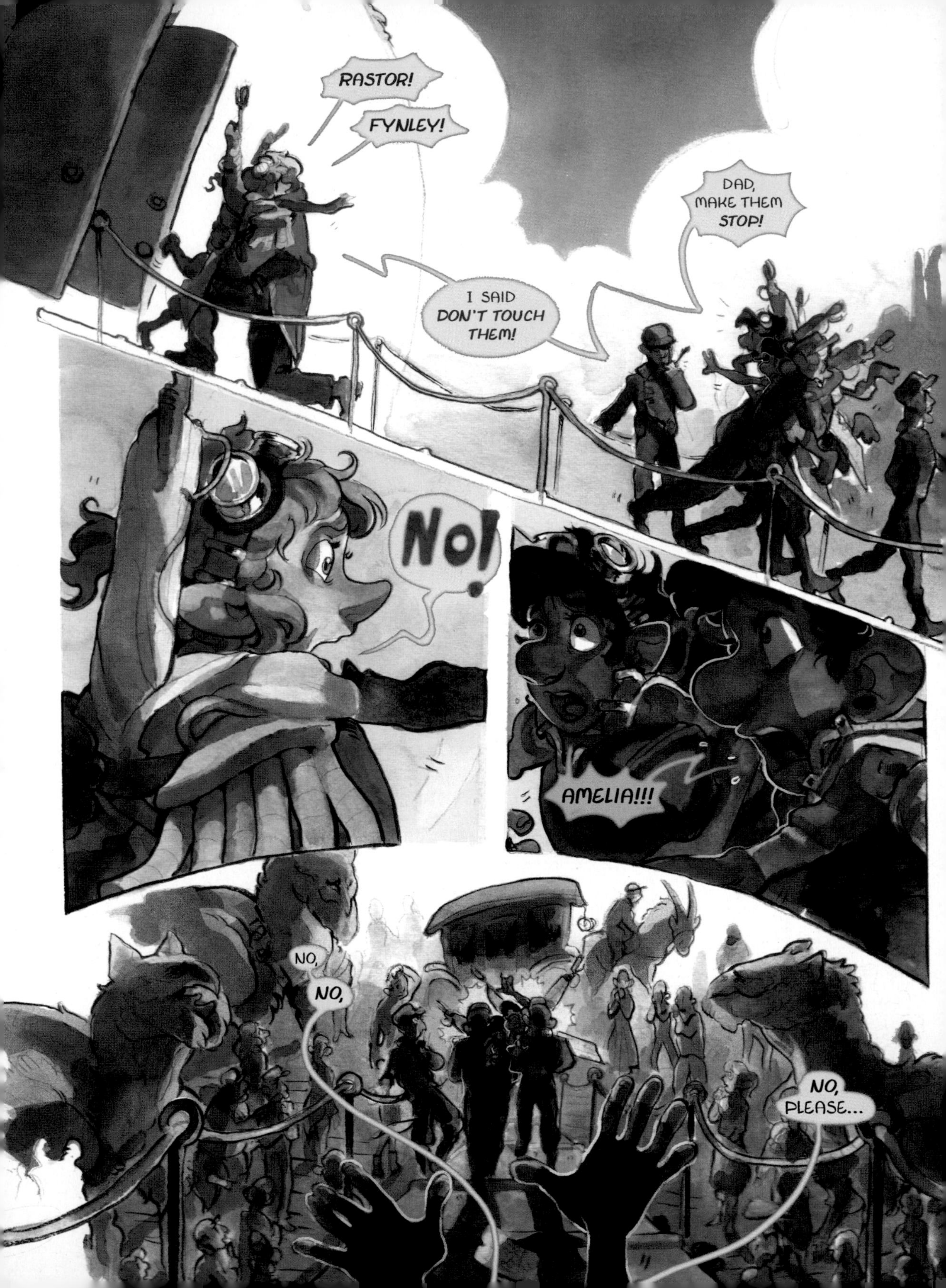
RASTOR!
FYNLEY!
DAD, MAKE THEM STOP!
I SAID DON'T TOUCH THEM!
NO!
AMELIA!!!
NO,
NO,
NO, PLEASE...

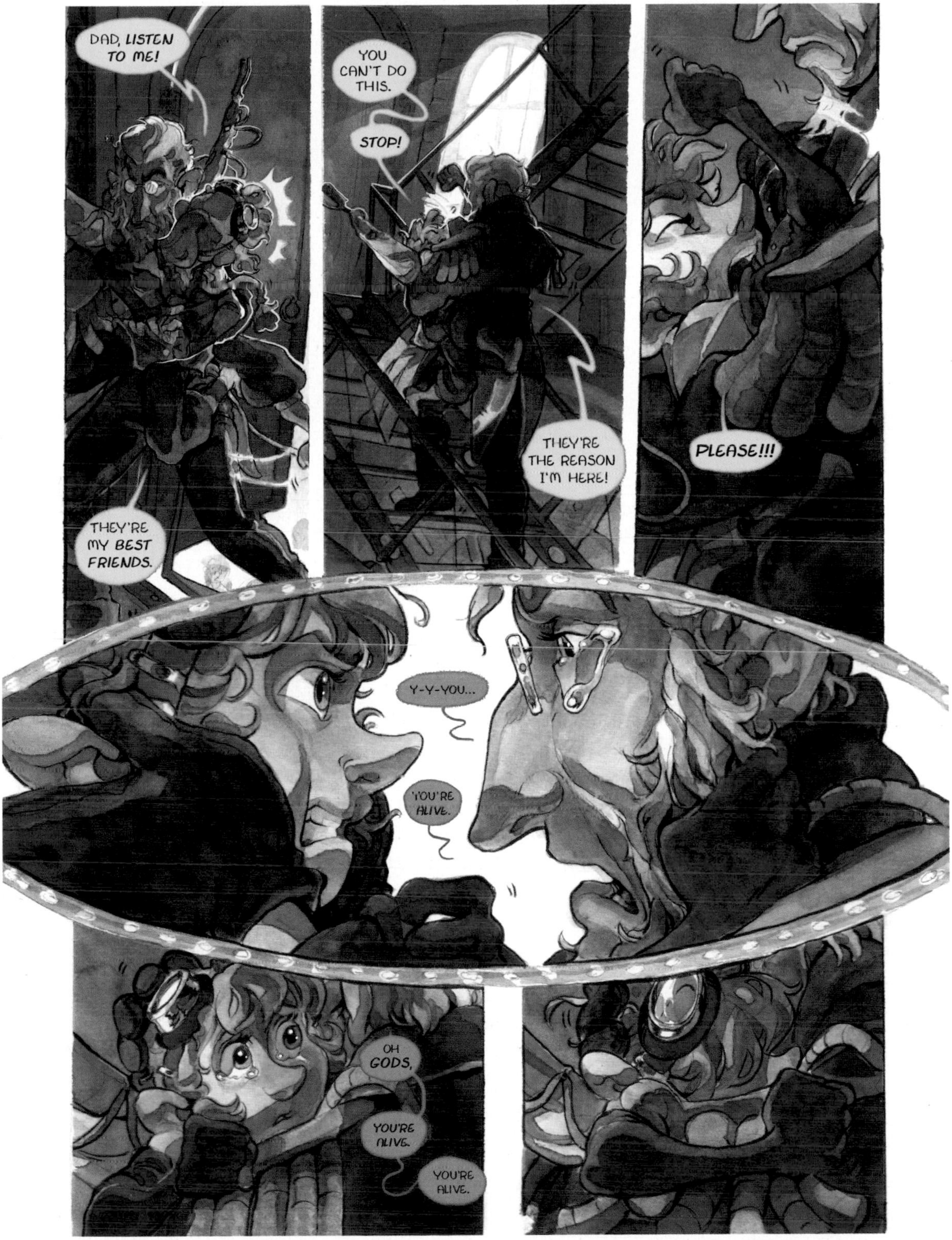

DAD, LISTEN TO ME!
THEY'RE MY BEST FRIENDS.
YOU CAN'T DO THIS.
STOP!
THEY'RE THE REASON I'M HERE!
PLEASE!!!
Y-Y-YOU...
YOU'RE ALIVE.
OH GODS,
YOU'RE ALIVE.
YOU'RE ALIVE.

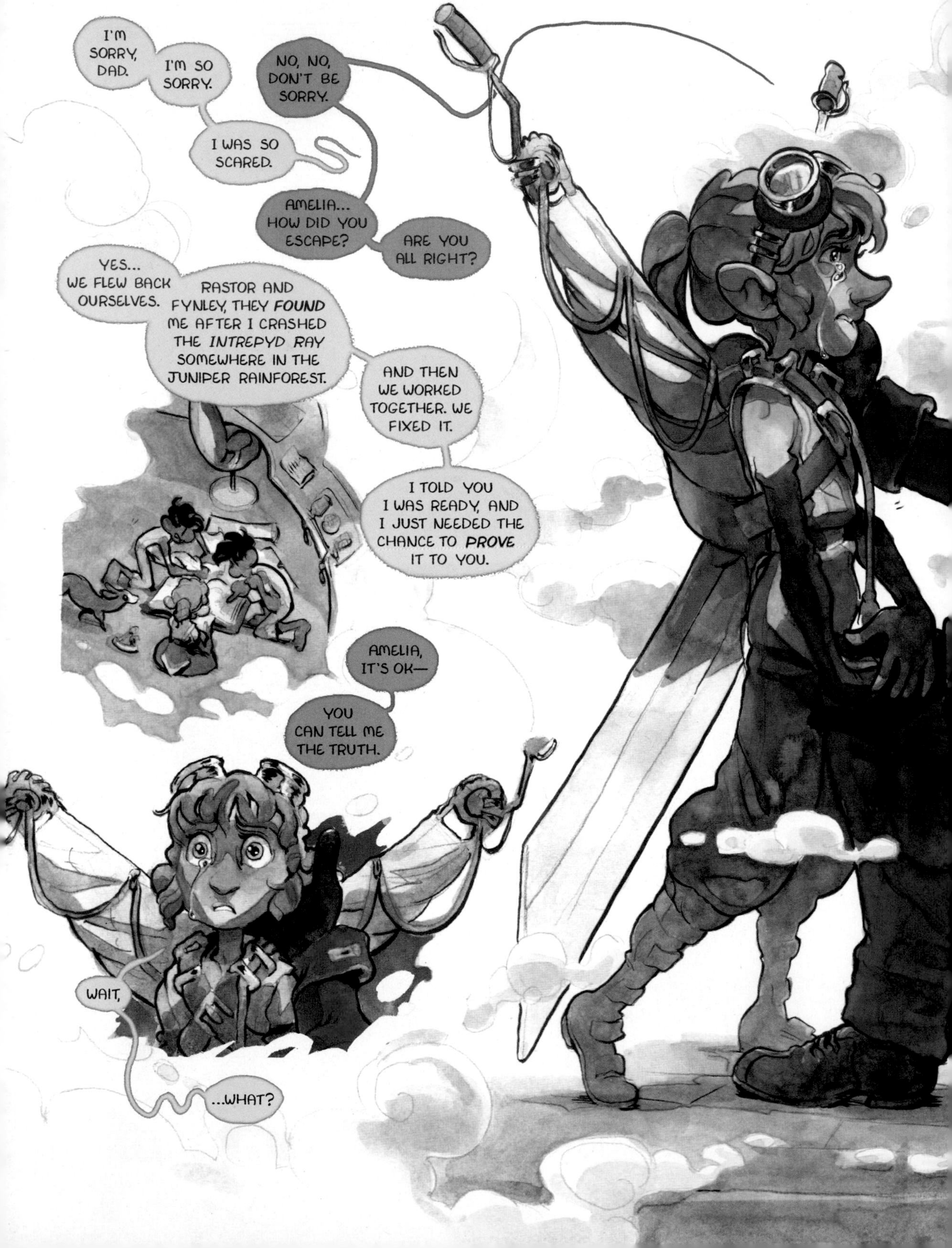
I'M SORRY, DAD.
I'M SO SORRY.
I WAS SO SCARED.
NO, NO, DON'T BE SORRY.
AMELIA... HOW DID YOU ESCAPE?
ARE YOU ALL RIGHT?
YES... WE FLEW BACK OURSELVES.
RASTOR AND FYNLEY, THEY *FOUND* ME AFTER I CRASHED THE *INTREPYD RAY* SOMEWHERE IN THE JUNIPER RAINFOREST.
AND THEN WE WORKED TOGETHER. WE FIXED IT.
I TOLD YOU I WAS READY, AND I JUST NEEDED THE CHANCE TO ***PROVE*** IT TO YOU.
AMELIA, IT'S OK—
YOU CAN TELL ME THE TRUTH.
WAIT,
...WHAT?

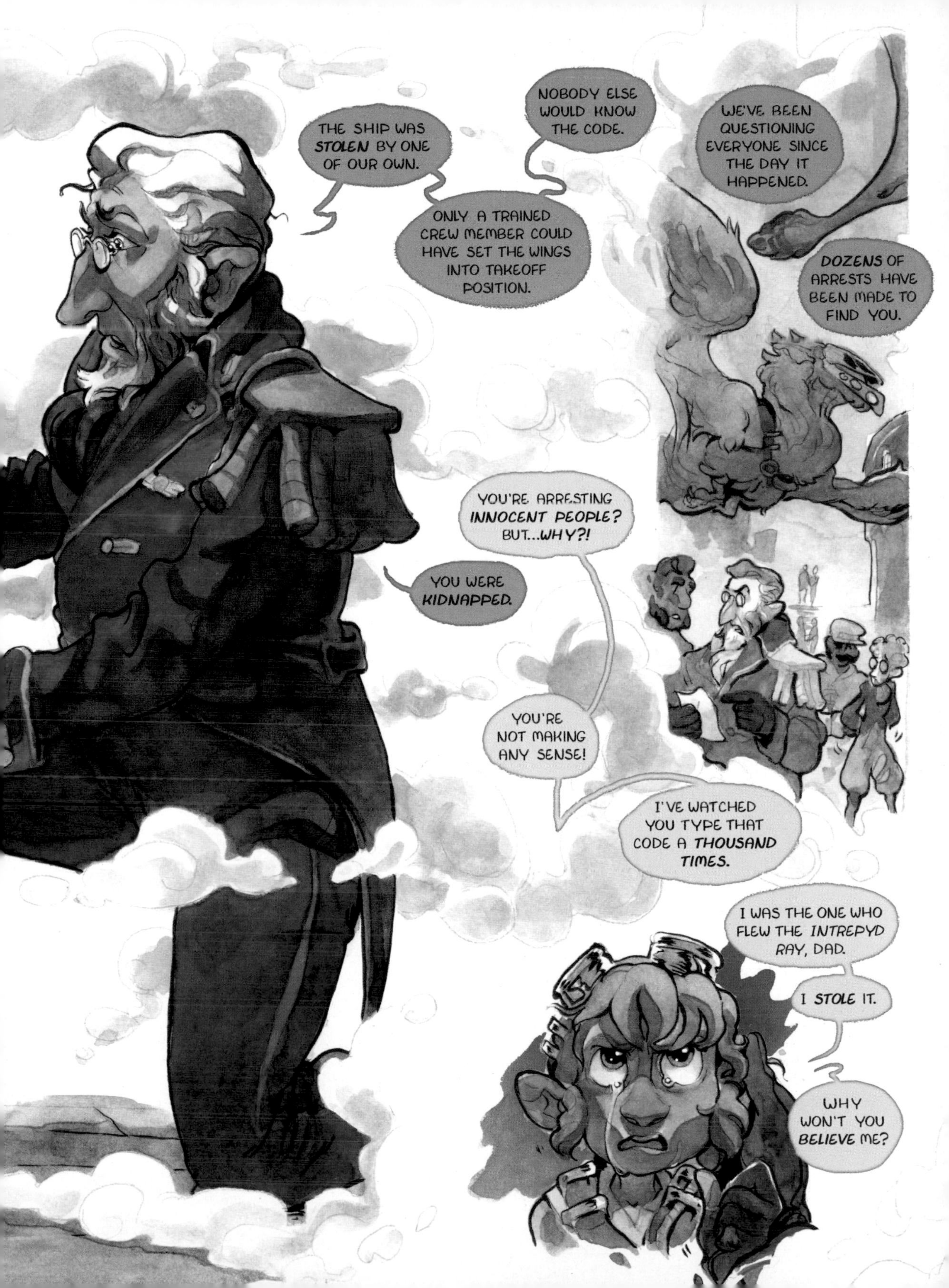
THE SHIP WAS STOLEN BY ONE OF OUR OWN.
NOBODY ELSE WOULD KNOW THE CODE.
ONLY A TRAINED CREW MEMBER COULD HAVE SET THE WINGS INTO TAKEOFF POSITION.
WE'VE BEEN QUESTIONING EVERYONE SINCE THE DAY IT HAPPENED.
DOZENS OF ARRESTS HAVE BEEN MADE TO FIND YOU.
YOU'RE ARRESTING INNOCENT PEOPLE? BUT...WHY?!
YOU WERE KIDNAPPED.
YOU'RE NOT MAKING ANY SENSE!
I'VE WATCHED YOU TYPE THAT CODE A THOUSAND TIMES.
I WAS THE ONE WHO FLEW THE INTREPYD RAY, DAD.
I STOLE IT.
WHY WON'T YOU BELIEVE ME?

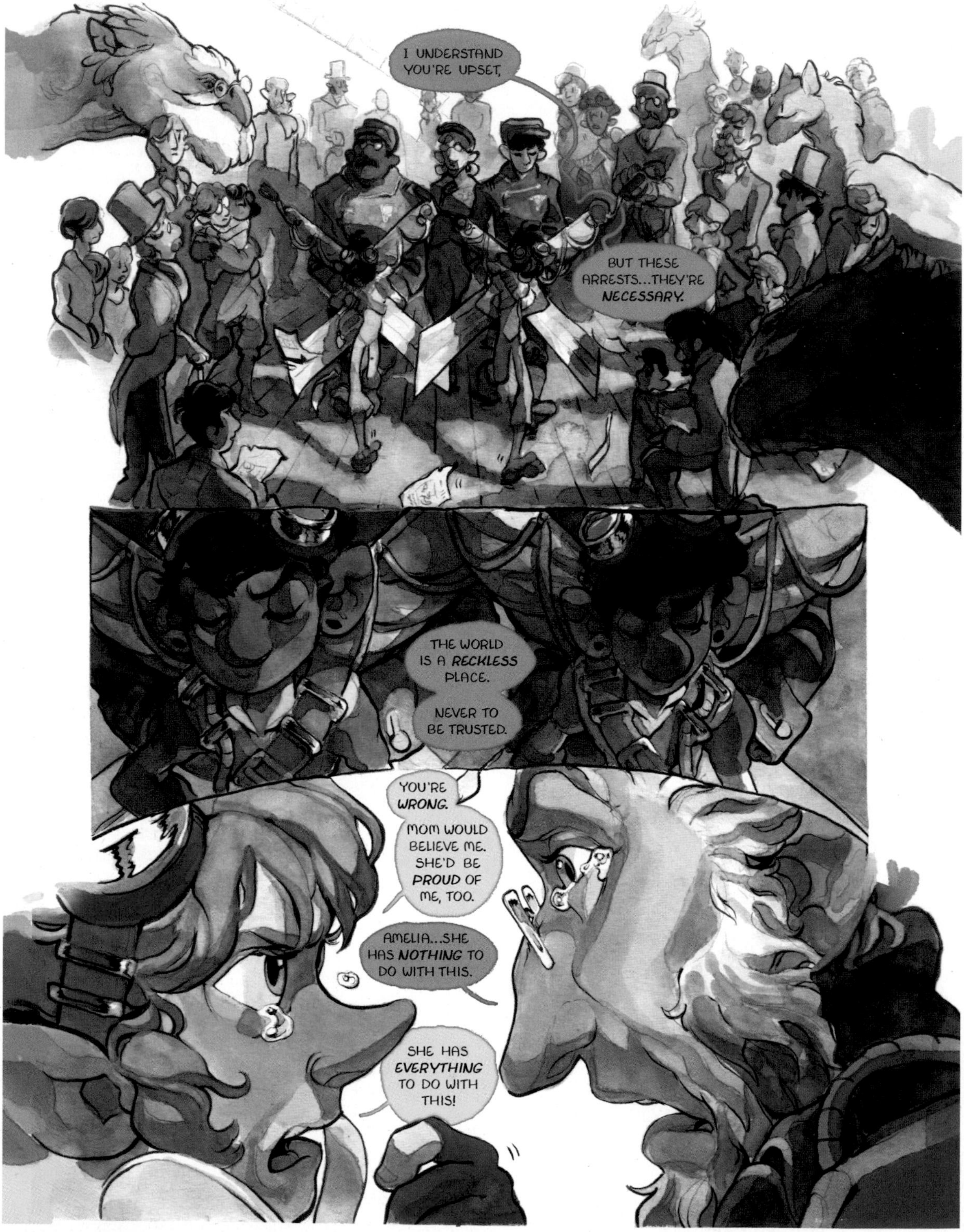
I UNDERSTAND YOU'RE UPSET,
BUT THESE ARRESTS...THEY'RE NECESSARY.
THE WORLD IS A RECKLESS PLACE.
NEVER TO BE TRUSTED.
YOU'RE WRONG.
MOM WOULD BELIEVE ME. SHE'D BE PROUD OF ME, TOO.
AMELIA...SHE HAS NOTHING TO DO WITH THIS.
SHE HAS EVERYTHING TO DO WITH THIS!

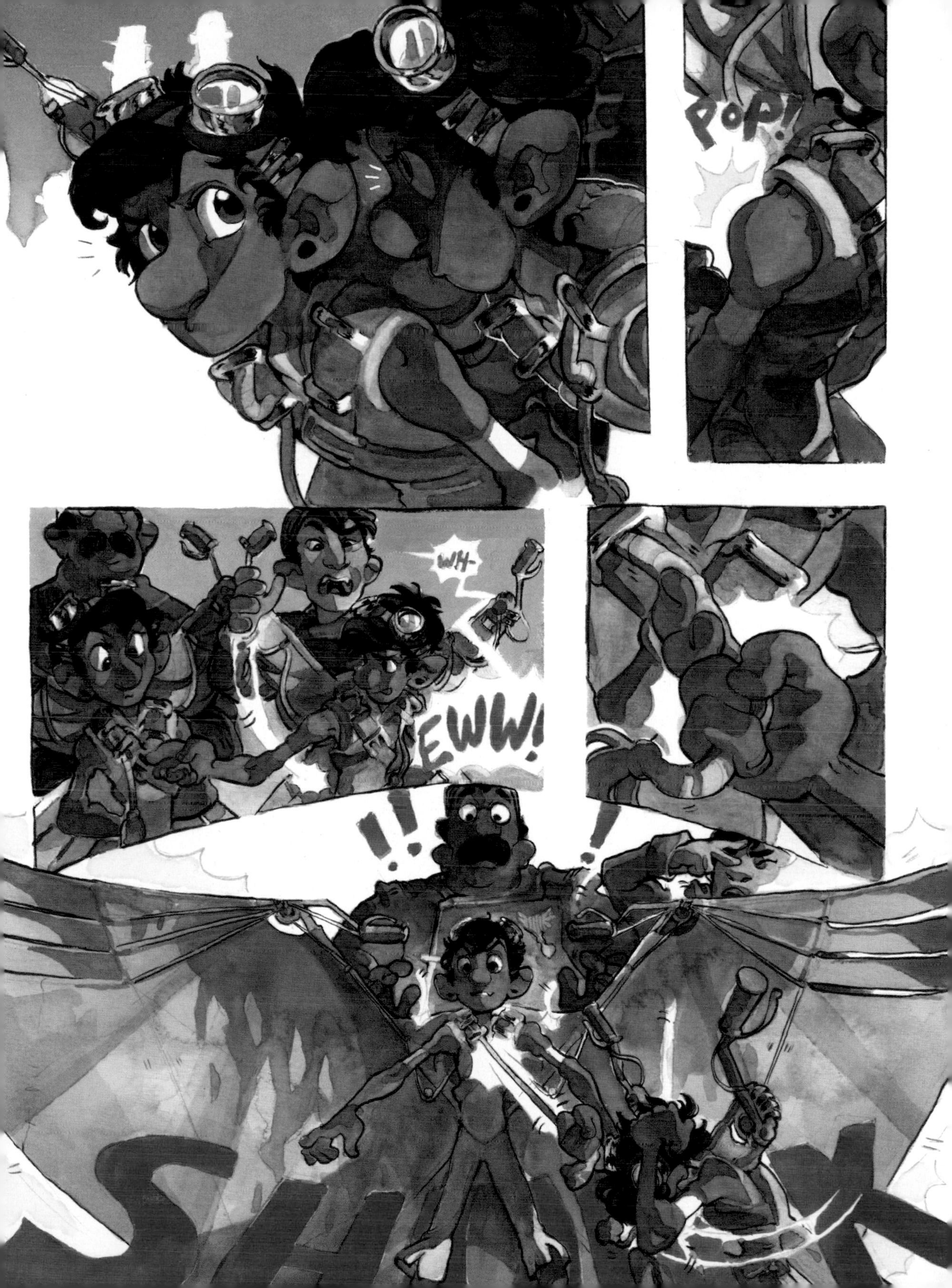
POP!
WH-
EWW!
!!
!

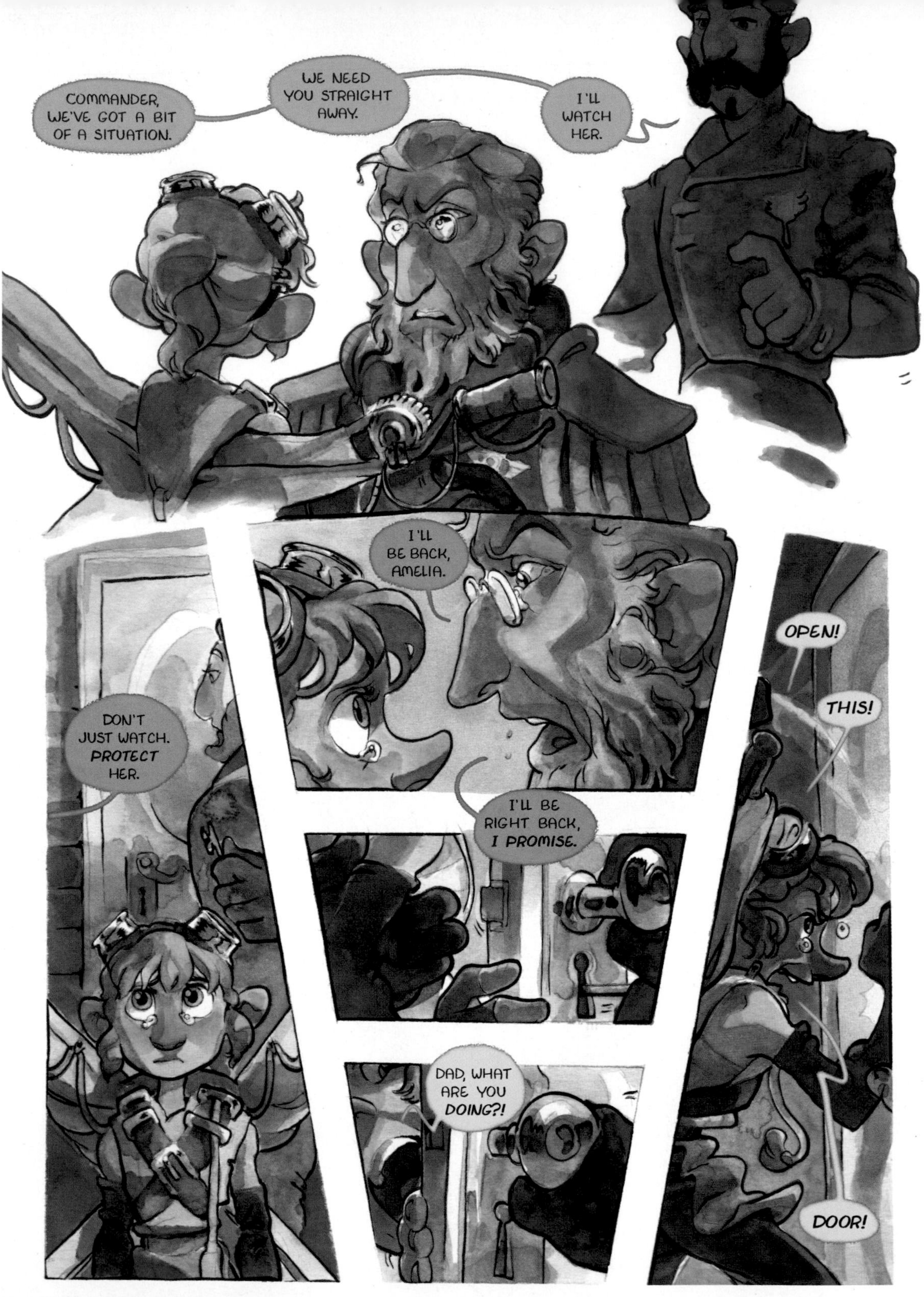
COMMANDER, WE'VE GOT A BIT OF A SITUATION.
WE NEED YOU STRAIGHT AWAY.
I'LL WATCH HER.
DON'T JUST WATCH. *PROTECT* HER.
I'LL BE BACK, AMELIA.
I'LL BE RIGHT BACK, *I PROMISE.*
DAD, WHAT ARE YOU *DOING?!*
OPEN!
THIS!
DOOR!

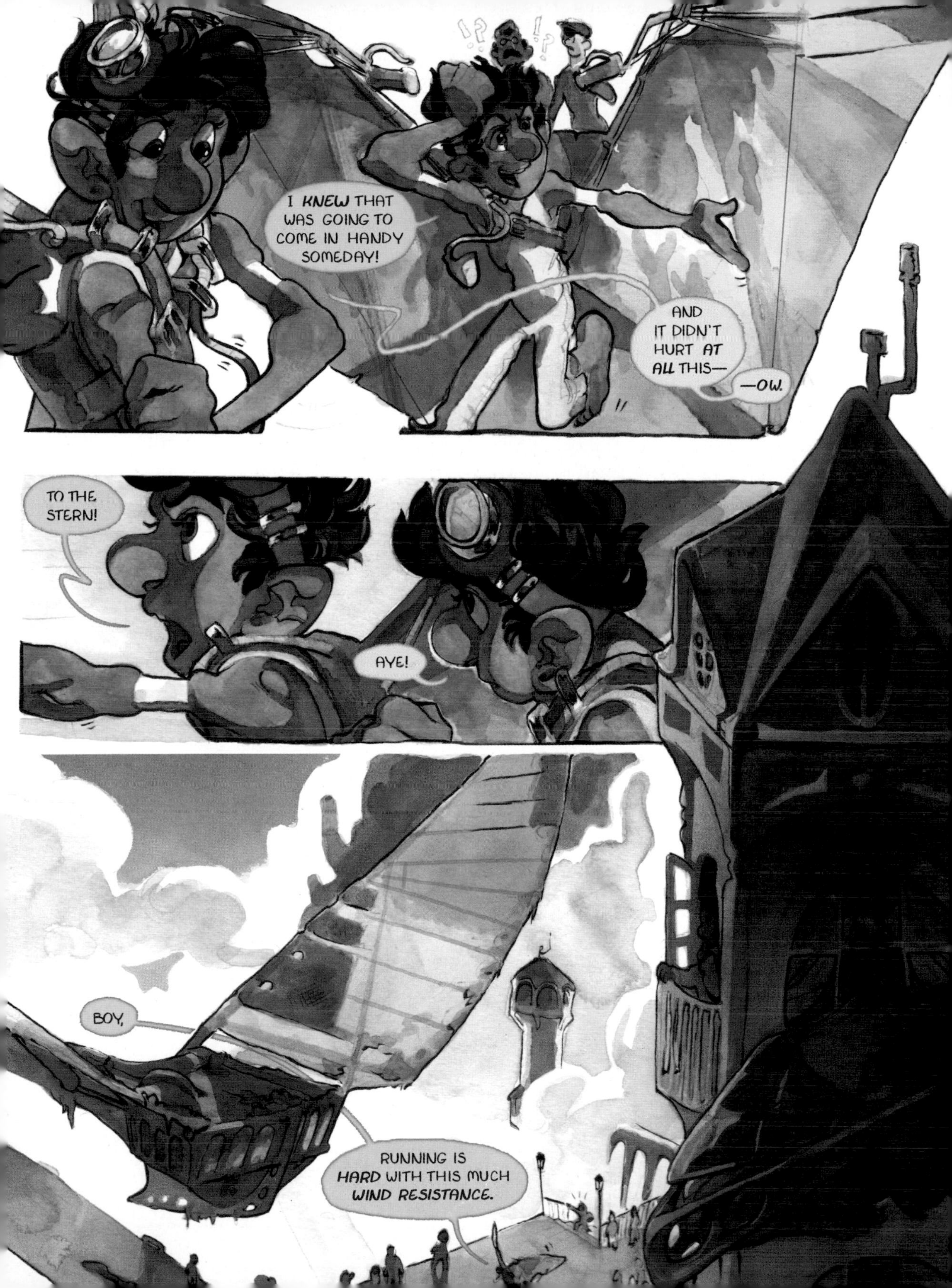

!?
!?
I KNEW THAT WAS GOING TO COME IN HANDY SOMEDAY!
AND IT DIDN'T HURT AT ALL THIS—
—OW.
TO THE STERN!
AYE!
BOY,
RUNNING IS HARD WITH THIS MUCH WIND RESISTANCE.

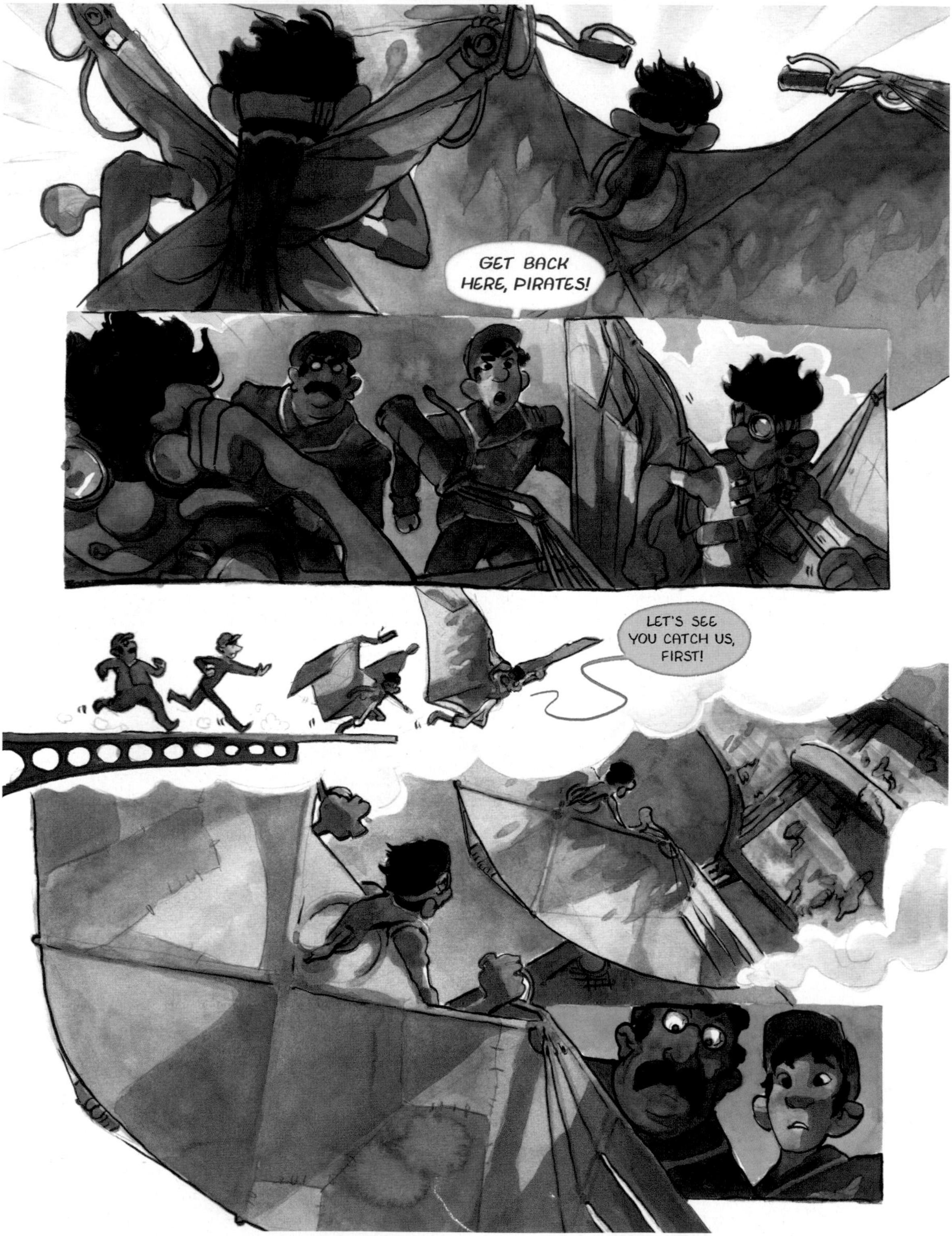
GET BACK HERE, PIRATES!
LET'S SEE YOU CATCH US, FIRST!

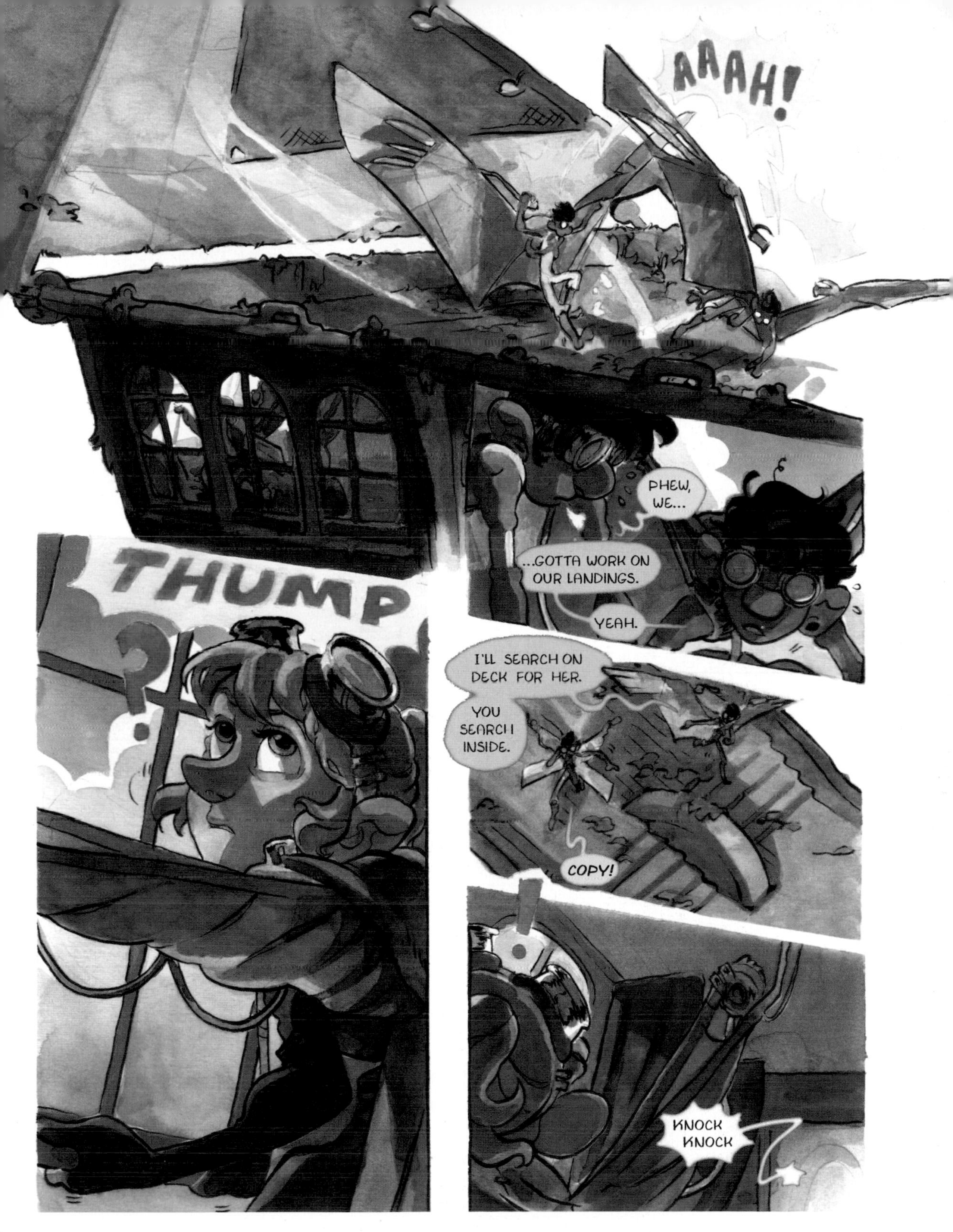
AAAH!
THUMP
PHEW, WE...
...GOTTA WORK ON OUR LANDINGS.
YEAH.
I'LL SEARCH ON DECK FOR HER.
YOU SEARCH INSIDE.
COPY!
KNOCK KNOCK

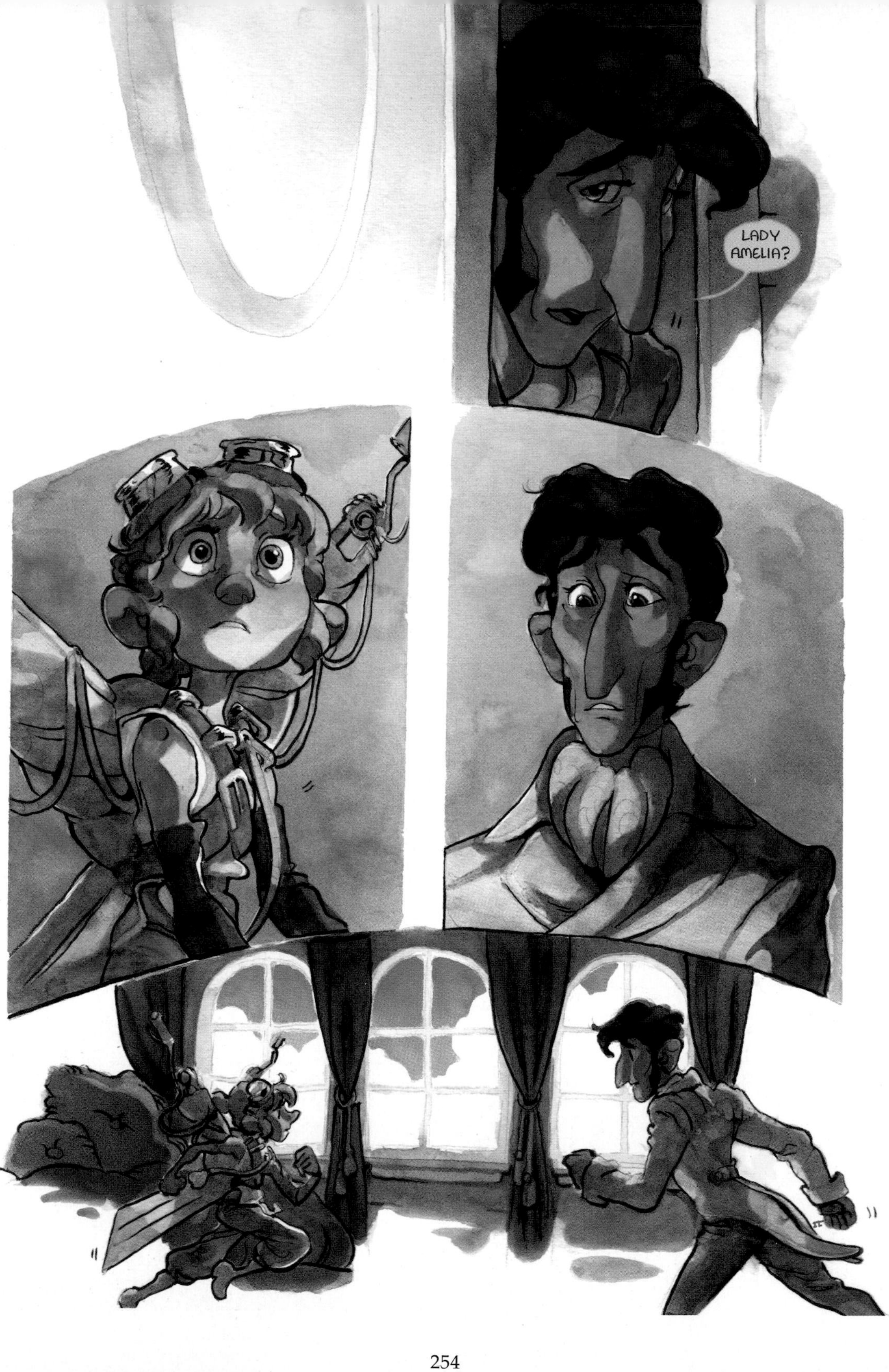
LADY
AMELIA?

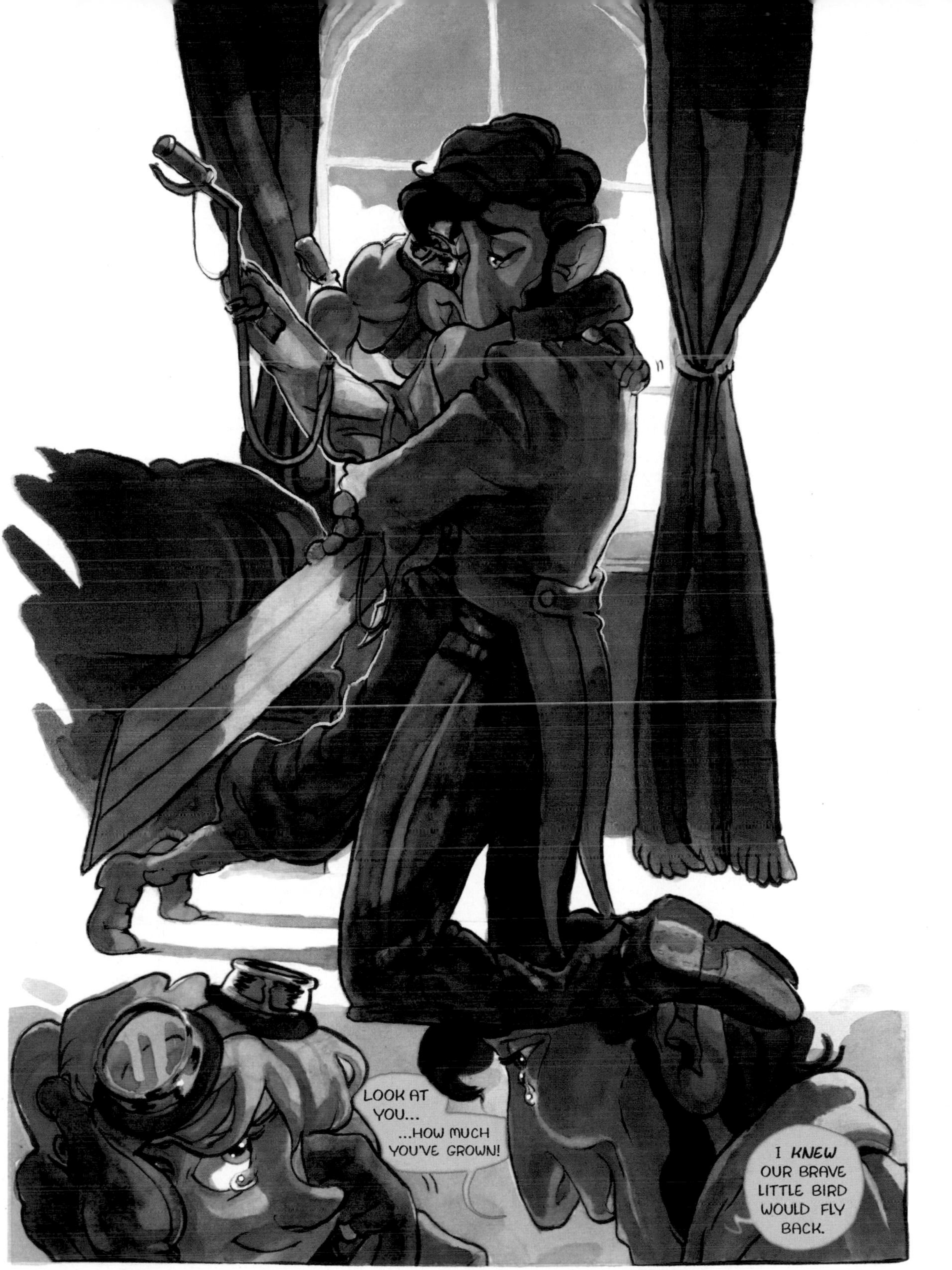
LOOK AT YOU...
...HOW MUCH YOU'VE GROWN!
I KNEW OUR BRAVE LITTLE BIRD WOULD FLY BACK.

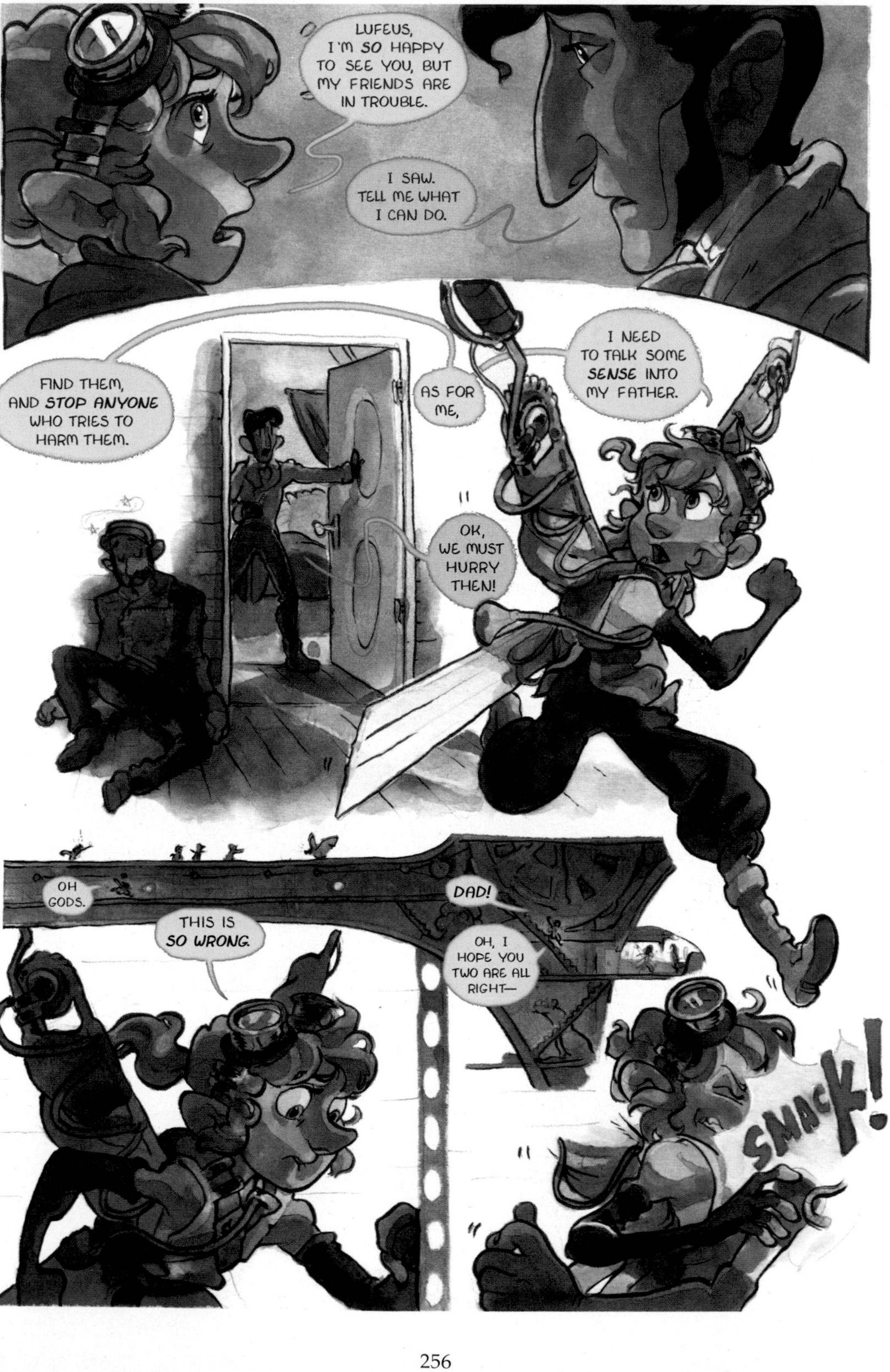
LUFEUS, I'M SO HAPPY TO SEE YOU, BUT MY FRIENDS ARE IN TROUBLE.
I SAW. TELL ME WHAT I CAN DO.
FIND THEM, AND STOP ANYONE WHO TRIES TO HARM THEM.
AS FOR ME,
I NEED TO TALK SOME SENSE INTO MY FATHER.
OK, WE MUST HURRY THEN!
OH GODS.
THIS IS SO WRONG.
DAD!
OH, I HOPE YOU TWO ARE ALL RIGHT—
SMACK!

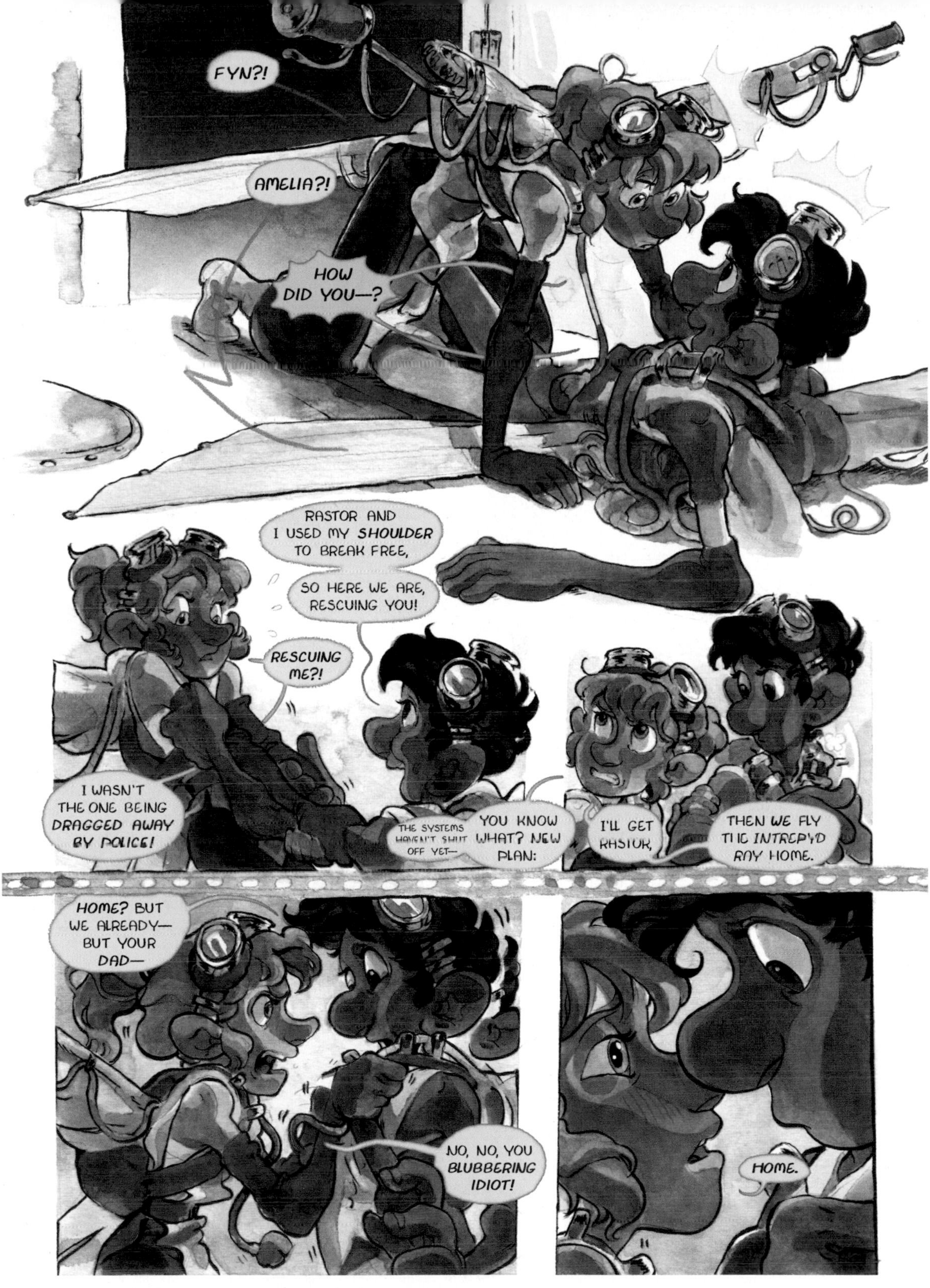
FYN?!
AMELIA?!
HOW DID YOU—?
RASTOR AND I USED MY SHOULDER TO BREAK FREE,
SO HERE WE ARE, RESCUING YOU!
RESCUING ME?!
I WASN'T THE ONE BEING DRAGGED AWAY BY POLICE!
THE SYSTEMS HAVEN'T SHUT OFF YET—
YOU KNOW WHAT? NEW PLAN:
I'LL GET RASTOR,
THEN WE FLY THE INTREPYD RAY HOME.
HOME? BUT WE ALREADY— BUT YOUR DAD—
NO, NO, YOU BLUBBERING IDIOT!
HOME.

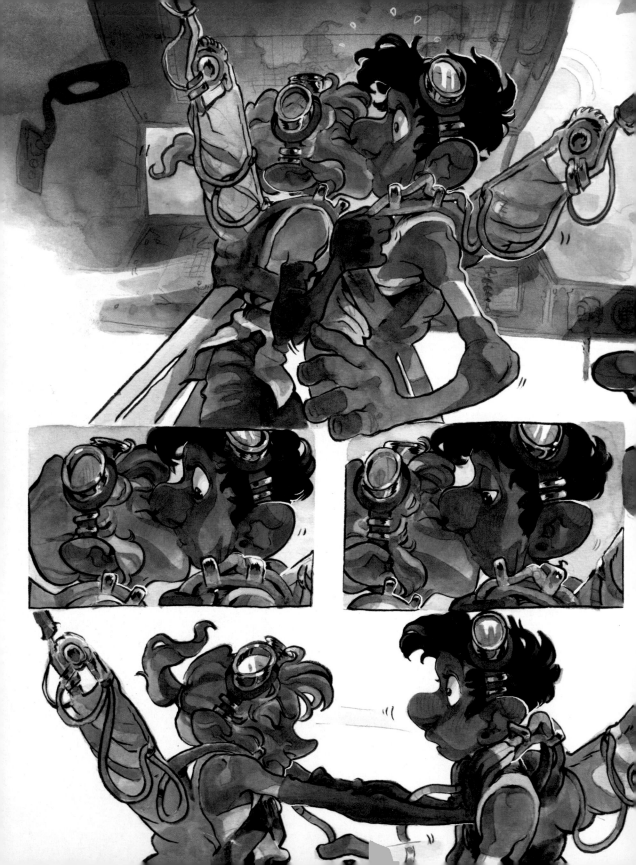

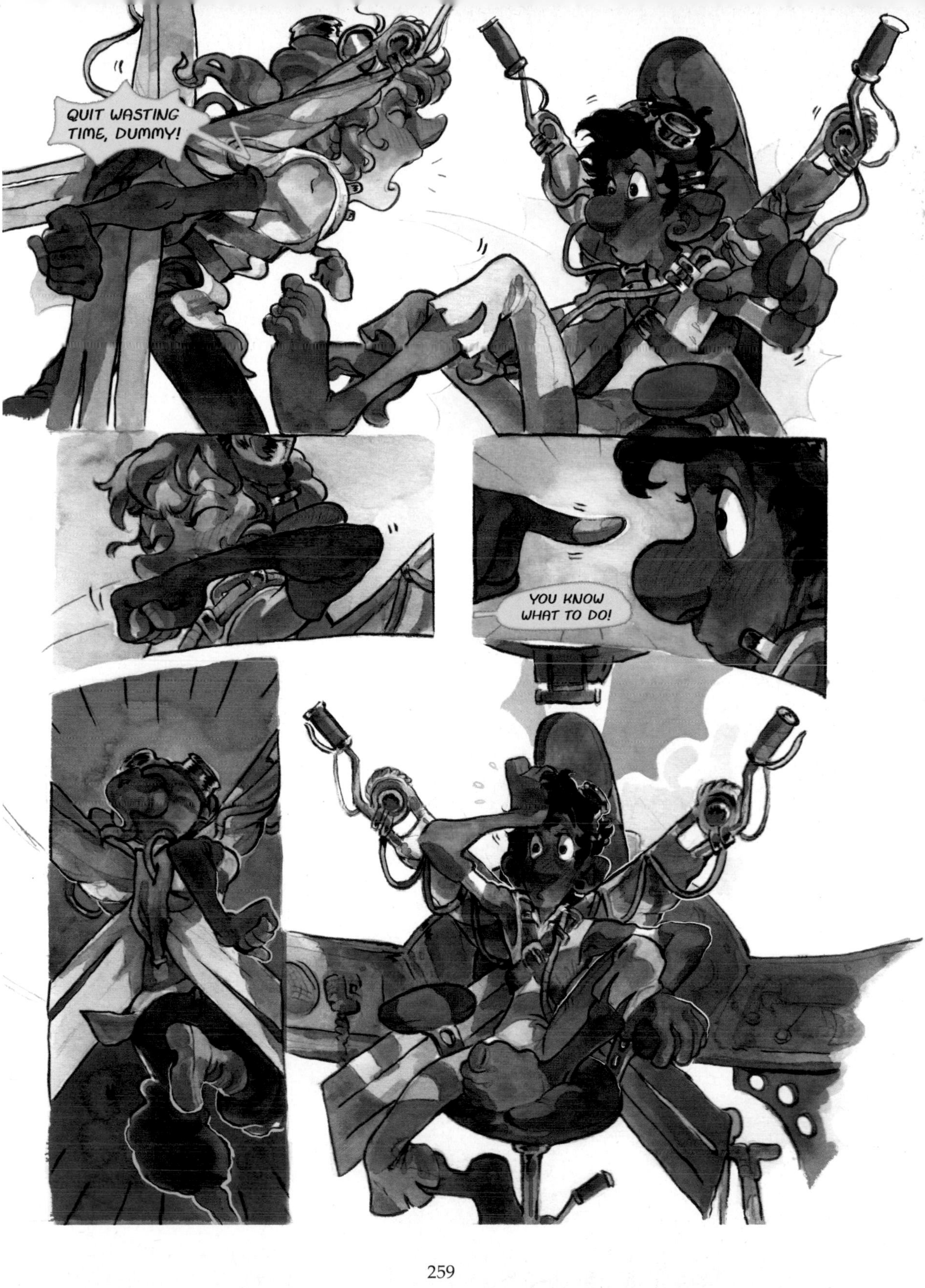
QUIT WASTING TIME, DUMMY!
YOU KNOW WHAT TO DO!

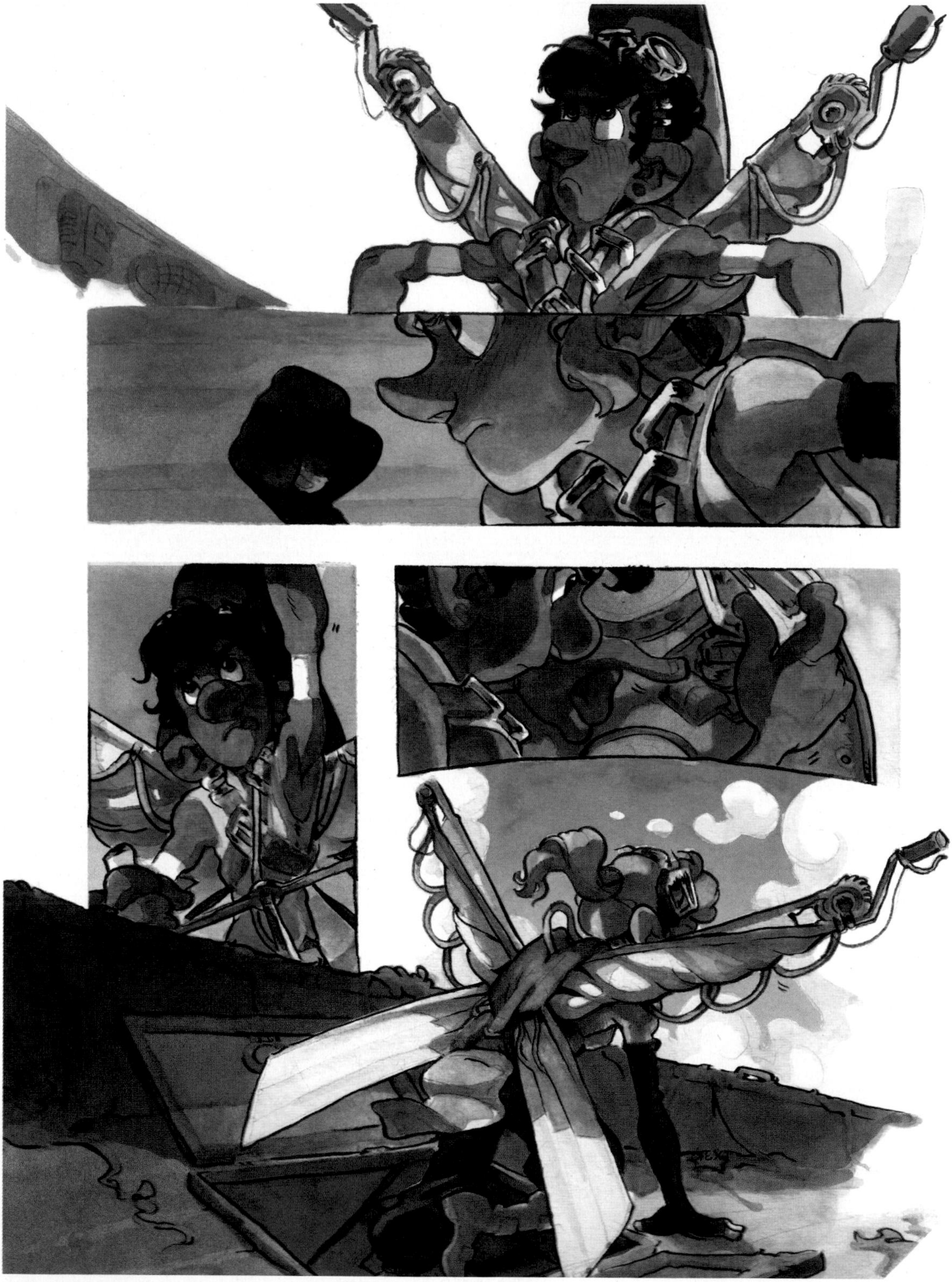

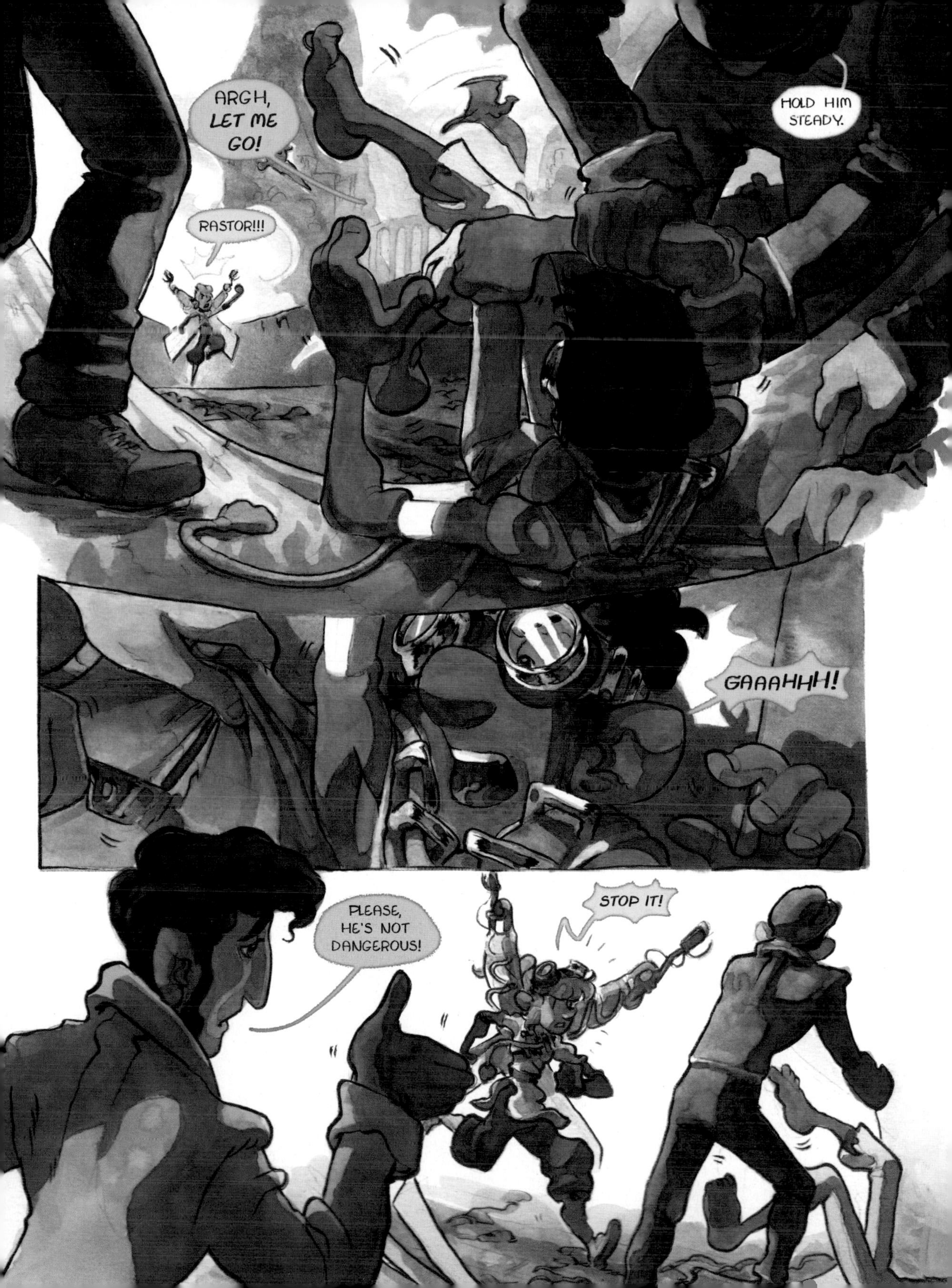
ARGH, LET ME GO!
HOLD HIM STEADY.
RASTOR!!!
GAAAHHH!
PLEASE, HE'S NOT DANGEROUS!
STOP IT!

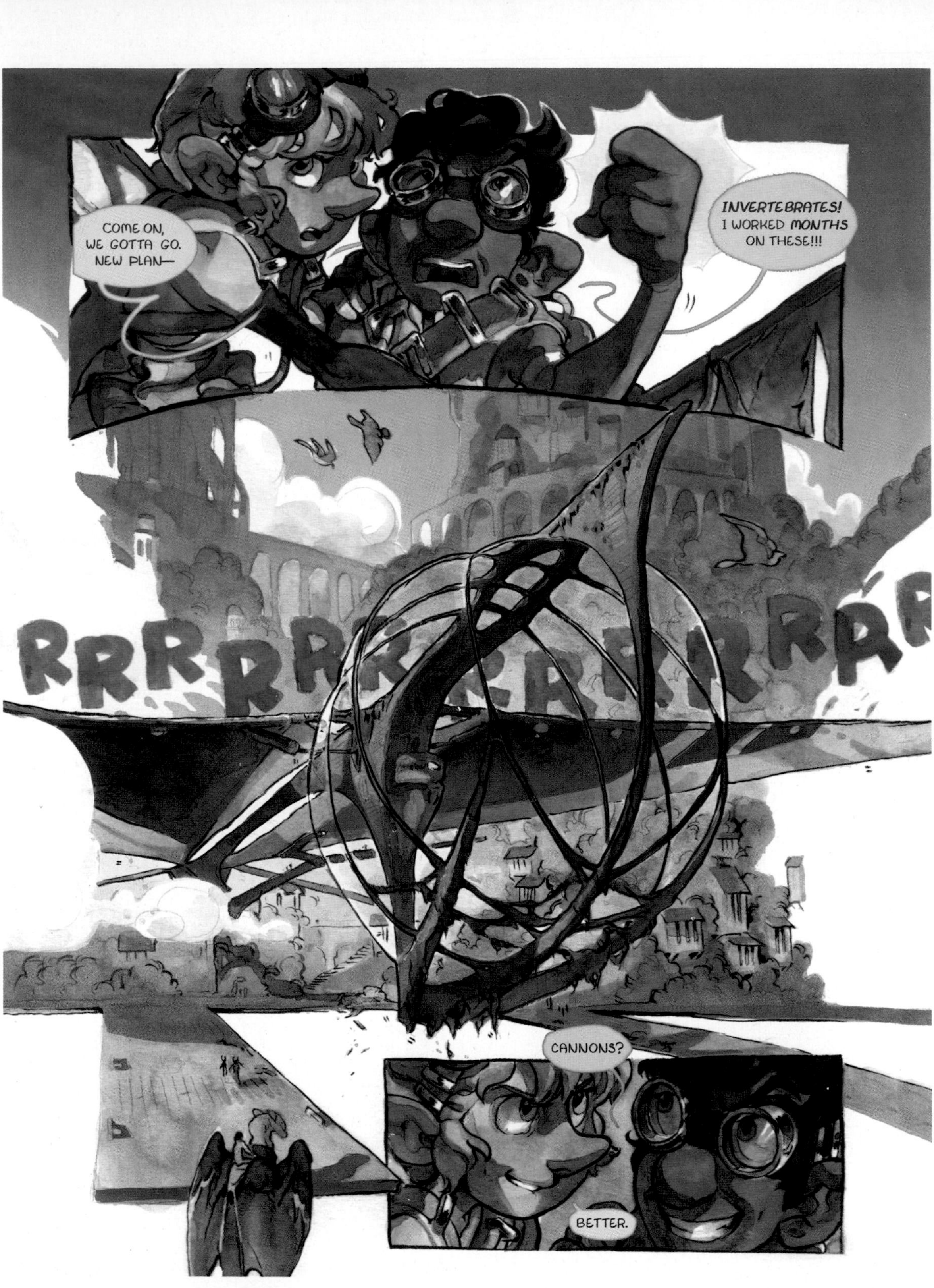
COME ON, WE GOTTA GO. NEW PLAN—
INVERTEBRATES! I WORKED MONTHS ON THESE!!!
RRRRRRRRRRRRRRRRR
CANNONS?
BETTER.

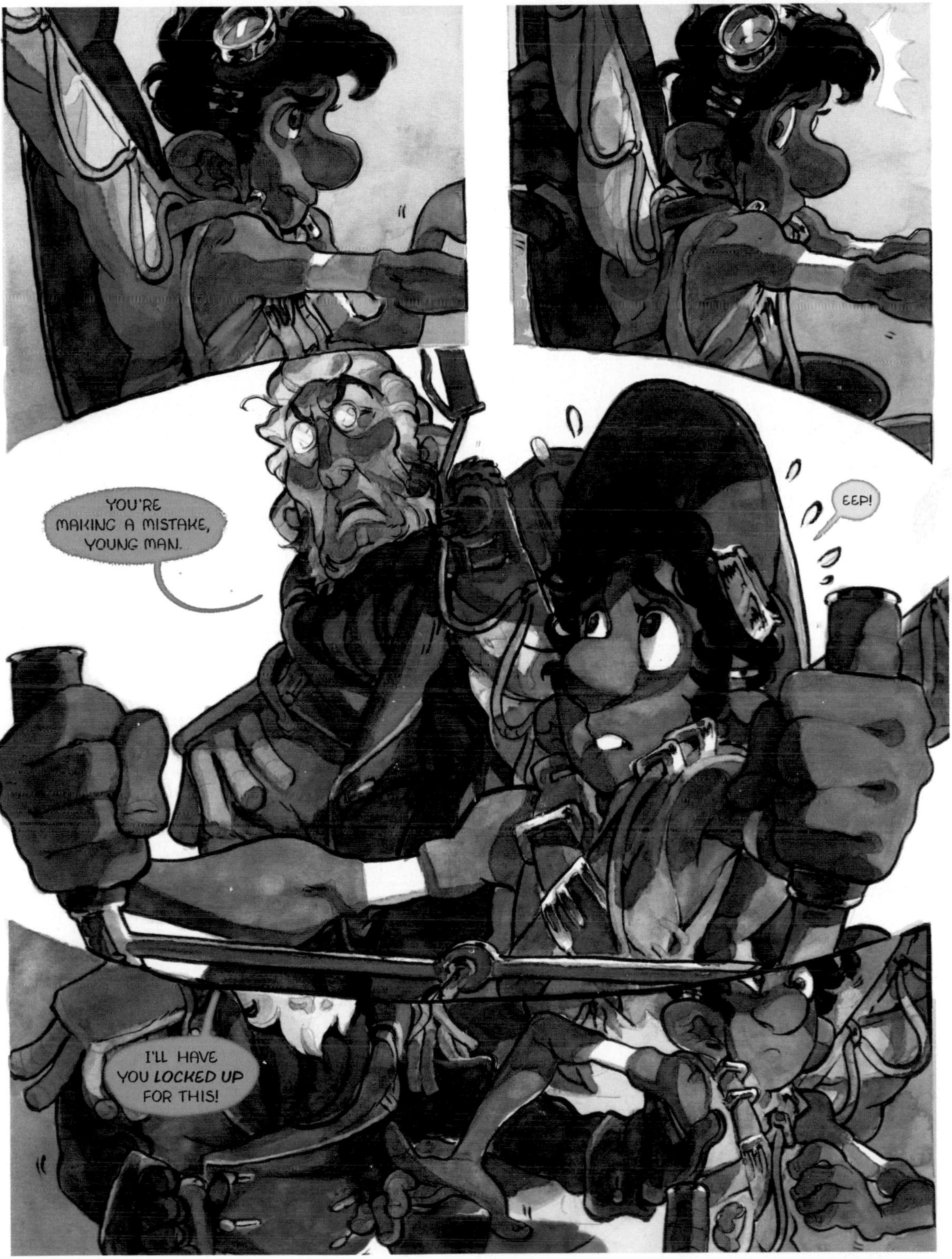
YOU'RE MAKING A MISTAKE, YOUNG MAN.
EEP!
I'LL HAVE YOU **LOCKED UP** FOR THIS!

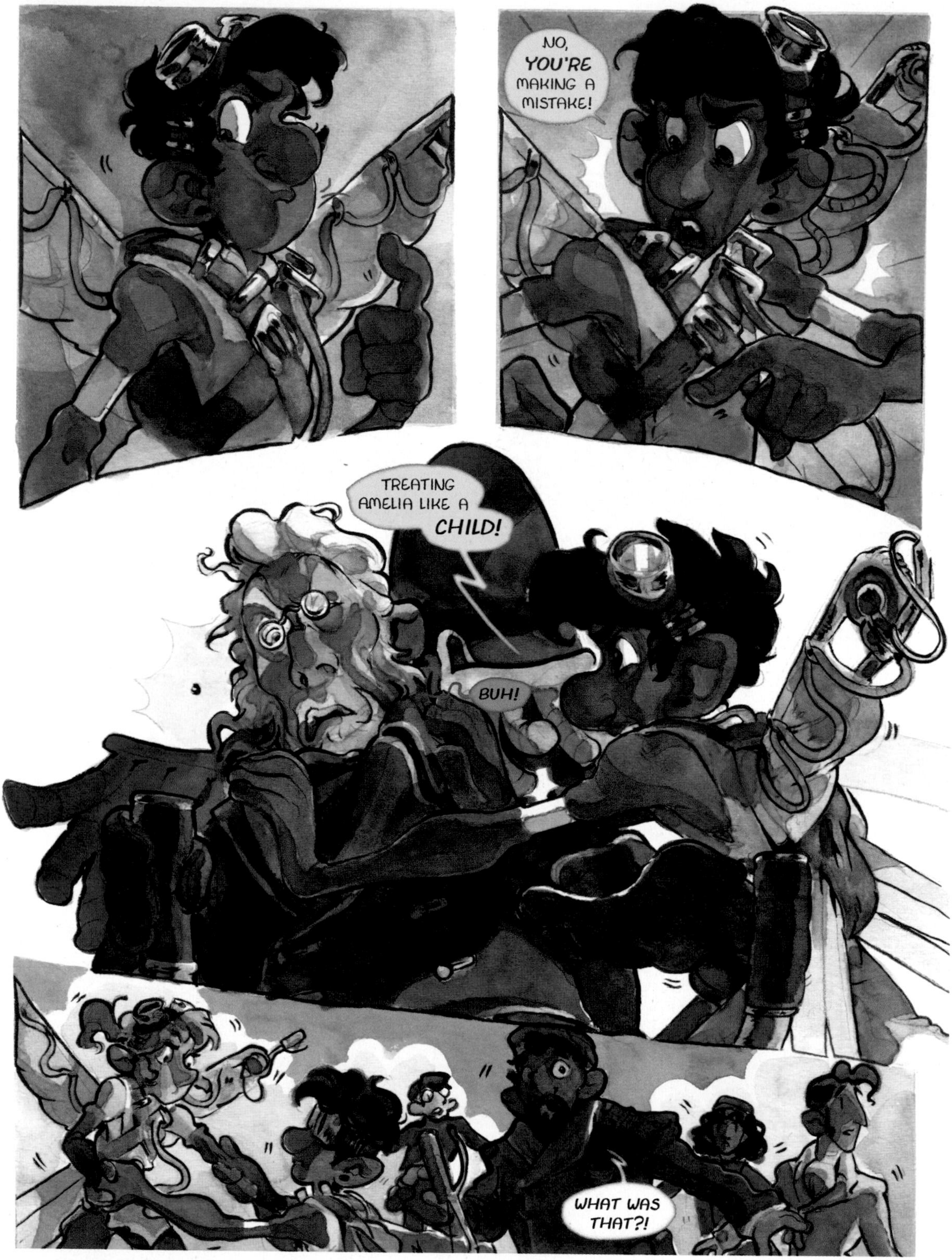
NO, YOU'RE MAKING A MISTAKE!
TREATING AMELIA LIKE A CHILD!
BUH!
WHAT WAS THAT?!

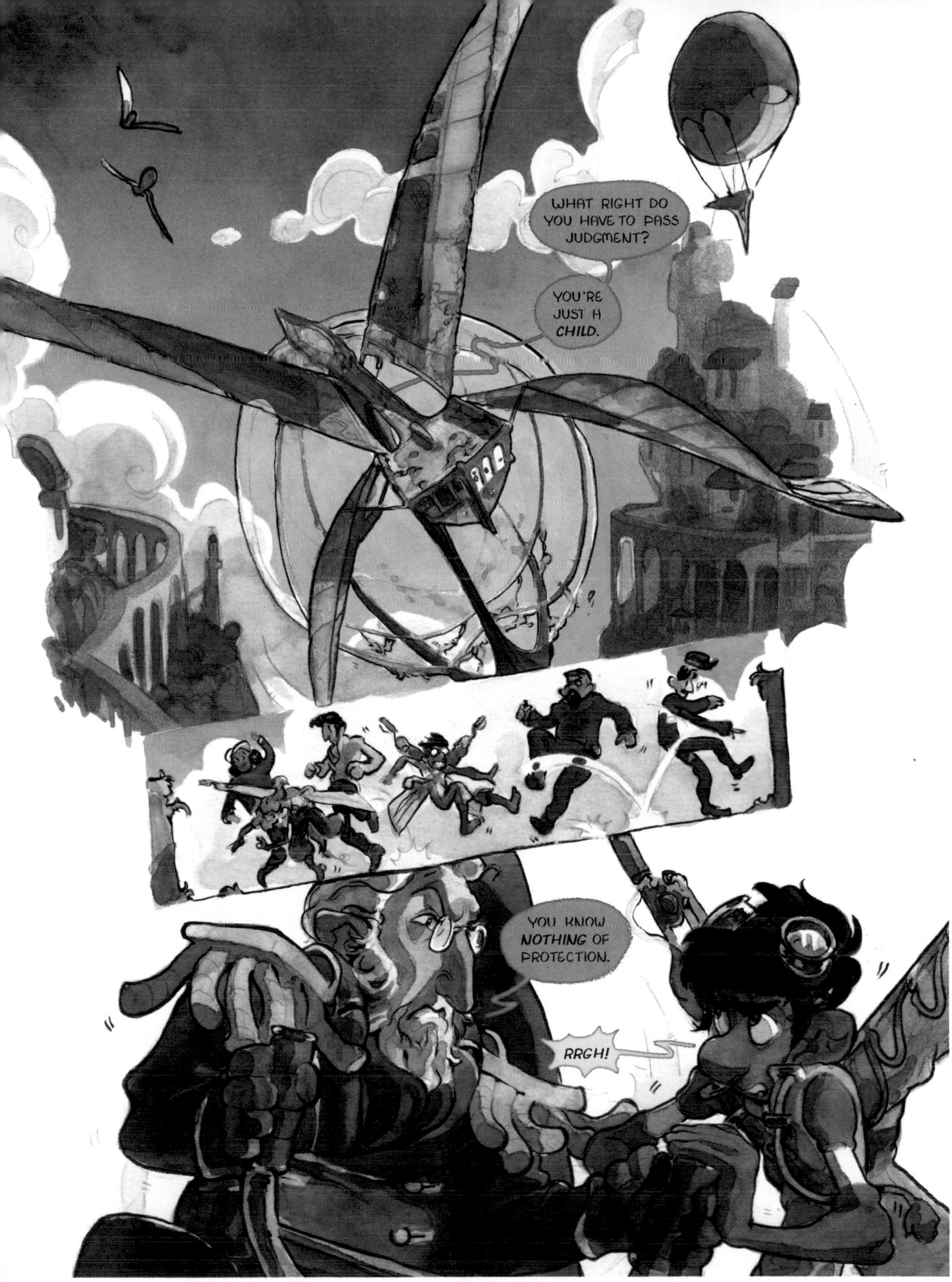

WHAT RIGHT DO YOU HAVE TO PASS JUDGMENT?
YOU'RE JUST A *CHILD.*
YOU KNOW *NOTHING* OF PROTECTION.
RRGH!

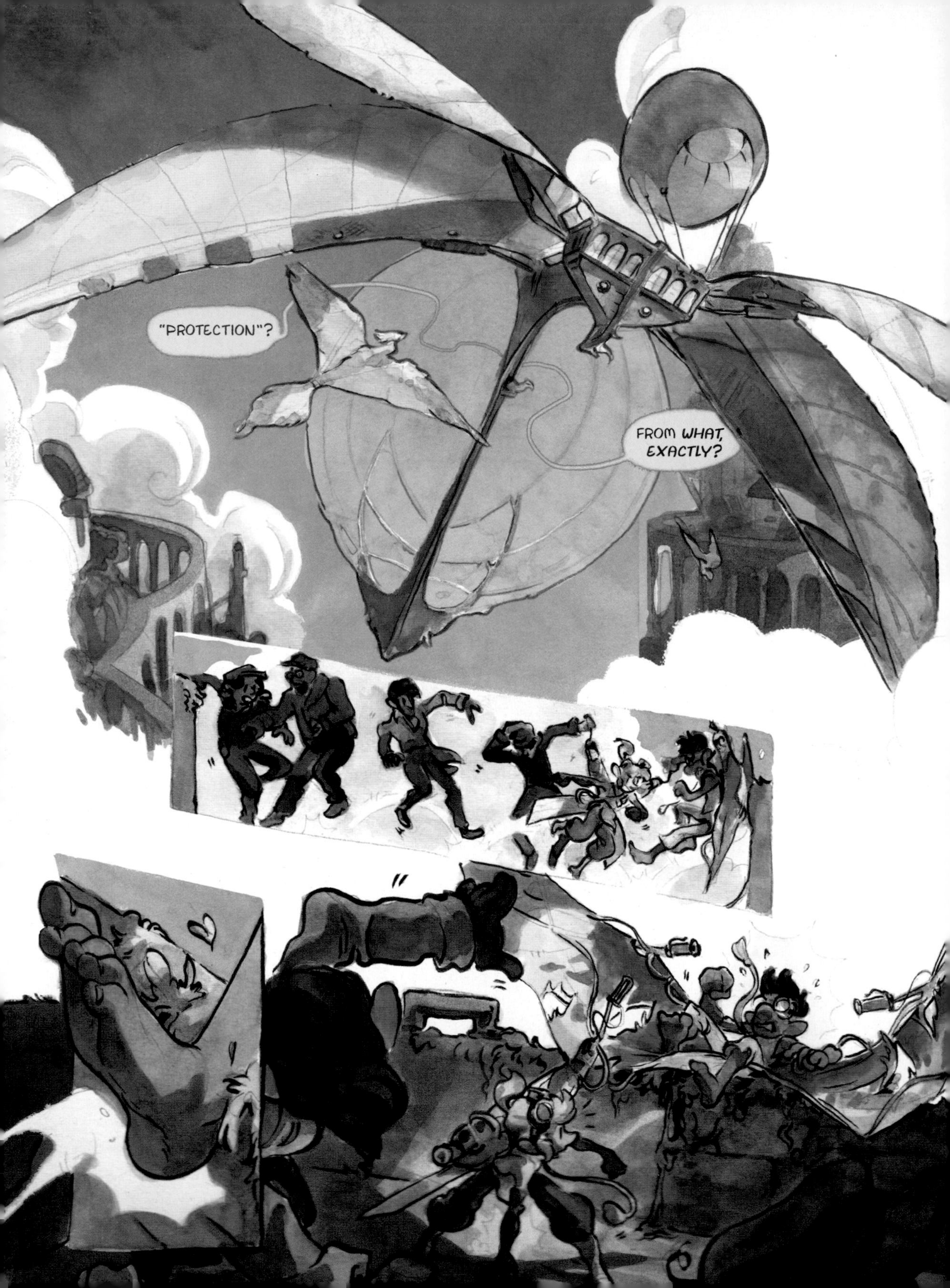
"PROTECTION"?
FROM WHAT, EXACTLY?

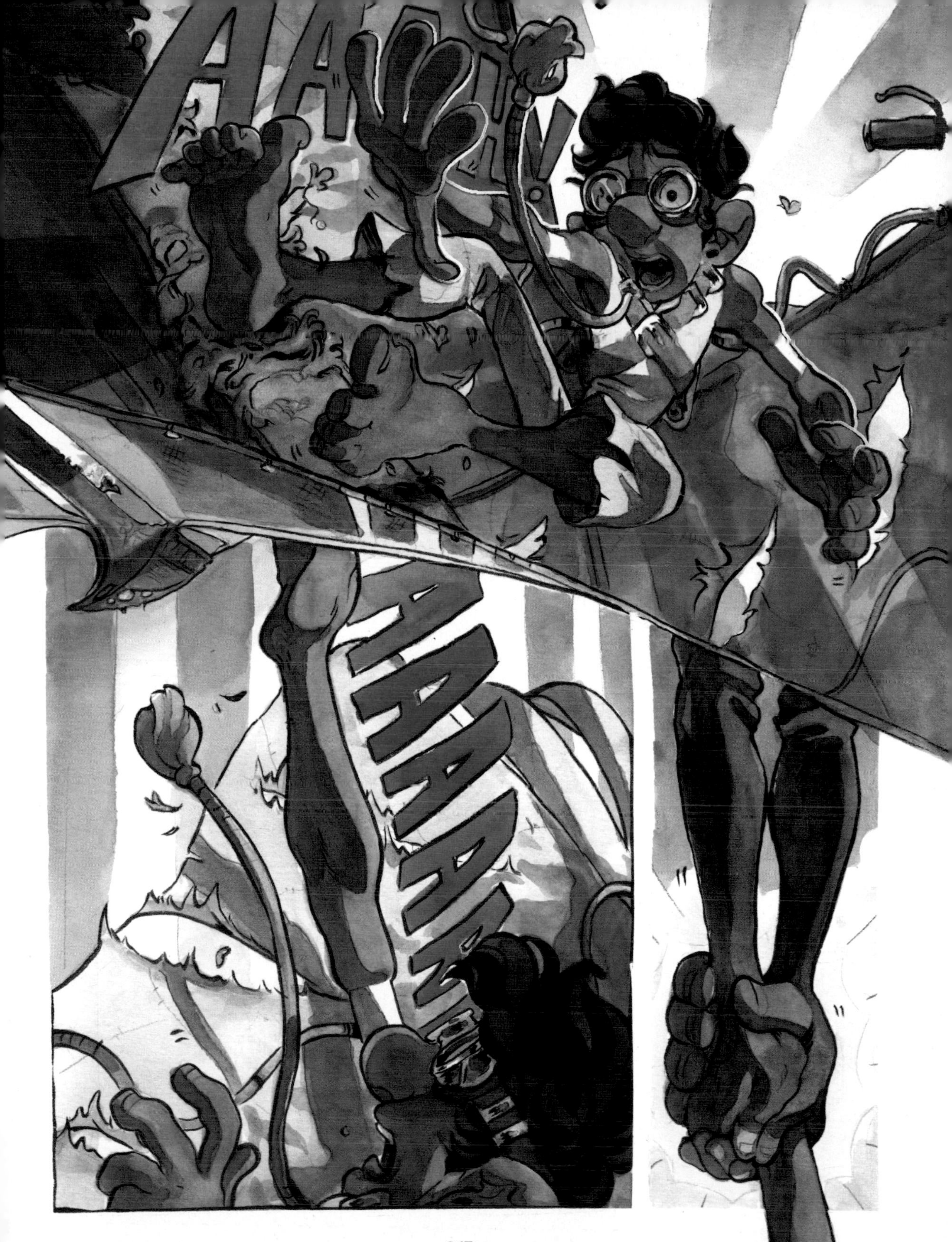

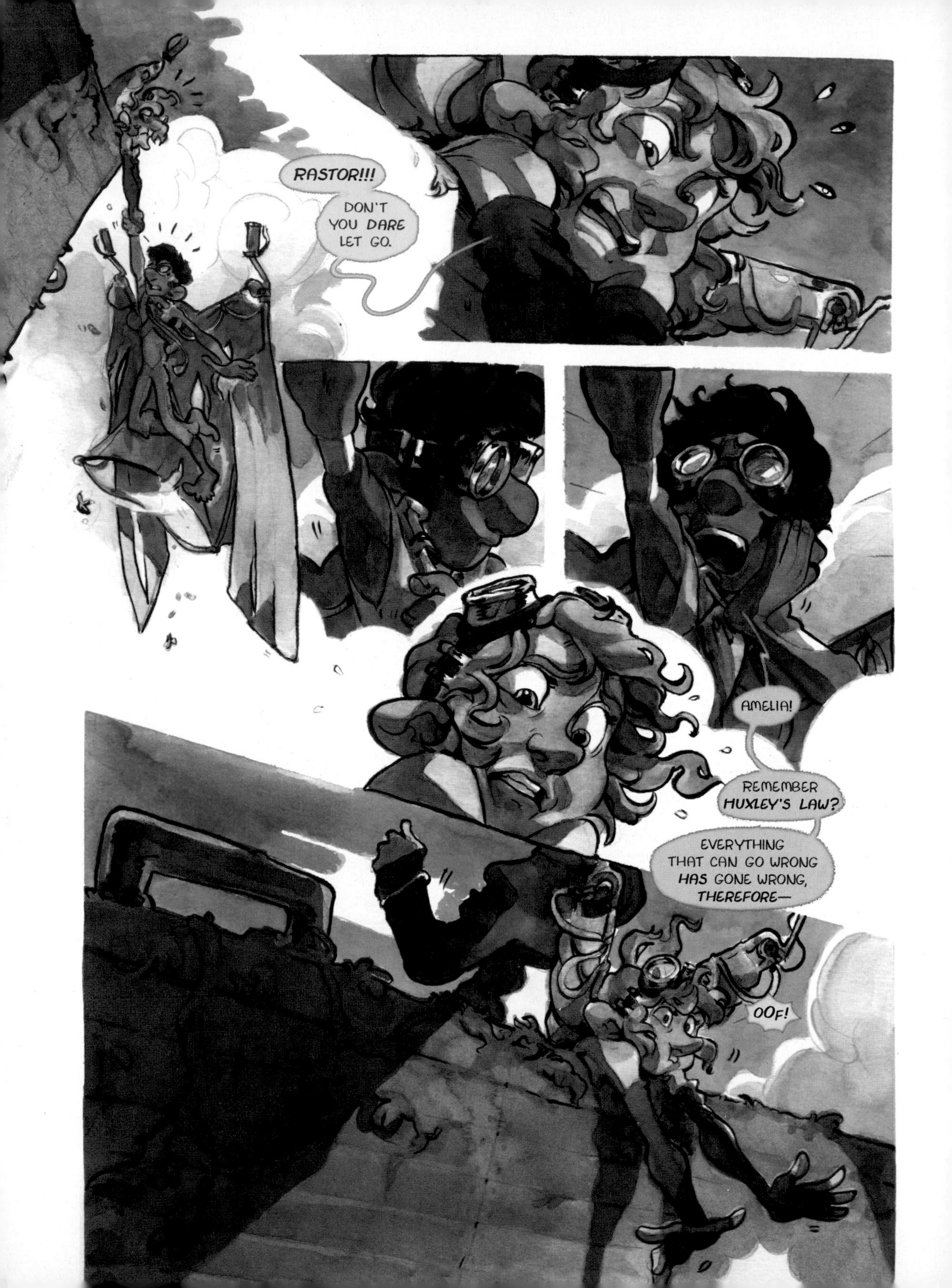
RASTOR!!!
DON'T YOU DARE LET GO.
AMELIA!
REMEMBER HUXLEY'S LAW?
EVERYTHING THAT CAN GO WRONG HAS GONE WRONG, THEREFORE—
OOF!

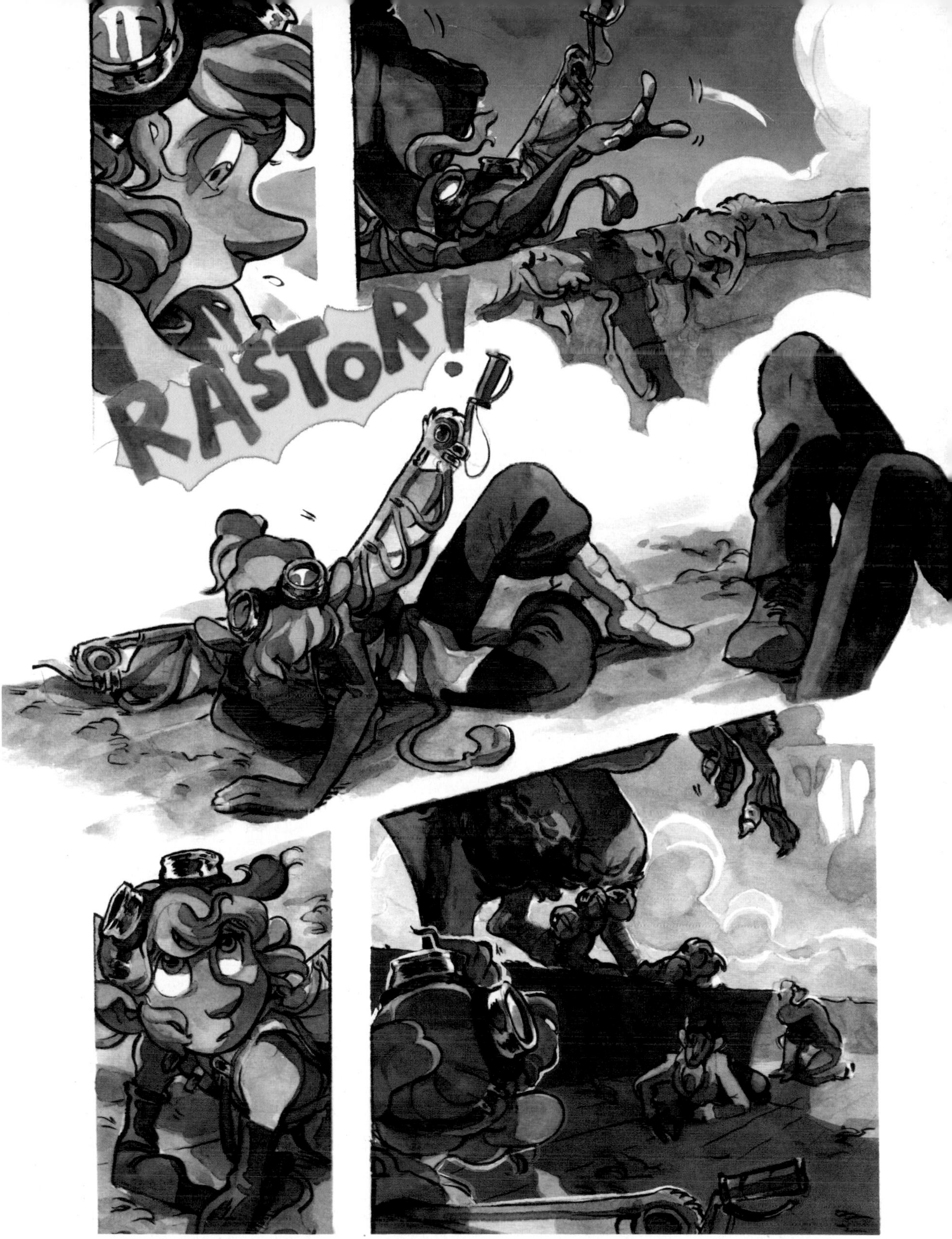
RASTOR!

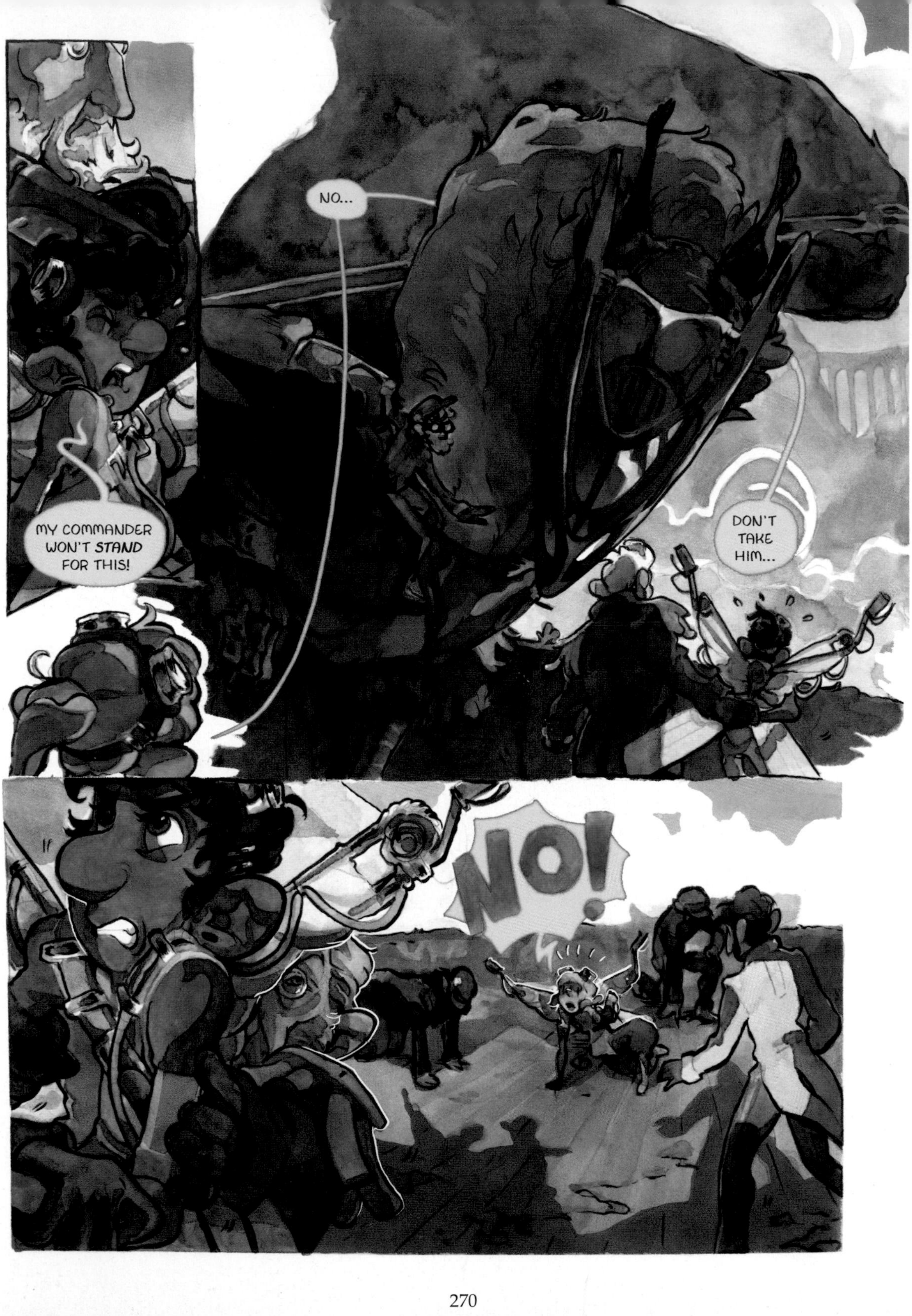
MY COMMANDER WON'T STAND FOR THIS!
NO...
DON'T TAKE HIM...
NO!

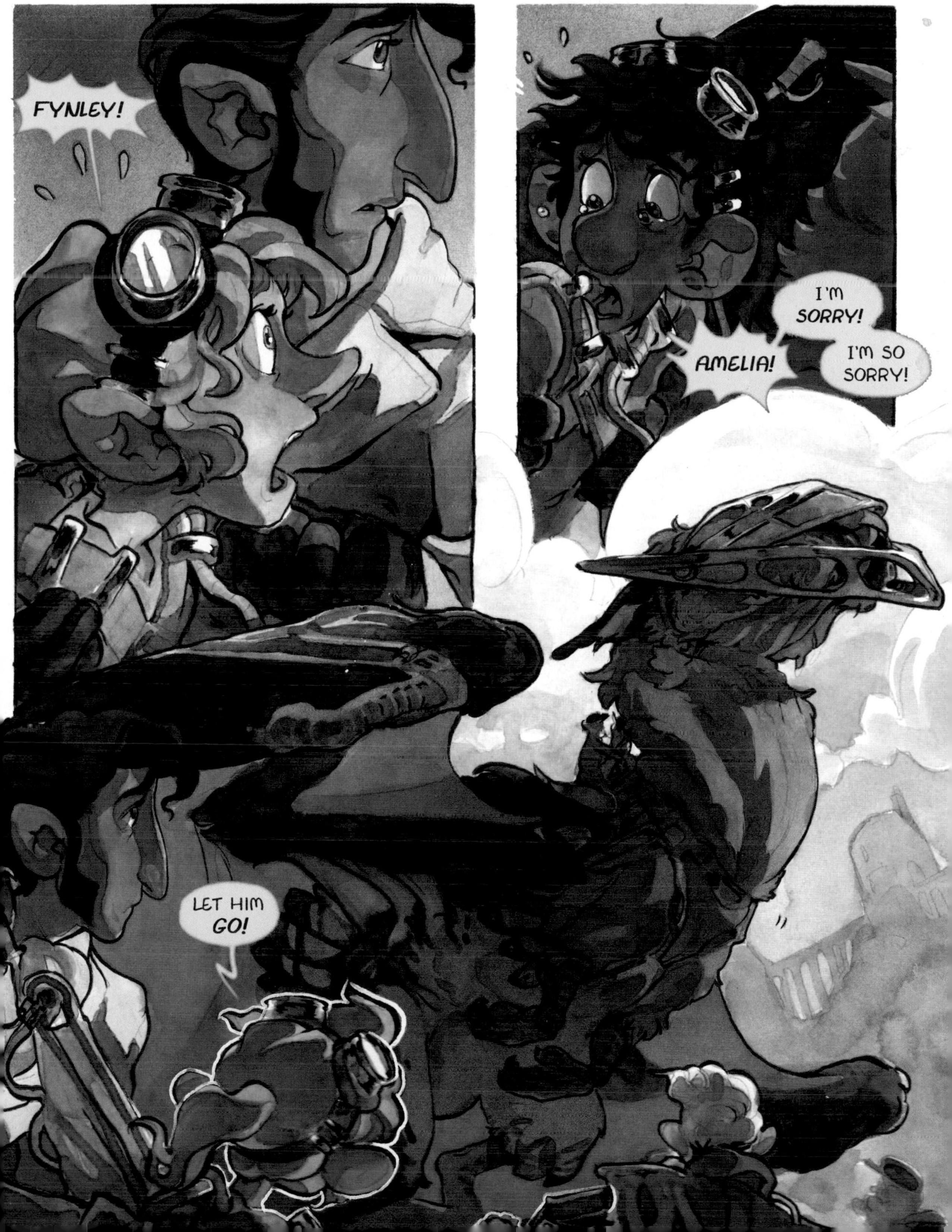
FYNLEY!
AMELIA!
I'M SORRY!
I'M SO SORRY!
LET HIM GO!

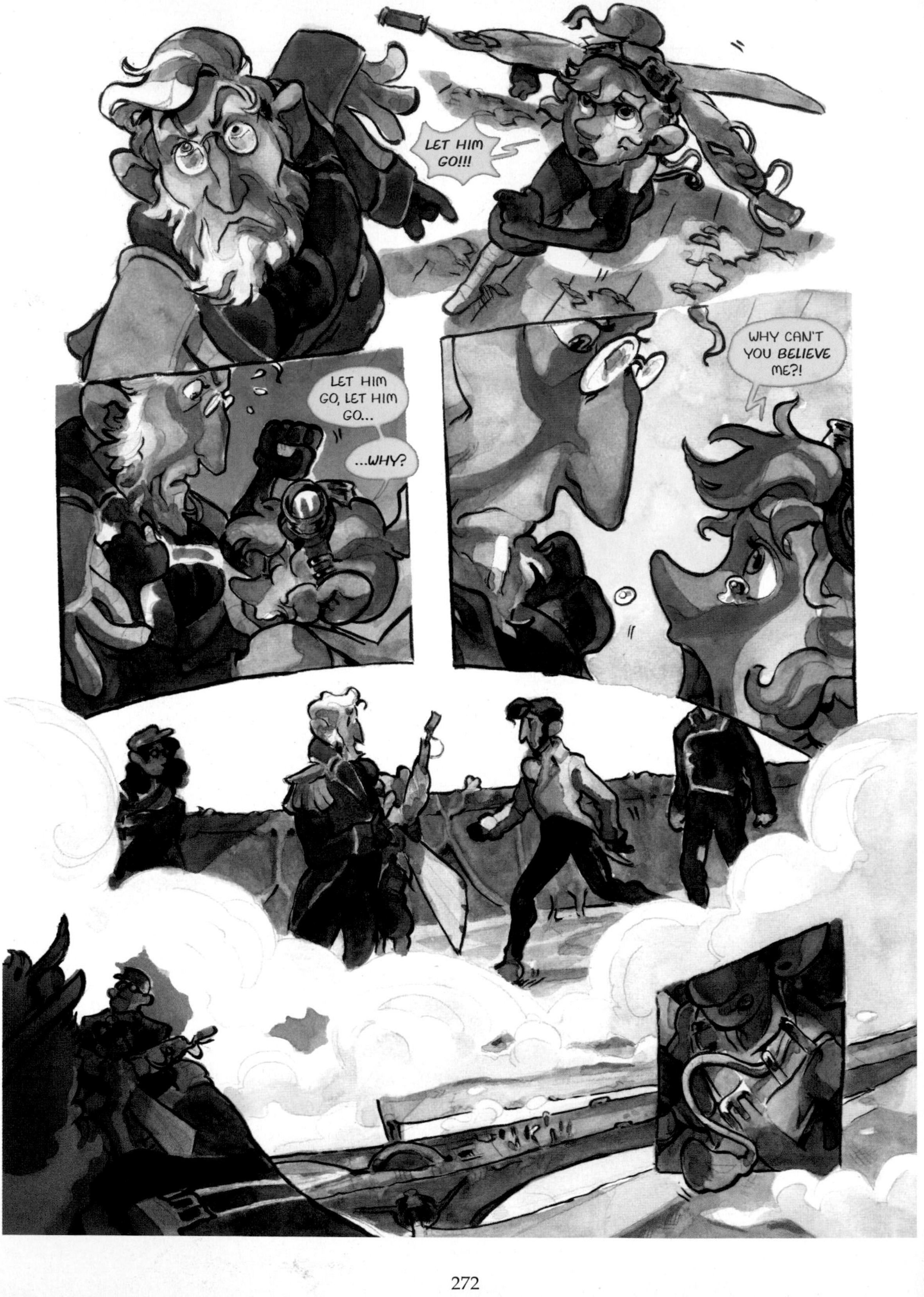
LET HIM GO!!!
LET HIM GO, LET HIM GO...
...WHY?
WHY CAN'T YOU BELIEVE ME?!

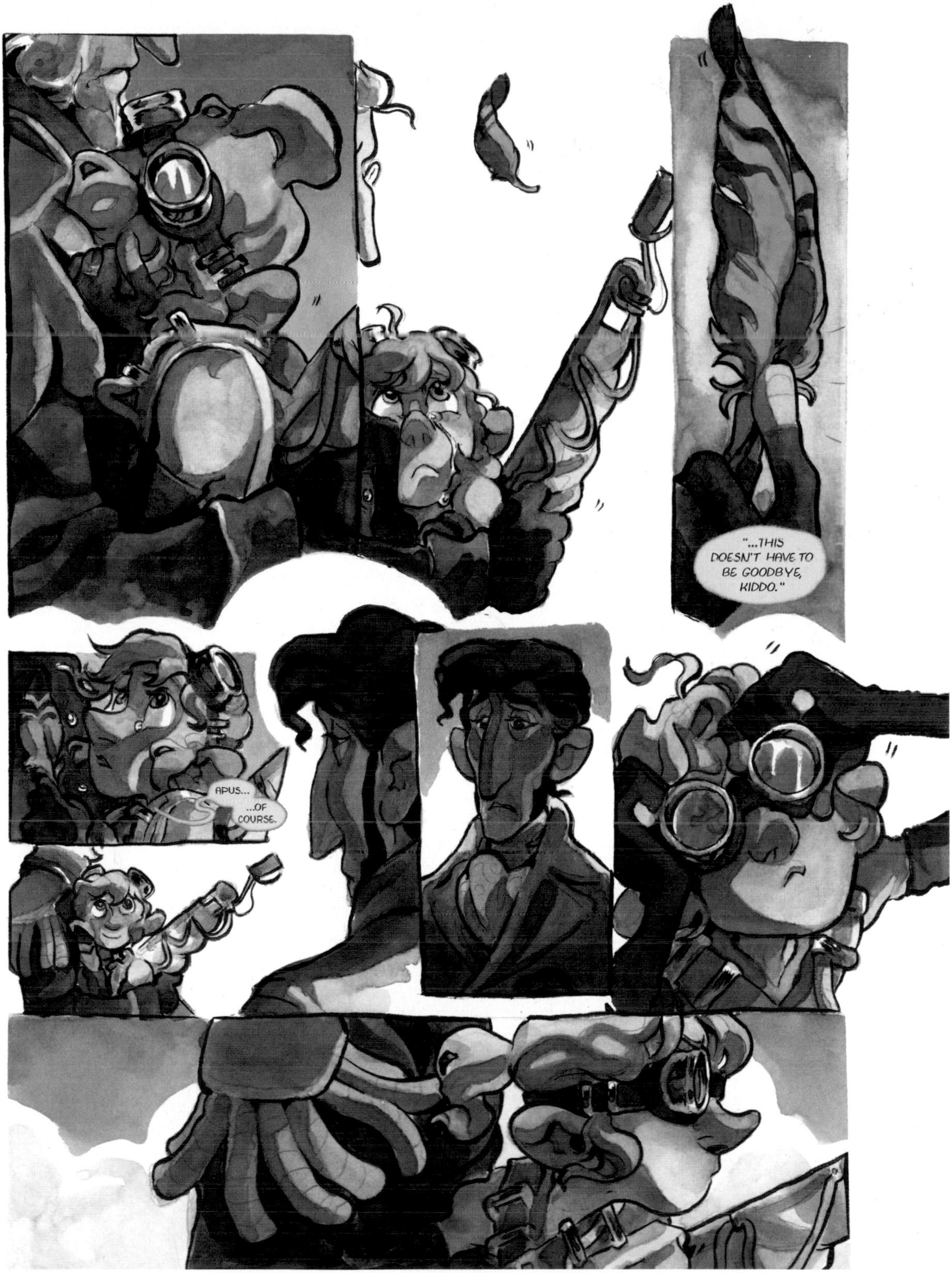
"...THIS DOESN'T HAVE TO BE GOODBYE, KIDDO."
APUS...
...OF COURSE.

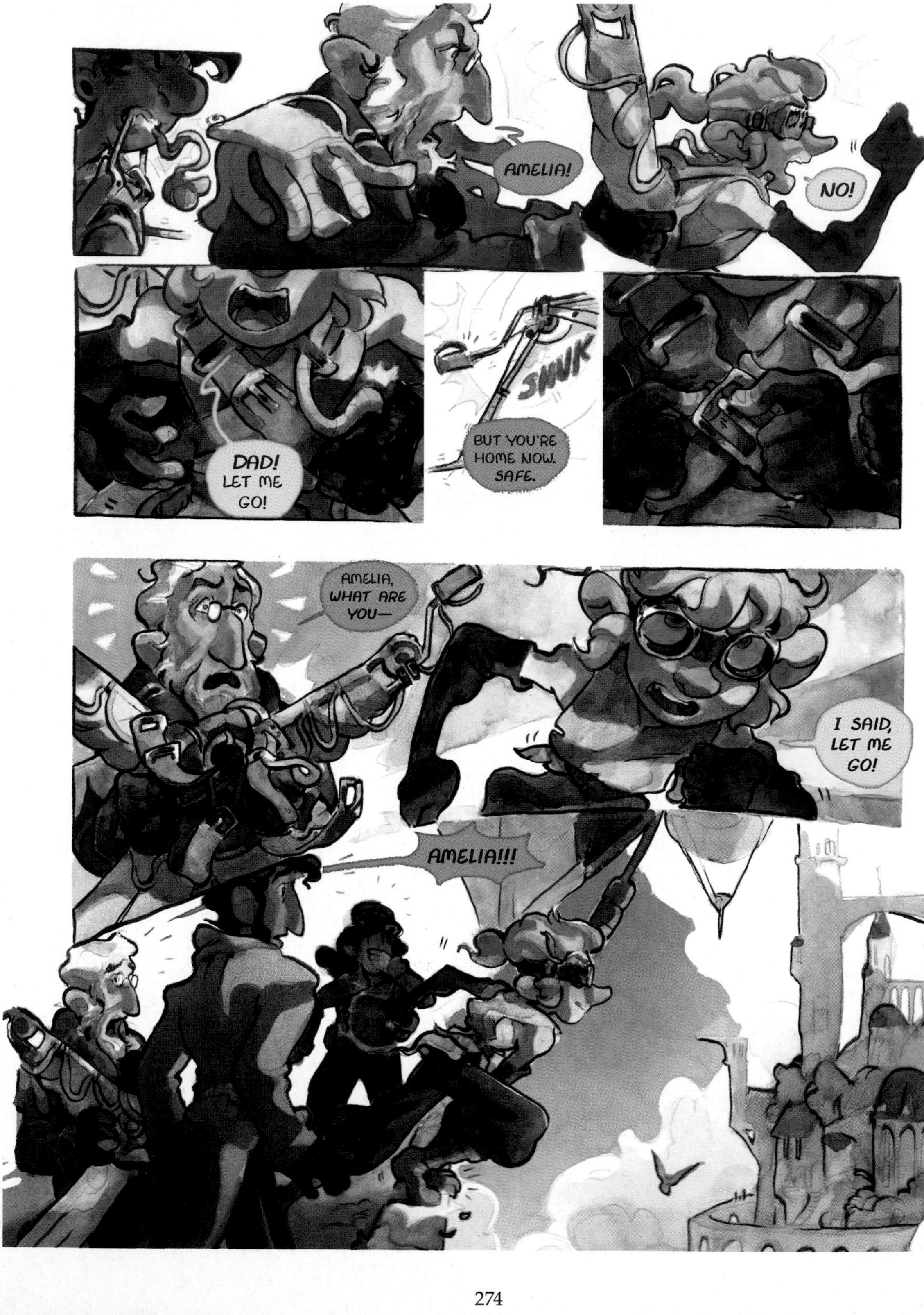
AMELIA!
NO!
DAD! LET ME GO!
SNUK
BUT YOU'RE HOME NOW. SAFE.
AMELIA, WHAT ARE YOU—
I SAID, LET ME GO!
AMELIA!!!

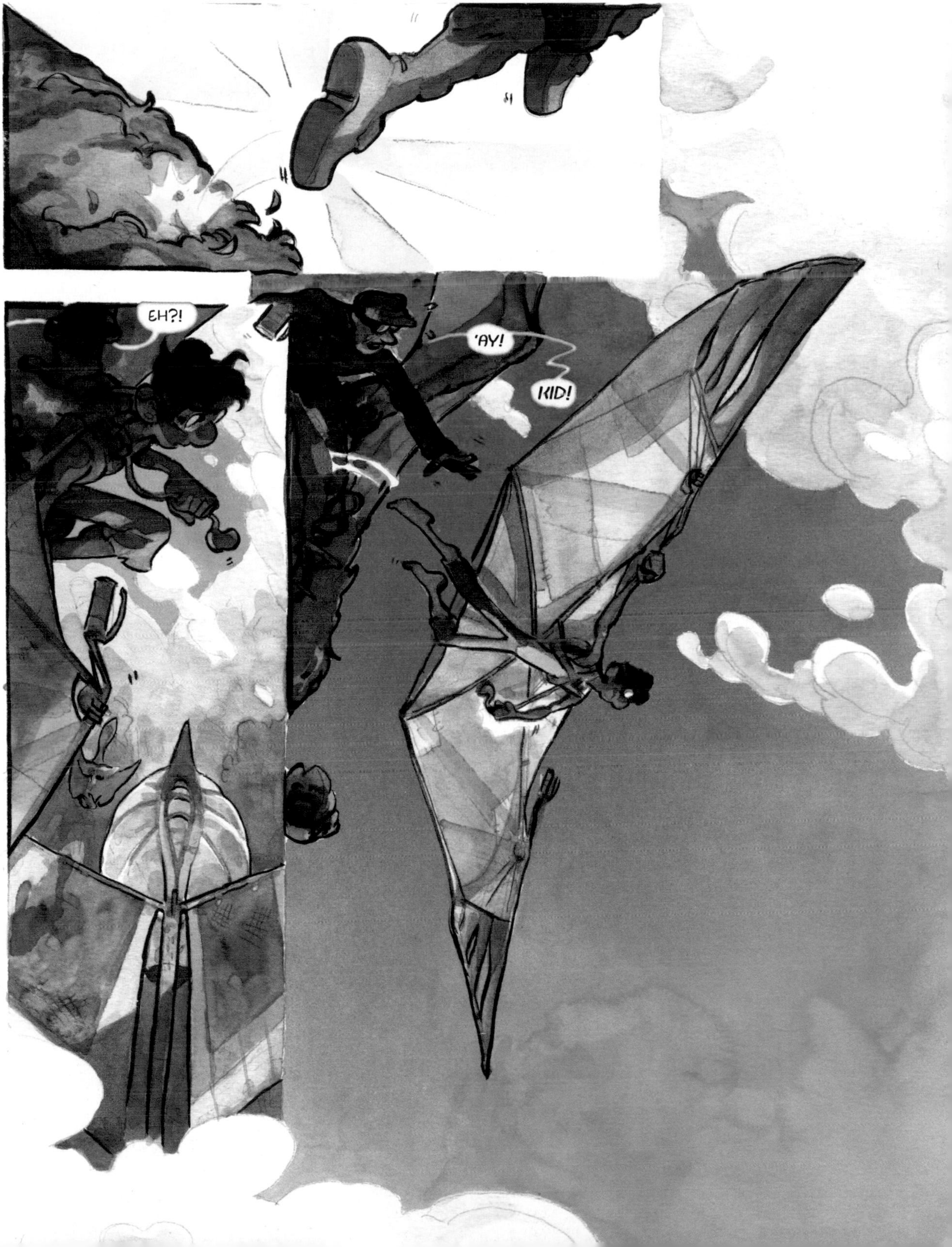
EH?!
'AY!
KID!

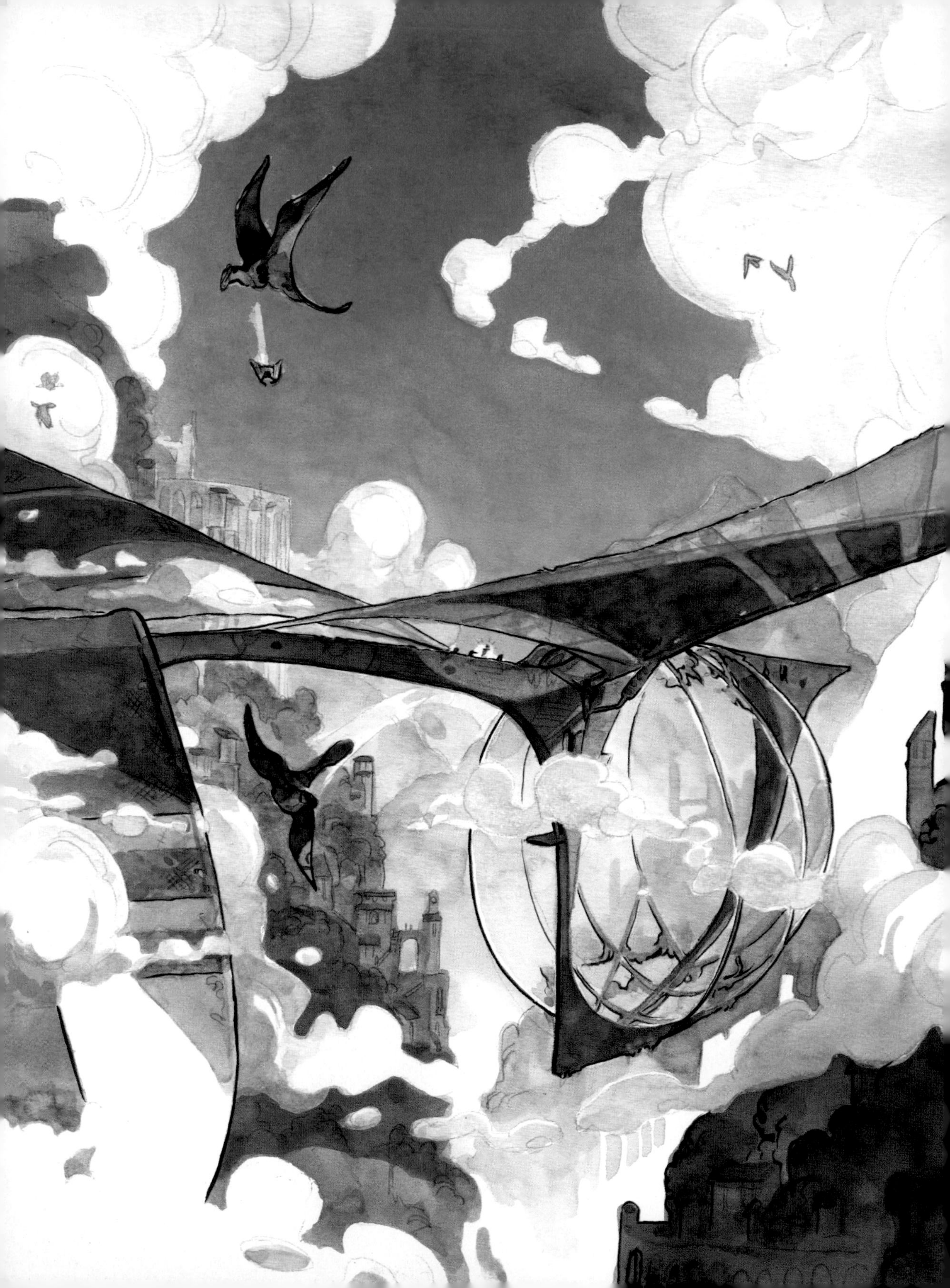

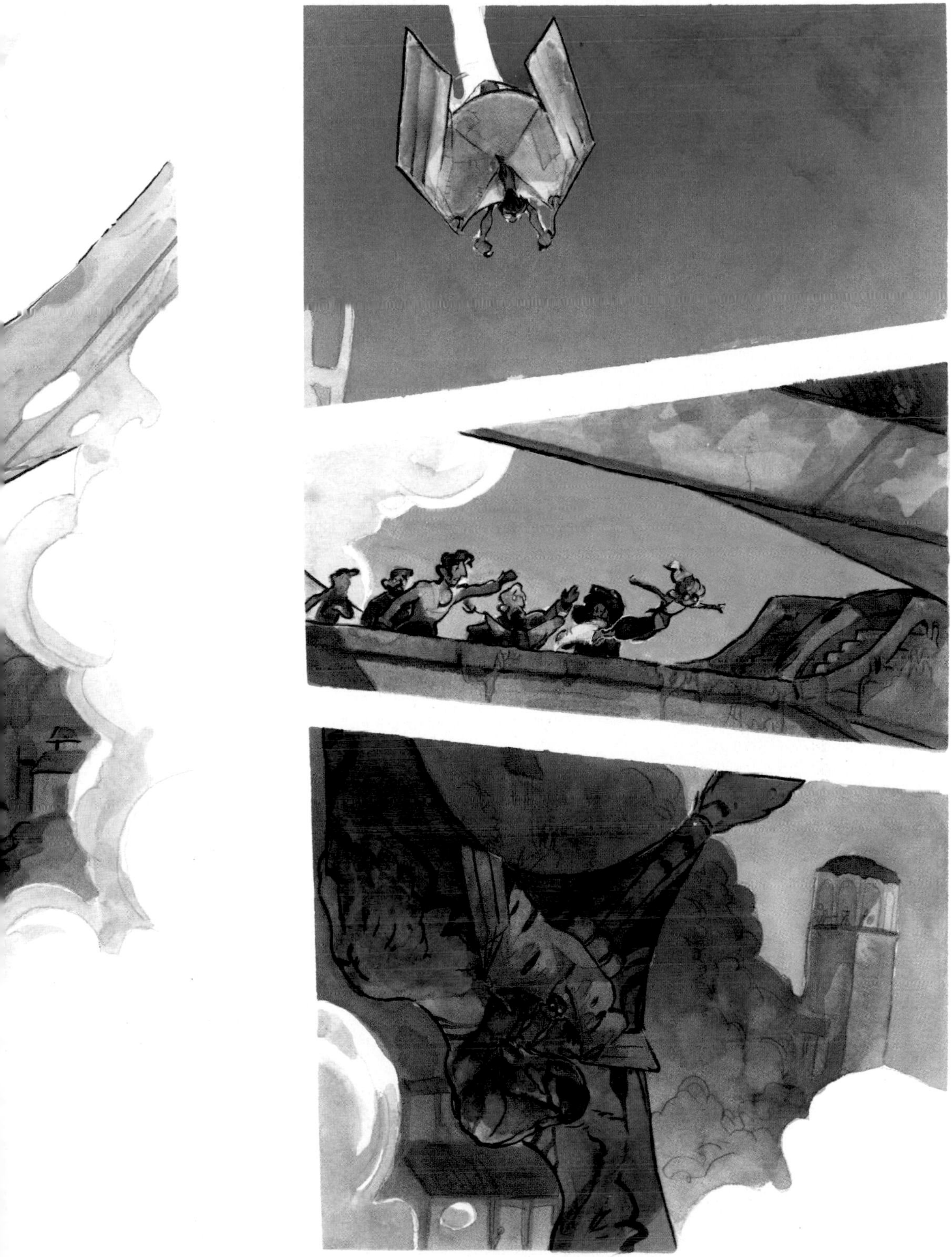

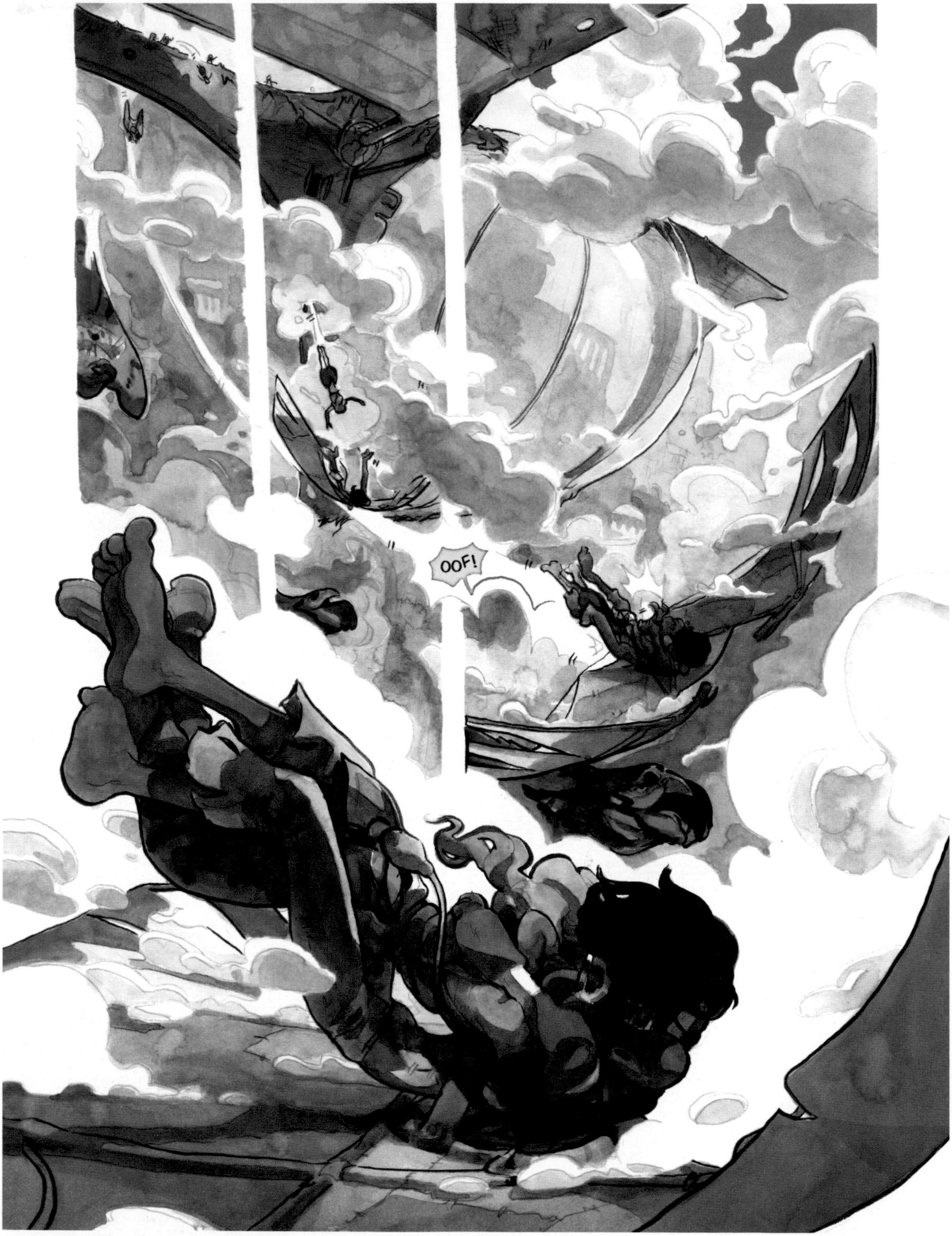
OOF!

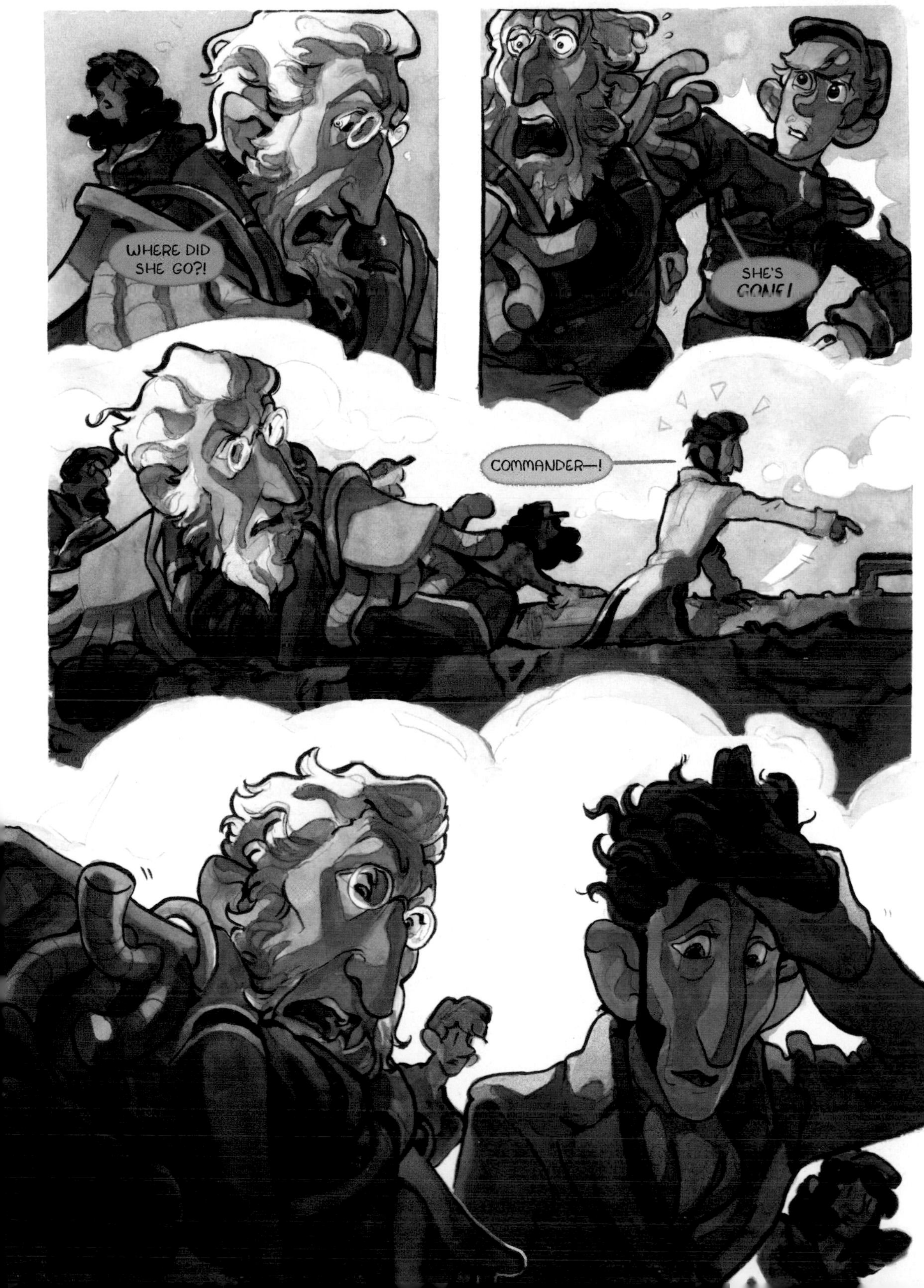
WHERE DID SHE GO?!
SHE'S GONE!
COMMANDER—!

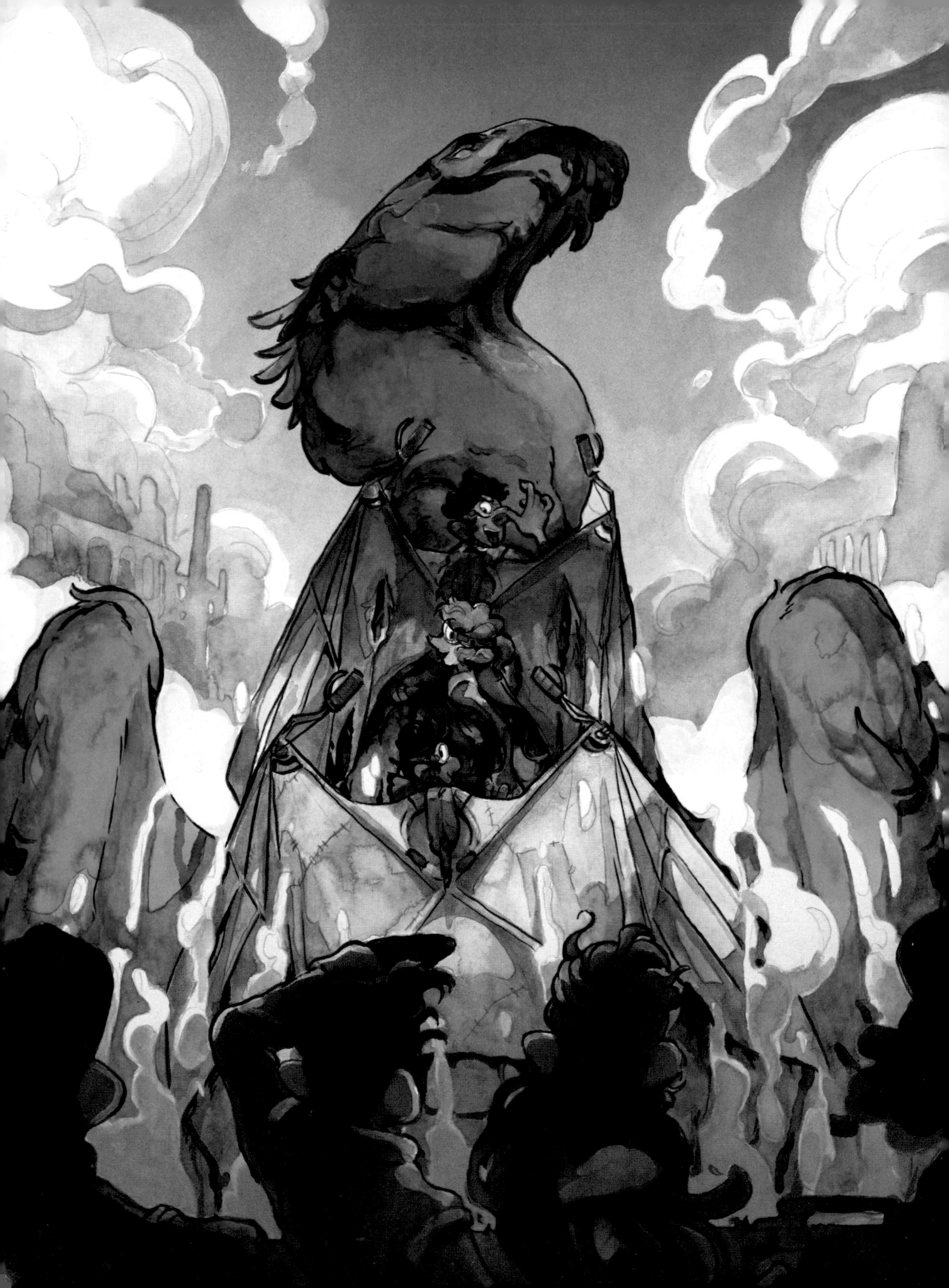

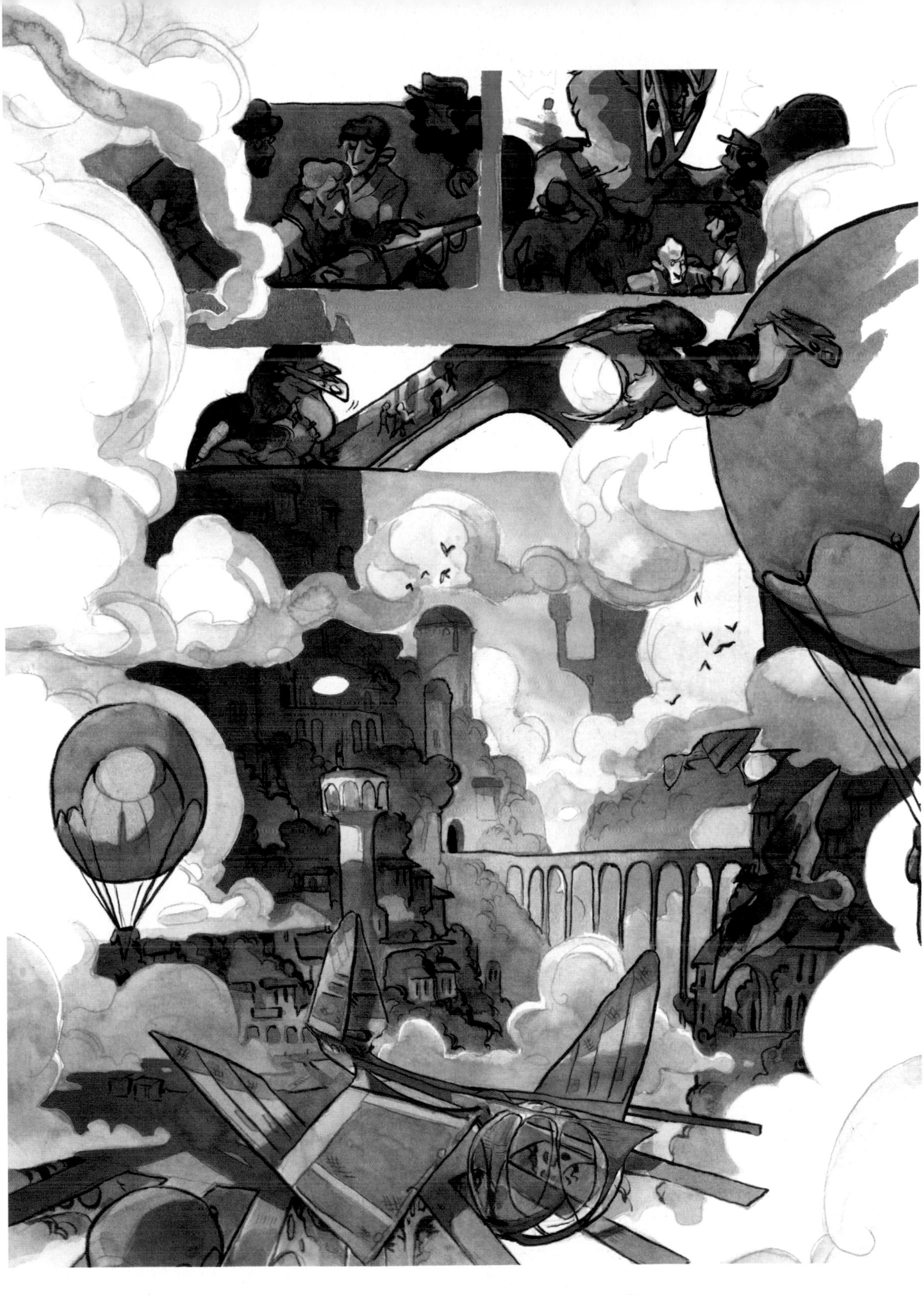

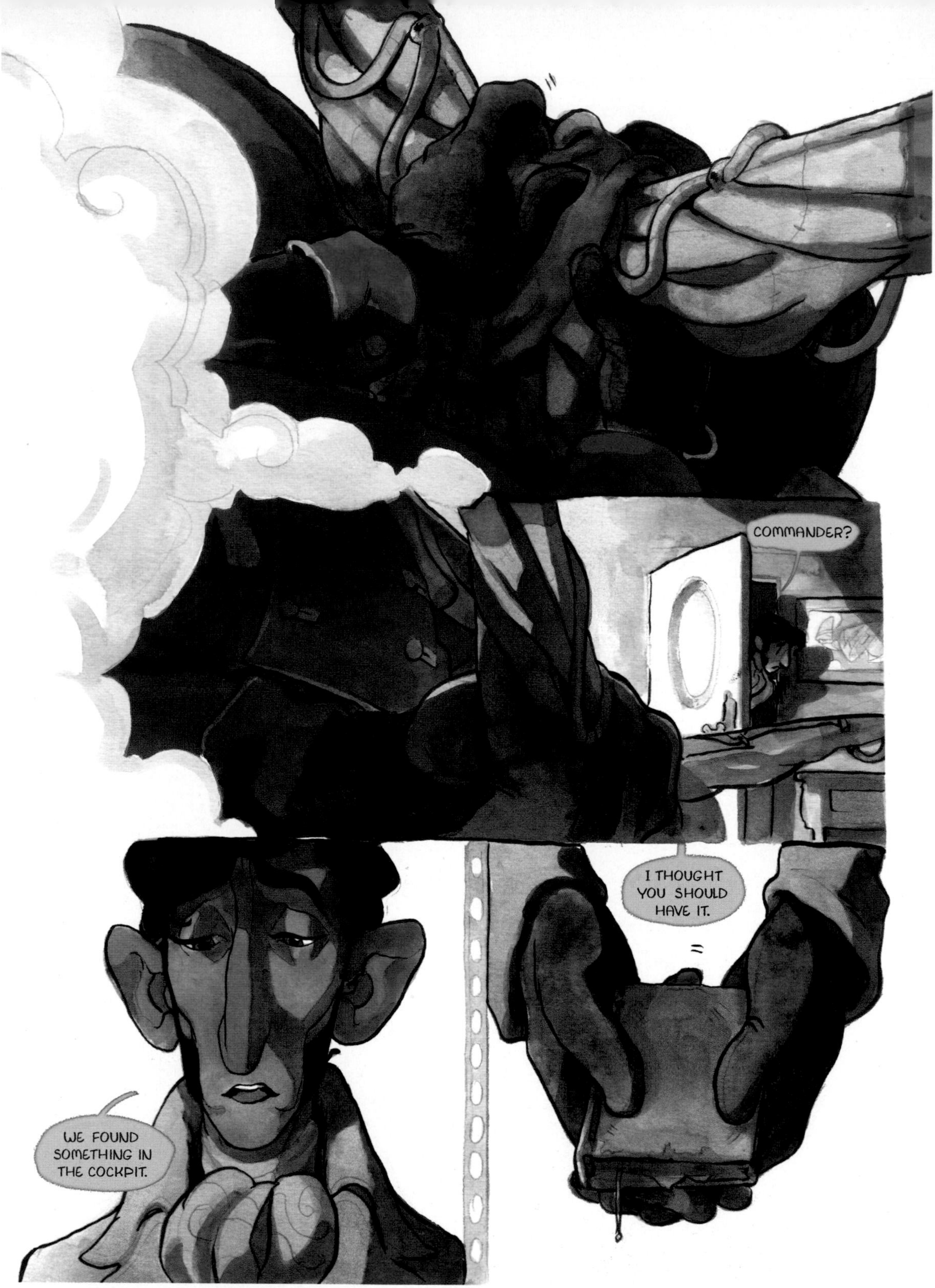
COMMANDER?
I THOUGHT YOU SHOULD HAVE IT.
WE FOUND SOMETHING IN THE COCKPIT.

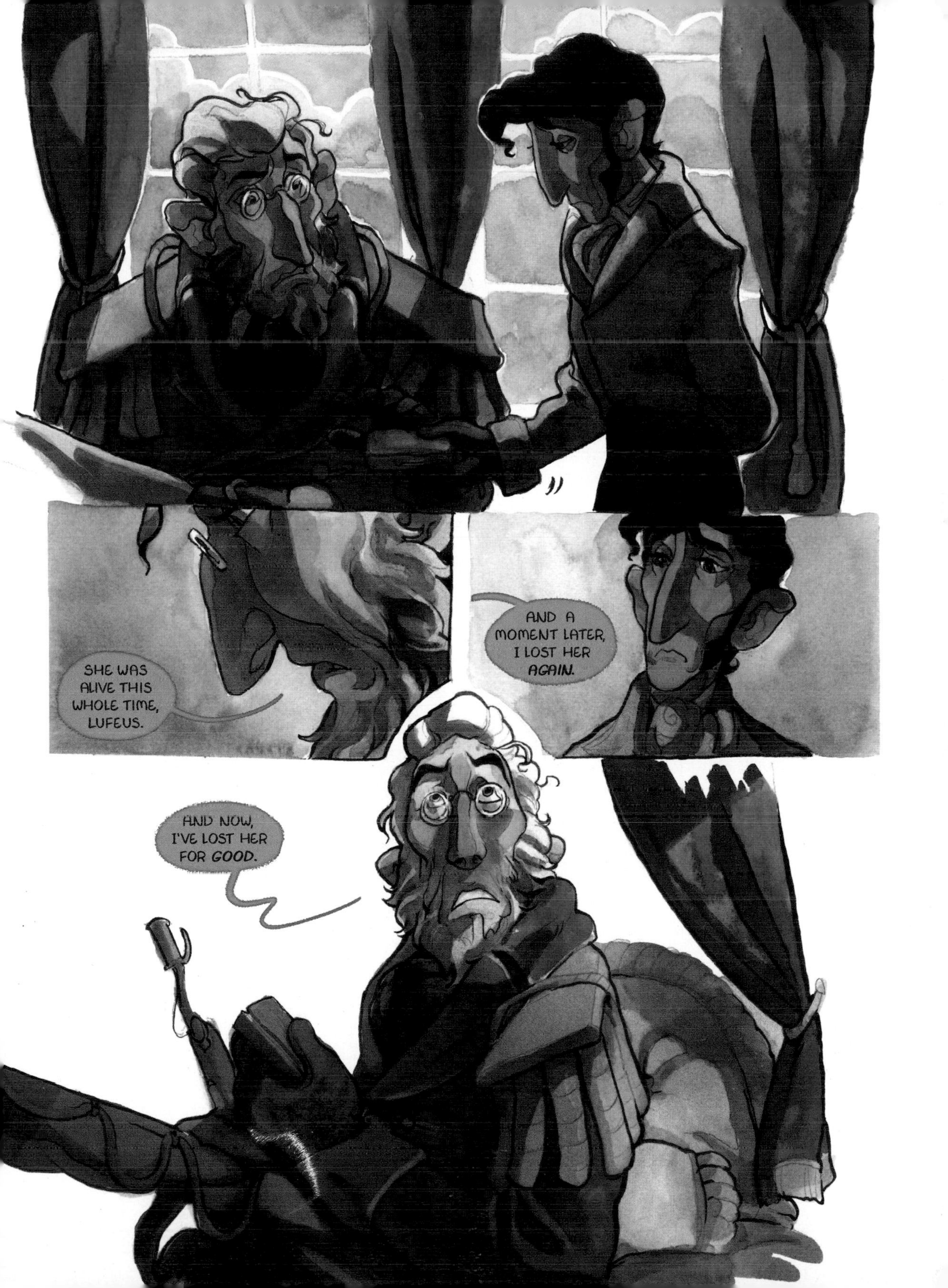
SHE WAS ALIVE THIS WHOLE TIME, LUFEUS.
AND A MOMENT LATER, I LOST HER AGAIN.
AND NOW, I'VE LOST HER FOR GOOD.

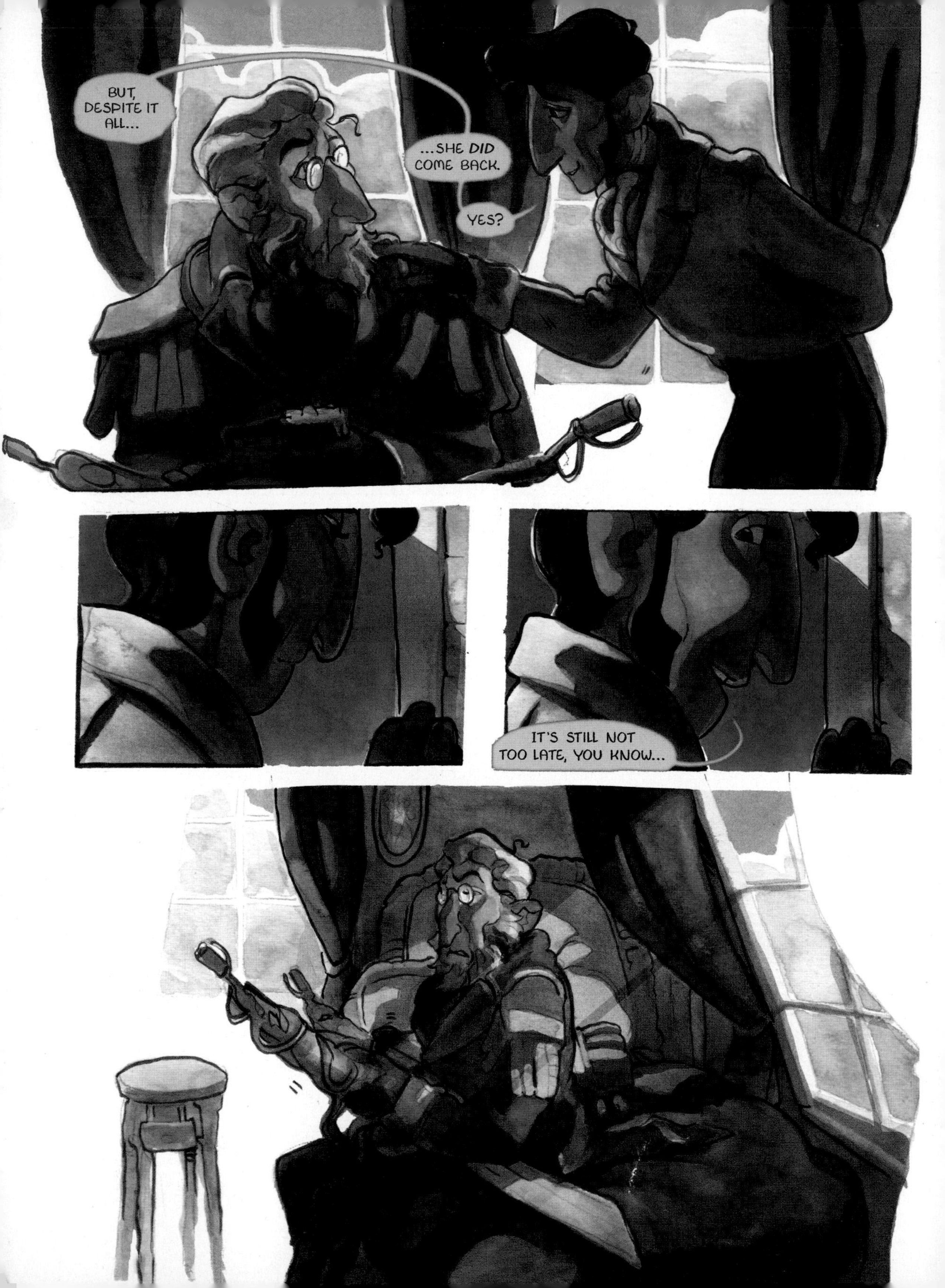
BUT, DESPITE IT ALL...
...SHE DID COME BACK.
YES?
IT'S STILL NOT TOO LATE, YOU KNOW...

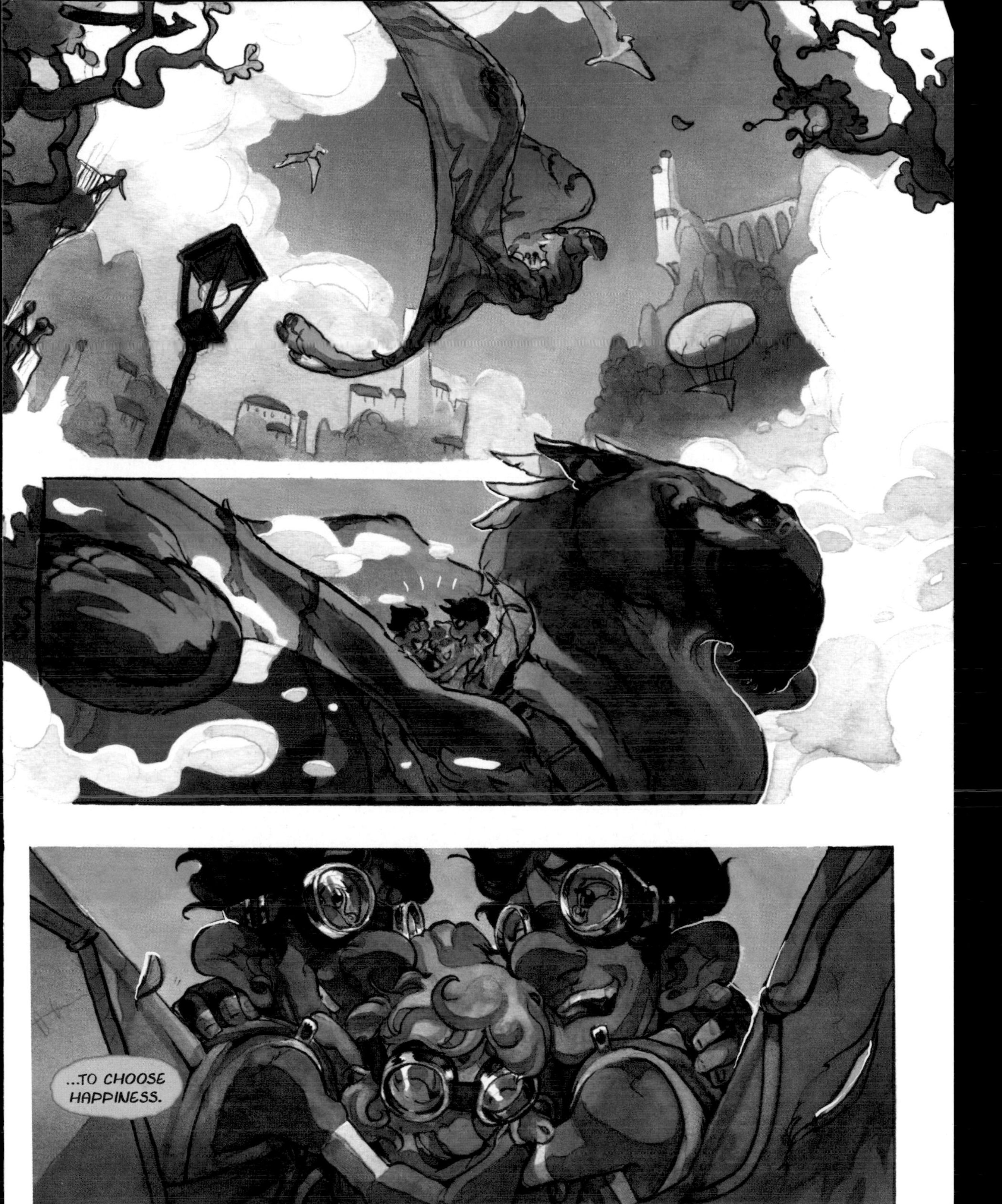
...TO CHOOSE HAPPINESS.

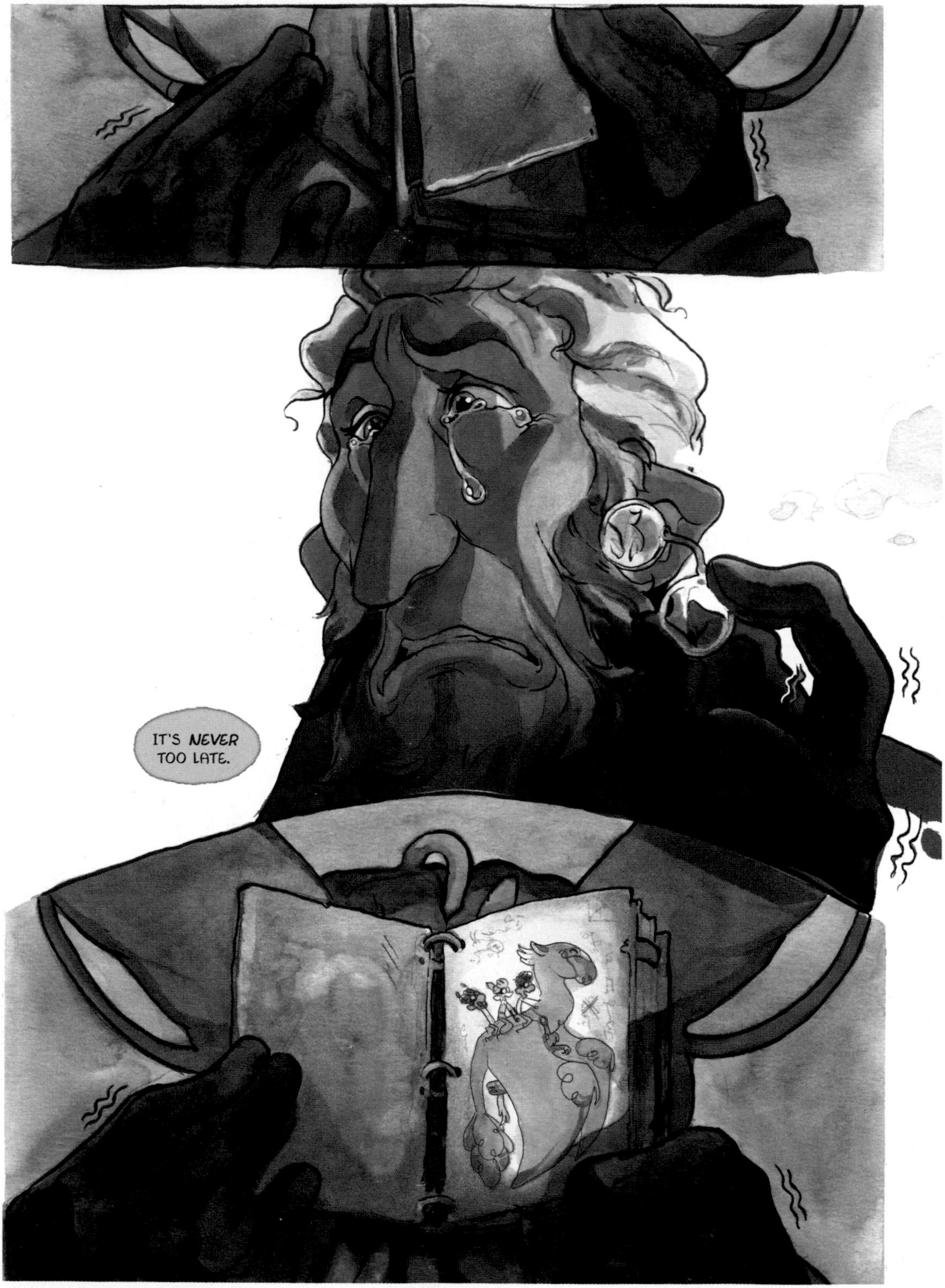
IT'S NEVER TOO LATE.

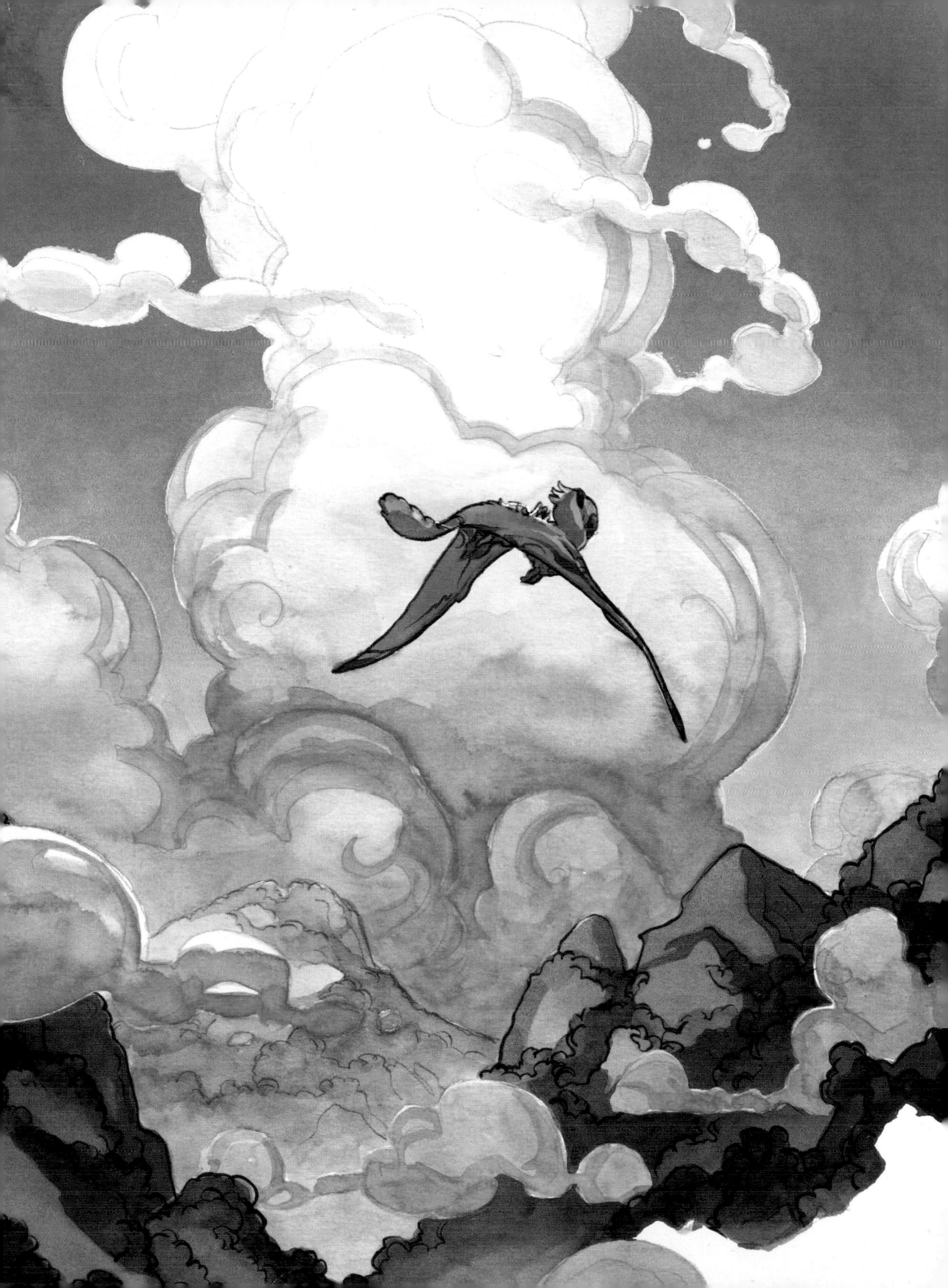

B. C. PETERSCHMIDT has dreamed her entire life of being a visual storyteller. She was born and raised in Minnesota and began her career as a freelance illustrator, later graduating from Pratt Institute. She has illustrated book covers for Diana Wynne Jones's *The Islands of Chaldea* and Naomi Shihab Nye's *The Turtle of Oman*. Her work is published in Marvel's *New York Times* bestselling anthology *Out of the Past* and also appears in Frank Beddor's Hatter Madigan series. B. C. Peterschmidt now makes her home in California.

A NOTE FROM THE AUTHOR

Visiting the Smithsonian Air and Space Museum as a kid, it amazed me how tenacious the pioneers of aviation could be when it came to rising from failure. Consider this book to be a love letter to all the brave souls and their flying machines who aren't covered as much in the history books as they deserve, such as the Aldasoro brothers and Otto Lilienthal.

Inspired by them, I wanted the ornithopter to be based in real science. The flywheel, for instance, was directly based off of a steam locomotive drive wheel; the piston and counterweight work together to create momentum. While I can't say for sure that the *Intrepyd Ray* would be able to fly, it's fashioned on sound engineering principles, and I even built prototypes to make sure that what I conjured held some basis in reality.

The next time you fly, as you look out the window at the ailerons gracefully maneuvering up and down on the ends of your wing, consider all of the love that went into this gift of flight we now have.

ACKNOWLEDGMENTS

I'd like to thank the following people: my agent, Allen Spiegel, for seeing my vision from the get-go; my story therapist (editor), Adam Rau, for pushing Amelia to a place that was way better than I could have imagined; my publisher, David Saylor, for all of the late nights considering the deepest intentions of the story; the Scholastic designers, Phil Falco and Steve Ponzo, for making the book beautiful in spite of my endless adjustments; my mentors, Giuseppe Castellano, Pat Cummings, Dawn Duwenhoegger, Julie Hintsala, and Luke Peterschmidt, for your unconditional support over the years; Libby Wambheim, for workshopping this story with me since high school and being a great friend; Olga Andreyeva, for your Photoshop magic and steady friendship; Caitlin Critchfield, for teaching me how to fly (literally); Nidhi Chanani, for being a beacon of light into this next chapter; my engineering consultants, Eric and Max Peterschmidt (the ornithopter became scientifically feasible thanks to you two); my life consultant, Bugs Peterschmidt, for everything else, really—I'm glad you're my mom; and to my partner, Katie Morrison, for the many late nights patiently waiting for me to finish working (each of the little animals hidden in this book are for you).

Special thanks to my dear cousins, Daniel, Matthew, and Thomas Peterschmidt, for reminding me every day how good it is to be true to yourself. Don't change.